THE

MANIAC FATHER,

OR, THE

VICTIM OF SEDUCTION.

A ROMANCE OF DEEP INTEREST.

. BY THE AUHTOR OF " ELA, THE OUTCAST," " ANGELINA," " ERNESTINE DE LACY,"
" EMILY FITZORMOND," " THE DEATH GRASP,"
" ROSALIE ; OR, THE VAGRANT'S DAUGHTER," " THE BRIGAND ; OR, THE MOUNTAIN CHIEF,"
" AGNES THE UNKNOWN ; OR, THE MENDICANT'S SECRET,"
" WIFE'S DREAM ; OR, A PROFLIGATE'S LESSON," " EVELINA, THE PAUPER CHILD," &c., &c.

"When lovely woman stoops to folly,
And finds too late that men betray,
What charms can soothe her melancholy?
What tears can wash her guilt away?"
GOLDSMITH.

LONDON:

PUBLISHED BY E. LLOYD, SALISBURY-SQUARE, FLEET-STREET.

MDCCCL.

PREFACE.

For the idea of the present tale, the Author feels it necessary to state that he is indebted to Mrs. Opie's beautiful story of " FATHER AND DAUGHTER," but for the idea only ; the first part of " THE MANIAC FATHER" only bearing the least similitude to that work, and all the other portion of the matter being entirely original.

The tale above mentioned embraces only one incident, which, however beautifully wrought out and skilfully treated, is abruptly brought to a termination at the very time when the interest is most excited.

The object of the writer of the present narrative has been to show the numerous miseries which a dereliction from the path of virtue is sure to entail upon the unfortunate ; but how, by repentance and remorse, and a strict adherence afterwards to rectitude, are sure to defeat ultimately the designs and machinations of the guilty, and to be rewarded by future happiness.

In the career of Adder, the Author has endeavoured to show the continual cares, disappointments, and anxieties that guilt is sure to bring upon itself, until, in the end, defeating its own purposes, it is brought to a premature death of ignominy and violence.

How far he has succeeded in achieving these objects, the Author must leave to the judgment of the reader, who he is bound to believe he has at any rate amused, by the remarkable sale " THE MANIAC FATHER" has enjoyed from the commencement, for which patronage he returns his grateful acknowledgments, and begs leave to remain

THE PUBLIC'S MOST HUMBLE

AND OBEDIENT SERVANT.

October, 1850.

THE
MANIAC FATHER;
OR,
THE VICTIM OF SEDUCTION.

[THE MANIAC OCCUPIED IN SKETCHING A TOMB.]

CHAPTER I.

THE SEDUCER.—THE ASSIGNATION.

It was evening, and the moon was sailing majestically through an ocean of fleecy clouds, tinging the scenery around with a silvery hue, when Rosabelle Montalbert was seated at a window in the spacious and elegant apartment, which was the favourite sitting-room of her and her father. A deep melancholy seemed to have stolen upon her senses; she leant her head upon her hand; er whole demeanour was sad and pensive, and the sighs that frequently escaped her bosom, clearly evinced that sorrow lay heavy at her heart.

There could not be imagined a more lovely object than Rosabelle Montalbert, and to every perfection of face and form, she united all the graces and elegances of mind that can be inherited by her sex. Nor was she the less remarkable for the sweetness and gentleness of her disposition; and in the country town in which she resided, she was held up as a pattern of virtue, and universally admired and beloved.

"Beresford, dear Beresford," she soliloquised

at length, and her beauteous blue eyes beamed orth redoubled lustre as she mentioned that name, "alas! what a change has come over Rosabelle since first we met; what hours of rapture, yet of intense melancholy, have I endured. How often, ere we become acquainted, have I resolved never to marry, but to live single for the sake of my beloved father; that father whose virtues have rendered him the admired of all; but oh, can I help thinking that he is now unjust and capricious, or why should he encourage a prejudice against Beresford? A prejudice which he is himself unable to account for. Who can dislike Beresford? —young, amiable, and accomplished; graceful in person, elegant in manners, noble alike by birth and nature, to see, and not to approve of him, were irreligion against love. Oh, Alfred, dear, dear Alfred, you have gained that ascendancy over my heart which I am certain nothing can ever destroy."

As she gave utterance to these observations, she took from her bosom a miniature, which, having gazed at for a few minutes in transport, she pressed vehemently to her lips, and tears, tears of mingled joy and sorrow, flowed from her eyes. She was aroused by a gentle tap at the door, and having desired the person to walk in, Martha, her waiting-maid, presented herself.

"Colonel Beresford, Miss, requests permission to see you," said Martha, in reply to her lady's interrogatory, as to what had brought her thither.

Rosabelle started at the mention of that name, and turned very pale and blushed alternately, while her bosom heaved with much emotion.

"Is it possible that Beresford can have been so imprudent as to come at this hour?" she said; "should my father become acquainted with his clandestine visit, how angry would he be. Still, can I refuse to see him? Oh, no, so strong is the hold he has of my heart, that I cannot deny him anything. But are you sure my dear father is not in the way?"

"I am quite positive, Miss," answered Martha, "for master has gone down to Mortimer's, his steward, to give directions about the festivities that are to take place to-morrow, which is the anniversary of your birthday. Oh, it will be a delightful day. My dear master is resolved that all work shall be thrown aside on that occasion, and that it shall not be his fault if there his a sad heart in the neighbourhood. Ah! Heaven bless him! if ever there was a good man, Squire Montalbert is one."

"Yes," exclaimed Rosabelle, as her maid quitted the room while her eyes beamed with love and fervour as she spoke, "well does my beloved father deserve those encomiums. If succouring the sick, and encouraging the poor; proving a father to the orphan, and a friend to the widow; rewarding the righteous, rescuing the sinner, make a good man, who is so well entitled to that name as my father?"

She was startled by some one laying his hand gently on her shoulder, and, turning round, she beheld Beresford standing before her.

Alfred Beresford was possessed of an elegant figure, and noble countenance; his manners were graceful, and his talents of the first order. Few could resist the fascinating powers of his conversation, and many were the female hearts that he had captived, deceived, and broken.

"Rosabelle," said Beresford, in a tone of sadness, "I hope you will pardon this intrusion; it may be my last. I have seen your father, have urged my passion to him, and solicited your hand; but he has proudly, unjustly, and contemptuously refused me. I but come here to have that refusal confirmed by you, and I leave these scenes for ever. Yes, I will wander to others, less dear, perhaps, to my heart, but less fatal to my peace—less alluring to my fancy, and less deceitful to my hopes."

"Oh, Beresford," replied Rosabelle, reproach-fully, "how can you be so cruel and unjust? Think you I can impugn the conduct of a father, who, till now, has never cost me a pang, or awakened an emotion, save of pleasure and tranquility? for, whatever may have been his conduct, I have ever received you with kindness and sincerity; never professed more than I felt, nor meant less than I professed."

"Forgive me, Rosabelle, for the observations that I made in a moment of irritation," said Beresford, "I will not, cannot doubt you; but this no place to enter into explanations; your father cannot be long ere he returns, and refusing to sanction my addresses, he will not be disposed to look kindly on my attentions; promise to meet me at midnight, in the garden, and I will disclose myself fully—the welfare of your life depends upon that hour. I have matters of the utmost moment to reveal. You will not—you cannot deny me! On my knees I ask—I implore it!"

"An assignation, Beresford!" ejaculated Rosabelle; "can Rosabelle Montalbert honourably consent to an assignation with any one, however beloved and respected? What would my dear father say, were he to know his child concealed a thought from him?"

"Your father!" cried Beresford, vehemently; "he is the enemy of your happiness, of your love; can you expect, then, that he will smile on any step, however unexceptionable, that you may take to secure it? Refuse me, and I will tare myself away from you for ever—consent, and a life of obedience to your wishes, of devotion to your will; of unbounded love, shall recompense the blest compliance. Rosabelle, adored, beloved Rosabelle, speak but the word then; it is my first, my only poor request; let it not by your cruelty prove my last."

As he spoke, he knelt before her, and taking her hand, pressed it to his lips, and looked up in her face with an expression of the most earnest supplication. The maiden trembled; a variety of conflicting feelings rushed for a moment to her heart, and she paused and hesitated.

"How shall I act?" at last she observed, in tones she did not mean Beresford to hear; "the instant expectation of my father's return, the still small advocate that pleads for him in my heart! Oh! I cannot hesitate! I may be wrong, but I cannot be cruel. Beresford," she added aloud, while deep blushes suffused her cheeks, and rendered her ten times more ravishing to his sight,—"I will not be inexorable—I must, I do consent."

"Ten thousand, thousand thanks!" cried Beresford, energetically, and his eyes sparkling with delight; "this repays me for all your father's scorn, your——"

"Pray begone!" interrupted the agitated and trembling Rosabelle, "he will return,—will discover us,—let me entreat,—let me beg."

"Well, then, at twelve—in the gardens."

"I will be waiting," hastily replied Rosabelle.

"Angelic, enchanting girl—she's mine! she's mine!" said Beresford, aside; then turning to Rosabelle, he ejaculated, in a tone of the utmost fervour, "farewell, dearest maiden, farewell!"

"Farewell—till midnight," said Rosabelle, and Beresford tore himself from her presence.

The moment he was gone, the most agonizing thoughts distracted the bosom of Rosabelle, and her heart was agitated by a thousand fears. What had she done? No—no—she had no alternative. Her beloved father, whose pride it had hitherto been to anticipate her wishes, now disappointed her in the one most dear to her. Surely her love and duty merited not such a denial?

The tears filled her eyes as these thoughts occurred to her mind, and she covered her face with her handkerchief and wept. So completely absorbed was she in the sorrowful reflections that tortured her brain, that she did not notice the entrance of her father until he spoke to her.

"In tears, my Rosabelle?" he said, in a voice of deep affection.—"but too well can I divine the cause: I met Beresford as I entered. Why will my darling girl still cherish an affection for one who never can insure her happiness? Believe me, I speak, love, more in sorrow than in anger. Beresford's income is precarious, is slender; he cannot be either constant or domestic; brought up in an idle profession, and accustomed to habits of intemperance, expense, and irregularity."

"Oh, my father!" exclaimed Rosabelle, with feelings of powerful emotion, "spare me, spare your Rosabelle!"

"I will forbear, my poor child," said her father, kissing her cheek;—Rosabelle Montalbert, I am certain, will never accept the addresses of a man, whose father, he himself owns, will never sanction them with his approval."

"I have no plea but one—I dare not urge," returned the maiden, "unbounded love!"

"You would not wed without a father's sanction, Rosabelle?" said Montalbert, solemnly.

"Oh, no—no—no; never!" she replied.

"Then," said her father, seriously, "encourage not that in another which you would forbid in yourself. I am only prompted to urge this by the earnest, the ardent wishes I have for your future happiness. Think not that I would endeavour to oppose your love whenever your affections were placed upon a worthy object; and, although it will be a severe trial for me when you are taken from me, I will not be so selfish as to wish to continue my happiness at the price of your's. Still in tears?—nay, my love, I cannot bear to see you weep. You know that tyranny is foreign to my nature. Time and absence may have the effect of eradicating this unfortunate passion from your heart; at any rate, I must advise you to try what effect they will have; and should you, after due trial, not be able to succeed in vanquishing your love for Beresford, even though it is sorely against my inclination, I promise you that you shall receive my consent to your union on one condition only ; namely, that the consent of the father of Beresford is also obtained. But I do my child an injustice to imagine for a moment that she would ever agree to be united to any man in a clandestine manner. Her heart would revolt from such an idea."

"It would, it would, my dear sir!" returned Rosabelle, vehemently ; "believe me, I will never do anything which is not sanctioned by you, or might cause you unhappiness."

"That promise re-assures me," said Montalbert, "but I must exact yet more from you, my dear child. You must assure me that you will not see Beresford again, and I am satisfied. He has a wily serpent tongue, and if—"

"Does, then, my father suspect," said the damsel, "that Rosabelle would ever be seduced to violate her duty, or endanger her honour?—Oh, sir, think better of your child, nor wound her heart by such unkind suspicions."

"I spoke in haste, my child," said he; "forget it and forgive it. The night advances; the morrow brings with it a busy round of pleasures; we shall need less to encounter their sweet labour. I will no longer keep you from your couch than to solicit my favourite strain. I have been somewhat ruffled; it will soothe my troubled spirits; come, then, my Rosabelle; thy voice has that sweet power that can charm to rest the darkest, moodiest passion. Kind Heaven hath given it its own seraphic sweetness; and as thou singest, the ministering angels stand in the porches of the eternal palace, and fancy echo gives them back their own celestial songs of praise and love. Sing, sing, my child."

"With joy, my father," said Rosabelle;

"though it were my last breath, it were sweetly breathed to pleasure thee."

As Rosabelle spoke, she drew her chair closer to where her father was sitting, and while she listened to her with breathless attention, she sang to him a song he chiefly delighted to hear. It was a simple, plaintive ballad, and she sung it with such taste and melodious sweetness, that

"Might have created a soul
Under the ribs of death."

The following lines Mr. Montalbert always listened to with particular pleasure and attention—

"Oh! never could that darling child,
    Her aged parent loved so dear,
Cause in his cheek the blush of shame,
    Or in his eye excite a tear !
A comfort to his old grey hairs,
    A solace in his hours of woe ;
Woe brought not on by sin of her's :
    Could she e'er grieve his heart? ah! no!"

"No, no, my sweetest," said Montalbert, straining his daughter fondly to his bosom ; "never will you, never can you My dear Rosabelle will live to be a comfort to that father who loves her so fondly ; and never, he is confident, will she give him cause to feel a moment's anguish. Good girl, good girl ; and now, then, good night. I have a sad weight on my soul, and yet to-morrow should bring smiles and joy. It must be our late conference that has affected me. We are not used to differ, Rosabelle. God bless thee child; a father's prayer act like a charm upon thee, and shield thee from the perils of the night. Good night—good night."

Again and again did Mr. Montalbert embrace his beloved daughter, and seemed loath to separate from her. A terrible foreboding of he knew not what haunted his mind ; and when Rosabelle responded to his wish, and he had reached the door, a sudden impulse made him return ; and again enfolding her in his arms, he ejaculated—

"Again let me press thee to my heart, my child. God bless and shield thee; for on thy precious welfare hangs thy doating father's life should aught befal thee. Why yield I to these thoughts? 'tis strange! let me shake off this weakness ; 'twould seem as if some spell forbade my leaving thee, and yet a few short hours of sleep, and we shall meet again. Why, what a fond, weak fool has nature made me; once more, good night; good night, and Heaven preserve thee, child !"

The old man once more hugged her to his bosom, parted the silken tresses from her forehead, and kissed her fervently ; a tear fell from his eye upon her cheek ; and at length, with a powerful effort to conquer his feelings, he tore himself from her embrace and rushed out of the room.

"Stay, stay, my father," cried Rosabelle, as the idea of the manner in which she was about to deceive him, for the first time flashed across her conscience; "but why should I recal him?" she added ; " what thoughts are these that dart across my brain?—his unusual tenderness—Beresford—Beresford, I cannot, I dare not meet thee. Not meet him? Am I, then, so weak in resolution that I fear to trust myself? I were unworthy of security were I unable to withstand temptation. I will not think so slightly of myself ; besides, have I not pledged my solemn word, and can I break it? No, Beresford, I'll at all hazards meet thee; the hour is almost come ; one last look at this dear scene of all my childhood's pleasures, and I go. This is my father's favourite apartment, and doubly is endeared to me for that. Farewell! farewell!"

As she thus spoke, she cast a sad, last lingering look upon the apartment, and then pensively quitted it. With a melancholy heart, she bent her steps towards the spot where she had promised to meet her lover. At the door of her father's chamber she again paused and listened; the tones of his voice met her ear; he was breathing his evening prayer to Heaven, and she heard him implore the protection of the Almighty for her. Her heart faltered, a trembling came over her, and she felt half inclined to abandon her purpose, and to retire to her chamber; but a secret and irresistable impulse urged her on; and breathing a blessing upon the head of her beloved parent, she hurried from the place.

CHAPTER II.

THE ELOPEMENT.

WITH feelings of exultation the profligate and unprincipled Beresford quitted that fair girl whom he was seeking to make the victim of his guilty and disgusting passions. And when he had left the house, after encountering Mr. Montalbert, with whom he only exchanged a few words, he gave vent to his sentiments upon the subject in the following expressions—

"So, then, she has consented to meet me, and I triumph; she will be mine; the old dotard. Montalbert, to believe me serious in my offer of marriage to his daughter. Marriage! ha! ha! it would ill suit my roving inclination; besides, it would disappoint all the ambitious prospects I have formed for my future life, and bring on me the eternal displeasure of my father, Lord Mornington. 'Twas a masterly stroke of policy my hinting at the necessity of the marriage being kept secret till my father's consent should be gained. I did not think old Montalbert had so much pride in him, though; I never was so cut up since I met my tailor in Bond-street, the day after the non-payment of my last bill forced him into the Gazette; but I shall have my revenge. Rosabelle is irrevocably mine; admiration, gratitude, respect, esteem, pride, all combine to keep her so. She admires my person; is grateful for the distinction of my attentions; respects the superiority of my acquirements; esteems my outward virtues; and is proud of my birth and expectations; what, therefore, is to prevent me obtaining full possession of her? I will convey her by a forged tale to London; feed her with promises till I have obtained the summit of my wishes; and having satisfied my love, by procuring a handsome mistress, make a necessary sacrifice to prudence, by looking out for a wealthy wife. Ha! ha! ha! nothing could be more admirably arranged, and so certain of success!"

With these words the heartless libertine hurried home, and gave instructions to his valet Adder, to procure him a rope-ladder, and to have a post-chaise ready by twelve o'clock, and to be waiting near the house of Mr. Montalbert.

Punctual, of course, to his appointment, Beresford made his way to the gardens attached to the residence of Mr. Montalbert; Adder following at a short distance with the post-chaise, and everything in readiness for the nefarious plot; and he had scarcely reached the spot of assignation, when Rosabelle appeared at the balcony; and, in a timid voice, repeated his name.

"My love! my life!" exclaimed the deceiver.

"Beresford," said Rosabelle, "I have, with many struggles, kept my word; prize well the moments of this meeting, for never must it be renewed. My father has been speaking of our union; he has forbidden all further intercourse between us; has stated reasons, alas! too strong, too convincing, why we should never be united, and has for ever refused his consent to our marriage without the consent of your father."

"Selfish, cruel man," observed Beresford, with warmth; "see you not, my adored one, that his rejection of my offers does not proceed from any dislike of you marrying me individually, but from an unfeeling and interested design of preventing you marrying at all."

"Can such be my father's motives?" said Rosabelle; "impossible, Beresford; I cannot believe it."

"What others can he have?" interrogated the libertine; "is not my character unexceptionable? are not our habits, our inclinations, our ages in unison? What possible objection can he have?"

Rosabelle paused for a few moments, and it was evident, from the agitation she evinced, that the most tormenting thoughts racked her brain.

"It is but too true," at length she said; "I am unwilling to believe it of my father, yet cannot blind my judgment to the justice of your argument."

Beresford, with difficulty, could repress a smile of satisfacton and exultation at the ready manner in which Rosabelle was falling into the snare he had laid for her, as he thus observed:—

"Why not at once defeat his machinations, then, and secure my happiness and your own, by eloping with me to Scotland? Time, necessity, and our parents' affections, will soon secure us their forgiveness. Never may we find another opportunity: to-night either makes us wretched, or blest for life. I have a chaise-and-four at hand; this rope ladder you may descend in safety; and, to-morrow, the blessed day of your birth, will prove the still more auspicious day of your nuptials."

"A clandestine marriage!" ejaculated Rosabelle; "can Rosabelle Montalbert ever so descend? Ah; she who listens to the dictates of pride, can know but little of love besides its name;—oh, Beresford, Beresford, cease to tempt me to my ruin."

"I do but urge you to your happiness; pause not, beloved Rosabelle, I conjure you; think of the dreadful agony your loss will cause me; think of my despair, nor burden your pure soul with the dread weight the consciousness of my destruction would heap upon it. Oh, let my tears, my sighs prevail upon you. I call on every sacred power to witness I will be all your fondest thoughts can wish me—your faithful and adoring slave for life; will live, will die for you. Consent, then, Rosabelle; seal thine own happiness for ever, and rescue me from everlasting wretchedness. Coy opportunity has lent his wings to these brief moments; oh, seize them, ere they fly for ever from us."

"I dare not deliberate," said Rosabelle, with much emotion; "Beresford, thou hast triumphed; I yield me thine for ever. Great Heaven, that gave me all a woman's weakness if I have erred, oh, judge me as a woman, nor blame me for the absence of that strength which thou hast not bestowed upon me."

"This ladder, Rosabelle," returned the delighted Beresford, throwing it into the balcony; "this ladder leads thee to love and liberty; a moment will convey thee to my arms."

"My trembling hands can scarce perform their office," said Rosabelle, as she prepared to affix the rope-ladder to the balcony, according to the instructions of Beresford. "Now, for the first time, home of my father, peaceful shades of my early joy, to quit your fostering shelter."

She descended the ladder, and at the foot, the libertine was waiting, with open arms to receive her.

"Support me, Beresford," she said, in trembling accents; "I sink, with unknown terror. Should I be acting wrongly—but 'tis too late receding; I am all thine, Beresford. Farewell, my home! farewell, my father! Ah! my eyes grow dim, my senses fail me, my limbs refuse—oh!"—and with a sigh she fainted in the arms of the deceiver.

"She faints!" ejaculated Beresford, as he clasped the senseless form of the maiden to his bosom, and gazed with a feeling of indescribable transport upon her. "How beauteous in insensibility she looks! I could feel pity but that love overmasters all. Let me bestow my prize within the carraige, then off to town and rapture."

With these words he bore the insensible Rosabelle to the spot where Adder had the vehicle waiting, and after he had deposited her in the carraige, and placed himself by her side, it was driven off, without the least delay, in the direction of London.

CHAPTER III.

THE MANIAC FATHER.

Mr. MONTALBERT had been a widower for some years, and had no other child but Rosabelle, on whom he doated with the most ardent fondness, and was unhappy if she was out of his presence for any length of time. With all the sincerity and fervour which woman is capable of feeling, did Rosabelle return her father's affection; in fact, Mr. Montalbert was universally beloved by all who had the pleasure of knowing him;—to the poor he was a generous benefactor; and to the more wealthy an amiable companion, and a sincere friend. He never crossed the threshold of his door without having the blessings of all classes invoked upon his head, and, in fact, he was looked upon as a parent by those whom misfortune had placed in indigence. Rosabelle, too, was beloved and admired by all, for to the inestimable qualities of her father, she united all the gentleness of her sex, and was admitted to be a pattern of unsophisticated virtue.

Mr. Montalbert had been fortunate in mercantile speculations, and had retired some years with a handsome fortune;—and, certainly, never was fortune bestowed upon a more deserving individual, his chief study being how to alleviate the wants and necessities of his fellow-creatures.

Upon the education of his daughter, Mr. Montalbert had bestowed every attention and expense, and her numerous accomplishments could only be equalled by the natural graces of her mind.

The morning after the events took place which we have related in the previous chapter, was ushered in by every possible demonstration of joy and festivity; the village bells rang forth a merry peal, and everything seemed to augur a day of the utmost delight. At an early hour the peasants and domestics assembled on the lawn, and soon afterwards Mr. Montalbert, accompanied by several of his guests, made his appearance among them, and was hailed with every possible demonstration of pleasure.

"Mortimer," said Mr. Montalbert, addressing himself to his steward, "I must request you to go on a few errands for me, which will not detain you long; and you will be back in plenty of time to join our revelry."

The steward bowed and the master proceeded.

"Take five pounds down to the curate of the next parish, and kick out the lawyer Farmer Ironheart has put in there with a distress. Bid William Waggoner see that load of turnips off for the London market to-morrow morning, and let John Footman take that basket of broken victuals to the invalid in the green lanes; tell him to dismiss his doctor, and to prevent his ever having the disease of want again, I'll make his half-pay double; the veteran who has supported his country should never want support from his countrymen."

"I'll take care, sir," said Motimer.

"And, harkye; let Giles Gammon have his wages as usual; 'tis illness and not idleness, that keeps him from labour, and we should not make the v situation of Heaven heavier by unnecessary privation."

"Heaven bless your kind heart for that, sir,"

said the steward; "I'll not lose a moment, I warrant."

The steward hastily departed on the missions of charity and benevolence upon which he had been despatched by his master, and the latter then turning to the humble guests assembled, said—

"Welcome, welcome, my honest friends, I rejoice to meet you thus;—Goodman, my friend, accept my warmest greetings; as for your daughter, ther fair Miss Emily here, I would fain claim of her a gay salute, in token of our ffiendship, but that I know my young friend Rattleton, is such a miser of her charms, he'd grudge a kiss even unto her father; and, one to me?—oh! he'd grow down right jealous!"

"You are pleasant, sir," observed the fair Emily, who was leaning on the arm of her lover, the gay and thoughless Rattleton.

"Yes,"returned Montalbert, "I am not so old but I can still be gay at seasons."

"Gay!" repeated Rattleton, "why you have always been a gay man; nevertheless, I would sooner trust Emily with you, than with our staid justice or even the vicar and churchwarden, who dart an ogle through a demure eye, just as the angler does a hook through a May-fly, when he wishes to tickle up a trout, and find the bait swallowed the more readily in proportion as the danger of it is less apparent. Wip me such sanctified rogues, say I."

"The same merry Rattle as ever," said Montalbert. "I have began this day with the performance of a pleasing, but pensive duty. I have been laying the first stone of an asylum for those unfortunates, who, through calamity and disappointment acting upon too keen a sensibility, too sanguine an imagination, may experience a temporary derangement of intellect; feeling, in my own frame, the evils of a mind too sensitive,—too feelingly alive to the crosses of the world, I have not been unmindful of it in others. The loss of reason, under misfortune, is what I have ever dreaded: I was not born for suffering over-much; but I grow gloomy. Where—where is she, who will enliven all—where is my child—my Rosabelle?"

"She has not left her room yet, sir," remarked a domestic.

"Nay then, fie on her for a sluggard," remarked her father; "let some one tell her we are waiting for her."

"Be that my task, sir," said Rattleton, "if Emily will not be jealous?"

"Jealous of my Rosabelle!" exclaimed Emily, "oh, no, no;—in serving her, you will best woo me—run Rattleton, I am longing to embrace her."

"Egad! and so am I," said Mr. Goodman, "although I am an old man."

"Well, then," observed Rattleton, hurrying away into the house, "I'll content myself with embracing the opportunity of pleasing all parties and offending nons;—so here goes."

Rattleton was not long gone upon his errand, but when he returned to the lawn, his face was pale, and his manner altogether exhibited the greatest confusion.

"Rattleton," cried Mr. Goodman, impatiently, "that hurried step—those pale looks—that agitated air—what means all this?"

"Oh! my foreboding soul!" gasped forth Montalbert—"where is my child?—where is my Rosabelle?—speak for mercy's sake!"

"How can I tell it?" answered Rattleton, in accents of anguish—"yet, how can it be hidden? Summon your fortitude, and arm your soul with courage. Rosabelle has fled, and——"

"Ah!" suddenly interrupted Montalbert, staring wildly, and in tones which completely startled every one who heard them; "my Rosabelle left me! Fled! But no, it cannot be; they would deceive me! Great God you surely mean it no;

you must be mistaken; she has but wandered forth, and will return again; she is but missing for a time, no more! We will make search in every direction."

"Would that she were but missing," remarked Rattleton, in a melancholy tone; "there is but too good proof that she has fled—the ladder from her window, the writing left."

"Destraction!" exclaimed Montalbert, "but I will not believe it—you are but merry with me. Come, come, you do but jest, though you do look so grave; I am unused to pleasantry like this; but, doubtless, 'tis brave sport to prey upon a parent's feelings for his child. Young man, I am a lone, weak, doating father!—here, on my knees, I pray you undeceive me.—Say 'tis a jest, I'll bless, I'll worship you!"

The poor old man as he thus spoke, dropped on his knees, and with clasped hands, and supplicating looks, gazed in the face of Rattleton, while the tears at the same time gushed from his eyes, and streamed down the furrows of his cheeks.

"Alas! sir," said Rattleton; "happy should I be, were it in my power to undeceive you. I'll gladly bear the odium of the folly of such a jest, could I relieve you from your present agony; your daughter, sir, is gone—is eloped!"

"Villain!" vociferated the distracted father, in wild accents, and rushing fiercely upon Rattleton, "thou liest! thou art ten times a liar for that word—eloped! Gone, gone! then she is dead—she could not leave me living. Eloped!—she elope?—then are the angels false. She was as pure as are these seraphs who stand the nearest Heaven's eternal throne; she was as chaste as marble in its strata; chaste as the bud whose leaves have not yet opened. If she be false, spring's lilies are all lustful, the dove a cheat, and virtue but a name."

"Oh, I pray you, sir, to calm this transport," said Mr. Goodman, "let your friends advise you."

"Where is my child?" shouted Montalbert, deliriously, "talk to the howling tempest, Rosabelle, my child! my all! Oh, hear me, answer me—not speak? not come! Great God! preserve my reason; my head grows giddy, my senses wander; my brain is on fire; where is my child? Rosabelle! my child, my child!"

With a wild and frenzied laugh, the wretched Montalbert sunk into the arms of Mr. Goodman and Rattleton.

"All pitying powers!" exclaimed the gentle Emily, "the shock has hurt his reason!"

"Nay, my love," observed her father, "let him have his own way; the first burst o'er he will be calm again."

"Who says I'm mad?" cried Montalbert, suddenly arousing himself, and looking with a vacant stare upon those around him; "I am not mad! No, no, I'm not mad! I do but wander; I am not mad; try me we with subtle questions; my reason shall make answer same as yours; I hear, I see, I feel—would that I did not. When men are mad they rave, foam at the mouth, and wildly stare; know all things—nothing—cease to know themselves, but I am calm; I do but know the truth. I've lost my child, she's gone, she's dead! Beresford has destroyed her. Give me the knife! Treason's abroad; but we'll convert our ploughshares into swords, and mow the damned traitors to the earth."

"Alas! dear father," said the terrified Emily, "he raves—secure him in pity."

"I am not mad," repeated Montalbert, in a still more vehement tone than before, and looking round upon the different persons assembled. "I know you all; you are old Honesty," (to Mr. Mortimer, the steward, who had returned a few minutes before,) and you his fellow, (to Mr. Goodman,) and you—you are, (to Emily.) But, no, you are not my child; but you," he added, with increased violence, addressing himself to Rattle-

ton, and grasping him fiercely by the collar, "ha! have I found you? You are Beresford, you have murdered her. Villain! resign your prize—restore my child. I'll hunt thee on the horses of the night, lash thee with meteors, hire the fiends to scourge thee, and night and day pursue thee for my Rosabelle. Ha! have I caught thee? this, then, to thy heart. What! dost thou shrink? Thou art not, then, all flint, though thou couldst rob a father of his daughter. He bleeds, he bleeds; he totters, falls, he dies, and I am happy. Ha—ha—ha!" and with an hysterical laugh, which was truly awful to hear, the wretched Montalbert sunk into the arms of Mr. Goodman and Mr. Mortimer, and became insensible. He was conveyed with all possible expedition into the house, and medical assistance immediately sent for, but his reason had fled; he had become a wretched maniac.

———

CHAPTER IV.

THE PROFLIGATE.

WE will pass over the manner in which the villain Beresford contrived to gain his lustful and guilty desires, and to effect the ruin of the unfortunate Rosabelle, and follow their footsteps to London, where the libertine took handsome apartments, and did all he could to reconcile her to her fate, and make her forget the guilty step she had taken; but this was no easy task; and there were times when the remembrance of her poor father, and the peaceful home she had quitted, would rush to her memory in such vivid colours, that it almost drove her to madness. Beresford endeavoured to appease her anguish by a promise of marriage; and so well did he act the hypocrite, that Rosabelle had no suspicion of his truth.

It was evening, and Beresford and some of his profligate associates were assembled in the parlour of the former, drinking and carousing, and indulging in such rude ribaldry as was their wont to do upon occasions of this description.

"Come, come, another bumper, Beresford," said Captain Mowbray, who was one of the guests upon the occasion; "another bumper, and I'll give you a toast you'll not refuse to drink, I'll warrant me. Fill—fill!"

"No," said Beresford, hiccupping, "I'll drink no more to-night; I am more than flushed already."

"This toast you will, for a thousand," returned Mowbray. "Gentlemen, charge your glasses. Come, Beresford, you smuggle her up very slily; yet, notwithstanding, I'll give you pretty Rosabelle Montalbert, with three times three."

"Pretty Rosabelle Montalbert! Hip, hip, hip, hurrah!" exclaimed the other guests, clamorously, and drinking.

"Gentlemen," said Beresford, "I thank you in Rosabelle's name for the honour you have done her."

"We would rather be thanked by herself," returned Mowbray. "Psha! man, don't be so fearful of letting her be seen; surely you have sufficient confidence in your own attractions to prevent your being jealous of us. We sha'n't run away with her. Come, come, introduce us—introduce us."

Beresford was confused, and scarcely knew what to offer in excuse; but after a few moments hesitation, he said—

"The fact of it is, Rosabelle is at present absent; were she not, you would not have been invited. She has some old fashioned notions of propriety, which I am unfashionable enough to indulge her in—retirement, books, needle-work, and my society she deems better suited to her taste and situation than either public places or private parties. Never but as my wife would she presume to meet the blic eye."

"I'll see her, though, for all that," muttered Mowbray to himself.

"I don't know how the devil you manage it, Beresford," remarked Lord Saunter, a foppling debauchee of the first water, "but you certainly get into the books of a tradesman and the good graces of a pretty girl quicker than any other man in the guards: you must positively be a devilish clever rascal."

"Your lordship flatters me," replied Beresford.

"Why," continued Lord Saunter, "I have heard that you have absolutely ruined more old men and seduced more young women than any officer of your age in the kingdom; but you must leave off all this sort of thing now you are going to be married."

"Nay," interposed Mowbray, "he will have more occasion to follow all this sort of thing than ever, marrying, as he does, merely for money. What are the accomplishments of this intended Miss Rochdale of yours?"

"Sixty thousand!" laconically answered Beresfard.

"A desirable women, faith," said Lord Saunter, "if she didn't come from the city. But pray, if it is not too impertinent, tell us how you contrived to prevail upon Miss Montalbert? I had always heard her cried up as a perfect mirror of virtue."

"The thing was simple enough, my lord," returned Beresford; "fine words and fast promises got her into a post-chaise a hundred miles on the northern-road; then the pretence of a pocket-book left behind, inveigled her to London, where, by one plausible excuse or another, I have amused her to this moment."

"Devilish well contrived, and equally well managed, Beresford," observed Lord Saunter. "I must give you every credit for the manner in which you devise and put into execution your amours. I must positively take a leaf out of your book, I think."

"Your lordship is disposed to flatter me," said Beresford, smiling.

"Oh, not at all, I can assure you, my dear fellow," returned the other; "in fact, in all matters of this kind I must yield the palm to you, and yet, you know, I am not reckoned an unskilful libertine."

"Very true, but your lordship does me great honour."

"Honour?" repeated Lord Saunter, with a satirical grin; "that is a very convenient word for us gentlemen of the care-for-nothing fraternity. It may be all very well in theory, but d—n the practical part say I. However, I must rattle off to Brooke's, so good-bye; we shall meet at one of the subscription-houses, I dare say. Come, come, Mowbray."

"I am ready to attend your lordship," said Captain Mowbray; "but," he added, again muttering to himself, "I will soon return, for I am determined to have one peep at this said Rosabelle; I dare say she'll be in soon. I can coax Saunter to come. I am entirely at your lordship's disposal. Good night, Beresford."

"Good night, empty-headed fools, puppies!" cried Beresford, as the profligates quitted the apartment; "I am very glad to think they are gone, for I was fearful that they would have stayed until Rosabelle returned, and in that case they might have blown more than would have been exactly pleasant to me just now. Should they have thrown out any hint about my affianced bride, it would not have been altogether well-timed."

Having thus spoke, the villain Beresford sat himself down at a table and commenced writing a letter.

We will pass hastily over the various machinations that were devised by Colonel Beresford to triumph over the virtue of Rosabelle; the solemn vows and protestations he made to her that she should become his wife; the many torturing pangs which she, poor girl, endured when she thought of the too fond parent she had abandoned, and the ruin she had most probably brought upon him. We will draw a veil as quickly as possible over such scenes as these, that can only excite anguish in the reader's breast, and draw the tear of pity for human frailty from their eyes. Suffice it to say, that Beresford succeeded but too well; that Rosabelle's virtue was not proof against his importunities and tender asseverations; that he triumphed, and Rosabelle became lost for ever.

For awhile after she was awakened from the fatal delusion which had stolen upon her senses, she was quite inconsolable, and it required all the skill, the ingenuity, the sagacity, the duplicity, and the rhetoric of Beresford, to calm the violence of her feelings. She raved incessantly of her father; called herself his murderess, and uttered a determination of flying from the roof of Beresford, and seeking that home in which she had passed so many years of virtue and happiness. To appease her anguish, and to prevent her putting her threats into execution, her seducer pretended to send messengers down to the place in which her father resided, and who did everything that his invention could suggest to wean her affections from the good old man, by not only assuring her that he had expressed very little or no emotion at her elopement, and that he was not only now quite happy, but was about to enter into a second marriage. The scheme succeeded; and Rosabelle, who was in transport at the thought that her father suffered no misery on her account, became more calm and resigned.

Weeks and months passed rapidly away, and the love of Rosabelle increased tenfold when she found that she was likely to become a mother; but the idea that the little innocent she would shortly give birth to would be the child of shame, filled her bosom with the greatest agony. Again and again did she urge her seducer to fulfil those vows he had so frequently given utterance to, and make her his wife, but he had always some plausible excuse to offer for the delay, and was so accomplished in sin, that he found it no very difficult matter at any time to quiet her fears, and to drown her suspicions.

On the evening we have been describing Beresford to have been honoured with a visit from his wild and dissipated associates, Rosabelle had taken a walk, and returned just after Lord Saunter and Captain Mowbray left the house in a melancholy mood. Beresford greeted her with his usual fervour and apparent sincerity, and taking her hand eagerly, and pressing it to his lips, he said, in a tone of rapture—

"My dear, dear Rosabelle, how anxiously have I been waiting for your return."

"Ah! Beresford," answered Rosabelle, while a tear trembled in her eye, "if I am indeed so dear to you, why not at once allay the anxiety, the misery, my bosom is at present the receptacle of, by making me your wife? Ere you last visited your father, you know you pledged a solemn vow that on your return it should no longer be delayed."

"I know it, my dearest love," returned Beresford, "my father's late illness was occasioned solely through fear that our marriage had taken place; he sent for me purposely to know the truth of it; and, on my assurances to the contrary forced me, unless I wished to kill him at once, to take a solemn oath never to marry you, but with his approbation."

"And did you take the oath?" demanded Rosabelle, breathlessly.

"What could I do?" said the deceiver; "my father's life was in evident danger if I refused; the dreadful certainty that he would put his threat into execution, of cursing me with his dying breath; and cruel as he is, Rosabelle, I could not help feeling he was my father."

"Wretch! deceiver! villain!" shrieked Rosabelle, sinking into a chair, "and is the return you make me for the sacrifice I had made to you? Did I not abandon my father, brave his curse for your sake, and now you talk to me of—— Oh, God! support me! or I shall go mad! An oath, too, that you will not wed me! Have you not sworn ten thousand oaths you would? Perjured seducer!—treacherous, heartless, Beresford!"

The wretched girl covered her face with her hands as she spoke, and sobbed convulsively. Beresford, long as his villainous plot had been concocted, was too much confused and bewildered for a several moments to utter a word in extenuation of his conduct, but suffered her to remain uninterrupted until the violence of her grief had, in some measure, passed over; then, with every appearance of truth, he said—

"Indeed, my dear Rosabelle, you are by far too hasty; true it is, that I have promised my father, nay, sworn to him, that I will never marry you without his consent; but, it is not too late to hope far the best yet; he may relent, and, indeed, had I not firmly believed that he would yield to my wishes in time, he would not have exacted the promise so easily from me, not even though it might be the means of saving his life."

Rosabelle smiled ironically as she answered, "Oh, no, Beresford, you do yourself an injustice; you are too kind, too dutiful a son, not to yield your consent without the least hesitation; alas! where shall we find a child so bad, so very bad as I am?"

Again the bosom of Rosabelle heaved with the most violent emotion, and she sobbed hysterically.

"Compose yourself, my dearest," exclaimed Beresford, "and you will yet be forgiven; yes you will not only be pardoned, but restored to happiness if——"

"Happiness!" interrupted Rosabelle, frantically, "oh, let me go to this flinty-hearted parent, let him hear the tale of my wretchedness; let me say to him, for your son's sake, I have left the best of fathers, the happiest of homes, and have become an alien from society; let me bid him look at this care-worn cheek, this emaciated form—proofs of the misery that weighs upon my heart, and warn him to beware, how by forcing you to withhold from me my rights, he makes you guilty of murdering a poor deluded wretch, who, till she knew you, never lay down without a father's blessing, nor rose but to be welcomed by his smile."

"She cuts me to the heart!" said the libertine, averting his face, and feeling, for the first time, probably in his life, a ray of compunction dawn upon his soul. "In what manner am I to answer her? what can I say, in extenuation of my conduct? Ah! who is this approaching?"

Beresford was startled by the sound of approaching footsteps, and his confusion and chagrin may be easily conceived, when the voices of Lord Saunter and Captain Mowbray smote his ears.

"Confusion!" he exclaimed, "it is those two prying coxcombs, Mowbray and Saunter! What shall I do? You must not be seen by them, dear Rosabelle, so pray hasten away. Ah! they are already here, and your retreat is, therefore, cut off; but, here, in this closet, you can conceal yourself, and I will contrive to dismiss them soon."

"Alas!" cried Rosabelle in accents of the deepest melancholy, "to what am I reduced."

Beresford, with agitated looks of supplication, hurried her into the closet, and he had scarcely closed the door upon her, when the two profligates entered the apartment.

Captain Mowbray looked round the room with an expression of disappointment when he found that Rosabelle was not there; for he had been in formed by one of the servants that she had returned.

"My dear Beresford," observed Mowbray, "I must apologise for intruding again upon you, but his lordship omitted to say, that, being engaged upon a shooting excursion in Leicestershire, he will not be able to attend you on your projected visit to the seat of Lord Rochdale, the father of your betrothed Cecilia, and——"

At this moment, a piercing shriek was heard to proceed from the closet in which Rosabelle was secreted, and Beresford turned ghastly pale.

"Damnation!" cried he, "this will spoil all!"

"What's that?" inquired the captain. "I heard a scream."

"'Tis nothing!" answered Beresford, confusedly; "some one in the street, perhaps; but I must leave you."

"I say, Beresford," observed Lord Saunter, laughing, "that was a damned clever thing of your putting in the paper that old Montalbert is going to be married, when we all know if he isn't dead, he's in a far worse condition."

At this moment the distracted Rosabelle rushed from the closet, and, throwing herself at the feet of Lord Saunter, in tones of frenzy ejaculated—

"My father dying? Oh, my lord! my lord! for pity's, mercy's sake, acquaint me how and where, that I may fly to save him! Here, on my knees——"

"This intrusion, my lord," said Beresford, unable to conceal his resentment and confusion, "this intrusion is ill-timed. Miss Montalbert would be alone; I must beg of you to withdraw."

"Then I do see her at last," said Captain Mowbray, aside, and in accents of pity that could not have been expected from him; "alas! unhappy, betrayed, deluded girl!"

"Very extraordinary, upon my honour!" remarked the coxcomb, Lord Saunter, eyeing the beauteous supplicant with a mingled expression of stupid amazement and rude admiration.

"Rosabelle—Miss Montalbert," said the chagrined Beresford, laying hold of her arm; "you forget yourself; rise, rise."

"Does my father still live?" almost shrieked Rosabelle.

"Oh, yes, my dear creature," replied Lord Saunter, "I dare say he still lives—he's well enough in health; but his mind——"

"He lives—he lives!" ejaculated Rosabelle, still remaining on her knees before Lord Saunter, while her eyes seemed as if they would penetrate to his soul; "but oh, tell me, do you think he would pardon me?"

"Oh, there is not much doubt of that, I should think," replied Lord Saunter, "that is if——"

"Ah!" exclaimed Rosabelle, "I understand you; too well do I know what your lips would give utterance to. You would say if I would leave my betrayer and return; enough, enough; Heaven bless you for this, you have saved me from madness!"

"Very extraordinary," repeated Lord Saunter, with the same stupid expression of countenance, "very extraordinary, upon my honour."

"My lord," interposed Beresford, impatiently, and with much resentment, "I must entreat——"

"Good night, Beresford," said Saunter, taking the arm of his friend, and moving towards the door; "extremely sorry I cannot attend you to Rochdale Abbey; fine creature—devellish fine creature, egad!—Come, Mowbray."

They quitted the room, and Beresford turning to Rosabelle, took her gently by the arm, and, in a tone of supplication, called upon her name.

"Unhand me, villain," cried Rosabelle, "your touch is poison."

"This will not do," muttered Beresford to himself, "I must e'en brave it out, as I have often done many a similar affair to this before. Rosabelle," he continued, aloud, "what have you to complain of? The cheat I put upon you of your father's situation was meant in kindness; and though Cecilia Rochdale will possess my hand, my heart will still be yours:—I wished to keep you ignorant of this, and hold you as my greatest worldly treasure. Plague on this prating lord, he has overturned the prettiest arrangement that could possibly be formed. But, if you are determined that we shall part, I hope it will not be bad friends."

"Great God!" gasped forth Rosabelle, "surely my ears must deceive me; I cannot be awake; is it possible that such back-hearted perfidy can exist in the world? And for a wretch like this, then, I have abandoned the poor old man who gave me being, and whose sole happiness was centred in mine? But be not deceived, sir; understand me right, Mr. Beresford, and think not, fallen and degraded as I am, that I will stoop to become the mistress of a wretch like you! No, sooner will I perish with the poor child I now carry in my womb, than I will receive protection or support from you. You have made me guilty, it is true; but, you have not yet, sir, quite obliterated my horror for crime, or destroyed my veneration for virtue; and now, in the fulness of my contempt, I tell you that we part for ever."

"Say not so, dear Rosabelle," returned the libertine; "at any rate, you will remain here to-night? This the first time we have quarrelled, Rosabelle, and the quarrels of lovers. you know, are only the renewal of love; and, therefore, for the present, I will take my leave, trusting, by the morning, you will be in a better humour."

Thus speaking, Beresford kissed his hand to his unfortunate victim, and hurried out of the apartment.

"Horrible monster!" cried the frenzied Rosabelle, as he disappeared; "my God! how have I been deceived! How easily have I been made the dupe of his perfidy! My brain his feverish, and yet my heart is cold, cold as ice! Would that I could go mad, that I might be unconcious of the poor ruined, degraded, despised wretch I now am. But, shall I remain under this accursed roof? No, no, no, not an hour, not an instant! I will arise and go to my father's house, and tell him I have sinned; when he sees his child, his penitent child return, worn out, heart-broken, unprotected, to beg at once his pity and forgiveness, he surely cannot, will not refuse to pardon me. Let me instantly away while my resolution is firm."

She quitted the room, and had descended one flight of stairs, when a terrible faintness came over her, and she must have been precipitated to the bottom, had not, at that moment, a female domestic happened to be ascending the stairs, who received her in her arms, and conveyed her to her chamber. Before the morning dawned, Rosabelle Montalbert brought into the world a beauteous cherub boy.

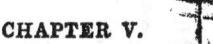

CHAPTER V.

THE FLIGHT.—THE PENITENT AND HER CHILD.

WEEKS glided on; weeks of horror to Rosabelle, for she was still confined to her bed, and to the horrors which the knowledge of the treachery of Beresford, and that the little innocent who reposed in unconcious tranquillity upon her bosom was the child of shame; that he must never breathe his father's name, would never receive a father's blessing, was added the misery of being compelled longer to remain beneath the same roof as her betrayer, whose sight was now odious to her, and for what attention she received in this time of retribution, to be compelled to be beholden to him. And then the dreadful account she had heard of her unhappy father's situation, completely distacted her brain, and for several days the medical gentlemen who attended her, despaired of her life. During this time, she raved incessantly of her home—her broken-hearted parent, and called down curses upon the head of her seducer.

"Take the child away," she would exclaim, looking wildly upon her attendants; "slay it; destroy it;—is it not the child of shame? Is not the curse of its guilty mother entailed upon it? Let it not live to be the mockery and scorn of the world; to have the finger of opprobrium pointed at it; or, perhaps, to turn out as great a wretch as its father; —father did I say? There's mockery in the name. He has no father; he has no father."

Then, after a pause, she would start suddenly up in bed, and appearing to listen attentively, she would say to her attendants—

"Hark! do you not hear them? There again! What a merry peal they are ringing. Do you not know what it is for? It should be for the nuptials of Rosabelle and——. I must not speak that name now! It is for he—yes, he, the traitor, the deceiver, they are ringing! But they shall not be united. No, no; I forbid, in the name of Heaven! Wretch! what have I now to do with Heaven? Am I not an abandoned, degraded being? Take me hence. I cannot bear the light of day! Hide me! bury me in the bowels of the earth, where darkness universally reigns. Let no one know that Rosabelle still lives. Hide me from myself. Shut out the knowledge of my infamy! Hide me! hide me! hide me!"

Thus, in tones that were piteous to hear, did the unfortunate girl continue to rave until completely exhausted, when she would sink back on her pillow without sense or motion.

Colonel Beresford came but seldom to the house, for his conscience upbraided him; and not being entirely callous to the better feelings of nature, he could not bear to contemplate the work of his destruction; the fair temple of beauty and purity his guilty hands had razed to the ground! and he would willingly have made any sacrifice could he have restored Rosabelle to that virtuous and happy condition from which he had so heartlessly betrayed her. Yet although it was in his power, in a great measure, to make her reparation for the wrongs he had done her, and for the sufferings he had caused her, by bestowing upon her his hand, pride made him revolt from such an idea, and he was resolved that nothing, at the same time, should deprive him of her but death; he could not think of parting with her with any degree of patience, and he flattered himself that, after the first violent paroxysms of her grief were over, he should easily be able to persuade her to pardon him, and rather consent to become his mistress, than to abandon the father of her child.

He ordered that every possible attention should be paid to her, and that no expense should be spared towards effecting her recovery, and then left the house and went on an excursion in the country for a few weeks, hoping in the interim, Rosabelle would be restored to convalescence, and that he should find her, on his return, ready and anxious to assure him of her forgiveness, and to accede to his proposals.

He went down to the country estate of his father, whom he found in a very indifferent state of health, but most eager for his nuptials with the lady he had selected for his future partner. To say that Beresford loved the lady, would be to tell a falsehood, and to say that she felt the least affection for him in return, would be equally wrong. It was, in fact, an alliance of interest, and not of love; an alliance formed between the parents of the young people, who had but seldom seen each other, and when they did, beheld one another with a feeling of coldness, amounting to absolute contempt. Never were two young persons more ill-calculated to come together; dissimilar in behaviour, tastes, and dispositions; the lady grave, dull, and sedate; Beresford, gay, volatile, thoughtless, giddy, and dissipated. More than this, she had bestowed her affections upon another man, a member of the church, and she had inwardly resolved rather to suffer anything than to grant her hand to a man whom she could but barely esteem. She had candidly avowed her repugnance to the union repeatedly to her parents, and declared her resolution; she had also confessed to Beresford that she could not love him, and that another possessed her heart; but it was all to no purpose; her parents were obstinate; they had fixed their minds upon the match, and was determined it should take place; and the lady was too wealthy a prize for Beresford to wish to resign her to another, although the only sentiments he could possibly entertain towards her, approached very near to aversion.

During the time Beresford was away from London, Adder transmitted every particular relating to Rosabelle; who was slowly recovering from her accouchement, and the effects of the shock the discovery of his treachery had caused her; but, against him she uttered every malediction that her outraged feelings could suggest, and declared that nothing should ever induce her to forgive him.

"She will alter her tone," said the libertine, after he had perused his valet's letter, "she will alter her tone when she again beholds me, and listens to the tender asseverations and protestations I have in store for her. The first ebullition of her resentment and grief abated, she will again behold me with re-kindled, re-doubled passion, and hug the chain my powers of deception have placed upon her. Beauteous Rosabelle, I am all anxiety to see you again; to enfold you in my arms; hear my forgiveness pronounced by those lips I so ardently long to press once more, and to learn that Rosabelle resigns every thought, every care to the love of him for whom she resigned innocence, virtue, and happiness!"

Thus did Beresford soliliquise; and full of these vain thoughts and sanguine expectations, he sat down and wrote to Rosabelle a letter, soliciting her forgiveness, and making the most solemn protestations of the continuance of his love, and declaring that nothing should ever prevail upon him to cease to be her "protector," while he continued to exist.

This letter he despatched immediately, and in two days afterwards, when he was anxiously waiting in expectation of an answer, it was returned to him unopened. Shortly afterwards, he received a communication from Adder, informing him that Rosabelle continued unchanged in her manner, and he firmly believed, that, as soon as she could gather sufficient strength, after the severe illness she had suffered, she would seize the first opportunity of escaping from the house.

"Ah! that must not be," exclaimed Bereford, when he had perused the letter; "the bare idea of my being deprived of her, and now that the birth of the object of out mutual love renders her doubly interesting, drives me to madness."

He, therefore, immediately wrote to Adder, and in reply, strictly enjoined him to use such measures as he might deem necessary to prevent her from putting those designs into execution, which he suspected she had in contemplation; and told him that he should hold him responsible for what might happen after having given him this warning.

It was now the depth of winter, and piercing cold it was; and two months had elapsed since Beresford had seen the victim of his treachery, when a circumstance took place which caused a wonderful revolution in his sentiments, and filled his bosom for a short time with chagrin and disappointment. Miss Rochedale contrived to elope with the object of her choice, in spite of the care and vigilance of her parents; and before they could be discovered, they were indissolubly joined in wedlock.

Enraged and ashamed to remain in a place where he had been so truly jilted, Beresford sought permission of his father and hastened to London, filled with sentiments of increased affection for the unhappy victim of his duplicity, and resolved at her feet to beg her pardon.

Beresford did not drive direct to the house upon arriving in London, but putting up at an hotel, after partaking of a bottle of wine, although it was a bitter cold night, and the snow was rapidly descending, he proceeded to the place where he expected to behold Rosabelle, on foot. When he had arrived within a few yards of the house, a faintness came over him—his heart throbbed violently against his side, and he paused a few moments until he had recovered himself, laying hold of the railings. A feeling, such as he had never before experienced, had suddenly come over him, and although he made a strong effort to shake it off, it was some time before he could succeed in doing so.

"Psha!" he at length exclaimed, arousing himself, "I am a child, thus to give way to such weakness. Rosabelle will forgive me;—I feel confident that love for me is too strongly engraven on her heart to be eradicated but with death. I see the lights moving in her apartment. Dear, dear Rosabelle! little do you think that Beresford is so near."

He reached the house—he approached the door, and raised the knocker; again the palpitation of the heart seized him more violently than before, and he found it impossible to conquer the melancholy forbodings that crossed his mind. The door was opened in a moment by a female servant, who started back in amazement and confusion when she beheld him.

"Is my valet, Adder, in?" he demanded, hastily, and walking into the parlour.

The girl replied in the affirmative.

"Then send him to me immediately," said Beresford, taking off his gloves and throwing himself into a chair.

In a few minutes Adder entered the room, and from the paleness of his countenance and the agitation of his manner, it was very evident to Beresford that something more had happened than his sudden and unexpected return to London.

"Ah, Adder!" he hastily exclaimed, "you do not look well—you are pale. Has anything taken place to alarm you?—Tell me where is my Rosabelle?"

"Alas! I know not, sir," replied the valet:— "she is gone——"

"Whither?" demanded Beresford, breathlessly, and starting from his chair.

"Heaven only knows," answered Adder. "She left the house this evening amid the storm."

"Villain! traitor!" cried Beresford, fiercely:— "did I not strictly enjoin you to watch her narrowly, and to take effectual means for preventing such an occurrence?"

"And so I did, colonel, I assure you," said the valet. "I made her an absolute prisoner in her apartments; and how she contrived to escape I am at a loss to conjecture, unless it was by the treacherous connivance of one of the servants."

"But the child?" cried Beresford.

"She has taken with her."

"Gone!" gasped forth Beresford, in a tone of agony — starting, and striking his forehead.— "Rosabelle gone! Through storm and tempest, fled from me! Great God! should she—ah! what but deepest guilt could nurture such foreboding? Should consciousness of shame and misery have led her to despair—should my foul treachery have—— Hah! Rosabelle a suicide! I am a MURDERER! a double murderer! Traitor to love and nature! Outcast of Heaven and man! Seducer, destroyer, a perjured lover, and a blood-stained father! Oh, villain! damned villain! Rosabelle!—Rosabelle! I knew not half thy value till thy loss!"

"We can make search for her, sir," said Adder, "meanwhile, to dull the anguish of her flight. Think how the world——"

"The world!" interrupted Beresford, passionately. "My world was in my Rosabelle! She lost, I have no other! All here is hell perverted by my guilt! Rosabelle!—Rosabelle! Oh, that I could recal thee! But 'tis in vain—too late! 'Tis now that fortune crowns my hopes, and there remains no obstacle to my making her my bride'"

At this moment there was a loud knock at the door, and soon afterwards a letter was placed in the hands of Beresford, sealed with black, and which bore the crest of his family. He broke it open, and the instant his eye fell upon the first few words, he exclaimed—

"Ah, my father is no more! He suddenly expired soon after I quitted him, and I am now Lord Ravensford! But wealth comes to mock me!—rank to brand and cheat me! What are they, if not shared with her but curses? Much-wronged old man!—ill-starred Montalbert! Oh! that the pitying madness which, on thy loss, came kindly to rob memory of its tortures, would now, in mercy, seize upon my soul! Shut out each sense, and drown each fell reflection! Such fate were bliss: but 'twill be mine to live and know my loss! My villany! Worst curse of life! Go, Adder, go. Spare no toil—no gold. Search everywhere; nor back return till thou canst bring some tidings.—Away! I am on racks!—in agony!"

Thus saying, the distracted Beresford despatched his valet in quest of the fugitive, and then hastened into her apartments, to see whether he could discover anything there which might give him a clue as to whither she had directed her flight: but he was disappointed. Rosabelle had taken nothing with her but her wearing apparel and some jewellery which belonged to herself: those trinkets which he had given her were left behind, and she had not so much as left him a line in farewell.

"My God!" cried Beresford, again striking his forehead with intense anguish. "what will become of the poor girl? Exposed to all the inclemency of the weather and the darkness of the night, how poignant will be her sufferings!—to what dangers will she not be exposed! Besides will she not die of want and exhaustion on the road—scantily supplied, as I know she must be, with cash? And whither will she direct her footsteps? Towards that spot where she first drew breath—that once happy home, which by my guilt, is rendered desolate? Will she seek out her father, the light of whose reason my tre chery and cruelty has extinguished? Alas! what horrors are in store for her gentle mind! Wretch! monster that I am to have caused all this misery!"

He threw himself in an agony of despair upon a sofa, and there gave vent to the heavy grief anp compunction that afflicted his heart.

CHAPTER VI.

A NIGHT OF HORROR.

IT was with feelings of the utmost impatience and anxiety that Rosabelle had waited her restoration to convalescence, when she was determined, at all hazards, to quit that hated roof where everything reminded her of the treachery of Beresford and her own shame. Had it not been for the maternal cares that were excited in her bosom, the instinctive promptings of nature towards her child, she verily believed that she should never again have been restored to reason; and had it not been for that fond tie, how thankful would she have been to Heaven to have remained in such a state of unconsciousness! But to what a sense of horror was she awakened! What a poor, deserted, fallen creature she was: one who could only expect to meet with the scorn and reproaches of

mankind. and who must inspire disgust and abhorrence in all well-disposed minds, for the misery she had brought upon one of the best of fathers. And yet, when she pictured to herself all this horror, notwithstanding she knew Beresford to be the guilty cause of all that had taken place, there were times when her heart could not help relenting towards him, and she found it impossible entirely to banish from her heart those germs of passionate fondness with which he had inspired it.

"Is he not the father of my child?" she would exclaim; "and can I—dare I curse him? Nature seems to revolt at the idea; and yet, is he not the murderer of my poor father's peace—the destroyer of my happiness? Wretch, guilty wretch that I must be, to continue to harbour any other sentiment than that of detestation towards him!"

Thus violently did the poor girl struggle with her emotions, and awful was the penalty she paid for the dereliction from the paths of virtue she had made. When she beheld the letter which Beresford had sent to her while he was in the country, she was half tempted to open it and peruse the contents; but a second thought prevented her, and with a sentiment of disgust, horror, and indignation, she hastily enclosed it in an envelope, and returned it to him in the manner we have described.

Her strength now gradually increased; and being at length entirely restored to convalescence, she determined to endeavour to put the project she had formed of escaping from the house into execution. She made up her mind to return to her home, to seek out her father, to throw herself at his feet. seek to awaken him once more to reason, and to obtain his forgiveness. He surely would not—could not long be deaf to the pleadings, the supplications of that poor girl (now truly penitent), whom he had ever loved with such devoted, such ardent fondness.

To escape from the house, however, was a task of not such easy accomplishment as might be imagined, for Adder strictly obeyed the injunctions of his master, and kept her confined to that suit of apartments that were appropriated to her use, and the windows were all properly secured, so that she had no means of making any one acquainted with her situation outside. At length, however, she did manage to tempt the humanity of a female servant to assist her, and on the very night that Beresford returned to London, the woman had contrived, by some means or the other, to obtain a duplicate key of the rooms, and while Adder was busy about something in another part of the house, she unlocked the doors, and Rosabelle, clasping her infant to her bosom, left the house.

She wrapped her cloak close around the sleeping innnocent, for the wintry blast howled fierce around, and the snow lay thick upon the earth; and then hurried on she scarcely knew whither. At any other time, and on any occasion but the present, Rosabelle would have severely felt the horrors of the night, but she noticed them not; her mind was too fully occupied with other thoughts, and with feelings of delight, to think she was once again at liberty, and away from that place where contamination seemed to breathe around; and yet with that feeling was mingled one of intense sorrow and regret, when she thought of Beresford and her early love, and looked upon the cherub countenance of her sleeping babe, whose features so strongly resembled those of his guilty father.

"Oh! mayest thou, my poor child," she cried, hugging him closer than ever to her breast, while all the warm feelings of a mother for her first-born rushed impetuously to her heart; "oh, mayest thou not inherit his vices with his resemblance; mayest thou never live to become the villain that he is now; sooner would I behold thee perish immediately in my arms. But no, thou wilt not, my darling babe. Something whispers to me that thou wilt live to be a comfort and a blessing to thine unfortunate mother. Heaven grant that my surmises may be verified, or stretch thee a corpse, my child, this instant, on thy mother's bosom!"

The sum of money she had with her was very inconsiderable; but, at length, remembering that she was no great distance from the Golden Cross, Charing Cross, and that it was the time when the coach started for B———, which was little more than fifteen miles from her native place, she made up her mind to hasten there without any further delay, and ride as far as she had the pecuniary means to enable her; the remainder of the journey she would, of course, be compelled to prosecute as well as she could upon foot.

The pavement was like glass with the frost, and, therefore, she found much difficulty in walking, and could not make the progress she wished, and had she been a minute later at the coach-office, the vehicle would have been gone. Fortunately, too, she did find that there was one inside seat at liberty, and she therefore stepped in, with a mingled feeling of satisfaction and regret, and the coach was soon far away from the scene of her misery.

She avoided entering into conversation with her fellow travellers, and concealed her features as much as possible from observation, to hide from them the agitation of mind under which she was suffering; but the deep sighs that frequently escaped her bosom, in spite of all her struggles to the contrary, frequently drew their attention towards her; and although none of them took the liberty of making any remarks to her, it was very clear to be seen that she had in no small degree excited their curiosity.

The whole of that night they continued to travel, and about breakfast time the coach stopped for such of the travellers as liked to partake of refreshment. Rosabelle now knew that her finances would not permit her to remain any longer an inside passenger, and she, therefore, thought it prudent to change her appearance, not only to defend her from the pitiless pelting of the storm, but also to prevent her from being known by any of the passengers again. In order to effect this the more securely, accordingly, she exchanged her own handsome silk cloak for a large, thick, coarse grey one, and put her feet into a pair of clumsy soled shoes; and having well wrapped her baby up in flannel, and tied a handkerchief across her bonnet and under her chin, there was such a change made in her appearance (she looking like some humble rustic's wife), that it would have been quite impossible to recognise her.

It was piercingly cold on the outside of the coach; and, notwithstanding the manner in which Rosabelle was wrapped up, the wind seemed to penetrate to her heart, and she shivered as though she had the ague. Her heart was full, almost to bursting, but she mastered her feelings as well as she was able, and rocked her child to sleep upon her bosom. It was a weary, a toilsome, a miserable journey, and sometimes the limbs of our heroine were so benumbed, that it was with the utmost difficulty she could save herself from falling off the coach. The roads, too, were in such a dreadful condition with the frost, that the coach could not proceed without considerable difficulty and danger, and then it was very slowly, so that by the time it had arrived at the place at which Rosabelle was to cease riding, darkness had veiled the earth, and the prospect before her was shocking to dwell upon. She partook of a scanty repast, for money she had now very little, and by the time she had done that, and warmed herself by the fire, she heard a clock strike eleven, and, therefore, was confident that even if she exerted

herself to the utmost, for she was very much exhausted already, she could not reach the place of her destination before the morning. But nothing could alter her determination to proceed, so anxious was she to behold her poor father, and to learn the truth concerning his situation; and to throw herself at his feet and seek his pardon, that had she even had tenfold greater horrors and vicissitudes to encounter, she would not have shrunk from them, sooner than she would have delayed it another day.

It was Rosabelle's intention to proceed to the cottage of old Meriel Marygold, who lived on the estate of her father, and had been her nurse, where she might, in all probability, ascertain all she wanted to know, and thus be better enabled to come to a determination in what manner it would be advisable for her to proceed towards the furtherance of her anxious wishes. Surely the sufferings, the horrors to which she had been exposed in that dreary journey, would be received by Heaven as some atonement for the offence of which she had been guilty, and that she would find her father, not mad, as he had been reported to be, but ready to pity and pardon his penitent child.

Notwithstanding, however, she sought all that was in her power to strengthen this idea, many doubts, fears, misgivings, and apprehensions would steal into her bosom, and every blast of wind which howled around her seemed to come fraught with the moanings of despair. She had travelled about three miles from the place at which she had quitted the coach, and was upon a dreary waste, where there was nothing to protect her from the fury of the blast and the fast falling snow, which drifted like a shroud around her. It was a most awful spot, and, in spite of her resistance to fear, she felt the most indescribable sensation of horror creeping through her veins.

"My God!" she exclaimed, "my weary and benumbed limbs will not support me much further, and yet, if I pause, nothing but death stares me in the face. How awful is the darkness around, and here am I placed alone, and fated to endure all this toil and wretchedness. Could I but hear the sound even of a human voice, methinks it would be transport to my soul. This silence is appalling. When I was gay and cheerful, and innocence was mine—whenever I had occasion to cross this wild heath, I always felt the most irresistible terror; it is indeed a fit place for the perpetration of the bloody crimes which report says have been committed here, and I do not wonder that people should shun it after nightfall in dread; but I knew not guilt at that time. Oh, no! Now, alas! how awful is the change; I am a wandering, wretched outcast—a mother without the sacred name of wife. My child, dear witness of my love and shame, thy mother's limbs fail her; I can no longer bear thee. My God! do not desert me in this dreadful moment. Oh! I remember there is an old out-house not far from this spot; could I but reach that, it would afford me shelter until my recruited strength will enable me to proceed on my journey. The storm increases; what will become of me? Thou sleepest in peace, my child, nor heedest the bitter blast; would I could sleep like thee. The snow falls faster than ever; I must proceed ere its heavy flakes conceal my track. Protect me Heaven!"

Trembling in every limb, and her knees smiting each other, Rosabelle forced her way through the snow, as well as she was able, in the direction of the old out-house, which she at length perceived at no great distance from her; and so completely exhausted was she, that had she had to have proceeded many yards further she must have sunk to the earth. It was an old red wooden building, broken in many parts, and known by the name of the *Lover's Resting Place*, which it had gained from a legend which was very popular in that neighbourhood, and was, that two lovers, whose vows had been opposed by their parents, met there by appointment, and having resolved to die together, they at the same moment plunged a knife into each other's hearts, and being found there dead, and weltering in their blood, were interred upon the spot where they had so tragically ended their existence.

This story gave the place a kind of fearful interest; and there was one period when Rosabelle would not have ventured within its precincts, but now she thought nothing about it; she thought only of her weary and exausted state, and the benumbed limbs of her poor babe, who, although he was so well wrapped up, and notwithstanding she kept him nestled so closely to her bosom, by the cries which he uttered, showed that he had not been entirely shielded from the severity of the weather. She reached the wretched place, and found no obstruction to her entrance, the door having long since been torn off its hinges; and she, therefore, staggered into the place, and threw herself, exhausted and breathless, upon a heap of rubbish in one corner, to rest herself for a few minutes, ere she could see what was best to be done for her accommodation for the night. The out-house was divided into two compartments, and one of these was in much better condition than the other. There, then, Rosabelle determined to remain till day-break; and gathering together some pieces of old boarding which had fallen from different parts of the building, and a heap of straw, which she found in one corner, she retired into it, and contrived to make herself up some kind of a rude pallet, piled all the old rubbish she could find against the door which opened into this division of the out-house, and then imploring the protection of Heaven, she wrapped her infant more closely to her bosom, and laid down.

Completely wearied out, it was not long ere she was about to sink off to sleep, when she was suddenly alarmed and astonished by hearing a noise outside the building, and soon after a light glimmered between the crevices, and the horror and amazement of Rosabelle may easily be conjectured, when she caught a glimpse of the shadows of two men, bearing something which seemed to be very heavy between them. They moved stealthily and cautiously round by the side of the building towards the entrance, and Rosabelle had not the least doubt but that they were coming there; in another second her conjectures were confirmed, and she heard them deposit their burthen in the adjoining shed to that in which she was.

How shall we attempt to pourtray the terror of Rosabelle at this circumstance? She did not venture to breathe scarcely, and screwed herself into the smallest possible compass in the corner, for fear that the men should discover her there; but, from a small hole in the boards, she could perceive all that was passing. "My God!" she thought, "what can be the purport of these men? Certainly no good, at such an hour. Heaven send that you may sleep soundly, my dear boy, for, probably, on that depends the life of thy mother and thyself; shouldst thou utter the least cry, thou wouldst betray us to these fellows, and if their design is a bad one, there can be little doubt but that they would murder us both!"

Rosabelle placed her eye to the hole in the boarding, and perceived that they were two tall and powerful formed men, dressed in long smock-frocks, and as the rays of the light fell upon their countenances, she shuddered at their forbidding aspects. They had placed the sack upon the floor, and began digging up the earth with a couple of spades which they had brought with them. A deadly chill fell upon the heart of Rosabelle when she beheld this, and she could scarcely repress a scream, as a dreadful idea shot through her brain.

"Horror! horror!" she reflected, "the wretches have surely been committing murder, and have come hither to bury their unfortunate victim."

"There, we shall soon be able to make a snug lodging for him," said one of the villains, taking up a spade and preparing to begin to dig, "and and no one will ever know what has become of him. How nicely we gammoned the old fool to take up his lodgings with us."

"You're right," said the other, "it was very well done, and I must give you the credit of doing the best part towards it. If the friends of the old grazier look for his return home with the brads, how woefully deceived they will be."

"Ha! ha! ha!" laughed the first villain, "indeed they will. Well, we have got a very tidy booty from this job."

"Yes, it will pay us for the trouble we have been at," was the answer; "but I'll warrant that we shall circulate the blunt a little more freely than the old fellow would have done. We must not be in England many days."

"As soon as this job's over we will quit the spot," returned his companion, "and it shall be many a long day ere we will re-visit this neighbourhood again. We couldn't have fixed upon a much better place than this to deposit the old fellow's remains in; but, I say, there is a door yonder, which seems to lead to another part of the out-house; suppose we examine that, and see whether it will serve better to conceal the body of the murdered man than this."

"Great God!" thought Rosabelle, "I am lost; they will discover and murder me and my infant. By what horrible fatality were my footsteps guided to this place?"

"Psha! what's the use of talking in that manner, Gordon?" said the other ruffian, to whom this proposition was addressed; "we have no time to spare; besides, we have half dug the grave here, and I dare say the old chap will lie as contented here as he would a foot or two off. Come come—let's finish the business and begone, for I am almost tired of it, and if we remain here much longer, there's no knowing but that we might be discovered."

"Oh, very well," said Gordon, as the other man had called him, "it matters very little, so let's go to work."

"I think we have given him depth enough," remarked the other wretch, "and he'll not pop up again in a hurry by himself. Come, out with him, and let's finish the job at once."

This, as may be imagined, was a moment of unutterable horror to our heroine, who had watched the proceedings, and listened to the conversation of the assassins with the most breathless attention; and a shuddering seized upon her frame, which she found it impossible to resist. It would, however, be useless to attempt to describe the relief she felt when she heard the observations of the first ruffian, by which he was persuaded from entering the place in which she was concealed; but every moment that they prolonged their stay increased her terror and anxiety, for fear that her infant should awake, and, crying, betray them.

After having untied the mouth of the sack, they drew it nearer to the edge of the grave they had been digging, and turned out the body of a stout, but aged man, whose long grey locks were matted together with large clots of blood that had issued from several deep wounds in the scull. Horror enchained all the faculties of Rosabelle, and with distended eyelids, she fixed her straining eye-balls upon the dreadful spectacle, and pressed her babe with a sensation of the most terrible and indescribable apprehension to her breast. Her blood seemed turned to ice, and her heart appeared almost to cease its pulsation. Should the wretches find out that she was there concealed, and had been watching them, and overheard the acknowledgment of their dreadful crime, the death of herself and her infant would be certain to follow. And yet, in a moment, the thought darted across her brain, and with the most distracting feelings, did she reflect upon; why should she, guilty, miserable wretch that she was, wish to cling to life? What had she to expect but perpetual misery, and the weight of a parent's curse to rest upon her head? Yet, there is a tenacity of meeting death, and especially in so awful a manner,—a terrible dread of being suddenly ushered into the presence of that Almighty Judge, whom, our conscience tells us, we have offended,—which impresses itself upon the minds of some persons, that even under the most wretched circumstances, and in the most appalling situations, they cannot contemplate it with any other sentiment than one of the greatest awe and consternation. And thus it was with our heroine; she felt herself too miserable a sinner to meet the presence of her Maker, and wished for life for the sake of her child, with the hope of again seeing the parent she had so much injured, and to make all the atonement in her power for the offence of which she had been guilty.

These reflections passed rapidly in the mind of Rosabelle, as she watched, in a state of the most breathless suspense, the actions of the murderers, as they, in the most callous manner, tossed the body of their wretched victim into the grave they had dug for its reception, and commenced filling it up, occupying the interval, during the disgusting scene, with the most ribald conversation, which smote the heart of our heroine with horror as she listened to it.

"There," exclaimed Gordon, as he placed the last spadefull of earth into the grave of their murdered victim, "that job's finished, and a long and sound rest to the old grazier. This business has been performed throughout in a tradesman-like manner, and no suspicion can ever attach itself to us."

"Suspicion!" reiterated the other, with a laugh, "oh no, we might almost as well imagine that somebody had been watching us all this time in this lonely place, as to suppose that even the shadow of an idea of we being the murderers of the old man could attach itself to us."

"Ah!" exclaimed Gordon, "your observations have started an idea in my mind, and, had you attended to my suggestion in the first instance, we should have been secured from any danger of the sort."

"What mean you?"

"What mean I? why, that door, which, as I before observed, no doubt, communicates with some other part of the outhouse, and it is not at all unlikely that some weary traveller may have taken up his lodging there, or sought shelter from the storm, and been listening to our discourse all this time. Should such be the case, we shall not go far without falling into the hands of the traps, depend upon it. I will examine the place."

"Bah! why, you are growing worse than a child, Gordon," said the miscreant's companion. "I never heard such improbable ideas to strike a fellow in all my life Do you think any person could have been watching us all this time without betraying some signs of terror?"

"You may laugh at me if you like, Jack," returned Gordon, "but I am generally pretty correct in what I fancy, and I don't think I shall be far out in this instance. Here goes to see."

We must fail were we to make any attempt to pourtray the feelings of our heroine, as the ruffian, Gordon, approached the door, and tried it. Such was the violence of her agitation, that cold drops of perspiration stood upon her forehead, and it was only by a complete miracle that she could prevent herself from screaming. It was, also, a most fortunate thing that her child slept so soundly, or otherwise their fate must have been speedily determined. Gordon tried hard to push the door open, and swore when he found the obstruction; and at that moment, when Rosabelle had nearly given herself up for lost, some noise on the outside of the building arrested the attention of both the villains, and Gordon immediately quitted the door, much to the relief of our heroine.

"Hist!" muttered Jack, in cautious tones, "did you not hear a noise outside, Gordon?"

"I fancied I did," was the reply.

"Extinguish the light," commanded the other, "and I will reconnoitre."

Gordon immediately did as his companion directed him, and Jack cautiously opened the door and looked out. As he did so, Rosabelle could hear that the storm had increased in violence, and immediately afterwards she heard the voice of Jack observing—

"Oh, the coast is quite clear, as far as I can see, and, therefore, it could only have been fancy; but, notwithstanding, Gordon, I do not see the policy of remaining here. We had much better, on the contrary, make our escape as speedily as possible, while we have the opportunity; for, should we be discovered here, and the fresh earth upon the new made grave, we should be bowled out to a dead certainty. It's madness to suppose that anybody but ourselves have been here during the time we have been performing the funeral obsequies for the old man. Come, come, no more of this foolery, but travel's the word."

And "travel" was not only the word, but the action of the wretches, much to the relief of our heroine, who had almost given her mind to despair; and after a short time had elapsed since they had quitted the place, and Rosabelle, by attentive listening, had assured herself that they were not near the spot, first, with eyes brimful of tears, and clasping her unconscious child, with all the fervour of maternal fondness to her breast, having returned her thanks to Providence for her deliverance from that death which she at one time imagined was inevitable, she removed the rubbish which she had piled against the door, and left the place in which she had been concealed.

What an inexpressible feeling of terror smote her breast, when she passed the grave of the murdered man!—Her limbs trembled so violently that it is surprising how she was enabled to support herself, and she mentally offered up an involuntary prayer for the repose of his soul, and that his barbarous assassins might be brought to punishment for their inhuman violation of the laws. It was a second of two before she ventured to quit the place; but having listened at the door, which the ruffians had closed after them, and hearing no other sounds than those caused by the fury of the storm, she ventured to open it and look forth. The scene was awful enough, as a pitchy darkness obscured all around, save when, at intervals, the flashes of lightning succeeded the deafening thunder-peals. The rain also descended rapidly, and all around presented a scene of the most appalling horror. But awful as it was, to Rosabelle it presented not half the terrors of the old out-house, which now contained the mangled remains of the poor old man, whom the monsters, Gordon and Jack, had murdered; and could she have been convinced that by so doing she would have been restored to all her former state of innocence and happiness; had she been certain that her reward would have been the forgiveness of her father, and his restoration to peace, she was confident that she could not have undertaken to remain there another half hour. An idea also struck her immediately on the departure of the assassins, and that was to make her way with all possible dispatch to the nearest town, which was the one to which she was going, and, giving notice of what she had seen, enable them to go in immediate pursuit of the perpetrators of this dreadful crime.

Defending her still sleeping infant, as well as she was able, from the fury of the storm, by wrapping him in her cloak, and covering that with the skirt of her gown, totally regardless of herself, our heroine issued forth, and emerged into a wood which was not very extensive, and only a short distance from the place of her destination. She had not, however, proceeded far, when a strange noise, like the clanking of fetters, smote her ears, and by the lurid glare of the lightning, she beheld what she imagined to be the figure of a man approaching along one of the avenues. She was transfixed to the spot with alarm, and almost immediately afterwards, the man, who seemed to have beheld her at the same instant that she had seen him, instantaneously vanished from her view, as if he was equally as frightened at the sight of her, as she had been at the sight of him. But another idea occurred to her, and that was, that it was not a man at all, but either the clanking of a gibbet, which she knew stood not far from that place, or some animal that was grazing on the spot. She, in consequence, became less daunted, and went on her way. Not many yards, however, of her course had she pursued, when she again heard the clanking of what she imagined to be a chain, and directly afterwards once more beheld the form which she had thought she had perceived before, coming towards her. Suddenly it paused, and our heroine paused also, and with a feeling of extreme terror, which the circumstance was very well calculated to excite, she watched it with breathless attention, and was unable to move either one way or the other. Suddenly, however, her courage revived.

"I will not give way to this alarm," she observed, "which, after all, may be perfectly groundless. It is as likely as not, that he may be some unfortunate, shelterless wanderer, like myself, who would not attempt to harm me. I will, at all events, venture up to him, and trust to Providence for the result."

She did as she said, and having advanced to within a few paces of him, she once more, to her extreme alarm, heard the clanking of the chain, and shrunk back, as the impression darted upon her mind, that this was some poor unhappy wretch who had escaped from prison. As well as the vivid flashes of lightning would at intervals permit her to discern, she saw that the man was attired in a dark, rude suit; his head and neck were bare, his beard neglected, his hair matted and dirty, and his whiskers suffered to grow in such wild exuberance, that it was utterly impossible to recognise him. One stocking had fallen, exposing his naked leg, and from his waist hung a heavy chain, which dragged upon the ground.

"It is some guilty wretch escaped from justice," she gasped forth; "oh, save me, Heaven; or myself and boy may fall victims to his cruelty."

At this moment the man advanced nearer towards her, and as he did so, judging from the wildness of his demeanour, Rosabelle altered the opinion she had previously formed, and believed him to be some unfortunate maniac who had contrived to elude the vigilance of his keeper. In this she was the more confirmed by the wildness and ludicrousness of his antics, as he come towards her; and fearful that he might inflict some injury upon herself and child, she tried to avoid him. The nearer he came, the more hopeless did the chance of passing him appear to be, and she heard him talking in a strange manner to himself, and at intervals, laughing in tones of wildness that made the woods re-echo again. Then he looked round quickly, as though he heard some one whom he had cause to fear approaching, and paused, looking intently into the deep obscurity beyond.

"Ho—ho—ho!" laughed the maniac, for such it appeared now that he undoubtedly was: "so they thought to catch me!—Ha—ha—ha!—Fools! slaves! villains!—But I have broken away from their dungeons! I have escaped from them—I am triumphant!—Ha—ha—ha—ha!"

Rosabelle shuddered, and a more powerful feeling than that of pity shot through her heart. She could not speak; and even had death been the consequence of the same, nothing could have empowered her at that moment to move. Directly afterwards, the maniac seemed to fancy that some persons were moving near the spot, for he started, and then in the same hollow tones exclaimed—

"Ha, I see them ; there they are, but they do not see me. Softly, softly, they pass me; they tread the thicket; six sturdy rogues; I'll hide me in yon cowslip; ha! they are gone; I'm free, I'm safe again; where is my horse? I'll live no more in England."

"Poor unhappy wretch," mentally ejaculated Rosabelle.

"No, no," continued the man, "I'll to Siberia; it's snows, less chaste than she, will better shroud my child than these false flakes which melt as they surround me, like the world, and leave me cold and naked. Ha! a spy," he added, as his eye encountered Rosabelle. "Wretch, thou shalt perish; thus I strike."

As the maniac thus spoke, he seized the broken branch of a tree, and wielding it in the air, was in the act of felling her to the earth, when she exclaimed in frantic accents,—

"Oh, spare me! spare me!"

"A woman!" cried the lunatic, "and in my power!" He let fall the branch of the tree as he spoke, and after gazing at our frightened heroine for a second or two, with intense earnestness, "'tis well, or I would crush thee. Answer me; whither have they gone? What course have they taken? The wretches!—the thieves!—the villains! But I was too cunning for them! Ha! ha! ha! I outwitted them. I escaped them! Ha! what noise was that? It sounded like the cry of a child!"

As the maniac thus spoke, the loudness of his tones and the clanking of his heavy chain, awoke Rosabelle's infant, and which began to scream; he fixed upon it such a look of wildness, that our heroine shrunk back in the most terrible consternation, and in accents of fear and supplication, she thus ejaculated—

"My child! oh, do not harm my child!"

"A child!" reiterated the maniac, fiercely, and once more seizing the branch of a tree, advancing closer to Rosabelle, and grasping her arm with great strength; "a child!—there is hatred and horror in the name. Murder it—murder it, I say. Ah! dost thou hesitate? Give it then to me, and I will place my fingers in its throat! It will be a goodly deed, and thou shouldst thank me for it. They are only fools that do not detest children: if we place our affections upon them do they not abandon us? If we place our reliance in them do they not deceive us? Yes, yes—they do, they do. Give me the child and let me kill it."

At this moment it would be utterly impossible to do adequate justice to the feelings of the distracted Rosabelle; for she perceived the maniac's eyes glowing with the utmost expression of ferocity, and his whole demeanour was sufficient to inspire the most resolute with consternation. As the unfortunate man wielded the branch of the tree in the air, she shrieked, and raised her hand to avert the impending blow, then, in piteous accents, she implored his mercy. She appealed to the feelings of one who understood her not. Still did the child, who had been terrified at the sight of the maniac, scream loudly, and all the efforts of his nearly-frantic mother to quiet it were unavailing. And in that dread moment, when the death of her little innocent offspring seemed inevitable, for she had not strength to cope with that of the man, our heroine experienced more soul-harassing anguish than she ever remembered to have suffered before, even in her most trying moments. But just at this critical juncture, when all hope seemed at an end, a sudden noise caused by the wind, startled the maniac, and releasing the arm of Rosabelle, he looked quickly around him, and fled with the utmost precipitation into the wood.

Pressing her infant closer to her bosom, Rosabelle would now have retreated from the spot, and the danger she might be placed in by the unhappy maniac, but some secret and indefinite power seemed to rivet her to the place, and rendered her incapable of moving. There was something too in the voice of the unfortunate being, which forced its way to her heart, and inspired it with a feeling for which she was totally at a loss to account. While she thus stood, she once more heard the clanking of the unfortunate man's chain, and saw him returning hastily; and as he advanced towards her he laughed long and loud. He came close up to her, and placing his hand gently on her arm, fixed his wild eye on her face, and cried—

"Again I, have eluded them;—fools, idiots, slaves, villains! Ha, ha, ha! They thought to take me ;—I. the king of the moon, and emperor of the stars! But I strode across the lightnings flash, and escaped them. Hast thou got enemies—wretches thou woulds't avoid? No, no, no, thou art a woman, and they never abandon anything but their too-fond and doating fathers. Ah! what is that you have got in your arms?"

"Oh, God, my poor boy! Mercy! mercy!—spare my child!" exclaimed Rosabelle, and she pressed the infant still closer to her bosom, and endeavoured to shield it from the gaze of the maniac.

"A child!" he cried, in a terrible voice, grasping the arm of our heroine more vehemently. "Ah! cast it from thee, and trample it in the earth, I tell thee; it is an adder nurturing in thy bosom but to poison it. Oh, once I had so sweet a child myself, but she is no more—she is in the cold grave; but the liars—the wretches, they abandoned me—that she deserted her poor father for a lover. 'Twas false as hell!—she died. Oh, she was too kind, too fond, too virtuous to desert the parent who doated on her. Besides, did I not see her buried? Fiends—liars, to invent so base a falsehood to calumniate one so fair, so pure, and to torture the soul of the poor old man. Can you keep a secret?—I have such a one to impart to you, but be sure you do not tell it to any one. I made my escape from their clutches last night. I burst through my prison walls, and I am now seeking for a spot where repose the remains of my poor child. Come, come, if you like you shall accompany me. Hush—hush, tread softly, lest you crush the sweet flowers that blossom o'er her grave. This way—this way—I will guide you to it."

"Gracious God—what is it I forebode?" cried Rosabelle, in a voice of horror, as she looked closer into the countenance of the maniac; "what painful feeling is it that penetrates to my heart? It is—it must be he. I cannot bear this torture—this suspense; and yet the darkness that prevails——"

"At this moment a vivid flash of lightning darted over their heads and rendered the features of the unfortunate man perfectly visible, and Rosabelle screamed aloud, and threw herself into his arms, exclaiming—

"Great Heaven! my conjectures are too well confirmed ;—it is—it is he! Father;—dear dear father! Oh horror!"

The wretched Montalbert (for he it certainly was) laughed idiotically, and played like a child with the straw which he had twined around his girdle. The storm in the mean time had increased, and the scene altogether, and at that dismal hour, was a most appalling one.

"Ha, father!" at length said Montalbert; "no, no, I am not a father now—the name is mockery to my ears. But I was a parent once ;—yes, I had a daughter: oh, she was such a beauteous girl! But she abandoned me—she left me—went off with the rank fiend, seduction. Wouldst thou believe it, when I loved her so fondly, I would have shed the last drop of my heart's blood for her? But she left two precious comforter's behind—Poverty and Despair; and I have daily feasted with both since then.—Ha, ha, ha!"

"Horror! horror!" groaned the distracted Rosabelle; "even thy flinty heart, Beresford, couldst thou behold this, would——"

"What!" cried Montalbert, fiercely, and his eyes gleamed like two balls of fire. "Beresford! monster! miscreant! seducer! robber! Where is he? Give him to mine eyes! I have two daggers, and they shall drink his blood! Revenge hath been with me, and she hath promised to turn my grasp to iron when I meet him. Give me my daughter, monster! I will have no struggling, slave! My knee is on thy breast. Down, down, and let me tread thy life out! There, wretch, there; below the surface of the earth I've crushed thee, and I can smile again! Ha! ha! ha!"

"Alas! alas! what a sight is this!" sobbed Rosabelle, weeping bitterly; and taking her father's hand, she pressed it in a wild paroxism of agony to her lips; "can a whole life of tears wash out the deep remembrance of this hour?"

Montalbert seemed to be again aroused by her words; and looking earnestly in her face, he passed his fingers through her tresses, and in accents that sunk deep into the wretched girl's soul, he said—

"Ah! what is this? There are tears upon thy hand! You are weeping ;—poor girl! poor girl! But tears are now strangers to me, I have not cried for such a while—never since the time when they bore my child to her final resting place. For she is in the grave; is she not? Come, come, come, you will not leave me, will you?"

"Oh, never! never! death alone shall again separate us," replied our heroine.

"Death!" reiterated Montalbert, passing his hand across his forehead, as if seeking to bring something to his recollection; "death! Oh, yes, I remember now ;—my child is dead, and we will hasten to the spot beneath which she reposes; the snow has hidden it, but we shall find it soon. I say that snow's less pure, less fair, less cold than her dear bosom: 'tis a brave winding sheet—cold! cold; cold! We shall find it soon—a plain stone only, and a little dust. Ah! those snow flakes—see! they mock at these grey hairs; they say my child deserted me, and every other for her must die!—Prepare!"

With these words, Montalbert spurned her fiercely from him, and she sunk on her knees, while he once more raised the branch of the tree in the air, and prepared to strike his defenceless daughter.

"Oh, father, spare me!—help! help! for mercy's sake!" screamed Rosabelle, and springing on to her feet, having placed her child on the stump of a tree close by, with desperate strength occasioned by the horrors of her situation, she seized his arm, and endeavoured to avert the maniac's deadly purpose. A violent struggle ensued, but another moment and Montalbert must have overcome her, when she heard the voices of men close at hand, and in an instant he let fall the branch of the tree, and throwing himself fearfully into her arms, vehemently supplicated her not to let the men take him away.

"Ha! we have caught you, have we?" said one of them. "Come along." "Oh, hide me! hide me!" implored the Maniac Father, clinging still closer to Rosabelle. "If you are men," exclaimed Rosabelle, in accents of intense agony—"if there is one spark of humanity in your breasts, do not take this wretched unfortunate man from me! —I am his daughter, and you need not fear to leave him in my care. Thus on my knees——" "Oh, you are his daughter, are you?" said one of the men; "but suppose you are, it is not in your power to assist him, I dare say, and you should think yourself lucky that you will not be troubled to look after him." "Oh, do not! do not let them tear me from you!" said Montalbert, aside to Rosabelle, and looking imploringly in her face. "So this is your father, young woman, is it?" said the keeper; "you are the daughter, then, I suppose, that brought him to this pass? Ay, ay

you may well weep, but your tears come a little too late, my fine lady; come, boys, bring him along." "You shall not tear him from me," frantically ejaculated Rosabelle, clinging to him desperately; "I have deserted, left him once, but now I'll die ere I resign him." "Stand off!" exclaimed Montalbert, bursting from their hold —"stand off!—the first who stirs, my bolts shall lay him lifeless!—Oh, villains! murderers! Off! off! off!" "Spare him for mercy's sake!" implored Rosabelle, with clasped hands; "he is my father—I alone can cure him; leave him with me, and I will ever bless you!" "Oh, yes," returned the keeper; "that would be a pretty joke, truly; hows'ver, I don't think it will be long first before you are with him, or in the same prison with him; for I'm blest if I don't think you are almost as mad as he is—poor devil! Come, lads, drag him along."

CHAPTER VII.

THE WEDDING.—THE INTERRUPTION.

THE day before these circumstances took place, Meriel was anxiously waiting in her neat and clean little cottage parlour, the arrival of her faithful lover, honest Gilbert Batchelor, whom, we believe, we have before introduced to the reader as a husbandman, working and living upon the estate of the unfortunate Mr. Montalbert. "Well I wonder whether Gilbert will succeed this time," said Meriel, "and whether we shall be married at last, or not? Dear me! dear me! so many disappointments!—It quite tries one's patience." She hastened to the door, and opening it Gilbert entered joyfully, and kissing Meriel affectionately, he exclaimed—"Huzza! Meriel, lass, I ha' gotten the money! squire ha' kept his word; so we shall be married now at all events. Squire Rattleton be going to be married to-morrow, so the parson may make one job on it." "So he may, Gilbert," observed Meriel, "but, I say, we'll be married quite private like, Gilbert,

for neighbours have been so often made fools of by us before, that we should only be making ourselves fools by asking them again." "True, Meriel," said her lover, "we'll get it done when Miss Emily's is all over; and instead of asking neighbours to wedding, ecod, we'll invite them all to our first christening; sure not to disappoint them then. Oh, here comes Miss Emily." Emily Goodman entered as Gilbert spoke, and greeted her humble friends with that kindness and familiarity for which she was so remarkable. She looked more lovely than ever, and Meriel and Gilbert greeted her with a profusion of courtesies and bows. "Good day, Gilbert," said Emily; "have you been fortunate enough to obtain any tidings of the unhappy Rosabelle?" "No, my lady," answered Gilbert, "but she be still living in cog, I believe they do call it." "In cog, Gilbert?" returned Meriel; "law, no they be living in a square." "Ill-starred, but still beloved girl," said Emily, "I cannot refrain from being anxious for thy welfare. How different is thy fate from what our youthful fancy pictured! you were to be bridemaid to your Emily, and she was to have been the same to you. Oh, that she could be! What tears it still might save. Gilbert, Meriel, you will visit the hall to-morrow evening; there is to be a ball and you can be partners."

"Thank you, Miss," said Gilbert, bowing; "we do mean to get parson to cast off too couple instead of one, and make Meriel and I partners for life."

"Married!" ejaculated Emily.

"Yes, my lady, only we don't mean to tell neighbours of it till it be all done, because we ha' been so often disappointed like, they wouldn't believe us as it were."

"No, Miss," remarked Meriel, courtesying; "but as winter be coming on, and nights be getting lonely, Gilbert and I are going to get married, just for company, if you please; but do'ee just walk into the next room and refresh yourself before you go; there be some nice home-made bread and some clouted cream, and a famous fire. Run, Gilbert, into the garden, and get some fresh logs, and I'll go and get everything ready while you be gone."

Thus speaking, the kind-hearted but simple Meriel vanished.

"Ay, that I will, lass," observed Gilbert, "how prattily we do agree; surely it were quite a shame we should ever be separated, that it were."

Gilbert then hastened to obey the instructions of Meriel, and Emily was left to herself.

"Hospitable creatures!" she soliliquised, "I must watch over their fortunes, if only for thy dear sake, my Rosabelle. Blest with the approving sanction of my father, to-morrow weds me, 'midst every luxury, to the husband of my choice; while thou, my Rosabelle, whose prospects once were brighter far than mine, thou art an exile from society, thy friends, thy reputation lost! thy father in a mad-house; thy fortune gone; thy fair hopes blighted in the world for ever! But still, the victim of an artful villain—thou'st yet one bosom that will defend and succour thee: one heart that loves thee for thyself alone!"

She was interrupted by Meriel re-entering, and informing her that she had prepared the humble repast, and Emily thanking her, retired into the little back parlour.

The following day Emily Goodman and Mr. Rattleton were united in the indissoluble bonds of matrimony, and never was a day celebrated with more festivity. Old and young, rich and poor, were alike invited to share in the mirthful scene, and the mansion and grounds of Mr. Goodman were thronged with delighted guests. There was everything provided that the heart could wish for, and not a sorrowful countenance could be seen among the vast assembly, and the day passed away, and the night set in with the utmost gaity, notwithstanding the storm that had arisen, put a stop to the festivities in the gardens. The hall was fitted up for a ball, and brilliantly illuminated, and the harmonious tones of the music, were gracefully and gaily accompanied by many feet.

Rattleton, his new-made bride, and her amiable father, were seated together at the upper end of the hall, and the joy of the latter was never more powerfully evinced than it was on this auspicious occasion.

"Rattleton, Emily," he ejaculated, "a father's blessing hallow your sacred nuptials. Now, then, for merriment."

"Ay, now for the fiddlers," said the bridegroom in a tone of hilarity; "if a man can't be merry on his wedding day it's very hard: Emily, my love, you look grave—I hope you don't repent your bargain?"

"My dear, dear Rattleton," said Emily, looking affectionately in his face, "I was reflecting upon poor Rosabelle; and——"

"My darling Emily," ejaculated her husband, "that thus e'en in the moment of rapture, can gem the goblet of joy with a tear of pity for the woes of others. But we must drive away these thoughts, that, while they do honour to the head and heart, prey too deeply on the soul. Come, gentlemen, strike up; my friends will sing a little epithalamium, sir, they have kindly composed for the occasion."

Mr. Goodman expressed his thanks in the most fervent terms, and then a few friends of the bride-groom sang the following words; most of the company joining in the chorus—

"If on earth there's one spot more endear'd than
    another,
If in life there's one moment more gay than the
    rest,
'Tis the home of two hearts newly joined to each
    other,
'Tis the moment we first meet to heighten their
    zest.

'Tis the home and the moment in which we're now
    moving,
And may he who would waken with riot's rude
    breath
The peace of two hearts so beloved and so lov-
    ing,
Ne'er slumber in rest till he slumber in death.

CHORUS.

Hail, Emily, hail! our hearts echo our voices.
    Love give but the down of his dust to thy
    breast;
And hail to the youth, who the youth of thy choice
    is,
    Long, long, may you live in love, rapture, and
    rest!"

"Thank ye, thank ye, gentlemen," ejaculated Rattleton, fervently. Hearts as light as our's will communicate some portion of their quality to the heels; so, what say you gentlemen, to a dance?"

"Bravo! bravo! a dance! a dance!" cried twenty different voices.

"Clear the room, then," said the merry Rattleton, preparing for action; "and do you, musicians, as you look for full skins of Burgundy and bridecake, move your elbows to some tune. Emily my love, as you're my partner for life, let some one else have you for a partner in the dance, while I—don't be jealous—choose out the prettiest girl I can find as a substitute."

Emily smiled sweetly upon her volatile husband, and the dance commenced.

Meriel and Gilbert Bachelor were also present, but they did not look near so cheerful as they might have been expected to do on so joyful an occasion.

"Ecod, Meriel," said Gilbert, when he overheard the observations of Rattleton; "but nobody else shall have you for a partner besides Gilbert Batchelor; for, though parson hadn't time to marry us to-day, and we were disappointed for the ninety-ninth time, he ha' promised to do it for us to-morrow, you know."

"I wish he'd ha' done it to-day, though, Gilbert," said Meriel.

"Father," asked Rattleton, after the first dance was over, "you'll make one?"

"Ay," said Goodman, with a smile, "though I have seen half a century, on this joyful occasion, I'll forget my gout and my years, and trip it away as nimbly as the best of you. It is a bleak night without; God help the poor wretches who have to encounter the pitiless peltings of the storm. Have you given orders that all shall be open house?"

"I have, sir," replied Rattleton.

"We have done our duty, then," said Mr. Goodman, "and may make merry."

"Ay, ay, lead off!" said Rattleton, and once more the happy company moved cheerfully through the mazy windings of the dance; but, suddenly, they were all startled and aroused by hearing a loud shriek, which proceeded from without; the next moment the folding doors were thrown back on their hinges, and Rosabelle with ghastly countenance, dishevelled hair, and her child in her arms, rushed wildly into the hall amidst the whole of the astonished guests.

"As you are christians—as you are human beings," supplicated the unfortunate girl, "succour and save my child!—He dies! he dies! but for your aid! Oh, pardon a wretched mother's darling!"

Rosabelle had wandered to the hall, unconscious at the time by whom it was inhabited, or the scene that was going forward; but when she recognized those who had formerly been her dearest friends, she covered her face with her hands, and groaned aloud with the intensity of her anguish.

"Gracious powers!" ejaculated Emily, "Rosabelle Montalbert!"

"The Lady Rosabelle!" cried Meriel and Gilbert, with equal astonishment.

"Emily!—Meriel!" screamed Rosabelle; "hour of unutterable shame and agony!—Cover me, earth—but save, oh, save my child!"

She could say no more, but overcome by the power of her emotions, she had but time to place her infant in the arms of Meriel, ere she sunk insensible on the earth.

"Lost! lost! unhappy woman!" cried Mr. Goodman; "but bear her to a chamber, and let everything be administered that may tend to her recovery; that accomplished, she must leave this house: I cannot give shelter to abandoned women and unnatural children!"

"Oh, my father," exclaimed Emily, bursting into tears.

"No more, Emily," interrupted her father, resolutely, "I will not listen to anything in excuse of her conduct: my orders must be obeyed."

With these words, Mr. Goodman walked away, and the sports were resumed, although the circumstance served to depress the spirits of most of the guests greatly. Rosabelle was conveyed to a chamber, whither Emily would willingly have followed if her father would have suffered her, and her gentle heart was distracted with grief at the melancholy manner in which she had encountered that unfortunate woman she had never expected to behold again.

CHAPTER VIII.

THE COTTAGE.—THE REQUEST.—THE MAD-HOUSE.

WHEN Rosabelle recovered her senses, she found herself in Meriel's cottage, and that goodhearted girl leaning affectionately over her. Rosabelle hid her face, overcome with shame and confusion; but Meriel, in her usual manner, but to the best of her abilities, endeavoured to comfort her.

"Nay, my dear young lady," she said, "pray do not give way to this violent grief: recollect that, although you have sinned, as you are now, I am sure, sincerely penitent, Heaven will, no doubt, pardon you for——"

"Pardon! pardon for a wretch like me!" interrupted Rosabelle, with a look of despair, and a groan of mental anguish. "Forgiveness for she who hath destroyed the reason of her fond and doating father? Oh, no—no! there is no hope—there is no hope!"

"Oh! say not so, miss," said Meriel: "there is hope for the greatest o' sinners—at least, so I have heard the parson say, if they only endeavour to make 'tonement for the offences they have committed, and why not, then, for you? But no doubt you take it more to heart, since your visit to Mr. Goodman's; and, to be sure, his treatment was very harsh and severe, and such as I never expected from him, seeing that he is such a kind and benevolent gentleman."

"Mr. Goodman acted perfectly right, Meriel," said our heroine. "Fallen and degraded as I am, I must not expect the virtuous and irreproachable to look upon me with anything but disgust and detestation."

Meriel made no reply to this; and having desired her, if she felt able, to join her at the mornings repast, she took her leave, and descended down stairs.

She had not been below many minutes when Gilbert Batchelor made his appearance with a most rueful expression of countenance.

"A very pretty thing this is, Meriel," he observed, taking a seat; "here am I, disappointed of being married again, and by you, too, Meriel. Dang it, but this be worse than all: it be more than any man can bear!"

"My dear Gilbert," answered Meriel, "place yourself in my situation: is not our dear young lady in trouble, and perhaps in want too? Do I not owe all I have to her? and can I think of marrying when my means and services may be necessary for the comfort and support of her and her dear baby? Alas! the day that ever I should live to see the Lady Rosabelle in want of that help she was always so ready to bestow on others!"

"It be very true, Meriel," returned Gilbert, dolefully, "and yet it be very provoking for all that. Thee hast a kind heart, that I mun say for thee, lass; and when I do get thee, thou'lt make a main good wife; but I be such a desperate long while about it, that I begin almost to despair. But hang faint heart: the Lady Rosabelle may find friends, recover her father's property, and, who knows, be a better friend to us by-and-by than ever."

"Hush, hush!" said Meriel; "she is coming this way. I was in hopes, after the dreadful fatigues of yesterday, she would have slept some hours. How pale she is to what we once beheld her: yet still she looks both lovely and a lady!"

At this moment Rosabelle, who had thrown by her own clothes, and appeared in a humble dress belonging to Meriel, entered the room.

"Oh, my dear young lady," said Meriel, handing her a chair, "I did not think you would rise so early. Was anything amiss? Things be very humble, to be sure, but they be heartily at your service—ben't they, Gilbert?"

"Yes, that they be, Meriel," replied Gilbert, with sincerity. "Dear heart!" he added, aside, "how sad she do look, surely; it do quite cut my heart to see her, like. Be there anything, Madam Montalbert, that I can do for you? I'll go to the end of the world to serve you; ay, and so will Meriel too. Won't you, Meriel?"

"Yes, that I will, Gilbert," answered Meriel.

"Kind, generous creatures; such behaviour to one so lost and fallen is more than I had a right to expect," exclaimed our heroine, energetically—"alas! what return can I ever make for such unexampled kindness? Meriel, you ask me why I arose so early, but of what use was it my remaining in bed when I could not sleep!—Sleep has not fallen upon my eye-lids all the night, or at least, since that state of insensibility into which I fell on my visit to the hall of Mr. Goodman. Sleep? how can a wretch like I am expect to sleep; my mind racked as it is by a thousand images of horror! my unhappy father! that dreadful recontre with the friends of my youth! Every one's horror at my presence! Mr. Goodman's reproachful looks! Only my Emily's pity, and your kindness to support me! But now to my first task! Ah! who's there?"

It was a knock at the cottage door, and on Me

riel opening it, a servant entered, in the livery of Mr. Goodman, and having said, "A letter for Miss Montalbert; there is no answer," he immediately departed.

Rosabelle took the letter with the most indescribable astonishment.

"A letter, and for me!" she cried—"who writes to one like me?—Ah! what do I see?—My Emily's hand!"

With a trembling hand she opened it.

"Ah! do my eyes not deceive me? An enclosure! and for twenty guineas! Merciful Providence! Writing too, with blotted tears. 'For my still beloved Rosabelle.' Generous, generous girl! I am not then quite forsaken!—Eternal blessings on her, for this deed!—This will at least prevent my being a burden on your kindness. I am a poor guilty creature, nor would I venture to solicit your kindness so far as I have done had I not already suffered severely for the crime I have committed, and come to the resolution to spend the rest of my days in compunction and by honest industry."

"Oh, Miss Rosabelle, it cuts me to the heart to hear you talk in this manner," said Meriel; "not venture to solicit my kindness? nothing that I may do, can be sufficient to repay the acts of kindness you have bestowed upon me."

"Meriel, understand me rightly," said Rosabelle, with mournful earnestness, "that woman who hath strayed from the path of rectitude and virtue, whatever her station in society may be, has no right to presume to intrude herself on the society of those whose morals are uncorrupted, and whose virtues are unsullied, let them be in ever such a humble grade of life; and so firmly am I convinced of the truth of these observations, that nothing, only the thought of having one friend who would commiserate my misfortunes and my sufferings, could induce me to seek your kindness, or the shelter of your happy, but humble dwelling. I hope, however, by honest labour, soon to be able to support myself and child; and I trust that, as my repentance is sincere, so will Heaven deign to pardon me. Mr. Goodman, I believe, is one of the governors of the asylum where my poor father is, and to him I am this day going to——"

Rosabelle paused, for the power of her feelings choked her utterance.

"The asylum raised by the bounty of your father, Miss," said Meriel; "Mr. Goodman is so strict in his notions of propriety, that he may treat you harshly, he may——"

"And why should I shrink from such treatment, if he does?" demanded our heroine, with a deep sigh. "Have I not deserved humiliation? oh, yes; and, therefore, let me not shudder to meet it. It is but a just punishment for my offences. But Mr. Goodman has a humane heart; his daughter Emily, too, was once my dearest friend, and she, I know, will not suffer him to trample on the fallen. I can meet with success in the plan I have concocted only by humbling myself."

"What plan, my dear lady?" asked Meriel.

"You, probably, would disapprove of it, Meriel, were I to make you acquainted with it," answered Rosabelle. "But I will tell you all on my return; farewell awhile, watch over my boy, and should I die—which may be but too soon—be—be a mother to him.

"Ay, that I will," said Meriel, fervently: "but cheer up, dear lady, all may yet be well, and we may all soon again be happy. Heaven bless you."

"Farewell! farewell!" cried our heroine, with deep emotion; and having hastily finished the repast, she put on her cloak and bonnet, and quitted the cottage.

"Dang it, how queer she ha' made my eyes," said honest Gilbert Batchelor: "they be just for all the world like as if I had been chopping onions, they be so full o' water."

"And so be mine, I'm sure, Gilbert," said Meriel, crying.

"But, I say, Meriel," said Gilbert; "we shall be married after all; you see Miss Rosabelle do find friends. Twenty guineas already; she'll get back some of her father's money, I dare say, and be as rich as ever she was: poor soul, all went to rack and ruin after she left. But she'll be happy after all, and so shall we, when we do get married."

"Yes," returned Meriel, "so we shall, Gilbert."

With a heavy heart, poor Rosabelle bent her footsteps towards the town, and as she proceeded, every object she encountered recalled to her memory, in vivid colours, some painful reminiscence of the past. When last she was a rambler among these scenes, she was a happy, innocent girl; without a care to haunt her mind; surrounded by every enjoyment, and blest with the love of a most affectionate father, whose only prop and source of earthly happiness she was. Now, alas! how dreadfully changed her circumstances; she shuddered with horror when her memory reverted to it. She was now a poor, guilty, fallen wretch, scouted and despised, scouted and detested, by those who had formerly courted her friendship, and felt honoured by her smiles. That father, too—he, the fond, the doating father—the benefactor of the poor, the honoured of the rich—was now a wretched maniac, the inmate of that asylum his bounty had been the means of raising; his property destroyed; everything made desolate, ruined!—Bitter, bitter, indeed, were the pangs that shot through her heart, as these reflections flashed upon her brain, and she groaned aloud with mental anguish. As she approached nearer the town, her agony increased, and she was half inclined to return again, and abandon the project she had formed; for how could she again encounter the reproachful glances of Mr. Goodman?—how meet Emily, after the recent act of generosity which she had performed towards her, and which she had so ill-deserved? But she combatted these objections after a while, and proceeded on her way.

And what was the project the poor penitent had formed?—She had determined to ask Mr. Goodman, as one of the governors of the asylum, to exert his influence to procure her a place as servant in that establishment; so that she might be near her unfortunate father; watch his actions—attend to his wants—talk to him, pray with him—and, perhaps, through the mercy of heaven, be enabled to re-illumine the light of reason her guilt had extinguished. This hope it was that sustained her through all the humiliating circumstances with which the scheme was beset, and added speed to her footsteps.

"Yes," she cried, "I will not shrink from my task and its difficulty, and the degrading circumstances attending it will be no more than a fitting punishment for one who hath so deeply sinned."

She had now reached the town, and was hastening towards the house of Mr. Goodman, when suddenly her attention was arrested by a burst of wild and delirious laughter, which seemed to proceed from several voices, and looking up, she beheld herself standing near a large stone building, the iron-barred windows of which denoted it to be a prison.

"Poor things," said a decent looking woman who was standing next to our heroine; "how shocking, how very shocking it is, I think, to hear those laugh who have so much cause to weep. Did you not hear their wild mirth, young woman?"

"Who do you mean, my good woman?" demanded Rosabelle, trembling at the same time that she put the question.

"Why, the poor mad people," replied the woman ; "ah, I see you are a stranger to this neighbourhood, or you would have known that this is the asylum for lunatics. There is a very awful circumstance connected with the history of this place ; the poor gentleman, Mr. Montalbert, who founded it, was the first unfortunate to become an inmate of it. Ah! poor gentleman; he was one of the best of men; a real Christian, whose greatest pleasure was in making the hearts of the poor and afflicted rejoice. He was driven out of his mind by the cruelty of his only daughter, upon whom he doated, but who eloped with an officer in the army, and has never since been heard of."

A deadly faintness came over our heroine, and she could scarcely repress a groan. With much difficulty she walked on, without stopping to exchange another word with the woman.

And now she had arrived at the house of Mr. Goodman, and again a deadly sickness came over her ; her limbs trembled, and pausing for a few minutes, she was obliged to hold by the railings that surrounded the house, to save herself from sinking to the earth.

"My God !" she ejaculated, "with what different feelings to those I now experience, I once used to cross this threshold ! But then I was innocent ;—spotless !"

After a painful struggle with her feelings for a few moments, she once more rallied, and ascending the steps, knocked at the door.

At this time, Emily and her father were in the parlour of the mansion, and they had been having some rather warm words upon the subject of the unfortunate Rosabelle ; Emily maintaining that her father had been too severe, in so abruptly ordering her to be removed from the house.

"Nay, but my dear father," said Emily.

"Don't tell me Emily," returned her father, "I insist that I was right."

At this moment they heard the hall-door opened, and immediately followed the voices of two persons in altercation.

Oh, I implore you," said one, in the accents of a female, "but for a moment will I detain him."

Emily started from her seat, and approached the room-door.

"I know that voice," she exclaimed, "oh, yes, it must be she !—Let me hasten to——"

"Stay where you are, Emily," said Mr. Goodman, stepping between her and the door, and opposing her departure ; "I also know that voice. —Emily, fallen, degraded women, and unnatural children, shall not find an asylum beneath my roof."

"But oh, my dear sir," appealed the affectionate Emily, "will you allow it to shelter for a moment the unfortunate and the penitent ? Father, my dear father, I entreat you to see this poor Rosabelle, and if possible, assist her.'

"To tolerate vice is to encourage it," said her father, "but since you desire it so earnestly, I will see Miss Montalbert directly; and assist her if I can, without any discredit to myself."

"Ah! now you are indeed like my dear father," said Emily, in joyful, grateful accents.

"Retire for awhile, my child," said Mr. Goodman. "I would speak with the poor unfortunate alone."

"Oh, pray be gentle, my dear frther, for my sake," supplicated Emily, as she retired into an adjoining room. Mr. Goodman nodded, then, opening the parlour-door, he said—

"I desire Miss Montalbert to walk in."

Rosabelle, trembling and very pale, was ushered into the room by the servant, who, having set chairs for her and his master, retired.

Mr. Goodman looked steadfastly at our heroine for a second or two, and then said—

"Miss Montalbert, what are your commands ? Young lady, you tremble, you look pale—be more composed—I would not wish you to distress yourself unnecessarily ; the heat is somewhat oppressive—you seem faint—sit in this chair."

"Well, sir, may I tremble, and look pale," said Rosabelle, in faltering accents ; "well, sir, may I feel faint, when every object around me rouses some memory of past joys, lost through my guilt, that come like fiends of vengeance to reproach and madden me. It was in this very house a father was a daughter's all—supplied a doating mother's loss—anticipated every wish, and left no virtuous desire unsatisfied. 'Twas here that daughter fled—plundered, betrayed that father—left him to woe and want—to loneliness and madness : that father was Montalbert—that daughter was the kneeling wretch before you."

Mr. Goodman was evidenly deeply affected, and gazed at her with all his wonted kindness and commiseration.

"Be comforted—be comforted," he said ; "rise, I beseech you, rise. Anchor your woes on hope—life's last, best stay."

"Ah !" ejaculated Rosabelle, while tears of anguish and remorse stole down her cheeks, "dare I do so, and not fear a wreck ? In you, sir, is my haven. I have one hope—one dear, one only hope : never did storm-toss'd mariner cling to rock or mast as I do cling to that ;—in you, sir, it is centred ; refuse me not—restore a sire to reason, and yield repentance prospect of forgiveness !"

"All I can and may do shall not be refused," said Mr. Goodman, compassionately, "but you speak in riddles—what is it that you would ask of me ?

"My father, sir," sobbed Rosabelle ; "my dear, unhappy father. You know how late I met him : he knew me not, but yet seemed calmed at moments by my presence. Could I be with him, I might restore him haply to his reason."

"Miss Montalbert !" exclaimed Mr. Goodman, in accents of astonishment.

"Let me become a servant in the asylum; let me watch o'er him, tend on him, wait on him! My assistance, my presence night——"

The idea appeared to strike Mr. Goodman most forcibly, and he hastily interrupted her.

"It shall be so," he said, "you shall be near your father; you shall watch over and console him. I will rejoin you presently, and take you thither at once ;—the resolutions of repentance shall never be checked by me. Wait here for a few minutes, when I will attend you; and heaven grant your efforts may prove successful."

"Ten thousand, thousand blessings for this !" cried our heroine, sinking on her knees at the feet of Mr. Goodman, and clasping her hands. Mr. Goodman raised her gently, smiled benignantly upon her, and then left the room.

Emily, from the adjoining apartment, had overheard all that had passed between her father and Rosabelle ; and while at the same time she was delighted to hear the merciful tone and resolution Mr. Goodman had come to, she could with the utmost difficulty resist the temptation she felt to rush into the parlour and embrace her once dearest, fondest friend.

"Oh, my father," she observed, when Mr. Goodman entered the room in which she was, after leaving our heroine, "how can I ever sufficiently thank you for your kindness and mercy to the unfortunate, but repentant Rosabelle ? How can I ever enough applaud her affectionate resolution ? Oh, let me hasten to her, to assure her that she has still a heart warm and affectionate which throbs for her welfare ; and one attached being who hopes to see her restored to happiness, her father to reason, and that joyful condition from which, in a moment of weakness, she was the cause of hurling him. Let me go, dear father, and——"

"Hold, child !" desired Mr. Goodman ; "this'

i cannot, I will not allow. It is not until Miss Montalbert has proved by her conduct beyond all doubt that she is sincerely penitent, that I can allow my daughter again to embrace her as a friend. Besides, the interview would but distress her, and unfit her for the trying scene to which she will shortly be exposed. Stay where you are, my love, and rest assured that for the sake of my unfortunate friend Mr. Montalbert, all the assistance I can render her in the furtherance of her designs, shall not be wanting."

Emily very reluctantly bowed with submission to the will of her father, who, having prepared himself for his journey to the asylum, returned to the parlour in which he had left our heroine.

He found her on her knees, with upraised hands and tearful eyes, before a portrait of Montalbert, imploring the mercy and assistance of Omnipotence in the scheme she had formed, and so totally absorbed was she that she did not for a second or two notice his entrance : when, however, she did, she hastily arose, and, apologizing, declared herself ready to attend him.

Mr. Goodman had gazed upon her with unusual interest, and taking her hand, he pressed it in a most vehement manner, plainly testifying the compassion and affection with which he viewed her. Then, without saying another word, he led her from the room, handed her into the carriage which was waiting at the hall door, and they were immediately driven off towards the asylum.

They conversed but little on the way thither, for neither of them were so disposed, being too much engrossed by the various melancholy thoughts that crowded upon them, and they soon reached the asylum. A terrible sensation came over our heroine as she gazed upon its gloomy walls ; and casting her eyes over the doorway, she beheld there inscribed the name of her father as the founder of the institution. She clung involuntarily to Mr. Goodman with a shudder of horror, who guessed, and fully appreciated the cause of her violent emotion.

"Nay—nay, Miss Montalbert," he observed, "pray be calm, and prepare yourself for the dismal scene your eyes will shortly have to encounter. But, if you do not feel yourself prepared to undergo the trial this day, we will return, and postpone this painful business to a future period."

"Oh, no—no," said Rosabelle, eagerly, "pray let us proceed. It was only a momentary weakness, and I am better now. I—I am fully prepared to encounter whatever may take place."

Thus assured, Mr. Goodman handed her from the carriage, and they entered the asylum. They proceeded along many passages, and through numerous apartments, in each of which there was some scene of misery ; until they reached one in which the keeper stopped, and addressing himself to Mr. Goodman, said—

"This is Montalbert's cell, sir."

"Gracious heavens!" exclaimed our heroine, as she gazed around her, "what a place of horrors."

The walls of the wretched cell were bare, and here and there were seen rudely sketched, various drawings of tombs, on which appeared the words, "Here lies Rosabelle." On one side was a small bed, with a rug and a blanket ; on the other a rude table, on which was placed a vessel of water, near it a plain wooden chair. At the back was seen a door, secured by strong iron gratings ; on the left side of the door was a window, guarded in like manner by strong iron bars. The wretched maniac was, at the time of Mr. Goodman's and Rosabelle's entrance, occupied in sketching another tomb. After a while he threw away the pieces of coal with which he was drawing, and with hurried steps paced the cell. At one moment he laughed, and at another fell into a deep reverie : at length, fixing his eyes upon one of the tombs he had been sketching, he spoke.

"Yes," he said, "it is thus I will construct it for her—raise it of costly marble—exhaust a fortune on it. But where is she? She's dead! But yet I shall find her. Oh, yes—oh, yes! what can escape a father searching after his child? Rosabelle!"

He again fell into a deep reverie, and walked slowly to his seat.

"Rosabelle—beloved Rosabelle!" he ejaculated, "hear thy father. Where art thou now, my child? Oh, leave thy gay seducer and his costly domes. Come to thy poor old father, and these wretched walls!"

He arose again in great agitation.

"Ah, no—no—no," cried he, "she is dead: this is her tomb! But she did not fly from me; 'twas in these arms she died."

"God—God! support me through this dreadful scene," groaned Rosabelle.

"Pray compose yourself," said Mr. Goodman, "lest you disturb him."

"You may come in," said the keeper, "you'll not disturb him: when he is wrapped up in his meditations an earthquake would scarcely rouse him. 'Tis ever so after his fits of meditation. The other morning we had no sooner secured him than he slept calmly for above an hour."

"That," observed Rosabelle with a deep sigh, "was at least some respite to his sorrows. See, he recovers ; what is he about to do?"

Montalbert aroused himself hastily, ran to the table, took up a piece of coal, and began to sketch as before.

"These," said the keeper, "are designs for a tomb he purposes to erect for some one he calls his Rosabelle. You see they are all of his own drawing."

"And this," groaned Rosabelle, "this is my doing! Wretched, guilty Rosabelle!"

Montalbert seemed pleased, smiled, and walked cheerfully about.

"He smiles," observed Mr. Goodman; "does not that augur well?"

"It does—it must," ejaculated our heroine; "may I not go forward and address him? Who knows what effect my presence may produce?"

"Have a care you do not anger him," cautioned the keeper.

"Ay, do not dare too much," added Mr. Goodman; "we will draw back, and stay at hand to aid you."

Mr. Goodman and the keeper drew back, and Rosabelle advanced unseen by Montalbert.

"Oh!" said Rosabelle, "and is this the dreadful home I have provided for my father? Is this the recompense bestowed on him by the daughter he loved and trusted for years of unparalleled fondness and indulgence? Horrible—horrible!"

As she thus spoke, Montalbert turned suddenly round, and seeing Rosabelle, uttered a cry of joy and ran towards her.

"Ah! 'tis she!" he cried frantically. "But no no, it cannot be! Fool—fool, she died within these arms!"

He then returned to the table.

"He does not recognise me," said Rosabelle; "still I will hope. Let me observe him."

She drew back, and Montalbert began to hum over in a low voice part of the song he had been so fond of—

"Oh, never could that darling child,
    Her aged parent loved so dear,
Cause in his cheek the blush of shame,
    Or——"

"He sings!" exclaimed Rosabelle: "then there is hope."

Montalbert, after having in a low voice made various attempts, in the manner of one who endeavours to recollect something pused yn1 broke forth with transport—

"Oh, never could that darling child,
Her aged parent loved so dear,
Cause in his cheek the blush of shame,
Or——"

"Ha!" ejaculated our heroine, "it is the song that oft in happier days he loved to hear me sing." Montalbert resumed.

"——In his eye excite a tear.

I have forgotten the rest; but do you not recollect it?"

"Oh, yes, yes," eagerly replied Rosabelle; and she sung—

"A comfort to his old grey hairs."

"Ay, so it is," said Montalbert; "I had forgotten comfort, but it is no wonder, for she is dead—cold—gone—oh!" He groaned, then added "go on, go on, sing; for the love of heaven, sing again."

"I will, I will," eagerly cried Rosabelle: and then in a voice of plaintive sweetness she sung the following words—

"Oh, never could that darling child,
Her aged parent loved so dear,
Cause in his cheek the blush of shame,
Or in his eye excite a tear.

A comfort to his old grey hairs,
A solace in his hours of woe;
Woe brought not on by sin of hers:
Could she e'er grieve his heart? ah, no!"

"Ay, so it was my Rosabelle used to sing it," said the maniac; "but oh, so sweetly! But I shall hear her no more now, for she is in the cold, cold grave. Let us go look for the sod which covers her; you will not leave me, will you?"

"Leave you—never!" exclaimed Rosabelle, with a burst of agony.

"Poor girl! poor girl!" said Montalbert gazing earnestly upon her.

"That earnest gaze!" observed our heroine; "he will—he must remember me!"

"How pale you are, poor thing!" continued the maniac; "but oh! she was so blooming. Don't go—don't go: stay here, and talk of Rosabelle."

"And is she, then, still dear to you?"

"Still dear to me!" reiterated the wretched Montalbert, quickly; "when can a father cease to remember with unbounded affection his child? Vipers have stung, and vulture gnawed my breast —drunk up my blood—cut in my sinews—half destroyed my mind—but they've not reached my heart. No, no; 'tis whole and healthful yet. Feel how it beats: one—two—I can't keep count."

"And thinkest thou that thou shouldst recollect her wert thou to see her again?"

"Recollect her!" reiterated Montalbert in a loud voice; "oh, when can I forget her?—Ha!—I see her now?"

"Where! where?" cried Rosabelle.

"Here! look how she stands, arrayed in virgin white, her golden ringlets playing luxuriantly o'er her snowy brow. Oh! see those heaven-blue eyes, that seraph form! Would she but speak to me! Ah! she is gone! Yes, she is there," (pointing to the drawing of the tomb) "Dead! dead! and gone!"

"Oh, no, no," sobbed forth our heroine, "here at thy feet she kneels, penitent, and imploring to ask thy pardon and confess her crime!"

"'Tis false; 'tis false!" cried the maniac, spurning her from him: "yes, were she at my feet I'd strike the wanton lifeless to the earth, and show the terrible revenge of injured fathers. I'd tear—"

At this moment the keeper walked hastily down, and addressing himself to Rosabelle, said—

"Young woman, you have aroused his anger; 'twere better now to leave him for awhile."

"Thou weepest," said Montalbert, in softened accents, and gazing upon our heroine earnestly; "thou weepest:—it would give thee pain? Then I'll not kill her! No, no, I'll bless—I'll pardon her; my child! my child! but she's dead. Yes, yes, I know it all."

"He'd pardon me!" sobbed our heroine, with much emotion; "oh, blessed sounds! Thou art balm to my racked soul!—Oh, what a weight has that taken from my heart; he'd pardon me, and I am happy."

"Come, lady" said the keeper, impatiently.

"I will, I will," replied Rosabelle;—"farewell, my father: God bless you, and restore you!"

"You must leave him now," urged the keeper.

"Leave me!" repeated Montalbert, looking hastily around him, "you shall not go; you shall not go; no, no, I will not let them tear you from me!"

"Do you hear that?" exclaimed our heroine, with an air of transport, turning to Mr. Goodman, who had been standing by and watching the proceedings with the most intense interest, while his bosom overflowed with soft compassion for the sufferings of the penitent daughter; "did you not hear that?" she repeated; "my presence still is dear to him; oh, joy, joy unutterable! Farewell, farewell, my father."

"Father?" reiterated Montalbert—"what means she? Who calls me by that name, and with that voice? 'tis long since last I heard it—again! again!"

"Father! dearest, dearest father!" again ejaculated Rosabelle, approaching nearer to him.

"Ah!" sighed the unhappy maniac, "sweet music, sweet music; but she's dead, and this is mockery. Ah! that I could see clear! but no, all's dark! dark! But you'll come again?"

"Or die! farewell!" solemnly replied Rosabelle, as she followed Mr. Goodman and the keeper up the steps that led from the cell.

"Die! die!" murmured Montalbert,—"she is dead; ah! she is gone! has left me, has left me again! left me to double madness! No, 'twas a dream! And yet I heard her voice, and saw her form; they cheated me. Barbarous traitors! See see; they grin, they mock at me! She's dead, she's gone. Oh, wretches, but I'll be revenged; lost, lost Montalbert!"

Thus speaking, the unfortunate gentleman ran to the grated door of his cell, which he shook furiously. The keeper forced him away, and throwing himself on the floor with an air of despair, he apparently became unconscious of all around.

Deeply impressed and affected by the melancholy scene we have been describing, was Mr. Goodman; and convinced of the penitence of the unhappy Rosabelle, his heart relented towards her; and as they left the prison, he turned upon her a look of the utmost compassion, as he said—

"Miss Montalbert, you have erred, greatly erred, but to a mind so susceptible as that which I am convinced you possess, the punishment you are now enduring, is fully adequate. I do believe your repentance is sincere, and heaven forbid that I should sternly discard the penitent sinner. Let your heart still continue in the same course, and rest assured that in Mr. Goodman you shall find as warm a friend as ever he was to you and your unfortunate father."

Tears burst involuntarily from the eyes of Rosabelle, and for a few moments choked her utterance She could only look earnestly in his countenance and by her expressive glances evinced the gratitude she felt. Mr. Goodman, with much emotion extended his hand to her, which she pressed vehemently to her lips.

"Oh, sir," she sobbed, "this is more than I deserve; this is too kind. You will then aid the wretched Rosabelle in her endeavours to restore the wandering reason of her ill-fated father?"

"Aid thee, my poor girl?" said Mr. Goodman,

kindly; "oh, how willingly, how gladly will I do all I can to further your worthy designs; and may Heaven in its infinate mercy crown your efforts with success. You shall visit him daily and——"

"Oh, this is indeed kind," again ejaculated Rosabelle; "may the Almighty bless you for your compassion to the poor penitent."

"I merit no thanks, Rosabelle," said Mr. Goodman, who was deeply affected by the earnestness of our heroine's manner; "I am doing that only, which is a duty incumbent upon every true Christian. Charity is one of the brightest attributes we possess."

Rosabelle could not return any answer: her heart was too full. Rattleton had listened to all that had taken place with the utmost commiseration, and he was delighted to find Mr. Goodman disposed to view with clemency one for whom he had ever indulged the greatest esteem, and to whom he knew that his dear Emily was so warmly attached.

"From this interview with your father, Miss Montalbert," said Rattleton, "I augur the most favourable results; "but it will, doubtless, take some time to effect so desirable an object as that which you have in view."

"Oh, was he not moved to tears?" said our heroine eagerly; "did he not recollect me? I'm sure he did."

"He will in time," replied Mr. Goodman; "some gleams of recollection often broke upon him; so long accustomed to regard you dead, he cannot all at once resign the thought;—besides his present habitation, your present sad appearance, altered by grief and suffering; this menial dress—all, all forbad his perfect recognition."

"True," said Rosabelle, with a deep sigh "true; but Heaven, I trust, will not abandon the poor penitent in this design. To you, sir, I can but repeat my unbounded gratitude for your kindness; and there is one, who—but, no, no, I will not mention her name now; I—I will leave you, sir, if you please. This is my way."

"Stay, Miss Montalbert," said Mr. Goodman, gently taking our heroine's hand, "we must not part thus; the sincerely penitent must not be left to complete destitution. As a friend of your poor father, I am anxious to see what can be done towards your future provision."

"Mr. Goodman," said Rosabelle, solemnly; "think not that I will be dependant upon any one for that. No, my own weakness and indiscretion has brought me to poverty, and it is fit that I should alone suffer for it. I am resolved in future to endeavour to support myself and my child by honest industry: and my heart, I am certain, will feel no greater satisfaction than it will should I have an opportunity of accomplishing my wishes."

Mr. Goodman looked at her with the most earnest pity and admiration, and scarcely knew how to answer.

"At any rate, Miss Montalbert," he said at length, "at any rate you cannot support yourself until you obtain some employment, and until you can, I must request you to suffer me to assist you."

"Oh, no, no. never!" cried Rosabelle, "believe me, sir, your kindness is duly felt by me, and I shall ever remember it with the deepest sense of gratitude; but I cannot—will not avail myself of your offer. Indeed, I am not at present in want of it. One dear friend to whom I would have acted the same under singular circumstances, has already afforded me assistance; but from this time, as it is my own guilt alone that has plunged me into misery, so shall it only be my own industry that shall extricate me from my wretchedness. Farewell, sir, and may Heaven pour down upon your head its choicest blessings for your kindness!"

As Rosabelle thus spoke, she hastily curtseyed to Mr. Goodman and Rattleton, and with a violent burst of grief she hastened away, and bent her footsteps once more towards the cottage of Meriel. Mr. Goodman had noticed the observations of Rosabelle respecting the assistance she had received from a kind friend, and immediately guessed to whom she alluded. His heart told him that it could be none other than his amiable daughter, Emily; and a thousand times he mentally blessed her for the act of charity she had thus performed.

Mr. Goodman was a gentleman of the most unbounded urbanity and benevolence. Humanity was one of his greatest characteristics; and if he had at first behaved with what may be considered unnecessary harshness, he had done so more from what he imagined to be his duty than as his own heart prompted him. But now, when he beheld the sad ravages which care and compunction had made upon her face and form—once so fair, so blooming—and recollected how meekly, how mildly she had even comforted herself in the days of her prosperity, to those inferior to her in station—how she delighted in executing those acts of philanthropy for which her father had been so celebrated, his bosom could not but yield to all its natural sensibility; and although he applauded the resolution she had formed, he could not but regret that she had declined his assistance. Rattleton, too, reproached his sentiments, and secretly determined that, in spite of the determination which Rosabelle had expressed, she should not be left entirely to the mercy of the world, and the caprices of misfortune. He knew full well how readily his dear Emily would enter into the views he had formed, and adopt some plan by which they might put their wishes into effect.

The reader, may, perhaps, deem it necessary to be made acquainted with the circumstances that so reduced the unfortunate Mr. Montalbert, and ruined his once ample fortune. It can be soon explained. Sensitive as were his feelings, and doatingly fond as he was of his daughter, it need not be wondered that, after her elopement, he had entirely neglected his business, and was continually talking of his misfortunes. He recovered from the temporary insanity into which he had fallen, when he became acquainted with her flight; but it was very evident to all who knew him, from the deep impression the melancholy events had made upon him, that his mind would soon again become a total wreck. He turned a deaf ear to the entreaties of his friends, who advised him, by strict application, to endeavour to repair the injury he had already done to his property, and seek to redeem some serious losses he had recently sustained in his business. He was reckless, careless to everything; he was abandoned by that daughter for whom alone he had strove to accumulate wealth, and now he looked upon poverty with an eye of indifference.

"Heaven," he often observed, "has severely, but justly humbled me, for I was too proud of my Rosabelle, and by that means I offended it."

As time with rapid wings flew on, as week after week, and month after month passed away, and yet nothing of Rosebelle could be heard, the malady of Mr. Montalbert became stronger; his melancholy gained greater ascendancy over his mind, his pecuniary difficulties daily increased, and, at last, he became a bankrupt; and no sooner did this take place, than he was made acquainted, from a source that he could not doubt, that Rosabelle—the daughter whom he had so fondly loved, that child in whom all his happiness was centred—was living with Colonel Beresford as his mistress. The intelligence was too much for him; his reason, which had long been tottering, again fell; he became a complete maniac, and his friends were compelled to get him admitted into that very asylum of which he was the founder.

Notwithstanding the precautions taken to prevent his escape, he eluded the vigilance of his keepers, as has been seen, on the night when Rosabelle met him in the wood.

*　*　*　*　*

Rosabelle bent her steps towards the cottage of Meriel. Her mind was filled with anguish by the scene that had just taken place when she reflected that she was the cause of so much misery, but after a violent struggle with her feelings she aroused all her energy, and endeavoured to bury in oblivion the painful reminiscences of the past, and sought to indulge in hope for the future. Indeed, the distant recollection which her father seemed to have of her, was sufficient to authorise the supposition, and after reflecting for a few moments, she became comparatively tranquil and resigned; and when she reached the cottage of Meriel, she had become so changed that the poor girl was quite surprised and delighted to see it.

She pressed the boy to her heart, and kissed him with all the strength of maternal fondness.

Meriel was quite delighted at the difference she exhibited in her manner, although, of course, she was unacquainted with the cause. True, she knew that she was going to Mr. Goodman, but upon what errand she had declined telling her; and, therefore, did she feel the more surprised and agreeably disappointed, inasmuch as she had expected, from the strict, and in some instances, the stern morality, of Mr. Goodman, that she would have met with insult, from the objection he had made to her calling upon him.

"Oh, Miss," said Meriel, in accents of pleasure, "how glad I am to see you return. I have been all in such a pucker since you have been away; for I know well what sort of a gentleman Mr. Goodman is; though a better Christian, I firmly believe, or a better meaning man, I do not think there is in the universe. Still, you know, he is so precise and particular, that—that—I thought——"

"I know what you would say, Meriel," inter-

rupted our heroine with a sigh; "but Mr. Goodman is a gentleman that all should admire. Oh, he has behaved very kind to me: kind—ah! how much more kind than I merit. Oh, Meriel, I have seen him once more, and he nearly recognised me; he will, I feel convinced, recollect me altogether in time; and then he will regain his reason and happiness will again light upon me."

Meriel, who had no idea whither she had been beyond Mr. Goodman's, looked at her with amazement and alarm, and began to fear that the intensity of her sufferings had turned her brain; but Rosabelle quickly banished her alarm, by recounting to her all that had taken place, and the sanguine hopes she had now ventured to indulge.

Rosabelle then mentioned to her the ideas she had formed of gaining her future livelihood; and poor Meriel, who shed torrents of tears at the idea of "her dear young lady" being brought to such a state as actually dependant upon her for

the means of obtaining a subsistence, expressed her entire approbation of the resolution she had come to, and assured her of her determination to render her all the assistance that was in her power.

"Ah!" said Meriel, "it is a sad thing to think that you, my dear young lady, at whose wedding I once expected to dance so merrily, should be thus situated; and only a day or two since, the bells were ringing so cheerfully for the nuptials of Miss Goodman; and such a fuss, too, they made; such preparations, as though it were the first time that a wedding had taken place in the world."

Rosabelle sighed; and took no particular notice of the manner in which she delivered herself, as she was confident that she was prompted entirely by her feelings towards her, than by any ill-will which she could by any possibility entertain towards Emily, who had ever behaved so kindly to her.

"Ah! my dear young lady," continued the honest creature, while tears of pity and regret trembled in her eyes; "I hope you will pardon me for my boldness, but I would not attempt to make use of the observations, were I not certain that you are convinced they spring from the best of motives. It cuts me to the very heart to think, and many a tear I have shed, I assure you, upon the subject, that just the same kind of merry-makings, and festivities did I expect some day or the other to see on your nuptials; but now—but, bless me, where is my thoughtless tongue leading me?—But yet I hope that the day will yet come when I shall have the pleasure of dancing at your wedding."

"Meriel," exclaimed Rosabelle, with deep emotion, "pray do not continue this subject; I am certain you would not if you knew how it tortured me."

"Well, well, I will not, my dear young lady," answered Meriel; "it was very wrong of me; very wrong, indeed, to take such a liberty; but I hope you will excuse me."

"No more, Meriel," said our heroine, "I know you will never give utterance to anything that you think will distress my feelings, and that whatever you say or think is only dictated by the love you bear me. Ah! Meriel, there was a time when I fondly hoped that all you have expressed would be realized. But I trust that my dear Emily will never have cause to repent the choice she has made."

"And so do I, and sincerely, too," returned Meriel; "but I think she has made a very good match, and Mr. Goodman is, I understand, quite proud of it."

"And may his sanguine expectations never be disappointed," said Rosabelle; "may her numerous virtues meet with that reward which they deserve. But now, Meriel, I wish to talk to you upon another point, which must be settled at once. You are already aware of my determintion henceforth to live entirely, and support my child, by my own industry."

"Oh, my dear madam," observed Meriel, tenderly.

"Nay, Meriel, do not utter any expressions of regret; it is what I have a right to do, and if I can only succeed in my plans, I ought to consider myself happy. I have erred—I have brought misery upon myself, and it is fit that I should feel the effects of my indescretion."

"No, no, Miss Rosabella," remarked Meriel, "it is not you that should suffer, nor your poor child either, but that bad man who—"

"I know what you would say," interrupted our heroine; "but I must not listen to it. I feel my own guilt sufficiently to know that nothing that I can suffer can be an adequate atonement for the irremediable misery I have caused. And who am I, that I should shrink from the performance of that which honest poverty is daily subjected to? Meriel, I know your heart, and that you would readily make any srcrifice to serve me, but I cannot, I will not permit it. You are about to be married?"

Meriel blushed, and half smiled, and then replied—

"Why, to be sure, madam, I believe that is about to be the case at last, although you know that me and Gilbert have been so many times disappointed before, that I will never be too sanguine again until the marriage is celebrated. But I do somehow think that it will take place at last, for Gilbert is determined, and he has got the money; and I expect him here every minute with the wedding ring."

"Well, then, my good girl," said Rosabelle, with a melancholy smile at the simplicity of her companion; "of course, when you are married, your husband will live with you?"

"Why, yes, Miss," answered Meriel, laughing outright, but blushing deeply; "I should imagine he would."

"Certainly," continued Rosabelle; "and this cottage is small, and has only sufficient room for you. I had once hoped to have been able to—but I am again wandering into a painiul subject. The fact is, Meriel, that when you are married, I should be an intruder that would put you to a great inconvenience; so, as I have before hinted to you, it is my intention to take a lodging, and—"

"A lodging, my dear young lady!" interrupted Meriel; "bless my soul, what would you and your dear infant do in a lodging?—And how would you support yourselves?"

"Why, upon that subject I have a proposition to make to you;—I depend upon you for the accomplishment of my scheme."

"What mean you?"

"Simply this: you are, I know, an excellent dress-maker, and have plenty of business. I, of course, am not ignorant of the use of my needle, and I have been thinking, that, witnout injuring yourself, you might probably be able to give me some employment."

"Employment!" reiterated Meriel; "oh, my dear young lady, that I should ever live to hear this; to hear you, who were ever so kind and benevolent, asking assistance from that humble being who—"

"Again I entreat you to desist from observations of this kind, Meriel," said Rosabelle, with much agitation; "why should I, who am now sunk lower than the most humble individual, shrink from honest labour? Will you grant my request, Meriel?"

"Oh, why do you ask me, my dear young lady?" said Meriel, sobbing; "there is nothing I would not do to serve you, but—but—"

"There must be no buts in the case, my good Meriel; so there ends the matter. I will immediately look out for a lodging."

"And will you then leave me?"

"What alternative have I? But I will call and see you every day."

"Will you though? Oh, that is indeed kind of you. Oh, miss, you to be thus necessitated, while Emily——"

"Hush, Meriel," interrupted our heroine reprovingly, "I must not hear another word from you upon this subject. It seems as if you regretted Mrs. Rattleton's happiness."

"You there wrong me, my dear young lady," observed Meriel; "I do not regret her happiness, but I cannot help repining at your misfortunes, when you had once every prospect of doing even better than she has done. Ah! she is an amiable lady, but lor', there is no comparison between her and you, then——"

"True," interrupted Rosabelle, "there is, indeed, no comparison between us. I am now unworthy to be compared to her. But my own guilt hath produced the change."

"And, therefore, ought we the more to regret it," returned Meriel.

Although Meriel had meant not to convey such a meaning, this remark was very severe, and keenly did poor Rosabelle feel it. She could not make any reply, and fortunately at that moment there was a hasty tap at the door, as if proceeding from some person who was anxious to communicate his pleasurable feelings to others.

"That's Gilbert, I'll be bound," said Meriel, joy sparkling in her eyes, as she hastened to open the door. "I wonder if he has got the wedding ring, which he went to the town to purchase this morning?"

She opened the door, and Gilbert bounded into the room, with his countenance elated with pleasure.

"I have done it, Meriel!" he shouted joyfully;

"I have done it at last. There will be no disappointment this time, at any rate, and——"

"Hush, Gilbert," interrupted Meriel, blushing deeply, "do you not see that Miss Montalbert is present?"

"Oh, I beg your pardon, miss, I'm sure," said the honest rustic, doffing his hat; "but I did not observe you, or I would not have been so bold. But then, you see, I have been to purchase the wedding ring, and now I have got that, I think there be some chance of I and Meriel being married at last. Here it be, all pure gold, as pure as our love, Meriel."

Rosabelle sighed. "Simple, but happy creatures," she mentally ejaculated, "what reason have I to envy ye your fate?"

"Yes, my lady," continued Gilbert, "I and Meriel have been disappointed a great many times; but the banns have been put up, the day after to-morrow the ceremony shall take place, I am determined on it. But, eh, Meriel, what are you looking so dull about?"

"Why, Gilbert," answered his sweetheart, "our wedding is fated to be the signal for us to lose Miss Montalbert."

"Lose Miss Montalbert!"

"Yes; as there will not be room in this cottage to accommodate her, she is going to leave us and take a lodging."

"Take a lodging! what Miss Montalbert, our dear young lady, take a lodging! That I am sure she never shall."

"Why not, Gilbert?" demanded Rosabelle. "What am I to do? This place is too small to accommodate us all, and why should I put you to an inconvenience? Besides, there cannot be any disgrace in one humbled as I am, and have no other means left than to live by honest industry, taking an humble apartment. It will be quite as much as I can afford, and for that even, or at least the means to obtain it, I shall be indebted to Meriel."

The honest rustic turned away his head a moment, and drew the cuff of his coat across his eyes.

"Ah!" at length he said, "never did I expect that it would come to this; but yet, as you say, miss, this place is very small, and we could not make you so comfortable as we should wish. But I declare, only a few minutes ago, I was so happy at the thoughts of being married to my dear Meriel, but this will put quite a damp on the wedding. If it were not for another disappointment, I'll be hang'd if I would not put it off again."

"I thank you sincerely for the feeling you entertain towards me, good Gilbert," said our heroine, "but such a decision on your part would be complete folly. Besides, I dare say I shall not be far from you, and I will not fail to see you and your Meriel every day."

"That is very kind of you, miss," observed Gilbert, "and I'm sure neither I nor Meriel will ever be unmindful of it. And now I think me of it, poor old Dame Martlock's cottage, who died of late, is to let, and that will just suit you. It is small and cheap; and so, if you like, miss, I will go over and speak to the bailiff about it directly."

"Not now, Gilbert," returned our heroine, "we will talk further of it to-morrow."

Thus saying, Rosabelle, taking her child in her arms, hurried to her own room, where she gave free indulgence to the many painful thoughts that distracted her brain. And poignant cause for reflection she had; and the hope that she had so lately indulged that her father would be restored to reason, gradually became weakened. The manner in which she had been treated by Mr. Goodman, however, had been a great relief to her; to find that he had relaxed in that severity which he had at first shown towards her, and was disposed to aid her views, was a great consolation to her, and she hoped that in time he would even permit her to speak to his daughter, and once more to call her by the name of friend.

"But no," she reflected, "it is presumption in me to think such a thing! I, who am so disgraced in the world's estimation—who have so disgraced myself—must never dare hope again to associate with so much virtue and worth."

Then she recalled to her mind the kind and commiserating looks of Emily on the night when she so suddenly made her appearance before the wedding-guests; the affectionate letter she had sent her; and the entreaties she had overheard her make use of, when she last applied for an interview with her father; and her heart completely overflowed with gratitude, and tears filled her eyes.

"Kind, too kind and generous Emily!" she exclaimed: "oh, that it had been permitted me to congratulate her on her happy union with the man of her heart. But no, it is better that it is not so, although nothing could afford me more pleasure than to assure her of my thanks for her kindness, and the sincerity of the love I still bear her: and I should return feel gratified by being received by her in a manner which would show that she is really still my friend—it would distract the poor girl's mind, and render her miserable by contrasting the difference of her own situation and of mine; and, therefore, I will endeavour to banish such a wish from my thoughts."

She gradually became more composed after a little reflection, and, harassed with what she had undergone during the day, she retired early to repose. The following morning, she having reflected upon Gilbert's proposal, requested him to go and inquire the particulars concerning it; and the terms being very low, they immediately settled about it. This business being arranged to their mutual satisfaction as regarded the reasonableness of the place, Rosabelle bent her way, as she had received permission to do, towards the prison in which her unfortunate parent was confined.

Her heart drooped every step as she proceeded, and she was frequently obliged to pause, as a faintness came over her. It happened, unluckily for her, that in her way to the prison she must pass by the house of Mr. Goodman, and just as she came within sight of the building in which she had passed her early days of happiness, but which had now fallen into the hands of Mr. Goodman, she beheld a train of carriages drawn up to the door, and the whole had a very gay and splendid appearance.

"What can be the meaning of this?" said Rosabelle, as she approached nearer the house, and then paused, and leant against a stile, as a trembling sensation came over her. Then she remembered that the day before some conversation had passed between Mr. Goodman and Rattleton, from which it appeared that it was the intention of the latter, his lovely bride, and their friends, to depart this day for the country seat of Rattleton's father, where they purposed passing the honeymoon; and not a moment had this recollection rushed upon her memory, when she beheld the bridegroom appear at the door and hand Emily to the carriage, while Mr. Goodman, also, made his appearance, his countenance animated with delight; and every action betokening the happiness which reigned within his breast.

The sight was agony to the bosom of our wretched heroine, and, with a deep groan, she hastened from the spot with all the precipitation her strength would enable her to use; and at length gained the prison.

But now that she had arrived at this abode of misery, and contrasted it with what she had just been gazing on, how shall we attempt to analyze her feelings? We are confident we have no occasion to do so, as it must occur to every susceptible mind in the most vivid characters. She looked up at the dark stone walls and grated windows of the prison, and reflected that this was the place inhabited by her father—the place to which her guilt had consigned him; while the magnificent abode she had just past, and which had formerly belonged to him, was now in the possession of Mr. Goodman; her heart was full to bursting, and, turning away with a a shudder of horror, she gasped forth—

"This day, and the thoughts it awakens, are too horrible for contemplation:—father, father, thy wretched daughter cannot, dare not this day behold you."

A cold perspiration bedewed her temples as she spoke, and she trembled so violently, that she could not preceed for a few minutes. At length, having recovered, she made her way to the cottage of Meriel. Being too much occupied with the dismal thoughts which the event we have just been describing had given rise to, Rosabelle made an hasty excuse to Meriel, and hastened for the last time, to the little room which had been appropriated to her use, since she had been staying with Meriel, and passed the remainder of the day in deep and melancholy rumination.

But Rosabelle's heart would, no doubt, have been lightened of half its care, had she known that Emily's bosom so deeply sympathised with her, and that, in spite of the gaiety by which she was surrounded, she was far from being happy, when she though of the miserable condition of the once fortunate Rosabelle.

"But I shall hear from her," she said, "oh, yes, my still dear Rosabelle, the friend of my heart, surely will not neglect to send me a letter, or something in remembrance of me? Oh, full wel l can I judge her feelings by my own, and they convince me that her prayers will ascend to heaven for my prosperity and peace. Would to God that in quitting this spot I did not leave her in the misery it is her lot at present to endure."

Before Emily stepped into the carriage which was to convey her away, she left particular injuctions with the domestics that if any letter should come from Miss Montalbert, they were to be sure to forward it immediately to her. But they had no occasion for this, as none arrived; and if Emily had been aware of the motives which prompted our heroine to this conduct, her admiration of the poor unfortunate would have increased.

CHATER IX.

THE LIBERTINE'S DESPAIR.—REMORSE.—THE ATTEMPTED SUICIDE.

WE have beford described the remorse and despair of Lord Ravensford, (late Calon l Beresford), when he foun d that Rosabelle had left him. and that was increased when week after week had elapsed without his being enabled to gain the least clue to her, although both himself, and the fellow. Adder, had made the most vigilant inquiry in every direction which they thought at all likely they might hear of her. Lord Ravensford had gone himself to the coach office, and being well known to the people there, likewise Rosabelle, from their having once or twice stopped there, he mentioned the day, or rather the evening of her flight, and inquired whether she had booked a place there for her and her child, to go to a certain village, naming the native place of Rosabelle. But they could afford him no information there, which was easily accounted for, she having, as we have before stated, taken a place in the coach at the very moment it was about to commence its journey, so that the coachman and guard where the only individuals who had any knowledge of it, and it was not very pro-

bable, had the idea to question them upon the subject occurred to his lordship, that they would have remembered anything at all about it owing to the time which had elapsed. Thus again disappointed, his misery became the more intense, as the idea became stronger, that the unfortunate girl had destroyed herself and child. But now did his compunction come too late; his remorse was completely unavailing, and he knew not what course to adopt. On every side he turned his mental vision, despair stared him in the face, and at times he was half driven to madness. Adder, in vain, attempted to banish his agony, and upon one occasion he even ventured to insinuate the probability that Rosabelle had found another protector, with whom she had eloped; but he repented of this stratagem to drive the unfortunate victim of his master's treachery from his thoughts; for Lord Ravensford became perfectly furious, and it was not without considerable trouble that he was again pacified, or the resentment which he (Adder) had excited against himself could be appeased. The excitement which this event had caused in his mind, at length brought on a complete delirium, and Lord Ravensford was unable to rise from his bed, and was pronouced by his medical attendants to be in a most dangerous and alarming state.

In this manner he remained for several weeks, but at length a youthful and robust constitution prevailed over the malady, and he was again enabled to leave his couch. But although he had been restored to comparative convalescence, a melancholy of the most intense description had settled upon his mind, and at times his grief reached to such a pitch, that his attendants feared a relapse of his most alarming illness. When he thought upon Rosabelle (and when was it that she was not present to his memory?) he was nearly driven to madness. What a guilty, heartless wretch he must be, he would reflect, to have betrayed such innocence as her's. And how happy might he have been had he not so basely played the hypocrite, but have made her his bride. Now that she had left him, he, for the first time, discovered her real value, and there was no sacrifice he would have hesitated in making could he but have had her restored to him, and be assured of her forgiveness. But that could never be; never could she (if she still lived) pardon that man who had inflicted upon her such an irremediable injury! who had treated her with such cruelty and deceit. Never could he have hoped to be reconciled to that unfortunate girl, whose fond father he had worse than murdered. Then his child, too—his sweet boy, on whom its unfortunate mother bestowed such unlimited fondness and attention: should he never behold that again? Alas! he feared never; and all a father's feelings rushed to his brain, until his manhood gave way to their influence, and he wept like a child. These were the corroding cares that racked the mind of Lord Ravensford; such were the feelings with which he was constantly tortured, and which, amid all the splendour of rank by which he was surrounded, sought after, honoured, and flattered with the bland smiles of adulation, rendered his life one of the most poignant and perpetual misery.

His confidential valet, Adder, whom it will be seen was a deep, designing, crafty villain, knew well by this time that Rosabelle had returned to her native village; but that fact he was most careful to keep a profound secret. Adder had a great fear of his master settling down into a quiet, domesticated, married man, for then would he lose a considerable portion of those profits which he now gained by aiding and abetting him in his different nefarious transactions; and the change he had noticed in his master's sentiments towards our heroine with much alarm, and he had, therefore, determined, at all hazards, to prevent their meeting again and effecting a reconciliation, if possible. He did all that he possibly could to make him continue the belief that Rosabelle and his child had perished, not by the hands of the former, but in the snow storm, which took place on the night she quitted the "protection" of Lord Ravensford. In this he succeeded too well; Lord Ravensford did believe it, and all his former gaiety gave way to the deep gloom and despair which this belief created in his breast.

It is a matter of astonishment that the idea should never occur to his mind, to make inquiries at the native village of Rosabelle, which would at once have been the means of setting his doubts and surmises at rest, and brought about that result for which he had so anxiously prayed, since remorse had terrified his heart. But the villain, Adder, who was almost constantly with him, always took especial care, when his lordship made use of any observations that were likely to suggest such a thought to him, to change the subject of conversation, and diverted his attention to something else. He sought to induce him to enter into society, but in vain; his mind eschewed all those former follies which the world call pleasures, and he could not think of his former giddy and dissipated companions without disgust.

"Weak fool that I was," he would soliloquise, "ever to be be seduced by their empty words, and hollow smiles, to be tempted to join them in their wild and reckless career, and exult with them in the indulgence and triumph of our sensual desires. What a wretch has it made me; a hated, despised wretch, amidst all my splendour and greatness. What a treasure has it lost me!—Oh! God! the thought is madness!"

Thus would Lord Ravensford incessantly rave; and had not Adder taken care to be seldom out of his presence, there cannot be any doubt but that he would have committed suicide.

In the midst of this, Adder was very well pleased to hear that Lord Ravensford had made up his mind to try to get some relief by change of scene, and fixed upon going to Bath. Adder applauded his resolution, and in less than a week afterwards they quitted London.

Nothing occurred to them on the journey to Bath worthy of finding a place in this narrative, and they took up their residence in one of the mort fashionable purlieus. But after they had been there for a few days, Adder was vexed and disappointed to observe that not the least change took place in the spirits of his master, unless it was, if anything, for the worse. He also began to dislike society altogether, even that of his valet, who, in fact, only reminded him of his vices, in which he had ever found him so ready an abettor. He would leave home for hours together, and wander about in the suburbs of the city, buried in deep and melancholy meditation.

Adder felt very uneasy at those solitary rambles, and as his master would never listen to him with any degree of patience when he wanted to accompany him, he frequently followed him at a distance, and watched his actions.

Upon one of these occasions, however, business had called the valet away from home, and Lord Ravensdale, more melancholy than usual, walked forth almost immediately after Adder had quitted the house, and took with him a loaded pistol. He wandered to some distance into the country beyond the city, unheedful of the romantic scenery which surrounded him, nor paused until he reached the borders of a silvery stream. There he suddenly stopped, and casting a hasty glance over its glassy surface, exclaimed, as an agonising thought seemed to flash across his brain—

"It is too clear—Rosabelle and her child have perished, and I, wretch, am be murderer. Herself scorned and deserted by her seducer; her father mad and impoverished! What firmness could survive it? But—but I will search for her poor remains, and in a splendid monument perpetuate her virtues and my villany—her repentance and my despair! Adder is continually telling me to seek some relief. Relief! how?—rush from folly to folly; mix with the heartless world; the pale, cold form of Rosabelle for ever at my side; hear her accusing voice in every breeze; see her reproachful look at every board—poisoning my pleasures—shutting out my peace—drag through a lingering round of weary, hopeless years, and die the execrable victim of my vices, with the corroding consciousness that Rosabelle's parting breath breathed curses on me! Oh, 'tis too much! my soul shrinks from the prospect! One bold step ends this anguish! She has gone before, and I will follow! Rosabelle, I come!"

As the wretched man thus spoke, with an air of desperation, he raised the pistol to his head, but in a moment his arm was arrested by some person behind, and a well-known voice exclaimed—

"Hold, madman! What is it you would do?"

Lord Ravensford turned quickly round, and to his astonishment, confusion and shame, beheld in the person of the man who had frustrated his guilty design, Rattleton, supporting on his arm the graceful form of Emily, his beauteous bride.

"Ah!" cried Rattleton, "by heaven it is Beresford, the seducer of Rosabelle."

"Yes," rejoined Lord Ravensford, in the most dismal accents: it is indeed that guilty but unfortunate wretch, but who now would die for her as she has died for him."

"Rosabelle dead!" ejaculated Emily; "forbid it heaven! She lives, I trust, to bless us all,"

Lord Ravensford started hysterically, and the pistol dropped from his hand.

"What!" he cried, "Rosabelle living? then I am not a murderer. But you would deceive me!"

"My Lord Ravensford, for such I believe is now your title," said Rattleton, sternly and haughtily—"we are no deceivers—it is yourself that must claim the honour of that title. Miss Montalbert still lives, I repeat."

"Oh, where—where? Tell me, I beseech you. Do not rack me; where shall I find my Rosabelle?"

"In her native village, attending upon her unfortunate parent, whom your base villany and treachery have consigned to a madhouse," answered Rattleton.

"In her native village!" reiterated Ravensford; "ah, then Adder has deceived me. Fool that I was, not to see through the designing hypocrite before. Oh, God! I thank thee; then I am not an assassin. Oh, my friends, surely you have not abandoned the poor girl in her adversity? She was not to blame; it was my wily tongue that did it all. But you will not desert her? Oh, in mercy speak for me—plead for me. I implore ye plead for me with my unhappy victim. I am a penitent, heart-broken man. Every bar to our union is removed; let me then make every reparation in my power, and restore her to that rank in society from which my guilt seduced her."

"Can this be sincere!" ejaculated Rattleton, looking earnestly at his former friend.

"It is—it is!" answered Lord Ravensford, hastily, "and you would not doubt me, did you but know the bitter pangs of remorse which I have suffered."

"This," said Emily, "this does indeed look like penitence!" and a smile of gratification animated her lovely features

"But will you promise me?' eagerly demanded Ravensford.

"I will—I will!" replied Emily; "you must assist me, my love," she added, speaking to her husband.

"Assist you, dearest Emily?" returned the latter, cheerfully; "ay, that I will. I am a thoughtless, volatile fellow, laughing at every folly as it rises; but though many may say that I have a very little head, I trust no one can deny I have a heart. Your repentance, Ravensford, I need not say affords me the most superlative delight, and I trust that we shall be able to arrange everything in the manner we wish. We are staying here for the present with our father; for you, of course, are aware that Emily is now Mrs. Rattleton. I will make Mr. Goodman acquainted with all; and having considered what is best to be done, by to-morrow, at latest, I have no doubt I shall have the pleasure of sending for you to the house at which we are staying, when everything will be arranged to our general satisfaction. Till then, farewell; and may your sentiments remain unchanged."

"Oh, blessed thought!" cried Emily, as tears of joy filled her eyes; "he once again her friend, the world will quickly follow."

Rattleton pressed the hand of Lord Ravensford, and they immediately separated. For a few minutes after their departure, the latter stood as it were transfixed to the spot. The whole appeared to him a dream; it was too pleasing to be real. But when he was convinced that his senses had not deceived him, his feelings so overpowered him that he laughed and wept alternately. Then, with the utmost rapidity, he returned home, where the first person he encountered was Adder. His eyes flashed the utmost fury and indignation upon the treacherous valet, who, perceiving that something unusual had happened, and stung by a guilty conscience, shrank abashed, and turned deadly pale.

"Villain! wretch!" cried Lord Ravensford, grasping him by the throat; "thou hast deceived me!"

"My lord," exclaimed the affrighted valet, struggling violently to extricate himself from his hold; "unhand me—what means this violence?"

"Miscreant! Rosabelle lives, and you have all this time been misleading me," shouted Lord Ravensford, as he spurned Adder from him.

"It is you who would deceive yourself, my lord," retorted Adder.

"Villain!" shouted Ravensford, choking with indignation, "I tell you again she lives. I have seen Mr. Rattleton, who informs me that the unfortunate victim of my baseness is now in her native village, of which circumstance you must have been fully aware, had you made an inquiry. Begone from my sight, wretch, and never more dare to enter my presence."

"I go my lord," said the valet, as he turned away, "and I wish you joy with your Rosabelle, the woman who once lived with you as your mistress. Ere long, you may repent having thus behaved towards your faithful myrmidon."

"Miscreant! dare you threaten?" exclaimed his lordship; but Adder was gone, and lost not a moment in leaving the house.

"So," he soliloquised, as he quitted the house, "my treachery is at last discovered, and Lord Ravensford, after having been with him so many years, has discharged me? Well, no matter; I have taken especial care to pay myself very well for all that I have done since I have been with him, and I am much mistaken if I have done with him yet. At any rate, I will have revenge! How confounded unfortunate it is that we should come to the very place where this Rattleton is staying. But I must contrive some method to remove Rosabelle. Yes, he must not see her again; or, at any rate, not until any attempt to effect a reconciliation must be entirely hopeless. I will lose no time in hastening to the village, and see what can be done. She is a lovely creature, and I have often envied my master his happiness.

Let me now see whether I cannot adopt some scheme or the other to make her securely mine. Ha—ha—ha! that would be glorious revenge, for it would entirely preclude all possibility of her ever becoming the bride of her seducer. It shall be done. I never yet failed, scarcely, in any scheme which I have concocted, and it is strange indeed if I do in this. Rosabelle Montalbert instead of being led to the altar by the penitent Lord Ravensford, thou shalt become the mistress of his discarded valet! I go to put my threats into immediate execution."

Thus speaking, the miscreant Adder hurried on his way, and having reached the coach-office, took his place in the first vehicle which he found going to the place of his destination.

In the meantime, the feelings of Lord Ravensford may be imagined;—sometimes he gave way to all the wild extravagance of delirious transport, and at others he became calm, and returned his thanks to Providence that Rosabelle still lived. Again his mind became tormented with doubts, and fears, and surmises. Would Rosabelle ever pardon him, after the base manner in which he had behaved towards her? Must she not scorn, despise, loathe, and curse him? He, the destroyer of her father's reason—the seducer of her innocence! Oh, yes, assuredly she must, and his anguish would be redoubled instead of being diminished. Then he pictured to himself the unhappy girl attending in the dismal cell of her poor maniac father: listening to his wild ravings, and trying, but hopelessly, to soothe him into recollection and calmness. His anguish increased to an insupportable degree. Again he thought upon the misery she must have endured since she had fled from him; the scorn, the opprobrium, that had, in all probability been levelled at her by the world; and he could scarely confine his feelings within the bounds of reason.

After his meeting and interview with Rattleton and Emily, he was unable to rest, but passed his time in traversing his apartment, in a state of the most violent agitation, and giving utterance to broken and disjointed exclamations. Sometimes hope sprang up in his bosom, that all would happen exactly as he wished, and then again despair would fall upon his heart, and he would writhe in mental agony. Oh how impatiently did he await the following day, that he might once more see Rattleton, and hear his and Mr. Goodman's opinion upon the subject; although, at the same time, he felt a sort of repugnance in meeting the latter, whose stern virtue, he felt convinced, would view his penitence with so suspicious an eye, and who would probably reproach his past conduct so severely. One moment he was almost determined immediately to go to the village, and endeavour to gain an interview at once with Rosabelle, and settle his doubts and suspense altogether. Then again, when he remembered the friendship that had ever subsisted between the family of Mr. Goodman and the unfortunate Mr. Montalbert, he became more powerfully convinced than ever of the influence they must possess over Rosabelle, if they thought proper to exercise such influence, and he resolved to await the result of their advice. He drew from his bosom the miniature which Rosabelle had presented to him in happier times, when she had believed him to be all honour and virtue. As his eyes became fixed upon it, and admired the admirable skill with which the artist had depicted every lineament of her beauteous countenance, tears, scalding tears, filled his eyes, and he beat his breast with the most indescribable emotion. With frenzied fervour he pressed it to his lips, and then implored Heaven to grant the realization of his hopes.

All that night Lord Ravensford found it impossible to sleep, such was the state of his mind; and when the morning dawned, he left his couch, and walked into the garden, anxiously awaiting the arrival of any messenger that might come from Mr. Goodman. The morning's repast was scarcely over, when his hopes were realised, a note of invitation being brought from Mr. Goodman by one of the servants of that gentleman. He immediately ordered his carriage, and in a few minutes was rattling off to the mansion at which Mr. Goodman and his family were staying.

We will not describe the interview which ensued between Lord Ravensford and Mr. Goodman. The latter gentleman had been assured, prior to the meeting, from the description given of Ravensford's behaviour, of the sincerity of his penitence, and he was prepared to receive him accordingly. To say that it was a source of the utmost pleasure to Mr. Goodman, would be superfluous, as his character must be so well known to the readers of this narrative; and he resolved that no exertion should be wanting on his part to bring about the result so much desired. With this determination, he made up his mind to return to —— with the least possible delay, and thither, of course, Lord Ravensford would accompany them. On their arrival, the first thing to be done was to effect an entire reconciliation with Rosabelle in the best manner that could be devised, and as to the results, Mr. Goodman and his son-in-law entertained the most sanguine expectations. In regard to the reason of Mr. Montalbert, Mr. Goodman also expressed strong hopes, that by the attentions of his daughter, it would be restored to him.

"Heaven send that it may!" ejaculated he, "that he may be witness to the joyful events which we anticipate!—and, moreover, because I entertain strong hopes of being able very shortly to arrange his affairs. A scheme has flashed upon me, which, on our return home, I will lose no time in putting into execution. I will have his favourite room in my house altered to represent his cell; will change his dress while sleeping, and convey him thither unknowingly:—have Rosabelle attired as she was wont to be—take his senses; thoughts of past times will all recur again;—he'll know his daughter;—bless her; forgive you, Ravensford, and make us all happy."

"The scheme is excellent!" observed Rattleton, while the charming Emily was unable to restrain her tears at the happy picture which her father had drawn.

"Goodness and virtue meed you, dear sir," ejaculated Lord Ravensford.

"I will see about the preparations immediately on our return," said Mr. Goodman; "by the day after to-morrow, all my arrangements will be complete, and then if it suits your lordship, we shall be ready to depart from hence without any delay."

"Oh, immediately; this very hour am I ready;" ejaculated Lord Ravensford. eagerly.

"Mark me, Ravensford," observed Mr. Goodman, "you must learn patience in this business, for it will not do to be too precipitate, lest we should thwart the scheme we have at heart."

"I will be guided entirely by you, my dear sir," answered his lordship.

"Do so, and all will, doubtless, terminate as we wish," said Mr. Goodman; "I am certain, my lord, that not even you can be more anxious than I am to bring this painful event to a happy conclusion."

After some further conversation, they separated, and Lord Ravensford returned to the place where he had been staying, with a lighter heart than he had possessed before for some time before. The words of Mr. Goodman inspired him with confidence, and he could never feel sufficiently grateful, he was certain, to that gentleman for his kindness, and the deep interest he took in the business.

CHAPTER X.

THE RECONCILIATION.—THE RETURN OF REASON.

In the meantime, Meriel and honest Gilbert Batchelor were united, and in their happiness, Rosabelle saw, with the most agonized feelings, a painful contrast to her own forlorn condition. She was a daily visitor at the asylum; she attended upon her poor father with the most unremitting care, but watched in vain for the dawning of reason once more upon his shattered intellects. Sometimes, indeed, she could almost fancy that he had some recollection of her, but such a supposition was only transitory. He would quickly relapse into insensibility, and give vent to his wild ravings and dismal lamentations over the supposed tomb of his Rosabelle.

The cottage in which our heroine resided, was close to that of Meriel and Gilbert, so that they were still almost the same as if they had resided together. Meriel and her husband were unremitting in their kind attentions to her, and seemed never so happy as when they had it in their power to render her any little service. She got sufficient to employ her time from Meriel, whose business increased, and thus rendered it better for both parties. And as her business, and the profits arising from it, rapidly advanced, so did the energy of our heroine strengthen, and all those hous which were not passed with her unfortunate parent, she closely applied herself to habits of exemplary industry; every day she became more saving; and at last would scarcely allow herself the common necessaries of life, toiling at the same time night and day. This very much astonished Meriel, who could not account for it, seeing that Rosabelle had no one but herself and her child to maintain, and she could not conceive for what purpose she was hoarding up her money.

"My dear miss," said Meriel one evening to her, not being able to restrain her curiosity any longer; "what has come to you lately, that you are so saving as to be absolutely very little better than starving yourself?"

Rosabelle looked at Meriel for a moment, and then burst into tears.

"Meriel," she said, "you have often heard me remark that one thought has always occupied my mind more powerfully than any other besides; and that is that my poor father may some time or other be restored to reason. If I could only once more hear him call me by name, and give me his benediction, I should have nothing more that I would wish to live for in this world, and I could view death without a single pang of regret. I cannot often times help thinking that my anxious wishes will be one day realized, and that we may yet pass a happy and contented life with one another."

"Heaven grant that your prayers may be heard, my dear young lady," ejaculated Meriel, "but this does not fully account for the change which has lately come over you."

"True, Meriel," returned our heroine, "but I will explain my motives to you, and I am convinced you will approve of them. Of course you have heard of the rules of the asylum in which my unfortunate parent is confined; but lest you should not, I will inform you. Five years is the time allotted for a patient to remain in the prison; and then if he is not cured, he is removed to another part of the building, appropriated to those whose cases are hopeless, and there they remain for life, upon his friends paying a certain sum annually for his support. But he is restored to the care of his friends if they prefer it."

"Well, my dear lady," said Meriel, who remarked with surprise the unusual expression of delight that sparkled in the eyes of Rosabelle through her tears as she spoke;—"and what of that?"

"What of it!" repeated Rosabelle, "why, will not my father at the expiration of the time allotted for the confinement of patients, either be restored to his senses, or to my care, and who can then tell what the result may be?"

"Oh, yes!" returned Meriel, who was unwilling to damp the ardour of our heroine's anticipations, or to crush the sanguine hopes it was quite evident she had formed, although, for her own part, she saw much trouble and anxiety in the plan which Rosabelle had conceived;—" oh, yes, it may be so indeed, as you say—there is nothing impossible to Heaven, and I only hope that the day is not far distant when your cares will be set at rest by the restoration of your poor dear father to reason, without his having to remain five years in the asylum."

Rosabelle made no answer, and soon after relapsed into that state of profound meditation in which she was usually buried. And often did the thoughts of our heroine wander to Emily and Mr. Goodman; and many were the prayers she uttered for their happiness. Well did she feel convinced that the former did not forget her; she could read the sentiments of her as well as if she had been present to her and giving utterance to them; she could judge her feelings at all times by her own. They had now been several months away, and Rosabelle frequently breathed a sigh of regret at their absence, and longed for the time for them to return;—but why should she do so?—She should never be allowed to associate with them again, she reflected, and, therefore, it was a matter of indifference what distance divided them. Little did she imagine what had taken place at the time these ideas occurred to her, and what was about to happen, or happiness might once more partially have been hers.

But in the midst of all these reflections, other thoughts would rise to torment her; those occasioned by her ill-requited passion. Many indeed were the hours she passed in giving vent to the anguish this created in her breast. Nor can it be wondered, that she who had loved so fondly, as to sacrifice all her happiness to the object of it, could not once erase from her heart the remembrance of that man on whom she had placed her warmest affections, but who had so cruelly deceived her. No: such an idea would be as unnatural as it would be wrong. It was not likely that she could easily forget the one her heart had chosen;—the father of her offspring. There were times also, although fully convinced as she was, how despicable a being his guilt had made him, when she could not help recalling him to her memory arrayed in all those virtues and allurements in which her fondest imagination had clothed him.

These recollections, however, we often overwhelmed by others of a contrary description; and when her reason could dwell calm and dispassionately upon the subject, her seducer would appear to her imagination in all his odious colours; she would contemplate him as a wretch—libertine—debauchee—heartless profligate, and the destroyer of all her hopes and happiness;—as a villain who at the very time he was most apparently sincere in his protestations, was seeking her ruin. He never having made any inquiry after her or her child, although she had left the place where they lodged in the depth of winter, with her unfortunate infant in her arms, and without any one to protect them, he had left them to their fate, and was evidently indifferent as to what became of them; this placed him in the light of a monster, whom it would be " base mockery to call a villain." But in these suppositions, as our readers must be aware, Rosabelle did her seducer an injustice.

When these thoughts took possession of the mind of our heroine, they sometimes drove her to a state bordering upon madness and unable any longer to remain in her humble dwelling, she would hasten forth, and seek in society to banish the recollection of them. But more often did it happen that her inclinations led her to the abode of honest poverty; to those poor persons, to whom when she was in prosperity, she had ever been so bountiful, so kind a benefactress, and who, not unmindful of the same, were now alway delighted to see her; and whenever they met her in her peregrinations, made her the only grateful acknowledgment in their power, by invoking a blessing upon her head.

Rosabelle's return to her native village, had no sooner reached the knowledge of these former recipients of her benevolence, than she was followed wherever she went by them, and in the hour of her adversity, received even more respect from them than she had even done in the hour of her happiness. And a great relief was this to her heart; for she felt that there were yet those who could esteem and pity her; that there were those who beheld her with confidence; while there were other beings in the world filling a far different station, and who had ever been foremost in offering her their fulsome adulation, who now looked upon her with the eye of scorn, and who were the readiest and most severe in their censures of her conduct. But yet, upon more mature reflection, she could see but too good reason for their censure, for had she not, by throwing herself in the arms of her seducer, and abandoning her father, violated one of the most sacred duties; and not only that, but it had caused her also to violate the duty which she owed to the poor, yes, to her they had looked, upon as a benefactress, and she had deserted them and thus did all the dreadful consequences of her guilt became more apparent to her. These feelings for a while distracted the mind of our heroine, but in time their severity was abated, and she sought to make all the reparation she could by once more extending her charity towards them, as far as her limited means would allow her to do. Indeed, in a pecuniary point of view, she had it no longer in her power to assist them; but she could perform those acts of benevolence which often possess as great a benefit, namely, she could commiserate in their misfortunes, and afford them her advice and consolation. and this the poor creatures estimated beyond all price, as they viewed, with unbouded gratitude, one so far above them by birth and education, take so much care of them, and interest herself so much in their humble affairs. Night after night did she watch by the couch of the sick and dying, and by her gentle soothings rendered the nauseous medicine more salutary; and offer up a prayer to the throne of mercy for the departing souls of the suffering. Thus then did Rosabelle in the midst of her misery find a source of consolation and gratification of the highest order, and one which fully compensated for the loss of pecuniary means, for from it she derived the blessings of a self-approving conscience, and those of the objects of her benevolence.

And now was our heroine to receive an additional cause of gratification. She had a letter form her dear Emily, couched in the most affectionate language, and sent by the sanction of her father. This was proved by one being enclosed from him also; in which he wrote to her with much kindness, commended warmly her exemplary industry, of which he had received a full account; desired her to persevere in her laudable conduct, and that she might depend upon it. in him she would ever find a warm friend. He added in a few days it was his intention to return from Bath, when he should wish to see her at his house.

To say that Rosabelle was delighted with these letters, would be to speak too lightly of her feelings. A hundred times she kissed them both, pressed them to her heart, and invoked blessings upon the heads of those who had written them. But her sentiments received some check, when she reflected on the melancholy situation of her father; when she ruminated that he was now unconscious of her receiving those marks of attention and esteem which would have afforded him so much delight; and that he was also unconscious of her being anything but the degraded being she was while the mistress of her seducer.

"Yet, still," she reflected, "I will not give way entirely to despair; no—no, I will hope that the time will come when that most in-

ROSABELLE ELOPES WITH CAPTAIN BERESFORD.

estimable of all blessings, the restoration of my poor father to reason, will be granted to my incessant prayers."

As she uttered these words, her bosom became the abode of a feeling she had not for some time experienced, and she shed abundant tears of joy and gratitude. Again and again did she peruse the letters of Emily and her father, and every time she did so, she saw some fresh cause for joy. The idea of their return to the neighbourhood, filled her mind with transport, and then the intimation of Mr.

Goodman, that he should wish to see her at his house, excited in her bosom additional hope.

"What can he want with me," she soliloquized, "unless it is to assure me of his entire forgiveness? My dear Emily too, will she—will her husband suffer us to meet again as friends? Something assures me that they will; and then, with what increased energy shall I renew my painful task in endeavouring to recal the wandering senses of my poor father! But let me not be too sanguine, lest if I am doomed to be disappointed, it should fall more heavily upon me."

The delight of poor Meriel and her husband when they were informed of this circumstance, was scarcely less than that of our heroine, and they augured from it quick approaching happiness to that " dear lady," to whom they were both so warmly attached.

Rosabelle waited with the utmost impatience the arrival of the day on which Mr. Goodman and his family were expected to return home; and at length it came, and a joyous one it was in the neighbourhood; the tenantry and neighbours of Mr. Goodman being determined to give him such a reception as his numerous good qualities justly merited.

Rosabelle had arisen that morning at a very early hour, and attired herself in her best; in fact, she could not sleep, her mind was too busily engaged with delightful anticipations to suffer Morpheus to descend upon her eye-lids. A hundred times she went to the casement of her cottage, from which she had a full view of the road along which they must pass, thinking to see them : but each time she was doomed to be disappointed. She did not like to venture forth towards the spot, a felling of delicacy and timidity prevented her ; and indeed, under these circumstances, it would have been highly imprudent in her had she done so, and it was with the greatest difficulty she could resist the temptation which at times prompted her to it. Meriel, who called upon her early in the morning, at her request several times walked towards the main road to notice if she could see anything of their coming, but always returned with an answer in the negative. At length, the village bells struck up a merry peal, and then Rosabelle felt certain that they were near at hand. And now a sudden faintness and trembling came over her. She remembered in happier times how often she had listened with rapture to the village chime; how often their merry peal had sounded of the anniversary of her own and father's birth-day ; and a dreadful pang shot through her heart when she reflected upon the dismal change that had now taken place. He for whom they had so often rung, was now the inmate of a mad-house, shut out from, and unconscious of the cheerful sounds; while she—but she endeavoured to banish the thought, for it drove her to madness. Shortly

afterwards, while she stood at the casement she could see the distant carriages as they drove gaily along the high road; her ears were greeted by the joyful shouts of the persons assembled to welcome back to his home an indulgent landlord and a liberal benefactor. The sight overpowered her; it brought with it too many reminiscences of former times, of the days of her prosperity; and covering her face with her hands, she hastily quitted the casement; threw herself upon the bed, and burst forth into a paroxysm of convulsive sobs and tears.

Meriel did not offer to interrupt this ebullition of her feelings, for she knew it would relieve her, but stood looking on with the utmost sympathy.

At length Rosabelle became more composed, and drying up her tears, she said—

"It is very silly of me thus to give way to grief, when it is a circumstance at which I have rather so much cause to rejoice. Dear, dear Emily, and shall I then once more be allowed to see you ?—Be permitted to call you friend, and receive your embrace ?"

She paused a moment, and then added:

"I wonder if they will send for me to-day ?"

But as a sudden thought flashed across her brain, she said—

" But no, they have too much compassion for the wretched outcast than to invite her to a scene where her presence would probably be considered an insult, and which could only add to her misery."

This day was one of mingled pain—hope—pleasure—and suspense to our heroine ; but at length it passed away, and night came on. Her rest, however, was disturbed by troublesome dreams, and she was glad when the morning dawned. She arose, and busied herself in tidying up the place, and preparing her frugal repast prior to her sitting down to her daily employment. Her mind was too much harassed with contending thoughts to suffer her to eat much, and she had but just finished her meal, and cleared the things away, when Meriel came running into the cottage with breathless haste, and surprise depicted in her countenance, and after two or three efforts to speak, she said—

"Oh, my dear young lady; such a surprise ! prepare yourself—for just now as I was returning from the field, where I had been to take Gilbert his breakfast, I met Mr. Goodman's carriage in the road, and it strikes me very forcibly that it is coming in this direction."

Rosabelle turned very pale, and trembled violently, and Meriel walking up to the casement, looked out, and presently exclaimed—

" Ah ! it is just as I expected ;—see, Miss, here it comes."

Rosabelle, in a state of great agitation, tottered up to the window, and beheld the vehicle rapidly approaching towards the cottage. In another second or two it stopped at the door, at which the footman knocked loudly.

"But why should I suffer my emotions thus to overpower me?" said our heroine, endeavouring to regain her composure; "why should I fear to see him now any more than at our last interview; especially after the letters I have received from him and Emily?—Meriel, your arm; I feel very faint."

She leant upon the arm of Meriel, and with a heart palpitating with hope, fear, and anxiety, she descended the stairs into the little parlour. Here she sank into a seat, and motioned Meriel to open the door. No sooner was this done, than Mr. Goodman, his countenance beaming with kindness, presented himself, and was immediately followed by Rattleton and Emily. Rosabelle no sooner beheld the latter, than she started from her seat with a cry of surprise and delight, and before she could give utterance to a syllable, Emily rushed into her arms, and enfolded her in a warm embrace.

This scene lasted for several minutes without any one having the power to speak, while Mr. Goodman and Rattleton stood by, gazing upon them with looks of deep emotion and admiration. As for Rosabelle, the shock was so sudden. that she was for a few seconds in a state of complete stupefaction, while Emily wept and sobbed upon her bosom. Meriel raised her hands and eyes to Heaven in mute astonishment and delight.

"Oh, Emily, dearest Emily, friend of my youth: constant companion of my thoughts," at length ejaculated our heroine, withdrawing herself gently from the embrace of the former; " can this scene be real, or is it only imaginary? Am I once more granted the felicity of calling you friend; and——"

"You are, you are, my dear Rosabelle," said Emily in reply, "and never for one moment have you been estranged from my thoughts; never have you ceased to occupy the same place in my affections that you ever did. My dear father, to him is this blessing due."

"And is then the unfortunate Rosabelle, the——"

"No more, Miss Montalbert, I entreat," interrupted Mr. Goodman, kindly, advancing and taking her hand; " it is sufficient that your penitence—your exemplary conduct since your return to this place, and with which I am thoroughly acquainted, have at once interested me in your favour, and—but let us say no more here; my carraige awaits at the door, and you must accompany us back to the hall; we have much to say to you. There now, no tears, my poor girl—come, come!"

And as he spoke, Rosabelle having put on her bonnet and shawl, Mr. Goodman led her to the vehicle, into which he assisted her—and himself, Rattleton, and his fair bride, having followed, the coachman prepared to drive away. The poor people to whom Rosabelle had so much endeared herself, when they beheld the carriage draw up to the cottage door, were quite alarmed, for they imagined she was going to leave them again, and feared they should never see her any more. They therefore surrounded the vehicle, and when our heroine came out of the cottage, she was greeted with loud but respectful exclamations and inquiries as to whether she would return to them again.

"Oh, yes, yes," sobbed forth Rosabelle, overcome with emotion at their demonstrations of love and gratitude; and unable to give utterance to another word, she was handed into the carriage, and waving her hand to the humble group, it drove away.

As the carriage proceeded on its way to the hall, we need not attempt to describe the sweet interchange of friendly sentiments which took place between them—Mr. Goodman and his daughter needed no explanation from our heroine of her conduct since they had been away, for they had been furnished with every particular. They had visited the asylum, and there the account which the directors had given them of the devoted attention which Rosabelle had bestowed upon her father, being with him at every opportunity which she could steal from her employment, not only drew forth their warmest admiration, but tears of pity at the unhappy circumstances that gave occasion for it.

"Such care deserves its reward," continued Mr. Goodman, " and God grant that you may meet with it, Miss Montalbert, in the restoration of your father to his senses; but——"

"But—ah! you hesitate, sir," gasped forth Rosabelle, catching at Mr. Goodman's words, and the manner in which they were spoken; " you have your doubts, I see, that he will ever be restored! Tell me—is it not so?"

"Compose yourself, Miss Montalbert," returned Goodman; " I said not so. The fact is, I have seen Doctor Winter, who has informed me that he fears nothing can be done for him in the asylum, and that the only hope he entertains is for him to be taken out and placed under skilful treatment; and even then he says that you can do more for him than——"

"Ah!" exclaimed Rosabelle, eagerly laying her hand on Mr. Goodman's arm, and looking earnestly in his face, " say you so?—Oh, tell me how!—What means shall I adopt? Even the sacrifice of my life would be to purchase such a blessing cheaply."

"From what I have seen myself," said Mr. Goodman, " and what I have been told, he seems, unquestionably, happy when you are with him, and when you are doing any little kindness for him; therefore, it is not at all improbable that when he is restored entirely to you—that is, when he resides with you——"

"Resides with me!" gasped forth Rosabelle, her bosom heaving with the most violent emotion, and her whole frame greatly agitated;—"what mean you? For the love of Heaven—"

"What I mean is simply this," interrupted Goodman—"that I have come to the resolution to take your father out of the asylum, and remove him to my house, formerly his own; that, if you object not, there you shall reside with him, and adopt as much of your old plans as possible. He must be left to resume all those ways he was formerly accustomed to; and, by living in the same house, taking his usual walks, letting him hear his favourite songs, and being as much in his society as possible. if you are not the means of completely restoring him to reason once more, you may contribute, at least, to his happiness."

"Contribute to his happiness!" repeated Rosabelle, in the most dismal accents; "alas! alas! it will never be my lot again to contribute to his happiness, though once I——"

"Nay, dear Rosabelle," said the gentle Emily, "do not thus give way to despair. He will be happy—I am sure he will—when you are near him; and, by degrees, the light of reason will once more break in upon his now darkened and desolate mind. Something whispers confidentially to me that it will be so."

"Dear comforter!" ejaculated our heroine, "the blessings of the Almighty descend upon your head for these words, and all the innumerable kindnesses I have experienced from you. And you, my dear sir—oh, how can I ever sufficiently express to you my gratitude? But tell me, when will you put this design into execution?"

"I will delay it no longer than the day after to-morrow," replied Mr. Goodman, "in order that I may have sufficient time to make the necessary arrangements."

"Oh, thanks! thanks!" uttered our heroine, in accents that showed at once her sincerity. "Hope again begins to dawn upon me! Could I but restore him to his senses, and hear my pardon pronounced by his lips, my every wish would be gratified, and I would not care to live another moment."

"But your child, Rosabelle," observed Mr. Goodman.

"Oh, yes, yes" eagerly cried Rosabelle hugging the child closer in her arms; "for thee, my poor boy, I hope that my life may be prolonged, or that the same moment may summon us both to eternity."

Many other observations of an equally interesting and affecting description took place between them as they proceeded, and at length the carriage arrived at the Hall.

What pangs shot through the heart of Rosabelle as she once more crossed the threshold o that house in which she passed the halcyon days of her youth, and contrasted that happiness with the present misery she endured; she was obliged to avail herself of the support of Mr. Goodman's arm to sustain her trembling form; for with such rapidity did conflicting thoughts crowd upon her brain that they almost overwhelmed her, and she was ready to drop with agitation. What joyous, what rosy hours had she passed beneath that roof, when she was the pet of a doating father, and her virtue was pure and unsullied. Now, alas! how awfully changed was everything! She was a poor, degraded, miserable wretch, her father the inmate of a madhouse. As she entered that parlour where had she so often sat and sung to her father the ballad he so delighted to hear, she could almost imagine she saw his wild eyes glaring reproachfully upon her, or heard his lips breathe a curse upon her head, and a deadly sickness came over her, which she had not the power to shake off Mr. Goodman, who noticed our heroine's emotion, endeavoured to console her, and whispered to her words of comfort and encouragement, and at length he succeeded. When he repeated his designs as regarded Mr. Montalbert, her eyes brightened, and hope once more irradiated her mind.

"Oh, yes, yes," she ejaculated, "he will be restored—something assures me that he will; and I shall at length be blessed with that result for which I hourly pray. He will pronounce his pardon on his poor unfortunate daughter; and then, should death immediately be my portion, I should meet my fate with calmness and resignation."

"Although I would not have you be too sanguine, Miss Montalbert," said Mr. Goodman, "lest disappointment should be more painful that you now endure, I must say that I entertain very great hopes of the success of our scheme. The scenes he has been in the habit of mingling amongst—the words, the songs he has been accustomed to hear—the same faces his eyes formerly constantly encountered—may arouse his sleeping memory, and rekindle the fire of reason in his mind. I look forward to the time of trial with as much impatience and anxiety as you can possibly do; but we must not be too premature. Our plot can only be effected by degrees, and by extreme caution; and ultimately we may have our efforts crowned with all the success we can wish."

"Heaven grant that your prognostications may be verified, my dear father." ejaculated Emily, her eyes filling with tears of compassion; "I am sure no one can more earnestly and sincerely pray for such a result than I do."

"I know it, my dearest Emily," said her husband, kissing her fondly, "and it is that conviction which makes me love you better than ever. If I am giddy and wild, I will not yield to any one in existence for sympathy in the misfortunes of my fellow-creatures. For my own part, I am quite deligbed with the plan upon which Mr. Goodman has hit, and if it does not succeed, say that I am no philosopher, that's all."

"I think that no one would be bold enough to deny that you are a laughing one, at any rate," observed Mr. Goodman, with a smile.

"And, in my humble opinion, sir," said Rattleton, "that is the best species of philosophy, after all; at any rate, nothing can be more conducive to happiness and health. I wish I could instil a little of the quality into Miss Montalbert, and I do not despair of being able to do that in a short time."

Rosabelle smiled faintly, and the conversation and behaviour of her friends was well calculated to ameliorate the anguish of her mind. When she thought upon the kindness with which they treated her—the interest they took in restoring her to peace, and how undeserving she was of such attention—her eyes filled with tears of gratitude. She looked in the countenance of the gentle Emily, and there she read consolation and commiseration. After some time passed in conversation, Rosabelle requested permission to walk over the different apartments; Mr. Goodman yielded his consent; and Emily having offered to accompany her, they both quitted the room together, leaving the gentlemen to themselves.

Our heroine and her companion ranged through every apartment the house contained; and as the former perceived that the furniture in some of the rooms had not been disturbed, and that, in most instances, the place had undergone very little change since it had been inhabited by her and her father, her heart swelled almost to bursting, and she was obliged frequently to pause, and give free indulgence to her feelings; and Emily did not offer to interrupt her, for she well knew that it would all tend to relieve her overcharged bosom, and soften the anguish of her mind. In one room was a full-length portrait of her father, as he looked when happiness, reason, and content were his—so kind, so amiable; the poor penitent knelt before it, and, as her lips breathed a prayer for the consummation of her wishes, in which Emily cordially joined, she wept torrents of tears. Every little thing she gazed on brought to her mind some tender reminiscence, and recalled all the bright and sunny visions of former days. She could have gazed on them for ever; and from them culled a lesson which severely punished her for the error of which she had been guilty.

From the house they walked into the garden, and here again was food for deep and melancholy reflection. In this garden her father had taken great delight, and the flower had been carefully attended to by her. But now, al-though it was still well arranged, it was very different to what it had been then, and the flowers seemed to droop their heads, and to have lost half their freshness. Here was the little alcove, looking upon the crystal lake, in which Rosabelle and her father had so often delighted to sit, and where she had passed many of the happiest moments of her life—moments, it was to be feared, that were never fated to return. Here had she often struck the strings of her harp, and warbled songs of bliss; but now, alas! everything seemed changed to gloom, misery, and despair. It did not look like the same place, for the master-spirit was gone.

Rosabelle loitererd for some time here, absorbed in dismal reflection, and unable to leave it; but at length Emily, fearful that she might give too free indulgence to her feelings, gently forced her away, and going into the house, returned to the apartment in which they had left Mr. Goodman and Rattleton.

In the meantime Lord Ravensford, who had returned with Mr. Goodman and Rattleton, was all impatience and anxiety—the victim of alternate hopes and fears. Had it not been for the advice of Mr. Goodman, he would not have procrastinated his meeting with Rosabelle one hour; but when the folly and imprudence of such a course were pointed out to him, he reluctantly yielded to persuasion, and submitted to be guided entirely by Mr. Goodman. The latter gentleman found this task not so difficult to accomplish when he informed Lord Ravensford that their meeting should not be delayed longer than the following day. While the circumstances were going forward which we have been describing, the latter was in the adjoining apartment to that in which Rosabelle and the others were seated, only waiting a signal to rush forward and clasp her to his heart, and beg her forgiveness. With what mingled feelings of melancholy and rapture did he listen to the well-remembered tones of her voice, and hung upon every word; and how did he long once more to gaze upon her features! The time appeared almost insupportably tedious to him, and he could not help thinking that Mr. Goodman protracted the decisive moment beyond all reason. When Rosabelle and Emily quitted the parlour, he had an opportunity of issuing from his concealment and remonstrating with his friends, and he earnestly begged that they would bring about the event at once, if they did not wish to drive him mad, or to tempt him to overstep those rules of prudence they had prescribed. Mr. Goodman promised faithfully to do as he requested, but at the same time once more urged upon him the necessity of his using the utmost caution in his behaviour, or the sudden surprise, in Rosabelle's present state of mind, might otherwise be productive of the most dangerous consequences.

Lord Ravensford, who saw at once the absolute necessity of this, promised to obey, and when he heard Rosabelle and Emily approaching the parlour, he returned to the room in which he had hitherto been concealed, and there awaited the eventful moment, his heart palpitating violently with mingled feelings of hope, pleasure, and apprehension.

"I have looked upon each well-known spot, examined every place that was dear to him," said Rosabelle, when they had returned to the parlour, "and, although they have caused many pangs in my bosom, I now feel more at ease, and hope begins to hold more powerful sway over my mind. With a beating heart I wait the event; could I but once more hear him call me by name, and bless me with his forgiveness, I should die in peace."

"I must not, will not hear you talk about dying again, Miss Montalbert," observed Rattleton; "trust me, you have many years of happiness in store yet."

"Oh, yes, I feel that there are," said Emily; "dearest Rosabelle, we yet may pass our days in peace together. Should your father recover, but one thing will be wanting to complete your happiness—Lord Ravensford's penitence and reparation!"

"Oh, name him not!" ejaculated Rosabelle, "he is a wretch—a villain, unworthy of a thought but such as is prompted by disgust and detestation."

"Be not too severe, my dear Miss Montalbert, I entreat!" said Mr. Goodman. "I am ready to admit that Ravensford has been a villain, but what if he were a repentant one?"

"He is the murderer of my peace and honour, the destroyer of my parent, the ruin of all my prospects," observed Rosabelle.

"But still he is the father of your child," returned Mr. Goodman.

"He is my seducer," retorted our heroine.

"But he will be your husband," exclaimed Emily, eagerly.

"My husband!" repeated Rosabelle, "impossible! Is he not the husband of another?"

"No," replied Emily, "every obstacle to your union is removed—his father is dead, and his heart is alive to penitence and virtue."

"Is he not in London," said our heroine incredulously, "brooding over some fresh schemes of villany, doubtless; and plotting the ruin of emale chastity?"

"No," returned all three in a breath; "Ravensford is here!"

"Here!" shrieked Rosabelle, starting up with astonishment, and turning ghastly pale and red alternately.

In an instant Ravensford threw open the door, and rushing into the apartment, fell at Rosabelle's feet, at the same time exclaiming—

"Yes, behold him at your feet!—Oh, Rosabelle, my adored, my injured Rosabelle, can you forgive a wretch like me?—the source of all your errors, all your woes!"

Rosabelle heard him not; surprised, thunderstruck, shocked—she no sooner beheld him, than she sank upon the floor in a state of insensibility. With the most heartfelt agony did Lord Ravensford raise her from the floor, press her to his heart, and imprinted kisses many and fervent upon her pale cheeks; called upon her name, and implored her to forgive him. It was with the utmost difficulty Mr. Goodman could persuade him to resign her to the care of his daughter, who used such restoratives as she had handy, and which shortly proved efficacious. Rosabelle recovered, and, passing her hands across her temples, she said—

"What a strange vision has haunted my imagination; I dreamt that I was in the presence of my seducer; that he knelt at my feet; talked of penitence, and begged my forgiveness."

"Much wronged, angelic Rosabelle," exclaimed Ravensford, once more coming forward, "it was no vision; behold your penitent lover is here to beg your forgiveness for the sorrows, the disgrace he has caused you, and to make you all the reparation in his power."

"Reparation, Ravensford!" said Rosabelle, "what can ever repair the injuries, the dreadful injuries, you have been the cause of? Can any atonement, which you can make, restore the reason of my poor father?—Can it——"

"Rosabelle," interrupted Ravensford, "for the love of heaven, do not distract me. I know—I feel—I deserve all that your reproach can heap upon me; but in pity do not destroy the hopes that have been so recently engendered in my breast. Oh, most severely have I suffered for my crime, bitter has been my compunction. Driven to despair, but for the interference of these dear friends, my hands would have put a period to my existence; do not, then, I beseech you, driven me again to madness, but pardon me, and my whole, my future study shall be to make you happy."

Rosabelle looked on him with a bursting heart; utterance was for a few seconds denied her; these seconds were as so many hours to the impatient and anxious Ravensford, who still knelt at her feet and looked up in her face with the most earnest looks of supplication. At length, as her eyes filled with tears, she exclaimed—

"Ravensford, cruel, guilty, wretched, penitent Ravensford—partner of my crimes—my heart—"

"There now, I'll not have another word said," interrupted Rattleton, in his usual volatile manner; "your hearts are agreed upon the subject, and whatever you may say, does not signify a button. Ravensford, I wish you joy in this double accession to your honours, and your honour; Rosabelle, I shall soon wish you joy on your nuptials, for if I have any influence in the business, you shall be married without any further delay. Emily and I have been foolish enough to commit matrimony, and we must have somebody to keep us in countenance. Now, now, embrace at once, and end this matter, of which I am quite tired."

"Oh, Rattleton, · Mr. Goodman," cried Ravensford, "my heart is too full for thanks. Rosabelle, still dear, dear Rosabelle!"

"Truant, Ravensford—Husband!" cried Rosabelle, as she threw herself into his arms, and wept upon his bosom. We must pass over the scene which followed, for no pen can do justice to it. Again and again they embraced, and mingled their tears together; and then Lord Ravensford pressed his offspring to his heart, and bestowed upon him all a parent's fondest caresses. There needed no further explanation; the looks, the manner of Lord Ravensford, all proved the sincerity of his protestations; and Rosabelle gazed upon him with glances as affectionate as those occasioned in the spring time of their love. She felt that he was then all her heart could wish him; that he was truly penitent, and should the plan prove successful in restoring her father to his senses, her sorrows would be at an end, her happiness would be complete. And hope, in all her gayest smiles, assured her that her wishes would be verified; that by her sedulous attention, and that of Mr. Goodman and Emily, her poor father would be restored to his senses. Oh, yes, the scene of all his former pleasures, the fond partner of his blissful moments, must recal his scattered reason, and when he was assured of the penitence of both her and Ravensford, and the anxiety of the latter to make all the atonement he could, she was confident that the happiness of her father would be fully restored to him. Nor would he be awakened to reason to find himself a ruined man, as, thanks to the friendly assiduity and strict integrity of Mr. Goodman, his affairs were in a fair way of arrangement, and there was not the least doubt but that in a few weeks they would be finally and satisfactorily settled; more particularly as Mr. Goodman was in hopes that he should be able to recover a large sum of money owing to Mr. Montalbert, and which would be of itself sufficient to liquidate nearly the whole of the demands upon him. But for the remembrance of her father, poor Rosabelle would now have been extremely happy; the truant had returned to her—her first, her only love, was aroused again to honour and virtue; she could no longer doubt his sincerity, her honour would be retrieved, and her boy, her beloved child, would not be fatherless! As she gazed upon her lover, and marked the fond delight which animated his features when she had pronounced his forgiveness, she felt all her former passion return with even more than its original strength,

and she could scarcely believe that he had acted towards her with that cruel treachery, which had exposed her to so much suffering and so many painful vicissitudes. But now that his repentance was, she felt convinced, sincere, she was ready to bury the past in oblivion, and felt satisfied that, should her father be restored to his senses, he would freely and gladly grant him his pardon, when assured of what he had suffered by remorse, and how willing he was to make reparation. Of one thing, however, Rosabelle was determined, and she expressed the same resolution to Lord Ravensford and her friends, which was that she would never consent to become the wife of the former, until either death closed the sufferings of her ill-fated father, or he regained his reason, and pronounced to Ravensford and herself his forgiveness. This determination was too reasonable for Ravensford or the others to offer any objection to it, although the former was so impatient to make every atonement for his guilt, that he would have been glad that the marriage rites should be solemnized without any delay.

The remainder of the day was the happiest that Rosabelle had lately experienced, and in which feeling Lord Ravensford and the others fully participated, and the time flew away on gossamer wings, night arriving before any of the party had anticipated it. Emily and her father would have persuaded our heroine to remain there for the night, but she thought it would be better for her to return home, and after arranging her little affairs first thing in the morning, to give up the cottage and return to the hall, the home of her early youth. Having come to this arrangement, our heroine, accompanied by her friends and Lord Ravensford, returned in the carriage of the latter to the humble dwelling she had lately occupied, and there, after an affectionate farewell, and promising to send the vehicle for her early on the morrow, they separated.

Notwithstanding it was getting late, Meriel had not retired to rest; in fact, she had been all impatience and anxiety to learn from "her dear young lady" the particulars of what had occurred to her; and, consequently, she no sooner saw a light in the casement of our heroine's hut, than she hastened to her, and after greeting her with her usual kindness, she put a multiplicity of questions to her regarding the adventures of the day, what Mr. Goodman and his daughter had said and done, and what they purposed doing for her; whether they had behaved kindly to her, and a variety of other interrogatories to the same effect, and all prompted by her hearty wishes for Rosabelle's welfare. Although our heroine was not much disposed to be communicative that night, being tired, yet she was willing to gratify the poor woman's anxiety, appreciating as she did the motives from whence it sprung; she, therefore, briefly as she could, detailed what had taken place, and which, when Meriel heard it, afforded her the utmost pleasure, more especially her reconciliation with and the compunction of Lord Ravensford, and to hear that in future she was to reside with Mr. Goodman, and be again the lady she was formerly. Meriel, also, could never sufficiently express the satisfaction and admiration she felt for the plan which Mr. Goodman had formed for the restoration of Montalbert to his senses, and expressed her most sanguine hopes of its success. She left Rosabelle quite elated with joy at the days occurrences, and promised to be with her early in the morning to assist her in the adjustment of her affairs, previous to her departure to the hall, and, merever, she was fully resolved herself to be near the madhouse, to see Mr. Montalbert brought away from the asylum.

Need we describe the feelings of Rosabelle after the joyful, the totally unexpected events which had that day taken place? We are certain we need not: the reader can fully imagine them. Now that she had again seen Ravensford, and been assured of his repentance, and his willingness to make her every reparation; when she had once more listened to his tender asseverations, and was convinced of their sincerity, she felt her heart throb with all the strength of that unbounded love she had at first entertained for him, and a load of care was removed from her bosom that had before so heavily oppressed it. She dwelt upon every word he had uttered to her; recalled to her memory his tender, his ardent expressions, and the more she did so, the more was she impressed with the firm belief of his truth. And should but her father be restored to his senses, she was certain that his forgiveness would be awarded to them both, that happiness would again dawn upon them. These thoughts calmed the turbulence of those feelings that had before distracted her mind, and she had several hours of most refreshing sleep, and awoke at an early hour in the morning, in better health and spirits than she had experienced for some time before, and fully prepared for the duties of the day. Her affairs were soon settled, and, by the time they were completed, Lord Ravensford and Mr. Goodman drove up to the door, and Rosabelle bade adieu to Meriel, she inviting, and the latter promising to call at the hall every day, to inquire after the health and circumstances of "her dear young lady."

The carriage was not long in reaching the hall, where it put down Lord Ravensford, it being thought advisable that he should not be seen by Montalbert for the present, and it then proceeded direct on its way to the asylum.

On the way thither Mr. Goodman and our heroine conversed but little, they being too much occupied with their own thoughts, which were of a similar description, and the heart of Rosabelle beat quick with the conflicting sentiments of hope and fear.

Meriel did not forget to make the poor people, who were so fondly attached, acquainted with the particulars of what we have been detailing, and the purpose upon which she was gone to the asylum, and when they heard it, they simultaneously raised their voices towards heaven in purest but fervent supplication for success in her undertaking. Had their prayers indeed prevailed, upon her arrival at the prison, she would have found her unfortunate father not only fully restored to reason, but ready to clasp her to his bosom, and imprint his assurance of forgiveness upon her lips. However, when they did arrive at the asylum, and were introduced to Montalbert's cell, they found there was not the least change for the better in him, although it seemed to afford him great delight when he was told that he was going to ride in the same carriage with the "pretty lady," which was what he always denominated our heroine, and he took his seat between her and Mr. Goodman with much apparent pleasure.

As nothing of importance took place on the journey from the asylum to the residence of Mr. Goodman, we shall not detain the reader by any description of it. Mr. Montalbert was very passive on the way, and when he alighted from the vehicle and saw the house, his satisfaction seemed unbounded; he clapped his hands, and laughed heartily, from which both Mr. Goodman and our heroine augured the best results, as it appeared to them that some recollection of the place had dawned upon his scattered memory. Mr. Goodman had thought it advisable to have one of the keepers to sleep with him, but it was only with him he behaved in the most untractable manner, he having great trouble in making him keep to his couch, and he was often compelled to knock for Rosabelle, who slept in the adjoining chamber. When Montalbert saw her he immediately became perfectly tranquil, and did not offer to oppose her wishes, but on the contrary, seemed most anxious to obey them. Lord Ravensford most sedulously avoided the presence of the unhappy maniac, for fear the sight of him might be attended with bad results, and, in fact, so deeply was he stung with remorse when he reflected that he had been the cause of bringing him into that awful condition, that he revolted from the idea of encountering him with horror.

A most gratifying but melancholy sight was it to mark the care of Rosabelle to her father. Well aware as she was that nothing whatever that she could do for him, could repair the dreadful wreck she had occasioned, that poor amends indeed would be all that she could now do for it, yet was it truly heart-rending to behold how fondly, how attentively she accompanied him in his rambles when he chose to walk forth from the house, and how she laboured to make him appear as he was wont to do in his person; but even had she not done so, and notwithstanding the change which his awful malady had wrought in him, the appearance of the unfortunate Montalbert was noble, was gentlemanly.

And there were times, too, when the change was so little visible, and her father looked so much like what he was before he was deprived of his reason, that the imagination of Rosabelle was so powerfully worked upon by the delusion, and, for the moment, she would forget herself entirely, fly towards him, and grasping his hand with the most eager anxiety, she would call him father, and talk to him the same as if he had been in a rational state of mind. But soon, alas! the spell would be broken, and she awakened to double misery. He would gaze at her vacantly for a second, laugh idiotically, and exhibit all that phrensy which disordered his brain.

In spite of all these disappointments, however, it certainly was a source of infinite gra-

THE KEEPERS TEARING THE MANIAC FATHER FROM ROSABELLE'S ARMS.

tification to our heroine to observe that he really recognised and was pleased at the attentions she paid him. But then a mist was before his eyes, and a cloud was upon his brain; he recognised her, and was pleased with her attentions, it is true, but he knew not who she was that bestowed them. He knew not that she who was incessantly with him, to comfort, succour, and watch by him, was that poor girl whom he believed to be dead, or guilty of the most cruel ingratitude. He heard her, but she was unknown to him; he beheld her, but in her he recognised not the child of whom he had been so doatingly, so passionately fond; and this it was that racked the brain, and tortured the heart of Rosabelle more than all, and deteriorated from that hope she would otherwise have indulged in.

Rosabelle had engaged the gardener, who had been her father's servant, to make the walks look as much like what they formerly did as possible; a task which he executed very well, with the exception of leaving some straggling flowers on the path which he had forgotten to tie up. The following morning after this was done, Rosabelle, Emily, her father, and Montalbert, walked into the garden, with which he seemed extravagantly pleased, dancing, laughing, and cutting all sorts of antics, until suddenly his eye rested on the flowers before mentioned, and addressing Rosabelle, he said, in tones quite rational:—

No. 6.

"Do you not see those flowers trailing along the ground? Bind them up—bind them up—you should not leave them thus."

In her days of happiness, before Rosabelle had absconded from her father, to attend to the flowers in the garden had been one of her most favourite employments; and Montalbert had imagined that no one could attend to them so well as her—guess, then, the transport, the hope, these observations must have excited in her breast, which she could not help thinking originated in his imagining that she and his daughter were in some way connected, had flitted across his mind. With what pleasure, with what ecstasy, did she immediately proceed to do as he desired, and Montalbert watched her actions with eager and approving eyes until she had completed it, when suddenly he drew her affectionately toward him, and ejaculating—

"Bless you! bless you!—thou art a good girl—a good girl!" he pressed and kissed her vehemently.

It would be impossible to describe the astonishment, the transport, the violent agitation of our heroine upon this; and her feelings completely overpowering her, she fainted.

She was quickly restored to sensibility again, and with much anxiety asked Emily and Mr. Goodman how her father (who was running too and fro), had acted when he saw the effect his behaviour had had upon her.

"Oh, Rosabelle, it was a most distressing scene," replied Emily. "He forced you from me, supported you in his arms, and would not let any one apply the restoratives but himself; but when you were recovering, you made use of the words 'dearest father,' which took an immediate and wonderful effect upon him: he stared at you for a minute quite aghast, turning alternately pale and red; then resigning you to me, he rushed from the spot, and commenced running about in the manner in which you now observe him."

"Ah!" ejaculated Rosabelle, joyfully, "your words fill my bosom with ecstasy. I am satisfied—quite satisfied, and at this moment experience indescribable happiness! It is evident that he remembered me;—I have again felt a father's kiss upon my cheek—received a parent's warm embrace, and I am happy. Then the emotion you tell me he exhibited when I was insensible, all serves to convince me that he knew I was his child. It has inspired my breast with the most sanguine hope that ere long his senses will be quite restored to him."

"Very likely he may," answered Emily; " and——"

"Very likely he may—and—" repeated Rosabelle, in a petulant tone; "I am certain —I know he will be quite himself again

shortly and those who are doubtful of the same are no friends of mine."

With these words Rosabelle left Mr. Goodman and his daughter, and hastened to rejoin Montalbert; they taking no notice of the manner in which she had spoken, well knowing the cause of it, and that she, in all probability, did not know at the time what she was saying. The perpetual care and misery which Rosabelle endured had taken a painful effect upon her temper, which was by no means to be wondered at; and having reflected until she had formed the most sanguine expectations of her father's recovery, she could not patiently brook contradiction upon the subject. But if ever, when she became more calm, she became conscious of having said anything which might cause offence to, or wound the feelings of any one, she was uneasy until she had made an ample apology, and effected a reconciliation with them.

The joy with which Montalbert received her on her return to him, drew tears in her eyes, and the maniac became once more terrified; and ejaculated "Poor girl! poor girl!" he threw his arms around her waist, and seemed to be apprehensive that she was again about to faint.

The exultation of Rosabelle knew no bounds, and, turning to Mr. Goodman and Emily, she exclaimed—

"There, there—did I not tell you?"

"God grant that your hopes may be realised, my dear Rosabelle," said Emily, seeing the folly of attempting to contradict her; and shortly afterwards, as it was getting dark, they returned to the house.

Day after day elapsed, and Montalbert's attachment to our heroine appeared to increase, and not only did he seem to be particularly fond of her, but also of her son, whose innocent gambols served constantly to amuse him.

Not an evening passed, if the weather was favourable, in which Rosabelle, her child and father, did not take those walks that had been the favourites of the latter when he was in his right senses; and those poor persons amongst whom he had so amply dispensed his benevolence would meet them with bows and courtesies of respect, and many were the prayers they uttered for the recovery of Montalbert, and the blessings they invoked upon the head of his daughter.

Mr. Goodman had at last, as the principal assignee, succeeded in bringing his affairs to a final adjustment, and nearly the whole of his property was recovered, so that Rosabelle was placed in the same condition that she formerly was; and, in fact, the house at present inhabited by Mr. Goodman he determined to resign to her, if she at any future time required it. This afforded Rosabelle no extravagant satisfaction, although it gave her great pleasure to think that, should her father be restored, he would not be placed in any of those difficulties which would retard, if not ultimately defeat, his complete restoration to convalescence.

Mr. Goodman and his daughter, as may be expected, did not escape the envenomed tongue of slander for the kindness with which they had behaved to Rosabelle; but Mr. Goodman generally treated any remarks of the kind with the most superlative contempt, unless the attack was brutally directed towards our heroine, when he would champion her cause with all that spirit which his manly feelings, and the regard he bore for her, prompted him to. An event of this description occurred, which it may be as well to mention in this place.

It happened that Mr. Goodman was invited to a party held at a lady's house in the neighbourhood, who had two bold, ignorant, vain, and extremely ugly daughters, who, in her prosperity, were ever most inordinately jealous of Rosabelle, and now took the opportunity of venting their spleen in the most virulent species of calumny whenever they could.

The eldest Miss Scanmag, who either did not, or pretended not to know that Mr. Goodman was so near her, addressed herself to her sister, and two or three other females that formed a coterie, observing, with a toss of the head, and a look which was meant to be expressive of much virtuous disgust, said—

"Is it not horrible that that abandoned creature, the daughter of Montalbert, should be countenanced in the town—nay, even sheltered beneath the roof of Mr. Goodman, where her paramour daily visits her? I wonder she is not ashamed to be seen in public; but then the impudence of such base hussies as her is abominable."

"That is a very true observation of yours, Miss Scanmag," returned another female who was sitting next to her; "they have face enough for anything. Why, I understand that Lord Ravensford turned her off in London because he found her flirting with some low fellow, and I think he must be mad to take her again after such conduct."

"It is very disgraceful of his lordship, to say the best of it." remarked the amiable Miss Scanmag the younger; "but it will not last long, I have no doubt, and then there is no other prospect for her but the town, the fittest place for such a minx as she is."

"Say, rather, Miss," interposd Mr. Goodman, in tones of the most ineffable contempt, "that Miss Montalbert is more likely not to trouble the world long. However, notwithstanding the error of which she has been guilty, her penitence makes ample atonement for it, and what she has suffered, and her praiseworthy conduct since her return hither, merits not only the deepest sympathy, but admiration."

"Admiration!" reiterated Mrs. Scanmag, the mother of the two amiable ladies who had before spoken, "admiration, indeed! what for one who has——"

"Whatever have been Miss Montalbert's faults, interrupted Mr. Goodman, with resentment, "she has done no more than many in high life, and other grades of society who yet pretend to the most inordinate virtues, and are the first to cry out against the indiscretions of those against whom their malice and envy have been excited. At any rate, he who caused her to sin is ready to make her reparation, and would undoubtedly be the best to select to defend her cause, and reply to the animadversions on her character that are so freely indulged in by many individuals."

"Oh, no doubt the girl can deceive weak-minded people," observed the elder Miss Scanmag, spitefully.

"Did she ever deceive you, miss?" retorted Mr. Goodman, sarcastically.

"No, indeed, I was never deceived by her," answered Miss Scanmag; "I always thought her a forward, bold slut, and my ideas were fully realised. But she had always a very smooth tongue in her head, and some persons are silly enough to be cajoled by any tale. I am really surprised, Mr. Goodman, that you should countenance such a girl, and even allow her the shelter of your roof and your protection."

"And it is for the very reason that I am her present protector, that I condescend to reply to some very ignorant and ill-natured observations," returned Mr. Goodman; "if the most untiring attention to her unfortunate father; if sincere repentance, prayers, and tears, can prevail, then most assuredly hath Heaven forgiven her, and she will——"

"Heaven, indeed! oh, the profanity!" ejaculated Mrs. Scanmag, turning up her eyes with a very solemn assumption of pious horror. "What can such a creature as that have to do with Heaven, I should like to know?—I am sure whenever I die, that, in the other world, I shall never be placed in such society as this Miss Montalbert."

"Certainly, madam," observed Mr. Goodman, "if an Almighty being views your faults as you view those of your fellow creatures, I can unhesitatingly declare myself to be perfectly of your opinion. But your remarks, I think, are rather out of place in a public company, and especially when it is well known that Miss Montalbert has my protection. However, as there may be many persons present who are not acquainted with the particulars of this melancholy history, I will, with permission, detail them, and the sensible and humane will then see how far Miss Montalbert has atoned for her errors, and not only whether or not she is entitled to their sympathy, but how infinitely she is above those base aspersions which are so lavishingly bestowed upon her by some individuals."

Mrs. Scanmag, her daughters, and the *amiable* coterie by which they were immediately surrounded, would willingly have dispensed with this recapitulation, but many of the guests, coinciding with Mr. Goodman's sentiments, and forming the more sensible and respectable portion of the company, having expressed a great desire to hear Rosabelle's melancholy story, Goodman proceeded forthwith to detail it as briefly as he could, but bearing most energetically upon the conduct of our heroine since her return to the town; her unremitting attention to her father;—her industry;—her incessant care, and sincere repentance; and many of the guests were affected even to tears, and expressed the utmost commiseration in her misfortunes, and uttered the most fervent wishes that her worthy efforts might be crowned with success, and that in the union with her seducer, now as well as herself, sincerely penitent, she might experience all that happiness she merited.

"Notwithstanding, in a moment of weakness, she listened to the voice of the seducer, still is she Rosabelle Montalbert; she who was ever the pride of the place;—beloved by the poor,—esteemed and honoured by the wealthy; whose hand was ever the first to dispense charity to the needy and distressed, and to lighten the sorrows of the afflicted."

These observations were eagerly and cordially responded to by several voices, and wound up to a pitch of almost insupportable malevolence, Mrs. Scanmag and her daughters became livid with rage; and were for some time so confounded, that they could not give utterance to a syllable in reply; at last, however, the malignity of Mrs. Scanmag found vent in the following words—

"Good gracious! the world has come to a pretty pass, indeed;—here are some persons who may do anything with impunity; nay, who may not only be guilty of the most shameful indiscretions, (as they are mildly denominated,) but who are actually praised for the same, as if they were paragons of virtue, and as though to be guilty of wantonness, and driving a parent out of his senses, were deeds worthy of the highest commendation. I doubt very much whether the daughters of other persons would meet with the same treatment. Miss Montalbert, indeed; it is quite sickening and disgusting to hear the creature's name. Before she ran away and deserted her father there was nothing talked of but Miss Montalbert. No one could do anything but Miss Montalbert; and yet I should like to know whether certain people's children couldn't do quite as much, and perhaps more, although they did not think so much of themselves, nor were

so fond of letting people see what they could do."

"To be sure not," exclaimed the younger Miss Scanmag. "had other people's children followed Miss Montalbert's example, they would have doubtless met with very little mercy at other persons' hands. But it is very well known that Miss Montalbert had always boldness and impudence enough to perform anything."

"To be sure she had," responded Miss Scanmag the elder, "and a very pretty and respectable condition it has brought her to; fact to—to—but the word shacks me."

"Miss Scanmag," cried Mr. Goodman, indignantly, "are you not ashamed thus to exult over the misfortunes of your fellow creature, and that one of your own sex?"

"Misfortunes!" screamed Miss Scanmag, in her harshest and most discordant tones; "and pray who brought on those misfortunes but herself? I have no patience with such abandoned fallen creatures."

"Miss Montalbert may have fallen," replied Mr. Goodman, "but how much more fallen must those be who refuse that Christian mercy to the errors of their fellow creatures, which is one of virtue's most noble qualities. In the midst of her prosperity, when surrounded by every luxury and happiness, never did Miss Montalbert refuse the tear of pity to the unfortunate, nor treat the faults of others with undue severity. It strikes me, miss, that you would have done well to have followed her example, and then you would never have given utterance to those sentiments, I regret to have heard you express this day."

"This is insupportable!" shrieked Miss Scanmag, almost choked with passion; "to talk to me about following the example of such a low degraded——but I will be calm—I am not in a passion; I will treat such observations as they deserve,—with silent contempt. She set me an example?—mamma, Euphemia, I can't sit in this company any longer to hear such creatures held up as a pattern to prudent and virtuous females!"

And with these words, her face completely livid with malignity and resentment, Miss Scanmag arose from the table, and bounded out of the room, in a towering rage, and followed by Mrs. Scanmag and Euphemia, amid the laughter, pity, and contempt of the persons assembled.

Although Mr. Goodman tried all in his power to keep from the knowledge of Rosabelle observations similar to those we have recorded, they often reached her ears; but she was fully prepared to encounter them, and they drew not from her a single pang. Her mind was too deeply absorbed in the one great task she had imposed upon herself; too much engrossed by her care and attention to her father to give scarcely a thought even to other subjects, and the hopes that had gained a place in her bosom of his ultimate restoration to his senses, haunted her imagination night and day.

With what mingled feelings of self-reproach, love, and sorrow, did Lord Ravensford watch her affectionate attention to Mr. Montalbert, and although he had never ventured to enter the presence of the latter, for fear the recognition of him should make him worse,—often did he secrete himself in the garden when they were taking their customary walks, and watch with the most poignant anguish the care and solicitude of Rosabelle; the innocent gambols of his son, and the wild antics of the Maniac Father. In such moments as these how bitterly did he upbraid himself for the crime he had committed; for his cruelty and treachery to Rosabelle, and which had been the cause of all the misery he beheld. There was no sacrifice which he would not willingly have made, could he have been the means of rekindling the light of reason in the mind of Mr. Montalbert; and no reproach that he could heap upon himself, which he could consider sufficiently severe for the manner in which he had behaved towards so noble-minded a woman. How anxious was he to make her his bride; and again and again did he urge her to assent that their nuptials should take place without any farther delay; but Rosabelle remained firm to the resolution she had formed, namely, never to become the wife of Ravensford until such times as her poor father should be restored to his senses, and would be able to give them his consent and benediction. What powerful reasons, therefore, had Lord Ravensford to pray for the speedy recovery of Montalbert. Rosabelle was convinced of the sincerity of his protestations, and although she found it impossible to forget the past, she sincerely pardoned him.

Montalbert was now dressed the same as he used to be formerly, and there were times when any one to gaze upon him would have scarcely believed that he was not in his senses, he looked so rational. But these moments of calmness only took place at intervals, and a wild laugh, or some extravagant distortion of the features, would in an instant do away with the delusion under which they had laboured, and Montalbert would again become all the maniac, rave of his daughter, mock at Rosabelle if she called him father; and when somewhat appeased, request her to accompany him in search of her tomb.

Day after day, week after week passed away, and month succeeded month, without any material change taking place, and alternate hopes and fears continually distracted the mind of our heroine, and preyed upon her constitution. Sometimes utter despair would fall upon her heart, and she would become, as it were, completely inactive and unfit for anything. Lord Ravensford became seriously alarmed for her health, and urged the absolute necessity of her resting for awhile from her arduous duties, and seeking change of scene. But Rosabelle could not listen to such advice with the slightest degree of patience, and declared that nothing should induce her to leave her father; that she would remain with him and watch him night and day, even though her life should fall the sacrifice to her assiduity.

Her lover and Mr. Goodman found it impossible to combat these arguments, and they were, therefore, compelled to drop the subject, and to trust in Providence for the ultimate completion of their ardent hopes and wishes.

In Emily, Rosabelle ever found a most delightful companion; and her gentle soothings and arguments often had the effect of recalling her from the very lowest depths of despair, and once more arousing her to hope. She would often accompany her with her poor father, and he always beheld her with pleasure, and seemed gratified when he saw her and Rosabelle in each other's company.

Mr. Goodman had thought it prudent to defer resorting to the scheme he had at first thought of until the last extremity, when all other plans had failed; and he had given strict orders, and taken especial care that Montalbert should not approach that apartment in which it had been resolved that the trial should be made, so that it might not lose any of the effect which it was desirable it should have. This apartment had been the favourite sitting-room of Montalbert in his days of reason and happiness; and here everything remained in precisely the same condition as it had been at that time. Not an article of furniture had been removed: the books—the vases, filled with flowers, fresh, 'tis true—the harp, whose chords Rosabelle had so often touched to charm him—remained the same as they were on the evening of that fatal night when she abandoned her home.

Now, when every other effort had failed, was the time when the plan should be put into execution, Mr. Goodman thought; and he mentioned his ideas to Rosabelle. She agreed with them with avidity, and the following day was appointed for the important event. The arrangement of the business was entirely undertaken by Mr. Goodman, whose bosom as the time approached was more and more elated with hope.

Before a door which opened into another apartment, a large frame had been constructed, so that Rosabelle, dressed as she used to be before she left her father, and seated at her harp, might look like a portrait. Before this a green baize was drawn, so that the objects beyond might be concealed until the moment when they wanted to bring the trial of their scheme to a conclusion.

It was about the middle of the day when they found an opportunity of commencing their plans. Mr. Montalbert had stretched himself on a seat in the summer-house, as was his usual custom, and had fallen into a sound sleep. Cautiously Mr. Goodman ordered two or three of his servants to convey him to the sitting-room, where he was placed upon a sofa without waking him; and behind which Ravensford, Rattleton, Goodman, and Emily were concealed, watching him, while the keeper stood on the opposite side, in case his services should be required.

Rosabelle had taken her station, and the feelings of agony, suspense, hope, and fear that agitated her frame and racked her brain, were more powerful than can be done justice to by description.

There was a painful pause of a few moments, and not a sound could be heard save the low breathing of the patient, who slept as calmly as an infant. The keeper and Rosabelle had never observed him so comfortable and composed before—a circumstance which greatly added to the sanguine expectations they indulged in.

"I think it will be better for you not to be present," said Mr. Goodman, addressing the keeper; "the sight of you might spoil the effect of our stratagem. We have got everything ready, I believe. Do you think he will be waking soon?"

"It is near his time," answered the keeper; "sleep is mechanical with him—it has been rather a habit than otherwise of late."

"Away—away, then," said Mr. Goodman, hastily; "if I don't prove a good doctor in this case, I'll never take out a diploma for insanity, but confess myself more mad than my patient. We will commence operations directly—see, he arouses himself."

Montalbert awoke, and raising himself on his elbow, passed his hand across his eyes, and then, in solemn accents, ejaculated—

"Sleeping! would I could sleep like her! In her lone cell she sleeps the sleep of death; how long will this continue? I had a dream of days long past, bright days! would it would come again! Great Heaven! what change —what place is this? Oh, I should know this spot! Is reason dawning?—or is madness coming? No cell—no chains—no straw? No, no, I am not mad! Who's that? —who's that?"

"A friend!" answered the overjoyed Rattleton, stepping forward, and followed by Mr. Goodman and Emily, whose feelings may be conceived, but cannot be pourtrayed as they merit.

"A friend!" exclaimed Montalbert, fixing his eyes searchingly upon the speaker. "Have I, then, a friend? No, no! she was snatched from me by the damned artifices of a human fiend, who called himself my friend! No, no! 'tis false—I have no friend!"

"Beresford, stung with remorse," eagerly ejaculated Mr. Goodman, "and eager to repay the wrongs he has wrought you, now comes to give her to your arms again, and to crave your blessing on their union."

"For shame—for shame! old man!" said Montalbert, "falsehood but ill becomes that hoary head—age should be mate to truth."

"By Heaven, I—" cried Goodman.

"You mock me, sir," interrupted Montalbert; "I tell you, she is dead—poor Rosabelle. Yes, cold! cold! cold!—Oh! that I could again behold her!"

This was the important moment; the heart of Rosabelle throbbed violently against her side, and her blood rushed tumultuously through her veins as Emily drew back the curtain, and discovered Rosabelle in the attitude we have before described, seated at her harp, and attired in white.

"Has not this portrait some resemblance to her?" asked Emily, with the greatest anxiety.

Montalbert bent his eyes in the direction to which she pointed, and as they became fixed upon the form and countenance of his daughter, his frame became dreadfully agitated, he staggered towards it, and, clasping his hands, vociferated in delirious tones—

"Ha! what do I see? The shade of Rosabelle? Father of mercy, do not thus deceive me! In pity mock not a wretched father —cheat not mine eyes with fantasies of her I ne'er shall see again. Bring not back thus bright memories of past joys—gone—lost for ever! shut not out returning reason—still there! Then I must fly! I feel despair, rage, madness, agony! all, all, returning; they rise, they rage within me. One last, last look, and thus I turn myself away from this bright mockery! proof to the sorceries that would ensnare my soul. Yes, yes, there is no tarrying here. Away, away!"

Montalbert covered his face with his hands as he spoke, and groaning deeply, he was rushing towards the door of the apartment, when Rosabelle struck the strings of her harp, and in tones rendered doubly plaintive by the circumstances under which they were called forth; she sung the ballad he had always been so delighted to hear.

The words and the air in an instant arrested his attention; he paused, his bosom heaved, his countenance became pale and red alternately, his lips quivered, and his eye-lids were distended, while he exclaimed—

"That voice, that song! and yet, no. But still that form! oh, tell me, art thou real, or sent by hell to tantalize my soul?"

Rosabelle arose in the fame, and stretching forth her arms, in a paroxysm of wild, delirious transport and emotion, she ejaculated—

"Father! beloved father!"

"Ha!" cried Montalbert, rushing towards her, "it is no illusion, each sense assures me. My heart throbs with confirmation of their truth; oh, bliss beyond mortality! all, all, proclaim thee living. I know—I feel 'tis thou—my long lost child, my much-loved, erring, and forgiven Rosabelle!"

With frantic delight too powerful to be described, Montalbert and Rosabelle rushed into each other's arms, while the repentant Ravensford came forward, and taking his child, the child of Rosabelle by the hand, he knelt at Montalbert's feet, and in tones of the most earnest supplication, implored his forgiveness. We must draw a veil over the scene which followed. Suffice it to say that Montalbert joined the hands of Ravensford and Rosabelle, and invoked a blessing upon their heads.

———

CHAPTER XI.

THE WEDDING.—THE INTERRUPTION

As may be expected, it was several days after the happy restoration of Mr. Montalbert to his senses, and the joyful results we have recorded in the preceding chapter, ere the actors in this eventful drama were restored to anything like composure. Mr. Montalbert's frame and constitution had been greatly impaired by his long sufferings, and it required the greatest caution to appease the too violent indulgence of his feelings, lest the delirious transports of his joy should occasion a relapse of his fatal malady. Upon Rosabelle the consummation of her hopes, her wishes, had an effect that afforded her friends the utmost satisfaction; her ecstasy was not expressed by any extravagance of behaviour, but she seemed at once to resume all her former happiness and calmness, while her soul ascended in gratitude to Heaven for having so mercifully listened to her prayers, and rewarded her cares, her anxieties, her contrition, by so joyful a result. Scarcely a minute could she bear to be out of her father's sight, and bestowing upon him all those fond endearments, and unbounded attentions she had been in the habit of doing in the early days of their happiness. She felt that unlimited felicity which language is by far too weak to depict. Often, as she gazed upon his mild and benevolent countenance, now beaming with pleasure and content, she could scarcely persuade herself that anything had occurred to interrupt their peace, and the past would seem to her only as some frightful vision. Then when she heard Montalbert again and again express his forgiveness of

Ravensford, and evince the greatest impatience for their nuptials, her feelings would almost overpower her, and she would think that the Almighty had been more merciful to her, and showered down upon her more happiness than her errors had deserved. But when her father was informed that she had for so long a time been constantly with him, attended upon him, and watched with feverish impatience the least signs of returning reason, and he not to know her, his heart became full, almost to bursting, and he would clasp her to his bosom with convulsive emotion, and press a thousand kisses upon her lips. All that he had endured, all that was past, her crime, were forgotten in the transport of the present, and daily he regained strength and health. The little Alfred, too, shared his most unbounded love, and in his innocent gambols, he always found a balm for any corroding cares that otherwise might at times have been recalled by painful reminiscence to the bosom.

Mr. Goodman had made it one of his most especial cares to see to the arrangement of Mr. Montalbert's affairs as expeditiously as possible, in case the happy event of which he was in hopes should take place; so that upon his restoration to his senses, Mr. Montalbert found himself in the same situation that he was before his misfortunes, and had but a vague idea that anything had occurred to disarrange his affairs, no more than what might be supposed to be consequent upon such a misfortune as that which had occurred to him. Mr. Goodman had removed from the hall; all the old tenants lived upon the estate; and everything had the same aspect as if nothing had taken place to alter it.

But none more rejoiced at the restoration of Mr. Montalbert than the poor people, to whom he had been a father, and those persons in the neighbourhood who had had the honour of his friendship. A day of rejoicing was got up, and never were more more cordial or sincere demonstrations of delight and gratitude exhibited than on that occasion. Mrs. Scanmag and her two daughters were so chagrined that, finding no one to participate with them in their sentiments, they quitted the neighbourhood, expressing their determination never again to come near a place where modest women were surrounded with contamination, and in which immorality and shameless vice were patronized and lauded to the skies. They carried with them the utter scorn and detestation of every sensible and well-disposed person in the town.

Great indeed was the pleasure of honest Gilbert Batchelor and Meriel his wife, at the consummation of their "dear young lady's" wishes; and had she been connected with them by the ties of consanguinity, they could not have been more sincere in their satisfaction and gratitude. Nor did our heroine and her father forget to reward them for their kindness and services to the former: they were placed in a commodious little house, an annuity fixed upon them for life, and Gilbert promoted to the office of gardener to Mr. Montalbert—a situation of which he felt not a little proud, and declared often that he would not resign it to be made Lord Chancellor of England.

Mr. Goodman and his daughter, with her husband, were almost constant guests at the hall, and in their society Mr. Montalbert and Rosabelle passed some of the happiest moments of their lives.

Daily did the affection of Lord Ravensford for Rosabelle increase, and he seemed to think that nothing he could do or say could ever repay her for the many sufferings he had caused her. Innumerable times did Rosabelle assure him of her entire forgiveness, and avowed for him all that strength of passion with which he had at first inspired her. Now, repentant, fond, sincere —the father of her child—could it be expected that she could feel otherwise?

Lord Ravensford had purchased a handsome estate not far from the hall, so that when they were united they might constantly, or as often as possible, be near Montalbert; for Rosabelle could not endure for an instant the idea of being separated by any material distance again from him; well knowing, if he was deprived of her society, his happiness would be at an end, and that in all probability, he would relapse into that melancholy state of mind from which he had so recently been recovered. Often her father would look mournfully in her countenance, and, sighing deeply, would say—

"I know not how it is, my Rosabelle, but at times I cannot divest my mind of an impression which will, in spite of all my efforts, get possession of it, that this happiness is not destined to last. I would that I could shake it off; but surely heaven has sufficiently punished me for my errors, and will not again visit me with its wrath. You will not leave me, Rosabelle, will you?"

"Leave you, dear—dear father!" sobbed Rosabelle, "oh do not torture me by such horrible ideas!—Death, and death alone shall again separate us."

"I do believe you, my sweetest," her father would reply, regaining in some measure his composure, and kissing her fervently;— "pardon me; long suffering hath impaired my nerves; I will endeavour to conquer this tormenting feeling; and oh, may the Almighty in His infinite goodness, avert any evil that may threaten us."

As the strength of Mr. Montalbert daily increased, and the mind of Rosabelle became settled, Lord Ravensford urged the celebration of the nuptials, and Mr. Goodman giving it as his opinion that the sooner they were solemnized the better as the voice of scandal might

otherwise put a wrong construction on their motives for further delay, Mr. Montalbert acceded, and the day for the celebration of the auspicious event was appointed. And seldom had their been an event looked forward to with greater delight, expectation, and impatience in the neighbourhood, than that, and although both Ravensford and Rosabelle would much rather that the wedding had taken place as private as possible, so eager were the gentry and poor people to testify their joy and congratulations on that occasion, that Mr. Montalbert was induced to yield a compliance with their wishes, and to give instructions for it to be celebrated with all possible festivity. The cheerful note of preparation had been heard for many days before, and it was a general holiday in the neighbourhood, the hospitality provided being welcome to all who chose to go and partake of it.

At length the day appointed for the nuptials dawned, and a lovely morning it was. Not a cloud was to be seen in the clear blue sky, and the sun shed his warmest and most effulgent rays upon the earth. Nature itself seemed to rejoice at the coming event. The village bells rang forth their merriest peals, and all in the neighbourhood was bustle and joy.

Mr. Montalbert had been able to sleep but little the previous night, and when he did, his rest was disturbed by troublesome dreams, which recalled the events of the past to his mind, and rendered him feverish and uneasy.

He left his chamber sooner than he was wont to do, and descended to the parlour, where he found his daughter and the bridemaids already assembled, and attired for the joyful event that was shortly expected to take place. Montalbert approached his daughter, and as he fixed his eyes brimful of tears upon her, the recollection of that fatal day when she had been torn from him, rushed upon his memory with such force, that it almost overpowered him. He threw his arms around her in silence, and clasped her with the most indiscribable feelings of transport to his heart. His emotions were too strong to suffer him to give utterance to his feelings.

Rosabelle, though pale, looked as lovely as she did in the days of her greatest happiness; she was dressed in white, in the most simple but elegant manner, and no one could gaze upon her without admiration. On her right was Emily, her faithful her attached friend, who filled the capacity of one of her bridemaids, and whose sparkling eye, and the expression of her countenance, fully evinced the delight she felt on the occasion. It was an event she had looked forward to long before her own nuptials had taken place; but now that Rosabelle had been enabled to surmount all the heavy trials to which she had been exposed, the pleasure of it was more than doubly enhanced.

Shortly afterwards the bridegroom arrived, and he was received with the greatest enthusiasm.

Montalbert took the hands of Rosabella and Lord Ravensford, and placing them in each other, raised his eyes towards heaven, and in solemn and fervent accents, exclaimed :—

"The day has arrived which bestows my Rosabella upon one whom I firmly believe loves her, and will cherish her as she deserves !—Vouchsafe, Almighty Father, to crown their union with thy blessings; grant that no future cares may occur to interrupt their happiness, and all the wishes of thy faithful servant in this life will be gratified. My children,—my children, bless ye !—bless ye !—bless ye !"

The prayer and the blessing of Montalbert were responded to by all present; and the tears that were shed, best testified the impression his words had made upon them.

We will now request the reader to accompany us to the ornamented lawn before the mansion of Montalbert, where a gay posse of villagers were already assembled, and evincing the utmost joy upon the occasion, more especially three humble couple, who had resolved to be married on that morning, and upon each of whom Mr. Montalbert had promised to bestow

RESPECT OF THE VILLAGERS SHOWN TO MONTALBERT AND ROSABELLE.

a small sum of money, and a cottage, in honour of the nuptials of his daughter.

"Ay, ay," observed Mortimer, the steward, addressing the villagers in his usual jocular manner, "nobody doubted you'd be in time this morning; though among you there are some who are ever backward in coming to work, I must do you the justice to say, none are more ready in coming forward when there's a feast. There, there, you needn't throng so ; the eatables won't be on the tables yet awhile, and there will be more than enough for all of you, I'll warrant. But where's Robin Maydew, who is one of the three young men who are going to be married this morning ? I do not see him among you."

"Why he's waiting 'till the village schoolmaster writes out his epitaph-alarm-em, Master Steward," answered one of the villagers.

"Epitaph !" repeated Mortimer, "why, is he going to be buried then ?"

"No," replied the rustic, "he's going to be married you know."

At this moment there was a noise of music and loud shouts at no great distance from the lawn.

"Hey day," said Mortimer, "what noise of fiddling, drumming, and haloballooing is all this?—As I live, that silly scapegrace, Robin Maydew, decked out in ribbons and posies with a whole troop of fiddlers and pipers at his head ; Rosa Cowslip at his side, and all the village, man, woman, and child, tag, rag, and bobtail at his heels : why, what means all this ?"

"It is only Robin's bridal procession, I suppose, sir," returned one of the villagers.

"A *Bridewell* procession you mean," observed Mr. Mortimer; "ecod! you ought all to be sent to Bridewell, if it was only to get you out of the way; here they come !"

And there they did come, sure enough, and a very pretty assemblage they were when they made their appearance; Robin Maydew and his sweet-heart Rosa Cowslip, preceded by several fiddlers and pipers, and followed by a whole troop of rustics, decorated with large wedding favors, making as much noise as their lungs (which were none of the weakest) would allow them, and dancing and capering in the most extravagant and ludicrous manner.

"Hurrah! lads, thank you!" said Robin Maydew, as soon as he could obtain a hearing, "thank ye, that will do nicely. Master Steward, be the squire coming; for I be ready to be married, you see, and so be Rosa; ben't you, Rosa ?"

"That I be, Robin," said Rosa, with a simper and a blush.

"Ay, ay, the deuce doubt you," returned Mortimer, "always ready for mischief, that I'll warrant; the squire and gentry are coming this way now—but have the decency to wait until his lordship and our young lady are united, before you think of troubling them with your affairs : let them banquet on matrimony first, and then your wedding will serve by way of entertainment afterwards."

"Ah! a sort of a dessert, like," said Robin, laughing.

"Dessert, rogue," returned Mortimer, "if you had your desert, you'd be led to a halter at the cart's tail, and not an altar in a church."

"I don't value waiting an hour or two, Master Steward," observed Rosa, "so long as we do but manage to get married to day at last."

"At any rate, there's nothing like making sure, lass," said Robin; "here Gilbert Batchelor can answer for that; look at the many disappointments he had before he could get married."

"Ay, Robin, you may say that," returned Gilbert; "but we got over the job at last, didn't we, Meriel? thanks to Miss Montalbert, and Mrs. Rattleton."

"Yes, Gilbert," replied Meriel, "we were married safe enough at last; and what is more, I do not think that either of us have had any reason to repent of it since."

"No, inneed we haven't, my wench," returned Gilbert; "and I would recommend steady well disposed young women, not to stand dillydallying and considering on the brink of matrimony for any length of time, but to make the plunge at once."

"I like your advice vastly, Gilbert," said Robin, "and depend upon it, I will follow it as closely as I can; I will make the plunge, if I sink by it."

"Now, now, clear the way, clear the way," said the steward, "for you see the carriages have made their appearance, and the wedding party will be out directly. Hollo! who is this coming? Another madman, I declare. It is Giles Jolter, dancing and shouting, as if he had lost his senses. Well, I verily believe all the people are gone crazy this morning."

"Giles is another votary for wedlock, Mr. Steward," observed Gilbert Batchlelor, "and I dare say he has heard some good news, as he is so merry over it."

"Well, every person in this neighbourhood seems marriage-struck," remarked Mr. Mortimer; "the mania seems to spread so fast, that I am fearful if I remain in it much longer, I shall be seized with it myself. But here comes Giles."

At that moment the simple rustic alluded to, entered dancing about, and sing and laughing, and shouting alternately, in the most extravagant manner.

"Hey dey, Master Jolter, what's the matter now?" inquired the steward.

"Don't speak to me, Master Steward," replied Giles Jolter; "don't speak to me; the only relation I have in the world is just on the point of death, and I'm the happiest dog alive. I dare say she's giving her last kick now. Hurrah! hurrah! tol de dol!"

And with that Giles recommenced dancing and singing in the most ludicrous manner.

"Well," said Mortimer, "this is the first time I ever heard losing his only relation was a way to make a man the happiest dog alive; but you've not been at work to day?"

"Work!" repeated Giles; "work! no, I should think not; I shall do no more work till I am married. Tol de dol!"

"You married! ha! ha! ha!" laughed every person present.

"Yes, I married," repeated Giles; "and I should like to know what there is to laugh at in that ?"

"You say right, Giles," observed the steward. "Marriage is not always a thing to be laughed at: it often turns out to be a very serious affair."

"Well, that may be true, Master Steward," returned Giles; "but I do not think that will be the case with me. But I'll tell you all about it. You all know that, like Gilbert Batchelor, here, who got married at last, I have been going to be married at least a hundred and fifty times, but some unlucky accident has always occurred to prevent it."

"Ay, ay, we know all about that, and have laughed at it often enough, Giles," said Mortimer.

"Though one of the best *husband*-men in the kingdom," continued Giles, "I never could get a wife; because why?—I never would have any wife but Kitty Selwood, and her friends wouldn't let her have any husband that had not got a little money beforehand, to support the live stock she might present him wi'h."

"But what has all this to do with your marriage now?"

"Why this—my old aunt, Dorothy Scrop, was seized last night with the rheumatiz. Doctor said she couldn't live till morning. I'm the only heir to her fortune. There's above seven pounds a-year in house and lands, and Kitty be gone over to see if it be all over wi' her. She were a main stingy old toad; but though she never did any good in her life, she'll make it up by her death. Yes, she'll be buried, and I shall be married. Yes, I shall be married to a dead certainty. Hurrah! hurrah! Here she comes! Tol de dol!"

As Giles Jolter spoke, Kitty made her appearance, looking very sorrowful, at which the former evinced much pleasure, imagining that the result was as his wishes would have it.

"Well, Kitty," he exclaimed, eagerly; "is it all over?"

"Yes, Giles, it be all over," was Kitty's mournful reply.

"Be there no hope of Aunt Dorothy?" asked her sweetheart.

"None—none," she answered.

"I thought it must be all up wi' t' old woman by this time," said Giles, joyfully.— "But I mun appear to be a little down-hearted, like, at her loss—it will be but decent, like. Yes, I'll follow Kitty's example—though, ecod, Aunt Dorothy's death do set I all alive. But come, lass—cheer up. Never grieve: though Aunt Dorothy be gone, she ha' left her house and lands behind her. Seven pounds a year! and if she hadn't ha' died, you know, we couldn't ha' been married. All our neighbours, here, will gladly go for mourners, I warrant, if it be only for the sake of throwing the stocking wi' us afterwards."

"Throwing the stocking, Giles!" interrupted Kitty, in sorrowful tones. "Married! Why Aunt Dorothy ha' had a relapse, and be better than ever she were!"

"Aunt Dorothy better!" repeated Giles, quite chop-fallen. "Wheugh! Why, then, here's another disappointment, and we shan't be married after all!"

Poor Giles said this in such doleful strains, that every person present laughed outright.

"Ha! ha! ha!" mimicked the disappointed rustic; "I should like to know what there be to laugh at?"

"I don't know," replied the steward, "but there's nothing to cry at, Master Giles. As your aunt has got better, you'll not want us to be mourners, you know. Very sorry it's all over—regret there's no hopes of her; ha! ha! ha! Poor Giles Jolter!"

"Dang it, I don't care for myself," said Giles, "but the poor lass there, she'd set her mind on it so, like."

"I'm sure, Giles, I don't value it a pin, for my own sake," observed Kitty, blushing, and her looks fully contradicting her assertions; "but you know you were all agog to be married, Giles."

"I'll go to work again, now, Master Steward, since I can't be married. Heigho!"

"Heigho!" responded Kitty.

"Oh, no, you had much better stop here and partake of the festivities," said Mr. Mortimer, "for although our good master hates idleness, and there is nothing like labour for driving love out of the heart—this being the day of Miss Rosabelle's wedding, on such a joyful occasion labour is held in abeyance in this neighbourhood, at any rate. But ah! who is that stranger?"

The attention of the steward had been attracted to the person of a man, enveloped in a large mantle, as though he sought concealment; and who, having first walked up to the spot where the carriages were standing awaiting the wedding party, and looked inside them, and then up at the house, stalked away; and at the time the steward spoke, was hurrying among a deep cluster of trees at the further end of the grounds, and adjoining the principal walk, as if he were desirous of escaping observation.

"Why, that's the very man I saw as we came here," said Gilbert Batchelor; "and when he saw me and Meriel, he walked out of the path, and turning a corner, we lost sight of him all in a moment. I don't half like the appearance of the fellow; for where people behave themselves in such a mysterious manner, we have a right to be suspicious."

"Did you observe his face?" asked the steward.

"No, he took good care of that," replied Gilbert; "he concealed it beneath his cloak when he saw me, and sneaked off like a thief."

"His conduct is rather strange, certainly," said Mr. Mortimer; "but perhaps, after all, we wrong him by supposing that he has been brought hither by any other motive than that of curiosity. But stand aside, lads and lasses—here comes the wedding party."

As the steward spoke the bride appeared, supported by Montalbert and the bridegroom; and the shouts of the persons assembled, as the wedding party stepped into the vehicles that were to convey them to the church, rent the air.

At the moment that the carriages were driven off, the steward again observed the form of the man that had before excited his curiosity, standing in the centre of the path they were pursuing; but when they came near him, he once more retired among the trees, and was concealed from observation. The gates were thrown open, and the vehicles had passed out into the road, when every person assembled was alarmed by the loud report of a pistol, and a simultaneous rush was made towards the carriages, which stopped immediately on the report of the pistol being heard. Mr. Goodman and the others had alighted, and were anxiously surrounding the vehicle which contained the bride and bridegroom, and the father of the former. Upon arriving at the spot, a sight presented itself which filled every beholder with pain and alarm. Lord Ravensford was being supported in the carriage by Montalbert, bleeding profusely from a wound in his side, while Rosabelle had fallen into the arms of Emily in a state of total insensibility.

"Good God!" exclaimed Montalbert, "are our troubles never to cease? Thus, thus, are my melancholy forebodings realised. Oh, let us hasten to the house with all possible haste, and get immediate advice, or Ravensford will bleed to death. Rosabelle, my poor child! Alas! she hears me not; I fear this will be to her a death blow."

"Who could have committed this atrocious act?" said Mr. Goodman.

"I know not," returned Montalbert, "but I plainly saw the person who did it, although his features I could not exactly recognise; he was enveloped in a large mantle, and immediately upon discharging the deadly weapon, he retreated from the spot, which, in the hurry and confusion that prevailed, he was easily enabled to do."

"Ah! it is the very man we have observed lurking about the grounds, this morning," said Mr. Mortimer, the steward; "my lads, hasten in different directions in pursuit of the villain."

The rustics who had met there for the purpose of celebrating the bridal festival, immediately obeyed, and the vehicles returned to the house, where medical assistance being sent for, Lord Ravensford was put to bed, while Rosabelle was conveyed to her own chamber, and attended by Emily and her father, who having seen the surgeon arrive, and learned from him the condition of his patient, which he was happy to find was not dangerous, although serious, could not rest a moment from the couch of his daughter.

The wound of Lord Ravensford having been dressed, he quickly regained his senses, and, although suffering the most acute anguish, his first words were to inquire after Rosabelle, whom he had feared might have fallen a victim to the murderous miscreant. When informed that she had escaped, his joy was unbounded, and he expressed himself quite content, even should his wound be attended with fatal results.

In the course of time Rosabelle was restored to sensibility; and, on being assured that Lord Ravensford still lived, and that the wound he had received was not mortal, she became more composed, and would have arisen from her couch to hasten to the chamber of the wounded man, had not her father persuaded her to the contrary.

The persons who had gone in search of the man who had attempted to assassinate Lord Ravensford, returned in an hour or two, having been entirely unsuccessful in their endeavour to find him, and the guests who had there assembled for celebrating the nuptials of our heroine and Lord Ravensford, then separated, and thus terminated that which had been expected to be a day of rejoicing. Silence reigned throughout the mansion; the bridal favors were removed, the feast remained untouched, and everything gave painful note of the dismal change which only a few short minutes had wrought.

CHAPTER XII.

THE PLOT OF VILLANY

THE event which has been recorded in the previous chapter, had a very alarming effect upon the spirits of Mr. Montalbert, and there were times when Rosabelle and Mr. Goodman, who were almost constantly with him, were fearful that it would be the cause of his relapsing into that awful state of insanity from which he had been with such difficulty restored. His ideas dwelt continually upon the dismal forebodings that had distracted his mind before the events of which we have been writing took place, and what caused it to make a deeper impression upon him than it probably otherwise would have done, was, that they had inadvertently selected the very day for the union which was the anniversary of Rosabelle's birth, and the day on which she had eloped with Lord Ravensford, leaving her father to despair and madness.

"The curse of Heaven seems to have descended upon me and mine," he exclaimed, when alone with Mr. Goodman; "this day which should have been one of universal joy, is thus changed to one of mourning, and there is something which seems to whisper to me that this affair will not terminate as it is. There is more misery, more trouble yet in store for us; more bitter care for the poor old man; more suffering for his unfortunate daughter. Oh, God! I do earnestly implore thee, not to again deprive me of my reason, but rather to take me at once to thee. That dreadful cell, those galling fetters, the wretched straw pallet, the stern looks of the gaoler, the terrific yells of the poor wretches confined in the prison, all, all, recur to my recollection, now I have been aroused from that long, long, sleep, and smite my heart with horror! Oh, let me not be doomed to that awful fate again; and yet I feel my brain already growing unsteady. Goodman, dear friend, instruct me, counsel me what to do—I will be guided entirely by you."

"Then, my dear sir," said Mr. Goodman, "the advice I have to give you is this, to dismiss from your mind the impression it has received, and to endeavour to compose your feelings, for your own sake, for your daughter's sake, and that of all those friends who have your interest so much at heart. Time will, doubtless, unravel the mystery of this affair, and the perpetrator of the deed brought to justice. But has not Lord Ravensford been able to form any conjecture as to who the villain is?"

"You have heard what he has said, my dear friend," returned Montalbert, "he has not the least idea who the ruffian can be, and what could induce him to endeavour to take his life; for that he was the intended victim, there cannot, I think, be any reasonable doubt."

"Every inquiry must be made that is likely to throw any light upon this subject," observed Mr. Goodman, "and a strict search be made after the attempted assassin. I propose, also, that a large reward be offered to anyone who can give such information as may lead to the detection of the guilty party."

"That, of course, will be done," said Montalbert, "but I fear that it will not meet with any success, no one having seen the features of the man. It is a great pity that Mortimer, who saw him lurking about the house and in the grounds, did not take the immediate steps to discover who he was, and what what was his purpose there; that might in all probability have been the means of preventing that which has taken place."

Mr. Goodman coincided in the opinion of Montalbert, but at the same time thought that Mortimer's neglect was excusable, as on a day of that description, when there was open house to all, he had no just cause to suppose that the man had come thither for any other purpose than that of the rest of the guests, namely, to share in the hospitalities provided.

The arguments of Mr. Goodman had their due effect upon Montalbert, and he became more composed, more especially when he understood that Ravensford was doing well, and that Rosabelle, having been restored to tranquillity after the accident, was enabled to leave her chamber, and had suffered no ill-effects from it.

But, although Rosabelle, for the sake of her father, struggled against her feelings, and appeared to be composed, she, as may be supposed, suffered really the most intense anguish, and was continually questioning the medical attendant of Lord Ravensford, as to the actual condition in which he was placed, and whether there was any cause to apprehend danger from the wound. She was constantly in the chamber of his lordship, and her affectionate solicitude relieved him of half his anguish. In the attentions she paid him, he read the purity and sincerity of her sentiments towards him, and the ardour and sincerity of that passion he had one time abused, and for which he was now rendered still more anxious than ever to make her reparation; he, however, as well as Rosabelle, felt the event more keenly, as it seemed as if some fatal spell were upon them, and that fate had ordained that they should never be united.

The event caused the utmost excitement and indignation in the breasts of all who heard of it, and all means were adopted to find out the villain who had committed the sanguinary deed; but all their efforts were ineffectual, and it did not appear probable that any clue would ever be obtained to him; the more so, as Lord Ravensford, after racking his brain for a considerable time, had not been able to form the slightest conjecture upon the sudject, he not knowing any person to whom he could have given reason for such a blood-thirsty attempt upon his life.

Had his lordship, however, recalled to his recollection the circumstances under which he discharged his former steward, Adder, and the villany of his character, his suspicions would have been immediately excited, and justly too; for Adder was the miscreant who had committed the outrage, and his object had been to take the life of his former master. From the moment he was discharged from the service of Lord Ravensford, his bosom yearned for vengeance, which was increased by the guilty passions the charms of Rosabelle had excited in his breast; and he resolved at all hazards to gratify both passions. Nothing less than the life of Ravensford, and the possession of Rosabelle, would satisfy him; and, in the execution of the infamous projects he had formed, he was determined to lose no time. We have before informed the reader that, on quitting Ravensford Castle, he made his way to the neighbourhood in which Rosabelle resided, to watch an opportunity of waylaying and bearing her off. He waited, however, for some time, and fate did not throw in his way a chance of accomplishing his designs. In the meantime, he had the chagrin to hear of the arrival of Ravensford, his reconciliation with Rosabelle, and the subsequent events which brought about the circumstance of the time being appointed for the union.

His rage at this exceeded all bounds, and he resolved to prevent the nuptials taking place, even if he sacrificed his own life in so doing. He watched diligently for a chance to put his diabolical designs into execution, but none presented itself; neither could he find a chance of getting our heroine in his power, as she never left the house unless she was accompanied by several persons. At length, wound up to desperation, he resolved to make the inhuman attempt on the morning appointed for the union, and he thought, in the confusion and the number of persons that would be congregated on that occasion, he might easily effect his escape. He obtained access to the grounds disguised in the manner we have described, and how he succeeded the reader has already been informed.

Exulting in the sanguinary deed he thought he had fully accomplished, the villain left the spot with all the precipitation he could, and threw the cloak in which he had disguised himself after he left the place in which he was lodging at, into a stream which he passed, quite satisfied that he was secure from detection, as he had never let his features be seen, and it was very evident that no suspicion could rest upon him, as he had not been recognised by any of the persons who were assembled at the mansion of Mr. Montalbert.

By this time it will be clearly perceptible to the reader, that Adder was a most consummate, deep, designing villain, and one who was not at all likely to be diverted from his purpose when he had fixed his mind upon anything. Inured to vice, of naturally depraved habits, he had from boyhood moved in every scene of profligacy, until crime had become perfectly familiar to him, and he was out of his element unless he was committing some nefarious action. He had been in the service of Lord Ravensford from a boy, and his father had been steward before him, and had set him a most base example ; so that no wonder he should become the miscreant he afterwards turned out to be. His father had been steward to the estates during the lifetime of the present Lord Ravensford, and having received some offence from the youngest son of his master, who had detected him in some act of dishonesty, and threatened, if repeated, to make it known to his father, old Christopher Adder vowed revenge. Like his son, he was not a man to forget to put into execution what he promised as soon as possible, and the young gentleman had soon good reason to know that. Christopher Adder was a very great favourite with his master, who placed the most implicit and unlimited confidence in him, and the former, than whom no one could better act the hypocrite, did not fail to take every advantage of this. Unfortunately the young man had formed an attachment for a female of the most amiable qualities, but in

humble circumstances, and although he felt assured that his father would never give his assent to their nuptials, such was the powerful hold she had obtained of his affections that, let the consequences be what they might, he found it would be impossible for him to shake them off.

This fact, the hoary villain Adder determined to take advantage of, and accordingly seized every opportunity he could to introduce the subject to his master, and while he pretended to take the part of the young man, and to endeavour to prevail upon his master to take a more favourable view of the attachment his son had formed, he took good care to introduce such side notes that would tend to exasperate him more than ever against him; until he at length commanded his son, on the pain of his eternal displeasure, to discard the young girl from his heart, and for the future to avoid her presence. Herbert would willingly have obeyed his father had not the voice of love pleaded far more powerfully, and knowing how worthy of him the object of his affections was, he could not bear to think of abandoning her; knowing that by so doing he should break her heart, and probably bring her to a premature grave, he sacrificed self-interest to love, and the consequence was a secret marriage.

Never did Christopher Adder exult more than when this circumstance came to his knowledge, and he had the opportunity of being the first to go and make his master acquainted with it, and by the most crafty and insidious methods, inflame those feelings of rage that already raged with such violence in the bosom of the old gentleman. His villany succeeded better than he had even anticipated — his master instantly discarded the young man, and appointed his elder son his sole heir. The latter was a man whose sentiments were in perfect unison with those of the steward, and consequently he never forgot him for this piece of service. On the death of his father he retained him in his service, and amply rewarded him for the guilty part he had acted, and for pandering to his vices in more respects than one. As for the younger son he quitted England with his wife a short time after the union, and was never afterwards heard of.

Thus, brought up in the midst of vice, with nothing ever but folly and dissipation before his eyes, as we have before observed, it is no wonder that Adder should become the wretch he was—and a worthy scion of his parent he was. There was scarcely any crime, but that of murder, of which he had not been guilty, and it has appeared even from the perpetration of that his heart would not revolt, when it was to gratify his vengeance. Beresford had not been naturally vicious ; his principle failing was an inordinate love of pleasure, and of this Adder took every advantage, and it was not long ere he contrived to wean him exactly to his wishes. He supplied him with cash to support his extravagances, well knowing that he had every opportunity of repaying himself tenfold, and encouraged and applauded his errors. In fact, he acted the part of the tempter, and to him, Lord Ravensford might truly be said to be indebted for all the vices and follies of which he had been guilty, and all the misery he had brought upon himself and others.

When it is recollected that Adder's situation was a most lucrative one, and that he had an opportunity of carrying his practices to a very great, to an almost incalculable extent, it will not be wondered that his utmost rage and vengeance should be excited when he found himself detected in his villany, and so abruptly dismissed, or that he should be determined to follow up his evil designs to the fullest extent. Nothing but the life of his late master could satiate him. and that he resolved to sacrifice, even though he lost his own in acomplishing it.

But what more than all urged him to the speedy execution of this diabolical deed was, the near approach of the nuptials of Lord Ravensford with Rosabelle Montalbert, whose charms had excited the most ungovernable passions in his bosom, and of whose person he was determined to obtain possession by some means or the other. That she should be his, he vowed no earthly power should prevent, and any belief in a supreme being he did not entertain.

When Adder learned that although severely wounded, Lord Ravensford was not dead, but on the contrary, likely to recover, he was very much enraged and disappointed, but on more maturely reflecting upon it, he felt satisfied at having been the means of preventing the union taking place for the present, and likewise exulted with all the malice of a fiend, in the suffering he had been the cause of inflicting upon his lordship; moreover, in the long interval which must elapse before Ravensford would be restored to convalescence, he had not the least doubt that some opportunity would present itself for him to get Rosabelle in his power.

How he laughed in fiendish triumph when he heard of the consternation which the attempt on his late master had caused in the minds of all those who heard of it; and when he saw the bills offering large rewards for any person who could be the means of bringing the villain to justice, he triumphed in the security he had afforded himself, by the scheme he had adopted ere he made the sanguinary attempt.

Although he was daily in the vicinity of the mansion of Mr. Montalbert, watching the opportunity for which his soul panted, he always so disguised himself that it would be impossible for any person who knew him to recognise him, and he used every precaution to prevent his appearance or conduct from exciting any

suspicion, and in this he was equally successful as with all his other acts of villany. But, although he never missed a day in wandering about those places where Rosabelle walked forth, he could never see anything of her. In fact Rosabelle kept herself almost entirely secluded to the house, seldom walking farther than the gardens. Her whole pleasure was the society of her father and Emily, and in watching the progress which Ravensford made towards recovery. Her mind, too, was too much oppressed with care at the mystery in which the attempt upon the life of Lord Ravensford was involved, to think of anything else during those moments when she was alone, and she felt no inclination to leave the mansion.

The recovery of Lord Ravensford was very slow and tedious, but his pains were greatly ameliorated by the kind, the unremitting assiduities of Rosabelle, who was almost constantly his companion, and in her sweet manner, holding out hopes to him of the happiness of the future, and seeking to banish from his memory the pangs and upbraidings which any reminiscence of the past might occasion him. However, notwithstanding that she affected to hope for the best, and even tried to persuade herself that she was not too sanguine, her mind was far from receiving any such impression; on the contrary, she could not help fearing that there was yet more unhappiness in store for them. But from what source it was to spring, she was at a loss to conjecture; that Ravensford would again deceive her she could not for a moment do him the injustice to think—there could be no doubt, now, at any rate, of his sincerity. But then the attempt upon his life had filled her bosom with the most uncontrollable alarm. That he had a secret and bitter enemy, she could not for a moment doubt, but who that could be, she of course could not be expected to be able to form any idea, when Ravensford himself was at a loss to imagine. It is remarkable, after the behaviour of Adder, and the manner in which they separated, that no suspicion should ever enter the mind of Lord Ravensford as regarded him. This was the more singular, when it is remembered that he must so well have known the character of the villain, and that he was a man capable of committing such an act. But Ravensford never so much as bestowed a thought upon him, and thus the wretch had an opportunity of triumphing in his guilty machinations, and escape himself unscathed.

There were times, too, when a horrible idea would dart upon the brain of Rosabelle with such force, that she almost sunk beneath its influence. and had the most extreme difficulty in banishing it from her thoughts. This was a terrible dread that the sanity of her father would only be temporary, and that something was about to occur which would reduce him to his former pitiable condition. There were times, too, when the same idea seemed to take possession of his mind; for, after watching her with the most intense affection for a few minutes, he would suddenly seize her hand, and press it vehemently to his lips, sigh heavily, and bursting into tears, would exaim—

"What can this emotion mean? What strange feeling is it that seems to take possession of my imagination? what fearful foreboding of some other calamity yet in store for us? The present appears like a vision, too bright to last, and—Oh, God! if it be Thy will that I should never again experience permanent peace in this world, in mercy take me to Thyself,—but oh, let me not become a wretched maniac; extinguish not again the light of reason from my poor brain."

At such times as these, agonised, deeply agonised as the feelings of Rosabelle were, to find her father's thoughts in unison with her own, she made the most violent efforts to stifle her own emotions, and to endeavour to banish the dreadful idea from the mind of Montalbert. And she was generally successful; Mantalbert would listen to her with the most profound attention, and her soft, her gentle tones, her fond persuasions seldom failed to soothe him.

Thus passed away several weeks, and Lord Ravensford continued to mend, and was at length able to leave his chamber, and the first thing he urged when he could get about was that the union of himself and Rosabelle should take place without any further delay. To this Montalbert readily gave his consent, for when he could see his daughter under the protection of a husband, he thought he should be happy. Our heroine had no objetion to the offer, but she requested that the marriage should take place as privately as possible, a plan she considered by far the most advisable, as there was no knowing whether or not that the secret enemy of Lord Ravensford might avail himself of that opportunity to make a similar attempt to the one he had made before. Although Lord Ravensford did not entertain any idea that such precautions should be taken, yet, as he had no wish to use any ceremony upon the occasion, he agreed with the wishes of Rosabelle, and it was settled that the nuptials should take place at the house in the presence only of their private friends, while the poor people and the tenants were to be regaled at the principal inn.

A few days after this arrangement was made, the ceremony was accomplished, and Rosabelle became the bride of that man who alone possessed her most ardent affections. It was a day of the most pure, the most unbounded delight to Montalbert, and as he pressed his daughter and her husband to his heart, he invoked a thousand blessings upon their heads, and wept tears of ecstasy. At that moment he felt that he had lived to see accomplished all that he could wish for, and could have been content, had it been the will of heaven, to have resigned his life into the hands of his Maker. Rosabelle too, in the supreme happiness she felt at that time, forgot for awhile the melancholy, the torturing thoughts that had before worked upon her imagination, and looked forward with hope to days of bliss. Tears of transport gushed to her eyes, when she saw the little Alfred pressed to her husband's heart, and heard him lisp forth the name of father, a title she feared he would never have been permitted to use. She looked in the countenance of her husband; he read her thoughts in a moment, and hugging her to his bosom, pressed warm kisses of affection and inexpressible delight upon her lips. It was the most blissful moment he had ever experienced in his life, and never did vice appear to him more hideous than it did, by, at that time, contrasting the miseries it is invariably productive of, with the happiness he felt at having performed an act of justice and of virtue.

It would be impossible to describe properly the rage of the villain Adder, when he heard of the marriage; and he had been foiled in every attempt he had made to waylay and seize upon Rosabelle. Disappointment had but increased the strength of his base desires, and he could not think of her as the wife of Ravensford with any degree of patience. But still he determined to leave no plan unadopted that might further his wishes, and place Rosabelle in his power; and well tutored in the school of villany, well skilled in every base stratagem, it was not long ere he contrived to concoct a scheme, which, although it would take time to carry it into effect, in his imagination, offered every prospect of ultimate success. This vile plot will be made fully apparent to the reader in the course of a short time.

Lord Ravensford and his lady had made up their minds to pass their honeymoon away at Ravensford Castle, which was a fine Gothic structure situated about a hundred miles from the place of their present residence. Mr. Montalbert, although he regretted quitting those scenes which were so endeared to him, even for a short time, could not bear the idea of being separated from his daughter, and, therefore, gave his assent to accompany them.

Adder heard of this, but fearful that some one in the neighbourhood of the castle might know him, and be the means of thwarting his schemes, he resolved not to follow them thither, but to let the business rest until they returned, as he could occupy the interim by ripening the plot he had devised to get possession of Rosabelle, and gratify the revenge which Lord Ravensford had excited in his breast.

Ravensford Castle was most delightfully situated, and covered an immense space of ground; it was many hundred years old, and seemed likely to bid defiance to the ravages of time for many years to come. Rosabelle and her father were very much pleased with it, and the change of scene had a very salutary effect upon their spirits; but the demon was at work to disturb their tranquillity.

They had not been at Ravensford more than a week when his lordship entered the sitting-room where Rosabelle and her father were together, rather abruptly one morning, holding a letter in his hand, and his countenance evincing considerable uneasiness.

"This letter," he said, addressing himself to his wife, "was given to me just now by mistake—it is directed to you, Rosabelle, and is in a male handwriting too, that's evident."

A deadly sickness fell upon the heart of our heroine, as with a trembling hand she took the letter from her husband, and in a tremulous voice ejaculated—

"A letter? and directed to me! from whom could it come? It must be a mistake.

THE RESTORATION OF THE MANIAC FATHER TO REASON.

Take it back, my lord, and peruse the contents. I cannot do so."

"Nay, my love," said Lord Ravensford, in a tone that sounded strange and suspicious to the ears of Rosabelle, "the contents of his epistle may be intended for your eye alone, and of course I do not wish to pry into anything that you may wish to keep a secret from me."

"Alfred," exclaimed Rosabelle, in a voice of the deepest reproach, and with a demeanour such as conscious innocence can only assume; "surely my ears must deceive me; it never could be you that made use of those observations. Can you believe me capable of having any secrets from you? What dark suspicions do your words convey? Read the letters, I beg of you; it cannot contain aught addressed to me, which I should not wish you to be made acquainted with."

"Ah!" cried Montalbert, who had gazed at his daughter and her husband alternately, in stupified amazement, "what fresh trouble is impending o'er our devoted heads? I thought our joy was too great to last long. I feel my head begin to grow giddy—I—I am very weak, Rosabelle——"

"My dear, dear father," said Rosabelle, with the greatest emotion and alarm; "oh, pray compose yourself; do not suffer any groundless apprehension to take possession of your faculties. I do not fear the result of this event."

No. 8.

"Well, well, child," said Montalbert, rising; "I will be advised by you; I feel better now; I will retire for awhile; but come to me soon, and let me know if any danger threatens us."

"I will, dear father," replied our heroine, "and fear not but that all will be well."

Montalbert kissed his daughter fondly, and supporting himself on his stick (for his long sufferings, as may be supposed, had very much enfeebled him) he tottered from the room. After he had gone, there was a pause of silence between Lord Ravensford and Rosabelle, during which interval the former was minutely examining the superscription of the letter, and he seemed to be enduring considerable agitation.

"Rosabelle," at last he said, "I would much rather that this letter should be destroyed, for I am fearful that the contents will be productive of unhappiness to us all."

"Destroy it, Alfred?" hastily returned our heroine; "oh, no, no, not for the world; it would be an act of cruelty, of injustice to me. But why do you hesitate? why should I dread to hear the contents of that letter, which, though directed to me, I am certain has only been done so in a mistake, and that it is intended for you. Read it, I beg, without any further delay."

"The hand-writing seemes familiar to me," said Lord Ravensford, still hesitating, "and yet I cannot think at the moment who I have seen write it. I know not how it is, Rosabelle, but yet I tremble at the very thoughts of breaking the seal. It strikes me forcibly that my fears are not without some cause."

"Oh, Ravensford," cried Rosabelle, with increased emotion, "this is distracting; if you have any pity for me, do as I desire, as I implore you. My poor father, too, he will never be able to endure this painful suspense."

Lord Ravensford made no answer, but conquering his feelings he broke the seal of the mysterious epistle, and hastily, but with a trembling hand, unfolded the letter. No sooner had his eye, however, fallen upon the first two or three words, than his countenance became ghastly pale and red by turns; his chest heaved violently, and with a stifled groan, when he came to the conclusion, he sank into a chair, and dropped the letter upon the carpet.

Rosabella had watched the workings of her husband's countenance during the brief space of time he was thus occupied, and her terrors were augmented grately when she beheld the dreadful agitation he betrayed; but she could not form any idea of the nature of the contents, although she imagined that her surmises were just, as to the letter being intended for Lord Ravensford, only misdirected, and that it contained some bad news. When, however, she saw her husband sink back in his chair, and cover his face with his hands, a different, a

madening sensation came over her, and rushing forward, she snatched up the letter, and hastily glanced her eyes over it. Judge of her surprise —incredulity—shame—indignation, and horror when she read the following—

"Dearest, and lovely, my own Rosabelle; for such my angel, I must still call you, although you are another's. I take this opportunity of writing to inform you that I shall be in town in a few weeks, when I will take the earliest chance of flying to your arms, and renewing those blissful moments we have so often enjoyed. Oh, my adorable Rosabelle, how my soul pants to enfold you one more to my bosom, and again to press soft and delicious kisses upon your lips. I cannot believe that the change in your circumstances can ever alter the sentiments of regard you have so often vowed for me. I will take care to contrive so that our meetings may take place without the suspicions of Ravensford being in the least aroused.

"Yours, ever adoringly,
"SAUNTER."

Astounded—horrorstruck; poor Rosabelle with the utmost difficulty read the contents of base, this cruel letter, and then with a scream of the most intense agony, she sank insensible at the feet of her husband.

Lord Ravensford, aroused by hearing her fall, looked at her for an instant with a vacant stare, then raised her in his arms; but recollecting the words the letter contained, his pity and love changed to hatred and disgust, and placing her again at his feet, as if there were contamination in her touch, he clasped his forehead, and groaned in the bitterness of his anguish.

"Good God!" he cried, "can this really be?—Can any man be guilty of such heartless perfidy; or is it possible that one so fair, so apparently innocent, should act with such deceit, and so shamelessly play the wanton? The thought will drive me to madness! Rosabelle, Rosabelle, you have inflicted a blow from which I shall never more recover. This is indeed a terrible punishment for the effences of which I have formerly been guilty! But no—no—it cannot be! Reason denies the truth of it! Rosabelle—my love—my life! Speak to me, and one word of yours shall convince me of the falsehood of this base scrawl!"

Thus speaking, Ravensford again raised his wife from the floor, and parting the hair from her pale forehead, kissed her fervently, and let fall a tear of anguish on her face. Rosabelle at length heaved a deep sigh, and opening her eyes, fixed them for an instant on Ravensford's countenance, and then burst into a paroxysm of sobs and tears.

"Oh, Ravensford," she cried, "that fatal letter! What monster, what fiend hath done this? Who is it that would destroy our happiness?"

"Rosabelle," returned Ravensford, still pressing her to his bosom; "for the love of Heaven answer me one question; when did you last see Lord Saunter?"

"Never but once," replied our heroine, gasping for breath; "oh, Alfred, I see you doubt me; this—this is more than I can bear! I swear by all my hopes here and hereafter, that never but once did I see the man whom you call Lord Saunter, never but once, and that was on the evening you must well remember, in London, when by his means I learned that you were about to be married to another."

"Is it possible that there can be villany of so black a dye?" cried Ravensford; "but this letter I could swear is in Saunter's handwriting!"

"It is a base, a murderous fabrication throughout; and no doubt the invention of the same secret enemy who made the diabolical attempt on your life," ejaculated Rosabelle; "oh, Alfred, can you, will you be so cruel, so unjust as to believe me the shameless deceitful wanton which this letter represents?"

"Never, by Heaven!" cried Ravensford, "never! It must be as you say, my much injured Rosabelle. It is a cruel fabrication, no doubt, occasioned by jealousy, and dictated by revenge. But I will immediately seek out the heartless libertine, Saunter, and wreak my vengeance on his head."

"No, my love," observed Rosabelle, "not so. I beseech you to let the matter rest for awhile as it is, and by silence, you may be able to discover the actual author of this wicked plot, and fully exonerate me from any of those awful suspicions that were gaining such rapid hold upon your mind."

"Enough, my dear Rosabelle," said her husband, "it shall be as you say; but let the miscreant or miscreants tremble at my vengeance, should I discover them; although I feel but little doubt that it is Saunter who is the villain, for well do I know his character. Compose yourself, my Rosabelle, and let us hasten to your father, who I think it will be as well not to make acquainted with the real contents of the letter, lest it should take too powerful an effect upon his spirits."

Rosabelle approved of the suggestions of her husband, and having with a powerful effort nearly regained her tranquillity, she took the arm of Lord Ravensford, and they walked to the room of her father, who they found awaiting them with the utmost anxiety, and who, on their entrance, looked eagerly at their countenances, to see whether he could discover there any symptoms that might lead him to conjecture the nature of the letter's contents, but they had so well regained their composure, that Montalbert's fears vanished, and his mind was completely set at rest, when Ravensford informed him that it was he who had made the error, having mistaken the superscription, the handwriting of which was not very legible, that it was directed to him and not to Lady Ravensford, and that it related to a little private business of no importance to any person but himself.

Of course, the reader will have guessed that the originator and author of the letter we have been mentioning, was the heartless and deep designing Adder, and he was already exulting in the fancied success of his plot. His object was to distract the mind of Ravensford with jealousy, and to bring about a separation between him and Rosabelle; and he flattered himself that he could not have hit upon a better scheme in the world to effect that design.

Adder was a man who possessed talents, which had they been applied to a different purpose, would have made him an ornament instead of a blot upon society. He had received a moderate education, which he had himself improved by study, and he possessed most extraordinary conversational powers. He had more than once been guilty of acts of forgery, and, therefore, found it no difficult task to commit one more on the present occasion, to suit his purpose. He was very well acquainted with the handwriting of Lord Saunter, and he determined to select him as the tool by which to obtain his object. He thought he could not have hit upon a more fit person, for his character for debauchery and licentiousness was so well known, that it would carry conviction immediately to the mind of Ravensford. Nursing himself upon the anguish, the bitter agony it would cause his late master, Adder sat down, and in a short time had composed the letter so often alluded to, and which he immediately forwarded to Ravensford Castle.

Singular enough, on the following day, Adder accidentally met Lord Saunter, who, on seeing him, addressed him familiarly, and expressed his surprise that he should have been discharged so abruptly by Lord Ravensford, especially after the many good turns, or rather bad turns, he had done him in his different amatory peccadilloes.

"You say right, my lord," returned Adder; "I was discharged in a most abrupt and ungentlemanly manner. But his lordship is very ungrateful, and I only wish he may get one to suit him better, or to have his interest more at heart than I had."

"By-the-by, as for that, my dear fellow," said Lord Saunter, smiling, "I dare say you did not forget to study your own interest as well as your master's, and no doubt his lordship bled pretty freely. But what was the reason of your separation?"

Oh, it was all owing to that Miss Montalbert, Ravensford's former *chere amie*," answered Adder.

"Indeed!" remarked Saunter, "how so?"

"His lordship suspected me of deceiving him respecting her, and turning rather squeamish after his former behaviour towards her, he turned me off, without giving me an opportunity of explaining my conduct."

"Which you no doubt could have done, in the most satisfactory manner," said the other sarcastically.

"Most unquestionably," was the reply, with a laugh; "however, his lordship has quite reformed now, and my services would be useless to him;—he has become a sober, sedate, domestic man, and will be in future, I dare say, held up as a perfect paragon of virtue."

"By Jove!" exclaimed Lord Saunter, "I almost envy Ravensford his happiness; Rosabelle is a very charming creature; and I was a good mind to set my cap at her myself, only I didn't like to do the unhandsome towards my friend."

"And if I must speak candidly, my lord," said Adder, whom a sudden thought at that moment struck, "if I must speak candidly, I do not think you would have found much difficulty in making a conquest of her."

"No," cried the fop, with a self-conceited chuckle, "why, you don't mean to say that the damsel was struck with my person? I never remember to have been in her company but once."

"Well, whether you were or not, my lord," rejoined Adder, elated at the success of his stratagem, "that once was quite enough, in my opinion, to make an impression upon the lady, from what I noticed afterwards."

"Well, you quite surprise me," observed Saunter.

"I dare say I do," thought Adder.

"And yet, by Jupiter, now you speak of it," added Saunter, "I do recollect that on that occasion she eyed me very earnestly."

"No doubt of it, my lord," returned Adder; "she was captivated with you, it is my firm belief."

"What are your reasons for thinking so?"

"Because I once or twice overheard her mention your name in the most affectionate manner, when she thought no one was near her; and she never could endure the sight of Ravensford afterwards!—you know she very shortly afterwards eloped from him."

"I do; but has she not married him now?"

"True; but I firmly believe she loves him not."

"Then why grant him her hand?"

"For what many females in her situation have done before—*to save her honour!*" answered Adder, ironically.

"But do you really think that Lady Ravensford loves me?" demanded the conceited nobleman, eagerly.

"I feel certain of it," answered Adder.

"Oh, blissful sounds!" ejaculated Saunter, rapturously; "and fool that I was not to observe

it. But there is no hope for me now, she is the bride of Ravensford, and as such her duty forbids her to think of me."

"*Her* duty!" repeated Adder, with a sarcastic grin; "the sensualist and the wanton think little of duty. I tell you, my lord, and I'll wager my life that my words come true, if you think proper to persevere, you will meet with all the success you could wish."

"Your words inspire me with hope."

"Then why hesitate?"

"Will you assist me?"

"Willingly."

"Your hand; it is a bargain;—I will well pay you for the job."

"You will, I dare say, find the prize well deserving of a liberal outlay."

"Where are they now staying?"

"At Ravensford Castle."

"Whither we will depart without delay."

"Not so; precipitation will spoil the sport; the game cannot be run down unless caution is used; besides, in a few days they will return from Ravensford to this neighbourhood. Will you be guided by me?"

"I will."

"Enough, then; you may calculate upon the most signal and certain success."

"Something seems to assure me that your words will be verified," said the elated Lord Saunter; "but you have made me all impatience and anxiety; where shall we meet again?"

Adder immediately thought of a place where it was not likely they would either of them be known, and fixed upon it for the spot of assignation.

"Then to-morrow I will again see you?"

"At what hour?"

"At twelve in the forenoon."

"I will be punctual."

"Enough; farewell, my Lord Saunter."

"Farewell, Mr. Adder; be faithful in this affair, and I will make it the best job you have had for many a day."

"You may trust me, my lord," returned Adder; and Saunter once more bidding him farewell, took his departure.

"Fool!" laughed Adder, scornfully and triumphantly, as he disappeared, "you are well entrapped, and shall pay dearly for your presumption, after you have served my purpose. Lady Ravensford your mistress!—Vain booby! No, she is destined for these arms, or I will perish in making the attempt."

Thus speaking, the villain hastened away.

CHAPTER XIII.

THE LIBERTINES.—THE DUPE.

EXULTING in the plot he had formed with Adder, and vainly imagining that all he had heard was quite true, and that Lady Ravensford really was struck with his graces and accomplishments, the unprincipled and weak-headed lord hastened to the tavern, where he had been accustomed to pass many of his hours since his residence in the neighbourhood, and was so elated, that he partook more freely than even he was wont to do of wine, and was unusually merry among his giddy associates, indulging to excess in amatory and ribald jokes, and laughing most immoderately at everything he uttered, whether good, bad or indifferent. Lord Saunter was the lion among his party, who, although he thought himself remarkably sagacious, was an easy victim, and had plenty of money to squander away. Lord Saunter's greatest failing, if he had one more strong than another, was the most inordinate vanity, and he had such an excellent opinion of his own pretty person, that he considered himself as graceful, and as elegant as Appollo Belvidere.—And then, with the fair sex (because a few courtezans who lived upon his purse flattered him highly) he imagined himself a general favourite, and that every female who looked at him was in love with him; consequently it will not be wondered that he was so easily cajoled by the crafty and designing Adder, and the more so, when he recalled to his recollection the particular manner in which Rosabelle had addressed him on the evening when they had met in London. She had pointedly appealed to him; nay, she had even invoked the blessing of Heaven upon him; and he was only surprised that he had not given this subject his attention before. Had he not been an arrant fool, he reflected, he might easily have persuaded her to place herself under his protection at that time, and then she would never have become the wife of Lord Ravensford. He could not help thinking that he had missed a very capital opportunity of gratifying his libidinous passions. Still, he doubted not that even now, with the aid of Adder, his success might be reckoned as almost certain.

"That Adder is a famous fellow," he reflected, "a devilish clever fellow—an invaluable fellow; it was a fortunate job I happened to meet with him, and I must take good care to retain him in my service, and my success in affairs of gallantry will take the shine out of all my companions By Jupiter, I shall become a perfect luminary in the world of fashion! the pride of the fair sex, the admiration and envy of all the men."

These were the thoughts that passed in the mind of Lord Saunter as he bent his way to the tavern, and here he became, as we have before stated, remarkably cheerful, so much so that he completely surprised his companions.

"Why, Saunter, my dear fellow," said Captain Mowbray, "what the devil is the matter with you this evening? I never saw you so gay and so facetious in my life before; something particular must have occurred to you of a joyful nature, that's very certain."

"His lordship's lucky star is in the ascendant, I presume," observed another.

"Egad you may well say that, Sir Harry," returned Saunter; "my fortunate star never shone with more brilliancy than it does at the present time."

"And may I make so bold as to ask what planet it is?" inquired Mowbray.

"Venus, to be sure," replied Saunter, with a self-conceited chuckle—"Venus—that is my lucky planet, you know—the star under which I must positively have been born, to judge from the uncommon success that invariably attends my amours."

"You are a devilish lucky fellow, upon my honour," remarked Sir Harry Spangle, picking his teeth; "another affair of gallantry, eh?"

"Yes, another amour to the thousand and one adventures of the kind which I have had," answered Lord Saunter. "Now Lord Ravensford has cut our society, I shall positively surpass you all. You will none of you stand any chance with me—not the least."

"No; I think we must yield the palm to your lordship, undoubtedly," returned Captain Mowbray, with a sly wink at his companions, from which it might very easily be inferred that he thought decidedly different. "Ah! Ravensford was certainly quite a devil among the women. But he has become a sober fool; —and then to marry the woman who had been his mistress! What a silly fellow—and so will the world think too, or I'm much deceived. Doubtless he will not be long before he becomes a contented cuckold!"

"Well, positively I was just thinking so," said Saunter, laughing and winking his eye, with much affectation of sagacity.

"And I for one," observed Sir Harry, "would not mind making him so. Lady Ravensford is a beautiful woman."

"Delicious creature!" returned the booby lord.

"Such brilliant eyes!"

"Such lovely skin—fair as snow, and soft as velvet!"

"Such a graceful and elegant figure!"

"Pretty little foot!"

"Beautifully turned ankle!"

"Such exquisite features!"

"And such pouting, kiss-inviting lips!"

"Ha! ha! ha! laughed Mowbray; "well, upon my word you give a very glowing description of her; and I should say his lordship would not feel very highly pleased if he were to hear you. I am ready to agree with you, however, that Lady Ravensford *was* a very beautiful woman."

"Was!" exclaimed Lord Saunter, hastily—

"*was* !—she is now a most beautiful woman! She's a perfect angel—a complete divinity !"

" Lady Rosabelle Ravensford is not quite so young as she was," said Mowbray.

" Her beauty is as young and fresh as ever," was the rejoinder from Saunter.

" Then she is too pensive, too melancholy—bears upon her countenance the ravages of care."

" For the very reason, I have no doubt, because she has no one to care about," said Lord Saunter.

" Why, does your lordship mean to insinuate that she has no attachment towards her husband ?" demanded Captain Mowbray.

" That is exactly what I mean," Saunter replied.

" That is a bold assertion, at any rate," returned Mowbray.

" His lordship would not make it, I dare say," remarked Sir Harry, " unless he had proof of the truth of it. But pray, my lord, who is the fair damsel whom you have chosen to honour with your attentions at present ?"

" The very damsel of whom we have been speaking," answered Lord Saunter.

" Lady Ravensford !" exclaimed the others, in a breath.

" Lady Ravensford," responded his lordship.

" Impossible !—your lordship must be joking," observed Mowbray.

" He, he, he, he !" chuckled Saunter, " and a demmed pretty joke I intend it to be. But I repeat what I have before said—Lady Ravensford is the lady I mean to honour."

" But with what prospect of success ?"

" Every prospect."

" How ?"

" Simply this—the lovely Rosabelle is actually smitten with me."

" Smitten with you !"

" Not only smitten with me, but positively stark-staring mad in love with me," said Saunter ; " and if it had not been for my own folly and blindness, she would have been under my protection at this time, instead of being the wife of Lord Ravensford."

" How know you this ?" asked Mowbray.

" I will tell you," answered Saunter, " and then you will, I think, agree that I do not exaggerate the case, neither am I too sanguine in my expectations."

" Ay, let us hear all the particulars, I beg of you, my lord," said Sir Harry Spangle, in a tone of impatience.

Lord Saunter then related, with many little additions and embellishments of his own, the particulars of his meeting with Adder, the late valet of Lord Ravensford, and what he had told him of the behaviour of Rosabelle, which he said could not suffer a doubt no remain upon the mind of any person who heard it, but that

he was the object of her affections ; and the principal cause of her melancholy was occasioned by her fate being linked to that of a man whom she had only married from a wish to retrieve her lost honour.

Although the associates of Lord Saunter, who possessed a considerable deal more sense and penetration than he did, only smiled at these vain observations, and saw very clearly that Adder was making a dupe of him, for some sinister purpose, they did not express themselves to that effect, but, on the contrary, they heaped upon him a double allowance of flattery, and encouraged the extravagant hopes he had suffered to take possession of his mind.

" It's a conquest—a safe conquest, my lord," exclaimed Sir Harry. " By Jupiter ! you are a fortunate fellow, and I should like to stand in your shoes. Poor Ravensford ! what a devil of a fluster he will be in when he loses his Rosabelle for the second time."

" And serve him right too," remarked Mowbray, " for being so foolish as to turn Benedict, and suffer a parson to walk off with Lady Caroline Rochdale and the cool sixty thousand."

" He will go mad," said Sir Harry.

" I should say he was mad already," retorted Lord Saunter, " or he would never have married a woman who had formerly been his mistress —a fact which had become so notorious, owing to the particular circumstances by which it was followed."

" What a sensation it will cause in the world of fashion," remarked Sir Harry.

" Terrific !" rejoined Saunter, rubbing his hands with much satisfaction. " Elopement in high life—noble and fashionable gallant—the lovely Lady Rosabelle Ravensford—and——"

" Action for *crim. con.*," added Mowbray drily. " Damages for the plaintiff, five thousand pounds."

" No, no, no—omit that part, if you please, captain," said Saunter ; " although, positively, if I were to incur damages of fifty thousand, I should not begrudge it in such a cause, and for such a prize."

" Your lordship is a bold adventurer," said Sir Harry, " and you deserve success."

" Which there is not the least doubt he will meet with," answered Mowbray ; " his lordship is a most irresistible fellow !"

" Positively, quite irresistible," responded Sir Harry. " We'll drink the beauteous Lady Rosabelle, the future mistress of Lord Saunter."

" The beauteous Rosabelle, gentlemen—that must be the toast," said Captain Mowbray ; and the glasses were charged, and the toast drunk with the most riotous enthusiasm, Saunter having been worked into a very agreeable mood by the flattery of his friends.

" And when is it expected that this grand

elopement will come off?" again asked Sir Harry.

"Can't say, exactly," replied Saunter; "but at the very earliest possible period. I am all impatience till it does take place.—They are at present at Ravensford Castle, spending the honeymoon; and when they return, I shall commence operations directly, and no doubt they will very soon be completed and carried into effect. Rosabelle will not require much persuasion, I flatter myself, and there will be plenty of opportunities for our meeting. But you must all of you use caution, and upon no account let a word of this drop, for then it would be all blown, and we should make a devil of a mess of it."

"I wonder your lordship should think it necessary to give us that caution" observed Captain Mowbray, "when you know very well you can trust us. Nay, more—should you require any assistance, I, for one, am at your service at any time."

"And I for another, as his lordship knows," said Sir Harry—who, it must be mentioned, had made up his mind to borrow four or five hundred pounds of Lord Saunter before they separated; and the way to success, he well knew, was by flattery, and in acquiescing in everything, however silly and preposterous, which he said.

"I thank you most cordially, gentlemen,' said Saunter. "I thank you most cordially for your kind offers, but too many might spoil sport. Besides, I have got the aid of Adder, and his ingenuity will accomplish everything. He is an inestimable fellow."

"Truly he is a most accomplished villain," remarked Sir Harry.

"And, therefore, just the man for his lordship," rejoined Captain Mowbray, rather sarcastically.

"Oh, you flatter, captain," said Saunter, with a simple and self-approving smile.

"Oh, no, I assure you I do not," returned the other, with a low bow. "But whither do you intend absconding to?"

"I have not made up my mind to that, yet," replied Lord Saunter. "I must consult Adder upon that point; although I should think Paris would be the place."

"Too public," observed Mowbray; "Ravensford would discover you in no time, and the consequences that might follow would probably not be altogether agreeable to your lordship. Ravensford is a capital shot, and I believe you do not pride yourself much upon that point."

"Demme, Mowbray, you positively are provokingly insulting this evening," said Lord Saunter, with much anger. "Do you mean to impeach my bravery?"

"By no means, your lordship," replied Mowbray, who received a nudge from Sir Harry Spangle, he fearing that he had proceeded almost too far,—"that was not at all my design, I assure you: if I thought so, I should consider you unworthy of the Lady Rosabelle, since none but the brave deserve the fair. I merely meant to ask your lordship whether you did not doubt your skill compared with that of Ravensford?"

"Why, positively I must confess," said Lord Saunter, "that I am not the best shot in the world, and that such a meeting would not be altogether pleasant. Duelling may be all very well in theory, but devilish bad I think it is in practice. I can't say that I fancy a leaden bullet for breakfast—it is so devilish hard of digestion. But if his lordship acts wisely, he will rest himself quietly over the matter, and let the affair die away. I will provide well for the lady, and as she does not like him, why it will take a great deal of trouble off his hands."

"A very pretty arrangement," exclaimed Sir Harry.

"Capital!" responded Mowbray; "and his lordship has my best wishes for his success."

"Thank you—thank you," said Lord Saunter. "Now then, repledish your glasses, gentlemen; we will have a jovial night of it, of that I am determined—another bumper, and then I will give you a song, which I think is very appropriate to the occasion."

The glasses were once more charged, a toast given, and drunk with boisterous cheers, and then his lordship, who had a very good voice and some judgment, sang the following

SONG.

Oh! life has not a single joy
  In our brief passage hence,
But will on repetition cloy,
  And pall upon the sense.
Love in its birth, its being ends,
  Wine only keeps its power;
For every glass we take with friends,
  But makes us wish for more.
Ambition is a weary dream,
  And power a toilsome gain;
The halcyon rests but on the stream—
  That stream's the ruby main.
Then drain the flowing bowl like men,
  And, laughing at life's pother,
Drink off a bumper glass, and then—
  And then—then drink another.

This song was received with loud applause, and, at the conclusion of it, the drinking was renewed with increased spirit; and so elated did they all become that they were forced to remain at the tavern the whole of the night, for their swimming heads fully convinced them that they could place no dependance upon their feet at all.

In the meantime Adder had concocted the whole of his plot, and was ready to commence operations as soon as it might be deemed prudent. In entrapping the simple lord he had gained a double point—he had in him a fit tool to work out his own designs, and moreover, he should have an opportunity of extorting from him large sums of money as a reward for his services. Besides, what glorious satisfactio n it would be to him to know that Lord Ravensford was suffering all the pangs of jealousy and disappointed hopes.

"The hour of my triumph is at hand!" he soliloquised—" my revenge shall be satisfied, and the beauteous object who hath excited my desires shall be in my power ere many weeks have elapsed. The scheme I have laid is such a deep one that she cannot escape me; and then will Ravensford deeply repent the hour he discharged and insulted me by his opprobrious epithets and accusations. As for the fool, Lord Saunter, when I have fleeced him of all I can, I can easily get rid of him—but not a chance shall he have of accomplishing his wishes with Rosabelle. Soft fool! did he possess the least sense in the world he would easily perceive that I have been cajoling him. But it is well—if there were not these idiots in the world, one half mankind would starve. And now, no doubt, Ravensford is suffering the most poignant anguish, owing to the contents of the forged letter I sent him—little suspecting who is the real author of it. May anguish the most bitter continue to harass his mind, and it shall not be my fault if he be not tortured to distraction. He ought to have known Adder, so long as he had been with him—he ought to have known that he will never brook an insult, but would be sure to be amply revenged. But there is one consolation to me, to know that I have not been idle since I have been with him, and that I have always contrived so that we should share his fortune between us."

Not one of our readers, we dare say, will doubt that Adder spoke the truth, and, in fact, he might have said that Ravensford's former fortune had been more than divided between them, or, at any rate, that the valet had taken to himself by far the greater share. Adder had contrived to make himself very rich, and at one time he was the principal cause of his master being nearly ruined, and it was astonishing that Ravensford should so long put up with it, when he must have been fully aware that he was swindling him daily and hourly to a great extent. In fact he did know it; he was positive of it, but he had become so used to him, and he was always so successful in any stratagem which he undertook for him, that he could not bear to encourage the idea of parting from him. Moreover, he was absolutely afraid of him while his father was alive, he being entirely in his power, and knowing

that he could inform his father of many things that might prejudice the latter against him or, perhaps, cause him to discard him altogether; and he was, therefore, compelled to submit to many degrading circumstances, and to brook insults from which his pride revolted. Adder well knew upon what a slight tenure his connection with Ravensford hung, and he was, therefore, fully determined to make the most of it while it did last. But we must return to the part from which we have thus slightly digressed.

Lord Saunter was true to the hour of appointment the following morning, although his face was still flushed, and his head ached from the effect of the last night's debauch. He greeted Adder with the familiarity of a friend and an equal, a condescension which the former did not acknowledge, but on the contrary, to any person would have appeared to look upon Saunter with the most superlative contempt.

"To judge from your lordship's appearance," said Adder, "I should say that you had not slept much last night."

"Sleep, my dear fellow?" replied Saunter; "who the deuce do you think could sleep after receiving such information as that you gave me? I positively do not think I shall sleep again until I have the lady in my power. The fact is, I kept it up rather, last night, with Captain Mowbray, Sir Harry Spangle, Mr. Twitts, and two or three others, and—"

"I hope you did not mention anything about the business to them," said Adder.

"Why—why—yes, I did," faultered out Saunter; "but there could not be any harm in that."

"The devil!" ejaculated Adder, who was fearful that the more penetrating friends of Saunter would see through his plot and thwart it; "did I not bag of you to use more caution?"

"Well, so you did; but there is nothing to fear from them, my dear fellow," returned Saunter; "they are all my bosom friends, you know."

"Friends," repeated Adder ironically and with emphasis; "they may not betray us, but still it would have been better not to have trusted to them."

"Well, so it would," said Saunter, "but it can't be helped now, and I don't suppose any harm will come of it."

"What did they say about it?—what did they seem to think about it?" inquired Adder.

"Why, they admired the plot vastly," answered Lord Saunter, "and wished us success in it."

"'Tis well," returned Adder; "but I caution you not to make any other person the depositary of our secret. Are you still prepared to go on with the scheme, my lord? do yeu think the Lady Rosabelle a prize worthy of running any risk for?"

"Worthy of running any risk for!" repeated Lord Saunter: "why, the little divinity—I declare I should think no danger too great to encounter in getting possession of her."

"Very well, keep in that temper," said Adder, scarcely able to conceal the exultation he felt at having got Saunter so completely in his power—"keep in that temper, and I prognosticate that all will go on as well as you can desire, and in less than two months Rosabelle will be under your protection, and far away from Lord Ravensford."

"Extatic assurance!" ejaculated the delighted Saunter.

"But I must be well rewarded."

"Can you doubt me, Adder?"

"It is a very troublesome piece of business, and attended with no little danger," said Adder, "and your lordship will please to bear in mind that, had it not been for me, you would still have remained in ignorance of the sentiments that the Lady Rosabelle nourishes towards you."

Never shall I be satisfied till I hear those sentiments pronounced by the lips of the angelic woman," said Lord Saunter.

THE NUPTIALS OF RAVENSFORD AND ROSABELLE.

"You may depend upon the truth of what I have asserted, my lord," said Adder.

"Doubtless I can," returned Saunter, "but the other is a felicity I look forward to with impatience. But to remove all doubts from your mind, take this purse as a guarantee for what I intend to do. It is not a few hundreds that I will hesitate to give, if you will only exert yourself to serve me in this business."

Adder weighed the purse in his hand, and finding it very well filled, he altered his tone, and, with a smile of satisfaction, said—

"I hope your lordship will excuse me for my boldness in speaking to you; not that I doubted but that you would behave handsomely to me, but in matters of this kind it is always

best to give some encouragement by way of starting. Now, then, I am your servant to command."

"But what is the plan you have concocted?" interrogated his lordship.

"It is unnecessary for me to detail it at present," replied Adder, "let it suffice that it is a most subtle one, and if you only abide by my instructions, its success is certain."

"But can you not contrive to obtain for me an interview with Rosabelle on their return to this neighbourhood?" asked Saunter.

"That all depends upon circumstances," answered Adder, "but if it can possibly be done without any danger of being the cause of frustrating the whole plot, you may depend upon it I will manage it. Until the time, however, appointed for the elopement, you may rest assured that I will contrive for you to correspond with each other."

"Do this, my good fellow," said his lordship, "and I will be satisfied. I shall require you to take a very active part in the abduction."

"Leave that to me, I will manage all that," returned Adder; "it is not the first time I have had the arrangement and the execution of a little affair of this description, and I always contrived to get through the business with satisfaction to myself and those who employed me."

"You are positively a pink of a fellow, Adder," said Lord Saunter, admiringly.

"I feel extremely honoured by your lordship's compliment," replied Adder, "I always endeavour to give satisfaction to those who place confidence in me."

"I know you do, Adder," observed Saunter, "and a great genius you have—a wonderful genius in this line. Such a man as you is worth a mine of gold to a young man of fashion."

"Your lordship flatters me," remarked Adder, with difficulty repressing a laugh of scorn.

"No, I do not, positively," was the reply of Saunter; "demme! if you are not the most accomplished rascal I ever met with. I beg your pardon, I mean only that as a well merited compliment to your superior abilities."

"And as such it is taken, my lord," answered Adder, bowing obsequiously; "but we are straying from the immediate subject we came here to discuss."

"Well, positively, so we are," said his lordship; "suppose we succeed in bearing Lady Rosabelle away, whither do you think it would be best and most secure to convey her?"

"No place can be better than some obscure town in France, my lord," replied Adder.

"Well, well, I'll leave it all to you, Adder, I'll leave it all to you."

"You will find it to your advantage by so doing, my lord," returned Adder. "But now I wish to engage your attention to something else."

"Name it, my good fellow," said Saunter, eagerly.

"In order to prepare Lady Rosabelle to meet you, or correspond with you when she returns to this part of the country," observed Adder, "it will be necessary that you should write to her a letter, stating the nature of your sentiments, and which I shall take care shall reach her hands in safety."

"I admire your suggestion," said Lord Saunter, eagerly, "and am anxious to do as you wish immediately. In writing the state of my heart, I shall feel a great relief, and shall almost fancy I am in her presence. Pens, ink,

and paper, Adder, immediately—I will write without a moment's delay, and while the ardour of my feelings are at their full pitch."

"Your lordship's promptitude augurs well for the success of our stratagem," ejaculated Adder; "write boldly, forcibly, and eloquently, and fear not the result. I will wager my life, that ere many days you will receive an answer from Lady Rosabelle, fully confirming all that I have informed you of, and satisfactory to your hopes and wishes."

"I do believe you, Adder," returned his lordship; "and place the utmost reliance and most unlimited confidence in all you say or do. Let me at once, I again request, do as you have advised."

Adder immediately placed pens, ink and paper before the deluded Lord Saunter, and looked over his shoulder with an expression of the greatest exultation and triumph, while his dupe wrote the following extravagant epistle—

"Ever adorable Rosabelle,

"You, who alone possess my heart, and without your love that heart must cease to beat—how shall I express my transport to know that you return the ardent, the unextinguishable passion which glows within my breast, and forms a portion of my very existence? Alas! no language can ever paint it. Time and your own dear self, loveliest of women, alone can prove it. But a short time, my angel, and I hope to clasp you in my arms, breath my vows upon your lips, and release you from the power of a man who is unworthy of you, and whom I know you both hate and despise. Bear with your fate a short time longer, my dearest love: and, above all, endeavour to conceal your repugnance from Ravensford, lest he should become suspicious, and take steps to frustrate at once our hopes and intentions—bear with your misery, my adored one, I implore, and until the blissful time arrives when we shall again meet, seek consolation in the assurance of the unalterable, the fervent affection of

"Your devoted
"SAUNTER."

"Capital! excellent!" exclaimed the designing villain Adder, when he had finished perusing the letter; "you lordship has entered into my ideas exactly. It is brief, but nothing could be more pointed, or to the purpose. This letter must have the effect desired."

"Then you think Rosabelle will give me an answer?" demanded Lord Saunter.

"Undoubtedly she will," replied the wretch; "and happy enough she will be when she receives this, or say I have been deceived altogether. Now, my lord, entrust the letter to me, and I will see that it is forwarded to her without delay."

"Here it is," said Lord Saunter, giving Adder the note, after having carefully folded, sealed, and written the superscription to it;

"and if the same success attends it as you prognosticate, I shall be the happiest man in Christendom."

"And nothing will afford me more infinite satisfaction," returned Adder, putting the letter carefully away in his writing-desk. "One thing I hope you did not do—that is, tell any of your friends where I was at present staying."

"I did not," replied Lord Saunter,

"That was right," said Adder; "now another thing I would advise you to do is this —keep yourself as retired as possible, and report that you have left the neighbourhood for another part of the country."

"It would be useless doing that," observed Lord Saunter, "since I have told my companions about the scheme I have in view. They would feel confident that I was deceiving them, and probably, out of spite, upset the whole stratagem."

"Why, yes," said Adder, "that certainly is reasonable enough, and more than ever convinces me that you acted exceedingly imprudent in divulging your mind to them at all. You see you have placed yourself in their power, and are at the mercy of their caprice or envy."

"I cannot deny the justice of what you say," said Lord Saunter; "and I regret that I did so. But after all, I do not much fear them: they are already greatly in my debt, and if I do not say anything about what they owe me, and object not to accommodate them again occasionally until our plot is executed, I think we may reckon ourselves pretty secure as regards them."

"I hope it may turn out as your lordship surmises," said Adder; "but as there is nothing like using precaution, I will be upon the look-out, and should I observe anything that may excite my suspicions that all is not right, I will take timely steps to frustrate any designs that they may have against us."

"Thanks, good Adder," said Saunter; "this caution is extremely prudent on your part; and while I have such a guide as you, I do not entertain any apprehension. Come, we must drink success to our plot."

"With all my heart, your lordship," answered Adder; "and now I think we have arranged everything to our mutual satisfaction."

"Perfectly to mine," observed Lord Saunter.

Wine was now ordered, and the two worthy and amiable beings sat down to regale themselves, and partook of many deep libations ere they separated.

"Ha! ha! ha!" laughed Adder, when his noble dupe had made his departure, "how easily the shallow-pated booby has been gulled, and how great will be his rage and disappointment when he finds it out. By hell, I could not have hit upon a better scheme, for by it I shall make money, gratify my revenge, and gain possession of her who hath excited my desires. I am all eagerness to commence the work of mischief. The poor lord will be finely laughed at by his companions, and will be unable to show his face into society again.. Ha! ha! ha!"

Having thus spoke, the villain hastened to forward the letter to Ravensford Castle. Adder had hit upon another scheme to forward his diabolical views, and to render the torture of Lord Ravensford still more exquisite; and this was, to forge the handwriting of Lady Ravensford, and address a letter as if coming from her in answer to the one Lord Saunter had sent her. This, he felt assured, the foolish lord in his drunken moments would not fail to exhibit to his companions and others; and the consequence would be, that in all probability the circumstance would reach the ears of Lord Ravensford, and, confirming the cruel suspicions excited by the two letters sent, would drive the unfortunate nobleman to distraction, and take off all conjecture as to in whose power Rosabelle was.

The wretch glutted on these ideas with demoniac satisfaction, and lost no time in setting about putting his diabolical designs into execution. Even the arch-fiend could not have gloried more in doing evil, and working misery to others, than this man; and, unfortunately, for awhile his nefarious schemes were attended with too much success.

CHAPTER XIV.

RAVENSFORD CASTLE.—THE LETTERS.

WE have before described the demoniacal exultation of Adder at the success of his diabolical stratagem; and we will, therefore, now leave him, and return to Ravensford Castle, where, although the bride and bridegroom had become more composed after the reception of the mysterious letter, they were yet far from being entirely composed. There were times when Lord Ravensford felt the pangs of jealousy and doubt gaining powerful ascendancy over his mind, and he found it often no very easy task to conquer his feelings sufficiently to disguise them from Rosabelle. Those who have themselves been deceivers are always the readiest to suspect others of deceiving them, and so it was with Lord Ravensford; and, although he tried to persuade himself that he believed the letter all a base fabrication by some person envious of his happiness, he by no means succeeded. The handwriting, which he felt confident was Lord Saunter's, more than ever convinced him that there was more in it than he had at that time an opportunity of ascertaining; but he determined to stifle his real feelings as much as possible, and having by that means elicited either a confirmation or a contradiction of his surmise, to wreak an ample vengeance on the fopling lord, whom he now blushed to acknowledge he had once owned as a friend. At the bare idea of Lord Saunter's having aspired to the affections of Rosabelle, especially after she had become his (Lord Ravensford's) bride, his blood boiled with almost ungovernable resentment and offended pride; and he felt that, if his fears should happen to be realised, nothing but the blood of the offender could wash out the remembrance of the insult: and that he resolved, at all hazards, to accomplish.

Rosabelle also, although she behaved with the becoming dignity and composure of conscious innocence, by no means felt easy. Her feelings had received a severe shock by the contents of the letter, and although she strove hard and successfully to conceal her real thoughts from her husband, in private she endured many hours of the greatest excitement, anguish, and suspense, and in vain tried to divest her mind of the melancholy forebodings which had taken possession of it, and which seemed to assure her that her troubles were not yet half over. In vain did she rack her brain to endeavour to surmise who had been the actual author of this base plot to seek to destroy the mutual happiness of her and her husband; she could not form even the slightest conjecture. She knew not that she possessed an enemy in the world who could feel any interest in trying to do her so great an injury; and if it were really Saunter he must be possessed of more consummate villany and insolence than she had imagined could ever belong to the human race. From the tenour of the letter, whoever the person was who had written it, it evidently boldly insinuated that they had been keeping up a correspondence for some time; and yet, of course, her conscience entirely acquitted her of having ever harboured a thought towards any other man than her husband, which innocence might blush to hear, or she to acknowledge. It seemed, therefore, altogether impossible for any person, particularly one who was almost a stranger to her, to be base enough to endeavour to trample on her peace of mind, of which she had so long been deprived, in so heartless a manner.

But with more acute agony than all, and in spite of his efforts to conceal the fact, did Rosabelle notice the emotions of her husband, and the look of mingled suspicion, doubt, and fear, with which he would occasionally contemplate her; and at such times she was ready to go distracted, and sinking at his feet, implore him at once to assure her of his confidence in her integrity, or to end her life and misery by acknowledging to her that he believed her to be an adultress. These suffer-

ings were rendered the more painful as she was compelled to keep them confined to her own breast, and in the presence of Lord Ravensford and her father to appear calm and contented, and even cheerful, more especially as she feared that the latter's fears and suspicions would be aroused should she betray any particular emotion, and she knew that his keen and penetrating eye would detect the least symptom in a minute. She had always a terrible dread of causing any excitement in the mind of Montalbert, lest his reason should again be overturned, and it was, therefore, with the most anxious solicitude she watched his every action, and studied everything she could possibly devise to keep him calm and happy. And happy indeed was Montalbert, could he but see his daughter smile, no greater bliss could Heaven bestow upon him; or when excited by anything that might have been said, the roses would resume their place in her cheeks, and she would look as beautiful as she had ever done before sorrow and her were acquainted; and overcome by his feelings, and the number of reminiscences that rushed upon his recollection, the old man would snatch her to his bosom, and imprint numerous and fervent kisses upon her lips.

A few days had only elapsed after the circumstance had taken place, which had caused Lord and Lady Ravensford so much uneasiness, when Rosabelle's waiting-woman entered her dressing-room one morning, and delivered to her a letter, which she said had only just been brought. Rosabelle looked at the superscription which was directed to her, but a sickly faintness came over her, and her heart palpitated violently against her side, when she immediately perceived that it was written in the same handwriting as the letter sent before. She gasped for breath, and a cold tremor seized upon her limbs. She held by the back of a chair to support herself, and then again her eyes became fixed upon the letter, becoming the more convinced that she was right in her conjectures, the oftener she gazed upon the characters.

"Is there any answer, my lady?" asked Esther.

"Ah!" ejaculated Rosabelle, hastily. "Who brought this letter?"

"A footman in blue livery," answered Esther, "and if I am not mistaken, my lady, it is the livery of Lord Saunter."

"Do you know the man, Esther?" eagerly demanded Rosabelle.

"No, my lady," answered the maid; "I don't know that ever I saw him before."

"Is he waiting?"

"He was waiting in the hall, my lady, when I came up stairs," said Esther, "and I understood him that he would wait to know if there was any answer to the letter."

"Ah!" cried Rosabelle, her eyes brightening with hope and expectation; "then there is some chance of this painful mystery being solved. I will instantly go to the man myself."

"You, my lady!" said Esther, in a voice of astonishment, "I beg pardon, there is no necessity for that, I——"

Rosabelle interrupted her, and with an impatient wave of the hand, motioned her to silence, and then with all the haste which her agitation would permit, she left her chamber, proceeded along the gallery, descended the stairs, and entered the hall, but she saw no person there but one or two of the domestics belonging to the castle, to whom, upon her putting the question as to what had become of the man who had brought the letter, they informed her that he had left the place immediately after he had given the letter to Esther. Vexed and disappointed, Lady Rosabelle hastily inquired whether the man was known to any of them, but they answered in the negative, only reiterating the opinion of Esther, namely, that he was a servant of Lord Saunter, but who, they said, they did not believe to be in the neighbourhood.

"Should any of you know the man again?" demanded our heroine.

"Oh, yes," they all replied together.

"Did you notice which way he went when he left the castle?" asked Rosabelle.

"He turned to the right, as if he were going towards the common," answered one of the servants.

"Hasten two or three of ye in different directions," said our heroine, "and endeavour to overtake him. If you should see him, request him to come back, and if he refuses, even use force to compel him."

Wondering what could be the occasion of the violent agitation of their mistress, and the cause of the strict injunctions she had given them, the servants obeyed, and during the time they were absent, Rosabelle paced the hall with hasty and disordered steps, and her bosom was filled with the most intense agitation. Again she looked at the letter, and then the thought occurred to her—

"Shall I break the seal; or give it into the hands of Lord Ravensford as it is?"

It was a second or two before she could answer those questions in her own mind, and then she said to herself:—

"But no, why should I distract his mind more than it has been tortured already?—It is evidently the production of the same base hand which concocted the other infamous epistle; and according to all appearance, Lord Saunter is the villain who is the guilty author of the vile plot. Ah! should I not do wrong in concealing these suspicions, and the reasons I have for them, from my husband?—Yes, indeed I should, and——"

She was prevented from proceeding further by the return of the servants who had been despatched in pursuit of the man. They had been quite unsuccessful, not being able to see the man anywhere.

Rosabelle was very much chagrined and disappointed at this, and returned to her dressing-room, still holding the letter in her hand, and undecided how to act. At length, after a violent struggle with her feelings—she determined on perusing its contents, and breaking the seal: she glanced with eager haste at the writing, but had scarcely read three lines, when she uttered a loud scream, and immediately fainted away.

Lord Ravensford, during the time that these circumstances were taking place, had been in his own apartment, upon descending from which, he was informed by one of the most officious of the domestics of the letter being brought, and the great emotion which their lady evinced at the event.

"Ah! a letter!" cried Lord Ravensford, and a sickly foreboding rushed to his heart; "who brought it?"

"A man wearing the livery of Lord Saunter," answered the same officious individual.

"Confusion!" exclaimed his lordship, striking his forehead; "when,—where is he gone?"

"Oh, he has been gone about half an hour; he did not stay two minutes after he had delivered the letter to Esther to convey to her lady; and that was strange too, because I heard him say that he would wait to see whether there was any answer."

"Has Lady Ravensford received the letter?" asked Lord Ravensford.

"She has, my lord, and she came down stairs very much agitated, and commanded us to hasten in pursuit of the man; hows'ever, we could not find him."

Lord Ravensford did not stay to hear any more, but hurrying from the hall, he made his way with rapid strides, and in a state of mind which needs no description, to the chamber of our heroine.

"Well, I wonder what all this will come to," said the officious individual who had spoken to Lord Ravensford; "there is some mystery in this which I cannot fathom. I should like to know what business a servant of Lord Saunter's has coming here with letters for my lady?—Where there is so much secrecy, there cannot be much good."

"For shame, for shame, Jenkins," said another of the domestics; "these insinuations very ill-become you, and deserve to be reported to my lord. Inquisitive prying persons, always contrive to make mountains of mole-hills, and to suspect that guilt in others which they themselves possess."

Jenkins was evidently very much chagrined

at this home thrust, and it was several moments before he could return any answer.

"You are very ready with your insolent remarks, Thomas," he at length said; "that's what you are, if any body cared anything about them. I am no more peeping and prying than any one else, that I'm sure of, and perhaps if I was so sly as some folks, I shouldn't get that character. I say again, and I will maintain it too, that where there is so much secrecy, there cannot be any good intended."

"And pray what business is it of yours?" demanded Thomas; "you had better undertake to dictate to my lord and lady, and take upon yourself to censure them for what you might consider to be the impropriety of their conduct. No doubt they would feel highly honoured in having such a mentor. However, depend upon it, I will not fail to make them acquainted with the good opinion you have of them, if I hear any repetition of this."

"That fellow is a perfect monster—a complete rhinoceros; and has no more gentlemanly ideas about him than a Polar bear," observed Jenkins, as Thomas quitted the hall; "I must contrive something to get him dismissed, or I shall not be long here, I can see. I don't care what anyone may say to the contrary, but I still mean to say that this business has a very mysterious and suspicious look with it, to say the least of it, and I will find it out, if there be any possibility at all. Ah! I never expected there could be much happiness between my lord and lady after what happened; and I'm certain that a separation will take place before long; at any rate, they have commenced the honeymoon in a very promising manner."

Thus saying, the busy Mr. Jenkins walked away, priding himself greatly on his own superior skill at divination and penetration.

In the meantime, Lord Ravensford had ascended to the chamber of Rosabelle; and having knocked two or three times at the door without receiving any answer, he opened it and walked in; the first object which met his view was his wife, stretched upon the floor in a state of insensibility, and the open letter lying by her side, to which his attention was immediately attracted. Trembling with fear and resentment, he snatched it up, but before he had perused half a dozen words, his indignation was so great, that he crumpled it up in his hand, and striking his forehead vehemently with his clenched fist, he traversed the room in a state of disorder which the mind of the reader will possibly find no difficulty in conceiving.

"The villain, the base, the insidious, daring villain!" he exclaimed, as he stalked across the room; "yes, there is no longer any doubt, but that it is he. I will swear to his handwriting —his style, and—ah! his crest, too! Miscreant, damned miscreant, he shall pay for this with his life. But could he have presumed so much had he not received some encouragement? Ah! what maddening thoughts are these that take possession of my brain? My Rosabelle, a deceiver—my Rosabelle, false to me, and bestow her favours upon that senseless booby? Oh, never! never! There is base calumny in the bare idea! I will tear it from my mind; never will I do my own—my much wronged Rosabelle, the wife of my bosom, that injustice. Never will I suspect her truth, her constancy, her integrity. It is fabricated by the wretch out of a paltry spirit of revenge, because I have abandoned him and his guilty, unprincipled associates; but he shall not triumph, he shall not succeed in his infamous, his diabolical designs; and dearly shall he pay for his presumption!"

Having thus given utterance to his feelings, Lord Ravensford seized a smelling-bottle, which was fortunately close at hand, and raising Rosabelle in his arms, by the most affectionate attentions, endeavoured to recall her to animation. It was some time before he succeeded, but at length she opened her eyes, and seeing Ravensford hanging over her, her feelings overpowered her, and uttering a faint cry she almost relapsed into her former state of unconsciousness. Her husband, however, by the most tender asseverations, composed her, and gazing upon him with the most affectionate earnestness, she said—

"Oh! Ravensford, that letter—that fatal letter. Do you not believe its shameful contents? Do you not think me a guilty wretch, unworthy of anything but your scorn and hatred?"

"Cease—cease, beloved Rosabelle, I implore you, unless you would drive me to madness; your words torture me," exclaimed Ravensford; "and think you I could be so weak, so base, so cruel, so unjust, as to believe the contents of this letter, or think you untrue to me? Oh, Rosabelle, deeply do you wrong me by such a supposition. No, I see through it all; envy and malice have dictated all this; it is the work of the villain Saunter, and my former base companions. They are jealous of my happiness, and would willingly cause a dissension between you and me. But I will have my revenge: they shall not thus insult and try to torture me with impunity. Come, my love; dry up your tears. I cannot bear to see you weep."

"They are not tears of sorrow, Alfred, but tears of joy and gratitude," sobbed our heroine, throwing her fair arms around the neck of her husband, and looking tenderly in his face. "You do not doubt my truth, and I can, therefore, treat the vile machinations of the wretches with contempt. You know full well that I never beheld this man Saunter but once, and then it was in your presence."

"Oh yes, my love," said Ravensford, impatiently; "I know it all, and I should indeed despise myself could I doubt you. But I regret that the fellow who brought the letter was not detained, for from him we might have drawn a confession of the whole truth, and have forced him to state where his master is at present staying. But why do you tremble, Rosabelle?"

"Oh! Ravensford," said his wife, "I tremble at the thought of your having a hostile meeting with Lord Saunter; for, should you fall, what then would become of me, deprived, as I should be, of your protection?"

"Oh! fear not for me, my love," returned her husband : "Heaven and the justice of my cause will protect me. The villain shall not escape without punishment, depend upon it."

"He, indeed, richly merits punishment, I admit," observed Rosabelle; "but would it not be more advisable to let that punishment be inflicted by the strong arm of the law?"

"No," replied Ravensford; "the law would but inflict a fine, which, wealthy as Saunter is, would be no punishment to him at all. It strikes me forcibly that he is somewhere in the neighbourhood, and while we remain here, I will cause a strict watch to be kept up; and, should I discover his retreat, let the miscreant tremble."

Rosabelle sighed, but made no answer to it; and though she wished to see Saunter brought to some punishment for his unparalleled impudence and villany, she secretly prayed that her husband might not encounter him, fearful as she was that some accident might occur to him in the affray. Her husband read her thoughts, and kissing her fervently, endeavoured to banish her apprehensions, and requested her to try to gain her composure as well as she could before they joined Montalbert at the morning's repast. This Rosabelle sought to do, and succeeded better than might have been expected, but not so well as to be able to conceal the traces of her grief entirely from the observation of her father. He looked at her very earnestly for a short time, and then, in a voice of deep concern, said—

"Rosabelle, my love, your eyes are red—you have been weeping. What has happened to cause this? You are not happy."

"Oh! yes, my dear father," replied Rosabelle, eagerly, and forcing a smile. "I am happy, very happy, with you and my husband. What should make me otherwise?"

"I know not," observed her father, "but for some days past I have noticed that you looked pale and ill, and that your bosom was the abode of melancholy, which you were endeavouring to conceal from me. My heart, too, has been very much depressed of late; and although I have struggled hard, I have been unable to banish certain dismal forebodings from my breast. But, perhaps, it is the place that is the cause of it: we are no longer among those scenes we have been used to, and——"

"Oh, yes," interrupted Lord Ravensford, eager to catch at anything to prevent the necessity of explaining the truth; "that is it, my dear sir, depend upon it. This castle is so strange to you and Rosabelle, and everything about it is so new to you, that it is no wonder your spirits should be affected by it. Rosabelle, too, doubtless, wishes again for the society of her friends—for that of Mrs. Rattleton—while you miss your old companion, Mr. Goodman. We will leave here as soon as you deem fit, sir."

"You are very kind," returned Montalbert, who evidently coincided with his opinion as to the cause of the depression of spirits himself and his daughter felt. "I do believe what you say is correct, for were it the most miserable hovel to be seen, my old house at home would be dearer to me than the most magnificent palace. What say you, Rosabelle?"

"Oh! my dear father," answered Rosabelle; "well do you know my attachment to the home of my childhood. Your thoughts, your wishes upon that subject are also mine."

"I know they are, my love," said her father. "Then be it as your husband thinks proper: I am ready to depart from hence whenever it will suit his convenience."

"We have but few arrangements to make, my dear sir," observed Ravensford; "and, therefore, if it meets your approbation, and that of Rosabelle, the day of our departure shall be fixed for Monday next."

"That arrangement is perfectly agreeable to me," said Montalbert.

"And to me," remarked Rosabelle, who was, in fact, very much pleased to leave the place, on more than one account; but the principal of which was, that, suspecting Lord Saunter was somewhere in the vicinity of the castle, it would very likely prevent the meeting taking place which she so much dreaded. She did not, however, for a moment think but that it was quite likely when Lord Saunter found that they had left the castle, he would follow them, a conclusion which any one, who really believed him to be determined in the designs he had formed, would naturally come to.

Having thus settled that point, Montalbert and Rosabelle became perfectly restored to composure; and Lord Ravensford stifled as much as possible the resentment that filled his bosom towards Saunter, so that Montalbert might not observe anything which would be likely again to excite his suspicion.

This was on the Wednesday; and Ravensford, who could not rest until he had gratified his revenge, occupied the few days that intervened before the time they had appointed to leave the castle in instituting strict search and inquiries about the neighbourhood, to see whether he could learn anything of Saunter; but, of course, it was all in vain—no one had ever seen him, and, therefore, Lord Ravensford was at last obliged to arrive at the conclusion that he was not near the spot, and was compelled to conquer his impatience to inflict upon him a befitting chastisement for his audacity until he should encounter him.

We will now return to Adder and Lord Saunter, whom we left immersed in the business of their villanous plot. Adder fought his scheme and played his cards with the most consummate skill, and Lord Saunter, believing him to be heart and soul devoted to him and the nefarious object he had in view, loaded him with presents, and was continually in his society. How Adder now exulted at his success, and at every fresh present he received from his simple dupe! He laughed at him for a fool, and a vain, shallow-headed puppy. The reader has, doubtless, ere this, read the design of Adder: it was to rest all the *onus* of the guilty plot upon the shoulders of Lord Saunter, so as to remove any suspicion from himself, and enable him more readily to effect his design; and he resolved that very little time should elapse ere he would accomplish his wishes, and have Rosabelle in his power so securely that nothing could rescue her, or prevent his fully completing his base wishes.

"Yes," he reflected, "Rosabelle, your doom is sealed; ere many weeks have elapsed you shall be the mistress of the former servant of your husband. Oh, what torture will it inflict upon him to know it! What ample revenge will it be to me to know that he will believe he has been deceived, abandoned by the woman whom he imagined was perfection; but greater, far more exquisite will be his agony when he learns the truth, that he has wronged her, while that man whom he dismissed contemptuously from his service, has been the author of it all; the very man who hath succeeded in destroying his peace of mind and his prospects for ever. Ravensford, proud lord, you little imagined the misery you were bringing upon yourself, when you aroused the hatred and revenge of Adder. Nature has, indeed, bestowed upon me a very appropriate name; I am an adder, which never fails to spit its deadly venom against those who exasperate it."

In ruminations such as these the villain constantly indulged, and they were food to his base soul.

The man who had delivered the letter at Ravensford Castle, was a simple rustic, who knew nothing of Lord Saunter, so that Adder was aware he could not betray the plot by answering any questions that might be put to him. Neither could he tell from whom he received the letter, as he did not know his name, and Adder had laid the strictest injunctions upon him, not to satisfy any person who might question him, from whom he had received it, or in what part of the country, he (Adder) resided. He told him to act in the manner he had done, as regarded telling the servant at Ravensford Castle that he would wait for an answer, as that might perhaps prevent them putting any questions to him, and enable him to make his departure without any interruption, and, as it has been seen, the scheme succeeded as well as he could wish. The better to increase the suspicion that Lord Saunter was the sole guilty party, Adder had borrowed a suit of livery of the former, in which the countryman dressed himself, and thus it was that it was naturally concluded he was a servant of his lordship.

We believe we have before mentioned that Adder had prepared a forged letter as coming from Rosabelle to Lord Saunter, in reply to the letter he had sent her, and the day after the return of the man from Ravensford, he placed it in Saunter's hands, who was in such an ecstasy of delight, that he could scarcely contain himself. With eagerness he broke the seal, and having perused the contents half a dozen times, he pressed it to his lips, and devoured it wit kisses. His extravagant and ludicrous behaviour, so tickled the fancy of the crafty Adder, that he was obliged to turn away to laugh.

The letter, as may be supposed, was couched in the most romantic and affectionate language, and written with all the ability which Adder possessed. Any one, however, but such an empty fool as Saunter, would have considered the improbability of Rosabelle (unless he set her down for one of the most wanton and abandoned of her sex) sending such a letter to a man whom she had never seen but once before, and then under circumstances that it was not at all likely she should be smitten with him. But the vanity of his lordship, as has been fully shown, was equal to his ignorance, and he placed the most implicit confidence in the genuineness of the letter itself, and every sentence it contained.

"It is settled!—it's done!" he exclaimed, joyfully; "she declares she loves me, is ready to make any sacrifice for my sake: to abandon home, father, husband, all, and I am one of the happiest fellows alive. I'll take good care not to make such a fool of myself as Ravensford did. No, no, when I have got a prize I know how to take care of it;—and Lady Rosabelle is a prize, by Jupiter, it is well worth running some risk to obtain. Adder, my boy, you are an excellent fellow. I have reason to like you better than ever every day. Your hand, while I place a purse in it; you deserve a fortune for the manner in which you are managing this business, and demme, if you shan't have one too, if we are completely successful. True merit deserves to be amply rewarded."

"I am perfectly of your lordship's opinion," said Adder, obsequiously; "but you are too generous, my lord; indeed you quite overwhelm me with your kindness; it is a great deal more than any humble services I can render your lordship can possibly merit."

"Now, now, don't talk in that way, Mr. Adder," observed Saunter, "or you will positively offend me; you will, demme!"

"Oh, my lord, I would not do that for the world," said Adder.

"Then don't you attempt to run down your own abilities again," said Saunter, "for I positively won't have it."

"It is sufficient for me to know that your lordship appreciates them," returned the designing hypocrite; "and I cannot give sufficient expression to the happiness I feel at having been so fortunate as to meet your lordship's approbation."

"Approbation! demme! I can never cease admiring you. If it had not been for you, I should probably never have been made ac-

GILBERT BACHELOR AND MERIEL SURPRISED BY THE DISGUISED ADDER.

quainted with the sentiments which the lovely Rosabelle has imbibed towards me, and even if I had, I should, doubtless, have been at a loss to have brought about the completion of a design which now has every prospect of being consummated. To you, then, I repeat, I am indebted for everything, and you shall find that I am not unmindful of it. Egad! we must have a bottle of wine over this business."

Adder bowed, and rang the bell for the waiter; he liked to hear his lordship call for wine, for it was in such moments as these that he was enabled to wheedle him out of the most, Lord Saunter being, like many persons, particularly liberal when inebriated.

The wine was brought, and after taking a glass or two, Saunter once more went into perfect ecstasies at the contents of the letter, which amused Adder much, and who quite coincided with everything which his lordship said, although that everything was most superlatively ridiculous, and only in reality excited his contempt and disgust, and it required the utmost stretch of patience to endure it without evincing the real opinion he had of it.

"Read the letter again, Adder," said his lordship, once more thrusting it into his hand —"is it not exquisite? Is it not charming? Every syllable is a gem, and the whole worth more than the costliest diadem. Each word breathes the most ardent affection, and every sentence is so delightfully turned, that it is enough to entrance the soul to read it."

"Your lordship ought indeed to thank your lucky stars," replied Adder, after having pretended to read the letter; "a more beautiful epistle I never remember to have perused. '

"It is quite impossible that you or anybody else could ever have done so," returned the foolish lord, "for, by Jove, she writes like an angel, demme, if she don't. I'll treasure this letter next my heart, and never part with it while I have life. Adder, how long do you think it will be before they return to this neighbourhood? She does not say anything in her letter, and I am rather surprised at that, for I should have thought she would have been anxious to let me know."

"Why, I do not think there is anything very remarkable in her omitting to mention it," returned Adder, "for her thoughts were, as you may perceive from the tenour of her letter, too much occupied with the warmth of her feelings to think of anything else. But I do not consider it is at all probable that they will remain any long time there, as Mr. Montalbert is with them, and he is so much attached to his native place, that I am surprised they could prevail upon him to quit it."

"I am all impatience till the time arrives," ejaculated his lordship; "I long to clasp the beauteous woman in my arms, and receive from her own lips an acknowledgment of that love she has so glowingly expressed in her letter."

"A pleasure which you are never destined to experience," said Adder to himself.

"It is a fortunate job, is it not, Adder," said his lordship, "that Mowbray and Sir Harry Spangle have left this place, for they might have presented many obstacles in the way of our plot?"

"Yes, it is a good job they have left," replied Adder; "but still it is necessary that we should use the utmost caution; I would advise that we remove from the immediate neighbourhood, and that you still keep it a profound secret from every one as to whither you are going."

"I agree with you," said Saunter, "and will abide entirely by what you propose; but in the meantime, to set my mind at rest, pray endeavour to ascertain when it is likely they will return from Ravensford."

"I will do as you wish, my lord," said Adder; "but I must again request that you will not become impatient, as that will only retard instead of expediting our plans."

"Impatient, Adder?" cried Lord Saunter; "who the devil can help being impatient over such a business as this?—Who the deuce, do you think, can have the anticipation of so much beauty coming into his possession, and not grow impatient for the moment of his happiness to arrive?"

"I imagine, then, that your stock of patience will be pretty well exhausted," thought Adder to himself, "if you wait until your wishes are gratified in that respect. My lord," he said, aloud, "I do not wonder at your feelings, for the beauty of Lady Rosabelle is enough to inspire a stoic with rapture; but I must still urge that you will comply with my request."

"Oh, of course, Adder, my dear fellow," said Lord Saunter; "you are my Mentor, you know, and I have no wish to break through the rules you set down for my conduct. I will leave you to find a place where it is not likely that we may be known, and to fix upon the spot, only do not let it be far from hence; for, I protest, the very idea of being any distance from the Hall, gives me the horrors."

"In that respect," said Adder, "I will endeavour to gratify your lordship's desire as much as possible."

"Very well, then," said Saunter, "then that business we may reckon as settled; and now, my dear fellow, we must separate, for I have an appointment at seven, and it is half-past five now."

"Very well, your lordship," returned his myrmidon; "but let me beg once more to impress upon your mind the necessity of caution."

"Oh, yes, that's all right," said Saunter; "the thought of Rosabelle will be sufficient at all times to put me on my guard. I would not do anything which might be the cause of frustrating our well-concerted plot, not to be made emperor of the world."

"Upon that assurance I am satisfied, your lordship," said Adder; "and, I trust, you will also excuse my being so urgent, when the motives by which I act are taken into your lordship's consideration."

"There needs not the least apology, my dear fellow," returned Lord Saunter; "you can take what liberties with me you like, for I know that you have my interest at heart. There, there — that's enough; good-day, Adder; good-day: to-morrow we will meet again."

"Good-day, your lordship," said Adder, and the former then took his departure. When he had quitted the house, Adder gave vent to the feelings he had with such difficulty suppressed during the interview, and indulged in a hearty laugh.

"The fool has swallowed the bait more ravenously than I even anticipated," he cried. "I have him quite securely in my power, and will take good care that he does not slip through my fingers until I have accomplished all that I wish, and to do which he is so excellent a a tool in my hands. How the idiot will storm and rave when he finds that he has been so cleverly deceived; and yet shame and the other consequences that would follow, will prevent his making any fuss about it. By so doing, he would not only be exposed to ridicule, but much more serious consequences, in all probability, from the vengeance and indignation of Ravensford. How prodigal is the fool of that which he never laboured to obtain, and which has been wrung by his ancestors from the brows of the needy! Another well-filled purse has fallen to my share. Well, by the gods, the game goes on famously, and well repays me for my trouble."

Adder, during the time he was thus deceiving the lordly simpleton, was making every preparation for the reception and secretion of Rosabelle, when she should fall into his power, a circumstance he made fully certain of, so generally infallible had been the villanous stratagems of which he had been the author; and his exertions were redoubled when he learnt from one of the tenants on the estate, who did not know who he was, that they were expected to return about Wednesday in the following week. But it is not to be supposed that Adder could effect his wishes without assistance; he had several accomplices, whom he liberally paid for their services, and there are always wretches plenty, ready to the bidding of a scoundrel for lucre.

Although Adder had placed such strict injunctions on Lord Saunter, about using precaution, in his drunken moments he thought very little about them, and, in fact, he made no scruple at hinting the whole affair to some new acquaintances he had formed, contrary to the promise he had made to Adder, when Sir Harry Spangle and Captain Mowbray left the place; moreover, it was only the day subsequent to the one on which he had received the supposed letter of Rosabelle, that he absolutely read it to the said profligate associates, and boasted of the remarkable conquest he had made. He did not, however, divulge about Adder being his creature in the business: on the contrary, he took all the credit of the plot (if credit it could be) to himself.

Of course he did not make Adder acquainted with this circumstance; and when he became sober, and reflected upon what he had done, he was very sorry for it, and was fearful that it would be the cause of his meeting with some obstacle in the way of the accomplishment of his designs.

On the Monday morning early, Lord and Lady Ravensford and Mr. Montalbert, with their attendants, took their departure from Ravensford Castle: and although Rosabelle's feelings had received a very great shock by the affair of the letter, she had managed to become pretty tranquil, especially as her husband had placed such implicit confidence in her truth, and had so warmly expressed his sentiments of affection upon the subject. What she dreaded more than all was, that the circumstance should reach the ears of Mr. Montalbert, whose mind, should it do so, it would make a powerful and perhaps a fatal impression upon, weak and tottering as it was. Fortunately, however, this did not take place, and, for the present, our heroine was saved the heavy calamity of which she constantly entertained so great a dread.

We will pass over the journey from Ravensford Castle, which was performed without anything of sufficient importance occurring to demand any place in these pages, and bring them at once near the hall, from which a deputation, consisting of some of the oldest inhabitants of the neighbourhood, came forth to meet them, and to welcome them on their return. It was truly a gratifying sight to behold the young and the old, the rich and the poor, vie with each other in their demonstrations of friendship and esteem for Mr. Montalbert and his daughter. The former was affected to tears, and Rosabelle, who, mingled with her pleasure, felt a certain degree of pain and self reproach, when she remembered but too poignantly the unfortunate indiscretion of which she had been guilty, laid her head upon her husband's shoulder, and wept bitterly. He understood her meaning, but was unable to make any reply; conscience told him that he, in fact, was the most guilty party, and that, although he knew he had made all the atonement he could, he could never pardon himself for the misery of which he had been the originator.

Mr. Goodman, and Emily, and her husband, who had been most anxiously anticipating the time of their arrival, met them long before they reached the hall, and the greeting which took place between them needs no description from us. They were, however, greatly grieved to notice, in spite of her efforts to conceal it, the change for the worse which even the short absence from the hall had caused in the appearance of Rosabelle, and they could form a pretty shrewd guess in a moment that something had taken place more than they were acquainted with, to disturb her.

When the carriage had arrived within a short distance of the hall, Mr. Montalbert, his daughter, and her husband, alighted, and amid the acclamations of the poor but honest individuals who had come forth to testify their gratitude to those who had ever been to them such kind benefactors, they reached the hall, and once more found themselves beneath that roof where they had experienced so much joy and sorrow.

But there was one who came forth, and in secret watched the proceedings with very different feelings to those which the other persons experienced, and that one was Adder, who, having fixed himself in a place where he could notice all that passed without being observed himself, gloated upon the charms of her whom he had marked for his victim, with the most brutal desire, and as they passed close to the spot where he was standing, he could scarcely control himself within the bounds of reason. He watched them enter the hall, and long remained with his eyes fixed upon the place whence they had disappeared, unable to move. At length, he turned away, and clenching his fist in the intensity of the emotion which thrilled his bosom, he exclaimed :—

"Little dost thou think, proud and detested Ravensford, the deep plot which is being ripened into action by he whom thou has dared to offend, and who will not fail to have the most ample vengeance. Little dost thou suspect that the fair being, whom thou dost imagine to be solely thine own, is marked to be the victim of thy late servant! Ha! ha! ha! But thou shalt learn to feel and dread his power; the time rapidly approaches when thine heart shall be wrung, and when Adder shall have reason to exult in his triumph, and mock and revile at thine agony!"

Thus saying the villain turned away from the spot, and bent his footsteps back to the place where Lord Saunter was anxiously awaiting his arrival.

It had been with the utmost difficulty that Adder had succeeded in persuading Lord Saunter to remain at home on the morning of the expected return of Montalbert and his daughter to the hall, so anxious was he to catch a glimpse even of her whom he was infatuated enough to imagine was completely enraptured with his person; but at length he did contrive to induce him to remain at home, by pointing out to him the danger of his being seen abroad by any persons who might communicate the intelligence to Lord Ravensford or some of his friends, and thus, not only be the means of frustrating his wishes, but also of bringing upon him that resentment he had so much reason to dread. The booby lord was, therefore, at last prevailed upon to do as Adder desired, but it was not until he had exacted a promise from the latter to return as speedily as he possibly could and give him all the information in his power respecting our heroine, that he yielded.

Lord Saunter had much trouble, notwithstanding, in keeping his promise to Adder, and the time never appeared so long to him as it did on that occasion. Frequently he went to the window, and looked out upon the road to see if he could behold anything of him, but it was a considerable time ere his anxiety was gratified. At length he did behold Adder approach, and so great was his eagerness to learn all the particulars, that he could not wait until he had entered the house, but rushed forth to meet him.

"Adder, my dear fellow," he cried, impatiently, "the news—what is it? Has the dear, fascinating divinity arrived? Tell me immediately, or I shall go mad with impatience."

"My lord," returned Adder, "for the hundredth time I must warn you against your imprudent haste. Could you not wait until I had entered the house?"

"Wait! what a devil of a tedious fellow you are, Adder; but have they returned?"

"They have."

"Huzza! huzza! then, in a day or two, I may expect an interview, eh?"

"Not so; that would be too precipitate an attempt."

"More delay, damn it!—this is enough to try the patience of Job!"

"You must bear with it, unless you would render useless all that I have done already to forward your wishes."

"How provoking!"

"Probably it is, but yet it is prudent."

"Prudence again; I wish there was not such a word in the vocabulary."

"The felicity you will afterwards experience, my lord, surely is worth enduring ten times more to obtain than that you are complaining of."

"Why, that to be sure, is undeniable, Adder; but then it positively is a most severe trial, that there is no denying. And how long do you expect it will be now ere I shall be able to obtain an interview with the lovely Rosabelle?"

"I cannot say, exactly."

"Cannot say exactly! Damned aggravating!"

"No doubt of it; but it can't be helped."

"But may I not communicate with her?"

"I dare say I could contrive to get a letter conveyed to her if you were to write one," answered Adder.

"In which I could urge her to let the time of our meeting be at as early a period as possible."

"Exactly."

"Enough, it shall be done instanter," said the easy dupe, and taking the arm of Adder, they walked into the house, where Saunter having sat down and wrote another of those ridiculous letters, addressed to our heroine, of which we have already given the reader so fair a sample. Adder promised to get it forwarded without any delay, and after some further conversation, of too trifling a nature to deserve a place in these pages, the villain took his departure.

But although, to give a better appearance to his stratagem, and to prevent the suspicious of the consummate booby Saunter, the wily Adder had persuaded him to write a letter to Lady Ravensford, it was not his intention to forward it to her, thinking that he had already done sufficient to excite the jealousy and uneasiness of Lord Ravensford, and thus satiated his revenge, and imagining that something also might transpire if he sent too many epistles of the kind to lead his victim to suspect the truth, and thus render all his future plans abortive. Therefore was it, as we have previously stated, that the offspring of the puerile lord's brain was immediately committed to the flames by Adder, as soon as the former had turned his back.

The forgery which the villain Adder had concocted had all the effect he expected it would upon Lord Saunter, and not for a moment doubting that it was genuine, he was in perfect ecstasies.

"It is very clear that the dear, dear creature loves me—adores me," he soliloquised, "and is ready to make any sacrifice for my sake. I might have seen that from the very first moment I beheld her, only my modesty is so exceedingly great, that I am always very tenacious of arriving at such flattering conclusions. But that she should prefer me to the dull, insipid, sanctimonious Ravensford (which he now really is) is not to be wondered at. I am gay, volatile, devilish good looking, and— oh, it's as clear as the sun at noonday; the angelic creature is completely enraptured with me. This is one of the most enviable and triumphant conquest I have made in the whole course of my career, which has been a most extraordinary successful one, by the by. That Adder is a most inestimable fellow, as I have often asserted before; and when this business is completed I will make his fortune, if I don't, demme!"

Thus soliloquizing, the shallow-headed scion of nobility perused again and again the letter which he imagined had been sent to him by our heroine, and every time he did so his transport increased, and he was actually unable to keep it even within the bounds of reason. He erected to himself, in imagination, fairy temples of felicity, and Rosabelle became the sole empress of his fondest hopes and wishes. His sanguine thoughts anticipated every happiness that could fall to the lot of mortal; but never did he for a single moment think upon the dishonourable course he was pursuing with an idea of gratifying his guilty passions. Reflection, in fact, to him who possessed a heart that was entirely callous to all the better feelings of nature, was a stranger; and when, indeed, it was courted by him, it was only to exult over some act of iniquity of which he had been guilty. There was another feeling which predominated in the bosom of the ignorant nobleman, even more powerfully than the other, and that was the vanity occasioned by the thought of the talk and stir the affair would create in the world—at least, what he considered *his*

world—as, in fact, it was—namely, the giddy vortex of fashion. His gay, thoughtless, and unprincipled companions, he imagined, would set him down ever after as a paragon of fascination, a perfect adept at the art of seduction, a *rara avis* in the court of gallantry, and, indeed, the very epitome of seducers and ladykillers. Henceforward, he would be the star of all their meetings, the great card (as they have it in theatrical phraseology) of all their clubs; and to acquire such fame, in the opinion of his lordship, was to obtain more glory than all the victories which could laurel the hero's brow.

Saunter was a perfect exquisite, in his way; and the crafty and the designing, such as Captain Mowbray, and Sir Harry Spangle, had only to humour his vanity to make an easy victim of him. Yet, withal, they despised him in their hearts, and none were more ready than they were, when alone, to laugh at and ridicule his follies, and to treat him as they would a contemptible being, who seemed to be constituted alone to rob. Yet the poor victim could not see how they were imposing upon him, but, on the contrary, believed them absolutely to be sincere in all their professions; and his inordinate vanity, fed by such a supposition, instead of feeling, as he ought to have done, degraded by such an opinion from men actually beneath contempt, he became, in his own estimation, like some one superior to the general race of humanity.

Although, as we have before stated, Captain Mowbray and Sir Harry Spangle had quitted the neighbourhood altogether, the persons with whom Lord Saunter had since formed an acquaintance were equally profligate and unprincipled, and they, therefore, made as easy a dupe of him as others had previously done.

The letter which he supposed had come to him from Rosabelle, in reply to the one he had sent her, he, in his drunken moments, did not hesitate to exhibit amongst them, and to mention pretty freely what were his intentions, and what had already taken place. They most of them believed that he spoke the truth, and would have been ready enough to have made Lord Ravensford acquainted with the same, only most of them were unknown to that nobleman, and those that did know him, were tenacious of saying anything about the business, being fearful that it might be discovered by Saunter, who would in consequence be offended and withdraw himself from their society, which would deprive them of a victim, and a source of amusement they could but ill afford to lose. It happened, however, one evening that among the company assembled in the room of the hotel in which Lord Saunter was as usual, notwithstanding the precaution which Adder had given him, boasting of the conquest he had made, and reading the letter which had been forged by the latter, there happened to be a friend of Ravensford's, who had dropped in promiscuously, and who, happening to hear the name of his lordship bandied about so freely from one to the other, was induced to pay particular attention to the subject, and his astonishment almost exceeded all bounds, when he heard the manner in which Saunter spoke of Rosabelle. Could it be possible that Ravensford could be so easy a dupe, or that Rosabelle, whom he had heard lauded to the skies, could be guilty of such base, such unnatural duplicity? It seemed almost incredible, and so impatient did he become, that he had the utmost difficulty in retaining his temper within the bounds of prudence. Ravensford he had ever esteemed most warmly; he was also well aware of the painful circumstances that had taken place between him and our heroine; but he had always entertained the highest opinion of her character, and made every allowance for the indiscretion of which she had been guilty, through the persuasions alone of her present husband, and he could not, with any degree of calmness, listen to what he thought to be such heartless attempts at calumny. But when Saunter absolutely produced the letter, which he stated to have come from Lady Rosabelle, and which he (the friend of Lord Ravensford) could have sworn was in her hand-writing, his opinion began to waver, and he scarcely knew what to think. There was such a semblance of truth about it, that he found it almost impossible to doubt, and yet, for the sake of his friend, he would do so by a powerful effort. How his blood boiled as he listened to the manner in which Lord Saunter and his dissipated companions treated the subject. The levity with which they spoke of Lady Rosabelle, and the impudent confidence which Saunter expressed in the conquest he had made. Such depravity, especially in the female sex, the gentleman could scarcely bring himself to believe to exist in human nature, and yet the circumstances that Saunter mentioned, left him scarcely any further room to doubt. He took no part in the conversation that was passing among the profligates, and affected not to take any notice of it, pretending to be entirely engaged in perusing the paper; but not a syllable was lost upon him, and every observation that was made by Saunter was treasured in his memory. At the time this conversation was going forward, the wine was being circulated pretty freely around the board, and with every exclamation of exuberant delight, Lord Saunter took a fresh potation, so that at length he became almost completely insensible to what he was doing, and as the gentleman before alluded to perceived, but which was not seen by any other of the guests, he dropped the letter, without being aware that he had done so. To get possession of this was now the gentleman's object, and that he determined to accomplish by some means or the other. He put down the paper, and shifted his hat by the side of his lordship, where he dropped his handkerchief, as if he had done it accidentally, on the letter, and picking both up, conveyed them to his pocket.

Shortly afterwards, Mr. Wilmot (which was the name of the gentleman) made an excuse and took his departure from the place, and having made his way home, he more minutely examined the epistle, and so cleverly was the forgery done, that he felt convinced it was written by Lady Rosabelle. But was it possible, he ruminated, that our heroine could be so entirely lost to shame and delicacy, so utterly abandoned, as to avow an illicit passion for another man, and even to agree to secret assignations with him? That man, too, such an inordinate booby as Lord Saunter? It seemed so utterly opposed to nature and to reason, that although Mr Wilmot might be said to have the most unquestionable proof in his possession, he had his doubts upon the subject. But how should he now act? To reveal the circumstance to Ravensford would, he was certain, drive him to a state bordering upon distraction; and yet to conceal it from him, and to suffer him to be the dupe of his unfortunate, misguided wife, and Lord Saunter, would not be acting the part of a sincere friend. He, therefore, although he much dreaded the task at last resolved to break the subject to Lord Ravensford, but determined not to do so for a few days, in the hope that something might transpire to disprove the truth of the suspicions which circumstances had so forcibly stamped upon his mind.

When Lord Saunter missed the epistle which he had so much prized, he became much vexed and alarmed, lest his plot should be exploded, and his guilty views with regard to our heroine frustrated, and himself not only become an object of ridicule, but stand in danger of experiencing the full effects of the resentment of Lord Ravensford. He had not the least doubt but some one of his dissolute companions had purloined it of him, but he did not like to make any inquiry into the matter, as he was perfectly convinced that whoever had it they would be sure to deny it, and that he should only meet with derision and scorn. Of the real individual who had got it, however, his lordship had not the most remote idea. He was fearful lest the circumstance should by any means reach the ears of Adder, who, he had no doubt, if he should become acquainted with it, would immediately withdraw his services from him in disgust, and thus his schemes would all be at an end, and all his hopes of possessing Rosabelle crushed.

Adder had in vain endeavoured by every means to convince him of the actual necessity there was of keeping the place of their locality a secret; and although his lordship had promised to do as he desired, he almost invariably broke that promise nearly as soon as he had made it. He was, therefore, compelled to adopt another scheme; which was to write one more letter as if coming from Rosabelle, in which he artfully expressed a wish that Lord Saunter would by all means remove from the immediate neighbourhood of the hall, without any farther delay, and keep himself as much secluded for the present, as possible, as she was fearful, she having already noticed a change in the behaviour of her husband, that his suspicions were partly aroused, and that their designs might be frustrated if he did not that which she desired him. It was added, that she hoped the time would soon arrive when she could make an appointment to meet him with safety, until which time he was assured of her most unbounded and unutterable affection.

This letter had the desired effect; Lord Saunter again removed, and to a spot at some distance from that where he had latterly been residing, and he also forbore to visit his former companions, and kept himself so completely secluded, that no one could form any conjecture as to what had become of him.

In the meantime, the crafty and designing Adder was pursuing his own villanous stratagem with the most sanguine anticipations of success, and had almost got it ripe for execution. We have before mentioned that he had made the necessary arrangements for the abduction and security of his intended victim, and having so far proceeded, he was impatient to get it completed as quickly as possible, so that he might get rid of Lord Saunter, and have the game entirely to himself. That he should be able to accomplish all that he desired, he had not the least doubt, as he had ever been most successful in everything he had undertaken to perform, and since he had again seen the object of his guilty passions, after her return from the short sojourn they had made at Ravensford Castle, his anxiety to possess her had greatly increased, and he was, therefore, resolved to set all his energies to work to gain the consummation of his wishes as speedily as possible.

Although, of course, as must be imagined, our heroine had suffered much through the ravages of care, she was still transcendantly beautiful, and there was something in the melancholy expression which almost invariably stamped her features, which was particularly interesting. Hers was a beauty of no evanescent description; her charms alone could fade with death.

Although Lord Ravensford had endeavoured to acquit Rosabelle of anything wrong, there were times when the circumstance of the two letters they had received would occur to his memory so forcibly, that he had not the power entirely to resist their influence, and in such moments, he would imagine all sorts of things, which, perhaps, but a short time afterwards, he would reproach himself for having encouraged. But Rosabelle, the devoted, the fond Rosabelle, a deceiver — a wanton, and that too, to a man like Saunter—oh, it was impossible; he despised himself for even for an instant giving way to such an idea.

Although Ravensford was always most careful that his behaviour towards his wife should not be such as to give her cause to suspect the nature of the thoughts that occasionally, in spite of all his efforts to the contrary, took possession of his mind, she often observed a difference in his manners, and a certain restraint in her society, which filled her with care and anxiety; and she frequently apprehended that Ravensford, notwithstanding what he had said to her, and the general kindness with which he treated her, was far from being satisfied; but whether it was occasioned by the eagerness to meet with Lord Saunter, that he might seek an explanation from him, and the ill-success that he had hitherto met with, or whether it sprang from some other cause, she was at a loss to conjecture. She was, however, far from easy upon this point, and it was often the subject of her meditations when alone.

Lord Ravensford had used every means to find out the place where Saunter was staying, but he had not as yet been able to ascertain it. One day he was astonished on receiving a visit from his old friend and brother collegian, Mr. Wilmot, whom he had not seen for some time before, although they had formerly been on terms of the greatest intimacy. He was very glad of the circumstance, however, for Wilmot was a man whom he had greatly esteemed, for there were innumerable excellent traits in his character, and he had shared but little in the follies and extravagances which Ravensford had himself indulged in.

Mr. Wilmot was the only son of a very wealthy country squire, and was possessed of many accomplishments, together with a very pleasing exterior, and a gentlemanly address. He was, therefore, just the man that Ravensford could feel a pleasure in inviting to his house, and he would thus, at the same time, increase the social enjoyments of his domestic hearth.

The principal purport of Mr. Wilmot's visit to the hall, the reader will easily imagine; but now it came to the last, he shrunk from the delicate task he had imposed upon himself. When he beheld Lady Rosabelle, and noticed the urbanity of her manners, and the affectionate regard with which she seemed to regard her husband and child, he thought it utterly impossible she could have been guilty of such a base act of deception as the nature of the letter which Lord Saunter had dropped would convey an idea of; and he almost determined not to say anything at all about it. Surely Rosabelle and Ravensford had already endured misery enough, and why should he now wish again to steal upon their domestic quiet, and destroy the ideal temple of future happiness, which they had probably raised, at once ?— He well knew the despicable character of the idiot Saunter, and that he was capable of saying or doing anything to gratify his inordinate vanity and libidinous propensities, and he was half inclined to believe that the circumstance of the letter was entirely an invention of his own. Then, again, on the other hand, the letter was written in so plausible a style, that he could hardly discredit it, and having several times seen the hand-writing of Rosabelle, he could almost have sworn that it was genuine. At any rate, after some further deliberation, he determined to broach the subject to his friend, as he considered it would be an act of injustice to conceal the singular conduct of Lord Saunter from him, and it was, in his opinion, cruel in the extreme to suffer Lady Ravensford to remain under a stigma, which she could, most likely, quickly remove, if she had an opportunity afforded her of doing so. At length, his lordship and himself having walked into the garden, and Lady Rosabelle being engaged in the house with her father and child, Mr. Wilmot took the opportunity to inquire whether he had heard from Lord Saunter lately. Ravensford started at the question, and his cheeks glowed with the resentment which the bare mention of that man's name occasioned in his breast.

"The villain!" he exclaimed : "would that I knew where to find him; I have a long account to settle with him when we meet again."

"Ah!" ejaculated Mr. Wilmot, noticing the violent agitation of Lord Ravensford's manner, "then there probably is cause for the suspicions which——"

"Suspicions!" interrupted Ravensford; "what mean you ?—Mr. Wilmot, I beg of you to explain yourself as quickly as possible; for I plainly perceive by your manner, and by alluding to Saunter in the manner that you just now have, that you have something to say which concerns me."

"Compose yourself my dear Ravensford," said Wilmot; "it is true that I wish to talk to you upon a subject of a very painful and delicate nature ; a subject in which your honour, and that of Lady Ravensford, is involved; and it is only the long friendship which has subsisted between us, and the certainty that you would appreciate my motives as they deserve, which has emboldened me to broach it to you."

"Confusion !" cried Ravensford, striking his forehead with extreme emotion; "I shall choke. Mr. Wilmot, by that friendship to which you have just alluded, I implore of you to impart what you have to reveal to me as briefly as possible. What fresh trouble is in store for me ?"

"I must again beg that you will not give way to such violent agitation, Ravensford," said Wilmot, who half repented of the task he had imposed upon himself; "what I have to tell you, doubtless, will cause you much pain; but, at the same time, I cannot persuade myself but that you will easily be able to rebut the foul calumny which is afloat, and to chastise the author of it as he richly deserves. I must again repeat the first question I put to your lordship, namely, whether you have lately heard from Saunter?"

"Wilmot," returned Ravensford, with increased emotion, "I perceive clearly that you have heard something of a circumstance which has lately caused me much pain, and I will, therefore, in confidence, impart to you the particulars. Listen."

Mr. Wilmot did listen attentively, and Lord Ravensford, as calmly as the agitated state of his feelings would permit, detailed the circumstance of the two letters which had been addressed to Lady Rosabelle from Saunter, while they were at Ravensford Castle. Wilmot heard him with surprise, and when he had concluded, said, producing the letter which Lord Saunter had dropped a few evenings only before :—

"Do you know this hand-writing, my lord ?"

"Gracious Heaven !" exclaimed Ravensford glancing eagerly at the letter, and his countenance becoming ashy pale ; "why, these characters are written by Rosabelle ;—I could swear to them !—Good God ! I shall go mad ! —What feeling is this that comes over me ?— Can I read aright ?—Yes, yes ;—it is not mere idle fancy !—The letter is addressed to Saunter !—Every word seems to me like a brand of fire which scorches up my brain !— Oh, how have I been deceived !—Into what an abyss of misery have I plunged myself !— But let me seek the traitress !—let me——"

"Hold ! my lord ; be calm, be calm, and do nothing rashly, which you may sorely repent afterwards," remonstrated Wilmot, who seeing the violence of his manner, regretted having said anything to him about it ; "after all, this may only be a piece of base treachery, the contrivance of that wretch Saunter, for some sinister purpose."

"Psha ! I must be a weak, credulous fool, to believe such a thing," said Ravensford, as he paced backwards and forwards, in a state of the most uncontrolable rage. "Think you I know not her hand-writing ?—This, this at once confirms it all, and I am a miserable degraded being !—Oh, Ravensford, surely your repentance deserved a better fate than this."

He groaned aloud with mental agony, and struck his forehead violently. Then he again looked earnestly at the fatal letter, and once more ejaculated :—

"But she shall no longer triumph in her iniquity !—No, I will spurn the adultress from me !—She is no longer my wife, nor will I remain under the same roof with her. Where is she?—Let me find her, that I may heap curses on her head, and discard her for ever !"

"This violence is unreasonable, Ravens ford," observed Mr. Wilmot, "and will not do any good. In justice to Lady Ravensford, you ought to allow her an opportunity to explain, and exonerate herself if possible ; and somehow or the other, I cannot help believing that she will be enabled to do so with perfect ease, and in the most satisfactory manner. Guilt of such a nature as the contents of this letter would imply, surely cannot inhabit the bosom of one whom I had ever believed to be——"

"Enough, Wilmot," interrupted Lord Ravensford, passionately, "your words torture me. Think you I can be calm, and this

LORD SAUNTER IN COMPANY WITH HIS DEPRAVED ASSOCIATES.

damning proof of her whom I have made my wife's infidelity before me ?—This hour—this very minute shall decide all. Leave me, Wilmot. I must see Rosabelle alone."

"Excuse me, my lord," said Mr. Wilmot, "and do not deem that impertinence which is only dictated by pure friendship and esteem ; but in your present state of mind, I cannot leave you. I—ah, see, here comes the Lady Rosabelle."

At that moment, our heroine, who was surprised at the long absence of her husband from the house, and had come to seek him, entered the garden, and hastily approached the spot where Ravensford and his friend were standing. She looked in better spirits than usual, and a sweet smile overspread her features ; but her husband gazed at her with eyes that seemed to flash fire, and his whole frame was violently agitated.

"I have a good mind to chide you, Alfred," said she, in a tone of sweetness, "I have a good mind to chide you, I declare, for leaving me and our father in this manner. But, Heavens ! Ravensford, what is the matter with you ?—Why do you gaze so fiercely upon me, while your cheeks are pale, your brows contracted, and your lips compressed ? I never saw you look like this before ;—oh, tell me, I beseech you, what has happened to disturb you thus ?"

As she spoke she laid her hand gently on

his arm, and looked up supplicatingly in his face; but he spurned her roughly from him, and in a voice hoarse with rage, and the overwhelming fury of his feelings, he cried—

"Away, wretch! deceiver!—Abandoned woman, begone!—lest in the fury of my resentment, I strike you dead at my feet!"

"Merciful Heavens!" gasped forth the astonished Rosabelle, "he raves;—something has turned his brain!—Speak to me, my love, my husband, and explain to me the cause of this terrible agitation, Mr. Wilmot, what has happened?—what can have occurred to occasion this incredible and alarming change?"

"I have been the innocent cause of this, Lady Ravensford," replied Wilmot, "but, believe me, what I did was with the best of intentions. A foul conspiracy, some abominable calumny, has been——"

"It is no calumny," hastily interrupted the distracted husband; "have I not too fatal and indubitable proof of the truth of it?—Look, madam, at this letter,—the damning confirmation of your guilt, and my dishonour."

As Ravensford spoke, he held the letter towards Rosabelle, who took but one hasty glance at it, and them screamed with terror and amazement.

"Ah! does your conscience smite you, wretched woman?" cried Lord Ravensford; "can you, will you, dare you deny your own hand-writing?"

"Ravensford," ejaculated our heroine, struggling for breath, and her bosom heaving with agony; "Ravensford,—can you,—will you believe this?—My God! what fiends have conspired to ruin me; to drive me to madness? —Where, where did you obtain this diabolical forgery?"

"Lord Saunter dropped it in the room of an hotel in which I happened to be present, Lady Ravensford, where he had been perusing the contents of it to his dissipated companions," answered Wilmot.

"Oh, shame, oh degradation insupportable!" exclaimed Lord Ravensford. "The villain! But base as the miscreant even is, what must she be who——"

"Ravensford," interrupted our heroine, bursting into a wild paroxysm of tears, and sinking on her knees at his feet, "you surely will not, cannot believe me the abandoned, guilty wretch this base forgery would make me appear? Surely you will not believe that I am the authoress of that base epistle?"

"Unparalleled effrontery!" cried Ravensford, stamping with indignation; "can you deny your own handwriting?"

"Alfred," solemnly sobbed forth the distracted Rosabelle, raising her hands towards Heaven, "I swear that I did not write that letter, neither did I know anything of it, until you just showed it to me."

"You would swear to what is false!" returned her husband.

"By Heaven you wrong me, Ravensford; deeply, cruelly, wrong me," replied Rosabelle, with convulsive sobs; "if I am not innocent, may the most dreadful vengeance of the Almighty descend upon my head! May you curse, spurn, detest me; and may misery pursue me until death!"

"Ah!" cried Ravensford, moved by the solemnity and earnestness of her manner, "can this be true? and have I again been deceived by some fiend in human shape?"

"You have! you have!" replied Rosabelle, still remaining on her knees, and looking up in his face with an expression which was sufficient to bring conviction of her innocence home to the most obdurate heart. "Oh, Ravensford, think of my past life, my devotion to you and my child; my conduct since my return to my native place, and then ask yourself whether it is possible you can believe me to be the guilty woman some monster seeks to represent me? If I am no longer worthy of your confidence, oh, let me die; death would indeed be preferable to your hatred, and to be thought so basely of."

Mr. Wilmot, who was deeply affected by this scene, did not offer to say a word, thinking it would be much more prudent to suffer them, without interruption, to enter into a thorough explanation.

"Can I have been wrong?" observed Ravensford; "have I again been deceived? Oh, yes, I see it all now; what a wretch I must be to think that my Rosabelle could be so vile! The letter is an infamous forgery, and there must be more than one person concerned in this diabolical plot, evidently stipulated on by some feeling of revenge, although what can have excited it, I am at a loss to conceive. Rosabelle, can you pardon me? Alas! I was too headstrong, and have caused you much poignant anguish. Forgive me!"

Rosabelle burst into tears, and throwing herself into her husband's arms, sobbed her forgiveness upon his bosom.

"But is it not wonderful," observed Lord Ravensford, "to see the cleverness of the forgery? Whoever did this must be well acquainted with us both. Ah! a thought strikes me! How foolish I must have been not to have thought of it before.—Adder;—I remember he dared to threaten me, when I dismissed him from my service. Well, too, do I know his malignant and revengeful disposition, and the talent he possesses to carry out any guilty stratagem he may have formed. Perhaps the dolt Saunter and he have conspired together!"

"It is but too probable, Alfred," observed Lady Rosabelle, drying up her tears; "but oh, how inhumanly depraved that being must be who could concoct such a design as this."

"He must indeed, my lady," remarked Mr. Wilmot, "and no punishment could be too severe for him. I trust you will pardon me, and not think me too bold in having acted as I have done, been guided as I was by the purest motives. I will most willingly lend you all the aid in my power to discover the miscreants and bring them to punishment."

"I will not rest until I have traced the villains," exclaimed Ravensford; "you say, sir, that you met Saunter at an hotel in this neighbourhood; "do you know where he is at present residing?"

"I do not," answered Mr. Wilmot, "nor has he been seen for the last few days, and his reasons for thus concealing himself are very evident. However, I think he must be lurking somewhere near this place, and if caution is used, it cannot be long before we shall be able to discover him."

"I will leave no means untried to do so," said Lord Ravensford, "and then let the daring miscreant tremble; I will have ample satisfaction for the anguish he has caused us, and the irreparable injury he has endeavoured to do us. But come, my dear Rosabelle, pray forgive me for judging you so cruelly, and endeavour to regain your composure. Your father will begin to be alarmed at our long absence from him, and he must not see anything in our appearance and behaviour to cause him uneasiness; come, come, my love, let this fond embrace restore us to ourselves again."

Lord Ravensford pressed his wife to his bosom, and with a powerful effort to regain her equanimity, Rosabelle returned his embrace affectionately, and fixed upon him a look which expressed far more than words could have done. Ravensford thrust the infamous letter carefully in his pocket-book, and after the lapse of a few minutes to recover themselves, they hastened from the garden, re-entered the house, where they found Mr. Montalbert amusing himself by playing with the little Alfred, who had climbed upon his knee, and was passing his tiny fingers through the old man's gray hairs, while smiles of innocence and infant happiness lighted his lovely features.

"You have been sad truants, my children," said Mr. Montalbert, when his attention was diverted from the child on their entrance. "I began to think you were never going to return. The evening is very fine, to be sure, and the air in the garden is refreshing; but yet, Rosabelle, you look pale methinks, and your eyes are languid."

"Oh, my dear father," said our heroine "you are so watchful of my health, that you imagine me unwell at times, when I am not. The evening is sultry, and probably that may have taken an effect upon me."

"Besides, you know, my dear sir," added Ravensford, "Rosabelle has for the last day or two, been labouring under the effects of a cold, and that has, doubtless, driven the roses from her cheeks. May it not be so, my love?"

Rosabelle with a melancholy smile assented to the probability.

"Well, well, I dare say it is so;—but you must take care of yourself, Rosabelle, for my sake," observed her father;—"I begin to grow tired, and as you young people can doubtless dispense with the society of an old man, I will retire to my own chamber. Good night, Ravensford, good night, Mr. Wilmot,—Goodman, —all;—Rosabelle, embrace me, my love;—Heaven protect you from all harm, and shower its blessings upon you and your offspring."

Our heroine gave utterance to a responsive wish, and tenderly embracing her father, he shook hands cordially with Mr. Wilmot, Ravensford, and Mr. Goodman, kissed his grandson most affectionately, and retired from the sitting-room to his own apartment, where he immediately hastened to repose.

"Your father still requires great care and attention," observed Mr. Wimot, after Montalbert had quitted the room, " the least painful event preying upon his spirits; the smallest cause for excitement, I am fearful, would reduce him to the same melancholy condition from which he has been so recently recovered."

"Oh, yes, indeed, it would," returned Rosabelle, sighing deeply. "I am confident it would, and the dread, the terrible apprehension under which I constantly suffer, makes me continually unhappy. In spite of all my endeavours to the contrary. I cannot help thinking that his reason is not destined to continue, that we are once more doomed to see him suffer all those horrors from which he is now suffering a temporary respite. In fact, that is the impression upon his own mind."

"But, my dear Rosabelle," said her husband, "you must endeavour to conquer these apprehensions, and seek to arouse your father when he is giving way to such dismal thoughts. The most trifling circumstance, the most trivial act of thoughtlessness may destroy all that we have done, and plunge us all into a state of misery more hopeless and unendurable than ever. Your father is naturally very nervous, and the least excitement working upon a system like his, would doubtless be attended with the most serious consequences. Whenever we find his spirits drooping, in future, we must endeavour to devise some means or other to raise them, and to banish any dangerous thoughts from his mind."

"Ravensford says perfectly right," observed Mr. Goodman, (who we should have mentioned before, entered the hall as his lordship and Mr. Wilmot retired into the garden,) "and I would most earnestly impress upon your mind, Lady Ravensford, the necessity of following his advice to the very letter. The long confinement Mr. Montalbert endured, has taken a great effect upon his constitution, and until that is in some measure recruited, we must expect him to be weak, and easily agitated."

"The observations of Mr. Goodman I consider to be very just," said Mr. Wilmot, " and that was quite sufficient to have a most serious effect upon a frame even much stronger than that which Mr. Montalbert appears originally to have possessed."

"One thing I must particularly advise you to, my lord," remarked Mr. Goodman, "and that is, by no means to take up your residence anywhere else but at the hall for the present ; for perhaps only the most trifling separation from his daughter, even divided by so short a distance as you would be at the new estate you have recently purchased, and where Lady Rosabelle and her father could see each other every day, might bring about the unfortunate circumstance you have so much cause to dread. And you know by experience, that any removal from the scenes among which he had been used to mingle, might be productive of the same evil results."

"It is too true," said Lady Ravensford with a sigh.

Mr. Goodman fixed his eyes earnestly upon her, and after a minute's pause, during which he had seemed to be endeavouring to read her thoughts, he said—

"Perhaps you will pardon me, Lady Ravensford, but it strikes me very forcibly that something more than usual has occured to disturb you. I am certain that you will, as well as your husband, acquit me of being instigated by any other motives than those of solicitude for your welfare and happiness; and in this case, I am convinced within my own mind that my conjectures are not unfounded."

"Mr. Goodman," said Lord Ravensford, "for your goodness, and many disinterested acts of friendship towards both myself and Lady Ravensford, I can never sufficiently express how greatly I am indebted. By your counsel and assistance we have obtained all, I may say, that we now possess, and it would be a poor return for your benevolence, did we now hesitate to confide to you any circumstance that may trouble us. Rosabelle, I am certain that I have your permission."

"Oh, yes," answered our heroine, "I am anxious that Mr. Goodman should be made acquainted with everything, for much, indeed, may we need his valuable advice in this perplexing matter."

Lord Ravensford then having collected all his patience for the task, of which, in fact, he stood greatly in need, detailed to Mr. Goodman all that had occurred to them during the short time they were staying at Ravensford Castle ; the receipt of the two infamous letters from Saunter, down to the recent one which Mr. Wilmot had obtained possession of in so singular a manner, and which he had given to them.

During the time his lordship was detailing these particulars, he was frequently interrupted by an exclamation of surprise, disgust, and indignation from Mr. Goodman, and when he had concluded, he arose from his chair, and traversing the room with hasty steps, he exclaimed—

"Is it possible that there can be wretches so thoroughly debased and lost to all human feeling, in the world ? Unmanly villain! His object must be one springing from motives of envy, and with an intention to create misery and dissention between your lordship and your lady; but surely it cannot have had any other effect, Ravensford, than to fill your mind with just indignation and abhorrence against the persons who could contrive such a base and brutal stratagem."

Ravensford was much confused, and at first scarcely knew what answer to make, but at length, with candour he admitted the fact to Mr. Goodman, but at the same time expressed his regret that he had acted with such weakness and injustice towards his wife.

"And yet," said Mr. Goodman, "there is a singular mystery attached to this event which must be unravelled. There must evidently be more than one person engaged in this vile plot. Lord Saunter was all but unacquainted with Lady Ravensford."

"I never beheld him but once," said our heroine, "and then my husband knows under what peculiar circumstances."

"The forger of this letter, must have been well acquainted with your ladyship's handwriting, to enable him or her to imitate it so closely. Have you no suspicion of any person among your own domestics, whom it is likely would be in the plot?"

"I, myself, cannot suspect any one of such black-hearted treachery," answered our heroine.

"My suspicions, have, but a short time since, fallen upon one who I know to be capable of anything that is base," observed Lord Ravensford; "and it strikes me very forcibly that my surmises in the long run will turn out to be correct."

"Ah, who is that?" interrogated Mr. Goodman.

"My late valet, the villain Adder," answered Lord Ravensford; "you know that, finding he had been most scandalously deceiving me, I abruptly dismissed him from my service ; when he left me, he ventured to threaten me, and I know his disposition so well, that I am certain he would not rest until he had gratified his vengeance in some way or the other."

"Ah! this does indeed seem to be a very reasonable conclusion," said Mr. Goodman;

"and you think, then, that Adder and that inherent and unprincipled booby, Lord Saunter, are colleagued together?"

"I do."

"But was Adder acquainted with Lady Ravensford's hand-writing?"

"He had often an opportunity of seeing it," returned Ravensford, "and being an excellent scholar, would, I dare say, be enabled to copy it. I have seen several specimens of his abilities in that way."

"But what purpose could he have in concocting such a letter to gratify Saunter?" demanded Mr. Goodman.

"Doubtless he has made Saunter his tool to further his designs of gratifying his vengeance; and he would find no difficulty in persuading the latter to anything, so long as it was calculated to gratify his inordinate vanity."

"But have you no idea where Saunter or Adder are at present?" inquired Mr. Goodman.

"I have not," answered his lordship, "but I am determined to use every endeavour to find them out, and having elicited the truth, inflict upon them that punishment they deserve, if they are really the authors of this base plot."

"It is an unfortunate circumstance, that the man who brought the second letter while you were at Ravensford Castle," said Mr. Goodman, "managed to escape. Had he been detained, there can be very little doubt that the whole plot would have been explained, and many unpleasant events avoided that may now take place."

"That is true," said Ravensford, "and I have often regretted that the fellow contrived to elude us. But I trust, that with caution and secrecy we shall yet be able to discover the villains, and to make them repent the nefarious designs they have formed against us. Of course, I need not inform you, sir, that it is highly important not a syllable of this painful affair should reach the ears of Montalbert."

"Certainly not," replied Mr. Goodman; "I will be careful upon that point; I will also act in concert with you in endeavouring to find out the place where Saunter or Adder are concealed. In the meantime, I must request that Lady Rosabelle will not suffer the affair to weigh too heavily upon her spirits, for the eye of her father is very keen, and he would be certain to discover in an instant, the least demonstration of uneasiness, and become himself wretched and suspicious."

"Contented in the confidence of my husband," observed our heroine, "I will indeed endeavour to conquer my own emotions, and to trust to time to bring about a revelation of the circumstances connected with this disgusting and infamous affair. Firm in the conscious-ness of my own innocence, what should I fear?"

"Nothing, my dearest Rosabelle," replied Ravensford, kissing her fervently. "My Rosabelle deceive me? oh, how base and polluted must be the wretch who could dare insinuate such a thing. But come, pray let us drop this painful subject for the present. My friend, Mr. Wilmot, here, will I trust frequently honour us with his company. We are very old and intimate acquaintances, and the folly and extravagance of my conduct was the only cause of our not keeping up the same intimacy for awhile that we had formerly done."

"Nothing could affords me greater pleasure," returned Mr. Wilmot, "than to renew those terms of friendship which we cultivated in our youth, Ravensford; and I cannot sufficiently express the warmth of my gratification that there is no longer any obstacle to the free enjoyment of the same."

The friends now conversed together upon a variety of other topics, and by the time they arose to separate for the night, Lord Ravensford and Rosabelle had so far conquered the emotions which the trying event of the evening had given rise to, as to appear with nearly as much composure as if nothing at all had occurred to disturb them.

When Lord Ravensford had retired to his chamber, however, and our heroine had sunk off to repose, his mind again reverted to the subject of the letters, and his brain became racked with perplexing and distracting thoughts. Notwithstanding all he had said, and all he endeavoured to think, at times, even in spite of his reason, a dark suspicion would obtrude itself, which he found it no easy task to banish.

The woman who has once yielded to the insidious persuasions of her betrayer, is ever afterwards, in too many instances, viewed with an eye of jealousy and doubt by her seducer, even though he may have been entirely to blame, and even the most trifling, the most insignificant event in some minds is misconstrued and swelled by the jaundiced eye of the green-eyed monster into something of vital importance, and is the cause of the most painful results.

Probably Ravensford might possess, in a small degree, sentiments of this description, which for a short time might overcome his reason; but in a very brief space his better feelings would predominate, and he would feel astonished and ashamed of himself for having for a moment encouraged such ideas. Throughout his whole connection with Rosabelle, he held himself entirely to blame for the shame and misery he had brought upon her, by persuading her to the dereliction from the paths of virtue and duty, and during the time she had been under his protection, and since they had been united, her conduct had been most exemplary and irreproachable ; and when he became able to reflect more maturely upon the subject, there was something so outrageously preposterous in the idea of any intimacy subsisting between Rosabelle and Lord Saunter, that he was surprised to think that he should ever have viewed it in so serious a light, no more than to form a resolution to punish the authors of the plot for their villany and presumption.

Notwithstanding, our heroine sought all that she was able to conquer her wounded feelings, and to appear calm ; she really experienced the utmost unhappiness, which was greatly increased by the confidence which her husband had at first placed in the letter which had been forged for the purpose of doing her some serious injury.

"Surely I have not deserved such suspicion," she ruminated ; "what has there been in my conduct to excite his jealousy? what have I not undergone to prove the strength and sincerity of the love I bear him? Have I not endured tortures enough to make the human heart shudder? Have I not encountered difficulties, at the bare contemplation of which many persons would tremble? Has he not been the cause of all the anguish I ever suffered, the shame and contumely I have met with? and have I not returned the same with the most passionate fondness? Yes, there has not been a single action of mine towards him which I can look back upon with regret or self-reproach ; and, therefore, it was indeed cruel and unjust of him, for an instant even, to believe me capable of such base conduct as has been attributed to me. But I will endeavour to think no more about it. Ravensford will no more wrong me by such terrible suppositions, and the wretches who have contrived this infamous stratagem will have their diabolical plans frustrated, and uninterrupted happiness will then be ours. I will compose my feelings, and rise superior to such vile attempts to debase my character in the eyes of the world."

CHAPTER XV.

THE LIBERTINE DRESSED.—THE ABDUCTION.

THE day after these circumstances had taken place, Lady Ravensford confided to the bosom of her friend, Emily, the painful circumstances that had occasioned her so much uneasiness. Emily listened to her with the greatest concern and anxiety, and when she had concluded, she gave free vent to her astonishment and resentment upon the subject.

"A more villanous stratagem, my dear Rosabelle," she observed, "I never heard of, and you will, I know, believe me, when I assure you that I sincerely hope the wretches will not only be foiled in their views, but that something will shortly transpire to unravel the whole of the plot, and disclose and bring to justice the infamous contrivers of it. For the present, however, Rosabelle, I must concur in the advice of my father, and beg that you will endeavour to regain your composure as much as possible, so that you may not excite the attention and alarm of your father, for should such a thing take place, it would undoubtedly be attended with a fatal result, and probably place Mr. Montalbert in the same dreadful situation from which you have, with so much trouble and anguish, rescued him."

"It is my determination to try to do as yourself and your father have advised, dearest Emily," returned our heroine ; "but you must make every allowance for the effect which such a cruel plot must have upon my feelings, which, although before those to whom they might cause such poignant regret, I may struggle to conceal, to you, my ever kind and sympathising friend, I may ever give free expression to them."

"I can make every allowance, and deeply sympathise in the distress you must experience, Rosabelle," replied her friend, "and you can, I know, sincerely believe me, when I assure you that all the humble advice and consolation I can afford you shall be granted at all times with pleasure. Time and unanimity of thoughts and principles have rendered us sisters, and whatever troubles you so unjustly encounter, I must equally share with you."

"Alas!" sighed Lady Ravensford, "what innumerable miseries does one act of indiscretion bring upon us. Had I never sinned, the foul breath of calumny could not have dared to have thus persecuted me; had I ever have remained virtuous, the least attempt of this description could only have recoiled upon the heartless and unprincipled authors of it, and brought inevitable shame and execration upon them; but now—"

"Nay, my dear Rosabelle," interrupted Mrs. Rattleton, "I must not suffer you to treat yourself with such unnecessary severity. That you have erred, I must acknowledge, but it was in a moment of weakness, to which frail mortality are all liable; but how amply has your penitence and subsequent exemplary conduct atoned for it. Cease, then, I beg of you, to dwell upon the past, or if it does occur to you, remember it only as a painful vision conjured up to warn you against future error."

"Generous Emily," said our heroine, unable to resist a tear, "would that the censorious world were like you. Yet, for myself, I could bear with it, but for the sake of those whose happiness is far dearer to me than my own life, there is no sacrifice I could consider too great, could the past be buried in oblivion."

"It will, it will," exclaimed Emily, energetically; "the present circumstance is only like an April cloud, that will quickly pass away, and the sunshine of uninterrupted happiness will succeed it. Now, pray endeavour to banish the event from your mind, and trust to the goodness of Providence to bring about that consummation your friends must all so cordially pray for. See, hither comes your father; pray struggle with your feelings, and do not let him perceive those signs of care upon your countenance which may fill his breast with groundless fears."

Rosabelle did, by a powerful effort, recover herself as her father entered the room in which she and Emily were sitting, and approaching her, he threw his arms round her neck with even more than his usual affection, and kissed her.

"Bless you, bless you, my Rosabelle," he cried, in a voice of emotion, "bless you for your kind attention to me this morning; I felt rather indisposed, spiritless, and was not inclined to leave my couch so early as I am accustomed; but, strange as you may think the observation, I would think little of illness so that I always had the felicity of being attended upon by you. Poorly as I felt this morning, never did I enjoy a meal more, for it was presented to me by your hand. Oh, Rosabelle, how welcome would be the grave to me, were I to be deprived of your kind attentions."

"Heaven forbid that you should be, my dear, dear father," said Rosabelle, with energy; "but you seem unusually dull; has anything occurred to oppress your mind? Is there anything that I have forgotten to do to add to your comfort? Tell me, I beseech you?"

"Anything you have neglected to do for me, my child?" repeated Montalbert, and a tear of gratitude and unbounded affection started to his eye; "oh, no, no, no!—You are too good, much too attentive for your own health. Rosabelle, I am a troublesome old man, and—and——"

"My dear father," observed our heroine, eagerly, and with much emotion; "oh, do not, I pray you, talk thus. Can I ever think any trouble too much for your dear sake?—No!—Heaven is my witness, that I cannot. But something must certainly have happened to have occasioned in you this unusual depression of spirits. I am afraid you have caught cold, and are not well. You must take more care of yourself. Pray sit farther away from the draught of that window; the air is not quite so warm this morning as it has been; and——"

"Rosabelle," said Montalbert, "my long illness has made me singularly weak to what I formerly was, and I can feel age creeping on me apace. That which, at one time, would, in all probability, only have occasioned me a smile, now conjures up terrors. Last night, my child, I had a dream; it was a very frightful dream. Methought that we were seated in this very room. Ravensford was with us, and was seated by your side, smiling affectionately upon your child, and bestowing on you every fond endearment. Suddenly the place became convulsed as with an earthquake;—a loud peal of thunder shook the lofty roof, a wide chasm in the wall appeared, from which darted two black and hideous fiends, on whose brows, in characters of fire, appeared the words 'Jealousy' 'Slander.' They flourished their fiery brands above your head, and instantly the countenance of Ravensford became distorted with deadly rage, his eyes seemed to dart glances of terrific fury upon you, and raising his clenched fist in the air, he felled you to the earth. Immediately the room seemed to swim round;—the objects faded from my sight, and I awoke; my limbs palsied, and cold drops of perspiration standing on my temples. Such was the impression this frightful vision had upon me, that for several minutes, I could with difficulty persuade myself but that what had been conjured up by my imagination was reality."

"Oh, my father," ejaculated Rosabelle, whose feelings may be imagined while her father was thus giving an account of his dream; "this was indeed a frightful vision; but do not let it weigh upon your thoughts. It was caused, no doubt, from illness, and the too great anxiety you feel in my happiness."

"Rosabelle," said Mr. Montalbert, solemnly. "if I thought there was that being in the world who would dare to contaminate you with the poisonous breath of calumny, methinks, aged and feeble as I am, my indignation would give me a lion's strength to punish them. If I thought there could be that fiend in human shape,—I——"

"Father, dearest father," cried Lady Ravensford with the most powerful emotion; "I beseech you be calm; as you love me and would see me happy, calm, oh, calm these paroxysms. Come, come, your imagination is too strong for your weakened frame. Endeavour to forget that you ever had such a dream, or if you do recall it to your thoughts, remember it only as 'the baseless fabric of a vision,' and attach nothing to it of reality."

"If I may add my humble advice to that of your daughter, my dear sir," remarked Emily, "with whom I in all respects agree, I would beg of you to treat it merely as the effects of indisposition, or to drive it from your recollection altogether; it can have no other effect than that of making you seriously unwell, and cause in the bosoms of your friends the utmost affliction."

"With two such sweet and gentle pleaders, I must be adamant, did I not yield," said Montalbert, with a melancholy smile. "Yes, I will endeavour to forget it, and to look upon it only as the effects of my over-anxious love for you, my dearest Rosabelle. Give me your arm, my child; the morning is fine, and I have not yet paid my customary visit to the garden."

Rosabelle took one of the arms of her father, and Emily the other, and they walked forth from the house. As they proceeded, Montalbert seemed to revive, and as they walked down the different little walks, all arranged with such care and judgment, the gloom which had lately overshadowed his countenance, disappeared, and smiles usurped its place.

"The flowers nurtuerd by your hand, my Rosabelle," he observed, "bloom fresh and fair. How beautiful is that rose-tree, while the flowers seem to open their silken leaves, and to exhale their richest perfume, to welcome their gentle mistress. What hours of happiness have we passed in this little paradise!"

He looked fondly in the face of our heroine as he spoke, who could not resist a tear, at the many painful as well as blissful reminiscences his observations recalled to her memory.

"And many, many hours more of happiness, I trust, we shall pass together here, my dear father," she ejaculated; "hours rendered doubly sweet by content, and a forgetfulness of the many troubles that have intersected our moments of bliss."

"Amen!" vehemently exclaimed Montalbert, and raising his eyes devoutly towards Heaven, as he spoke. At this moment they were joined by Rattleton and Lord Ravensford.

"So, so, we have found the ramblers at last," said the former, in his usual gay tones; "Mr. Montalbert, really you ought to consider yourself a most fortunate man; for you not only monopolize the affections of every one who knows you, young or old, gentle or simple, but likewise the wives of we less fortunate young men."

"You say true, Mr. Rattleton," said Montalbert, with a smile, "I am willing to plead guilty to the charge; moreover, I trust that it is a monopoly which I shall always maintain."

"And if you do, my dear sir," returned Rattleton, "believe me, no one will feel more contented than your humble servant. But, if you are tired of your walk, Mr. Goodman would be glad of your company inside."

"I will attend my old and excellent friend immediately," said Mr. Montalbert; "oh, what a blessing it is, when we get old and decrepit, to have such a host of anxious friends around us; the shafts of care become blunted, and even pleasure receives a tenfold zest.

Mr. Montalbert having given utterance to these words, and our heroine feeling grateful to observe him become so much more composed, the little party returned to the house, where they found Mr. Goodman awaiting them.

Lord Ravensford had taken care to give early instruction to two of his most trustworthy servants to make every inquiry to endeavour to find out the retreat of Lord Saunter, or to ascertain whether his surmises were right as to Adder being his associate and colleague, but they could learn nothing which could give them cause to suspect that they were anywhere in the neighbourhood. Mr. Wilmot was also using exertions for the same purpose, and Ravensford trusted that ere long, these endeavours would be crowned with success. He had become far more composed upon the subject, and his behaviour to Rosabelle convinced her that he entirely acquitted her of any guilty connection with the plot; and that certainly relieved her mind of a weight which had been almost more than she could bear.

Several days passed away, and still nothing was heard of Lord Saunter or Adder. Ravensford had despatched persons to his estates in Westmoreland, and likewise to the metropolis, but in neither of those places could they obtain any intelligence of the former; and the mystery of his concealment became most unaccountable and tiresome.

The reader will be certain that Adder must have racked his ingenuity and perseverance to no small extent to be able to keep his silly dupe in this state of absolute seclusion; and an almost intolerable trial of his patience was it to his lordship himself. Adder, however, managed to keep him under control, by pretending to forward letter from Saunter to Rosabelle, and forging answers from her in return, and as much of his time as he could devote, apart from the furtherance of his own base designs, he passed with him. In the letters which Saunter supposed to come from Lady Ravensford, Adder always took care to beseech him to use the utmost caution, and to rely upon her, as soon as an opportunity presented itself for her to meet him, and every letter teemed with additional asseverations of the most powerful attachment. Any one but the most inordinate fool would quickly have seen through this plot, and would have discovered that Adder was a designing knave, who was only making a dupe of him to answer some secret purposes of his own. The very idea was absurd, preposterous,—to take for granted, upon the mere *ipse dixit* of Adder, that the wife of another man, a woman whom he had never seen but once, was so madly in love with him, that she was willing to sacrifice home, honour, happiness, everything for his sake. But the ignorant lord really did believe it, and well might Adder laugh at the idiot in his sleeves, and despise him for his preposterous credulity, and detestible vanity. But the longer the plot was kept in hand, the more was Adder gaining by it; for scarcely a day passed but he managed to wcedle Saunter out of a large sum of money; which, added to the money he had already accumulated, he reflected, would enabled him to live in future as a man of fashion, without pandering to the intrigues and follies of others. He also became acquainted with the circumstance of Saunter losing the letter, and he was fearful that it might have fallen into the hands of some one who would communicate it to Lord Ravensford; consequently, it became indispensably necessary that he should let the business remain in *statu quo* for awhile, until he could ascertain whether the suspicions of the inhabitants of the hall were excited.

Of this caution he very soon saw the wisdom, for he learned that inquiries had been made in the neighbourhood respecting himself and Saunter; and he, therefore, naturally concluded that something particular had transpired to

LORD RAVENSFORD'S BEREAVEMENT AFTER READING THE LETTER.

give rise to this. He now found it necessary to place his lordship under greater restrictions than ever; and when the latter got out of all sort of patience about it, the surest way in which he could appease him was by threatening to withdraw himself entirely from the design, and to leave him to accomplish it in the best manner he could by himself. This always had the desired effect, and Lord Saunter felt himself compelled to submit, although it was with an exceedingly bad grace that he did so.

"How confoundedly provoking it is, to be sure," observed his lordship one day to Adder. "I declare it is enough to tire the patience of that respectable old gentleman, Job himself.

But then the lady is such a rich prize, that it is impossible for me to think of abandoning my design, especially after I have gone so far; but positively, Adder, I think you might have managed this business in much quicker time."

"If I had been as precipitate as your lordship would be," answered Adder, "I should have mis-managed it long ago. The lady is securely yours, if you will only act according to my instructions; and, therefore, let that suffice you. But if you will not do as I wish you, I regret that I have ever mentioned the subject to you, and that's all about it; and sooner than I would make a foolish job of it, I will withdraw my servies altogether."

"Now, what a hasty fellow you are

Adder," remarked Saunter. "I did not mean to offend you, by no means; but you can make no allowance for a man who is desperately in love."

"I can make allowances for a man in love, your lordship," returned Adder, "but I cannot make any allowances for a man who would, if left to himself, be so desperately headstrong that he would render completely abortive all the plans which have cost me so much trouble in devising. Are you not satisfied with the letters from Lady Ravensford herself, in which she assures you that you possess her most ardent affection, and that the very first opportunity which presents itself, she will fly to meet you, and throw herself into your arms, to part no more?"

"Angelic creature!" exclaimed Saunter; "yes, those were her words;—here is the very letter!—There is music in every sentence. She must love me to madness, that's very evident. Gracious me! what a very powerful thing this love is, Adder; for it has made me, in the hope of gaining the ultimate possession of the object that hath inspired it, me, the gay and thoughtless Lord Saunter, who before could only exist in the midst of life and gaiety, a perfect hermit; shut up in a very indifferent apartment, like a wild beast in a cage."

"Your lordship pays yourself a very high compliment, methinks," said Adder; "but no matter: when our plot has ripened itself, and the chance presents itself, the wild beast will doubtless break forth to become the very lion in the court of Venus!"

"Ha! ha! ha!" laughed Saunter, "very good, Adder, devilish good indeed; you are a monstrous funny fellow, Adder. But what was that you were saying about Ravensford, eh?"

"Why, that he must have scented something of our designs," replied Ander, "for there have been many inquiries after both you and I, in this quarter, within the last few days. This must have been occasioned through your acting so imprudently at the places you were in the habit of frequenting in the evening, for all that I gave you such strict injunctions as to your behaviour; and if you had continued to go there much longer, everything would have been blown in no time, and the lady lost to you for ever."

"Why, I will not deny that I might have said a little more than was prudent, when I had partaken too freely of wine," returned Saunter; "but I am positive I never mentioned your name to any one, so that you could not have got into trouble by it. Oh, no, leave me alone; I will never draw any of my friends into a mess, whatever I may do myself. Honour, you know, is my maxim."

"Oh, of course, your lordship," said Adder, sarcastically, "no one for a moment would presume to question that your lordship is not a nobleman of the strictest honour!"

"You do me no more than justice by that opinion," said Saunter.

"I am certain of that," returned the wily sycophant.

"But after all, Adder," said Lord Saunter, "do you not think that we might contrive some readier means of accomplishing our plot? Let me see: could we not put Ravensford out of the way at once? Shoot him, for instance. That would remove the principal obstacle, rid Rosabelle of an incumbrance, and place her in my power."

"Yes, and ourselves in rather an awkward predicament, I fancy," added Adder. "Oh, no, the plan I have devised is the only safe and certain one, and no other will I undertake."

"Well," observed Saunter, "it seems you are determined, and so I suppose I must yield to you. But for Heaven's sake do not lose any time over it, or I shall go literally mad with impatience."

"I will be as expeditious as possible," answered Adder; "and if you will trust to me, depend upon it everything will be settled in perhaps a shorter time than you anticipate."

After some other trifling conversation, the two worthy individuals separated.

"I must rid myself of this noble booby as speedily as possible," soliloquised Adder, when left to himself; "he has answered the purpose for which I originally intended him, and now becomes too troublesome. He has, by my contrivance, taken all the onus of the amour, if so I may yet call it, from my shoulders, and I think that not the slightest suspicion can rest upon me; also he has bled freely, which makes the trick still more pleasant, but now he becomes an incumbrance, that I must shake off at the earliest opportunity. Poor fool! how disappointed he will be when he discovers the manner in which he has been cajoled. He have Rosabelle? Ha! ha! ha!—Mate an ape with an angel, it would be equally as reasonable. I have arranged my plot admirably, and ere many days have elapsed, if fortune does not deceive me, I shall be far away from this spot, with the beauteous Rosabelle securely in my possession. This, this will be glorious revenge for the manner in which Ravensford has treated me, and gratify the desires with which his wife has inspired me. Methinks now I can see the agony of the distracted husband when he finds his fair bride borne away from him, and imagines that she has been a willing party to the plot, for then the letters that have been sent to her by my means, and in such a manner as he was sure to become acquainted with them, will be, to his jaundiced mind, of her guilt 'confirmation strong as proofs of holy writ.'—He ought to have known me better, and been more cautious of offending me, for Adder never yet suffered any one to insult him without being fully avenged. I grow impatient for the consummation of my wishes, and shall not rest until my stratagem is completed. I now go to see my companions, and to arrange about the final settlement of the plot."

Having thus spoken, the villain left the house, and then hastened to meet the fellows whom he had engaged to aid him in his nefarious scheme.

Notwithstanding the promises which Lord Saunter had made to Adder, his impatience was equal to that of the latter, and he secretly determined to adopt some readier means to gain an interview with the woman, whom, in his gross ignorance and vanity, he imagined had imbibed such ardent sentiments towards him; and not thinking it was likely it would come to the knowledge of Adder, and also having some idea that he was using more procrastination in the affair than was absolutely necessary, he determined, without any more delay, to endeavour to prevail upon Rosabelle to meet him. After some time spent in trying to think upon a plan to further his desires, he came to the resolution of writing a note to her, unknown to Adder, and forwarding it to the hall by the same fellow who had conveyed the letter to Ravensford Castle. By the dint of a handsome reward, he prevailed upon the man to enter into his views, and to swear to keep the whole an inviolable secret. It was about a week after the conversation which we have just described, that he fixed upon to put his plot into execution; and having written a letter, he disguised himself, and one evening when he had been given to understand that Lord Ravensford was from home, he departed for the hall, having sent the man on before him. What subsequently transpired will be seen anon.

Lord Ravensford and his friends had been most indefatigable in their endeavours to discover the residence of Saunter, but as has been shown, hitherto without the least success. His eagerness and uneasiness increased with each disappointment, and in spite of all his endeavours to the contrary, there were times when he could not acquit his wife of any guilty knowledge of the affair, and at such times his feelings reached such a pitch, that he became almost distracted, and he avoided her presence, lest he should treat her, and perhaps unjustly, with a severity which would convince her of the real nature of his sentiments as regarded her. But although, as we have just said, he used the greatest caution, the penetrating eye of Lady Rosabelle quickly discovered that he was far from easy, and her own unhappiness soon suggested the cause. This, as the reader may well suppose, was the cause of her feeling

much misery, and she could not help inwardly upbraiding Ravensford, after the protestations she had made, and the confidence he had expressed in her innocence, for thus suspecting her, when, at the same time, also, he had had such very little cause for such suspicions, inasmuch as the whole affair was of too preposterous a description, in her opinion, to deserve any very serious attention. Many were the hours of bitter grief she passed when she was alone, for in the presence of her husband and her father, the latter more especially, she was constrained to disguise her real feelings, and to appear calm and contented, when, at the same time, her mind was distracted with the most agonizing thoughts. Her fate was really a most untoward one, for even admitting that she had erred, now that she had repented, and was ready to make every atonement for the past, something continually occurred to dash the cup of happiness from her lips, and to fix upon her suspicions altogether unjust, and of the most vexatious description. At every opportunity she could seize to be away from her father, and when Ravensford was from home, which he now often was, she would wander into the extensive gardens adjoining the hall, and sometimes venture into the woodlands beyond, where, left to her own meditations, she would give free indulgence to the perplexing ideas which circumstances created in her mind. To Emily alone she communicated her thoughts; and in her she ever found a kind friend and consoler. Although she could not but be of the same opinion as our heroine, for the behaviour of Lord Ravensford had not escaped her keen observation, she endeavoured by every means in her power to persuade Rosabelle that she had mistaken his ideas, and that the difference in his conduct was only occasioned by the anxiety he felt to discover the retreat of Lord Saunter, and get that satisfaction from him which the serious nature of the injury he had attempted to do him, deserved. This, however, had little effect upon our heroine, who knew full well that she had not deceived herself; she was too well acquainted with the character of her husband, not to be able to read the real nature of his thoughts in a moment; and although she felt sincerely grateful to Emily for her good intentions, her words had not the slightest power to bring about the praiseworthy design they were meant to do.

Thus passed away several days without any material alteration in affairs, and Rosabelle pursued her solitary rambles as often as she had an opportunity, without feeling any abatement of her uneasiness, more especially as she remarked but little alteration in the behaviour of her husband. It was on a beautiful summer's afternoon, about a month after the circumstance of the letter had taken place, that

Rosabelle was seated in the garden, near the gate, wrapt in a deep reverie, when, suddenly, she was aroused by the plaintive voice of a female singing, and looking towards the gate, she discovered standing there the person of a gipsy girl of interesting appearance, and who sung the following words, to a simple, but impressive melody:

Oh, lady, turn thee not away,
   Though poor my garb and my estate;
Listen to the gipsy's lay,
   Pity, pray, the wanderer's fate.
By the lines upon your hand,
   By the mole upon your cheek,
I the past can understand,
   And the future can bespeak.
    Then, lady turn thee not away,
      Though poor my garb and my estate;
    I the future can display,
    And can read the Book of Fate.

Cold and hungry, and forlorn,
   The gipsy girl is doom'd to roam;
Meeting with the rich one's scorn,
   The humble tent her only home.
Life's luxuries she never knows,
   And her pleasures are but few;
Confidence in her repose,
   And kindly she'll remember you.
    Then, lady, turn thee not away,
      Though poor my garb and my estate;
    I the future can display,
    And can read the Book of Fate.

The young woman ceased, but our heroine had been so forcibly struck by her appearance and the manner in which she had sung the song, that she could not remove her eyes from her. The gipsy fixed upon her a glance of earnest supplication, and after a brief pause, she beckoned Lady Ravensford to come nearer to her, and after some hesitation, Rosabelle complied.

"Now, my poor girl," said our heroine, in accents of kindness, "what would you with me?"

"Do not fear me, lady," said the gipsy, "I would not harm thee even if I had the power. If you will cross my palm with silver, I will tell you by the lines in your hand what will befal you."

"Nonsense, girl," replied Rosabelle, impatiently, "I wish not to learn such absurdities. Here is half a crown for you, and keep your prognostication for some more credulous individual."

As Lady Ravensford spoke, she offered the gipsy the money, but the latter refused, with a lo k of disdain, and then, in a voice which instantly had the effect she wished it, she said:—

"Nay, lady, keep thy money, I will not accept it for nothing. Thou mayest treat me with incredulity, but if thou shouldst miss the present opportunity, thou wilt for ever repent it. I am no impostor, as I will quickly prove

to thee. Even now, lady, I can read thy thoughts. Thou thinkest upon thine husband, and believeth that he imagines thee inconstant to him. I can tell thee whether or not thou hast any just cause for such surmises, and what the result will be."

"Ah! mysterious girl," exclaimed the astonished Rosabelle; "what and who are you, and how came these things within your knowledge?"

"I have told thee my power," replied the gipsy; "if thou wouldst further test it, follow me."

"Follow you!" said Rosabelle; "whither, and for what purpose?"

"I have told thee."

"And why can you not impart what you say you know upon this spot?" demanded Rosabelle.

"For several reasons which it is unnecessary I should name," answered the girl. "Art thou afraid to trust me?"

"But where do you wish me to accompany you?" again asked Lady Ravensford.

"Merely to the valley a short distance from the hall, where we may not be observed, and need not apprehead any interruption," replied the gipsy.

"Are you sure you do not intend to deceive me?"

"What should I gain by so doing? I am not a thief."

Lady Ravensford again paused, and hesitated what she should do; but it was only for a short time; for noticing the apparent candour of the girl, and her curiosity being excited by what she said, although she was not by any means superstitious, she unlocked the garden gate, and motioned to the gipsy in silence to lead the way towards the spot she had mentioned. The girl smiled as if pleased with her compliance, and tripped lightly on before our heroine, every now and then looking back, apparently to see whether she was following her.

Lady Ravensford was so wrapped up in thinking upon the singularity of the adventure, and wondering how the gipsy could have obtained the knowledge she seemed to possess of her private domestic affairs, that she took no notice of the way they were proceeding, until she was aroused by noticing how dark the spot was, and looking up, she was surprised and somewhat doubtful when she found that, instead of the valley the girl had mentioned, they were in the wood.

"What is the meaning of this, girl?" she demanded, pausing; "you have deceived me; this is not the way to the valley of which you spoke."

"If I said the valley," replied the gipsy without exhibiting the slightest confusion, "I made a mistake. I meant a small glade close at hand, where there are two or three of our people, and—"

"Why, you told me that we were to be alone," interrupted Lady Ravensford; "I repeat you have deceived me, and I will not proceed any further with you."

"But thou hadst better, lady," said the gipsy, laying hold of our heroine's arm rather boldly, and with more strength than any person would have been led to suppose from her appearance she possessed. "We have not much further to go, and thou wilt repent missing an opportunity, which thou mayest probably never meet with again."

"Ah, girl," said Rosabelle, who now began to be alarmed by the manner of the gipsy, and repented that she had been so imprudent as to assent to accompany her. "Do you seek to detain me by force? This insolence I—"

"Nay, lady," interrupted the gipsy, "all that you can say or do is useless; you are far enough from the hall; there is no one at hand to aid you, and I have performed the task which I undertook to accomplish. You cannot escape."

As the girl said this, still retaining her hold of the struggling Rosabelle, she placed a whistle to her lips, and blew it loudly, and in an instant it was answered by another from a very short distance, and almost immediately afterwards, several men rushed to the spot, and seizing hold of our heroine, threw a cloak over her head, so as to prevent her from screaming for help, almost at the same time suffocating her; and raising her in their arms, she was borne hastily from the spot. In a few minutes she felt herself lifted into what she thought to be a post-chaise, and it was driven off as fast as the horses could drag it.

To seek to portray the terror of Lady Ravensford, would be a useless waste of time; indeed it was so great, that it was wonderful how she retained her senses. By whose orders had she been seized, and for what purpose, were the thoughts which naturally first occurred to her, and almost immediately the idea that Lord Saunter was the author of the base plot, flashed across her mind, and filled her breast with the most inconceivable anguish. Then the horrible thought of being dragged away from her home, her husband, her child, and father, almost drove her to madness. What would be their agony, their suspense, at the afflicting circumstance, but especially that of her father, whom she feared the sudden shock would occasion a relapse into his former dreadful malady; and then, indeed, would her misery be complete, and all hope of future happiness in this world would be at an end.

They had proceeded for some distance before the cloak was removed from Rosabelle's head, and then she discovered that she was seated in a vehicle which was moving along at a rapid rate, in company with three men, who had the appearance of gipsies, and whose countenances were ruffianly and forbidding in the extreme. The blinds of the chaise were drawn close, so that she had no opportunity of seeing the direction in which they were travelling, and the interior of the vehicle was only lighted by a lantern which one of the men carried with him, and which threw a dim reflection on their faces, that made them appear still more revolting than they otherwise would have done. They noticed the looks of terror which our heroine threw upon them, with an expression of the utmost indifference, and commenced talking to one another about subjects quite foreign to the one which was of the deepest interest to their unfortunate captive. Rosabelle, however, terrified beyond measure, implored them with tears in her eyes, to inform her at whose instigation this outrage was being committed, and whither they were conveying her.

"Oh, as for that matter, my lady," answered one of the men, "I believe it is very little consequence, as you will soon be made acquainted with every particular, and we should not be doing right perhaps, by telling you. If it will afford you any consolation, however, I can assure you that no harm is intended you."

"Oh, God!" exclaimed Lady Ravensford, "what cruelty is this? Oh, my husband, alas! my poor father and helpless child, what will become of ye?"

"I should advise your ladyship not to trouble yourself about them," said another of the ruffians, "for it's a chance if you see them again for some time, at any rate."

"Wretches!" cried Rosabelle, with a burst of agony, "release me, I command ye, and suffer me to return to my friends, or depend upon it you will be called to a severe account for this base action, and punished to the fullest extent of the law."

"Well, we must e'en take our chance as far as that matter goes," said the third fellow, with a laugh of contempt; "as for releasing you, we know better than that; we are to receive a handsome reward for our trouble, and are too *honourable* not to do our duty. But we would advise you not to be obstreperous, as it will do you no good, and will only compel us to treat you more roughly than we have any wish to do."

"Yes, you had better remain quiet," observed the man who had first spoken, "for in the part where we are travelling, there is no one near at hand who can render you any assistance, and if you make any noise, we shall be compelled to gag you."

"Gracious heaven, what will become of me?" exclaimed Lady Ravensford, wringing her hands and sobbing bitterly; "oh, if you have but one spark of humanity in your bosoms, take pity upon me, and yield to my entreaties. I promise you faithfully, nay, I am ready to swear, that you shall be forgiven for what you have already done, if you proceed no further in the shameful business."

"It is too late now to retract, were we even disposed so to do," said one of the men, "therefore it is useless to appeal to us."

"Almighty God protect me then!" ejaculated the unfortunate Rosabelle, and covering her face with her hand, she gave way to a violent paroxysm of grief, of which the three fellows took not the slightest notice, but resumed the conversation she had interrupted.

The vehicle continued on its progress with the same rapidity, and by its jolting it was evident that they were travelling along a wild and uneven road, and as it proceeded, at every additional yard they travelled, the despair and agony of Rosabelle increased, until she became in a state bordering upon distraction. The fearful thoughts that occupied her mind, were rendered still more terrible by the uncertainty as to whose power she was in, and for what purpose she had been so clandestinely seized; and the ribald conversation of the wretches in the vehicle with her, filled her mind with disgust and horror. But it was fearful to reflect upon the state of mind all the inmates of the hall would be in at her mysterious disappearance. She pictured to herself the despair of her husband, the cries of her child, and the frenzied grief, nay, most likely, the actual madness of Montalbert, until the imagination became too powerfully worked upon, and unable to support the intensity of her anguish, she threw herself back in her seat, and sunk into a state of complete apathy. The night, too, was intensely hot, and the carriage being so closed in, the heat was most oppressive. Feeling the inconvenience themselves, and doubtless knowing that there was very little danger to be apprehended from their doing so, the men at length opened one of the windows, and the breeze that was admitted in consequence was a great relief. Our heroine did become a little more composed, and looked out on to the country through which they were journeying. It was a wide and extensive common upon which they now were, and the moon riding majestically through a cloudless sky, rendered objects at a considerable distance as visible as if it had been broad daylight. But Rosabelle, as far as the eye could trace, could see nothing but a broad and open expanse, and the only sounds that met her ears was the occasional jingling of a sheep-bell, or the barking of the shepherd's dog. No hope of assistance thus presented itself, and she again threw herself back in despair, and became immersed in the dismal thoughts which her situation gave rise to. Some observations made by one of the men now attracted her attention, and from them she was convinced that Lord Saunter was not the

author of this outrage, as she had at first imagined, but who the actual villain was she was unable to ascertain; consequently the painful mystery in which the affair was wrapped, increased her anguish.

They had now been travelling for nearly three hours, and with the exception of once, had not stopped for the horses to rest themselves, and, consequently, they had become completely jaded, and were unable to proceed only at a slow rate.

"It's a pity we could not arrange it somehow to have a change of horses,' said one of the men, addressing his companions; "our horses are so confounded tired that we shall not be able to proceed much further."

"How much further is it across this heath?" inquired another of the fellows, calling to the driver.

"About six miles, I think," was the reply.

"A very pretty prospect, truly," observed the man who had put the question; "I expect the horses will lie down presently, and then we shall be under the necessity of taking up our lodging on the common, unless we think proper to walk on and leave the carriage behind us, which would not be a very convenient or safe method of travelling."

"If we can only keep them up till we get over the common," observed the first speaker, "we shall come to the residence of old Job Sommerton, who will accommodate us for the night."

"Yes, and for the next day too," added the second man; "for it will not be safe for us to travel in the daytime, and you know we received strict injunctions to that effect."

"True," said the other man, "and I don't know a better place than Job Sommerton's; 'for it is so retired that no one would ever think of looking for us there."

"Push on, driver, as well as you can," was the order of the man who had first spoken, and who appeared to be the leader of the party; "and hold the poor tired devils up, if possible."

The colloquy here terminated, and the driver, in obedience to the request of the ruffian, endeavoured to urge the horses on; but all his efforts were of little use, and they proceeded at a pace which rendered it extremely doubtful whether they would be able to go at all much longer.

Lady Ravensford had listened to this brief conversation with feelings of the greatest pain, for it afforded her not the least room to hope for any assistance, more especially when she heard the precautions that had been adopted by the ruffians, and could form a pretty accurate idea of the description of the house they were going to, and the possessor of it, from what the men had said: all that she could do was to resign herself to the will of heaven, and mentally to implore its divine protection. When the horror of her situation is considered, and the uncertainty of her destination, into whose hands she was about to be committed, or for what purpose, it is a matter of astonishment how she could retain her senses, or support it even with the firmness that she did; and, indeed, it would have been a kind respite from the most agonizing grief, had she become unconscious of her situation, or what was going forward.

But all the pain of what she was herself at present enduring, or what she had in all probability, yet to undergo, was trifling, compared to the anxiety and apprehension she experienced, when her thoughts reverted to home, and the anguish, the maddening anguish her friends must be exposed to. In her mind's eye she beheld the scene as vividly as if she were actually present with them; and it was perhaps more poignantly afflicting, from the additional colouring which her fevered imagination gave to it.

Upwards of another hour passed away in this manner, and then the driver suddenly stopped, and calling to the men inside the chaise, said—

"Thanks to my skill, we have very nearly reached the house you were speaking of; I can see lights glimmering in some of the windows."

"I am very glad to hear that," returned one of the men, "for I am heartily tired of our journey for to-night, and by what you say it is evident that Sommerton has not retired to rest."

"How do you know that he has not gone on his travels?" asked one of his companions.

"Why, didn't I tell you that I heard from him only a few days since?" said the other; "he has met with something that is much better than travelling about as a pedlar. You understand me?"

"Oh, right, I remember all about it now," observed the man, "but I suppose he does not intend to give up his old calling altogether? It was a very good blind."

"Capital," coincided the other; "oh, no, leave old Job alone for that; it was too profitable a business with him, and a devilish lucky one it has proved for him, for he has never so much as been suspected of anything wrong, and he must have made a good round sum in his time; but, hollo, here we are."

The vehicle, as the man thus spoke, stopped before a large wooden edifice, which, from its construction, seemed to have formerly been a farm-house. The driver alighted and knocked loudly at the door, and after a lapse of a few seconds, a head, surmounted by what appeared to be a woollen cap, protruded itself from an open window, and after seemingly surveying the vehicle with some astonishment and suspicion, demanded who was there, and what they wanted.

"What, Job Sommerton," exclaimed the fellow who always took the precedence in speaking; "do you not know me?"

"Why, it's not very easy to know a person in the dark," returned Job; "but, if I mistake not, that voice belongs to Michael Hernwood."

"The same," answered Michael, "and now, I suppose, you do not mind coming down stairs and admitting me my friends; we want to encroach upon your hospitality for to-night."

"Ay," remarked Job, as he took his head in, "what's the matter now?"

"Open the door and see," said Michael. The next moment a heavy footstep was heard descending the stairs, and shortly afterwards the door was opened by the old man, to whom Michael Hernwood spoke a few words apart, and then returned to the carriage, and told his companions to alight. They did so, and afterwards assisting Lady Ravensford to do the same, and Job Summerton having surveyed her inquisitively, and given instructions to the driver of the vehicle where to put the carriage and horses, the whole party walked into the house.

The appearance of the interior was anything but cheerless, more especially as a blazing fire crackled upon the hearth, and the room, although an old-fashioned one, was very clean and kept in good repair. It was also furnished neatly, and it was evident that it had the attendance of some industrious housewife. This opinion was shortly confirmed by the appearance of a middle-aged woman, of decent, motherly aspect, but in whose countenance there was a certain expression that deteriorated greatly from her appearance, and crushed the respect which she would otherwise have inspired. She was attended by a young woman who was particularly beautiful, and seemed fit to fill a much higher station. Her manners were gentle, and, in short, refined, and altogether she was a most interesting object. Rosabelle felt certain that she was not the daughter of Job Sommerton, for she was not the least like either of them, and her manners were so different and her general demeanour so superior. Our heroine could not help wondering what strange freak of fortune had placed her in a situation for which she was evidently so badly qualified.

Job Sommerton, although from the hints which Michael and his companions had thrown out, his method of living was extremely questionable, and his character by no means irreproachable, possessed far from an unprepossessing countenance. There was a certain good-humoured expression in his eyes, which at first filled the mind of Lady Ravensford with an idea that she would be able to interest him in her favour; but when she reflected that he was only an old man opposed to four ruffians of the most determined character, she was convinced of the fallacy of such a thought. Besides, it soon became evident, from his behaviour, that he agreed with

Michael and his companions; and, no doubt, expecting to be rewarded handsomely by their employer, for the accommodation he afforded, he paid them particular attention.

The elder female surveyed our heroine with much curiosity, and then exchanged a few words in a low tone of voice with her husband, who nodding his head, as if in acquiescence with something she had been saying, she returned to the table, where she commenced spreading the cloth, assisted by the young woman, whom they called Phœbe, and who contemplated Rosabelle with looks of astonishment, and as she thought with pity.

For a few moments the scrutinizing of these different persons drew the thoughts of Lady Ravensford from her own immediate misery; but at length being again aroused to a full and terrible sense of it, she threw herself on her knees before Job and his wife, and with clasped hands, and streaming eyes, implored them to take pity on her. Job and the woman made no answer, and turned their heads away, and Michael and his companions laughed, apparently in derision of the absurdity that had entered her mind that one man could render her any assistance when he had four persons to contend with, if he even had the will so to do. With a feeling of the utmost disgust, Rosabelle arose from her seat, and notwithstanding the night was so warm, she felt an icy chill come over her, and her limbs trembled. She left the table, on which a plentiful repast was now laid, and retired to a seat in the chimney corner, where she covered her face with her hands, and gave way to the overwhelming despair of her mind.

"Had you not better take some supper, madam?" inquired Job.

Our heroine only replied to him by sobs, but offered not to move from her seat.

"I should have thought that the journey would have sharpened her appetite," observed Michael Hernwood; "it has mine, at any rate, so I have no doubt I can eat the lady's share and my own too."

"And that of a third party also," retorted one of his companions.

"You can accommodate us here to-morrow as well as to-night?" said Michael; "we need not tell you why we have particular objections to travel in the day-time."

"No, I understand them very well," said Job. "Ay, ay, you can remain here for a week, if that's all; there's plenty of room in this house, and it is never troubled with many visitors. Perhaps the lady would like to retire to her chamber. Phœbe, she must sleep with you to-night."

Lady Ravensford could scarcely help giving utterance to the satisfaction which this arrangement afforded her, and she could perceive by the significant glances of Phœbe, that

she was equally well pleased. She, therefore, immediately expressed her anxiety to retire to rest, and Phœbe taking up a candle, desired her to follow her, and led the way to the room allotted for her repose, which presented a very comfortable appearance.

Phœbe placed the candle on the table, and turning to Lady Ravensford, she said in accents of sympathy—

"Lady, who you are I know not, but the clandestine manner in which you have been brought hither by those fellows, whom I shudder to look upon, convinces me that you are the victim of some cruel design. I wish it was in my power to assist you, but—"

"But you can, you can, my good girl, if you have only the will," eagerly ejaculated Rosabelle.

"Oh, tell me how," returned Phœbe, "and most willingly will I do it."

"If you cannot aid me to escape," said Rosabelle, "you might, perhaps, convey to my friends a note, in which I could inform them where I am, which will give them a clue to the route those who have me in their power have taken, and be the means of rescuing me. Say, will you, can you do this?"

Phœbe paused and reflected for a few seconds, and then replied—

"Why, madam, I think I can comply with your wishes, and oh, how happy shall I feel in doing so, and how sincerely anxious shall I be that the letter may have the desired effect. I have some knowledge of the guard of one of the mails that go to—"

"Does it go near M——?" eagerly interrupted our heroine.

"It does," answered Phœbe.

"Heaven be praised!" ejaculated Rosabelle, "then there is still hope. I will immediately write it, for here, I see, is pen and ink, and then if you will contrive to induce the person you have mentioned to leave it at Holly Hall, for Lord Ravensford——"

"Ravensford!" repeated Phœbe, with an expression of surprise, and turning very pale, "the same, whose name was formerly Beresford?"

"The same," answered our heroine, with equal astonishment; "he is my husband. But you seem to know him?"

"Know him!" reiterated Phœbe, "too well have I reason to know him! Your husband, my lady?"

"Yes; but what is the meaning of this emotion? Your words astonish me. Pray explain yourself."

"You then, Lady Ravensford, are that unfortunate woman whom he——"

"Formerly deceived," sobbed forth the blushing Rosabelle, "but for which he has since made every atonement."

"Alas! how deeply can I sympathise with

you in your misfortunes, Lady Ravensford," said Phœbe; "but pray pardon me; I am fearful that I have taken too great a liberty; I will leave you while you are writing your note, for perhaps they may feel offended at my remaining away from the supper-table; I will soon return."

And without giving Lady Ravensford time to say another word, quitted the room, and hastened down stairs, leaving the former in a state of the greatest surprise at her observations, and the manner she had evinced.

"Too well have I reason to know him," repeated she; "what can she mean? There is some painful mystery in this. Surely she cannot have been another victim to——"

She revolted from the idea which suddenly flashed upon her brain, and could not give utterance to it. With the utmost impatience she waited for the return of Phœbe; but at length, conquering her feelings as well as possible, she tore a leaf from her pocket-book, and sat down to write the note which Phœbe had promised to get conveyed for her to the hall. This assurance was a great relief to her mind, for it inspired her with a hope that her husband and his friends being informed of the road she had been taken, would be enabled to discover

THE LETTER FROM LORD SAUNTER DELIVERED TO LORD RAVENSFORD.

the place of her retreat, and quickly restore her to her liberty. She wrote every particular she could think of, and having ascertained before from Phœbe the name of the place where she then was, and given a description of the fellows by whom she had been seized, she folded up the note, and awaited again the return of Phœbe. She did not have to wait long; and the young woman having entered the chamber, she closed the door, and took a seat opposite to Lady Ravensford.

"My words, Lady Ravensford," she said, after a short pause; "my words have, doubtless, created your surprise, and, as I perceive, have excited your uneasiness; but do not mistake my meaning. Lord Ravensford never did me any injury, although he was the means of bringing into my presence one who brought upon me much misery and trouble, and but for my own firmness, I might have suffered the most irreparable shame and infamy."

Rosabelle sighed deeply, and looked upon Phœbe with greater interest than ever.

"Poor girl, I understand you," she observed; "but how did you escape the snares of the deceiver?"

"My story is too long for me to relate now, my lady," answered Phœbe, "but I have at my leisure moments written the principal incidents of my simple life; and if a humble narrative of facts, that I am certain inculcate a useful moral, will prove interesting to you, I will present you with the manuscript, which you may peruse when you are in happier circumstances."

Rosabelle thanked her.

"But surely you cannot be the daughter of these people?" she observed; "your manners convince me that you are not."

"I am not, indeed," replied Phœbe, with a sigh; "alas! my poor parents have long since slept in the peaceful grave. I have not a friend in the world, except Mr. Sommerton and his wife, who are distantly related to me, and who, to do them justice, have ever behaved with kindness to me, although I fear they have many sins to answer for; and to pity in general, they are quite callous."

Lady Ravensford felt more and more interested with Phœbe, and for a short time the keenness of her own sorrows was blunted.

"And how does this Mr. Sommerton procure a living?" she interrogated.

"That is a mystery which I am at a loss to unravel correctly," replied Phœbe, "although I can form a pretty shrewd notion of the truth; his ostensible avocation is that of a pedlar, and he is sometimes away for several weeks together, when he usually returns with a large sum of money, much greater, indeed, than his hawking could by any possible means, bring him in. I am afraid that he has some nefarious way of getting his living, which will some day or other bring him to a bad end. I can assure you, my lady, that I feel very uneasy at being placed in such a situation, and would not mind any one, however humble it was, so that I could alter my condition."

"But your manners are above the common order," remarked Rosabelle, "and you seem to me to be a person who has received a liberal education."

"For all that I possess I am indebted to the care and assiduous attention of two of the best of parents," replied Phœbe. "Alas! how often do I reproach myself for the many pangs I caused them, and which were so near bringing upon me ruin and perpetual misery."

The sparkling and expressive eyes of Phœbe became dimmed with tears, as she made use of these observations; and our heroine, who felt her words most keenly, for there seemed to be a great similitude between the fate of Phœbe and her own,—sat gazing at her for a short interval in silence, and with the deepest interest.

"From the observations you made a short time since," said our heroine, "it appears that you are acquainted with my melancholy history, and——"

"I am, I am! my lady," interrupted Phœbe, "but pray do not harrow up your feelings by dwelling upon that painful subject; if you have in one instance acted imprudently, you have, I firmly believe, made every atonement for it since."

"I have, I have!" hastily ejaculated Lady Rosabelle, "but yet it would seem that offended Heaven is not yet satiated, seeing the miseries that have lately befallen me, and this more particularly above them all."

"Would that I had it in my power to rescue you from your present situation," remarked Phœbe; "but there is no possibility of my doing so; the doors, and every outlet, are too well secured every night; and, besides, were I to do so, I know not what might be the consequences to myself, for they would be certain to say it was through my connivance."

"They would," responded our heroine, "and Heaven forbid that I should involve you in such danger. I feel equally as obliged to you for the sympathy you express in my misfortunes, and trust that this note, which you have so kindly undertaken to get forwarded to my husband, will have the desired effect, namely, that of enabling him to find me out, and defeating the base purposes of my secret enemy. Depend upon it, Phœbe, should I again be restored to my relations, you shall ever find a friend in Lady Ravensford."

"I feel convinced of that, my lady," answered Phœbe, "and Heaven ordain that you may shortly be delivered from the hands of your enemies, and restored to happiness."

"But have you no idea, Phœbe," asked Lady Rosabelle, "whither the men who hold me in their power intend to convey me, and by whom they are employed?"

"Not the least, my lady," answered the latter; "I never heard any mention of the affair until I saw you brought hither, and I do not believe that it was originally the intention of Michael and his companions to stop at this house, but they were driven to it by necessity."

"Have these men been in the habit of frequenting the house?" inquired our heroine.

"I never saw them here but once before," replied Phœbe, "and then I had no means of judging of their characters, only by their behaviour and appearance. But from all being so quiet below, I suppose that Mr. Sommerton and his guests have retired to rest, and had we not better follow their example? I am sure you must be completely worn out with fatigue and anxiety."

"I will do as you suggest, Phœbe," said Lady Rosabelle, "but I am convinced that my mind is too distracted to suffer me to sleep. Alas! what a scene of misery must be the home from which I have been so cruelly torn."

Phœbe again expressed her sympathy, and then prepared to assist our heroine to undress. In a short time afterwards they retired to bed, but Rosabelle sought to close her eyes in sleep in vain, and her companion for some time lay awake also, and endeavoured all in her power to console her. Above everything else, the probable situation of her father tormented the mind of our heroine. Weak as he was, this dreadful shock, she had too much reason to fear, would again overturn his reason, and should that be the case, all hope of his again recovering would, she felt convinced, be at an end. The fearful forebodings that had for some time haunted his imagination, recurred to her memory, and now that they were partly realised, what other conclusion could she come to? Then there was another idea which flashed upon her brain with overwhelming force, and that was what construction her husband would put upon her disappearance. Too well had she observed the state of doubt and uncertainty he had evidently laboured under ever since the fatal letter had been presented to him by Mr. Wilmot, and coupled as that was with other circumstances, might lead him to believe, after all, that the letter was no forgery, but had actually been written by herself, and that she was a willing companion in the flight with Lord Saunter. But surely he could never be so weak, so cruel, so ungenerous? If his love for her was really sincere, which she believed it to be, he would spurn with disgust such an idea. She made a powerful effort to banish the thoughts from her mind, for to suppose her husband capable of such conduct, was worse than death.

Phœbe had now fallen off to sleep, and Lady Rosabelle was left to the free indulgence of her own dismal thoughts. The hour of midnight had long since flown, and a solemn stillness reigned throughout the house, the inmates being all probably wrapt in the arms of sleep. Our heroine continued to think upon the misery of her situation, and to endeavour to conjecture by whose orders she had been seized, and what were his designs against her; but she was unable to arrive at any satisfactory conclusion, as the conversation she had overheard between the men, while they were travelling, assured her that Lord Saunter was not the enemy she had to dread. Towards morning, however, nature became quite exhausted, and Rosabelle fell into a deep slumber, but it was disturbed by troublesome dreams, so that when she awoke, just as the first golden streak of day illumined the eastern horizon, she felt very little refreshed from it. Phœbe had been awake some time, but she forbore to disturb her companion, and was glad to see her able to obtain some sleep, trusting that it would do her good, and in some degree compose her spirits. They remained in bed and in conversation for about an hour longer, when they arose, and Phœbe having assisted our heroine to dress, attended the summons of Mrs. Sommerton, to assist her in the preparation of the morning's repast. Rosabelle requested her to ask them to allow her to take what trifling refreshments she might feel inclined to partake of in the course of the day, in the room she at present occupied, and her wishes were acceded to, Michael Hernwood and his companions, no doubt, feeling her presence a restraint upon their conversation, and being glad to rid themselves of it until the hour arrived when they purposed resuming their journey.

We shall not enter into the particulars of the manner in which Lady Ravensford passed this day, which, as may very well be supposed, was a most wretched one indeed to her, and which all the sensible arguments and expostulations of Phœbe failed to render less miserable. The latter sought the earliest opportunity of leaving the house, and taking with her the note which Rosabelle had written, to deliver to the guard, in order that he might convey it to Lord Ravensford; and when our heroine was convinced that it was gone, and that the man had willingly undertaken to do as he was desired, she felt more composed. Often, in the course of the day, did she pray that something might occur to defer their departure from the house that evening, for, no doubt, his lordship would use the utmost possible despatch upon receiving the note, and before the following evening, could reach the house, and release her from the power of the ruffians who detained her. But, unfortunately, her wishes were not realised, and no sooner had the shades of the evening set in, than, the carriage having been got in readiness, they prepared for their departure. Phœbe parted with our unfortunate heroine with much affection, after having previously given her the manuscript she had promised her; and with the most horrible forebodings, Rosabelle was handed into the vehicle, the men quickly following her, and one of them carrying a bundle. The chaise went off at a brisk rate, and they were soon out of sight of the house where they had made their temporary stay.

The conversation of the men was quite foreign to that which was likely to attract the attention of Lady Ravensford, and she could elicit nothing whatever from it, which was at all calculated to enlighten her as to the place of her destination, or the person to whom she was being borne; but frequently, in the course of the journey, she appealed to them in the most forcible language, and endeavour to move them to pity; but her efforts were received in the same unfeeling manner as before, and she at length abandoned any further attempt in utter despair. After travelling in this manner a considerable time, one of the men inquired how much further it was to the "Royal George," from which it appeared to our heroine that they intended to put up there, and again hope for a moment gained possession of her mind; but it *was* only for a moment; for she soon learned by the observations which the fellows made, that the persons belonging to the house were perfectly aware of their coming, that they were in the plot, and that it was a place of resort for the most depraved characters. She likewise elicited that it was situated on the sea-coast, and, moreover, that there their journey on land would be at an end, as it was their intention to go on board ship. When she heard this, she could no longer control the feelings that rushed upon her, but wringing her hands, gave vehement expression to the violent grief and terror which oppressed her. Here, then, all the hopes she had formed of Lord Ravensford being able to trace the course they had taken, would be banished; for any idea of their going to such a distance, would never, she imagined, occur to him. She considered that she was lost; that her fate was sealed, and that nothing but horror and despair awaited her. But how deep-laid had been the scheme which had entrapped her; and what a time must it have taken to mature it, so as to attempt to put it into execution with any chance of success. She felt convinced that they had to combat with no trifling foe, but whether his designs were to gratify a feeling of revenge, or his brutal and sensual passions, she was unable to form a decided opinion. She was interrupted in the midst of these agonizing reflections by the carriage suddenly stopping, and looking forth from the window, she found that they were standing before a low tavern, and at no great distance off, she could hear the roaring of the ocean.

The house stood alone, and had anything but a lively appearance. The landlord met them at the door, and greeted Michael and his companions as they alighted from the vehicle. He was a tall, raw-boned man, with a low forehead, shaggy eyebrows, and a countenance very much sun-burnt, as though he had passed many years in a foreign climate.

As our heroine descended from the carriage, and fixed her gaze upon the landlord, who was scrutinizing her rudely, a deadly feeling of terror came over her, so that had it not been for the support of Michael, she must have fallen to the earth.

When she was about to ascend the step of the door, the loud shouts of laughter from the riotous guests smote her ears, and filled her with dismay.

"Take the female into my private parlour, Michael," said the landlord, "and then you can join me in the room up stairs. I see you have managed the business as it ought to be."

"Yes, nothing could be managed better, I flatter myself," answered Michael; "but leave me alone for that, I am the man that can do it, if anybody can."

The landlord nodded assentively to this, and the ruffian led, or rather forced our heroine into the house, for her faculties were so overpowered by terror and despair, that she had scarcely any use of her limbs, and she had no sooner crossed the threshold, than she uttered a piercing shriek, and immediately became insensible,

How long she had remained so, she had no means of judging, but on her restoration to consciousness, she found herself in bed, in a small room dimly lighted by the feeble rays emitted by a lamp, which stood on a deal table in the centre, and a stout, vulgar-looking female sitting by her side, with a bottle of hartshorn in her hand, which it appeared she had been applying frequently to her nose.

"Where am I?" she exclaimed, raising herself in the bed, and looking around her, "why am I brought hither?"

"Oh, you have recovered, have you?" said the woman, without returning any answer to her questions; "you'll do now, so I wish you good night. Should you require any assistance in the night, you will find a bell by the side of your bed."

"Oh, do not leave me, I beg of you," supplicated Lady Ravensford; but she asked in vain, for the woman had instantly quitted the room, and she heard her bolt the door after her.

Rosabelle looked fearfully around her; the room presented everything to heighten the excitement under which she suffered. It was badly furnished, the walls were dirty and damp and the whole place had a most gloomy and desolate appearance.

The occurrences of the last few hours had for a short time been banished from the memory of our heroine, but now they returned forcibly to her recollection, and her fears received additional strength from the remembrance. Occasionally she heard the rude mirth of the persons below, but gradually that subsided, and all was hushed in silence, save the ticking of an old clock in an adjoining apartment, which came with a dismal and monotonous sound to her ears. Shortly afterwards, it struck the hour of one. All kinds of frightful images flitted in imagination before the eyes of Lady Ravensford, and unable any longer to remain in bed, she arose, and walked to the only small casement there was in the room. It commanded a view of the beach, and Rosabelle could behold the dark waves of the ocean rolling beyond, from which proceeded a dismal, moaning sound, like the piteous cries of despair. To our heroine, in her situation, the sounds had an additional gloomy effect, and trimming her lamp, she sunk on her knees, and implored the protection of Heaven, and then once more returned to her couch, but not to sleep. Sleep, with the accumulated horrors that pressed upon her mind! That was utterly impossible.

So powerfully did terror work upon her imagination, that objects of the most awful description haunted her fancy, until unable any longer to combat their frightful influence, her senses gradually left her.

When she was again restored to sensibility, it was broad daylight, and she heard the people bustling about in the house. Her head ached dreadfully, and she felt parched and feverish. She attempted to rise, but in an instant a deadly sickness came over her, and she sunk back again on her pillow. Shortly afterwards, she heard some one ascending the stairs; then the bolts were withdrawn, and the same woman entered the room who had attended her the night before.

Rosabelle averted her eyes from her, with a sensation of disgust she found it impossible to resist.

"Come," said the woman, in an abrupt, vulgar tone, "you must get up; you have slept long beyond the time intended, and Michael and the others are waiting to depart."

"Oh, I cannot rise," returned Lady Ravensford; I am too ill, and—"

"Ill! ill!" exclaimed the woman, "nonsense; this must be all affectation;—come, come, do not be foolish."

"I have attempted to get up already," said our heroine; "but could not. Oh, if you have any humanity in your breast, give me some water, something to drink, to quench the burning thirst that is upon me."

"Here's a pretty job," ejaculated the woman; "was anything more provoking? Michael and the others will go crazy. I must go and tell master and them about it."

With that she fixed upon Lady Ravensford a suspicious look, and hastily quitted the room, taking care, however, to fasten the door after her.

"Good God!" exclaimed Lady Ravensford, when she had left the place, "what will become of me? Left to the mercy of such heartless wretches, and in such a pitiable condition, I shall die for the want of attendance! Oh, my husband! my poor boy! my father!"

She was left alone for about ten minutes, during which interval the excruciating pains in her head increased, and her eyes, which were bloodshot, seemed ready to start from their sockets. Shortly afterwards, the woman returned to the room, accompanied by a stern-looking man, who pronounced himself of the medical profession, and, after looking at her for a few moments, and having felt her pulse, stated that she was in a high state of fever, and ordered her to be kept particularly quiet. In the vain hope of being able to interest him in her behalf, Rosabelle was about to state the shameful manner in which she had been taken from her home and friends, but the doctor interrupted her by repeating his previous injunctions, and then abruptly quitted the room, the woman remaining behind to attend upon her, and evidently in no very agreeable mood, at the office which had thus so unexpectedly fallen upon her, every now and then complaining of the disappointment and inconvenience it had put Michael Henwood and his colleagues to.

The sight of this woman and her brutal behaviour, increased the illness of our heroine, and she continued to get worse every hour, until, at length, she became delirious, and raved incessantly of her father, Ravensford, and her child. She continued in this state for several days; but, at length, the strength of her constitution prevailed, and the fever left her; but she was so weak that it seemed likely to be some time before it would be safe for her to be removed.

She frequently inquired whether Michael and the others still remained in the house, and upon being answered in the affirmative, she expressed much disappointment and agony. But one thing distracted her more than all, and that was, she had heard nothing of her husband, whom she imagined might, from the delay caused by her illness, have found out where she was. But, perhaps the letter she had written to him had miscarried; the mail guard might have forgotten, or neglected to deliver it as he had promised, and her friends might remain in the same state of ignorance as to what had become of her as they were from the first. If such were really the case, all hope was undoubtedly at an end. These ideas had such an effect upon her, that she almost suffered a relapse; but, at length, by the perseverance of the doctor (who was really a very skilful man), she did regain sufficient strength to leave her couch, and Michael Henwood then sought an interview with her, and after complaining of the unfortunate delay which her illness had caused, told her that she must hold herself in readiness to go on ship-board the following day.

Again, in the most earnest and affecting manner, she implored Michael's forbearance, and begged of him to restore her to her friends, promising him not only forgiveness, but a handsome reward; but the villain remained inflexible, and smiled at her importunities, terming them absurd, and such as no person in their senses would think of yielding to.

Finding that all she could say was of no avail, she once more begged he would inform her whither they were going to take her.

"Why," answered Michael, after a few moment's reflection, "as you will soon be safe on board ship, I do not know that it can matter much whether I tell you the truth or not. We are going from hence to Jersey."

"To Jersey? Good God!" cried our heroine, with an expression of the greatest despair; "alas! who will think of seeking me there?"

"No, I don't think they will do that in a hurry, and that's the very reason that place was selected," replied Michael, with a look of exultation.

"Alas! what unheard of cruelty is this!" gasped forth the distracted Rosabelle; "what will become of me? Who is the villain that has been the instigator of this base plot?"

"I don't know either that it is of much consequence whether I keep his name a secret now," observed Michael.

"Tell it me, I implore."

"Do you know a gentleman of the name of Adder? He was formerly valet to Lord Ravensford!" returned Michael.

"Adder!" repeated Lady Ravensford, turning ghastly pale; "can it be possible? The villain!—the daring, the heartless villain! My husband's surmises were then too true; he is the infamous author of this cruel plot! Oh, what can be his motives for such base conduct?"

"Why, I believe they may be very easily explained," answered Michael, coolly. "The fact is, I understand, that Mr. Adder has fallen in love with your ladyship, and as there was no other means of getting possession of you, he has been led to adopt this measure, and a bold one it is too, and he well merits reward for his ingenuity in concocting the plot."

"Reward! yes, the gallows!" cried Lady Ravensford, with a look of horror and abhorrence. "The miscreant! what encouragement have I given him that he should thus presume?"

"Why, I can't say, madam," returned Michael, "that you have given him any particular encouragement; but then, you see, there is no accounting for the feelings of different persons, and, in some, discouragement only increases the strength of desire; that I dare say is the case with Mr. Adder."

"Great Heaven! shield me with thy almighty protection," ejaculated Lady Ravensford, clasping her hands; "give me strength to resist the persecution of this bad man, and to make his evil designs fall upon himself."

"As for that, young lady," returned Michael, it is all a matter of taste, to be sure; but, for my part, I do not see why you should have any particular cause to regret the change; Mr. Adder is quite as good-looking a man as Lord Ravensford, and loves you, I dare say, quite as well. Besides, he has got plenty of money; so, in that respect, you will have no particular cause to regret the change that I can see."

Rosabelle fixed upon the ruffian a look of pity and disgust, and made no answer, and Michael, after a few more observations to those we have quoted above, retired, and left her to herself.

Now that she was certain of the worst, notwithstanding her feelings of disgust and alarm may easily be conceived, Rosabelle became more composed, and endeavoured to prepare herself to meet the villain Adder with that fortitude and determination by which she could alone hope to be able to resist his nefarious wishes; but the deep-laid scheme the miscreant had formed, and the distant and obscure part he had selected for her concealment, filled her mind with the most serious apprehensions, and the thought of the despair to which her husband and father would be reduced by the mystery of her disappearance, and the uncertainty of her fate, occasioned her, if possible, more anguish than any danger or suffering to which she might be personally exposed. Alas! fate seemed to have conspired against her, for had the letter she had written reached Holly Hall, she entertained not the slightest doubt, owing to the delay which her illness had occasioned, that her husband would have contrived by some means to trace her out; but now, once on shipboard, all traces of her would be lost, and, probably, the idea would not occur to him to search for her on the sea-coast. She looked forward to the following day with the utmost dread, and her only hope of escape, for the present, rested in something transpiring in the interim. The day, however, passed slowly away, without any change taking place, and she was kept a close prisoner to the chamber in which she slept, no one visiting her, excepting the woman once or twice during the day. As night approached, her feelings became a little more tranquillised, and, on retiring to bed, she almost immediately sunk into a refreshing sleep.

She awoke at an early hour the following morning, and was about to rise, as she did not feel inclined to go to sleep again, when, to her astonishment, she found that her clothes were not in the room. Some person must have entered in the course of the night and taken them away, but for what purpose, she was at a loss to conjecture. This circumstance occasioned her the greatest uneasiness and perplexity, and she hastily rang the bell. The woman who had attended upon her ever since she had been in the house, shortly made her appearance, and, upon our heroine questioning her respecting the missing apparel, and who could have taken it away, she immediately replied that it was she who had done so.

"You!" repeated the astonished Rosabelle, "by whose authority did you do it, and for what purpose?"

"Why," answered the woman, "in the first place, it was by the orders of Michael Henwood I did so; and, in the next, because he wishes you to leave this house disguised. You will find your clothes quite safe when you are landed at the place of your destination."

"Disguise myself!" reiterated Lady Ravensford, with a look of indignation. "Good God! what new insult am I to be subjected to? In what disguise would the wretches have me appear?"

"In male attire," answered the woman; "it is necessary for their purpose, and you know it would be useless to seek obstinately to oppose them."

The deep blush of shame and resentment kindled in our heroine's cheek upon hearing this, and confusion and disgust, for a few seconds, prevented her from giving utterance to a word.

"Disguise myself, and in such a manner?" she at last exclaimed: "never! I will suffer anything first."

"We shall see about that," returned the woman; "but resistance will be all in vain; you are only required to assume it for the purpose of leaving the house, and you may change your dress as soon as ever you get on board the vessel, if you think proper."

"Oh, Heavens!" sighed the distracted Rosabelle, "this is past endurance; is there no pitying hand to save me from the degredation and misery about to be inflicted upon me?"

While she was thus speaking, the woman had quitted the room, and in a short time she returned, bringing with her a seaman's dress, in which she informed Rosabelle she must equip herself.

For some time Lady Ravensford remained firmly resolved not to comply with this disgusting order, but at last, finding that resistance would be useless, she, with the assistance of the female attendant, dressed herself in them, and underwent such a metamorphosis, that at any other time, and under different circumstances, would have excited her laughter; and then, after once more imploring the interposition of Omnipotence to save her from the wretched fate which threatened her, with a timid air, and the most painful feelings of outraged modesty, she followed the woman down the stairs, and entered the little parlour, where Michael Hernwood and his vile companions were waiting her arrival. With the deepest emotion, and while the crimson blushes of shame glowed in her cheeks, Rosabelle averted her face, to avoid noticing the rude glances which the men fixed upon her.

"You are now going on board the ship which is to convey us to the place of our destination, lady," observed Michael, "and I warn you, should we happen to meet any one on the way thither, that you do not offer to utter a syllable which may reveal your character, as you value your life. We are desperate men, and what we promise we will not fail to perform. Any appeal to those who will be on board will be useless, as the captain of the craft, and all those under him, are aware of your coming, and under what circumstances, the former being in the pay of the gentleman who has employed us. Mark me!"

Poor Rosabelle's heart was too full to render her capable of making any reply, and after the ruffians had bid the landlord of the house adieu, she suffered herself to be conducted forth, and they made their way speedily to the beach, where there was a boat waiting to receive them, without encountering a single individual, and in a few minutes the dipping of the oars in the water, arousing her from the kind of temporary stupor into which she had fallen, she found that they were making their way rapidly towards a small vessel which had cast her anchor at a short distance from the shore.

They were not long in reaching it, and having got on board, they found the captain, a rough, ferocious-looking man, who had more the appearance of a smuggler than a fair trader, waiting to receive them; and after he had eyed our heroine with the utmost insolence, and spoken a few words to Michael, he beckoned to a female who looked as disagreeable as the one at the tavern they had just quitted, and ordered her to show the lady to the cabin which had been allotted to her. The female desired Lady Ravensford to follow her, which mandate, completely broken in spirits, and bursting with shame and virtuous resentment, the latter obeyed.

The cabin she was ushered into was very commodiously fitted up, and there was everything placed for her use.

"Here are your own clothes, lady," said the woman, pointing to the same, "and if you think proper, you can change your dress. I dare say you feel uncomfortable in your present garb."

Rosabelle looked up, surprised to hear the woman speak with so much more kindness than, from her aspect, she had expected her to do; and having expressed her thanks for the suggestion, added—

"Oh, my good woman, surely you cannot have a heart quite callous to the feelings of your own sex when they are made the victims to cruelty. Pity my situation; torn from my home, my child, my husband, my aged father, and probably soon about to be subjected to—"

"Hush, madam," interrupted the female; "I am not quite so unfeeling as many persons might take me to be; but circumstances will not permit me to act as I could wish; but I am fearful that we might be overheard, and I should have to pay dearly very likely for what I have said. All that I can do to alleviate your anguish during the short time you will be on board, you may depend upon. Shall I assist you to dress?"

Rosabelle again thanked her; even the smallest symptom of pity, in her present wretched situation, came as balm to her deeply lacerated heart, and excited her fervant gratitude.

The female, having helped her to change her present uncouth dress for her own clothes, left her, promising to return shortly with some provisions.

Immediately after Rosabelle and the others had been received on board, the anchr was weighed, and the vessel scudded quickly on her way with a favouring breeze. During the voyage, our heroine was not permitted to leave the cabin, and the woman was almost constantly with her. From her she learned that the vessel was a smuggling craft, and that the captain was a friend of the villain Adder. She was the wife of one of the crew, and it was to a house belonging to the captain that she (Rosabelle) was for the present to be consigned, and where Adder would be waiting to receive her. Dismal indeed, then, was the prospect before her, and our heroine wept tears of the most bitter agony when she thought upon it.

We will not detain the reader by detailing the particulars of the short voyage. Nothing occurred worth recording. About midnight, the vessel reached the place of her destination, and running in between the rocks, cast anchor; and the smuggler captain, our heroine, Michael, and his companions, landed, and made their way on foot to some distance into the country, until they reached an unostentatious-looking dwelling, in a retired spot; and having give three distinct knocks at the door, and a boatswain's whistle, it was quickly opened by a man with a lamp in his hand. The light fell strongly upon his features, which Rosabelle no sooner beheld, than she recognised, and uttering a scream of terror, she sunk insensible to the earth. In that man Rosabelle recognized the features of Gordon, one of the murderers who had so terrified her on that awful night on which she sought shelter in *The Lover's Resting-place*, when on her return to her native place!

CHAPTER XVI.

THE MISTAKE.—THE JEALOUS HUSBAND.— THE FRENZIED FATHER.

THE man whom Lord Saunter had employed in the business by which he hoped to gain the completion of his wishes, probably fearful of the consequences that would be sure to follow, should the plot which he now suspected be discovered, resolved to betray him; and with that intention, having left the ignorant lord to await an answer to his letter, and who fully anticipated that Lady Ravensford would contrive some means to meet him, he hastened on towards the hall, where, on his arrival, he requsted to have a private interview with Lord Ravensford.

Ravensford was sitting in his study alone when this message was brought him, and was just beginning to feel surprised at the long absence of Rosabelle from the Hall. He desired the man to be ushered into his presence, and on his entering, he demanded his business.

The man made no reply, but delivered the letter which Lord Saunter had written into his hand. The moment Lord Ravensford's eye fell upon the writing, his face became inflamed with rage, and breaking open the seal, he hurriedly perused the contents.

"Who did you receive this from, fellow?" demanded his lordship in fierce accents. "Speak! —quick!—no equivocation!"

"I received it from the nobleman, whose name your lordship sees affixed to it," answered the man.

"To whom to be delivered?" said Ravensford, impatiently.

"The lady to whom you see it is directed," replied the fellow.

"And your reason for bringing it to me?"

"To reveal to your lordship the secret enemy you have, and enable you to thwart his evil designs."

"Good God! I shall go mad!" cried Lord Ravensford, clasping his forehead wildly. "Tell me, where is the villain?"

"He is waiting near the row of poplars, by the garden wall of this mansion, as your lordship may see by his letter," returned the man.

"Ah! then revenge is at last within my grasp!" exclaimed Ravensford, hastily seizing a brace of pistols which were close at hand, and rushing towards the door. "Follow me, fellow, and if you have deceived me, your life shall answer for it!"

With the impetuosity occasioned by the excitement of the moment, and the startling nature of the intelligence, as well as the plausibility which the absence of Lady Rosabelle from the hall gave it, Lord Ravensford rushed towards the spot mentioned by the man, and where he expected to meet the individual whom he had so long wished to encounter, and who had been the bane of his peace; the treacherous emissary of Lord Saunter followed, as we have before stated, but, at the same time, he nearly repented the part he had taken in the affair, inasmuch, as the conduct of his lordship, and the threats he had held out, led him to imagine a less profitable result than he had at first anticipated. Lord Ravensford had previously felt surprised at the protracted absence of our heroine, and his mind, inflamed by the circumstances that had for the last few weeks been a source of such annoyance to them, in an instant he conjured up all sorts of ideas, and could not keep conceiving that Rosabelle could not entirely be innocent or ignorant of the circumstance. Distraction had seized his brain, and he was prepared for the most desperate encounter.

"Which was the place you mentioned?" he inquired hastily of the man, as he darted precipitately across the garden; "the spot, I say?"

"By the row of poplars without the garden walls," answered the man.

"You have not deceived me?" was the demand.

"Your lordship can best prove that by the result," returned the man.

"Enough: then my deadly vengeance shall descend upon the miscreant's head," exclaimed Lord Ravensford, grasping the pistols more firmly, and hurrying towards the gate.

It was a beautiful moonlight night, and objects might be distinguished at a great distance as clearly as in the broad flood of daylight. As we have before stated, the man who had been employed by Lord Saunter and betrayed him, through motives of cowardice, and a hope

of getting better remunerated for doing so, repented sorely of the step he had taken, and would have been glad of having an opportunity to escape altogether, became more alarmed when he saw an object moving in the poplar walk, which he instantly knew to be that of Saunter. Ravensford's eye fell upon it at the same moment, and his passion now rose beyond control.

"By hell!" he exclaimed, "that is he; the miscreant shall not escape; die, damned villain, die!"

As he gave utterance to these words, he fired one of the pistols he had brought with him;

MR. WILMOT SECURES THE FORGED NOTE WRITTEN BY ADDER.

but the party, who had observed them, in a moment had taken to his heels, and was soon out of sight, before the contents of the weapon could possibly have reached him.

"Cowardly villain, stay!" vociferated Ravensford, bursting with indignation, as he darted precipitately forward in pursuit; but the deep enclosure of a neighbouring wood shielded the retreating party, and entirely concealed him from view, much to the satisfaction of the man, who flattered himself that the unpleasant affair he had engaged in was now at an end; but he was quickly disappointed, for Ravensford, having ran forward to some distance in pursuit of the fugitive, turned suddenly round, and grasping the former by the

throat with considerable violence, exclaimed, in a voice made hoarse by ungovernable rage and disappointment—

"Dastardly knave! this is but a mere trick. You have misled me; this was not Saunter, but some creature in this vile plot, and the whole has been a stratagem merely to give the wretch time to effect his nefarious object without interruption. Tell me, wretch, or I will drag the secret from thy bosom; where is Saunter? where is my deluded wife?"

"My lord," cried the man, seriously alarmed by his manner, "I assure you I have spoken nothing but the truth; it was Lord Saunter that you first saw, and who fled when he beheld us approaching; as I wish to be saved, I know nothing whatever of your lordship's lady, and——"

"Liar!" interrupted Ravensford, spurning the man from him; "but you shall pay dearly for this; what ho, there! this way! this way!"

The report of the pistol had alarmed several of the domestics at the hall, who now rushed towards the spot, and gazed with surprise at the scene which presented itself, namely, the man prostrate on the earth, and their lord standing over him with a pistol presented at his head.

"Convey this fellow to the hall," commanded Ravensford. "and see that he does not escape, and the rest attend to me."

A portion of the men laid hold of the man, imagining that he had been committing some outrage, or attempting robbery, and bore him away in the direction of the hall, while the others obeyed the mandates of Ravensford, and followed him, as he fled wildly into the wood, in the direction which the fugitive had taken.

In the meantime, Mr. Montalbert, who had been seated with Mr. Goodman in the parlour of the hall, upon hearing the confusion in the house, occasioned by the report of the pistol, and unable to learn whither Ravensford had gone, became violently agitated, and inquired the cause. Mr. Goodman was as much surprised as his friend, and his mind foreboded something wrong, but he endeavoured to stifle any display of his own feelings, and sought all that he possibly could to compose the alarm and agitation of Montalbert.

"It is nothing more, I dare say, than some little affray amongst the rustics outside; I—"

"Oh, no, no," interrupted Mr. Montalbert, impatiently, and his countenance becoming wild, "it is not that—it is not that;—something more serious than that has happened; I am certain of it. My mind has for some time entertained the presentiments of some impending calamity, and it has now taken place. Where is Ravensford? Where is my daughter? Rosabelle! where, where is she? She was not wont to leave us so long! Oh, God! what maddening thought is it that rushes upon my brain? Rosabelle!"

"My dear sir, for Heaven's sake, be calm!" expostulated Mr. Goodman, terrified at the wildness of his demeanour, for his eyes rolled fearfully, and his cheeks became flushed to an alarming extent. "Lady Ravensford has not yet returned from her customary walk, and you know——"

"I know," replied Montalbert, impatiently, "I know that you would deceive me! Rosabelle was not in the habit of leaving the society of her father so long since his recovery from that awful malady into which he feels himself now again about to be plunged! And Ravensford, too—that pistol! This strange confusion! Oh, I am certain that something has happened!

Madness is preferable to this state of uncertainty and suspense! I will be satisfied!"

As the poor old man thus spoke, he rung the bell violently, and, at that moment, while his hand was yet to the bell-pull, the servants who had the man that had been employed by Lord Saunter in their custody, rushed into the room unceremoniously, bringing him with them.

"What is the meaning of this?" demanded Mr. Goodman, while Montalbert gazed on in stupified amazement, and with an expression of countenance which plainly showed that his reason was on the totter—

"Why is this person brought hither, and what is the meaning of all this confusion!"

The man, whose loquacity was equal to his apprehension, quickly explained the circumstances, and no sooner had he done so, than Montalbert, starting wildly, rushed up to him, and seizing him fiercely by the throat, ejaculated—

"Ah, villain! miscreant! what is it you utter? My child again the victim of the seducer! Rosabelle an adultress! Wretch! dare not to utter a hint to that effect, or I will tear your heart out! But, yes, it must be so! for some time past I have noticed a change! Secrets have been withheld from me, from a feeling of charity. Where is Ravensford?—where is my daughter? I will have the secret unravelled! By Heaven! I will no longer be deceived! Oh, God! a fire shoots through my brain! in mercy to me, reveal all; do not again consign me to their dreadful dungeons! —I—I——"

"Mr. Montalbert," interposed Goodman, who became fearfully alarmed at the wild ravings of the former, and his general demeanour, "let me entreat you to calm this violence; it must be a misunderstanding; tell me, fellow, and at your peril attempt not to deceive me, or you will have dearly to answer for it, what really brought you hither, and by whose directions did you act?"

"I have told you the truth, I solemnly declare," faltered out the man. "I was sent here by Lord Saunter with a letter to Lady Ravensford, which Lord Ravensford has now in his possession, and he was waiting in the poplar walk expecting her to meet him, but thinking that Lord Saunter was acting a villain's part, I betrayed the affair, and Lord Ravensford rushed forth to inflict punishment upon my employer. He was waiting at the place I have mentioned, but fled on seeing us approach, and Lord Ravensford fired after him, which——"

"Fiend of hell!" shouted the delirious Montalbert, rushing upon the man, "recall your words, or I will crush you dead! My Rosabelle—oh, God! but where is she? Why is she not here to rebut the foul calumny? Calumny? no, it is not so; there is every damning proof of the truth of the assertion! My Rosabelle was never before so long absent from me till she fled with—Ah! the fiends are at work again! Yes, yes,—liars that they were, they told me that she was not dead! They deluded me with false tales;—they said that she was living—that she had returned to comfort—to make the declining days of her poor old father happy! But it is not so; it was a base, a heartless fabrication! My child—no, no, no, I have no child! She died! Fool that I was to believe them! Liars! liars! let me go forth!—unhand me!—chains shall not hold me! I'll snap them asunder as I would the bolts of Jove! Wretches! who shall restrain a father from visiting the grave of his child? Let me go, I say! Ha! ha! ha! Mockery! Ha! ha! ha!"

"Heaven's mercy light upon him," cried the deeply afflicted Mr. Goodman, "his senses are again gone. Bear him to his chamber, and call in immediate attendance."

"Off, off, ruffians!" shouted the wretched parent, "you shall not bear me to your cells—I have suffered too long—I have been whipped with rods of burning iron; see ye not my poor scarified flesh? Look at my gaping wounds! See, they bleed afresh as they were wont do do; but, no, I will ride the air and be at liberty! Softly, softly, it is only her tomb I seek—the tomb I reared for her; oh, it was such a costly one, with but one simple name upon it, the name engraven upon my heart, and imprinted in my life's blood. Nay, nay, I will not be held,—have I not a right to view my own handicraft?"

It needs not language to describe the emotions of the benevolent Mr. Goodman at this deplorable scene; he was so bewildered that he scarcely knew how to act. He, however, despatched a servant for the attendance of the unfortunate patient's medical adviser, and then taking the arm of Mr. Montalbert, in gentle and persuasive accents, he endeavoured to prevail upon him to suffer him to lead him to his chamber.

"Ah!" cried the maniac, looking vacantly upon Mr. Goodman, "I know you now; you will not harm me; no, no, you are the keeper that used to be so kind to me. But do you wish to see her tomb?—It is a goodly sight! It is the only memorial that a father could raise to his only daughter; but I did it all myself. Oh, yes, I cannot tell you how hard I laboured, and yet with such pleasure; for you know I loved her, and what was there that I could consider too much to do in her remembrance? She was so fair—so kind—so affectionate. But they told me she was not,—liars! —they sought to blast her fame—they said she fled from .... her doating parent, and threw herself into the arms of a villain! Monsters! fiends! to speak thus of one so kind—so

gentle—so lovely. But she is at rest now, and they cannot rob me of her cold remains. Come, come, we will pay a pilgrimage to her silent resting-place. It is my only haunt of pleasure; and the roses bloom so sweetly round the spot. But she is withered—she is withered! Come, come, I say, you and I will visit the tomb of the father's only one together."

Raising his eyes to Heaven, and mentally breathing a prayer for its mercy towards the unhappy sufferer, Mr. Goodman led, or was rather led by Montalbert to his chamber, where, by the time he had seen him into bed, the medical man arrived, and having left him to his care, he returned to the room he had just quitted, to interrogate the man further upon the unfortunate subject; but he could elicit no more than what we have already stated. His next inquiry was after Lady Rosabelle, and when she had last been seen. Her waiting woman informed him, that she had walked forth alone at her usual hour, as it was supposed, in the garden, and that she had not since been seen. Mr. Goodman then despatched persons in different directions, to make the strictest search after her, and shortly after he had so, Lord Ravensford returned, in a state of mind which language must fail to pourtray. In vain had he pursued the course which Saunter had taken; and now finding that his wife was still absent from the hall, his jealousy and suspicions were excited to the utmost degree, and he firmly believed that it was all a trick to mislead him; that the letter was merely sent for the purpose of carrying out that object; that it was not Lord Saunter he had seen at all, but that his wife, being equally guilty with the former, had entered into his plans, and eloped with him. In vain did Mr. Goodman expostulate with him, and endeavour to convince him of the utter absurdity of this idea, and the unjustice he did Lady Ravensford by such a supposition; his mind was too much excited to listen to the dictates of reason, and hastily ordering his horse, he started forth from the house, attended by two trusty domestics, vowing never to rest until he had discovered the place of her and her paramour's retreat, and wreaked his vengeance upon their heads.

In the meantime, the unfortunate Mr. Montalbert remained in the same melancholy condition, and raved in the same wild manner as at first. The medical gentleman considered it a a hopeless case, and feard that now, alas! his reason had fled for ever. Mr. Goodman could not be prevailed upon to quit the bedside of his unhappy friend for an instant, and having sent for his daughter, and apprised her of the melancholy circumstance, she came immediately to the hall, and they remained there the whole of the night.

At a late hour, the persons who had been in search of our heroine returned to the hall, without having been able to obtain to least clue to whither she had gone or been forced away, and the astonishment and alarm of all the persons interested in the melancholy and mysterious business, needs no description from us.

If it were possible, the feelings of Emily were more distracted than those of her father at the pitiable condition of Mr. Montalbert, and the unaccountable disappearance of Lady Rosabelle; but conjecture was exhausted in vain to form the most remote idea of the actual cause of the latter. That Rosabelle had eloped of her own free will was so opposite to reason, that she rejected it a moment, and in spite of the assertions of the man who had been the bearer of the fatal letter, she could not help firmly believing that she had been waylaid by the deep-laid designs of Lord Saunter and Adder, and was at present in their power. But oh, what agony did she feel when she reflected upon the probability of the misery that Rosabelle was at present enduring, the terrible calamity her disappearance had wrought at home, and the final blow it must be to her happiness when she became acquainted with the truth. All that care—that unremitting attention—that untiring assiduity—that deeply affecting trouble she had taken to gain the consummation of her happiness, the restoration of her father to reason, and which had been, after so much tedious anxiety, hours of half-formed hopes and despair been realised, and justice done to her by the man who had been the first cause of her sorrow, was thus in a few minutes crushed, and misery—hopeless, with tenfold power, had taken possession of that happiness they had fondly imagined would last for ever! As hour after hour passed away, and still nothing whatever was heard of Rosabelle or Ravensford, this agony increased, and it required all the firmness and self-possession of Mrs. Goodman and her husband to control it within the bounds of reason.

It was many years since Holly Hall had been such a scene of misery as it was upon that occasion, and the persons present looked upon each other with expressive glances, which seemed to forebode the worst for the future.

Mrs. Rattleton, as well as her father, could not be induced to leave the hall that dismal night, and the principal portion of the time she passed by the couch of the unfortunate and deeply afflicted Mr. Montalbert. It was truly heart-rending to hear at times the wild ravings of that ill-starred gentleman, and Mr. Goodman found it a very difficult task to keep him anything like within control. Sometimes, indeed, to such a pitch of wild delirium did his malady attain, that it required the aid of several of the servants to hold him in the bed, and Emily became so horrorstruck at the scene, that she

could only with the utmost preseverance contain herself.

"My child!" occasionally would the wretched maniac exclaim; "my Rosabelle! who has torn her from me? What monster has again deprived me of her? But no, no, she has not fled!—she has not fled! She is only at rest—yes, at peace; and yet her foul slanderers would insult her ashes by their base calumnies. The villains! where are they? Let me get at them! Let me but have them in my clutches, and they shall find how strong a parent is in the reputation of his darling child. Ah! see, who is that who scoffs at me? who derides me and points his envenomed dart at my Rosabelle's tomb? Demon! I know thee now. Yes, thy name is Slander! Thou and I art well acquainted—thou hast been my deadliest foe. Thou didst before trample on my peace of mind, and made that sear which would have been fresh and blooming; but I can grapple with thee now in all thy strength! I can defy thy utmost power. Ah! dost thou still mock me? Have at thee, then—down, down, monster, down! Ha! ha! ha! I have triumphed!"

"Great God!" exclaimed Emily, overcome by the power of her feelings, "surely thy visitations are too severe!"

"Silence, my child," remonstrated Mr. Goodman, although at the same time, his own emotions were almost overpowering, when he contemplated the lamentable scene, "arraign not the Almighty will. He who thinks now proper to visit with affliction these erring mortals, may shortly deem fit in His infinite mercy to spare them and restore them to happiness."

"Yes, my dear father," said our heroine, "I know it is wrong to question the dispensations of Providence; but oh, who with the least spark of humanity in their bosoms could behold such a sight as this unmoved? Who could think upon the second mysterious disappearance of Rosabelle with any other feelings than those of the most bitter, the most poignant anguish? Oh, God! what can have become of her, and what would be her agony, her insupportable agony, could she behold this distressing scene?"

"Endeavour to quiet your emotions, my dear Emly," said her father, "which I need not tell you I duly appreciate, and let me persuade you to retire to rest; this over exertion of mind and body will make you ill, and can do you no good; here are plenty to attend upon Mr. Montalbert already."

"Yes, my love," observed her husband, "be persuaded by your father, and hasten to repose; I will keep your father company till the morning."

"No," answered Emily, firmly, "if I were to retire, I could not sleep with the heavy weight of anxiety which is at present upon my mind, and I will therefore remain here; my wishes to render all the assistance in my power will sustain me; therefore, you need not be under any apprehension on my account."

"There, there, there!" suddenly exclaimed the wretched maniac, raising himself on his elbow, and pointing towards the door; "do you not see her?—no, no! she is not revealed to any other eyes than those of a parent—it is her pure spirit—oh how beautiful—how radiant her form, how angelic her countenance. See, how she smiles! Yes, it was so—she was wont to smile when alive! Hark! she speaks! Oh, these seraphic tones, they tell of Heaven! Ah! she is an inhabitant of Heaven now!—Who says she is not?—Base liar, whoever he be, I have a giant's strength to crush him!—Deceiver! adultress!—What fiend again whispers those shameful words!—'Tis false! 'tis false! See, there she is again! Why do you not let me approach her? Wretches, what right have ye to prevent a father from embracing his doating child? Off! off! off!

Here they had the utmost difficulty in keeping the unfortunate gentleman in bed, and it was at last found indispensably necessary to secure him to it by straps; after which, he remained calm for some time, and seemed to be holding a secret communion with his own thoughts. At length, he again opened his eyes, which he had before closed, though not in sleep, and looking once more round the room, he again ejaculated in subdued tones;—

"Soft, soft—she is there again! Once more the music of her voice vibrates on my ears;—hush, hush;—do not breathe a sound;—do not whisper a syllable, lest I should not hear her! Rosabelle, dearest, sweetest Rosabelle; best of daughters, why do you not come nearer to me? Oh! approach, and let your old father once more enfold you in his arms, and breathe warm kisses of adoration upon your cheeks! But no, it must not be! you are no longer of this earth! You are now an angel, and must not be approached by base mortality! Oh, how brilliant are those eyes that seem to penetrate my soul! Gone again! gone again, and I am once more wretched."

In these wild ravings no one attempted to interrupt him; but when he became more violent, Rattleton suggested the propriety of sending for the keeper who had had the former care of him, and who would be sure to know best how to manage him. This, however, Mr. Goodman strongly objected to, thinking that the very sight of that individual would recall all the horror of the past to the wretched patient, and render him worse; and as no one could attempt to dispute the reason of this argument, Rattleton's proposition was urged no further.

A dismal night, indeed, was this in the hall, Mr. Goodman, Rattleton, Emily, and two domestics continuing in the chamber of Mr. Montalbert, whose melancholy ravings continued with few intermissions thoughout the night, and the medical gentleman gave not the slightest hope of his being able to cure him of the terrible malady. It was a blusterous night, and the wind howled dismally round the halls and amid the foliage of the lofty tress that waved their lofty branches in the gardens that encompassed the house. None of the persons present felt inclined to talk, and in those moments when the patient was more calm, Emily listened with feelings that may easily be conceived to the wind's fitful gusts, and two or three times she suddenly started from her seat, and was hastening to the door, as her disordered imagination pictured to her the moanings of some person in distress; but recollecting herself again in an instant, she returned to her chair, and re-seated herself with a deep sigh. "Alas!" she thought, "where now is Rosabelle? Probably exposed to the most imminent danger, shame, and anguish, while every one, uncertain of her course, have it not in their power to render her the least assistance. And who has been guilty of this cruel deed? It must have been the emissaries of Lord Saunter, aided by the villain Adder;—oh, yes, for nothing shall ever persuade me that Rosabelle would abandon her husband and child; that husband and child to whom I am convinced she was so fondly attached, of her own free will. Oh, no, I should indeed be unjust could I believe such a thing."

Thus did Emily ruminate, and similar reflections were passing in the mind of Mr. Goodman and Rattleton, but they communicated them to each other only by their walks. But, anxious as the former gentleman was to lean to the side of mercy, in spite of all his efforts to the contrary, thoughts would arise in his mind, which impressed it with an idea that Lady Ravensford was not so innocent as she was generally believed to be, while at other moments, he would reject such a supposition as not only preposterous but illiberal, and he became completely lost in a labyrinth of conjecture, doubt, and uncertainty.

Persons were still despatched, as well as those who had accompanied Lord Ravensford, scouring the country in all directions, and every moment, every noise that stirred, they hoped to receive some information respecting her; but they were always doomed to some fresh disappointment, and at length their suspense became almost unbearable, being only diverted at intervals by the lamentable condition of Mr. Montalbert, and the expressions he gave utterance to. It is a melancholy task to watch in the chamber of sickness; every moment seems protracted into an hour, and all around appears to partake of the complexion of the feelings of the watchers; these, under ordinary circumstances, must have been the feelings that every person who has been placed in such a situation, must have experienced; but under such peculiar circumstance, such an accumulation of trying miseries, how doubly intense must have been the emotions of the persons by the couch of Montalbert! It was only now and then that they conversed together in low whispers, and then they were unable to afford one another the least hope or consolation. The midnight hour had long since passed, and those of the servants who were at the hall, had retired to their chambers, and were wrapt in sleep; there was not a sound to be heard, save the howling of the wind without, and the thick and heavy breathing of Mr. Montalbert, (for he had sunk into a temporary and uneasy slumber), and the air of everything around was sufficient to increase the heavy melancholy which depressed their spirits.

Emily walked for a moment from the side of the couch, and Mr. Goodman and her husband followed her.

"I fear there is no hope of receiving any intelligence of the unfortunate Lady Ravensford to-night," Mr. Goodman observed, in a low voice; "alas! I have racked my brain in vain to imagine what can have become of her. Can it have been her own voluntary act?"

"Oh, my father," returned Emily, "I am surprised to hear you, who are ever so generous, entertain such a cruel supposition. Surely you cannot be prejudiced by the unhappy indiscretion of former days, and for which she has subsequently made such ample atonement? A heartless wretch, indeed, must Rosabelle be, where she capable of entertaining even the bare idea of such a thing, knowing full well the circumstances of horror which must consequently follow such conduct."

"Lady Ravensford could never, I am certain, sir," said Rattleton, "could never become the unnatural creature that the confirmation of your suspicions would make her. Recollect the attention, and ceaseless anxiety she evinced in the restoration of her unfortunate parent to reason, and do you think she could be so callous to all feelings of humanity as to crush at one fell swoop what she had taken such pains to accomplish? The thought is too extravagant and unreasonable to be indulged for an instant; mark me, and be sure that time will prove it, the cause of Lady Rosabelle's mysterious disappearance, is all the effect of some deep-laid scheme of villany, which, in time, will be fully cleared up, and the perpetrator of it brought to punishment."

"Heaven grant that it may prove as you state," said Mr. Goodman, emphatically, "but alas! I fear that one blow is struck, which nothing can ever compensate for; the senses of Mr. Montalbert have, I have too much reason to apprehend, fled for ever; and should Lady Ravensford be restored, what think you will ever console her under this heavy and overwhelming affliction?"

Emily sighed at the true picture formed by her father.

"Lord Ravensford, too," she observed, "what will become of him? How will he act? It is plain enough to be seen by any person of penetration, that he entertains doubts of his wife's innocence, and under such circumstances, is not the worst to be dreaded? Terrible is the wreck caused by some fiends in human shape, in what might otherwise have been so happy a family."

"I am fearful that the impetuous and headstrong disposition of Ravensford, will induce him to commit some desperate act," said Rattleton, "and I am all anxiety to see him return to the hall."

"That you may depend upon it he will not do, until he has obtained some clue to the discovery of his much-injured wife," returned Emily; "it is clear that he will never rest, until he has obtained satisfaction in some shape or the other. Should he encounter Lord Saunter, I fear that death would be certain to be the portion of one of them; Ravensford has sworn to wreak his vengeance in the villain's blood, and he will not fail to keep his oath."

"But do you think that Saunter is the principal guilty party in this base stratagem?" asked Rattleton. "It seems to me to be too ingeniously contrived and executed, to have emanated from him, notorious as he is for being one of the veriest boobies in existence."

"No, I do not," answered Emily; "the suspicions of Ravensford lighted upon his late valet Adder, as being an accessary, or rather the grand inventor of the plot; and I think, (taking the character of the man into consideration, and recollecting that when Lord Ravensford dismissed him he held out threats to him), there is every reason to believe that this is a just supposition."

"And yet, although it is evident, and in fact, has been proved to have been the case, that they both must have been in the neighbourhood, or the immediate locality, for some time past, is it not strange that all endeavours to find them out were unavailing?" questioned Mr. Goodman.

Emily and her husband assented to the correctness of this, and Mr. Montalbert having awakened, the conversation dropped for a short time.

It was very evident, from the appearance of the patient, that he had derived little or no benefit from his disturbed slumber, and the alarming expression of his countenance seemed rather to have increased than abated.

They hastened to his bedside, and were seated around him, and alternately he fixed his eyes upon one and then the other of them, with a vacant stare.

"Who are ye all?" he suddenly articulated, "and what do you here?—Why is my privacy thus intruded upon, except by that bright form who is the constant companion of my thoughts? Ah! I know ye all now! Ye are the wretches that have so long oppressed me, and this the gloomy loathsome cell in which for so many years I have been incarcerated!—Release me from these galling fetters; unbar the doors that shut me from liberty.—Nay, I will not be kept down;—I will snap the chains asunder as if they were so many straws, and rush forth free and unshakled!—Who shall dare to attempt to prevent me from visiting that tomb where repose the ashes of my Rosabelle? Let me hence, let me hence! No power shall longer detain me!—See, my Rosabelle's shade beckons me to follow her!—I am coming, I am coming, sweet spirit, to that spot where the remains of my child repose within the narrow house death has provided for her!"

After the lapse of a few moments, during which he was struggling to release himself from the straps that confined him, completely exhausted, he once more sunk back on the pillow, and for a short time appeared to be entirely unconscious of all that was passing around him. Shortly afterwards they heard him in a mournfully plaintive voice, and in low, feeble tones, singing these impressive words from the song, which in their days of happiness it was his delight to hear our heroine sing to him, and which were so appropriate to their own melancholy circumstances;—

" Oh, never could that darling child,
    Her aged parents loved so dear,
  Cause in his cheek the blush of shame,
    Or in his eye excite a tear.

  A comfort to his old gray hairs,
    A solace in his hours of woe—
  Woe brought not on by sin of hers:
    Could she e'er grieve his heart? ah no!"

Then the poor old man wept, after which he burst into a loud peal of laughter, making the place resound again, and which at that solemn hour, (it was then past two o'clock,) sounded peculiarly awful. This having subsided, he once more became calm, talking incoherently to himself, and seeming to be engaged in reckoning something up by his fingers.

" One—two—three—six—no,—I cannot reckon now," he continued in under tones,—" but oh, what a long, long while it is since she died, and the roses bloom as fresh around her tomb as if they had only been planted yesterday. What strange, what wicked stories they told me of her too; what remarkable and cruel fabrications; but I believed them not; no, I only mocked at, despised, and scouted them! They told me that it was not true that she was no more; that she had fled from me, abandoned me, for a heartless deceiver! Psha! how weak they must be to think that I would believe them. Rosabelle abandon her doating father! No. no, no, perish such a thought! It is only

base and wicked children who desert their parents; and my child was so good, so kind, so gentle, so virtuous, and she is now an angel! But where are the monsters who have thus sought to caluminate my child; give them to me; let me but have them within my power, and I will inflict a terrible vengeance upon them! It is no use endeavouring to conceal them, for were they hidden in the deepest bowels of the earth, I would discover them, and drag them forth! Ah!—you are one—and you—and you!—Thus then do I annihilate ye all at a blow!—Ha! ha! ha!—I have triumphed now! —I have triumphed now!"

Thus did Mr. Montalbert continue alternately during the remainder of the night, and when the morning dawned, his malady appeared to have increased rather than abated. The most eminent medical men that could be found were called in, but they all pronounced it a hopeless case, and could only advise his being kept as quiet as possible, and to have some person constantly with him, but who was not to hold any more converse with him than he could possibly avoid.

In the forenoon most of the persons who had been sent in search of Lady Ravensford returned to the hall quite worn out, they having ridden hard, and without the least success, no one having been able to afford them the least information upon the subject. Thus was the perplexity and anxiety of all persons interested in the lamentable affair increased, and the excitement which prevailed in the neighbourhood of the hall, and for miles around, among those who were acquainted with the parties, was very considerable. Various and conflicting were the opinions formed upon the subject, and, as in all cases of a similar description, the busy tongue of scandal was not idle; and many prejudiced persons, judging only from the former event, when Lady Ravensford eloped with her present husband, did not hesitate to inculpate her conduct, and to set her down as the guilty party.

The man who had brought the letter from Lord Saunter was kept confined to the hall, and had been several times narrowly questioned by Mr. Goodman and his son-in-law, but he deviated not in the least from his original assertions, merely adding, that he was the person who had conveyed the letters to Ravensford Castle, on which occasions Mr. Adder had been his employer, although there could not be any doubt from the fact of his wearing the livery of Lord Saunter, that that dissipated nobleman was the principle in the plot, if not the inventor of it.

This statement was sufficient to show how deeply implicated the villain Adder must be in the stratagem, and that his actions were guided entirely by motives of revenge, the threats he had held out to Ravensford sufficiently proved. But there was another and important idea which the statement of the man excited in the mind of Mr. Goodman, and that was, whether the former was employed by Lord Saunter in the last affair at the house where he was staying? The man replied in the affirmative, and willingly offered to accompany him to the house.

"Had you but informed us of this before, it would have rendered an invaluable service, and have prevented the melancholy circumstances that have taken place, by frustrating the diabolical designs of the villains," said Mr. Goodman.

"I knew not of it myself, sir," answered the man, "until I was sent for thither to attend his lordship yesterday. He was living there incog, and from what I have elicited, I believe that Mr. Adder has been acting as his factotum."

Mr. Goodman having left the unfortunate Montalbert in the care of the proper attendants, accompanied by Rattleton, two servants, and the man who had given the information, left the hall, and hastened towards the house, where Lord Saunter was said to have been lately staying. When they arrived there, however, they were informed by the lady who belonged to the house, that neither Mr. Adder or Lord Saunter had been there since the afternoon previous, but that the latter had sent a porter for his portmanteau about two hours previous, and having also forwarded the balance of his account, he sent word to say that it was not his intention to return to the house. As Lord Saunter was not indebted to her anything, the lady in reply, said to Mr. Goodman, she, of course, did not take the liberty of questioning the porter as to whither he had to convey the portmanteau; but as Mr. Goodman and Rattleton afterwards observed to each other, it was far more probable that the lady was thoroughly acquainted with all the particulars, only she had been handsomely feed by Lord Saunter to keep the secret inviolable. Thus then was all prospect of gaining any intelligence of the two miscreants, Saunter and Adder, in that quarter, at an end, and Mr. Goodman and his son-in-law returned vexed and disappointed to the hall, taking care, however, that Burford, the man who had been employed by the silly and profligate nobleman to be the bearer of his letters, should accompany them.

On their arrival at the hall, they found little or no change in the patient, or if there was any at all, it was most unquestionably for the worse. He had, they were informed, raved almost incessantly, in the most wild and distressing manner, since their absence from the hall, and at times he had been so violent, that it was with the utmost difficulty, although he was strapped to the bedstead, that they could control him.

As for Lady Rosabelle, nothing whatever had been heard of her neither had Lord

Ravensford or any of the domestics that accompanied him, returned to the hall since they had departed on the evening before.

Mr. Goodman now began to entertain the most serious apprehensions respecting the latter, and a thousand vague thoughts rushed upon his brain, which, although they were many of them most improbable, he could not easily discard.

"Surely," said he, addressing himself to Rattleton, "the unfortunate nobleman cannot have been so rash, so overcome by the power of his feelings, as to have committed some desperate deed upon himself? My heart certainly misgives me when I recollect the state of mind in which he left us yesterday evening, and we so well know the power and impetuosity of his passions, as was fully exemplified at the time he was about to commit the act of self-destruction before."

"Oh, no, my dear sir," returned Rattleton, trying to laugh, though he was far from being in any mood to do so; "never fear—never fear; Ravensford will never be foolish enough for that, whatever he might have done before; then he knew himself the guilty party, and was conscience-stricken, now he supposes that his wife is the offender, and, thinking so, he seeks only retribution on the heads of her and her supposed seducer. He will return anon, or else I am much mistaken, and with some intelligence of Lady Ravensford too."

"I hope that your anticipations may be realised," said Mr. Goodman, "though, I confess, I am not very sanguine upon the subject."

"It is always best," observed Rattleton, "without giving way entirely to despair, to put the worst imagination upon uncertainties, as it then entirely protects us from disappointment; still, I cannot be shaken in the first opinion I formed, and which I have expressed. However, the whole affair is certainly a great mystery."

"And yet I think not, now, although I at first did certainly have a strong suspicion that Lady Ravensford was not altogether so innocent as many persons might imagine. There certainly appears to me now no doubt whatever that the whole is the contrivance of Adder and Saunter, the one from motives of revenge, and the other with the hope of gratifying his sinful passions. At any rate, no one can deny, that, whoever are the authors of the plot, it has been very cleverly managed throughout, and that there is more cause than ever, from such an enemy or enemies, to dread that the worst may befall the unfortunate and ill-starred woman."

"Your observations are very just, my dear father," exclaimed Emily, who at that moment entered the room, "and my terror for Rosabelle is more excited than ever."

"Let us beseech Heaven that things may not turn out so bad as we anticipate," said Mr. Goodman; "something strikes me that it will not be long ere we shall receive some intelligence of the hapless lady, and I sincerely pray that she may be fully able to repudiate any of the calumnies which the ambiguity of the affair is sure to give rise to, as it is now my firm opinion she will be able to do, to the satisfaction of her friends, and the shame and confusion of her enemies."

Rattleton and his wife heartily responded to this wish, and they then repaired to the chamber of Montalbert, who, they were glad to find, had fallen into a doze, and it was more calm than any he had had since the occurrence of the above affair. They seated themselves, and refrained from talking, except in whispers to each other, for fear of disturbing him. He continued to sleep for above an hour, and when he awoke, although he still occasionally raved most wildly, his general behaviour was more of a melancholy madness than the violence he had before evinced.

LADY RAVENSFORD'S HORROR UPON MEETING THE MURDERED GORDON.

CHAPTER XVII.

THE DASTARD LORD.—THE DISTRACTED HUSBAND.—THE LETTER.—THE DEPARTURE.

IT may now, perhaps, be as well to revert to Lord Saunter. On the evening when we sent Burford with the letter, which had caused so much excitement and alarm at Holly Hall, he felt far from being so easy as he had been on former occasions, and being naturally of a very cowardly disposition, his fears magnified the most trifling circumstances into subjects of the most vital importance, and what was suspicion only at first, by the aid of his own imagination became certainty. He fancied (and, probably, after what has been shown, not without very good reason) that Burford did not evince that sincerity of manner which would have been satisfactory to him, and more than once he repented having so far made him his confidant, or entrusted the business to him at all. Added to this, the behaviour of Adder on the previous day had far from pleased or satisfied him, and he had determined to keep a more watchful eye upon him for the future; yet, his inordinate vanity would not suffer him to suppose that there was any untruth in our heroine having conceived a violent and uncontrollable affection towards him, and that she was willing to make any sacrifice for his sake. He also firmly believed that the letters that had been forged and concocted by Adder, and purporting to come from Lady Ravensford, were genuine, and this it was that urged him on, or otherwise he might have been induced to abandon the whole business in despair, especially when the time was so protracted before the plot was sought to be put into execution. What tended to render his lordship more doubtful than ever of the fidelity of the crafty and designing Adder, was, that he had absented himself rather longer than was his wont, and that, when they last separated, they were far from being on such friendly terms as they usually appeared to be. Although, therefore, he had employed Burford to carry the letter and deliver it to Lady Ravensford, unknown to any one, he determined to be upon his guard, in case of any act of treachery. The time which Burford was gone to the hall, and during which interval he waited with the utmost impatience in the poplar-walk, appeared to Lord Saunter to be remarkably long, and tended not a little to make him watchful and wary. He paced backwards and forwards with uneven steps, frequently looking behind him, fearful of being surprised.

The fineness of the evening, and the brightness with which the moon shone, was all in favour of the profligate young nobleman's wishes, and it was a fortunate job for him that it was so, as his life would without a doubt have paid the forfeit of his audacity. For the better purpose of concealment, he at length placed himself behind one of the largest trees, and from whence he could watch all who issued from the principal entrance to the hall, with perfect ease. What followed, the reader is already made acquainted with. Lord Saunter, seeing the approach of Ravensford and Burford, immediately guessed what was the matter, and precipitately took to flight, without receiving any hurt from the pistol, the contents of which had been discharged at him by the man he had so seriously attempted to injure.

He was not so impolitic, however, as to return to the place at which he had been lately staying, feeling confident that Burford having already betrayed him to Ravensford, would not fail to make him acquainted where he could find him; he therefore plunged into the wood, as we have before described, and continued to run forward with the most breathless speed, fearing every moment to be overtaken by his enraged foe, and to encounter his most deadly vengeance, being thoroughly acquainted with the desperate character of Ravensford, and his own insignificance. He did not stop until he had reached a deep copse, full two miles from the hall, where he now paused to take breath; and after finding that he had outstripped his pursuers, he cut across the country, and having at length arrived at a cottage, pretending to have been benighted, he requested shelter for

the night, which the persons who belonged to it were ready enough to grant, seeing that he was a gentleman, and expecting they should receive an ample reward.

We need not inform the reader what a state of apprehension the dastardly nobleman was in the whole of the night, lest his retreat should be discovered; so fearful indeed was he, that he found it absolutely impossible to sleep, and he passed the time till the morning in cursing the treachery of Adder, and the man whom he had entrusted with the letter, also his own folly in being made so consummate a dupe as he found he had been, at least, so he now firmly believed he had.

In the morning he presented the man with a liberal reward, and after giving him strict injunctions as to secresy, he gave him a note to fetch his portmanteau from the house where he had been lodging, and to meet him with it at the coach office, to which he hastened, and having taken a place in the coach to Liverpool, in the course of the day he was on his way thither, from whence he embarked for Ireland, and did not consider himself out of danger from the vengeance of Lord Ravensford until he arrived in Dublin. There he assumed a different name, and endeavoured to forget the chagrin and disappointment occasioned by his late expected amour. For the present we will leave the cowardly scion of nobility at the latter place, and return to Holly Hall. At this place all was still in the greatest misery. Three days had elapsed since the disappearance of Rosabelle, and no intelligence had been gained of her or Lord Ravensford. Montalbert, too, remained in the same deplorable condition as at first, and he was obliged to be kept under the utmost restraint. Mr. Goodman and Emily, with her husband, were almost constantly with the unfortunate gentleman, and paid him all the attention in their power; they were almost indefatigable in their exertion to discover Lady Ravensford, and to learn what had become of her husband.

As day after day had elapsed, and still Lord Ravensford did not return to the hall, neither could they gain any tidings of him, their fears for his safety increased, and the apprehensions of Mr. Goodman that he had laid violent hands on himself, began to gain fresh strength, and to be entertained also by Rattleton and his amiable wife. At the end of a week, however, Ravensford suddenly made his appearance, pale, careworn, harassed by fatigue, and heartbroken. The melancholy situation of Mr. Montalbert appeared to make little impression upon him, and his mind was evidently more strongly impressed than ever that Rosabelle had proved faithless to him. It was in vain that Mr. Goodman and his other friends expostulated with him, and made him acquainted with the statement of Burford, which showed plainly the connection of the two villains Saunter and Adder, at the same time that they had pointed out to him the cruelty and improbability of such a supposition; he turned a deaf ear to all they said, and condemned Rosabelle in the most unmeasured terms. That prejudice seemed so foreign to the ardent attachment he had professed towards her, that they could scarcely credit the evidences of their senses when they heard of it, and then only imagined that it was excited by his excessive emotion at her loss, so that at times he scarcely knew what he said or did, and would be the first to condemn himself for his conduct when reason had resumed her empire in his mind.

This idea was, however, not doomed to be realised, and after the elapse of several days, Lord Ravensford was in the same state of mind as at first.

"Fool that I was to believe her," he soliloquised, "idiot not to be able to penetrate beneath the mask of hypocrisy she assumed towards me. But who could ever have thought that one so fair, and apparently amiable, could naturally be so base? Oh, curses light upon——"

"Forbear, forbear, my lord," interrupted Mr. Goodman; "madness surely must have taken possession of your brain!—Oh, how bitterly might you soon have cause to repent that malediction you were just about to invoke upon her head. Would you,—could you curse her who has suffered so much for your sake?—Could you curse the mother of your child?"

"My child!" repeated Ravensford, with a bitter smile, and biting his lips; "oh, agony! But he is motherless now! He must never know his wretched guilty parent—he must be brought up rather to despise and hate her! But where is the miscreant who has wrought all this evil? Every where that I could think of I have searched for him, but still he eludes my vigilance! Could I but meet with him, and satiate my wrongs in his heart's blood, methinks I could be more content—content, that alas! will never more be mine!"

"Nay, Ravensford," remonstrated Rattleton, "this is a weakness of which I could never have believed thou wouldst have been guilty. Wait with patience."

"Patience!" reiterated Ravensford, "talk of patience to a man situated as I am? Wronged deeply, irreparably wronged! Psha, the word is mockery! But I will hasten from this spot for ever; it has become hateful to me! I am debased, degraded in the eyes of the world, and will hasten to some place where my name and my sorrows are unknown, and there in seclusion, pass the residue of those days which the guilt of a wretched woman has rendered miserable and hateful to me for ever!"

"But your child, my lord," interposed Emily, "the little Alfred, what will become of him? Is he to be left to the care and the mercy of strangers?"

"No," hastily returned Ravensford, clasping his son affectionately to his heart, "my poor boy shall not suffer for the guilt of his unhappy mother. He shall go with me; he shall be my only companion, and in contemplating him, I shall be reminded of my own guilt, my own folly, and Rosabelle's crime. Of the kindness I have ever experienced from you, Mr. Goodman, and all of you, I shall ever, believe me, entertain a grateful remembrance; but, in a short time, we part for ever."

"Not so," answered Mr. Goodman. "I trust that the time is not far distant when we shall have everything explained to our mutual satisfaction, and that we shall yet pass many, many happy days together."

"Never," said Ravensford, in accents of the deepest melancholy and despair, "it is all over now; my fate is sealed, and happiness and I are henceforward strangers. When I had obtained, as I thought, the forgiveness of Rosabelle, and had made her my wife. I did indulge in the fond hope that our sorrows were at an end, and that our future days would be one continual round of felicity and content; but the delusion has vanished; the mist is banished from before mine eyes, and all my future prospects are dark and dreary."

Finding that all their endeavours to persuade Ravensford out of his present melancholy train of thought were useless, they desisted, and Mr. Goodman and Emily leaving him in the society of Rattleton and Mr. Wilmot, who had just come in, hastened to the chamber of their patient, whom they found in much the same condition as when they had last seen him, at times raving in the most frantic manner, and at others calm, but equally unconscious of all around him.

It was enough to lacerate the most flinty heart to behold the change that a few short days had effected among the inmates of the hall—a change which seemed destined to last for ever. Notwithstanding the exertions to discover the retreat of Lady Ravensford were redoubled, they were unattended with success, and the mystery seemed fated to become impenetrable. All the arguments which Mr. Goodman and the others could make use of continued to be lost upon Lord Ravensford, and for a day or two after his return to the hall, he avoided their society as much as possible, and passed the principal portion of his time in his study, engaged in writing. Sometimes he would take his son upon his knee, gaze at him passionately for a few minutes, and then snatching him frantically to his heart, kiss his smiling lips with all the fondness of a parent for his first, his only son; then, suddenly, he would put him hastily down, and turn from him with a look of peculiar and disgusting expression.

Lord Ravensford had now returned to the hall about a week, when, one morning, he observed a letter on the table, addressed to him. He snatched it up in a state of agitation, which may be easily conceived, when he found it was in the well known hand-writing of Rosabelle. With frantic haste he tore it open, and had only time to read the first two or three lines, when he let it drop again from his hand, sunk into a chair, and, covering his face, gave utterance to a deep groan, while the convulsive agitation of his whole frame plainly showed the agony which the letter had caused in his mind. It was some time before he could sufficiently recover himself to resume the perusal of it; but, at length, he did, and found it contained the following words—

"My lord, my husband—for such I must still call you, although I would fain blot out the title from my memory for ever—when this reaches you, I shall be far away, and we may never meet again. I have sacrificed honour to affection, but, if I am to blame, surely you are doubly culpable in having first set me the example. Ravensford, had you been sincere in your first vows of attachment to the unfortunate Rosabelle, you would not now have to upbraid me for that which you will, doubtless, term unparalleled deception, and cold-hearted profligacy; but recollect, my lord, that you, in the first instance, abused my woman's ardent love, and taught me what deceit was, and, although you afterwards repented and made me your wife, nothing could erase from my recollection your first action of cruelty towards me, when, by your systematic, cold, and deliberate hypocrisy, you drove me from that roof which had been rendered odious by the destruction of my virtue. I thought I had forgotten it; I endeavoured to persuade myself that I had forgiven you; but, after a short time, I found that another held the possession of those warm affections which were at one time yours and yours solely. Yes, Ravensford, I confess, and however you may curse my memory, still will I candidly acknowledge the truth, another now reigns master of those affections which you originally possessed, and so brutally betrayed. To prove the strength of that passion, which you know not yet the value of, I have only to adduce the sacrifice I have made. My father, my child, I forfeit all; I resign everything for the man who, I am confident, will repay me with unbounded affection and fidelity. That you may be happy—that Nature will prompt you to watch over and protect our child; and that you will not desert that father whom I have deserted through you, is the sincere prayer of her you will probably henceforth curse.

                              "ROSABELLE."

"Wretched, lost, abandoned woman!" ex-claimed the maddened nobleman, when he had arrived at the conclusion of the letter. "Good God! can I have eyes to see this damning proof of female guilt? Can this be the paragon of virtue which first took my youthful fancy! This the fond devoted daughter—the adoring mother she seemed to be? By Heaven! it is impossible! There cannot be anything so utterly base in human nature! Yet, why should I doubt? Is there not here the most incontrovertible proof? Oh, what an idiot have I been to be so easily deceived! Curses—curses upon my own credulity! Her father, too; to abandon him! She surely must be mad—mad as the unhappy being whom she took so much pains to restore to reason, as it were, to make his sufferings, his agony still more exquisite! The child, also, of whom she appeared so fond, that she would have considered the sacrifice of her own life a mere trifle, to save him a moment's uneasiness, and to protect whom she pretended that it was she combated almost every danger and degradation! I must be dreaming; and yet here is the damning proof! I hold it in my hands: her own letter; her own handwriting; Oh, torture most supreme—oh, agony insupportable! I cannot—I will not endure it! I have been made the sport of fortune—the mockery of those on whom I placed my whole affections; the temple of happiness I had erected to myself, has been at one terrible blow, razed to the ground; what then have I to do with life? It is a burthen to me—its very name is hateful! The grave is the only hope I have of finding an oblivion to my wrongs, my heavy sorrows! Oh, Rosabelle, cruel, heartless woman, you are not only the murderer of your husband, but your parent, and your child! But no, I will not die! it would be a weakness to rush by my own act upon eternity! I will live for revenge! Yes, upon that detestable miscreant's head who has been the primary cause of this event,, this unexampled scene of infamy, shall my most terrible vengeance fall! I will search him out, and though he be at the most remote corner of the earth, I will not rest until I have discovered him, and dyed my hands in his blood. I feel the fires of hell burning my brain, and rushing with the destructive violence of the burning lava through my veins! I am no longer human! No, nature has lost its influence over my passions! Vengeance, terrible and deadly vengeance occupies my whole thoughts! But where is the wretch? Who is the monster that has wrought this scene of ruin and misery? Saunter! Yes, by hell! here is his very crest upon the seal! Unequalled depravity! Oh, lost—lost, Rosabelle, to be guilty of atrocious conduct such as this!"

As he thus spoke, he sunk into a chair with a groan of the most intense agony, and for a few moments, covering his face with his hands, he became completely lost to everything around him, in the soul-absorbing torture of his own thoughts.

He was suddenly aroused by some one tapping him on the shoulder, and starting up, he beheld Rattleton by his side.

"Why, Ravensford," exclaimed the latter, "what in the name of conscience is the matter with you? Here you sit as if you were stupified; and if it were not so early in the morning, I should have been inclined to think that you had partaken too freely of wine. Mr. Goodman, Emily, and Wilmot, are below, and expected your presence, until tired out of all sort of patience, they at length prevailed on me to come in search of you; and here I have been knocking at your room door for nearly a quarter of an hour—in fact, till I was completely exhausted with waiting, so I took French leave, as you see, and have entered *san ceremonie*, and—but what the deuce ails you, my dear fellow? Something must have happened, even beyond the mysterious and painful event, which at present afflicts us all, to cause this."

"Rattleton," exclaimed Ravensford, starting from his seat, and staring wildly upon him, "I am mad—I am a wretched being! loathing life, and ready to curse all my fellow creatures. Who shall we trust, if not those who bear all the semblance of purity and sincerity? I have been deceived basely, cruelly deceived; my honour trampled upon—my penitence and affection made a mockery of!"

"What mean you?" demanded Rattleton; "what new cause for sorrow have you?"

"This letter," replied Ravensford, placing it in Rattleton's hands, and gnashing his teeth, "take it, read it, and convince yourself that if there ever was a human being in the world more base than another, that one is her I have the misfortune to call my wife; but who hath discarded me—abandoned me, her father, and her offspring, to become the mistress of a villain, an idiot, one of the most hateful and the most despicable of the human race!"

Rattleton took the letter presented to him by his distracted friend in the utmost amazement, and having hastily ran over the contents, he threw it from him with an air of contempt and disgust, at the same time exclaiming—

"Oh, shameless villany! monstrous iniquity! And can you, Ravensford, believe this base forgery, which alone emanates from the same polluted source as the others that have caused so much misery in this family? Shame on you for your weakness, my lord! shame on you for your credulity! This written and dictated by Lady Rosabelle? By Heaven it is as false as falsehood can be. Believe me, this is the work of that monstrous miscreant, Adder, as

time, I have no doubt, will satisfactorily prove. Compose yourself, Ravensford, and listen to the dictates of reason. Come, come, dissipate the deplorable feelings which this circumstance has occasioned, and by redoubled energy seek to discover the authors of the infernal plot, and bring them to that punishment which their crimes so richly deserve. Nay, I will not listen to anything against what—"

"But you must listen, Rattleton," interrupted Lord Ravensford, "or otherwise forbear to take any part in the affair at all. I have my reasoning faculties as well as yourself, and I am confident that there is more truth in this than you would seem to believe. Another day shall not behold me beneath this detested roof! True, I will search out the miscreant who hath laid waste my peace of mind, and seek satisfaction in his heart's blood. That accomplished, and all that I wish to live for will be at an end, and——"

"Psha!" cried Rattleton, endeavouring to rally his lordship out of his present mood; "this would tell remarkably well in a play, but it is immensely absurd and bombastical in real life. Come, come, let us to the sitting-room, and hear what our best friend, Mr. Goodman, has to say upon the subject."

"Oh, Rosabelle, beauteous, but guilty woman," groaned forth Lord Ravensford, almost unconscious of what was taking place, and suffering himself to be led by his friend from the room, "what a desert have you made of that heart, which none other has ever really held possession of but yourself."

Mr. Goodman and his amiable daughter, who had not long before left the chamber of the unfortunate Mr. Montalbert, who they imagined seemed to be more calm than usual, were alarmed and surprised when they saw the alteration in the countenance and behaviour of Lord Ravensford, and both looked towards Rattleton for an explanation, not doubting, from the time he had been absent from them, that he was made acquainted with the cause. He understood them, and observed—

"The fact is, our bitter enemies, at least, the bitter enemies of Ravensford, and she who has been torn from us in so ambiguous a manner, not content with the misery they have already wrought, have again been at work. A letter which Lord Ravensford has in his possession, and which purports to have come from Lady Rosabelle, will sufficiently explain all; but before you peruse it, which I have no doubt his lordship will permit you to do do, I premise that you will pronounce it one of the most heartless and self-evident forgeries that could possibly be concocted."

"Oh, no, nothing can persuade me to that," returned Ravensford; "everything is too clear for me to entertain the least doubt. Too long have I suffered myself to be deceived, but now the mist is banished which before obscured my reason, and everything appears to me with redoubled strength. Here is the letter, Mr. Goodman, read it aloud; I care not who hears my degradation and Rosabelle's guilt."

Mr. Goodman took the letter, and contrary to the desire of Ravensford, read it to himself, and then, without betraying any other emotion than that of the utmost indignation, he handed it to his daughter. She hastily read the contents, and then, with an expression of countenance which evinced the sincerity of her observation, she exclaimed—

"This the writing of my Rosabelle! Oh, as soon would I believe that it was dictated by an angel from Heaven. Believe me, my lord, this is nothing more than a contrivance on the part of the villain or villains, in order to drown suspicion, and also to harrow up your feelings. Lady Ravensford must, indeed, be a wretch unworthy the name of a woman, could she have written a letter like this. Alas! poor unfortunate Rosabelle, how great are the wrongs that are heaped upon you."

"You are precisely of my opinion, Emily," observed her father, "and depend upon it, ere long an opportunity will be afforded of proving our words to be correct. My lord, really it is too bad of you, and very unjust, I must say, to be so ready to condemn your wife upon such evidence as this."

"What evidence can be stronger?" demanded his lordship, his face glowing with the power of his feelings; "is it not her own hand-writing? I must be an idiot not to believe it, then."

"I will not believe but that letter, as well as the others you have received, is a forgery; or if it be indeed written by Lady Ravensford, it has been extorted from her by intimidation."

Lord Ravensford smiled bitterly.

"No intimidation, no threats, should have persuaded her to write such a letter as this," said he; "she ought sooner have suffered death than have consented to do an act which she must be certain would murder her own reputation, my honour and happiness for ever."

"Well, my lord," said Rattleton, "pray banish such suspicions from your mind until you have some stronger proof of the guilt of your wife. Rather redouble your exertions to discover the scoundrel Saunter, when you will be able to get a full explanation and satisfaction for the injuries you have sustained by his guilty machinations. How did the letter come?"

"I know not who brought it," answered Ravensford; "I found it on the table in my dressing-room this morning. I will, however, immediately make inquiries among the servants."

They were summoned one by one accordingly, and questioned closely, but all protested that they knew nothing whatever about it, with the exception of the housemaid, who had cleared out the apartment, and who stated that she saw the letter on the floor, and finding that it was addressed to his lordship, she placed it on the table, where he had found it.

"It is very clear," remarked Lord Ravensford, when the servants examination was over, "it is very clear that this letter was left behind on the evening of her flight, by the wretched guilty woman! Oh, Rosabelle, surely, deeply as I formerly injured you, I have not merited such heartless treatment as this!"

"By Heaven!" cried Emily in the most emphatic manner, "is the very acme of cruelty and injustice to suppose Lady Ravensford such a guilty being! I will never believe it; nothing shall make me credit it, unless I receive a confession from her own lips."

"Some one of the servants has spoken falsely," said Mr. Goodman; "there has been some deeper scheme of villany in this than we even at first suspected; one of the domestics is in the plot, depend upon it."

Rattleton and Emily were of the same opinion, and Wilmot also expressed the same idea. Ravensford, however, made no reply, and soon afterwards excused himself to his friends, and left the hall. When he had gone, they conversed for some time upon the painful subject which had lately so fatally engrossed their principal attention, but they could only arrive at the same conclusion they had at first, namely, that Lady Ravensford was entirely innocent of the base conduct of which her husband suspected her; that she had been forced away by Lord Saunter, aided by Adder, who, out of a feeling of revenge against Ravensford, had become the myrmidon of the senseless lord, and that the letter which had that morning been discovered by his lordship, was either a forgery, or else Rosabelle had been made to write it through fear. They were, however, seriously alarmed at the effect it seemed likely to have upon Lord Ravensford, and they were fearful from the impetuosity of his disposition, that he might, in the frenzy of his passions, be urged to commit some fatal act. Nothing could exceed the misery which this lamentable circumstance had occasioned, and was still likely to cause; and when Mr. Goodman thought of the deplorable situation of Mr. Montalbert, and the utter hopelessness there was of his ever being again restored, his anguish could only be equalled by that of his daughter.

Mr. Montalbert remained precisely in the same state, and the medical gentlemen who attended him, pronounced it to be one of the most determined cases of insanity they had for some time seen. It was enough to wound the most callous heart to hear the poor old man one moment talking calmly as if addressing his daughter, whom he imagined to be in his presence, and the next pronouncing her dead, and wanting to hasten to her tomb, that he might strew flowers over the spot he believed to contain her remains. Then he would suddenly burst forth into exclamations of the utmost wildness; raving and cursing against those whom he thought were traducing her fame, until completely exhausted, he would fall back on his pillow, and sink into a temporary state of torpidity.

Had Emily been his own daughter, she could not have watched him with more anxious care and solicitude, and it was with difficulty she yielded to the remonstrances and entreaties of her husband and her father, to leave him for any reasonable time to obtain that rest nature required; fearful as they were that she would impair her constitution.

Lord Ravensford did not return to the hall until the evening, and his pallid countenance, and sunken eyes, plainly evinced the suffering he had been enduring. He exchanged but a few words with Mr. Goodman and the other persons present, and then excusing himself, retired to his chamber.

The next morning they were surprised he did not make his appearance, although it was getting very late, and becoming rather alarmed, they despatched a servant to his chamber to ascertain the reason of it. The valet quickly returned and informed them that his master was not there, but that a note was lying on his table, open, and which was couched in the following words :—

"My dear friends—for dear and faithful friends you have been to me—I know not whether you will condemn my conduct, but I have been prompted to it by feelings which I found it utterly impossible to resist. I have left the scene of my misery, to which I shall never return until I have satisfied myself of the innocence of my wife, and punished those who have been the cause of all my sorrows. Should my suspicions of her guilt prove too fatally true, you will probably never see or hear from me again. I have taken my son with me, of whom, I need not assure you, every care shall be taken. If it be ordained that we should meet no more, Heaven bless you all, and render you happier than the unfortunate writer of this letter. This is the sincere prayer of your faithful and loving friend,

"RAVENSFORD."

This letter, although it did not surprise, very much grieved them all, and Mr. Goodman found himself again placed in the care of the hall, and the affairs of Mr. Montalbert, until something should transpire which might bring the whole business to an issue. It appeared that Lord Ravenford must have departed from the hall at a very early hour, taking with him his own carriage, his valet, and one of the female servants. The nurse was terribly alarmed on waking in the morning, to find that the child had been removed from the cot in which he had reposed, and until the letter which Lord Ravensford had left behind was explained to her, she was in the most terrible state of excitement and apprehension. It was impossible to tell what direction his lordship had taken, and pursuit, if even they had been aware of whither he had gone, they knew would be useless, as he was, doubtless, far enough off by that time, and moreover would not be likely to be dissuaded from the resolution he had formed, if even they should succeed in overtaking him. They were, therefore, compelled to let the matter rest where it was, and could only entertain the most fervent wishes that Ravensford would succeed in discovering the retreat of Rosabelle, and fully substantiate her innocence, also that no harm might come to him, or his child, in his endeavours to accomplish that object. They also determined to be indefatigable in endeavouring to effect the same, and something seemed to strike them that their efforts would ultimately be crowned with success.

Although the receipt of the fatal letter had been, no doubt, the cause of deciding the resolution of Lord Ravensford, they had every reason to believe that he had contemplated the step he had taken several days previously, as he had so well arranged his affairs, and this it would have been impossible to have done in a few hours; and thus they had no doubt he would strictly adhere to what he had stated in his letter: namely,—that if he did not succeed in discovering his wife, and establishing her innocence, they would not again behold him, as he would, in all probability, leave the country, and settle for the remainder of his days in a foreign land.

CHAPTER XVIII.

THE SMUGGLER'S HAUNT.—WOMAN'S LOVE.

LANGUAGE must fail to do adequate justice to the emotion of Rosabelle when she regained her senses, and found herself a prisoner in a large but very gloomy apartment, underneath the same roof as the murderer Gordon, whose forbidding features she had recognised immediately on his opening the door. Her horror was so great, that she was in danger of relapsing immediately into insensibility, had it not been for the timely application of some vinegar to her temples by an old woman whom she found in attendance upon her, but whose appearance was anything but inviting. In fact, at first sight, her real sex might be a matter of great doubt to the spectator, for her features were very masculine, her head was surmounted with an old tarpaulin hat, and her body was encased in an old immense pilot coat. Rosabelle gazed at this revolting looking being for a few moments with feelings of the utmost timidity, and then averted her head, and sunk into tears. Inconceivable was the agony she endured, and how many dreadful causes had she for such misery! Here she was in the retreat of smugglers and murderers, and securely in the power of a villain whose designs she could not for a moment doubt, and which she would have no power to prevent his accomplishing, as she had not a friend nigh who would step forward to protect her; and it could be no single arm which could defend her from the power of so many miscreants. The scene too, of misery, which was doubtless presented at that home from which she had been so shamefully torn— her distracted father—the horror, the doubts, the fears, and even suspicions which her husband was most likely enduring, all rushed in rapid succession upon her brain, and filled her with grief too powerful for description.

From these reflections she was suddenly aroused by the old woman, who seeing her recover, pointed to some refreshments on the table, and telling her in a surly tone that she might eat if she thought proper, she abruptly quitted the room. Our heroine felt relieved by her exit, for she could not contemplate that frightful specimen of the 'fair sex,' without a sensation of the greatest dread and repugnance.

The room in which our heroine found herself, seemed to have been used for a store-room, as well as a sleeping apartment, for there were several large chests piled one upon another,— empty casks, bales of goods, and other articles (which showed the contraband dealings of the men who frequented the house,) against the walls of the chamber. She observed, however, a door which was not quite closed on the left hand side of the room, and, advancing towards it, she threw the door back on its hinges, and found it to be an ante-room, smaller than the other, but much more comfortable and compact. She looked forth from the casement in this room, but the prospect beyond was as gloomy as could well be imagined, and was calculated alone to increase the misery which inhabited her bosom. She sat herself down in a chair, and again gave herself up entirely to the anguish of her thoughts. She recalled to her memory in the most vivid colours that awful night, when she had watched the wretch Gordon and his companion bury the body of their murdered victim in the old barn, or out-house; and as she did so, and reflected that she was at the mercy of one of the wretches, the horror which seized upon her was almost insupportable. What had she to expect from such a monster and those men who set all laws at defiance? And how base a villain must Adder be, who could associate with, and employ such men in his nefarious transactions. At the bare idea of Adder, Rosabelle felt a sensation of the most irrepressible disgust and indignation, and

she could scarcely believe that he could have had the presumption to have been guilty of her abduction to gratify his own purposes, but that he was merely the agent of Lord Saunter, which the letters she had seen from the latter, the more confirmed her in. But, however, as it was her prospects were equally fearful. So far distant as she was too from her home, the case became still more terrible and hopeless, and the chance of her husband or any of her friends discovering the place where she was confined, almost impossible. But to give way entirely to despair, under her present circumstances, could do no good, and might, on the contrary, effect greater harm; she, therefore, by a most powerful effort, so far vanquished her feelings, so as to become comparatively calm, and to form a resolution, to endeavour to meet the trials she would doubtless be exposed to, with that firmness and determination which could alone enable her to support them, and to resist the designs of her persecutor.

It was night, and yet she could hear from the loud and frequent bursts of laughter that proceeded from below, that the men had not separated, but seemed to be carousing merrily. Their rude mirth filled her with alarm, for she knew not what excesses such ruffians would hesitate to commit, especially when acting under the influence of liquor; indeed what could she expect from such a miscreant as Gordon? Again the dreadful circumstances she had encountered on that night when she was returning penitent to that home she had abandoned, rushed upon her memory, and in imagination, she endured a repetition of all the horrors she had at that time encountered. Once more she heard the unnatural expressions of the assassins; she saw them preparing the rude grave for the reception of the mangled remains of their murdered victim;—she heard them exult over the sanguinary crime they had committed; she again beheld the ghastly countenance and blood-clotted gray hair of the poor old man, as they turned the corpse out of the sack, and deposited it in the grave; then the subsequent terrors she had that night undergone, darted upon her recollection; her meeting with her father, and the scene which followed, and which could never be erased from her memory! Alas!— perhaps he was even now reduced to the same deplorable situation;—his reason might again be wrecked, and all hopes of being restored a second time, would be at an end. But she dared not dwell on the latter probability, or her senses would have fled. As it was, difficult was the task to keep up anything like a feeling of fortitude; and it was astonishing that she could so far conquer her tears and emotions as to act with the firmness she did.

One circumstance she greatly reproached herself for, and that was for not having made known to the proper authorities the awful scene she had been a spectator of in the *Lover's Resting Place*, which would, in all probability, have been the means of bringing the guilty wretches to justice and punishment. But notwithstanding the peculir nature of the event, in the constant state of agony in which her mind had been placed by the circumstances which followed the discovery of her father, and the care which continually occupied her thoughts, she had entirely forgotten it, and thus the assassins were suffered to escape, when they might have been apprehended and suffered the penalty of their crime in so miraculous a manner. It seemed as if it were a judgment upon her for having neglected to perform this duty, which had placed her in the power of one of the murderers, and this occasioned her more uneasiness than anything else. It also convinced her of the consummate villany of Adder, who was the employer, and, doubtless, the associate of such wretches. From such an abandoned man, she could not expect any forbearance.

At length the voices of the men ceased, and Rosabelle concluded that they had separated. She returned to the chamber, and then examined the door to see whether there was any fastening on the inside, so that she could prevent the entrance of any one, unless she pleased; and she was more satisfied and easy when she

LADY RAVENSFORD IN THE SMUGGLERS RETREAT.

found to her relief that she could both bolt and lock it.

She trimmed the lamp, and the fire burning briskly in the grate, the room had a less cheerless and desolate appearance than it had at first. Rosabelle felt not the least inclined for sleep, and, in fact, she dreaded to seek repose notwithstanding she felt that she was secure from the intrusion of any one, and drawing her chair closer to the fire, she resolved to sit up till the morning. Suddenly the manuscript history of her life, which had been given to her by Phœbe, recurred to her, and having safely preserved it, she determined to try to divert her thoughts from the painful subjects by which they had hitherto been occupied in a perusal of them. In this narrative she felt an unusual interest. Phœbe's observations convinced her that Lord Ravensford was in some way connected with it, and she therefore turned to it with the utmost eagerness. It was written in an elegant hand, and plainly showed in every sentence that Phœbe possessed a mind of superior order, and far above that station of life in which it appeared she had been born. As our heroine proceeded, she became most forcibly struck with the similarity of the story with her own; and in some of the passages, she could almost have sworn she was the original for whom the heroine was drawn. We will give the narrative in Phœbe's own words.

"Alas! who that has experienced the joys of a happy home, the fond endearments of the most affectionate parents—a father's fond caress, a mother's kiss and constant care and attention, could be tempted to abandon them? The writer of this has been that unhappy one! She, under some wild delusion, some unaccountable infatuation, listened to the persuasions of a villain, and deserted that home and those parents from which she ever derived the most unexampled bliss, brought herself to the very verge of ruin and destruction, and nearly broke the hearts of those to whom she owed her being. Deeply, however, has she since repented of that indiscretion, and been unceasingly grateful to the mercy of an allwise Providence, which recalled her to reason ere it was too late, and snatched her from that gulph, upon the brink of which she had long been tottering.

"Wealth,—rank! how great is your influence upon the inexperienced mind, the glittering baubles that too often lead the most virtuous astray, and bring them to misery, self-reproach, and despair. Happier, by far happier, is the peasant with a contented mind, in his lowly state, than the occupier of a palace; and often how much reason have those whom fortune hath placed so far above him, cause to envy him his lot. Would that I could always have thought thus, then I should never have erred, and the happiness of my parents would never have been disturbed. But I am doing myself an injustice; surely it was not pride, it was not ambition that caused me to commit myself; no, it was love, love for an object whom reason should have told me could never be mine. But I am wandering from my subject.

"My father was a farmer, in comfortable circumstances, which he gained by his own industry and exemplary conduct. I will not attempt to discribe him, for I should fail to do justice to his merits, eloquent, doubtless, as my affection for him would make me. Let it suffice that he was a man of superior education, having formerly moved in a different station of life, from which he had been driven by a long series of misfortunes, and his numerous virtues even by far exceeded his accomplishments. My mother was a complete counterpart of her husband, and never were two beings better formed to meet together. I was their only daughter, myself and a brother being the only offsprings they ever had. Every indulgence that child could wish or parent could think of, was bestowed upon me;—my every thought seemed to be studied by them, and there was not a single happiness which they had it in

their power to grant, which they seemed to think too great for me. Eternal blessings upon their memory! And if their bright spirits are permitted to look down upon this earth, and read the thoughts of its creatures, they will see with what ardent affection do I cherish their remembrance.

"Our home was the happiest in the neighbourhood, and it was the envy and admiration of all who knew it. Again when I think upon it, and how different my situation is now, I cannot help giving vent to my feelings; indeed, it is to indulge them that I have sat down to record the events of my life, although, in all probability, no other eyes but mine may ever behold it. Home, sweet home: there cannot be a theme upon which the mind of sensibility pauses with more peculiar delight than this. It is the cradle of our infancy and our age. Called from the house of our fathers to a far distant scene, it surprises us in the midst of enjoyment; and if sorrow and adversity cross our path, it comes upon us with double force, inspiring consolation and hope,—

"And as a hare whom hounds and horns pursue,
Pants to the place from whence at first he flew,
I still had hopes, my long vexations past,
Here to return and die at home at last."

"This feeling more particularly belongs to those who have emerged from the sequestered stillness of rural life, where refinement has not shed its influence, and the remembrance of the past is not wholly swallowed up in anticipation of the future:—

"Home's home, however homely, wisdom says,
And certain is the fact, though course the phrase."

"The seaman, amidst storm and tempest, in fair weather and foul, thinks of his native villige; the soldier that fights for kings; the merchant that dives for gain, are, alternately, stung with the thoughts of home; while the wanderer, that has followed pleasure, but found it a shade—that has bartered humble content for splendid misery, thinks of home with a self-accusing regret, that renders even a return to its enjoyments full of bitterness and remorse. Sensibly do I feel the force of these observations, and, therefore, have I digressed from my simple narrative for the purpose of indulging in them.

"I will pass over the early years of my life, which were passed in almost uninterrupted happiness, and come at once to that unfortunate circumstance which was the cause of my indiscretion, and occasioned me all that anguish I so severely felt afterwards.

"An accident brought Captain Beresford, (now Lord Ravensford) and his friend, the Earl Rosseville, to our house, from which the latter was unable to be removed for several weeks. Alas! it was a fatal day to me; the earl was young, handsome, and insinuating, and the very first moment I beheld him, my heart felt a sensation it had never before experienced, and too soon I was compelled to acknowledge to myself, that I had become deeply enamoured of him. Fatal attachment! Had I not been unpardonably thoughtless, I must surely at once have seen the folly, the danger, the hopelessness of indulging or encouraging a passion for one so far above me, and who would, probably, not feel for me a mutual sentiment, and have stifled it in its infancy. But it was not to be; I was to be taught reason only by dear-bought experience. At length, the earl being restored to convalescence, quitted our house, but I felt convinced it was with reluctance, and I noticed the looks he fixed upon me, with a sentiment of mingled delight and astonishment. The glances he bestowed on me were those of admiration—of love! How my heart bounded at this idea, I need not tell; but, alas! it should have been its greatest cause of anguish, and my pleasure was greatly increased when I learned that Rosseville, having expressed his delight at the neighbourhood, had taken up his abode in it for a short time; but Captain Beresford had made his departure some days previous to another part of the country. I frequently saw the earl, and he seemed anxious to say something to me, but had not an opportunity, as I was mostly in the presence of my parents; but I needed no interpretation of his thoughts; my own sentiments fully elucidated them, and the warmth of the glances he bestowed upon me. If it required anything to strengthen the affection with which Rosseville had inspired me, it was the amiable character he soon acquired in the neighbourhood, his chief pleasure appearing to be the performing of acts of benevolence and philanthropy, and the blessings of the poor were amply lavished upon him. Rash, thoughtless, girl that I was, I should have made my parents acquainted with the real state of my feelings, and sought their advice upon the subject; but, for the first time in my life, I was anxious to conceal my thoughts from them, and continued to encourage those passions which reason ought to have convinced me could never be requited by the object who had inspired them.

"It was about a month after the Earl Rosseville had quitted our house, that I arose rather earlier one morning than was my usual custom, induced by the fineness of the weather. I descended from my chamber, and entered the garden, which was very beautifully and tastefully arranged, and in which, as well as my father and mother, I took much pleasure. My whole attention, however, was particularly devoted to a rose tree, which I had myself planted, and I had frequently heard the earl express his admiration of it while he was remaining at our house. Could I but get him by any means to receive one how happy should I have been. This day I had resolved to make my father and mother a little present of some of these roses, which I knew they would receive with more delight by far than the most costly gift, coming as they did from me.

"'How sweetly my roses have opened,' I soliliquised; "they seem to know that they are destined to be the gifts of affection, and to smile with the delight I shall feel in bestowing them on those I love so dearly. So this for father, and this for mother.'

"I plucked two of the most beautiful, and had scarcely done so, when my father entered from the house, and greeted me with his usual affection.

"'Ah, father,' I exclaimed, 'I have such a gift for you and my dear mother.'

"'Indeed, my child,' returned my father, smiling fondly upon me.

"'Yes,' replied I, placing one of the roses which I had plucked in his hand; 'there,—is there a painting in any mansion in the country half so beautiful? What a name a painter would get who could only give a perfect copy of these roses, and, you see, I give you the originals for nothing.'

"'Dear girl, dear girl!" ejaculated my father, his eyes glittering with fondness.

"'And yet I do not give them to you for nothing, my dear father,' I added; 'for you give me in exchange those sweet smiles of affection, which are to me of more value than anything else in the world.'

"'Darling child,' cried my father, raising his hands above his head, and invoking a blessing upon me; 'the look of affection will always reward innocence.'

"After having thus spoken, he was about to depart, when I ran towards him, saying—

"'What! leave us so soon, my dear father? Prithee stay till the air grows cooler.'

"'My child,' answered my affectionate parent, 'these locks have withered in the hot sun. I have passed many years in toiling for others, and have never shrunk from its beam; and now, when it is partly for my darling girl I toil, the balm and comfort of my life, I cannot feel fatigue, and every drop that rolls down my weather-beaten forehead in such a cause, makes my old heart the lighter.'

"I threw myself once more into his arms, and he embraced me fervently, after which he hastened away. As soon as he had gone, I was joined by my mother, who, hearing my voice in the garden, had come to summon me to the morning repast.

"'So, my dear,' she remarked, 'old Mrs. Weston is likely to be better off than ever; instead of being ruined by the burning of her cottage, the Earl Rosseville is going to rebuild it at his own expense, and has made her a handsome present into the bargain.'

"At the mention of the earl's name, I blushed, and a sensation filled my bosom which no other name could have excited.

"'Indeed, my mother,' I observed, in reply to what she had stated; 'bless his kind heart! The whole village rings with his charities; and, whenever I see him, my heart beats so.'

"'Ah, child,' said my mother, 'it is a very bad sign when a young girl's heart beats at the sight of a good-looking young man. When that happens, she ought at once to get out of his way.'

"I felt uncommonly confused, and know I must have blushed deeply.

"'Nay, my dear mother,' at length I answered, 'to me a warning is superfluous; your daughter's affections live in her home. Is it possible she can find elsewhere what home will yield her?'

"As I afterwards learned, the earl and one of his attendants had watched the departure of my father, and at this moment the former descended from the bridge, and approached towards us. I started at his presence, and was much confused, especially as we had just before been talking about him; but, putting on one of his most affable smiles, he said:—

"'Pray don't rise. Don't let me disconcert you. Is Mr. Heywood within?'

"'He is but this moment gone into the fields, my lord,' answered my mother.

"'Indeed,' said the earl, with apparent disappointment, 'that is peculiarly unfortunate, for I have just now urgent occasion to speak with him.'

"'Urgent occasion,' repeated my mother, aside to me; 'what can it be? My lord, then I'll hasten after him; pray have the goodness to wait one moment.'

"'Nay,' said Rosseville, 'I am ashamed to give you the trouble; but being of importance——'

"'I'll make the best speed, and bring him to you immediately,' returned my mother, hastening away, and leaving me and the earl alone.

"Scarcely had my mother disappeared, when the earl, fixing upon me a look in which admiration and delight were blended, took my hand, and, in a voice of rapture, exclaimed:—

"'Phœbe, beauteous Phœbe! behold before you one who loves you to distraction.'

"Although my own feelings and observations had prepared me for this scene, I was so flurried and confused, that I could scarcely contain myself. My bosom heaved—my heart palpitated. Crimson blushes, I am certain, mantled in my cheeks; but yet was I unable to withdraw my hand from his hold, which he pressed vehemently to his lips, and then continued:—

"'Lovely Phœbe, pardon this abruptness; often have I longed for this opportunity, but in vain; never before have I had it in my power to declare how the first glance of that enchanting face——'

"'Oh my lord,' I faltered out, in tremulous accents, 'I must not listen to this—leave me, I beseech you.'

"'Leave you, angelic creature!' replied the earl, emphatically, and still retaining his hold of my hand; 'leave you! oh, there is madness in the bare thought! I cannot, I will not quit your presence till you have uttered some word of consolation—blessed me with some ray of hope!'

"I scarcely knew how to answer!—I could not behold the object of my love, kneeling at my feet, and soliciting my sanction to his vows, unmoved; the cold dictates of prudence would have told me instantly to give him a decisive answer, and to force myself from his presence, but my heart pleaded against its rigid rules. The earl noticed my emotion, and doubtless saw his triumph, for he continued in more fervent and emboldened terms.

"'But surely the gentle Phœbe cannot be so cruel as to bid one who is her devoted slave, despair? No—no;—she will impart to him a hope—'

"'Hope, my lord,' I interrupted, recollecting myself, and the remembrance of my mother's words, and my own assurance, rushing upon my mind; 'I am a poor girl, the daughter of a humble farmer, and have no right to listen to a man like you. Even were I no longer the mistress of my heart, I trust I am not yet so lost to principle, my lord, as to avow it where it might not be confessed with honour.'

"The earl arose from his knee, relinquished my hand, and walked away a few paces in much apparent agitation; then suddenly returning, he said in tones of mingled regret and reproach:—

"'Do you deem me capable of deception? Phœbe, it is to make you my wife, to give you rank and title, that I came. One word of yours can give splendour to the home you love, and make the heart that lives but in your kindness, happy!'

"As he thus spoke, his manner became more energetic, and I felt my heart gradually yielding!—I trembled, and longed, yet dreaded the return of my parents; while the earl seeing the hesitation of my manner urged his suit with redoubled determination.

"'Phœbe,' he exclaimed, 'there is not a moment to be lost! Can you doubt the sincerity of my protestations? Think you that I could be the base villain to deceive one in whom my very soul, my existence is wrapped up? Say but the blissful word; tell me that you will become my bride, the empress of my heart and fortune; — give me this sweet assurance, and——'

"'Oh, my lord,' I interrupted, in a state of confusion and agitation I will not attempt to describe, 'spare me, I implore you!—I—I——' and unable to finish the sentence, I turned away my head, and burst into tears. The earl again seized my hand rapturously, and encouraged by the emotion I evinced, his countenance became lighted up with an expression of delight, as he exclaimed:—

"'Oh, blessed moment! those tears convince me that I am not hated by her who hath taken possession of my whole affections. Blissful assurance! Ere another morn, my Phœbe, my loved, my adored Phœbe, will be my bride!—But time presses; we must away from this spot instantly.'

"And the earl attempted to place his arm around my waist, but surprised at his words and demeanour, I recoiled from him, and looking upon him with astonishment, I demanded:—

"'My lord, what mean you?—Leave this place?—Why, wherefore?'

"'Nay, my dearest Phœbe,' returned Rosserville, 'be not surprised or alarmed; my proposals are honourable; reasons of rank require that we retire to my villa in Buckinghamshire; our marriage must be secret and immediate, or it may be prevented. Once mine, I will lead you back in triumph.'

"'What,' I exclaimed, 'leave this place in doubt, in misery?'

"'Banish these childish scruples,' said the earl; 'your parents will applaud you when they know the truth. Come to the lover who adores you! Come to the altar which will pour forth blessings on those you love so tenderly! Come, Phœbe, come!'

"As the earl thus impatiently urged his suit, he attempted to lead me towards the bridge;—I felt my resolution getting weaker—I trembled,—and could offer but a faint resistance.

"'Urge me no more, my lord,' I cried, endeavouring to disengage myself from him;—'let me go—I dare not listen to you—farewell!'

"'Still inflexible,' ejaculated the earl, turning away from me, with a look of the most inexpressible anguish and despair; 'then is my doom sealed. I cannot, will not live without you, and thus I——'

"While he was thus speaking, he snatched a pistol from his bosom, and presented it towards his head! With a wild shriek of terror, I rushed into his arms, and arrested his fatal purpose. Some spell, some horrid spell came over me. I remember the last cloud of smoke curling over our ancient trees.—I—I've no farther recollection. When my senses were restored, and reason was permitted again to resume its sway, I found myself an inmate of the earl's villa, and far away from that home I had rendered wretched. Oh, God, how dreadful,

how agonizing were the thoughts that first crossed my brain! I upbraided myself for a wretch unfit to live—as one who had disgraced herself and destroyed the peace of the most affectionate of parents for ever; and whichever way I turned, a curse seemed to pursue me.

"Rosseville tried all that his eloquence could effect to console me; renewed his most tender asseverations, and repeated his promise to make me his bride. Strange infatuation!—I believed him;—I became tranquil—and if the thoughts of my parents and the home I had abandoned ever returned to my memory, they were quickly banished by the gentle soothings and fond protestations of the earl. Day after day passed away, and still Rosseville promised, but failed to keep his word. My humble dress was now exchanged for fashionable finery, and Rosseville visited me every day, repeating each time with greater energy the vows of love with which he had seduced me from my home. Every luxury—every enjoyment that could be wished was at my command; but could they yield me real happiness? Oh, no! The splendour I was now placed in, was purchased with agony; and my own feelings constantly reproached me for that offence of which I had been guilty. Some fated spell must have been upon me, or I must have soon been convinced that St. Clair was not sincere in his promises, or he would not day after day evade the fulfilment of them. But it was my fate dearly to purchase experience of my own weakness and of the earl's treachery. Several weeks elapsed in this manner, and still did the earl neglect to fufil the promise he had made me, while, at the same time, the ardour of his passion seemed to increase, and the excuses he made for delaying our nuptials, were so plausible, that I was deceived by them. Alas! the woman whose heart has become sincerely attached to any particular object, is made an easy dupe! Let me pass hastily over the time, until the anniversary of the day of my birth, at once the height of my misery, and the means of restoring me to reason and to peace. On that occasion, Rosseville had made the most extensive preparations, for celebrating it in the most spirited manner. Numerous guests were invited to the villa, and the peasants in the neighbourhood were also permitted to share in the rejoicings. Among other things, for my special entertainment, the earl had engaged a troop of itinerant players, who were in the neighbourhood, to perform a play in the grounds of the villa, which deserves particular mention, as it it was the means of recalling me to reason, and saving me from that gulph of destruction, upon the brink of which I stood.

"Seldom had I felt so melancholy as I did on that occasion; home and all its tranquil pleasures, came vividly to my recollection, and my heart was heavy. There was a song which was a great favourite in the village where I was born, and which described the pleasures of home in simple yet forcible language; and as it now came fresh upon my recollection, I could not help repeating the words. When I had concluded, I perceived that Celia, my waiting-maid, had entered the room, and had apparently been listening with much attention and admiration to me.

"'Bless me, Miss,' said the loquacious girl, "what a pretty song that was, and how prettily you sang it. Where might you have learnt it, Miss, if I might make so bold?'

"'Where I learnt other lessons I ought never to have forgotten,' replied I, with a deep sigh; 'it is the song of my native village—the hymn of the lowly heart which dwells upon every lip there, and like a spell-word, brings back to its home affection which e'er has been betrayed to wander from it. It is the first music heard by infancy in its cradle; and the villagers, blending it with their earliest and tenderest recollections, never cease to feel its magic, till they cease to live.'

"'How natural that is,' returned Celia; 'just like my nurse used to nurse me to sleep with a song, which I have never heard since without nodding.'

"'Has the earl been inquiring for me, Celia?' I asked.

"'He has been here this morning, and has only just gone,' replied the maid; 'but only see what lovely things one has left you, miss!'"

"And Celia displayed a costly dress, and several articles of jewellery, of which I expressed my admiration. But suddenly, gloomy thoughts again came over me, and while tears trembled in my eyes, I ejaculated:—

"'But can these baubles make me happy? Ah, never! The heart that's ill at ease is made more wretched by the splendour which laughs in awful mockery around its dreariness.'

"The presence of Clara embarrassed me; I wished to indulge in melancholy thought alone, but she seemed determined not to take my hints for her to leave me, and at last I only got rid of her by requesting that she would fetch me a book I had been reading the day previously. When she had left the room, with much agitation, I unlocked my cabinet, and took out the plain village dress I had worn when I quitted my my home. The sight of this tortured my brain, and while deep sobs of anguish almost choked my voice, I thus soliloquised:—

"'And shall I remain here, dazzled and betrayed by the splendour with which I am surrounded? Shall I still rack my parents hearts, and—I—will escape! Escape! no, no—I can brave the shocks of fate, but not a father's eye: to expose myself to his wrath—No, no! my heart's not strong enough for that.'

"I was interrupted by the return of Celia with the book, who, on seeing the village dress in the chaise, expressed the utmost astonishment.

"'Lor' bless me, Miss!' ejaculated the girl, 'what's this dress doing here?—Whoever could have put such trumpery in the way?'

"As she spoke, she snatched it up, and was going to throw it aside when I sprang forward emphatically, and hastily took it from her.

"'Give it back!' I cried, 'that humble dress was mine;—I cast it off—the splendour that has replaced it, is the source of the most bitter misery!—Oh, my forsaken parents;—Come hither, Celia;—I have no one here of my own sex to talk to—no one to listen to my sorrows. I——'

"'Pray speak freely to me, Miss,' observed Celia; 'though humble, you'll not find me insincere.'

"'Celia,' I remarked, 'if you knew what a home, what parents I had left, you'd pity me.'

"'I do pity you, Miss,' replied Celia, 'indeed I do. Better days will come; you'll be as happy as when you left them.'

"I sighed, and shook my head with a look of despair, and then detailed to Celia the particulars of my flight from home, and the promises which the earl had made, but had hitherto failed to keep his word.

"'Be of good cheer, Miss, I pray,' said Celia; 'he will keep it, depend upon it.'

"Celia spoke this with such a tone of confidence, that it forcibly struck me, and eagerly I exclaimed:—

"'Will he, Celia?—now don't trifle with me—tell me the worst at once!—Better is present death, than hope deferred; still lingering on, still doomed to be deceived.'

"'My dearest young mistress,' returned Celia, 'there is plenty of time before you think of dying; and, as a proof that the earl don't mean to deceive you, look here.'

"And with these words, Celia presented me with a miniature of the earl, elegantly set round with diamonds, at the same time adding:—

"'On a chamber-maid's penetration, this is nothing more nor less than an earnest of the original.'

"I took the miniature with transport, and my eyes became rivitted upon it with admiration. Nothing could be more true than the delineation.

"'Ah!' I said, 'precious to the fond one, is the semblance of the object held most dear. 'Tis the enchanter's wand, which gathers around it in a magic circle, sweet recollections and feelings which make memory a paradise! No, no!—treachery could never dwell in such a face—I'll trust him still. He cannot mean me false.'

"'Shall I put this away, miss?" asked

Celia, pointing to the village dress; 'I am sure the earl would be hurt to see it here.'

"'Yes, take it away, Celia,' I replied, 'I would not, for the world, do anything to make him uneasy.'

"Celia immediately obeyed, and she had not been gone many minutes, when St. Clair entered the room, and advanced joyful to meet me.

"'Ah, sir,' I ejaculated, 'why overwhelm me with gifts like these?—My humble habits shrink from such magnificence! This (pointing to the miniature,) is the only one I prize, the herald of a gift to follow, which shall restore me to my friends, my self-esteem;—my poor heart-broken parents.'

"The earl turned away his head, doubtless to conceal the embarrassment which my words occasioned him, and then, in a tone which showed that he wished to change the subject, said:—

"'This is your birth-day, Phœbe.'

"That word tore my wounds open! Oh! what a joyous day was it when I was at home! The farm seemed to be one smile of joy;— the sacred halo of a parent's blessing descended on me with the morning sun; and even my birds, my flowers, my young companions, all seemed to have a livelier look, and lift their heads rejoicing. These thoughts were too painful for my feelings, and I burst into a flood of tears."

Here Rosabelle was compelled to lay down the manuscript for a short time, to give vent to the emotions which the picture thus drawn, and which corresponded so well with her own sentiments and circumstances, gave rise to in her bosom. The similarity of Phœbe's adventures with her own, was most remarkable, and the circumstances recalled so forcibly to her memory what she had already undergone, and was most likely yet fated to endure, that she was unable to restrain her tears.

"Alas! my unfortunate parent, my wretched husband!—what intense agony are you doubtless now exposed to!" she ejaculated; and then she wrung her hands, and was altogether in such a state of affliction, that she was unable to resume Phœbe's narrative for several minutes. At length, she once more resumed as follows:—

"'Nay, Phœbe,' observed the earl, "cheer thee, love!—banish that woe; discard that dread; rely upon my promise.'

"'Heaven's smile repay that word,' I exclaimed fervently; 'the weight which pressed me to the earth is removed, and all around me breathes ecstasy.'

"'It delights me to hear thee say so, my dearest Phœbe,' replied the earl; 'go, sweetest, and put on your richest dress to celebrate this joyous day.'

"'That day,' I added, with enthusiasm, 'that day which gives me back to honour. It shall be done, my lord.'

"The earl kissed me affectionately, and left the room; and once more a cheering hope brought consolation to my-heart, and assured me of future happiness and joy. Alas! how soon was I to be awakened to the greatest agony! To more misery than I had ever before experienced.

"The festivities of the day passed off most brilliantly until the play commenced. The gardens in which it took place were brilliantly illuminated, and the temporary theatre was formed among the trees in the back. Just as the performances were about to commence, a servant entered and delivered to the earl a letter, upon perusing the contents of which, he excused himself to me and the numerous guests, it being necessary that he should be absent for a short time; but he begged that his absence might not interrupt their pleasure, as the village actors would amuse them with their humble efforts; and ere they had ended, he would return.

"When the earl had gone, I beckoned Celia over to me, and the play immediately commenced; but what were my feelings of intense agony as it proceeded, when I perceived that the plot, and every incident of the piece, so corresponded with my own circumstances, that it seemed as if they had actually chosen me to sketch the heroine from. A nobleman wooed a peasant girl; he vowed the most unbounded affection for her;—promised her marriage, if she would elope with him; she was persuaded; —she sunk senseless in his arms, and was conveyed away.

"During the time the piece was being played, my anguish was insupportable, and I was so worked upon by the power of each scene, that I could scarcely persuade myself but that it was reality.

"'Fatal resemblance,' I ejaculated, at the passage where the seducer bears his victim away; 'has there before been such another deluded being?'

"'Be calm, dear mistress, be calm,' said Celia, 'it is only a play.'

"But my thoughts were too intently fixed upon the scene which followed, to pay any particular attention to her words. The parents of the betrayed one, as represented in the piece, upon hearing the screams of their daughter, rushed on to the stage, the father demanding of his wife the meaning of the alarm, and the cause of the cries he had heard. The mother, looking round, and finding that her daughter was not there, exclaimed:—

"'My child;—my child!—A mere pretence —our darling—lost—escaped! Ah! there! behold the seducer bearing her away!'

"'Ah!' cried the father, frantically, 'what, fled? given up to shame?—Oh, art beyond belief! Have all your fond professions come to this? Oh, well-laid plan!—Lost! lost! —Oh, viper!—hypocrite!—I tear you from my bosom!—I sweep you from the home you have disgraced!—A father's curse——'

" With a wild shriek, as the actor gave utterance to these words, I rushed upon the stage, and falling at his feet, I vociferated, in tones that made the place re-echo again:—

"Hold! hold!—curse her not! She is not lost! She is innocent!'

" At this moment the earl entered, and the whole of the spectators seemed petrified to the spot with astonishment.

" ' Ah!' cried Rosseville, 'what do I see? —What is the meaning of this?'

" Celia raised me from the posture which I had assumed, and by the commands of the earl, whose confusion and chagrin were evident, she led me to my own chamber, while the guests quickly dispersed, and the entertainments abruptly ceased.

" After I had been taken to my own apartment for a few minutes, by the kind attention of Celia, I recovered myself, and addressing myself to her, said:—

" ' Thanks! thanks! a thousand thanks!— I grieve to have troubled you thus—'tis over now; 'tis nothing.'

" ' The earl, Miss! the earl!' exclaimed Celia, and the next moment Rosseville stood before me. There was an expression of sternness upon his brow which I had never seen before, and he seemed greatly agitated. I was alarmed, and advancing towards him, said:—

" ' Oh, my lord, how shall I apologise for——'

" ' No more of that,' he interrupted; ' 'tis past.'

" ' My lord!' ejaculated I, surprised.

" Leave us, Celia,' commanded the earl, and when the former had retired from the room, he turned to me, and the indignation of his looks seemed to increase.

" ' Oh, Rosseville,' I observed, 'how have I deserved this indifference? Is it my fault that the scene revived my sense of duty? Oh, my lord, it is those fatal feelings that have made me what I am.'

" ' I am weary of this parade of sensibility,' replied the earl, impatiently; ' you have called up against me the laugh of my tenantry and domestics—let that content you.'

" ' What does this change portend? This freezing look—this language of reproach?' I inquired.

" ' For your own sake and mine press me no further, Phœbe,' replied the earl; ' I would not have had the scene which has just past occur for millions. If you have placed yourself in unpleasant circumstances, common policy should at least teach you to shun the snares of the world; but it is over, and nothing can now be said which will not increase, instead of diminishing our mutual uneasiness.'

" A burning pang shot through my veins as Rosseville gave utterance to these words, and emphatically and hysterically I exclaimed—

" ' Am I deceived?'

" ' I cannot tell what childish hopes you may have indulged,' returned the earl, with the most freezing coldness, ' and I am only sorry that you should have been weak enough to deceive yourself.'

" ' Oh, no, my agitation has shaken my senses,' cried I, deliriously, and clasping my temples; ' he could not—no, no, Rosseville! in the name of all that you have professed, and I have believed, in the name of these vows which are registered on high, however man may slight them; and in that holier name of all, the name of Him, whose bolt hangs o'er the hypocrite, dispel these doubts and this suspense; restore me at once to my parents, or at once name the hour for that ceremony to pass, when, before the world, you acknowledge me as your wife!'

" ' Phœbe,' replied the earl, " since you will force me to be explicit, is it not strange that a mind so intelligent should fancy for a moment that it was possible for one in my rank to wed a girl in yours?'

" ' The oath!—the oath!' I cried, almost choking with emotion,

" ' My heart is ever your's,' returned the earl, " but of my hand, I have no power to dispose. Nay, you pass not hence.'

" ' Are there no pangs, that, like the dagger, kill the heart they pierce?' ejaculated I; ' I cast me at your feet in agony! 'Tis Phœbe kneels and supplicates! not for herself, but for the racked soul, and the gray hairs of age! For your honour and eternal peace, restore me to my parents.'

" The earl seemed suffering the most acute mental agony, and for a moment averted his head.

" ' Phœbe,' he said, in faltering accents, ' believe my heart unchanged—my unceasing love——'

" ' Monster!' I interrupted in delirious tones; ' darest thou still profane that sacred word? No, my lord, the mask is torn away,—the attachment which was my pride is now my disgust; 'tis past! I know myself deceived, but, thank Heaven, I am not lost! To you, my lord, the bitter hour is not yet arrived; but, 'tis an hour that never fails to guilt. At some unexpected moment, the blandishments of pleasure will lose their force—the power of enjoyment will be palsied in your soul; it will awake only to remorse. In that hour of retribution think of these words of warning,—think of the heart you've broken—think, my lord, and tremble.'

" Without waiting to give utterance to another syllable, I rushed from the room, but the voice of the earl tempted me to stop at the door and listen. He was apparently pacing the apartment in the most violent state of agitation, and thus soliloquising:—

"'The fatal truth curdles my blood like poison! I feel the hell in my bosom. Oh, what a heart I've lost! Why, splendid slavery of rank, must virtue be thy victim; why must affection be sacrificed to thee? The peasant mates him where his heart directs, and to his lowly bride brings happiness; his lord must fret, chained to some high-born fool; or either pine in vain for humble loveliness, or make its innocence a martyr to his choice. I was not

formed to be a betrayer. Wed! I cannot cease to love!'

"The words recalled my scattered reason, and I was almost tempted to return to the apartment; but a feeling of pride restrained me, and bursting with anguish, I hurried away to my chamber, where I was soon afterwards joined by Celia, who had been sent by the earl to watch me. I was at first almost insensible to her presence, and sat like a statue, with my eyes fixed upon the earth, and buried in deep and agonising meditation. The poor girl spoke to me, but, overcome with my emotions, I burst into tears, and threw myself on the couch, and

ROSSEVILLE ATTEMPTS TO SHOOT HIMSELF.

Celia, probably thinking that I should fall into a slumber, left me. My mind being so dreadfully fatigued by the sufferings I had so recently undergone, I did gradually fall to sleep, from which I was aroused by hearing some one moving in the adjoining apartment. The door was partly open, and I perceived it was Celia. Anxious to ascertain for what purpose Celia was there, I still pretended to slumber, and shortly afterwards, she stole softly to the door which opened upon my chamber, and peeped in.

"'Yes, she sleeps,' said she. 'Poor Lady, my heart bleeds for her. Why, this strange, unlooked-for adventure has created a fine confusion among all of us; for see—if one wouldn't think, by the state this room is in, that it had

turned the heads of the whole family. Scarcely a piece of furniture in its place, and my mistress's toilet, too. Here's confusion. But hold, Celia, that's your affair, so no complaining. I declare, I'm almost worn out with this bustle. Heigho! I'm ordered by the earl to watch my mistress here; but I'm sure I don't know what I shall do to keep awake. Suppose I finish the new drawing the Lady Phœbe honoured my humble talents by so much admiring—that's just the thing.'

"Celia placed the drawing-stand before her, and sitting down, applied herself to her task; but it was evident, by her frequent nodding, that her words would soon be verified, and I was most anxious for it to happen so, as I had formed a resolution to make my escape from he villa that night by some means or other. She once more approached the couch, and having apparently satisfied herself that I still slept, she returned to the drawing.

"'Oh, dear,' she exclaimed, with signs of excessive weariness, 'oh, dear, my eyelids are so very heavy, they stick together whenever I wink, and I can scarcely force them open again. My poor drawing will never get finished at this rate. However, I must try once more what it will do to keep me from sleeping at my post.'

"She again endeavoured to keep herself awake, but her efforts were all useless; she nodded, and nodded, until at length she fell back in her seat, fast asleep.

"I now hastily arose, and attired myself in the village dress I had gazed at with such feelings of pain and regret in the morning. I approached Celia on tip-toe, and being certain that she was really asleep, I soliloquised—

"'Yes, she sleeps! Now is the only moment! I thought I could not brave a father's eyes; but there is a courage in despair, which makes the weak frame wonder at itself. I have written this letter to the earl, and here are all his gifts—his diamonds—his detested wealth. Now, methinks, my heart feels lighter. Yes, like the prodigal, I will turn my steps where a child may always look with confidence. I have been imprudent, but am not guilty. Heaven receives the offering of the sincerely penitent, and can a parent's blessing be denied when Heaven forgives?'

"The apartment upon which my chamber opened, and in which Celia was, was a very magnificent one. On one side was a large French window, through which the distant country could be seen far away beyond. Outside was a balcony overhanging the road. I undrew the curtains softy, and opened the window. It was a fine moonlight night, and the distant landscape could be seen as distinctly as at broad day. I took a scarf from the shoulders of Celia, which she wore, fastened one end of it to the balcony railing, then returned, made an appeal to Heaven for protection, and blew out the candles. With more firmness than might have been expected, I then began my perilous descent, and gradually letting myself down by the scarf, alighted in safety below. Fear of being re-taken lent speed to my feet, and I flew with the greatest rapidity across the country, to which, however, I was a complete stranger. I scarcely abated my speed for a distance of five miles or more, when I was obliged to pause, in order to rest myself. I looked fearfully around me to see whether or not I was pursued, and then reflected upon what course I should pursue. I feared to travel at that hour, and, indeed, it would have been most dangerous to a young girl, especially; I, therefore, resolved to proceed for some distance

further, and then to seek shelter at some cottage till the morning. I then resumed my lonely journey in a state of fear and agitation it is unnecessary for me to describe. After walking for above an hour longer, I arrived at a small and obscure hamlet, and by the light which I perceived in several of the cottage windows, I was satisfied that some of the inmates had not retired to rest.

"Here, again, I paused, for uncertain of the reception I might meet with, I almost feared to knock. At length, I approached the first one, and having first listened at the door, and hearing only the voice of an old woman, apparently in prayer, I became more confident, and having waited till she had ceased, I knocked, and shortly afterwards, the voice of the old woman demanded who was there, and what they wanted. I informed her, and begged that she would admit me. It was some time before she complied, and seemed to be consulting within herself the propriety or safety of doing so, but having put several more questions to me, as to whether I was alone, &c., she at last ventured to open the door, and eyed me narrowly from head to foot. She was a very clean, motherly woman, whose appearance called the tears to my eyes, she was so much like the parent to whom I was returning.

"'Good gracious, child,' she said 'what causes you to be out at this time of the night, and from whence do you come?'

"'I am a stranger in this part of the world, my good dame,' I replied; 'have recently made my escape from villany, and crave a shelter in your cottage till the morning. I have sufficient to reward you for your trouble.'

"'As for reward,' returned the old woman, 'I require none; and if your story be true, you are heartily welcome to the humble bed I have to offer you.'

"I thanked the poor woman most sincerely for her kindness, and entered her clean little parlour, where the remains of the humble repast she had been partaking of was still upon the table, and of which she requested me to eat, but I declined. Judging from her manners and appearance that she was one in whom I could confide, I gave her a brief account of my situation, and upon what purpose I was bent. She listened to me with evident commiseration, and applauding the resolution I had formed, after some short time spent in conversation, she conducted me to the room in which she was able to accommodate me, and after bidding me good night, left me to myself. Fatigued with the events of the day, it was not long ere I fell asleep, and I did not awake until the old woman aroused me in the morning.

"Having been prevailed upon by her to partake of her humble meal, and offered her some remuneration for her kindness, which she persisted in declining, I took my leave of her, and made my way to the coach office, to which she had directed me. I met with no interruption on the way, and succeeded in obtaining a place in one of the coaches just about to start for my native village. I alighted from the coach a short distance before it reached the place of its destination, having made up my mind to walk the remainder of the way.

"I cannot adequately pourtray the nature of my feelings as I approached the home where I had never known anything but happiness until my meeting with Rosseville; alternate hopes and fears racked my bosom. It was a beautiful morning; the sun shone forth in full meridian splendour, and all nature seemed to wear a smile of gladness. When I came within sight of the village, my heart felt ready to burst, and suddenly the sound of pipes and tabors vibrated on my ears. Presently afterwards, a bridal procession approached towards the spot where I was, and stopped before the doors of one of my female companions, Ellen Greenley, and George Ashburne, who had long been her acknowledged lover. My heart beat quick at this sight, and I concealed myself from observation as well as I could. Having hung flowers at the door of each cottage, they joined together in singing the following chorus, which I had often heard before, upon occasions of a similar description.

"'Open, open lover's eyes,
    Hours of bliss are dawning,
Wake and see what glowing skies
    Gild your bridal morning.'

"When the chorus was finished, Ellen Greenly and George Ashburne came from their cottages, and were greeted by the acclamations and congratulations of the honest villagers. Oh, what ecstasy should I have felt, could I have mingled with them, as I had been wont to do.

"George Ashburne having thanked his friends for their kindness, the father of Ellen joined them.

"'Good morning to you, my dear child,' said Mr. Greenley, kissing his daughter affectionately, and smiling upon his son-in-law elect, kindly; 'may this prove a blessed day to you both. Go, lads and lasses, and gather the flowers to celebrate the ceremony.'

"The villagers departed, and Mr. Greenley continued—

"'I'll try if I can't prevail upon Mr. Heywood, the unfortunate father of Phœbe, to come to your wedding; poor fellow! he may be compared to the ruined wing of the crazy old mansion-house he has converted into a farm, that looks down in gloomy silence upon the bright and smiling landscape which everywhere surrounds it. Ah! that sad girl! the

flowers they go to gather are less frail than she has proved. My children, be virtuous if you would be happy.'

"Thus saying, the old man re-entered his cottage, but his words had been as so many daggers to my heart.

"'Phœbe's father,' observed Ellen, when her father had left them; 'ah! if our poor Phœbe herself were only here now, how her heart would rejoice in our happiness.'

"'Don't name her, Ellen,' said George, 'don't name her; a virtuous girl's lips ought not to be sullied by the mention of her name.'

"'Ah! George,' replied Ellen, 'pity becomes the virtuous, and the more she is fallen, the more she deserves to be pitied.'

"'Psha!' cried George, 'can't you talk about something else?'

"'A sad day it was when she went away,' continued Ellen, 'everybody was downcast, as if some great affliction had befallen the village.'

"'More fools they,' was George's abrupt retort; 'if you or I had gone, indeed, it might have afflicted them; now, Ellen, you shall not talk any more about her. Come, come, let us be going.'

"Suddenly accumulating all my fortitude, I emerged from the place where I had concealed myself, and called upon Ellen by name. Both she and her lover started, and the former exclaimed in a tone of astonishment and alarm:

"'Bless us! what's that?'

"'As I live,' said her lover, 'it is Phœbe Heywood, or her ghost!'

"'Do not be alarmed, Ellen,' I said, 'but one word with you.'

"'No, it's she herself, as I'm alive,' ejaculated Ellen; 'but oh, how changed.'

"'One word, dear Ellen,' I repeated.

"'I am not satisfied upon this subject,' said the timid George, 'so, as you seem resolved to stay here, I shall be off.'

"'Ellen,' I repeated, as soon as George had departed, 'have you forgotten me?'

"'No, Phœbe, no,' answered the affectionate girl, 'nor ever shall forget you. I was even talking about you, as you called. Ah! Phœbe, you're sadly altered; and so is everything since you went away. Such a day as it was, when you left us!—There wasn't a dry eye, nor a cheerful word spoke in the village. Your poor father——'

"'Well—well!' I hurriedly interrupted.

"'I see it grieves you,' said Ellen; 'I didn't mean to make you sad—you look as if you had suffered enough. This is my wedding-day, Phœbe.'

"'Your wedding-day, Ellen?' I repeated; 'blessings on it, Ellen!—blessings!—blessings!—Oh, if there be heaven on earth, it is the heaven of virtuous love, by virtuous bonds united!'

"Ellen sighed, and for a moment averted her head.

"'Yes, Ellen,' I resumed; 'I wish to see my mother, and to see her privately. She would not, perhaps, admit me to her presence, if she were forewarned. You can oblige me greatly, if you will induce her to come to me, by saying that a stranger desires to speak with her.'

"'That I will, with all my heart,' said Ellen, 'and may it turn to good. Oh, may all the realization of her hopes attend the returning wanderer. But where shall I find you?'

"'I'll follow you,' I answered, 'go round to the front door; I'll take the opposite side, and meet you at the yard-gate. And Heaven will help the heart determined to retrace the paths of rectitude and honour,' I cried, as with a heart beating with hope and dread, I made my way towards the house of my parents.

"Oh, never shall I forget the feelings with which I entered the gate.

"'Here is my home!—my blessed, blessed home!' I reflected; 'a frowning form appears to guard the threshold, shrieking in my ear— 'Hence! thou shalt not enter!' But can I linger here?—I seem to tread upon the earth like a criminal. I must, I will approach! Now, now, now!'

"Having at last made a violent effort to conquer my emotions, I rushed down the steps into the yard, and then exclaimed triumphantly:—

"'Once more, I am surrounded by all that is dear to me!—Father! mother!—your unhappy child, sorrowing, imploring, returns to you!—And hark! I hear hear the song of my childhood floating on the air. How acutely doth its accents strike upon my heart in such a scene as this, around whose every tree and flower some recollection of infancy's entwined.'

"My heart rose to my mouth, as I ventured, seeing the coast clear, to approach the house, and even to peer in at the parlour-window. I trembled; and an indescribable pang shot through my frame, as I noticed everything that well-known room contained, and which had not undergone any alteration since I had last beheld it. But how shall I describe my feelings, when immediately afterwards, the deer of an inner apartment was thrown open, and the next moment my mother made her appearance with the breakfast things? With what eager fondness did I gaze upon her revered countenance, and yearn to be enfolded again in her embrace; and most severely did I reproach myself when I noticed the heavy marks of care that were upon her brow. The casement was partially open, so that I could hear all that passed, and my mother, having placed the breakfast things upon the table, sighed heavily, and observed:—

"'There, there!—There's the breakfast ready for my poor husband, and now I wish he would return. He has been out ever since daylight with his gun; it is the only thing that seems to attract his attention. At home, all day he does nothing but sigh, or,—if he thinks he is not observed,—weep. Oh, Phœbe! unthinking girl, you have too much to atone for! How long he stays.'

"My heart was ready to burst as these words reached my ears, and it was with the utmost difficulty I could avoid betraying myself. My mother now came to the door and looked anxiously out, but a little thatched summer-house close at hand concealed me from observation. Again she entered the house, and I overheard her, in tones of the deepest anxiety, exclaim:—

"'No, I cannot catch even a glimpse of him, yet my mind is never easy in his absence; his despondency sometimes makes me fear that— ah! surely yonder I see him moving mournfully among the trees. Yes, 'tis he—he is just at the bridge;—he comes!'

"Never shall I forget the sensation with which I strained my eyes in the direction which the observations of my mother instructed me in, and I thought I should have sunk to the earth with mingled feelings of the most intense anguish and awe, when my eyes once more beheld my father. But oh, how altered was he! Care had deeply imprinted its furrows on his cheeks, and his form was bent and attenuated. He walked with a feeble step, and at least twenty winters seemed to have passed over his head since I had last beheld him.

"'My God!' I mentally ejaculated, 'and are these the terrible consequences of my imprudence? Oh, my poor mother, truly did you say that I had much to atone for!—How can I ever make sufficient reparation for the misery I have occasioned?'

"My father at length reached the house, and my mother ran affectionately to meet him.

"'You were wrong to have wandered so far,' she said; 'you seem quite exhausted.'

"'No,' replied my father, ''tis only exercise that can divert my gloom; when the mind's disturb, the body does not feel fatigued. I'm late—I hope you haven't waited breakfast for me.'

"'I would not, certainly, breakfast without you,' returned my mother; 'but you are too much heated to sit in this parlour; the breeze is too keen for you; we will go into the inner apartment. Go, and I'll take the breakfast things for you.'

"'Well, well, as you please,' said my father. 'Where is Edwin?'

"'He has gone to make one at the wedding party of Ellen and George,' answered my mother.

"' A wedding!' repeated my father, with a deep sigh; 'ah!'

"My mother had by this time hastily gathered up the breakfast things, and left the parlour.

"'Poor, bereaved mother,' sighed my father, looking with the most poignant sorrow after her, 'she struggles with her grief, and endeavours to impart a joy which neither of us can know again.—No! no! peace of mind fled with my guilty daughter—never to return! Why did I repair the ravages time had made in this old mansion? Why strive to give an air of comfort to my habitation?—Because I deemed it would be the abode of bliss. She—my child, hath made it the cave of despair!—But no matter, a few years of neglect, desolation will spread around, and hearth, roof, and tree will be ruined, like my happiness, and broken as my heart!—My daughter!—my Phœbe! Oh! misery! She's gone! she's lost!'

"As he thus spoke he rushed from the room, and my agony was so great that I could not help groaning aloud.

"' Oh, God!' I exclaimed: 'what will become of me?—I shall go mad!—Would that I had not ventured hither; I shall never be enabled to withstand the scene!—Never can I find resolution sufficient to meet his reproaches. Alas! he is too strongly prejudiced against me, ever to be persuaded that I am guiltless!—But where is Ellen?'

"I had scarcely given utterance to the words, when the latter approached, and before I had time to speak to her, entered the house, observing me, however, and motioning me to remain where I was, and to wait patiently. I cannot do justice to the anxiety of my feelings, during the time I was waiting there. A thousand doubts, hopes, and fears, flashed across my brain, and every moment seemed to be an hour. At length, I heard Ellen in joyful accents exclaim, as she came from the house—

"'Joy, Phœbe, joy!'

"I sprang forward with rapture to meet her.

"'I have succeeded, my dear Phœbe,' said the generous-hearted girl, exultingly; 'she'll come to you. Wait in the summer-house, and she'll be with you presently.'

"'Thanks! thanks!' cried I, 'a thousand thanks, my dearest Ellen.'

"'She's coming,' observed Ellen, eagerly; 'go, quick. I pray for your success from the bottom of my soul.'

"Scarcely had I time to enter the summer-house, when my mother approached. Now was the moment of my trial at hand; a deadly sickness came over me, and it was with difficulty I could save myself from fainting. The next moment my mother entered the summer-house, and she no sooner beheld me, than she uttered a loud scream of astonishment, and became, as it were, paralyzed to the spot.

"'Mother—mother!' I cried, in frantic tones, 'if I may still call you by that dear name;—oh, pardon your imprudent, but not guilty daughter!'

"I could say no more, but sank at her feet. A pause of several moments ensued, my mother being too much overpowered by her emotions to speak; but at length with a voice choked with agony, she exclaimed—

"'Wretched girl! dare you again to approach that home, those parents whose hearts you have rendered desolate? Guilty, miserable girl—'

"'Oh, no, no,' I interrupted, hastily; 'imprudent, cruel, I have been, dear mother, but your child returns to you as pure as when she left you. I appeal to Heaven to attest my innocence. Oh, my mother, pardon the poor prodigal, who erred alone through youth and inexperience, and who is now ready to make all the atonement in her power.'

"'Can this be true? Have you indeed not endeavour to deceive me?' ejaculated my mother, eagerly, and her eyes beaming, fixed with a penetrating glance upon my countenance, as though she would read all that was passing in my soul. 'But no, it is impossible. How can you be innocent, uncontaminated? Did you not abandon your home, your parents, and throw yourself into the arms of a villain, who—'

"'Oh, mother, believe it not,' I returned, with the tears streaming down my cheeks. 'I acknowledge that by the most base and subtle means, and in a moment of thoughtlessness and imprudence, Rosseville got me in his power, and bore me far away from my home. But I thought that he meant to act honourably towards me. He told me he would make me his bride. I was too ready to believe him, and day after day he made some plausible excuse to postpone the fulfilment of his promise. Think not, however, that during that time I suffered nothing—that you were ever absent from my thoughts, or that the fondly cherished recollection of my home, that home I had quitted, ceased to torture my mind. Bitter, indeed, were the pangs I endured. Ofttimes I would have fled the place and returned hither, but I dreaded to meet the reproaches of my parents. When, however, Rosseville threw aside the mask, I overcame that dread; and your unhappy daughter has come back to solicit your forgiveness, with her virtue as unsullied as when she left you."

"During the time I was speaking, the agony evinced by my mother needs no description; and when I ceased, in a paroxysm of delirious transport, she snatched me from the earth and enfolded me in her arms, exclaiming—

"'My child—my long lost Phœbe! Yes,

I do indeed believe you, and pardon you. Oh, this is a happiness that I never expected!'

"'Mother, dear mother!' I cried, in a tone of gratitude and delight which I cannot adequately describe, 'to be suffered once more to speak to you in this place—to hear those blest words—to know myself pardoned! My heart is so full. Thus—thus only can I thank you.'

"Again I threw my arms around her neck, and pressing me vehemently to her bosom, she wept tears of joy.

"'Unfortunate girl,'' at length she said, gently withdrawing herself from my enthusiastic caresses, 'I believe you innocent; but a mother's heart is more indulgent than the world. And, ah! there is yet one to be appeased. Hark! I hear footsteps. It is your father. Softly—stand out of sight! He comes, but must not know you yet.''

"Hastily throwing a veil over me, my mother urged me into the summer house, and the next moment my father and the father of Ellen came from the house. They were in conversation, and by the words which I overheard, it seemed that the latter had been endeavouring to persuade my father to join the wedding party.

"'But, at any rate,' said he, "for half an hour you might.'

"'No,' returned my father, mournfully, 'I should only mar the festal hour. I am the scathed tree of the heath that cannot drop. The bolt that struck off my branches has left my old trunk erect in wretched loneliness.'

"''Tis a shame, neighbour,' observed his companion, 'it is a shame, I say, for a strong mind like your's to give itself up to sorrow in this way. You might as well put a pistol to your head at once, for you will be sure to kill yourself by it, sooner or later, and self-murder in one form is quite as criminal as in another.'

"'When you have seen the being for whom you've lived,' retorted my father, 'the object of every solicitude—the child you've reared with unceasing watchfulness, wrenched from you by a villain's grasp, then come to me and talk of patience, and I'll listen.'

"'Well, well, I'll not weary you any longer, observed Mr. Greenley; 'from my soul I'm' grieved to see you thus abandoned to fruitless sorrow. Farewell, my friend, and may days be at hand when we shall see you smile once more.''

"Thus saying, and grasping the hand of my father most cordially, the father of Ellen retired through the gate.

"'Smile,' soliloquised the former, as his friend left him; 'smile! Oh, happy father!—happy to see his daughter safe in her native innocence—safe from the bane of wealth. I once hoped that such a fate would beam on me; but fate was jealous. Lost, lost, wretched girl!'

"While my unhappy father was thus speaking, my mother entered the summerhouse, and leading me forth, she placed her finger on her lips to enjoin me to silence. We stood aside, and watched him unobserved.

"'As I gaze there,' he continued, 'methinks I see her in her days of innocence, when first her little steps began; laughing, she ran, with arms extended towards me; then I trembled lest her young feet should fail, and she should fall. But she passed through those fearful times unharmed. She escaped those thousand dangers. Now she falls—falls to the earth, never to rise! She's gone—she's lost! My Phœbe! Oh, my child!'

"My heart was ready to burst, and I was choked with endeavouring to repress the heavy sobs that heaved my bosom. My father threw himself into a chair, and my mother advanced towards him and touched him on the shoulder.

"'A tear?' she observed, in gentle accents. 'Did I not hear our Phœbe's name too? Did not your lips utter the name of our child?'

"'No, no,' he replied, hastily rising; 'let us, if possible, not think or speak of her again.'

"'Well, well, dearest husband,' returned my mother, 'I will not urge it now; but here is a poor young creature, the daughter of—'

"'Away—away!' hastily and vehemently interrupted my unhappy parent. 'I have no daughter now.'

"'No,' replied my mother; 'but this repentant child, the daughter of a neighbour, is on her way to ask forgiveness of her offended father. She faints with shame and grief, and dares not meet him. Do speak a word or two of comfort to her, and teach her in what words she should address him to gain his blessing and to sooth his anguish.'

"'None,' replied my father, hastily, and his eyes becoming wild, 'none. Let not her presence insult the home her infamy has disgraced. Perhaps, too, she has a mother, rich in every virtue. Let her shun that mother, too, for contamination is in her touch. Virtue can hold no intercourse with vice, though vice, with double baseness, kneels affecting reverence for virtue.'

"I found it impossible to help groaning aloud, as I listened to my father's observations, and I threw myself into my mother's arms. He turned his eyes steadily upon me for a minute or so, and then resumed—

"'Yet hold! I will not judge too harshly; for there are shades of guilt, and hers, perhaps, may not be of so deep a dye as to preclude forgiveness. Perhaps her father was not affectionate. Perhaps (poor child!) he was morose and rigid. Perhaps neglectful, cold, unindulgent.'

"'Oh, no!' I sobbed, and sunk on my knees before him with clasped and upraised hands, 'he was most kind, affectionate, and good.'

"'What,' eagerly demanded my wretched parent, 'did he love you better than all the world?—did he rear you in domestic tenderness, and train you in the paths of virtue?—Did he clasp you to his doting heart, and in his foolish pride proclaim his child the paragon of earth?—and did you then blast all these fond hopes, and clinging to another, leave him in his storm of grief?'

"Again I groaned with the almost insupportable power of my anguish, and still remained on my knees before him.

"'Dearest husband,' said my mother, 'do not aggravate the dear child's misery. She is repentant—she is the shorn lamb, temper the storm to her affliction, but do not add another wound to a heart already too much lacerated.'

"'Well, well,' returned my father, 'be it so. I will forget my own, and try to sooth her griefs. Young woman, rise.'

"He raised me from the earth, and taking my hand tenderly, continued :—

"'What your miseries are, I can well guess; but what your sufferings are, I too well know. You fear to meet his eyes; you dread to hear his curse. A father's curse is heavy! Shall I paint this agonizing suffering to you, child? I can do so; for I have felt it. I have it now. I once had a daughter.'

"'Oh, sir, do not name her!' I cried, with a feeling of inexpressible agony, too powerful for utterance.

"'Oh, how I doted on that daughter,' he continued, and his countenance betrayed the terrible mental agony he was enduring. 'How I adored her, words cannot tell; thoughts cannot measure! Yet she sacrificed me to a villain,—her ingratitude has bleached this head,—her wickedness has broken this heart, and now my detestation is upon her! Oh, do not you resemble her—remain not a moment longer from your father—fly to him ere his heart give way, as mine does now—ere he curses you as I now curse—'

"'Oh, no more!' I interrupted, darting forward in excessive agitation; 'in mercy, oh, no more.'

"'Ha!' groaned my father, as he recognised me and retreated from me; 'away! away! away!'

"In a wild delirium of agony, I followed him on my knees, exclaiming in frantic accents,—

"'Your vengeance cannot make you deaf to the agony of a despairing child; behold me on my knees; I bring the sacrifice of a broken spirit. I do not ask your love till you know I am worthy of being beloved. I do not ask your confidence till you feel I can again be trusted; but do not deny me the shelter of your paternal roof.'

"My father spurned me violently from him, and as he did so, he cried in hoarse tones,—

"'Hence! hence!—I know you not! My sight rejects you—spurns you! If you have wasted all the spoils of guilt, there—there's gold; your idol, gold! for which you bartered all your hopes of bliss!'

"He dashed a purse furiously to the earth as he spoke, and hastened towards my mother, fixing upon me looks of scorn and hatred. Oh, Heaven! how each glance penetrated to my soul!—how every word burnt to my heart! It was wonderful that reason could retain her empire in that trying scene.

"'Father! father!' I implored, with redoubled vehemence, 'hear me, I beseech you.'

"'Husband, dear husband!' supplicated my mother, 'hear her, she is innocent,'

"'Innocent!' he reiterated, 'she innocent! No, no, it is impossible!—she left us; left her happy parents—her happy home—to follow a villain!'

"'Father, dearest father!' I cried, 'temper mercy, I pray you, with your severity. I am not the poor, guilty, degraded being that you suppose me to be. Your child is still virtuous—still unpoluted; her only crime has been in loving one too fondly, who sought to betray her! In the name of Heaven, I assert my innocence, and if I speak not the truth, may its most awful vengeance descend upon my head! But you cannot, you will not, longer doubt me. I see you will not! Oh, bless you for this, father, father!'

"I could say no more; but sobbing convulsively, I threw myself into his arms! He wept;—yes, I could feel his chest heave with the power of anguish, and the big round tear of sorrow fell from his eye upon my cheek; he pressed me with all the fervour he had been wont to do to his heart, and ere he pronounced it, I knew that I was forgiven.

"'My child! my Phœbe!' he at last cried, 'is it possible that I again hold you innocent to my bosom? But no, the bliss is too great to be real! And yet it is her! yes it is my child; it is her lips that have asserted her innocence, and appealed to Heaven to attest it, and I can no longer doubt! Oh, happiness supreme! My child! my long lost, reclaimed child! Good God, receive a parent's thanks.'

"He could say no more for a minute or two, but again did he clasp me with frantic ecstasy to his bosom, and wept tears of gratitude upon my cheek. Then he would, withdrawing himself from me, with an expression which I find it impossible to describe, gaze in my countenance, and clasping his hands together, raised them towards Heaven, in humble thanksgiving for its goodness in restoring me uncontaminated to his arms; while my poor mother's emotion was equal to his own, and she gazed on the scene with a sensation of the deepest gratitude and joy.

"'But where is the villain who has been guilty of this outrage?' he demanded, at length. 'Let me hasten to him, and demand satisfaction for the wrongs he has done us; the many days and nights of bitter misery he has caused your unfortunate parents! Tell me to what insult, what anguish did he expose you? I am mad to hear the guilty tale!'

"'Pray defer it, my dear husband, till your feelings are more composed,' said my mother.

"'No, no, no,' hastily ejaculated my father, and with the greatest impatience depicted in his countenance. 'I will hear it now! I will no longer hesitate!'

"In as few words as possible, I complied with my father's request, and related all the particulars of the earl's conduct to me during the time I was in his power. During the recital, the violent agitation of my father was plainly visible, and when I had concluded, he walked backwards and forwards for a short time, with disordered steps, and muttering incoherent sentences to himself.

"At length he turned to me, and clasping me vehemently to his bosom, exclaimed—

"'My child!—my own one!—my still innocent Phœbe! Can I longer doubt you? Oh, no! you are restored to my arms; guiltless as when in a moment of imprudence you were snatched away from your paternal roof! Oh, God! I thank you for this! The trial has been a heavy one! But my child has withstood the temptation, the artifices of the libertine, and the tempter, and I am again happy! Bless you! bless you, my Phœbe! Oh, I was too severe to imagine for a moment that you could be the guilty being I supposed you to have become! Bless you again! Here in this fond embrace!—this kiss of fervent affection, let me at once seal your pardon for the indiscretion of which you were guilty! We will never again part, till death shall interpose between us!'

"Thus saying, he snatched me fervently to his heart, and imprinted warm kisses upon my cheeks, my lips, my temples! How shall I describe the feelings that rushed through my veins at that moment? Language is by far too weak to do justice to them! They must be left to the warm imagination of the susceptible reader! I was unable to return any answer; emotion choked my utterance, and stifled the words of ecstasy that would otherwise have flowed from my lips! Again I felt the ardent embrace of that father whose forgiveness I had despaired of ever being able to obtain; once more I felt the glow of his kiss upon my lips, and heard him pronounce his forgiveness for the many, many hours of bitter agony, of doubt, of fear, I had caused him! Surely an age of anguish would have been trifling to purchase such a few moments of bliss, of exquisite transport, as those I then experienced. Again and again he enfolded me to his heart, and wept; like a child did the poor old man weep tears of inexpressible joy and gratitude upon my bosom. My mother, too; what pen could sufficiently depicture her emotions upon that occasion! She joined my father in the embraces he bestowed upon me, and then we knelt, and with hearts of sincerity, poured forth our gratitude to that Omnipotent being who had thrown the Almighty shield of His protection around me in hours of such eminent peril, and restored me innocent to the home wherein I had passed so many days of virtue and happiness, and which the wily seducer had endeavoured so artfully to make me disgrace for ever!

"'But I will seek out the villain,' cried my father, in vehement tones, after the first ebullitions of our joy and gratitude were over; 'yes, I will go to him and upbraid him for his base and brutal conduct, and demand of him all the satisfaction he can afford! The feelings of affectionate parents are not to be racked and insulted with impunity! No, by Heaven, he shall find, that in spite of his rank, he shall not escape the just indignation of those humble individuals whom he would have disgraced and rendered eternally wretched. To-morrow I will repair to the titled rake, and demand—'"

"'Oh, my dearest parent,' I interrupted, 'pray do not think of such a thing; rather leave him to his own conscience, which, depend upon it, will sooner or later, be a severe monitor to him, and amply punish him for his guilt. The journey is too long, at your time of life, and besides, the result of such an act, without affording any satisfaction, might be such as I dread even to think upon.'

"'Phœbe!' observed my father, 'think you I can tamely brook the injuries I have received from the Earl Rosseville? Oh, my child, did you but know, could you but form the least conjecture of the intense agony your disappearance, and the fears, the suspicions, that naturally resulted from it, caused both me and your poor mother, you could not thus advise.'

"'Alas! my father,' I returned, 'you do my feelings an injustice to suppose that I have not keenly, severely, felt the misery yourself and my dear mother must have undergone; in the midst of the luxury and magnificence that were displayed to ensnare me, it would rise in such vivid colours to my imagination, that many a time it surprises me how I could have retained my senses. Then would suspicion of the truth of Rosseville rush tumultuously upon my brain, and only that I had dreaded to meet your reproaches, long ere this should I have watched an opportunity to escape from him, and return to your fostering arms. Not able to form any conjecture of your sufferings! Oh, my father, the imagination constantly haunted me;—sleeping or waking, it was ever present to my mental vision; but Rosseville, with that deceptive art of which he is so consummate a master, never failed to use all the powers of his eloquence to soothe me, and by specious promises, day after day to quiet my apprehensions !   I will own my weakness : such was the powerful ascendancy he had obtained over my heart, that I was too ready to listen to him ; too willing to believe that he spoke the truth !   Oh, my beloved parents, do me not the injustice to suppose that I could for a moment learn to become insensible of the imprudence I had committed, or of the consequent anguish that I knew it would involve you in.'

"'And do you not love Rosseville now, my child ?' demanded my father, looking earnestly in my face.

"'Love him ?' I repeated, and the blush of indignation mantled in my face as I spoke ; 'oh how degraded, how fallen should I be, could I now feel anything but the utmost disgust and abhorrence for one who has acted with such duplicity towards me, and who would have destroyed the happiness of my parents for ever ! —No, my dear father, the youthful passions that are more powerfully excited in favour of any particular object, are more likely to become changed to those of hatred and scorn, when it is discovered that the being who has created them, has acted the part of the heartless traitor,—the deceiver !—It is thus with me !— Rosseville is torn from my heart for ever ; the place which his image once occupied, is replaced by the deepest scorn and detestation !'

THE DISCOVERY OF THE MURDERED EARL ROSSEVILLE.

"'My darling child !' cried my father, again clasping me in his arms, 'there is sincerity in every word you give utterance to.   Oh, how could I ever suspect that you would yield to the temptations of the guilty, and abandon those paths of virtue, in which you were ever brought up ?   This,—this indeed is a joyful day ; such a one as I never expected to experience again ! Come, come, my child, let us into the house ; let the blissful news be conveyed to all our neighbours, that this day restores a daughter, imprudent once, but guiltless, to her doating parent's arms.'

"'And let the past be forgotten in the happiness of the present,' added my mother, tears of ecstasy starting to her eyes;—'oh, Phœbe, you have returned at a time when joy predominates in the bosoms of those dear friends, with whom we have been so long associated.   Little did Ellen expect such a happy occurrence on the day of her nuptials.'

"Encircling my waist with their arms, my parents led me affectionately into the house, and in a short time I found myself seated at the breakfast table, and about to partake of that repast beneath the roof in which my infancy had been reared, and which I had been so near being discarded from for ever !   How shall I describe my ecstatic feelings on that occasion, or those, which, it was evident, from the expressive glances they fixed upon me, were passing in the minds of my father and mother. Should these records ever meet the eye of the susceptible, they will best be able to judge of them. I could scarcely bring myself to believe that I had ever undergone what I had;—that I had ever for a moment quitted my paternal roof! Everything was the same as on the eventful morning when I had been borne away, and the whole seemed like some fearful vison to warn me against the imprudent step of which I had actually been guilty. The charge effected in my father and mother in so short a time was most astonishing. The heavy care, the almost maddening anguish of my poor father seemed entirely dissipated, and was superceded by looks of the utmost joy and gratitude; looks of intense love and feeling which he constantly beamed benignantly upon me; while my mother could scarcely control her happiness within the bounds of reason.

"It might be imagined that my heart was too full, my transport was too unbounded to suffer me to eat; but it was not so,—on the contrary, I partook of the repast with a relish which I had never before enjoyed since I had quitted my paternal roof! I was again at home! in the home of my childhood! restored to the love and forgiveness of my dear parents; and never was the contrast of the pure comforts of a home of humble virtue, with the empty luxuries of wealth and magnificence, presented more powerfully to my mind. Oh, home! dear native home! the wayward child of fate must experience the trials I have undergone, duly to appreciate its blessings!

"Never shall I forget the supreme felicity I enjoyed on that auspicious day. In the course of an hour of two my brother returned to the farm. He had been delayed by some business on his way to the bridle party, and had, therefore, only a short time before been apprised of the happiness that was in store for him. He could at first scarcely credit it; but when, by repeated assurances, he was convinced that his friends were not deceiving him, he hastened with all the eagerness of an affectionate brother, to welcome my return, and from my own lips, gain a confirmation of my innocence. I must pass over the scene which followed; it was all that the warmest imagination can depicture! He embraced me again and again, and joined with our father and mother in expressing his gratitude to the Almighty, for the happy and unexpected termination of that event which had been the cause of so much poignant sorrow to them all. His indignation against Rosseville was equal to that of my father, and he joined him in giving utterance to a wish to hasten to the earl, and demanded an explanation of and satisfaction for the villany of which he had been guilty, and which was so near bringing the most irretrievable misery and dis-

grace upon our family. I urged upon him, by all the arguments I could make use of, to abandon the idea of putting his project into effect, and which could be productive of no actual good; but, although he became less violent, I could plainly perceive that both himself and my father were resolved not to suffer the matter to rest where it was.

"It appeared, that both my brother and father, for some time after my disappearance from the farm, had been most indefatigable in endeavouring to trace the earl, but without success; and so well had the latter contrived his plot, that it was generally imagined that we had both eloped to the continent.

"Ellen and George were united on that day, and when the ceremony was over, they hastened to the farm, to ascertain the result of the meeting between me and my parents. The pleasure they evinced, when they saw the reconciliation which had been brought about, and that I had proved beyond all doubt, that I had been able to escape the snares that had been so artfully and basely laid by the Earl Rosseville, to ruin me, convinced me more than any circumstance before, of the sincerity of the friendship they had ever possessed towards me. My return, and under the circumstances I have described, caused more unfeigned joy in the village than any event which had taken place for some time; and in the course of the day, most of our neighbours, with whom we had ever kept up the most cordial and friendly intercourse, came to congratulate us on the happy occurrences. The change from misery to the greatest happiness was almost too powerful for my feelings, and I could not but think that it was really more than I actually merited

"The day passed away, and at night, for the first time for some months, I retired to my chamber with the blessings of my parents. What ecstatic feelings thrilled through my veins, when I entered the little room where for so many years I had slept, and gazed upon every well-known object, which had undergone no perceptible change since I had before reposed in it. It seemed, indeed, to have been unoccupied since the time I had been from home; and every article I looked upon, appeared not to have been disturbed. There was the same clean little bed, with its furniture arranged with such admirable care and precision—the humble toilet—and everything the same as when I had last used it. There was the prayer-book, the one which had been presented to me by my father many years before, and in which was inscribed his name, with the leaf turned down at the particular prayer which I remember to have used the night before my elopement. With a heart overflowing with gratitude, I knelt down, and fervently breathed that prayer, and to it added one of thanks to Heaven, for the manner in which I had been saved from the sorrow and disgrace with which I had been threatened, and invoked its blessings on the heads of my parents and my brother. Then, with a lighter heart than I had experienced for many a day, I retired to my couch, and soon fell off into a calm slumber. No painful visions haunted my imagination that night; my dreams were those of bliss!—of the joys of home, and the affection of adoring parents; and in the morning, I awoke to a renewal of that happiness and content, which had ever been mine before I became acquainted with the Earl Rosseville.

"But what were my sentiments now as regarded Rosseville? Need I try to pourtray them? I am certain that I need not! They were fully embodied in the observations I had made use of to my father. The mask which the deceiver had thrown off, having shown me his character in its real light, I thought of him only with disgust and abhorrence, and had he even then have offered to make me all the reparation in his power, by bestowing upon me his hand, I felt confident that I should have rejected it with scorn. Great as had been my trial, and painful as had been the circumstances by which it had been attended, I felt that I had no cause to regret it now, but, on the contrary, to feel, in a manner thankful that it had occurred, as it had taught me a lesson I should never forget, and had afforded me that experience in the deceptive practices resorted to by the wealthy and unprincipled of mankind, which would prevent me for the future from approaching that precipice of destruction, down which I was so near being plunged.

"I arose the following morning at the early hour I had been accustomed, and found my father and mother, and my brother, already assembled in the little parlour, and the morning's repast spread upon the table. I could perceive, as soon as I entered, that they had been discussing something particular, and it was not long ere I was made acquainted with the subject. I found that my father and brother had come to the determination of going to the Earl Rosseville, in spite of my entreaties, and the observations I had the previous day made use of, to induce them to abandon their design, and such was their eagerness to see Rosseville, and demand an explanation of him, that they had resolved not to delay their departure any longer than the following day.

"'I fully appreciate your motives, my dear child,' said my father; ' but, after mature deliberation, I cannot consent to comply with your wishes. Were we to suffer the matter to rest where it is, it would be yielding a cowardly submission to guilt, which my heart revolts from; and, moreover, would give the foul tongue of slander an opportunity of propagating surmises derogatory to your reputation.

No, nothing will satisfy me, but a plain acknowledgment of his guilt and your innocence from his own lips, and a sufficient apology to satisfy the world at large. Were I to seek reparation in a court of law, his wealth and rank would be sure to be a protection to him.'

"'It would,' coincided my brother, ' and I see no other means of obtaining any satisfaction than the course we are about to pursue.'

"In this opinion, my mother coincided, and, much as I dreaded the consequences that might attend it, I was at a loss for arguments of any reason or weight to combat their resolutions. This day passed away in the same manner as the previous one, and the following morning, after a most affectionate farewell, my father and brother took their departure by the coach, for the mansion of the Earl Rosseville.

"After my father and brother had left, my mind underwent several gloomy presages, and although I perfectly agreed with the propriety of the arguments my father had made use of, I could not but sincerely regret that they had not abandoned their design.

"My mother endeavoured to soothe me by all the arguments in her power; and said that, doubtless Rosseville, for his own credit's sake, would be ready to make me all the reparation in his power.

"'Alas!' thought I, ' what recompense can he make me, for the injury he has inflicted upon my peace of mind?' Nothing can make amends for the pain of discovering that the only object upon which we have placed all our young heart's warmest affections is base, treacherous, and unworthy of that passion; and I now as thoroughly despised Rosseville as I had before loved him, for that he had thrown a blight upon my mind from which I could not thoroughly recover.

"We expected the return of my father and brother in about three or four days from the time they had left home, as they would have nothing to detain them after they had obtained the interview they sought with Rosseville, as they were fully aware that if they protracted their absence, it would excite our utmost alarm. The fourth and fifth day, however, elapsed, and still they remained absent. Our apprehensions began to be excited in the utmost degree, and all the fearful forebodings that had before haunted my mind, returned with redoubled force.

"In spite of all her efforts to appear to the contrary, the fears of my mother were, if possible, more excited than my own, and conjecture was exhausted in vain, to endeavour to account for the procrastination of their return.

"Another day elapsed in like manner, and yet we heard nothing of them, and then, indeed, our terrors were aroused to an almost insupportable pitch, and we no longer sought to disguise from each other the real state of our feelings upon the agonizing subject. I expressed to my mother all those forebodings I had before indulged in, and she could not but admit the too great probability of them. Now did she join with me in deeply regretting that my father and my brother had not yielded to my advice, or that she should have made one to urge the propriety of the course they had taken. What step to pursue we were at a loss to conceive.

"'I cannot wait in this horrible state of suspense any longer,' my mother ejaculated, when the seventh day dawned, and we heard no tidings of them; 'I will instantly take the coach for G——m, and learn at once the cause of this mysterious delay, and whether or not anything has happened to them. This dreadful state of doubt and suspicion is worse than the most terrible certainty.'

"She had scarcely given utterance to these words, when a knock was heard at the outer door, and a letter was presented to my mother, which she knew immediately to be in the hand-writing of her husband. Trembling violently with apprehension, she broke the seal, but had not read more than two lines, when, with a piercing scream, she fell senseless to the floor. I flew to her, raised her in my arms, and then, taking up the fatal letter, began to read the contents. The commencement of it was enough to smite my heart with horror; and it is marvellous how, under such trying circumstances, I retained possession for an instant of my faculties. My unfortunate father and brother were in gaol, accused of murder—— of the murder of my deceiver, the Earl Rosseville.

"My frantic cries soon brought the servants of my father to the room, who immediately conveyed my mother to her chamber, while I was reduced to such a state by the shock which my feelings had sustained, that it was found necessary to call in medical advice to me, as well as the former. I remained in a state of almost utter unconsciousness for several days, during which period I continually raved of the murdered Rosseville, and the awful charge which I would fain have believed my unhappy parent and brother were innocent of; but which, under peculiar circumstances, seemed, alas! but too probable.

"My mother had been restored to comparative composure much earlier than might have been anticipated from the violence of the shock her feelings had received; and when I regained my senses, I found that she had started the day following the one on which she had received the fatal letter, for G——m to seek an interview with her wretched husband and son, and to obtain an explanation of the horrible circumstances. The persons who attended me had the utmost difficulty in persuading me not to follow her; and it was only by the determined tone in which the medical man spoke, stating that the consequences of such a journey, in my then state of mind, might be productive of the most fatal results, that I was prevented from putting my wishes into effect.

"Too soon, alas! the horrible particulars reached my ears, which I will proceed to relate as they were afterwards detailed by my father.

"It appeared that after my father and brother had left home, they immediately repaired to the coach-office, where they had booked their places the evening before, and took their departure for G——m, whither they arrived in the evening without anything occurring worthy of being particularly noticed. As it was rather late, they resolved not to visit the earl till the morning, and accordingly took up their lodgings at an inn in the place. Not feeling disposed to go to rest for the present, they thought they would take a bit of a walk in the neighbouring fields previous to supper, and accordingly they walked forth, and instinctively directed their footsteps towards the mansion of Rosseville. They had proceeded across several fields, and had entered upon a dark and gloomy lane, which, they had been informed, led to his house, when suddenly they beheld, by the dim light of the moon, the shadows of two men before them, one of whom was a short way in advance of the other. They did not take particular notice of this at first, as there was nothing at all extraordinary in the circumstance ; yet, when they perceived that one of them still kept in the rear of the other, and that he was evidently fearful of being seen, they determined to watch his actions more narrowly. They, therefore, kept as close to the hedge as possible, so that they might not be observed, and yet cautiously kept advancing towards the two men, and taking particular notice of their actions. The one in advance made a motion as though he would turn round, when the other immediately stepped aside so that he could not be seen; and it then became very clear that he was after no good purpose, or why appear so anxious for concealment? My poor father and brother, therefore, redoubled their speed, entertaining strong suspicions that the fellow was a highwayman, and that they might be the means of preventing, probably, robbery and murder.

"They had not proceeded far when a turning in the lane hid them from observation, and directly afterwards the report of a pistol vibrated on their ears.

"Fearful, from all they had observed, that murder had been committed, they now ran with all their speed in the direction which the two persons had taken ; and having arrived at a dark and lonely spot, to which they were attracted by groans of agony, they beheld, by the faint light of the moon, whose rays now penetrated through the thick foliage above their heads, the form of a man elegantly attired, stretched upon the earth and weltering in his blood, while by his side lay the pistol with which the fatal and cruel deed had been committed, and which the assassin had left behind him.

"My father raised the unfortunte man in his arms, and the moonlight now streaming full upon his countenance, my brother suddenly exclaimed, in a voice of mingled astonishment and exultation—

"'Ah! by Heaven, retribution as overtaken the guilty! It is the villain, the betrayer, Rosseville.'

"The fatal words had scarcely escaped my brother's lips when a party of men, who had also been attracted by the report of the pistol, rushed to the spot; and having overheard what he said, and seeing the wounded nobleman stretched upon the earth, and my father and brother standing over him—the latter with the weapon of death in his hand, believed them to be the perpetrators of the bloody deed; and accusing them accordingly, and seizing them, in spite of their remonstrances and solemn protestations of their innocence, they bore them away to the nearest prison, while the wounded Rosseville was conveyed to his mansion.

"My God! how my very soul trembles when I recall to my memory this dreadful event, and my blood freezes in my veins with the most indescribable sensation of horror. Alas! who shall say that my sufferings have not indeed been severe?—It is really wonderful how I have found strength of mind to endure them all; how one so young, and, until lately, a complete stranger to misery, should be able to bear up under such an almost unprecedented accumulation of horrors. But my troubles were far from being yet complete.

"The unfortunate Rosseville was mortally wounded, and breathed his last before the morning, never having railied from the first, and having been unable to speak after he was first discovered. And here must I pause to reflect upon the terrible fate of the Earl Rosseville; as I do so, the remembrance of his faults, and his conduct towards me, are forgotten in the one strong and irresistible feeling of pity which inhabits my breast. His fate was marked by the most signal retribution of Heaven. The week following that of his assassination, he was to have been united to a young, beautiful, and wealthy heiress, to whom he had been paying his devoirs, at the same time he was pleading the most powerful passion for me, and most solemnly protesting, from time to time, that he would make me his bride. Ill-fated, but guilty Rosseville! Heaven pardon you for the deception of which you were guilty, as I now do.

"My father and Edwin underwent several examinations before the justices, and evidences of their guilt appeared so numerous, that few, if any, attempted to defend them. It was well known in what manner they were related to me, and the circumstances under which I had been placed with the murdered Rosseville, and, therefore, what had brought my father and brother to G———m, but to seek revenge?—Besides, it was proved by the landlord of the inn where they had taken lodgings, that they had left his house at a late hour in the evening together, and, that, previous to doing so, he had had a conversation with them, in the course of which they had asked several strange questions respecting the deceased Earl Rosseville, which were quite sufficient to strengthen the suspicions that were already excited against them; and more particularly they had made several inquiries as to the nearest way to the murdered nobleman's mansion, and had been directed the exact way in which they had been discovered. An inquest was held upon the deceased, the jury upon which unhesitatingly returned a verdict of wilful murder against my unfortunate father and brother; and ultimately they were committed to the assizes for trial.

"This was precisely the state of the affair, when we received the letter which was from my father; need it, therefore, excite any astonishment that our feeling were almost maddening? The circumstantial evidence against them was very strong, and alas! how many innocent persons had suffered under far less suspicious circumstances? The idea was enough to freeze the blood with horror, and here again did I find cause most bitterly to reproach myself for the one act of indiscretion which had thus been productive of all this awful misery, and might be the occasion of bringing my father and brother to an awful and ignominous fate, for a crime of which they were entirely innocent.

"The day after this, I received a letter from my mother, in which she described, in language I should fail to do adequate justice to, were I to try, the interview she had had with her husband and son at the gaol in which they were confined, but sought to inspire me with hope that something would take place to establish their innocence, and bring the real perpetrators of the horrid crime to justice. I tried to think so too. Never, I reflected, will the almighty suffer two innocent beings to suffer for the sanguinary crime of the real assassin! They will be saved, and the monster who has committed this atrocious crime brought to that punishment which his guilt merits.'

"These were but for a short time my reflections, then would the heavy weight of circumstantial evidence, which would be adduced against them on their trial, recur to my memory, and despair would again begin to settle upon my heart.

"My mother mentioned in her letter that

the assizes were expected to commence in about a fortnight, and that until the result of this awful affair was known, she intended to reside near the gaol, so that she might be enabled to visit the unfortunate prisoners every day. She added, that, if I thought myself capable of the task, and able to support an interview, I might also repair to the spot, leaving the farm for the time we were absent to the care of Ellen and her husband. To remain where I was, alone, with no one but Ellen to offer me the least consolation or advice, I felt would be worse than death; and, therefore, having made a powerful effort to conquer my emotions, I arranged the business with Ellen and her husband, and with the prayers of my friends for the happy termination of the trial, I set forth on my melancholy journey.

"What tongue could give utterance to the intense agony of my feelings, when the coach arrived at G——m, the place which I had so lately quitted to seek the forgiveness of my parents. Alas! under what different, what horrible circumstances did I now return to it. He who had first tempted me to act wrong had met with an untimely fate, and my father and brother the inmates of a prison, accused of his assassination. The reflection was almost too dreadful for human nature to support.

"The day after my arrival at G——m, I had an interview with my unfortunate relatives, but I must pass over that deeply agonizing scene; I cannot recall it to my memory without harrowing up my feelings. They both, however, attempted to appear more composed than I might have expected them to have been, and endeavoured to inspire me and my mother with the most sanguine hopes as to the result of the trial. We, however, could see but very little to excite any such ideas, and although, for the sake of calming their feelings, we pretended to place some reliance in what they said, we were very far from actually entertaining any such feelings.

"I will pass over the time which intervened previous to the trial, and come at length to the morning on which the fate of all my family, I might say, depended. The hall of justice was densely crowded, and the trial excited the most uncommon interest. Myself and my mother were accommodated with seats near the dock in which the accused were, and whenever, by chance, I happened to look up, I caught the eyes of the spectators fixed alternately upon me and my mother; but in the brief glance which I suffered myself to take, I beheld that the expression with which they contemplated us was more of pity than any other feeling.

"I know not how it was, but I felt a degree of firmness on that awful occasion which I never thought it would be in my power to assume, and my mother was perfectly calm and resigned. As for the prisoners, their whole de-

meanour showed the dignified firmness of conscious innocence, and a firm reliance on the goodness of Providence for the issue.

"The jury having been called over and sworn, the trial commenced, and the charge having been made, my father and brother both answered with a firm voice to the usual interrogatory put to them, as to whether they were guilty or not guilty—

"'Not guilty!'

"The trial then proceeded, which it is quite unnecessary for me to recapitulate here; the evidence against the unfortunate accused was, as I have before shown, entirely circumstantial, and even the facts which my father and my brother could advance, namely, the design which brought them to G——m, only strengthened instead of weakened the evidence against them, for it appeared in the opinion of the judge, that they had left their home with feelings of resentment towards the deceased, and to demand satisfaction of him, and they were consequently most likely to be excited to the perpetration of such a crime as that with which they were charged. Moreover, were they not taken on the spot, found with the bleeding form of the deceased? And then, my brother had been heard to make use of certain observations, which of themselves were quite sufficient to form a strong suspicion of their guilt, the words being of a nature from which it might be very readily inferred that he exulted in the accomplishment of that crime which he appeared to have assisted in perpetrating.

"The council for the accused made a most powerful and eloquent speech in defence, bearing with much emphasis on the principal points in the case, and pointing out in a clear and lucid manner the danger of admitting such evidence as that which had that day been heard, and the weight which would fall upon the minds of the jury should they return a verdict of guilty, and it should afterwards be proved that the unfortunate prisoners were innocent of the dreadful crime alleged against them.

"The jury retired to consider their verdict —and oh, God! what a moment of horrible suspense was that! All eyes were turned alternately upon me and my mother, and then the prisoners in the dock. But the latter were as firm as if they had only been spectators themselves, and frequently turned upon me and my poor mother glances that were meant to encourage us.

"My mother, as well as myself, I could perceive, struggled hard with her feelings, and endeavoured to evince a firmness she was far from, in reality, experiencing, and I could judge from my own sensations the poignant agony, the almost insupportable suspense, she was undergoing. Her cheeks were alternately flushed, and then became deadly pale, and several times she was obliged to apply to her smelling-bottle to save herself from fainting. Seeing the state of her mind, I endeavoured as much as possible to conquer the power of my own emotions, and by assuming an appearance of confidence, which was quite contrary to my actual feelings, I sought to inspire her with hope.

'The jury were absent about twenty minutes, which seemed so many hours to these who were so deeply interested in this important trial, and at length they returned into court. A death-like silence prevailed in an instant, and the lowest breath, the least sound imaginable, might have been heard at that critical moment. How I felt, it would be impossible for me to convey an adequate idea of. A deadly sickness came over my heart, and my limbs trembled as if I had been troubled with the ague. The suspense was but momentary; the jury having resumed their seats in the box, the ordinary question on these occasions was put to them, and the foreman of the same, in a deep, sonorous voice replied—

"'GUILTY!'

"An appalling shriek followed the pronunciation of the verdict; it proceeded from my mother, who sunk insensible into my arms. It seemed at that time as if I were endowed with superhuman power; my faculties were all restored to me, and I was enabled to support myself with a firmness that was most extraordinary. The verdict had fallen upon my ear, in a manner of speaking, with complete indifference, and it appeared as if a voice at that moment whispered to me hope instead of despair. But I feared to look at my father and his unhappy son. I was apprehensive that their bare glance of horror and despair would be sufficient to deprive me of my senses. With the assistance of one of the turnkeys, therefore, I was proceeding to convey my mother out of the hall, when my attention was suddenly arrested, and my purpose diverted by the officer of the court proclaiming silence while the awful sentence of the law was pronounced against the prisoners. What a moment of sickening horror was this. I resigned my mother to the care of the turnkey, for my strength was fast leaving me. I involuntarily turned my eyes towards the place where my father and brother stood. Their countenances were pale, but their demeanour was as mild and as undaunted as it had been from the commencement of the trial. The judge then having put on the black cap, proceeded to pass upon them sentence of death; but ere he had uttered half-a-dozen words, the whole court was thrown into the utmost state of astonishment, when a gentleman who had been seated on the bench by the side of the judges, suddenly arose from his seat, and with a countenance deathly pale, lips livid, and his whole frame powerfully convulsed with emotion, exclaimed—

"'Hold my lord!—proceed not to pass sentence on men who are entirely innocent of the charge brought against them, and whom the jury have but this instant unjustly convicted.'

"It would be an arduous task to attempt to describe the powerful sensation this address caused in the court; and all eyes were turned towards the speaker with looks of the greatest amazement and incredulity. A sensation, which I cannot pourtray, in a moment shot through my veins, and my bosom heaved with renewed hope, astonishment, and suspense. I gazed towards my father and brother, and beheld them very little moved by the singular and unexpected scene, the result of which they seemed to wait with the greatest composure.

"After a lapse of a minute or two for the court to recover themselves from the confusion into which this event had thrown them, the judge demanded of the gentleman the meaning of this interruption.

"'In a few words, it is this,' said the gentleman. 'You behold before you an unhappy wretch, who ought to have been placed in the dock now occupied by those much injured, and wrongly accused men. Nay, you may well be surprised, and it will doubtless be increased, when I tell you that in me you behold the actual murderer of the Earl Rosseville, and I, therefore, demand that justice be done upon me!'

"Nothing could now equal the extraordinary sensation which prevailed, and it was at first, no doubt, imagined by many that the gentleman's feelings who had thus denounced himself had been worked upon and excited by the circumstances of the trial, and that insanity had suddenly seized upon his brain; but they were soon convinced of the contrary, for the self-accused having paused awhile to suffer the excitement to subside, continued—

"'I see, my lord, and gentlemen of the jury, that you are disposed to discredit my awful assertion, and probably deem me mad; but I assure you most solemnly, and as I hope for pardon from that Almighty Judge, before whose terrible tribunal I shall most likley shortly have to appear, that I have only spoken the truth. It was this hand which perpetrated the hellish deed upon the unfortunate Rosseville, and upon a closer inspection of the pistol which was found by the side of the deceased, and which I accidentally left there, it will be seen that my initials and crest are engraven upon it.'

"The pistol was here handed up to the judge, and inspected by him and the jury, when the initials and the crest were found, exacily as the gentleman had described them. The case now had assumed a more serious and tragical form than had first been anticipated; and the judge, turning to the gentleman, whose name was Holland, put some further questions to him.

"'The awful tale is soon told,' answered the unfortunate gentleman.

"'The late Earl Rosseville and myself had been intimate friends from boyhood, and we had been companions at college. Soon after our return from the university, I formed an attachment to a young lady of considerable personal beauty and wealth, and was, after a formal declaration to herself and parents, permitted to pay my addresses to her. This courtship went on for a period of more than two years, when it was suddenly broken off, without assigning any cause for so doing, and the honour of my visits were in future declined by the young lady's parents. In vain I sought an explanation; none could I obtain, and, stung with chagrin and disappointment, I obeyed the commands that had been so peremptorily given me. Nothing more relative to this affair transpired till about a month ago, when, judge my resentment and surprise, to learn that the late Earl Rosseville was the admitted lover of the lady, and that their nuptials were actually fixed to take place upon a certain day. Burning with indignation, I immediately, on ascertaining the truth of this, sought an interview with the late earl, and demanded of him an explanation of such extraordinary conduct; but all that I could obtain in return, was a confirmation of the truth of the remark, and the most provoking raillery! I quitted the unfortunate nobleman burning with feelings of the most powerful resentment, and vowing the most dreadful vengeance. On the evening that I committed the hellish crime, I quitted my own house, with the pistols now produced in my possession, fully bent to way-lay and murder my rival. I knew the hour that he generally walked forth, and I was also aware that he must pass along the dark lane on his way home. There did I secrete myself then, and I had not been there long, when my intended victim made his appearance. He passed the spot where I was concealed, and I endeavoured to put my murderous intent into execution; but my courage failed me; my hand refused to pull the fatal trigger. I suffered him to get some considerable distance ahead of me, and then issued from the place where I had been hiding myself, and followed in pursuit, still unable to muster sufficient resolution to effect my inhuman purpose. Once he turned to look round, and then I hastily jumped into a dry ditch, and concealed myself from his observation. He resumed his journey, and acting under the influence of a sudden impulse, I presented the fatal weapon at him, and fired, just as he prepared to walk on. What followed has already appeared in the evidence brought against these two men, most wrongfully accused. No sooner had my victim fallen, than remorse seized upon my soul, and casting the pistols hastily from me, and

covering my face with my hands, to shut out from my sight the crime of blood my hands had perpetrated, I fled hastily from the spot. What I have since suffered, I cannot convey to you any adequate idea of. The image of the murdered nobleman was continually before me; and yet I had not the courage to resign myself into the hands of justice, even when I heard that the two individuals in the dock were taken up and committed for trial upon the charge. But, as the day of trial approached, so did my agony increase, and compunction began to obtain a most powerful ascendancy over my feelings. Could I be guilty of a threefold murder, by suffering these unhappy men to perish for the crime which I had committed? I could not; so, this day, I resolved to be present, and confessing my guilt, be the means of rescuing the innocent and suffering all the atonement I could, by expiating my terrible offence upon the scaffold. I admit that my resolution failed me so much, that I was unable to put this intention into effect, until after the trial had proceeded to the present length; but I have now acquitted my conscience of that additional and heavy sin, and I feel content to abide by the consequences. I repeat, that the men in the dock are entirely innocent, and that I only am the murderer of the late Earl Rosseville. I demand that justice be done, and thus give myself up to this tribunal to be tried and punished by the offended laws of my country.'

"A murmur of surprise, horror, and satisfaction ran through the hall of justice, at this remarkable confession, and, for a few minutes, the business was completely suspended. My mother had recovered, and overheard all that had passed. She was now standing with clasped hands, and eyes raised towards Heaven, with a look of the most unbounded gratitude; but her emotions were too powerful to suffer her to give utterance to a syllable. As for myself, I was completely paralyzed, and gazed upon the scene around me with the most inexpressible feelings of delight and unbounded admiration at the wonderful ways of Providence. My poor father and brother, too! What language can properly pourtray the different emotions that evidently filled their bosoms? They had sunk simultaneously upon their knees in the dock, and were puring forth their thanks for the wonderful and merciful interposition of the Almighty. But, suddenly, the court was aroused by the whole of the judges who were seated upon the bench, rising, and through the principal declaring it as their unanimous opinion that the two individuals who had been charged and convicted by the jury of the murder of Horatio, Earl Rosseville, were now shown to be clearly innocent, that the court, therefore, annul the verdict, and ordering them to be discharged out of custody, command

Richard Archibald Holland to be placed at the bar and indicted, upon his own confession, for the wilful murder of the said Horatio, Earl Rosseville.

"The sensation now created in the court was far beyond my powers of description; my father and brother were immediately released from the dock, and we once more enfolded them frantically to our bosoms; while, as a buz of admiration might be heard throughout the court, the unhappy man, who, by his own voluntary admission, was the real assassin, was placed at the bar, and was immediately put upon his trial. What took place, particularly on that occasion, I am unacquainted with, and if I were not, it would be quite unnecessary to enter into them here. It may be sufficient to state that the ill-fated Mr. Holland was, after a very brief trial, found guilty, and sentenced to suffer death.

"As for me and my parents and brother, as soon as convenient, we made our way from the court, outside of which a number of persons had collected, who hastened to congratulate us on the unexpected termination of the painful trial, and to commiserate with us in the great suffering and anxiety we had been so unjustly put to. We made our escape from the crowd

LORD RAVENSFORD GAZING ON THE FEATURES OF HIS SON.

as quickly as possible, and retired to an obscure part of the town, where we were not likely to excite the curiosity of the idle, and here, when alone, our feelings were allowed to have full vent, and our hearts arose with one accord to Heaven, in thanksgiving for the miraculous deliverance my father and Edwin had experienced from a fate which had appeared at one time to be inevitable.

"The following morning, we were on our way home again, when all our neighbours came forth to meet us, and to demonstrate their joy at the the termination of this awfully painful circumstance. The fate of Rosseville had made an indelible impression upon my mind, and I feared that I should never again know that happiness which I had once so uninterruptedly partaken of. My parents could well understand my thoughts, and they took especial care always to avoid that subject, and to endeavour to divert my attention to something else. In this, merely because I would not afflict them, I suffered them usually to imagine that they had succeeded; and, comparatively speaking, something like content began once more to smile upon us.

"But misfortune and I had got to be longer acquainted; and too soon her heavy afflictions came upon me with overwhelming force. The shock which my mother's feelings had undergone by the recent events, had made fearful inroads on her constitution, and it soon became too alarmingly apparent, that she was sinking under a rapid decline. All the medical advice that his means would allow him to procure; all the skill which his united resources would permit him to obtain, my father engaged, but they were all of no avail, and she at length yielded to the fearful malady, and she sunk as she had lived in Christian love with all her fellow-creatures.

"My father and all of us, were for some time inconsolable for her loss, but at length our grief was mellowed into resignation. This was one of the most severe blows I had ever experienced, but it was only a prelude to what I had to undergo. Only three months after my poor mother's death, my brother was seized with a violent typhus fever, which my father quickly caught of him; my care, my attentions to them were all useless; and how Heaven supported me through such a scene of affliction, is to me a miracle. A few short months only, consigned those two dear relatives to the grave also, and I was now left, as it were, alone in the world! Would that it had pleased the Almighty to take me also, then I should not have had to undergo the miseries, the degradations I have too much reason to fear it is yet my lot to suffer. Illness and incessant trouble had involved my father's affairs in difficulties, from which I found it impossible to extricate them. Let me draw my melancholy recital to a conclusion. Hard necessity drove me at last, to seek the protection of those relations with whom I am now living, and to place myself in a situation, at the thoughts of which my feelings revolt. But let me not murmur. It is the will of Heaven, and I must submit. When will happiness again be the lot of Phœbe Heywood? Alas! I fear, never!'

CHAPTER XIX.

THE ATTEMPT.—THE MAN OF BLOOD.

"Alas! unhappy girl!" ejaculated our heroine, when she had arrived at the conclusion of Phœbe Heywood's narrative; "yours has indeed been a hard fate, and let me not therefore complain of the severity of my troubles, while there is another in the world who has endured equally as many if not more severe hardships!—And yet, in how many instances does her fate and mine resemble each other! —Still is she not better off than I am? Oh, yes, to know that my poor father was no more, would not be so hard as to believe him living, and enduring all those horrors from the loss of reason he before did! My husband, too!—Oh, I cannot think upon his name without experiencing the most excruciating torment! What construction may he not put upon my mysterious disappearance? May he

not think me a guilty wretch!—One who has willingly abandoned him, home, father, child? —But no, no, I cannot,—I dare not—will not believe him to be so cruel—so lost to reason— to justice!—What cause have I ever given him for such dark suspicions?—None!—He cannot think that that woman who could forsake the best of parents, home, happiness,—to run the risk of losing name, honour, everything for him, could willingly desert him, now he has repaired the injuries he did her, by making her his wife! It were a gross libel upon human nature to entertain such an idea! And yet the dark suspicion and jealous fears which I noticed he did at times entertain, give fearful sanction to these surmises. Oh, wretch!— wretch!—to be guilty of such an outrage as this! Words cannot express the abhorrence and disgust which such a being excites in my mind!"

As the unfortunate lady thus soliloquised, she traversed the apartment in which she was confined in the greatest state of emotion, and at intervals her feelings were excited to such a degree, that she groaned aloud, with the intensity of her mental agony.

The perusal of Phœbe's narrative had taken her a considerable time, and daylight was just now beginning to peep in the eastern horizon. She walked towards the casement, and looked upon the uninteresting range of scenery which might be observed from it, with a vacant eye. The gray shadows that had before obscured the horizon at length entirely dispersed, and a broad expanse of gold succeeded. The sight was one which, at any other time, would have excited Lady Rosabelle's utmost admiration, but now it fell upon her sight without any power to charm.

Silence still reigned in the house, and it was evident that whatever inhabitants it contained, were they not yet stirring. One would have thought that the great fatigue she had recently undergone, and the circumstance of her not having been to bed all night, would have made her feel weary; but it was not so; the busy thoughts that crowded upon her mind, rendered her completely insensible to fatigue, and fear also lent its influence. More than an hour passed in this manner, and Rosabelle continued at the casement, until she heard a great bustle in the house, and soon afterwards, the outer door, which was beneath the casement of the room she was in, was opened, and a man of rough exterior, in whom she recognised the captain of the smugglers, emerged from it.

"You will not forget what I told you," Rosabelle heard him say addressing some person who was apparently standing at the door; "these were his orders, and you know best whether you deem it worth while to obey them."

"Oh, never fear, I will attend to them,"

said the other, in reply, and whom she directly knew to be the miscreant Gordon; "he is likely to be too good a customer to offend him readily."

"Ay, ay, so I should think," said the smuggler captain; "but he will be here this morning; at least, so he told me."

"Oh, very well," returned Gordon, "I shall be prepared to rece've him. I admire his choice! she is a fine woman, and I should not mind sharing with him in her favours. She is rather melancholy, to be sure, but I dare say he will find the way to cure that shortly."

"Oh, leave Adder alone for that," observed the smuggler; it is not the first job of this kind he has been engaged in by a dozen or two. Good morning; I shall not see you again until after we have had another trip! Keep a sharp eye after the Philistines; I have some idea that they will be down upon us shortly, and we must, therefore, be prepared to meet them on the same terms as we have done many a time before!"

"They must possess more sagacity than we are any of us willing to give them credit for," remarked Gordon, "if they prove too much for us."

"You're right, Gordon," replied the other; "but I must be going; it's broad daylight. Farewell!"

"Farewell!" responded Gordon, and the smuggler-captain walked on his way, with a hasty step, and was quickly hidden from view by a turning in the road, while Gordon re-entered the house, and closed the door carefully after him.

Our heroine had listened to this brief colloquy with feelings of fear and disgust; indeed the very tones of the villain Gordon's voice, when she recalled to her memory the dark doings in the old out-house, on the night when she there sought shelter from the inclemency of the weather, on her way to her once happy home, filled her with the most inconceivable terror! But to be an inmate of the same house with such a blood-thirsty and heartless villain, was enough to distract even stouter hearts than that which Rosabelle possessed, with the most uncontrolable alarm. The intelligence, too, of the intended visit of the villain Adder, although she had been prepared for it, now that it was so soon to take place, caused her the utmost uneasiness. She knew quite sufficient of his character to be fully aware how little she had to expect from his mercy or forbearance, and here at such a distance from her friends, and in the power of such depraved and guilty wretches, she could only look forward to the consequences that would follow, without her husband could be apprised of her situation, and take immediate steps to rescue her, her only hope of which being in the letter which Phœbe had promised to get forwarded to

Holly Hall, having reached there safe. The situation she was thus placed in, was one bordering upon hopeless; and there were moments when her despair would entirely gain the ascendancy over her mind.

In about an hour after the departure of the smuggler captain, the woman we have before mentioned made her appearance, and, addressing our heroine, said—

"I come to ask you whether you will take breakfast in this room? for I thought you might prefer it to having it in company with Gordon and his friends below."

Lady Ravensford contented herself by replying that she would rather take it in the apartment in which she then was; and the woman was about to depart, when, looking towards the bed, she exclaimed—

"Why, bless my soul! any one would suppose that you had not been to bed all night; and—no—as I live, I am certain this bed has not been entered since I made it yesterday morning!"

Rosabelle replied that she had not felt inclined to sleep, and had, therefore, set up the whole of the night, and the woman clasped her hands in amazement.

"Dear me!" she said, "I could never have imagined than any one in their senses would prefer sitting up all night alone, in a strange place, and which is none of the liveliest at any time, to retiring to a good clean bed like that. I couldn't do such a thing for the world, especially when I have very good reason to believe that——But I'm letting my tongue run too fast; and what's the use of frightening you out of your senses?"

"What have you reason to believe, my good woman?" inquired our heroine, whose curiosity was excited by her words.

"Oh, nothing particular," answered the woman, "but I must say that I'm pretty well positive I saw it one night."

"What do you think you saw?" asked Lady Raven-ford.

"Oh, nothing, nothing," answered the woman; "I might have been mistaken, to be sure; although, if all is true that I have heard has taken place in this house, it is no wonder that it should be haunted."

The woman did not wait to say any more, but left the room to fetch the breakfast. Her words had made but little impression upon the mind of our heroine, for she was not at all superstitious, and had been from childhood accustomed to laugh at the extravagant and frightful stories which the old people with whom she was acquainted had told her.

In a few minutes the woman returned with the breakfast things, which she spread before Lady Ravensford, and the latter partook slightly of the repast. Hoping to elicit something from the woman which might be of service to her in her situation, she returned to the supernatural story; but that the woman avoided, seemingly tenacious of dwelling upon it, and regretting, probably, that she had hinted at the subject.

"Why, you cannot have finished already, surely," said she, when our heroine turned away from the breakfast table; "I declare you haven't eat enough to feed a sparrow with! You are a perfect wonder, if you can do without victuals or sleep."

"When the mind is disturbed, neither sleep nor food afford their wonted pleasures," replied Lady Ravensford.

"Heigho!" ejaculated the woman, with mock gravity; "upon my word, if I am continued in my office to wait upon you, I shall grow quite sentimental. I suppose, however, when you and Mr. Adder perfectly understand each other, if you do not at present, you will live upon love entirely."

"Shame on a woman of your years to treat a circumstance which involves the happiness of so many, and particularly one of your own sex, who has been clandestinely torn from her husband, her offspring, her father, and her home—with such heartless levity," returned our heroine, with a feeling of disgust. "And can you so far forget the laws of christianity, and the danger you place yourself in, by associating with wretches like those you have described, in the performance of their infamous deeds?"

"Humph!" answered the woman, "this may be all very pretty for those who are fond of sermons, but I confess that my taste is widely different. I have been too long in this way of life to alter my course now, and it strikes me that I should gain little advantage by so doing."

"At any rate, you would gain the advantage of an approving conscience," observed Lady Rosabelle, "and that ought to be an advantage to you of more consideration almost than any other."

"Conscience!" cried the woman, with a sneer, "what have I to do with that? It never troubles me the least in the world."

"Some day or other, though, depend upon it, it will," returned Rosabelle, "and then it may be too late."

"Well, then," said the hardened old beldame, "I'll e'en wait till that time comes. But I have heard quite enough of this nonsense, and am tired of it; you would try to soften my feelings, but I fancy you would find that rather a tough job. After that, I shouldn't wonder if you were to try to persuade me to assist you to escape."

"I see you are inexorable," said our heroine, turning from the woman with a look of disgust; "but mark me—this daring and brutal outrage you will all have reason to repent. Most assuredly you will not long, any of you, escape the punishment which you so richly merit for it."

"Ha! ha! ha!" laughed the woman, scornfully—"they must first catch us; and we are pretty secure here. Besides, if there were any danger of your being discovered, I dare say we could find a certain remedy for that."

As the woman gave utterance to the latter words, a certain expression overspread her saturnine features, which Lady Ravensford could not mistake, and turning from her with a shudder of horror she did not offer to say another word to her. The woman, muttering something to herself, then left the room and our heroine to the indulgence of those feelings which her observations had excited in her bosom.

Lady Ravensford threw herself upon the couch, and tears came to her relief. The noise of some vehicle, apparently approaching the house, aroused her, and going to the casement, she beheld an open post-chaise, in which was seated Adder, advancing rapidly towards the door. She turned away with a feeling of the utmost dread; and trembling in every limb, she sunk into a chair, and mentally offered up a prayer to Heaven for protection.

She heard the outer door opened and closed again, and then all remained silent for a few minutes, but it was shortly interrupted by the sound of footsteps ascending the stairs. Rosabelle's emotion increased, for she had no doubt but that it was Adder; she was, however, quickly undeceived, for the room door was opened, and the woman of the house appeared.

"You are wanted below," said the latter abrupty; "Mr. Adder has just arrived, and requests an interview with you."

Lady Ravensford paused a moment to endeavour to conquer the feelings of wounded pride and indignation that swelled her bosom; then, as she suddenly felt imbued with fresh courage, she answered,——

"Yes, I will see the villain, and demand of him the cause of this brutal outrage. He shall find that he has no weak woman to contend with, who will tamely submit to his infamous stratagems."

The woman made no answer to these observations, and Lady Ravensford followed her out of the apartment to a room below, into which being escorted, she beheld Adder seated there, who arose immediately on her entrance, and advanced towards her with an air of hypocritical adulation, but she repulsed him with a look of ineffable scorn and dignity.

Adder was dressed in the very first style of fashion, and seemed to pride himself not a little upon his personal appearance. He assumed a supercilious smile, and seemed anxious to speak, but at a loss exactly how to begin; Lady Ravensford, however, whose firmness had increased, as she reflected upon the contemptible and detestable character of Adder, rescued him from his embarrassment.

"So, sir," she ejaculated, "you, then, are

the author of the infamous stratagem which has so long aimed at the destruction of my domestic quiet, and has at last been the means of tearing me from my home and friends. Think you that this shameful deed will go unpunished?"

"Beauteous Lady Rosabelle," answered Adder; "I know all the danger I have involved myself in, and am ready to encounter a thousand times more to secure the possession of her who has long been the idol of my soul,—the load-star, the magnet of my affections!—Yes, lady, mine is not the peurile evanescent passion of a day; it has glowed in my breast from the moment I first beheld you;—and when he. whose treachery in the first instance ought to have filled you with disgust towards him, left you to wander shelterless, houseless,—in vain I sought to find you, that I might avow the sentiments with which you had inspired me, and offer you the protection of an honourable hand and heart!— Perhaps you will say that such thougts, indulged in by one moving in the sphere of life I was then placed in were presumptuous; but love knows no distinctions of rank, and so it was with me. When I found that you had become the wife of Lord Ravensford, my regret,—I will not say my indignation, knew no bounds; and, urged on by the power of my love, I secretly vowed that you should not remain the treasure of a being I knew to be in every respect unworthy of you. It was then, indeed, I formed this stratagem, and determined not to rest until I had accomplished it, and—"

"Cruel, unprincipled, heartless man!" interrupted Lady Ravensford, unable longer to restrain the expression of those feelings which the boldness of Adder's manner had excited in her breast; "and can you thus coolly express your disgusting sentiments towards one whom you have already so deeply, and perhaps irreparably injured?—Are you not afraid of the terrible vengeance of Heaven, which most certainly will descend upon your head for this inhuman crime?—Think of the wretched husband, whom as a servant you betrayed, robbed of his wife; think of the poor old man, rendered now, perhaps, by your fiendish act a raving maniac, and tremble! My soul recoils with horror, even at the bare contemplation of such a miscreant as you are. Tremble, for rest assured, the hour is not far distant when a terrible retribution will descend upon you for this unprecedented act of villany."

Adder for a minute or two, shrunk within himself, abashed and confused by the dignity of her manner; but quickly overcoming his feelings, he replied :—

"Lady Ravensford, you have thought proper to assume a bold tone, but I can assure you, it will be of little service to you with me!—I would treat you with kindness; I would, in every sense of the word, act up to the protestations I have just made to you; but lest you should

flatter yourself that you can, by language such as that you have just used, intimidate me, it is necessary to inform you that I am fully determined to accomplish al I desire, and that any obstinate rejection of my suit on your part, will be quite hopeless, and complete folly. Here you are entirely in my power, and so well, and so secretly have I contrived my plot, that any discovery of the place of your retreat by your friends, is next to an impossibility. You will, doubtless, therefore, after this intimation, see the prudence of behaving less incourteously towards me, and you will find in me such a friend and protector, as will leave you no cause to regret the loss of the empty fool, Ravensford."

"Daring wretch!" ejaculated our heroine, her bosom swelling with resentment, and her eyes flashing glances upon Adder, that were sufficient to awe a more consummate scoundrel than himself, "have you the boldness, the disgusting boldness, to speak thus to one to whom you were a menial?—Rest assured you will have to answer dearly for this, and that my much injured lord will not fail to punish you severely for all you have done!"

"Psha!" cried Adder, scornfully; "the haughty Ravensford I scorn more than the veriest thing that crawls upon the earth!—I his menial?—Ha! ha! ha!—I tell you, Rosabelle, he was my slave. I was the lord and master of all his actions! and it was only because he feared my power, that he wished to escape his bondage. Who triumphs now? he whom you have called the menial, or the titled upstart? Oh, he shall yet learn that the man he has dared to insult, has both the power and the determination to wreak an ample vengeance. But, pardon me, lady, if you have forced me to make use of language of severity, when I would fain have used only that of love! Yes, charming Rosabelle, love! but even that is by far too weak a term for the sentiment with which you have inspired me! Were I to say that I adore you, I should not exaggerate. Oh, who could behold you and not—"

"Insolent man!" interrupted our heroine, while the sentiments of disgust that predominated in her breast were almost past endurance; "I will not listen to your infamous vows. Under any circumstance, my heart would revolt at the odious idea of having any connection with you. Suffer me to leave the room, I command you."

"Lovely Rosabelle," returned the villain, assuming an insinuating smile, which rendered his countenance still more sickening and disgusting to Lady Rosabelle, "lovely Rosabelle, I am sorry that I cannot comply with your request in this instance, because I am anxious to convince you of the sincerity of the sentiments with which you have inspired me. I was at first prepared to encounter your reproaches; but I do not despair of being ere long able to soften your heart towards me. Think, then, no more of Ravensford; scorn the slander of the world! Live only for love, and that man who now kneels at your feet, and whose soul idolizes you!"

Thus speaking, Adder bent his knee to the floor, and, in spite of the resistance of Lady Ravensford, seized her hand, and pressing it to his lips, devoured it with kisses. What pen could do justice to the feelings that raged in the bosom of our heroine at that moment! Could looks of indignation kill, those she fixed upon the wretch who knelt before her would certainly have effected that object. Her cheeks glowed with shame; her bosom swelled; she tried, but could not speak; and at length yielding to the powerful emotions that had struggled for vent, she burst into tears.

Adder arose, and looked at her with an expression of much apparent concern, but Rosabelle averted her head, and was so entirely absorbed by her own thoughts, that she was scarcely conscious of what he said, when he gave utterance to the following fulsome tirade:—

"Dearest lady, pray do not give way to grief; every tear you shed, believe me, goes to my heart; each pang you feel, inflicts a ten-fold anguish upon me. I will do anything to calm your feelings, and to make you happy, I will——"

"Oh, Adder," interrupted our heroine, in accents of supplication; and fixing upon him a glance sufficient to make an impression upon a heart of adamant; "in spite of all the suffering you have already caused me and my friends, let pity now enter your bosom; restore me to them, and I will freely pardon you. To tear a defenceless woman from her home, her husband and her child, is a deed of inhumanity of unparalleled magnitude; but do not, I beseech you, do not persist in your cruelty; consider, that it can only bring ultimate misery and destruction upon yourself; remember that the all-seeing eye of an offended God is upon you, and that His avenging arm is impending o'er you! Repent, suffer me to depart, and I will swear that no punishment shall accrue to you for the outrage of which you have been guilty; nay, more, that I will not even divulge your name to my friends."

"This appeal is madness," remarked Adder; "think you, then, Rosabelle, that the sentiments I have avowed are of so pusillanimous a description as to be so easily overcome: and that I will so readily resign the object, which, according to your own admission, I have run so much risk to obtain possession of? Psha! I should be a curse fool were I to do so! No, no, Lady Ravensford, if such I must still call you, I will do all I can to make you happy, but you and I never separate again."

"Good God!" exclaimed Lady Ravensford, in a voice of agony, and wringing her hands; "surely You will not suffer this! are there no thunderbolts of wrath to strike the monstrous perpetrator of this deed a corpse? Oh! my poor boy, husband, father, shall I not behold you again? My heart will burst. Adder, again I appeal to you: oh, mercy, mercy!"

And with looks of frenzied supplication, she sunk at the villain's feet, and clasping her hands, looked the very image of despair. He did, indeed, hardened as he was, feel moved at the vehemence of her manner, and gazed at her for a few moments without speaking. But he quickly conquered this feeling, and in a voice of assumed gentleness, ejaculated:—

"Rise, beauteous Rosabelle; it grieves me to see you in this posture. I may appear severe, cruel, unfeeling, because I do not yield to your supplications; but, indeed I am not so. It is the unconquerable fervour of my love for you, which prompts my conduct, and renders me inexorable. Part from you! resign you! after all the trouble and anxiety it has cost me to obtain possession of you? Oh, never! Sooner would I part from life. There is only one thing that I really regret, that I did not boldly confess to you the love I felt for you before your union with Ravensford, which would have prevented the necessity of the desperate step I have taken, and enabled me to have placed you in the honourable position in society, it would be my pride to see you move in. Ravensford, the deceiver; the betrayer; the hypocrite! Name him not! Banish him from your thoughts, or if he ever does occur to your remembrance, think of him only with detestation; as one who is totally unworthy of you!"

"Hardened villain! insensible alike to pity and to shame!" cried our heroine, rising hastily, "dare not to pollute the name of my husband with such base assertions."

"I repeat," said Adder, "that Ravensford is totally unworthy of you; that he loves you not!"

"Oh, calumny, most base!" cried Lady Ravensford; "are you not satisfied with what you have already caused, but you must endeavour to add to it ten fold by——"

"By speaking the truth," added the villain; "by undeceiving you, and showing you how little cause you have to feel towards that man who is, unfortunately, your husband, anything but disgust and hatred."

"What mean you?"

"That Ravensford loves another; and that—"

"Base libeller!" interrupted Lady Ravensford, indignantly. "I will hear no more!"

"I speak the truth, sweet Rosabelle," returned Adder, "and ere long I will give you sufficient proof that I do so. But, for the present, I will suffer you to retire to your own apartments, where you will have everything you require; every attention you can wish for. Left to your own reflections, I trust that, on mature consideration, your heart will not fail to relent in my favour, and that you will see the complete folly of opposing the will of a man, who, when he once fixes his mind upon the accomplishment of any particular object, will not fear to encounter any risk, any danger, to obtain it."

"Great Heaven!" sobbed forth Lady Ravensford, "is there no hope?—Must I be confined in this dismal place, so far away from my friends; in the power of a man to whom pity is a stranger, and beneath the same roof with Gordon, that man of blood, who—"

"Who, what?" eagerly demanded Adder, grasping her arm, and fixing upon her a keen and penetrating glance; "what know you of Gordon?"

"What know I of him?" repeated our heroine, with a shudder of horror that thrilled through her veins; then suddenly recollecting herself, and the danger she would in all probability incur by acknowledging what she really did know of the man, she added—

"I know that he must be a villain, or he would not become your accomplice in this nefarious deed!"

"Humph!" muttered Adder, releasing his hold of Rosabelle's arm, and walking for a moment across the room; "and is this all you know of him?—But why call him a man of blood?"

"My excited feelings caused me to call him so," replied Lady Ravensford; "but, perhaps, in that respect, I judged him wrongfully, though his countenance, which is generally the index of the mind, would proclaim him to be a man who would not hesitate to perpetrate any crime. But to be in the same house with such a man, and left to his mercy!—Oh, God! my blood chills with horror! Adder, again I supplicate your forbearance — your pity."

"Your terrors are groundless, Rosabelle," answered Adder; "no harm shall come to you here; and Gordon, who is in my power, for his own sake will not attempt to do anything which may offend you. Say but the word; confess that you do not hate me, and that you are willing to accede to my proposals, and we will instantly quit this place, and in some retired part on the Continent, where we shall be unknown, you shall have every comfort and luxury that your heart can desire. You turn away from me with a look of scorn, but I trust that you will shortly alter your sentiments. I have no wish to treat you harshly, but, on the contrary, to prove to you by my actions the sincerity of the love which I have avowed for you; but if you remain obstinate, you will compel me to a step which I shall deeply regret."

Adder, as he spoke, rang the bell for Cicely, the woman who had hitherto attended upon our heroine, and then continued—

"I will call upon you again to-morrow, when I hope to find you in a very different state of mind. Farewell, dearest Rosabelle, farewell!"

Here the villain again attempted to snatch the hand of Lady Ravensford to his lips, but with a look which awed him into immediate forbearance, she darted hastily away from him, and followed Cicely up the stairs, and having entered the room, and desired the latter to leave her, as she wished to be alone, she threw herself into a chair, and gave unrestrained indulgence to her feelings. What other prospect had she now but the most hopeless misery and suffering?—The villain Adder was an enemy whose power and determination she had too much reason to dread, and death would be preferable to the horrid fate to which she seemed consigned. She remembered every word that the miscreant had uttered, and they proved him to be a villain of the most infamous dye. The stratagem which had been contrived to ensnare her, and gratify his revenge against her husband, was one of the most consummate pieces of villany she had ever heard of, and never could she have believed human nature so base and crafty.

The letters which had fallen into the hands of Ravensford, and which purported to come from her, were now, she was convinced, forged by him, and that he had used Lord Saunter merely as a tool in the furtherance of his schemes, and to prevent suspicion falling upon himself, she felt equally certain; and, therefore, from a man who could concoct and execute such a plan as this, what had she not to dread?

Her heart sickened with horror in reflecting on it, and her brain was racked to distraction. She arose from her chair; she traversed the apartment in a state of the greatest mental agony; then she again sunk in a chair, and a paroxysm of scalding tears came to her relief. She remained in this state for several minutes; and then, by a powerful effort, becoming more tranquil, she arose, fastened the room door on the inside, to prevent intrusion, and throwing herself on the bed, fatigue overcame her, and she sunk into a deep slumber.

CHAPTER XX.

THE ROUE.—THE MEETING.—THE DUEL.— THE DEATH.

IT is a dark epoch in a man's life when sleep forsakes him; when he tosses to and fro, and thought will not be silenced; when the drug and the draught are the courtiers of stupefaction, not sleep; when the downy pillow is as a knotted log; when the eyelids close, but with an effort, and there is a drag, and a weight, and a dizziness in the eyes of man. Desire, and grief, and love; these are the young man's torments; but they are the creatures of time: time removes them as it brings them, and the vigils we keep, "while the evil days come not," if weary, are brief and few. But memory, and care, and ambition, and avarice—these are demon-gods that defy the time that fathered them. The worldlier passions are the growth of maturer years, and their grave is dug but in our own. As the dark spirits in the northern tale, that watch against the coming of one of brighter and holier race, lest, if he seize them unawares, he bind them prisoners in his chain, they keep ward at night over the entrance of that deep cave, the human heart, and scare away the angel sleep.

Thus it was exactly with the villain Adder; although he had gained what his avarice had so many years thirsted after—riches; notwithstanding he had succeeded in getting into his power the woman who had excited his most ardent desires; and in the possession of which he would also gratify his vengeance towards Ravensford; his mind was the constant abode of tormenting thought. Conscience brought to his remembrance the dark deeds of former days—deeds that have not yet been revealed, and drove sleep from his eye-lids. Night was to him, when others calmly reposed in peace, a time of dread and horror, and he more frequently than otherwise passed it away in dissipation, and sought to drown thought in the maddening beverage; but conscience would not be appeased.

He had done that for which he merited an ignominious death upon the scaffold, and was in constant dread lest his crimes should come to light, and he should be brought to that punishment from which his soul had shrank with all the coward fear of guilt. In the society of Lady Ravensford, however, he hoped to be able to meet that peace to which he had long been a stranger; and he determined that he would not wait long in endeavouring to gain her consent to the gratification of his wishes and lascivious passions, but compel her to yield by force.

"Yes, Rosabelle," he soliloquized to himself, after the interview we have described in the previous chapter, "you are securely in my power, and must become my victim. Oh, that thought causes my very soul to exult, when I think upon the agony which Ravensford will, and is now enduring! Revenge, thou art dear to hearts like mine, and I will ever cherish thee as my friend. How admirably have I managed this business throughout! Yes—and ere many days it shall be complete, and

Lady Ravensford, the wife of my late master, shall be the mistress of his discarded valet."

He laughed aloud in exultation as this thought crossed his mind, and he walked on towards the rendezvous where he had appointed to meet a portion of the smugglers—fit associates for so base a being.

Adder had for many years had extensive dealings with these traffickers in contraband goods, and they had a great portion of his property; and it was in connexion with them that he committed a deed of blood, which now preyed so heavily upon his conscience, and which he could not help fearing would some time or the other be revealed, and himself brought to condign punishment. The particulars of this atrocious event will be revealed at a future period.

We will now once more return to Lord Saunter, whom we left in Ireland, labouring under the effects of chagrin and disappointment. It was almost the first time in his life that he had been brought seriously to reflect, and the conclusion he was forced to come to was, that he certainly must have been a most consummate fool to have been so easily made a dupe of. Against Adder he was greatly incensed, and he inwardly threatened him with total annihilation whenever he encountered him —a threat, we need not inform our readers, that he would never have had the courage to attempt to put into execution. But not the least cause of his uneasiness was the fear of his being discovered by the much-injured Lord Ravensford, who he was certain would not rest himself until he had had ample satisfaction for the injury done to his feelings and his honour. It was not until several days after his flight that he was made acquainted with the disappearance of Lady Ravensford, and he felt confident that she had fallen into the hands of Adder, but how he had contrived to accomplish that ultimatum he could not form even the most remote idea.

After a few restless days and nights, Lord Saunter could not content himself that he was safe in Ireland, more especially when he encountered accidentally his former companions, Captain Mowbray and Sir Harry Spangle, from whom he expected it would be rather difficult to escape, and who, being acquainted with all the circumstances, he was fearful would make them rather more public than would be agreeable to himself, or conducive to his safety.

These two worthies were very glad to meet again with their former victim; for the state of the exchequer, as they facetiously termed it, had long been in a very low condition, and they hoped, by dint of "borrowing" what they never meant to repay, of the silly nobleman, that they should be enabled once more to enter into those scenes of vice and wild extravagance in which they had been so used to mingle, and which had, by constant practice, become a second part of their nature. Lord Saunter soon perceived that he could not shake them off quite so easily as he could wish, for they showed a determination to stick to him with all their former pertinacity, and he saw that he should find it a very difficult matter to leave the country without their knowledge, as they were constantly with him, and would not be denied his society. They rallied him upon his disappointment, and upon the manner in which he had been so artfully made the dupe of Adder : and, for the first time in his life, Saunter became heartily ashamed of himself,

and would willingly have sacrificed one half of his fortune, could he, by so doing, have recalled the past, or undone all that he had done.

"I must say, though, your lordship," observed Mowbray, with a look and tone of sarcasm which must have sounded anything but pleasant to the ears of Lord Saunter; "it must have been a sad disappointment to you, this same mock amour. It is very hard when one has made up his mind to anything, just at the time that we have reached the very pinnacle of expectation, to find all our hopes frustrated, and that we have been made the dupe, the laughing-stock of some crafty knave."

"Positively it is very provoking," added

ADDER RECEIVING LADY RAVENSFORD AT THE SMUGGLERS' RETREAT.

Sir Harry Spangle, in the same strain of irony; "and his lordship must really have the very patience of Job himself, or he could never put up with it so quietly."

"To lose such a beauteous creature !" quoth Mowbray, laughing; "such eyes !"

"Such features !" observed Spangle.

"Such lips !"

"Such grace !"

"Such elegance ! Yes, as you say, Sir Harry," remarked Mowbray, "it is a matter of the greatest astonishment to me that Lord Saunter can bear it so patiently. For my own part I verily believe that I should go raving mad with vexation and disappointment, espe-

cially after all the trouble and expense he had been to in making the necessary arrangements."

"Yes, and to be duped by that fellow, Adder, too !" remarked Sir Harry Spangle.

"Degrading !"

"The cunning knave ! to make a tool of Saunter, merely to forward his own elopement with the lady ! If I were in his lordship's place I would not rest until I had found out the rascal, and inflicted upon him a severe chastisement."

"I'd horsewhip him !"

"Clip off his ears !"

"Hang, draw, and quarter him !"

No 20.

"Gibbet him !"

"Damme, I'd annihilate him altogether !''

Poor Lord Saunter had, during this colloquy, sat biting his lips, but was unable to speak a word. His countenance expressed an opinion, notwithstanding, very clearly, that it was by far easier to threaten than to put the same into execution ; and he felt some strange misgivings when the subject of duelling or inflicting summary punishment upon any individual who had offended him was mentioned to him. Saunter (whether it was his modesty or not that was the cause, that we must leave to the judgment of the reader,) somehow or other did not entertain any very high opinion of his own prowess, and perfectly agreed with that immortal poet who says—

"He who fights and runs away,
Lives to fight another day ;
But he who is in battle slain
Can never live to fight again.''

Not that he had ever been particularly put to the test, always contriving by any means in his power to come to an amicable arrangement with his foes, to prevent their coming to so sanguinary a mode of settling their dispute, and being by no menas nice about making any concessions to come to such a desirable result.

"My dear fellows," he at last said, addressing himself to his two wild and unprincipled associates, "pray do drop this subject ; I must confess that it has positively cost me more pain and vexation than any other circumstance which I have encountered during my life.''

"But you certainly do not mean to let the matter rest where it is ?" said Captain Mowbray, who enjoyed the scene very much ; "you will not suffer this fellow Adder to first dupe you out of your expected mistress, and then to laugh at you with impunity ?''

"Most unquestionably not," joined in Sir Harry Spangle ; "his lordship would indeed be laughed at were he to suffer the fellow to go unpunished. He must not rest until he has found him out and fully repaid him for the trick he has played him. But of course his lordship will need no advice upon that subject : we well know his character for bravery.''

"Of course we do !" remarked Mowbray, with a smile ; "we cannot doubt but that he will have ample satisfaction ; more particularly as he will have to answer everything to Ravensford, whose temper we all know so well, that, we may be assured, he will not rest until he has demanded satisfaction of Lord Saunter.''

The rueful looks of the cowardly nobleman, fully testified that he was precisely of the same opinion, and which made him feel far from comfortable.

"Oh, yes, there cannot be any doubt," observed Spangle, who noticed the fearful looks of Saunter, and enjoyed the joke vastly ; "there cannot be any doubt but that that will be Ravensford's first step. He is a determined fellow when his indignation is excited, and there is not a better shot in the country.''

Lord Saunter could with difficuly suppress a deep groan, and Sir Harry Spangle continued,

"Lord Ravensford has had more experience in duelling than any other man I know of, and it would, I should say, be almost an impossibility for him to miss his man.''

Lord Saunter turned very pale, and his teeth gave symptoms of performing *a la castanet* ; he, however, endeavoured all he could to conceal his fears from the observation of his companions, and the smile with which he foreibly clad his features, was the most grim and melancholy looking thing imaginable.

"But Ravensford must first find out where his lordship is," said Captain Mowbray.

"True, ' answered Spangle ; "but, of course, Lord Saunter can have no wish or intention to conceal it from him. He will not hesitate to afford him all the satisfaction he may require, or who can say what might or might not be inferred from it ?''

"My dear fellow," hastily remarked his lordship, stammering, and looking most egregiously stupid and woe-begone ; "that is the very thing it is my particular wish to conceal. I—I—I—it is unnecessary for me at present to state what my motives are for so doing ; of course, it is not necessary for me, to assure you that fear of Ravenford has nothing whatever to do with it.''

"Oh, certainly," exclaimed Captain Mowbray and Sir Harry Spangle together, with a look of mock heroic solemnity.

"Under existing circumstances," added Lord Saunter, "such a meeting would be rather unpleasant at present.''

"Very unpleasant !" coincided both gentlemen sarcastically.

"There are times an seasons for all things, you know.''

"Oh, certainly, certainly.''

"And the time is not, perhaps, far distant, when my enemies may learn the real character of the individual they have to deal with.''

"Why, for that matter, my lord," said Spangle, in a tone of bitter irony, that could not escape the observation of Saunter, "few persons characters are so generally known, at present, as your lordship's. But, of course, you will leave Ireland then ?''

"No," answered Saunter, "if I can depend upon the secrecy of Mowbray and yourself, I do not think I shall ; I shall be quite safe as long as I can preserve my incognito.''

Lord Saunter thought and had determined to act quite contrary to this ; but he thought that by telling them so, he might deceive them, and have an opportunity of leaving the country without their being aware of the direction he had gone in. Their raillery had filled him with confusion and chagrin, and he felt greatly relieved when they informed him that they were going to a party that evening, and when he saw them arise to go.

"I wish your lordship a very good night," said Mowbray, approaching the door, "and whenever your meeting with Ravensford takes place, you will find both myself and Sir Harry at your command. We will do ourselves the pleasure of calling upon you again to-morrow."

"And, in the meantime," said his lordship, "let me once more beg of you not to let a syllable drop about me, or where I am at present staying."

"Certainly not," said Spangle, "you have known us before to day, and ought to have learnt to trust us without these injunctions. Mum's the word. Good evening to your lordship."

"Good evening! good evening, my dear fellows," said Saunter, impatiently.

Mowbray and the other moved towards the room-door, and where about to depart, when Captain Mowbray stopped and whispered something to Spangle, who turned back, and said aloud—

"Why, we have so often been accomodated by his lordship before, that I confess I do not ike to ask him."

"What is it you require?" demanded the ready dupe, happy to get rid of them on almost any terms. "Is there anything I can serve you in?"

"The fact is, Saunter," replied Captain Mowbray, with a bold front; "the fact is, we have both been devilish unlucky at play lately, and—but I am afraid you will think me making too free—could you—if you could, you would confer a very great favour upon myself and Spangle, if you would accommodate us with a couple of hundred for a month? Only for a month, mark that!"

"Yes, only for a month positively. I shall have plenty of money then; and will liquidate all we owe you! We have been devilish unfortunate lately, as Mowbray has told you; but who knows but that this very night we might be able to recover ourselves? Pay you directly."

"The money shall be yours," said his lordship, as he left the room for a few minutes, and shortly afterwards returned with a cheque for the amount, which he placed in the hands of Captain Mowbray.

"Thanks—thanks—a thousand thanks!" said Mowbray and Spangle, in a breath; "we'll pay you in a month at the very latest. Goodby; call again to-morrow! What a devilish fortunate chance it was which threw you in our way again."

"Curses light upon the moment!" ejacu-

lated his lordship, when they had quitted the house; "I must contrive some means to elude them, and to escape from this place, where, it is very clear, I am not safe for a moment. Courage may be a very good thing in its way; but I must candidly admit to myself, that I possess but a very small share of the commodity, and have not the least inclination to encounter either Ravensford or Adder, and sincerely regret that this affair which has placed me in such an awkward dilemma, ever occurred at all."

Wrapping himself in a large mantle, so as to conceal his person from observation, Lord Saunter now walked forth, and bent his way to a retired house a short distance from the city, where he had been accustomed to pass a great portion of his time, he being unknown to the frequenters in any other character than that of a private gentleman, and seldom mingling in their company. On the way thither, he reflected on the interview which had just taken place between himself and the two profligates, and he felt confident that, while they were near him, and acquainted with his residence, he was in the utmost danger, and the remarks they had made, and the manner in which they spoke, fully convinced him that as soon as he declined yielding to their extortionate demands, they would feel a gratification in disclosing all they knew about him, and in bringing about a rencontre of which he was so much in dread. He now regretted, when too late, that he had ever been so easily led astray, and that he should become so easy a dupe, made the complete laughing-stock to all who knew him, and in danger of that chastisement he could not but feel convinced he fully deserved; and readily would he have made any atonement that he could for that of which he had been guilty. But what means of doing so had he? What could ever atone for the deep, the irreparable injury he had been one of the principal causes of inflicting upon Lord Ravensford and the rest of the family? Would it restore the unfortunate Lady Ravensford to them uninjured? Would it restore the lost happiness of the family, or be enabled to remove the foul obloquy which the prejudiced and censorious world would be likely to attach to their victim's name? No, he was certain it could not, and almost for the first time in his life Lord Saunter became sensible to the voice of conscience.

The principal part of this young nobleman's vices, as we have, we believe, before observed, might be attributed more to the weakness of the head than the natural depravity of the heart. Left, when very young, in the possession of enormous wealth, and without any one to guide and advise him, he, like many others have done, became an easy victim to the votaries of extravagance and folly, and at length became so entangled in its giddy vortex, that he found it impossible to escape, and was too silly to take the trouble to reflect whether he was doing right or wrong. The progress of vice, especially when the votary of it has every means in his power to command the uncontrolled indulgence of his vicious propensities, is very quick, and so it was with Lord Saunter; and shortly after he had become acquainted with Captain Mowbray and his other profligate associates, tnose few vistues he had ever evinced were entirely stifled in his bosom, and he lived to be the curse of his fellow-creatures; the dupe and the scorn of his companions, and suspected by every one, admired by none. Now, however, as we before said, he did feel compunction for what he had done, and could he have met with any one who would know how to advise him, he might still have been reclaimed to society.

He in vain for some time endeavoured to think upon the course it would be most advisable for him to pursue, for, to remain where he was, he considered was fraught with great danger, yet how to get away without the knowledge of Mowbray and Sir Harry Spangle, he was at a loss. Nevertheless, he resolved to make the trial, and which he thought he could the more easily accomplish, he being only in ready furnished apartments, and he at last determined to make his way to Paris, the propriety of which determination, to say the least of it, we must consider rather questionable.

On his way home, deeply wrapped in thought, he had just turned the corner of a street, when raising his head, he beheld the tall and elegant figure of a man approaching him, with which he seemed perfectly familiar. A sensation of fear came over him, for which he could not exactly account, and he involuntarily wrapped his mantle closer around him, and almost buried his features in its ample folds. He soon perceived that his fears had not been excited without a cause; the man had got within a very short distance of him when he looked up, and the light emitted from a lamp close at hand fell full upon his features. Judge, then, the astonishment and alarm of Lord Saunter, when he recognised the man he so much dreaded to see, Lord Ravensford. The hasty glimpse he had of his features, showed the libertine they were ghastly pale and care-worn, out they were characterised by a determined expression which showed plainly that the thoughts of the heavy wrongs he had sustained were deeply implanted in his bosom.

It would be impossible to do adequate justice to the feelings of cowardice experienced by Saunter. He was so alarmed, indeed, that he could scarcely move, and he gave himself up for a moment for lost. To turn back and retreat would probably have been to betray

himself, and at last, covering his face with the folds of his mantle, and altering his gait, he walked to the other s de of the way, and had the satisfaction to find that Ravensford passed on and was quickly out of sight without, apparently, taking any notice of him. Once, and once only, did Lord Saunter turn round to look after his injured enemy, until he was completely hid in the darkness beyond, when the former walked, or rather ran, in the direction of the place where he was stopping, grateful that he had for the present escaped the calling to account which he so greatly feared, and fully determined that another day should not see him in Dublin.

Ravensford, then, must have obtained a clue to him; but by what means, or through whom, he was at a loss to conjecture; but had he ascertained the exact place where he resided? Had he been to the house during his absence? —he was coming from that direction; but no, he felt confident that if he had done so, nothing would have induced him to quit it again until he had seen him (Saunter). He, therefore, felt rather more easy on that point, and which was greatly increased when, on his arrival at the house, he eagerly inquired if any one had been asking for him, and he was answered in the negative. He hurried to his chamber, and there hastily packed up his portmanteau, being determined that the first streak of day the following morning should witness his departure, for which purpose he ordered his servant to get up at an early hour, and bringing the portmanteau with him, to meet him at a certain place at some distance from the city.

Lord Saunter's mind was to busily occupied to suffer him to have much sleep that night, and at daybreak the following morning, leaving a note on the dressing-table, apologizing for his abrupt departure, and partly explaining the cause of his going, he silently and cautiously quitted the house, and best his course speedily towards the place in which he had ordered his servant to meet him, and where he found him on his arrival. Having got into a vehicle, in a very short time they were a considerable distance from Dublin, and in the course of the same day, they had embarked on board a vessel and were on their way to the coast of France.

It was not until he was fairly on ship-board the pusillanimous lord could consider himself safe, and he then felt grateful for the success which had attended his scheme, and hoped that he was now out of danger of the wrath of Lord Ravensford, until such time as the affair might be finally and amicably settled.

Paris was about one of the worst places which Lord Saunter could have selected to retire to, much frequented as it was by the English nobility and gentry, and where, of all others, he was the most likely to encounter some one that knew him, especially among the gay and thoughtless with whom he had been accustomed to mingle. But this was only on a par with the other imprudent and silly things this unfortunate nobleman was in the habit of doing, and which had led him into such various dilemmas during his life; nay, more, he had not been in Paris many days when, encouraged by the hope of security, and tempted by the gaities and frivolities of the place, he banished his former apprehensions and precautions from his mind altogether, and launched forth into the course of extravagance and dissipation he had been in the habit of pursuing, visiting a l the places of fashionable resort, of the gay and the wild. His wealth, and the lavish manner in which he squandered it away in every species of debauchery, soon made him an object of attraction to those who aspire to pretensions to notice in preference to virtue and rectitude of conduct, and he had soon around him almost as numerous a host of acquaintances as he had had in England, and was soon the luminary in the fashionable world round which all the smaller plants revolved.

Fashionable pleasure! how empty — how insipid—how revolting is it to those who have no more than the means to enjoy the comforts of life without abusing them; who have felt the luxury of those domestic joys that are too frequently confined to the humble hearth. The utter mockery which the wild and un-principled call pleasure, is a creature of their own, a huge quack, got up for the purpose of deluding and destroying its unhappy votaries —the Juggernaut which lays waste and crushes beneath its ponderous weight the unhappy wretches who move beneath it. The votary of folly leads a life of incessant care, of pain, of self-reproach, and madness. Let him be roll-ing in all that wealth can purchase, still is he not half so contented—so happy as the humble husbandman who toils hard all day and finds his only happiness centred in his humble cottage, his frugal housewife, and his healthy, rosy children. There are moments when even the most callous, the most insensible must reflect, and happiness and content can only be the lot of those who know the happiness of a self-approving conscience.

Lord Saunter verified the truth of the above observations; for weak and foolish as he was, there were moments when conscience would speak in a voice which must be heard, and when he suffered all the torments we have described. Those were moments when even the maddening wine-cup failed to have its usual influence upon him, and when the remem-brance of our heroine, and the injuries he had not only sought to do her, but those which he had, in all probability, actually been the cause of her enduring, would rush upon his brain with the most powerful effect, and when the image

of Ravensford and the dread of his fury, would become present to his mind's eye, and fill him with the most unqualified compunction and apprehension. His constitution, also, had suffered much from the life of intemperance he had for so long led, and although at one time really a good-looking young man, he was now brought to a premature old age, and his features were swollen and disfigured with the effects of the pernicious draughts he swallowed with such frenzied gusto.

One thing we had almost forgotten to men-tion, which is, that Saunter had taken the pre-caution to go in an assumed name, and was known among the giddy circles with which he now mingled, as Sir Waldegrave Weston. In this he acted wisely, for his name would soon have reached England, and the whole secret have been exploded. In Paris he had now been for six months, and neither hearing nor seeing anything of Lord Ravensford, he thought himsel quite secure; but he was soon doomed to be undeceived, in a manner he had least expected, in order to explain which, we must return to the distracted Ravensford.

We have before described the feelings which tormented Lord Ravensford, when he quitted Holly Hall. Jealousy, revenge, despair, and maddening rage contended in his breast, and it was remarkable that his reason did not sink beneath it. In spite of all his endeavours to the contrary, he could not help yielding to the painful and fatal delusion that Rosabelle had deceived him, and was the willing partner of Lord Saunter and Adder in their flight, and he was fully bent upon not resting until he had obtained either a confirmation or indisput-able contradiction of his surmises, and had gratified his revenge against the guilty parties.

"Not even the most remote corner of the world," he soliloquised, "will I leave un-searched, until I have found them, or learned what has become of them. They surely cannot long elude an injured husband's eye! The retributive power of Heaven will direct me to the spot where the wretches have concealed themselves at present from my fury. Oh, Rosabelle, too beauteous but faithless woman; after all we have endured together; after your many vows of eternal love, of adoration, never did I imagine you could thus cruelly, dis-gracefully act!—Good God! is it possible?— Rosabelle, my wife, the mother of my child; —her whose whole, whose only crime I had believed originated with me,—so abandoned as to desert her home, husband, father, off-spring, and throw herself into the arms of another man! Oh! I cannot believe it!— Would that I could think to the contrary, but alas! is not black suspicion arraigned too powerfully against her? The letter! that fatal, that cold-hearted letter, in which she acknowledges, yes, shamefully acknowledges her guilt, ought to be efficient proof ; and why should I longer doubt? Oh, agony, supreme! —Oh, conviction, most excruciating ! The torments of the damned cannot equal those I now endure! But where is the wretch ! the fiend in human shape, who has done this?— Why am I not allowed to encounter him, that I may wash out the stain of my honour in his blood ? My brain is on fire till I meet with the miscreants who have wrought me this heavy evil, who have thrown a blight upon my happiness for ever! And thou, my poor child! must thou be left without a mother's fostering care ?—*My* child, said I !—Ah ! even in that **may** she not have deceived me ? But, no, no, base and cruel as I now suspect her to be, I cannot believe that she could be so entirely lost as that ! No, the cherub looks of the sweet innocent appear to offer a contradiction to it. I will not imagine thy mother guilty of this for thy sake.''

Indulging in these and other similar sorrowful ruminations, Lord Ravensford continued to caress his unconscious son, as the vehicle proceeded rapidly from the neighbourhood, and the anguish of the poor girl he had taken with him in order that she might look after the child, was fervent and sincere. Once she even ventured to inquire of her lord whither they were going, but she was awed from doing so a second time by the severity of the answer he gave her, and the impatience he evinced.

They stopped twice only to change horses and to take some refreshment; and then they resumed their journey in the same manner as they had hitherto proceeded. It was quite dark in the evening, after crossing an extensive wood, that they stopped at the door of a cottage, where Lord Ravensford bade the post-boy alight, and knock. It was quickly opened, by a clean, matronly looking dame, who appeared to have expected them, and ushered them into the parlour, which was also very clean, and neatly though humbly furnished, and by the fire-side sat an old man, who arose upon the entrance of Lord Ravensford, and paid his respects to him. Ravensford threw himself into a chair, and sunk immediately into a deep reverie, from which no one ventured to disturb h m and the old woman, upon a motion from her husband, bustled about, and quickly spread a frugal repast upon the table, of which she desired the female to partake, at the same time she ventured to observe, that the homeliness of the fare would not suit his lordship. Ravensford merely shook his head, and relapsed into thought, and the young woman who had accompanied him attended to the cottager's request, and partook slightly of the evening meal. When she had finished, Lord Ravensford suddenly arose, and addressing himself to her, said :—

"Your journey with me terminates here; I can manage the boy myself during the short time he will be in my possession. Here I desire you will lodge for the night, and these good people will accommodate you, and show you the coach-office, if you think proper to return to your friends. To Holly Hall I desire you will not go, unless you should hear further from me. Here is money for you, and I caution you not to tell any one who may inquire the particulars of our journey, or in what direction we travelled. Do you mind what I say ?''

The woman looked astonished, while Ravensford threw a purse of money into her lap.

" Gracious me, my lord!'' cried the former, " what are you going to do with the poor dear child ?''

" It matter not to you,'' said his lordship, impatiently, " he is going where he will be well provided for. But do you promise me what I ask of you ?''

" Oh, dear, yes, my lord,'' she answered, " but—''

" I must have more than your bare word,'' interrupted Lord Ravensford ; " it is of the utmost importance that this should not be known ; you must take an oath not to divulge it.''

The female, after some little hesitation, complied, and giving the old cottager some instructions aside, Lord Ravensford re-entered the chaise in which the little Alfred, who had fallen to sleep, was deposited, and the vehicle drove off in a contrary direction to that it had previously been pursuing ; and Ravensford, being left to himself, had an opportunity of giving the most unrestrained indulgence to the many conflicting thoughts that agitated his bosom. He had made every arrangement that he thought necessary for the plans he had in view, and the future care of his child. He had determined to place him with a humble but worthy couple, who had only one child of their own, and who had at one time lived in his service. They resided in a far distant part of the country from Holly Hall, and as it was his strict injunction that they should keep the circumstance a secret for some time, he thought it was not probable that any one would guess whither the boy had been conveyed. He had made arrangements to allow the poor people a handsome salary for the trouble they would be at, and he had not the least doubt but that they would pay as much care and attention to it as if it had been their own. His reasons for this extraordinary step will, probably, appear ultimately, until which time we must request our readers to suspend their curiosity. The cottage of Christopher Goldham, and his pretty young wife, was situated not far distant from the sea-beach, and the former had, since he had quitted Lord Ravensford's family, followed the humble occupation of a fisherman, but he hailed the introduction of the child of his late noble master beneath his roof with the most un bounded pleasure, not only on account of the honour, and the wish he had to render the latter all the service that was in his power, but because it would better their condition, and be the means of rendering his wife more happy, and increase their comforts.

Lord Ravensford having repeated his injunctions to these poor people, which they sincerely promised to obey, after caressing his child in the most affectionate manner, and invoking the blessings of Heaven upon his head, he took his leave of Christopher and his wife, and resumed his melancholy journey. He travelled the whole of that night, and the next morning put up at one of the principal hotels, where he intimated to the servants who attended him, that he should remain for a day or two to rest himself, and to consider his plans for the future, and cautioned them not to mention his real name, or whence they had come, and to keep themselves as much in-doors as possible. The men were two persons on whom he could depend, and, therefore, this caution was almost unnecessary. On the third morning after they had been here, they were surprised to find that Ravensford had departed; and from a note which he had left behind for them, as well as a well-filled purse each, they were informed that his lordship had no further occasion for their services, but requested them not to return to that part of the country from whence they had just come, where they would be immediately known and minutely questioned, and to keep every thing that had passed an inviolable secret in their own bosoms, until, if ever it so happened, they were at liberty to reveal it. The chaise they were ordered to return by strangers to Holly Hall, and thus put all fear of a discovery by that means at an end.

We will now further pursue the footsteps of the distracted Ravensford, who had determined, in various disguises, and on foot, to endeavour to gain that information on which his future happiness or endless misery depended. And language cannot do justice to the many cares, deep anxieties, vicissitudes and vexations, he underwent in the execution of that project; but he bore them all with much greater fortitude than could have been anticipated, and the alternate hopes he sometimes indulged in that his efforts would be crowned with success, kept up his energies, when they must otherwise have sunk under such heavy trials.—Bodily and mental fatigue he had become inured to, and night and day his mind could never rest, busy with the mighty schemes it was in possession of. Sometimes he attired himself in the garb of a mendicant, with tattered, patched up clothes, and unshaven beard, and in that disguise he would gain admission to various houses, where he endeavoured to obtain such information as might afford him a clue to the fugitives. At others he was disguised in female apparel, tottering with pretended age, and appealing immediately to the sympathies of the public. Then he would assume the dress of a countryman, and, in fact, he left no means untried; he was untiring and indefatigable in his endeavours, and often he pictured to himself the gratification he should feel in suddenly beholding those for whom he was in search, when they little expected he would be so near to them, and the consummation of all for which he now exerted himself. But for some time his labours, his anxieties, were unattended with any success. Not a word of information could he obtain of his unfortunate wife, or the villains who had wrought him so much misery; although he saw, from the accounts in the newspapers, that notwithstanding the great exertions that had been made for that purpose, no clue could be obtained to discover her, or the wretches by whom it was supposed she had been borne away. They also teemed with strange and romantic accounts of the no less singular disappearance of his lordship; and various were the conjectures they formed as to what had become of him and his son, and of the dreadful situation to which Mr. Montalbert had been reduced by the circumstances.

It may readily be imagined what agony rent the bosom of his lordship when he perused these melancholy accounts, which formed a complete romance of real life in the fashionable world. It was wonderful how his reason or constitution could support them; but, determined to set their minds at rest as regarded himself and the little Alfred, he found means to have a letter forwarded to Mr. Goodman, informing him of his own and the child's safety, and assuring them that he would not cease in his endeavours to unravel this dreadful mystery while he had life and strength to do so. He entrusted the management of his affairs, during his absence, to Mr. Goodman, and promised to give them further information whenever he had an opportunity so to do. He also managed to write a letter to Christopher and his wife, and to receive one in reply from them, making him acquainted with the welfare of his son, and the secrecy in which they had hitherto been enabled to keep him. He then renewed his researches with increased energy and determination.

The letter which had been entrusted to Phœbe, by Rosabelle, by some mischance never reached Holly Hall, a circumstance which will be hereafter explained, and thus one of the most certain means of disclosing the whole plot, and of tracing her, had been frustrated.

At length a circumstance occurred which raised the hopes of Ravensford, and made him anticipate the most favourable results. Notwithstanding he had gone in disguise to the different estates of Saunter, he had not at any of them been able to elicit any information to assist him in his purpose ; but, at last, by mere accident, he happened to drop into the cottage of the very man who had fetched the portmanteau of Lord Saunter from the place where he and Adder had been staying on the morning after the abduction. This man had removed to the part of the country he at present resided in immediately after that circumstance took place, and Ravensford, having taken an opportunity of alluding to the painful affair which was at that time exciting such a deep interest in the world, the latter said, in reference to it, that it was also very strange that Lord Saunter should also have disappeared about the same time, and that it should not be known whither he had gone ; and he then mentioned the circumstance of carrying the gentleman's portmanteau to the inn the morning after the painful event at Holly Hall, and that he had since ascertained that the gentleman who had employed him answered in every respect the description given of Lord Saunter. Snatching eagerly at this information, Ravensford questioned the man more minutely as to the coach in which the gentleman had departed ; and though he at first was reluctant to answer the inquiries, Ravensford at last thought it would be advisable to make a confidant of him, and revealing who he was, under an injunction of the strictest secrecy, he by the offer of a large reward at length prevailed upon him to tell him all the particulars he knew, and ascertained that the gentleman. whoever he was, had gone by the coach to Liverpool, from whence he had accidentally learned that it was his intention to proceed to Ireland. With breathless eagerness, Ravensford again and again got him to describe the gentleman, and it corresponded in every respect with the person of Saunter ; but more especially from a mole which the man had noticed on his right cheek, and that he had a slight impediment in his speech.

This was enough, and again elate with the most sanguine hopes, and burning with impatience to wreak his revenge on Saunter, who, it was clear, was deeply connected with the infamous and cruel plot, although he was not accompanied by any female, Lord Ravensford was the next morning early in the coach on his way to Liverpool, from whence he proceeded to Dublin. Here he arrived in due course, still sanguine as to the result of his adventure, and lost no time in making all the necessary inquiries, but with a caution which never forsook him in the most trying moments ; but for some time he was completely unsuccessful, owing to the steps which Saunter himself had taken for concealment. It will be remembered how Saunter encountered him, and what followed. The very next day Ravensford accidentally met Mowbray and Sir Harry Spangle. The meeting may be better conceived than described. The two profligates were at first ashamed to meet Ravensford, and probably remembered the manner in which the latter had deserted them after his marriage with Rosabelle ; but seeing the altered and careworn appearance of the former, indifferent as they were on most occasions to feelings of pity, they could not behold him, and know the manner in which he had been so unjustly served, without a sentiment of pity and commiseration ; and, such are the strange freaks of inconsistency which villany often assumes, they yielded to the earnest supplications of the distracted husband, and revealed to him the whole plot as far as they had been able to elicit from Saunter. With what feelings of disgust, agony, and indignation, did Ravensford listen to this painful story, and with what horror and bitter self-reproach did he find how cruelly and unjustly he had judged of his unfortunate wife ! The plot seemed too atrocious for anything but fiends to concoct, and for awhile Ravensford stood completely bewildered, and, as it were, paralysed to the spot.

" Oh, Rosabelle ! — deeply-injured, persecuted Rosabelle ! how shall I ever be able to repay the injury I have done you ?—What an unnatural monster I must be !—My God, do not deprive me of my senses !—Where is she— where is my wife ? Adder ! oh, villain !— miscreant unequalled ! dearly shall you suffer for this ! Saunter, too, where is he ?—Do not deceive me—you know !—Oh, pity me ; do not further rack that heart which is already almost broken !—Where is Saunter ?—Give him to my vengeance, that I may learn the truth from his polluted lips.'

Neither Mowbray or Spangle returned any immediate reply, although they were really moved by the intensity of his agony, and were uncertain how to act, being unwilling to betray Saunter, and yet anxious to grant Ravensford the information he required.

The impatience of Ravensford grew beyond all endurance, and his eyes burned like two balls of fire with the fierce emotions that racked his mind.

" Mowbray—Spangle !" he at length cried, " if you have any humanity in your breasts ; if you are not entirely callous to every feeling of pity, you will not torture me longer, by keeping me in this terrible state of suspense ! Oh. you will give me all the information in your power, and, in return, my everlasting gratitude, my friendship, nay, my fortune, shall be at your service. Ah ! I see you are not so base as you are represented to be ; you will not turn a deaf ear to my entreaties. What know you of the wretch Adder ?"

"Of Adder," answered Mowbray, "we know no more than what we have told you; and although we have been industriously endeavouring to ascertain whither he has conveyed Lady Ravensford (for that she is in his power, there can be very little, if any doubt,) we have not been able to succeed, the fellow has formed and executed his design with such ability."

Ravensford groaned aloud, and clasped his forehead frantically, then raised his eyes towards Heaven, as if imploring its aid.

"Oh, agony supreme!" he cried, "why am I thus punished? But tell me: Saunter—you know where he is? It is useless to deny it;

he is somewhere in this place, and you know it."

Mowbray and Spangle exchanged glances, which seemed to inquire of each other whether they should yield to the wishes of Ravensford, and betray that man who had so often befriended them, and that only the day before. But the agony of Ravensford prevailed over their scruples, and they informed him whither he would find that misguided nobleman.

"Ah, miscreant! wretch!" shouted Ravensford, as he prepared to rush deliriously from the spot to the place where they had informed him he would find the object of his revenge. "I have, then, at last discovered you! This

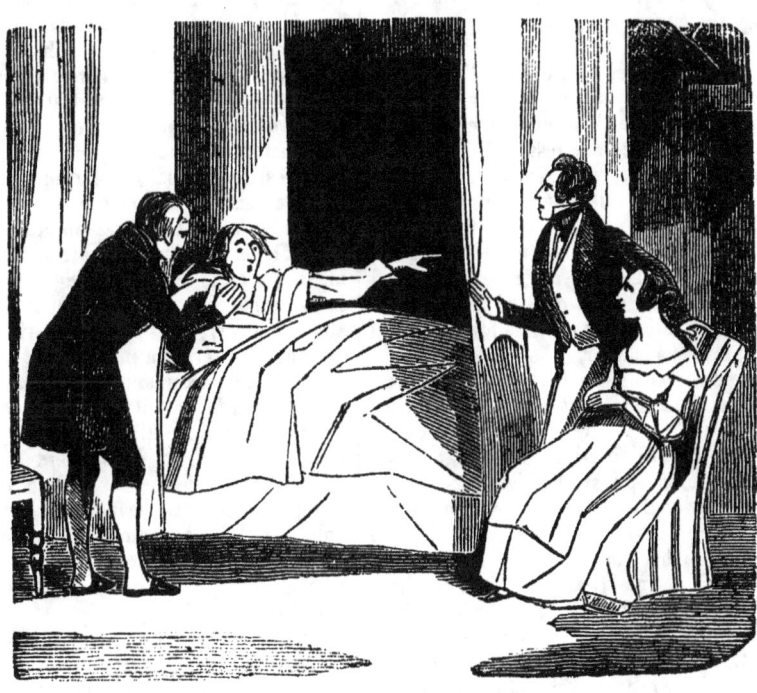

THE MANIAC FATHER RAVING OF HIS LOST ROSABELLE.

day, this very hour, you shall pay dearly for the wrongs you have done me and others!—I will have your heart's blood!"

"Hold, Ravensford!" exclaimed Captain Mowbray, laying hold of his lordship's arm, and seeking to detain him, "this must not be. Are you mad?—Would you commit a murder?"

"Murder!" repeated Ravensford; "has not the wretch murdered my happiness for ever? Mad!—yes, it drives me frantic when I think of the unparalleled cruelty to which I and mine have been made the victims. Unhand me, Mowbray; my blood's on fire, I will not be detained."

And with these words, the distracted

Ravensford tore himself forcibly away, and rushed towards the street in which they had informed him Saunter resided, they following him quickly, and almost repenting that they had given him the information, now they saw the consequences that were likely to ensue.

The wild demeanour and frantic manners of Lord Ravensford alarmed the female who opened the door to him, and her terror was by no means abated when he demanded in hoarse accents where the villain Saunter was (by which name she had not known him); and not being able to reply to him immediately, he repeated his question in yet fiercer tones than before. Recollecting, however, Mowbray and Spangle, she looked to them for an explanation, and was soon made to understand who it was the unfortunate gentleman wanted. Their astonishment was no less than that of Lord Ravensford, when the woman informed them that the gentleman they inquired for had gone away that morning early, in a very abrupt and mysterious manner ; and, from a note which he had left behind him in one of the apartments he had occupied, they were given to understand that it was not his intention to return again.

"Gone—gone !" cried Ravensford, wildly : "what cruel mockery is this ? You would deceive me. The villain is still in the house, but hears my voice, and would fain shield himself from my vengeance. Let me pass ! I will drag the miscreant forth, and tread him beneath my feet !"

"Hold—hold, Lord Ravensford !" remonstrated Sir Henry Spangle. "Pray calm this violence, and let us endeavour to ascertain the truth. Probably your mistress will favour us with a few minutes' converse, and will have no objection to explain this singular circumstance farther ?"

The female replied that she would make her mistress acquainted with their request ; and Ravensford, whose deeply-excited feelings had almost exhausted his strength, suffered himself to be led into the parlour, where he sunk into a chair, and, covering his face with his hands, groaned aloud in mental agony. By the time the lady of the house, however, had descended the stairs, he had become somewhat more calm ; and she, deeply sympathizing with him in his great distress, although unacquainted with the cause, readily gave them all the explanation in her power, and, to convince them, gave them the note which Lord Saunter had left behind him, and which Ravensford immediately recognised to be in the handwriting of Saunter ; but it gave them no idea as to whither he had directed his course.

Lord Ravensford was in such a state of excitement, that neither Captain Mowbray nor Sir Henry Spangle would leave him until they saw him to the hotel in which he had put up since his arrival in that city ; where nature could hold out no longer against the powerful emotion that raged in his bosom, and sinking on a sofa he fainted away, and was borne to his chamber, where medical attendance was immediately sent for, which, on arriving, pronounced him to be in considerable danger, and ordered him to be kept as quiet as possible.

Captain Mowbray and his friend attributed the sudden disappearance of Lord Saunter to the right cause—namely, his being fearful that they would betray the place of his retreat and his real name to somebody ; and they were vexed and disappointed that he had contrived to elude them so easily, and were resolved to use their utmost endeavours to find

him out. In the present instance they acted with more propriety and justice than they were frequently in the habit of doing, and took upon themselves to make the persons of Holly Hall acquainted with the circumstances as they had happened, and to inform them where he was at that time lying, and of the condition he was in.

Lord Ravensford remained for several days in a very dangerous state, and was quite delirious ; and when he recovered his senses, he was not a little astonished and gratified to behold Rattleton and Mr. Wilmott standing by his bedside. Eager as he was to know whether they had yet been able to obtain any information of Rosabelle, and of the state in which her father now was, the medical gentleman would not allow him to converse, and the patient was, therefore, compelled to suspend his agonizing curiosity and anxiety, the two gentlemen thinking the advice of the doctors perfectly just, and fearful that any fresh cause of excitement might cause him to suffer a relapse ; they, therefore, talked no more than was absolutely necessary, and after a short pause, his lordship dropped off into a calm and refreshing sleep, to the uninterrupted enjoyment of which they left him, and Mowbray and Spangle having evinced a very great alteration in their behaviour for the better, and expressed their readiness and anxiety to render all the assistance in their power towards the discovery of Adder, and the place where he, no doubt, held Lady Ravensford in confinement, they retired with them to the coffee-room, to hear from them such particulars of the behaviour of Adder and Lord Saunter as they were acquainted with, and to consult in what manner it would now be best to act.

In three days after this Lord Ravensford had almost entirely recovered, and heard from Rattleton with the most poignant regret, the melancholy state in which Mr. Montalbert remained, and of the little hopes there were of his ever regaining his senses any more. Mr. Goodman and Mrs. Rattleton still continued to behave to the unfortunate gentleman with the same kindness and attention that they had always done, and there were moments when they could almost fancy he knew them, but they were brief indeed, and such temporary lucid intervals were generally succeeded by the most awful and violent ravings. Rattleton gave a vivid description of the excess of their horror and grief, on receiving the letter which Captain Mowbray and Spangle had sent to Holly Hall, but it was somewhat ameliorated by the knowledge of where he (Lord Ravensford) was, and himself and their friend lost no time in hastening to him. The terrible information respecting Rosabelle, which left little doubt that she was in the power of the daring and heartless scoundrel, Adder, it is needless to say, had caused them all the greatest anguish and disgust, but additional exertions were being made, and large rewards offered to any person who could come forward and give any information upon the painful subject, and they had, therefore, very good reason to hope that the perpetrators of this vile act would speedily be brought to justice, and Lady Ravesford restored to his arms.

Lord Ravensford shook his head, and groaned deeply.

"Alas!" he exclaimed, "would that I dare encourage those sanguine hopes; but whichever way I look, nothing but horror and despair meet my eyes. Good God! how long is this state of anguish to last? Are we for ever to be made the sport of villany? Rosabelle, when I think of your name, and the probable sufferings and degradations to which you are doubtless exposed, my blood chills with horror! If you are, indeed, once more restored to my arms, it may only be after being exposed to that disgrace, at which my heart revolts! The wretch, Adder, little did I imagine when he threatened me with vengeance, that it would be inflicted in the dreadful manner he has chosen to gratify it, and in which, monster as he is, he has but too well succeeded. The heaviest malediction of the Most High descend upon his head, and may all the tortures he has inflicted upon others recoil with ten-fold severity upon himself."

Fearful that his feelings would again become too powerfully excited, and cause a relapse, Rattleton and Willmott again endeavoured to soothe him, and changed the immediate topic of conversation, the former taking the opportunity to inquire of Ravensford where he had placed his son, and what was his motive for so doing? To the first question Ravensford showed no hesitation in replying, but the second he begged leave for the present to decline; and finding it was no good to press him, they desisted. Lord Ravensford, however, gave his consent to little Alfred's being removed to the hall, requiring that his present nurse should attend him; and as there was nothing unreasonable in this, they did not endeavour to dissuade him from it. At the request of his friends, he wrote a letter to the appointed nurse of his child to that effect, which was immediately despatched, but little did they anticipate the answer they were to receive. In two days from the time Lord Ravensford wrote, an answer was returned by Christopher, which filled every breast with astonishment and horror;—the little Alfred had been taken away from the cottage three days before the receipt of his lordship's letter in a most mysterious manner, and not the least idea could be formed of the manner in which he had been stolen, or into whose hands he had

fallen. Lord Ravensford was so greatly shocked by this unexpected and afflicting intelligence, that he almost suffered a relapse; and Rattleton and Wilmott were so completely taken by surprise, and so grieved at the information, that they were scarcely in a better condition than Lord Ravensford.

"Good God!" exclaimed the latter, after a pause, during which he was undergoing the most dreadful mental torture, "what new calamities are in store for me? My boy!—my poor child!—oh, who has done this cruel deed?"

"Pray, calm yourself, Ravensford," at length Rattleton remonstrated; "do not give way to the violence of your grief, which will disable you from acting with promptitude and judgment in this most ambiguous affair. This, in my firm belief, is another of the villain Adder's deeds, to which he has in all probability been prompted by revenge or some other motive, which I cannot at present imagine. This must add fresh energy to our exertions to find out the place where he has concealed himself, and I have strong hopes that, by losing no time and the offer of a good reward, we shall succeed in finding him, and in wresting his victims from his power."

"The miscreant!" cried Lord Ravensford, clasping his forehead in despair; "I will not rest until I have found him and duly punished him for his hellish deeds. But my unfortunate boy: what has become of him? Should he have fallen into the hands of that wretch, perhaps, ere this, his innocent blood has been shed, and I may be bereaved of all that could make ——— to life."

"Come, come, Ravensford," observed Mr. Wilmott, "you must arouse yourself into action. Giving way to this state of despondency can effect no good."

Ravensford groaned, but made no answer. Shortly afterwards, however, he authorised Rattleton to write immediately to Holly Hall, acquainting Mr. Goodman and his daughter with the melancholy circumstance, and requesting the former to take such steps as would seem most wise to him. This Rattleton immediately did; and then, accompanied by Wilmott, went and made the event known to the different authorities, in order that a strict search might be made by the officers of justice after the lost child; and a very large reward was offered to any person who could bring them intelligence which might lead to the detection of the villain or villains who held him in their power, and cause his restoration to his wretched parent.

The following day Lord Ravensford and his friends left the place where they had been staying, and departed for the neighbourhood in which Gilbert and his wife resided, where they arrived on the day after. They found the poor people in a state of complete distraction; and, as they solemnly declared, they had not been able to sleep, eat, or drink ever since the shocking occurrence had taken place. Lord Ravensford and his friends questioned them narrowly, and the account they elicited was to the following effect :—

It appeared that for some days prior to the event taking place, a strange-looking vessel had been lying off the coast, and of which Gilbert formed no very good opinion. On the day before it happened, walking by the sea-beach, and leading the little Alfred by the hand, Janet had met with a very decently-dressed woman, who appeared to be very feeble, and who, taking notice of the child, got into conversation with her, in the course of which the old woman managed to elicit from her to whom the child belonged, although she had received such precautions from Lord Ravensford to keep secret upon the subject. She took no particular notice of the circumstance at the time, although the old woman was very inquisitive, and being a perfect stranger to her, she admitted that she had acted very imprudently, and for which she should never forgive herself. The next day, her husband being from home at the time, and the child having fallen asleep, she placed him in his little cot, and, having occasion to leave her cottage only for a brief space of time, she incautiously neglected to fasten the outer door. On her return, which was after the lapse of only a few minutes, her surprise and consternation may be easily imagined when she found the child gone, and could not perceive any trace of him. It would have been impossible for him, if he had awoke, to have got out of the cot by himself, and the horror of Janet was so great, that she was transfixed to the spot for a few moments, and gazing with despair at the empty cot, she was unable to move from the place. At length, partly recovering herself, she rushed frantically through the cottage, and searched every spot, but in vain, and she was about to leave the place, and with streaming eyes, and wringing her hands, hastening to make inquiries among her neighbours, when her husband returned. He was so astonished and alarmed, that he could scarcely believe his senses, but, after a minute or two, he rushed from the spot in one direction and his wife in another in search of the little lost one. But vain were all their inquiries, no one had heard or seen anything of the child, and they returned home in a state of mind bordering upon madness. They now remembered the circumstance of Janet meeting the old woman on the day before, and immediately the thought occurred to them that she was some spy or agent for the concoctors of this base plot, and that having watched Janet leave her cottage, had taken the opportunity to get possession of the child. They made known the circumstance to the nearest justice, and every prudent step was taken to detect the parties, but in vain. That same day the strange vessel before-mentioned was found to have disappeared, and a strong suspicion was in consequence excited, that the boy had been taken on board, and was then, doubtless, far away.

It would be impossible to depict as it ought to be pourtrayed, the intense, the almost insupportable agony of Lord Ravensford when he heard the terrible tale; he raved—he stamped —and, for a few minutes, he exhibited all the actions of the most decided maniac, and turned a deaf ear to the expostulations of his friends, who endeavoured to compose him, and to inspire him with a hope that something would in all probability occur to unravel the mystery in which the fate of his son was enveloped, and to restore him to his arms. But the idea of consolation to a man, who, whichever way he viewed the circumstances, could only accuse himself of being the primary cause of whatever dreadful fate might have befallen the poor child, was preposterous.

"Poor child!—sweet innocent!" he cried, "your cruel father has proved himself to be the most unnatural of parents, and whatever may have happened to you, must accuse myself, indeed, I am the author of it. Alas! why did I ever think of taking him away from the hall? Why did I not suffer him there to remain, under the protection of those who would have bestowed so much care upon him, and watched him with such affectionate solicitude? But some cursed infatuation! some infernal spell, has guided and gained full sway over all my actions of late, and will ultimately bring me to the most deplorable misery and ruin. Rosabelle! unhappy, much injured Rosabelle! wretched as no doubt thy fate is, if thou art still living, it is a mercy for thee that thou art spared this misery! The misery of suspense—the anguish of the uncertainty of the fate of thy first born, thy only one!"

"Nay, my lord," said Rattleton, "it is useless giving way to this violent paroxysm of grief; that will not recal the child; rather let us endeavour to devise some means of ascertaining what has become of the child!"

"Alas!" ejaculated Ravensford, disconsolately; "it is all to no purpose, we shall never see him again. He has fallen into the hands of the bitter enemy, who seems determined to pursue me to destruction, and I shall never see him again."

"Psha, Ravensford!" exclaimed Wilmott, "I am surprised at your giving way to this weakness, when at the same time there may not be any absolute necessity for the violence of your grief."

"What!" cried Lord Ravensford, impatiently; "no necessity for violent grief after such an event as this? Is it not enough, after the loss of my wife by such base, such monstrous means, and the traducing of her fame; is it not enough to drive me to madness, think ye, thus to be robbed of my child? Oh, God! the bare reflection is enough to turn my blood to ice, and to make every fibre thrill with horror! Rosabelle!—Alfred! Oh, Heaven! do not visit me with thy wrath more severely than I can bear! I have indeed deeply offended against thee, and deserve thy retributive wrath; but mercy!—mercy! do not try me beyond my strength!"

He beat his breast and traversed the cottage with the most agitated steps while he thus spoke; but neither Wilmott nor Rattleton offered to interrupt him; they had indeed little or no argument to offer under the painful circumstances. It seemed to them that the opinion of Lord Ravensford, namely, that the little Alfred had fallen into the power of the villain who had wrought the other afflictions that had befallen his lordship and his family, appeared to be too feasible to be disputed, and they had now, therefore, still greater cause than ever to endeavour all that was in their power to find out where Adder or Lord Saunter were concealed, although the latter simple nobleman, they could not help thinking, weighing all the circumstances together, was merely the dupe of the crafty and designing Adder, who had made use of him only to further his own diabolical schemes.

As for Christopher Goldham and his wife, after they had disclosed the lamentable circumstance to his lordship and his friends, sat quite mute and trembling, and expected every moment to have curses and reproaches heaped upon their heads.

"It was no fault of mine, your lordship," observed Christopher, after awhile, "for I was absent from home at the time; and I am certain that poor Janet would sooner have lost her own life than such circumstances should have taken place if she could have helped it."

"Ah! that I would, Christopher," sobbed Janet, "and I am sure I have never known what it is to have a moment's peace since this dreadful occurrence. He was such a sweet child, too, so handsome, so noble; oh! had he been my own, I could not have loved him more ardently than I did."

"Horror! horror!" groaned Lord Ravensford, who had, during the time these observations were being made, been traversing the room with the most disordered steps, and his hands clasping his forehead; "I shall go mad! My senses will leave me! Never—never can I support this double bereavement! Oh, Rosabelle!—oh, Alfred!"

"Be calm, be calm!" remonstrated Rattleton.

"Calm?" reiterated Ravensford, passionately; "who talks to me of calmness under such circumstances as these? Rather give me a pistol, and let me end my wretched life, since all that I prized in it has been taken from me! All has been lost to me, and through mine own blind obstinacy and impetuosity."

"We are losing time, my lord," observed Wilmott, "time which should be devoted towards discovering or endeavouring to discover where the child has been conveyed, and by whom; although I do not for a moment doubt Janet's affection for the child, I cannot help thinking that, in this instance, she acted with great thoughtlessness, to leave the door of the cottage unfastened, or even to leave the child at all alone."

"Yes, yes, I am, indeed, to blame," remarked Janet, weeping; "but who would have thought for a moment of such a circumstance taking place?—Who could have supposed for a moment, that any person could have been so base as to bear away the sweet little innocent? I shall never forgive myself, indeed I shall not!"

"Nor I," observed Christopher, "although I had no hand in the affair at all, and being away from home at the time it happened, cannot be supposed, in any way, to be responsible for that which has happened. I shall never cease to regret that such a melancholy event took place under my roof, and after we had been entrusted with so precious a charge."

"But what motives could any stranger have had in stealing the child?" said Wilmott.

"None, that I can see," returned Rattleton, "and, therefore, do I feel the more plainly convinced, that the same wretch or wretches who have been the cause of the abduction of the unfortunate and much injured Lady Ravensford, have also been the robbers of her child!"

"They have!—they have!" groaned Lord Ravensford, "and perhaps, ere this, the hapless innocent has fallen beneath the assassin's knife!"

"Oh, no!" cried Rattleton, "your fears draw too horrible an opinion of the circumstances; surely, there cannot be monsters enough to commit so atrocious a deed! And what should induce them to commit such a fiendish crime?"

"Revenge!" answered Ravensford; "the damned spirit of revenge with which Adder threatened me! Fool that I must be, not to guess who was my secret enemy; then might I not have been upon my guard, and have averted the horrible calamities that have since befallen me, through the guilty machinations of that demon in human shape."

"It is complete madness thus to give way to useless complaints and self-upbraidings," said Rattleton; "we had better lose no time in making every possible inquiry and search after the villain or villains that have committed this unnatural outrage."

"True," coincided Wilmott, "and every moment of delay but affords them a better opportunity of escaping, and of triumphing in their nefarious transactions."

"Search will be in vain," exclaimed Lord Ravensford, "the wretches are far enough by this time, and if their object was vengeance, which I have no doubt it was, the unfortunate child has, no doubt, been long since sacrificed to their barbarity. Oh, God! little did I expect this addition to my misery; and to be occasioned by my own headstrong folly!"

"My lord," said Rattleton, "you unnecessarily reproach yourself, and do but retard that which might otherwise be speedily accomplished. You say," he added, turning to Christopher; "that you made the circumstance known to the justices, soon after it took place?"

"Immediately, sir," answered Christopher; "you may be certain that I would not delay a moment, although I must confess, that I was so distracted at the time that I scarcely knew what I was doing."

"And they readily undertook to make all the necessary inquiries, and to adopt every means in their power to discover the perpetrators of the outrage, and to recover the child?" added Rattleton.

"Yes," replied Christopher, "I received every attention from the gentlemen, who immediately despatched officers both by sea and land, in all directions, to see if they could learn anything of the offenders or the child: and they have been gone ever since."

"And was it never ascertained for certainty, the real character of the vessel, which you say had been lying off here for some time before this melancholly and mysterious event, and which you say so suddenly afterwards disappeared?" inquired Wilmott.

Christopher answered in the negative.

"That is strange," remarked the former, "and gives the whole affair a more suspicious appearance."

"It does, indeed," said Christopher, "and I am afraid that it was some person on board that ship who has been the author of this diabolical plot."

Lord Ravensford groaned in the intensity of his agony, and throwing himself into a chair, covered his face with his hands, and rocked to and fro, with the power of his anguish. Rattleton and Wilmott again endeavoured to soothe his violent grief, but he was deaf to all their remonstrances, and continued to accuse himself of being the indirect cause of all.

"My child—my wife!" he exclaimed, suddenly starting from his seat, and pacing the room with hasty strides, "where are ye? Consigned to misery the most unspeakable—the most horrible! Oh, what punishment can be adequate to my guilt, in having by my unreasonable jealousy and insane rashness, been the occasion of such a catastrophe as this? And yet bitterly, dreadfully do I now suffer for it; yet not half enough—not half enough."

"Be more firm, my dear friend," said Rattleton, "and let us immediately set about the means of furthering the search which Christopher informs us has been already set on foot. It may not yet be too late to detect the villains and to gain re-possession of the child, but any delay is sure to be attended with the worst consequences. Where does the magistrate reside?"

"Not more than half a mile from this place," replied Christopher. "I will conduct you to him."

"Be it so," returned Rattleton, "let us away immediately; the sooner we have an interview with him, and consult him upon the matter, the better. Come, Ravensford, arouse yourself."

"Ay," observed Wilmott, "let us hasten to him without any loss of time."

"Alas!" ejaculated Ravensford, "I fear that all will be of no avail. Too much time has already elapsed to render it at all likely that the villains who have taken the child will be discovered. This, as well as the other abduction of my unfortunate wife, is, no doubt, the work of the miscreant Adder. Oh, that I could but meet with him, terrible should be the retribution which I would wreak upon his head. My wife—my child! Oh, God! I shall go mad!"

"Ravensford," expostulated Rattleton, "I am astonished at the weakness you evince but you must arouse yourself from it. Of what use are those bitter lamentations? They will not restore either your wife or child to your arms. Come, come—let us begone. Christopher will conduct us to Mr. Williamson's the magistrate, who may have heard something of the boy."

"I am afraid he has not," answered Goldham, "for if he had, he would, no doubt, have communicated with me immediately about it, knowing how anxious I must feel upon the subject. It is a dreadful thing, and to think that my wife should have been the cause of it."

"Oh, I shall never, never forgive myself," once more ejaculated Janet, "although, Heaven knows, that it was entirely accidental. I would sooner have lost my life than any harm should have befallen the dear child. But how was I to know or suspect that any person was lurking about in the neighbourhood for such a base purpose?"

"It certainly was very imprudent of you, Janet," said Rattleton, "to leave your cottage without fastening the door when the poor child was asleep in it. Indeed, you should not have left it at all, after the strict injunctions you received from his lordship; and your suspicions might also have been excited by the conduct of the woman, who you state yourself you saw lurking about the cottage for two or three days before."

"Oh, yes, I am very much to blame," said poor Janet, wringing her hands, and weeping; "I have been very much to blame, and never,

never shall I know peace again until the dear child is recovered. Greatly am I punished for my thoughtlessness. I tremble to look you in the face, my lord; I dare not ask you to pardon me."

Lord Ravensford's violent emotion had now somewhat abated, and glancing with a melancholy look towards Mrs. Goldham, he said—

"Janet, perhaps, through your imprudence, I may be doomed to perpetual misery; but I will not be too severe with you, knowing full well how poignantly you must suffer (if the expression of your sorrow is sincere), without my reproaches. I forgive you."

"Oh, my lord," cried Janet, and the tears streamed from the poor, simple, but good-hearted woman's eyes, " this is too kind, it is more than I deserve, and never can I sufficiently testify my gratitude to you for it."

" What a waste of time is this," said Mr. Wilmott, impatiently; " why do we procrastinate our departure to Mr. Williamson's for an instant?"

"I am ready to attend ye," said Lord Ravensford, rising from his chair; " but I still cannot be persuaded that the interview we may have with that gentleman will be attended with any beneficial results."

"At any rate we shall have the benefit of the magistrate's advice," observed Rattleton, "and he may be able to suggest some method of proceeding which might not occur to us."

"True," said Wilmott, " or he may have gained some clue which he may not have thought it prudent to communicate to Mr. Goldham."

" I pray to heaven that your sanguine hopes may be realised," ejaculated Lord Ravensford with a sigh.

"Come, come, I will have no more doleful faces, nor melancholy observations until we have seen the magistrate," said Rattleton, trying to smile; and taking the arm of Ravensford, while Wilmott laid hold of the other, they left the cottage, preceded by Christopher, and followed by the prayers of Janet.

Mr. Williamson was a gentleman of the most urbane and benevolent disposition, and was greatly esteemed in the neighbourhood where he resided for the philanthropic actions of which he was constantly the author. Unlike too many persons placed in a like official capacity, Mr. Williamson always tempered justice with mercy in his decisions, and he never suffered his temper to bias his judgment. In every sense of the word, he was a strictly impartial magistrate, and was an ornament to the bench, and admired and looked up to with the utmost regard in private life.

Mr. Williamson was a very wealthy man, and few individuals made a better use than he did of the gifts which fortune had bestowed upon him. The poor and the sick in him ever found a friend, and he seemed to delight in doing good. But he made no ostentatious boast of his charity.

" He did good by stealth,
And blushed to find it fame."

He was no sooner made acquainted with the afflicting circumstance of the abduction of the son of Lord Ravensford, than he sent officers in various directions with instructions how to act, and he had done everything in his power to trace out the villains who had been guilty of this base and inhuman deed, and to get the child restored. He had also, although a perfect stranger to Lord Ravensford, when he heard of the disappearance of Rosabelle, taken upon himself to send persons in various parts of the country in search of her, and the miscreant or miscreants who held her in their power; but his efforts had, unfortunately, been all unsuccessful.

He received the gentlemen with much kindness and cordiality, and expressed the most earnest commiseration with Ravensford in his misfortunes, and to his eager inquiries as to whether his endeavours had yet been attended with any favourable result, Mr. Williamson replied:—

" Why, my lord, I cannot say that I have yet been able to gain any clue to the authors of this cruel and infamous proceeding; but I have not the least doubt that the child is in the power of the same wretch or wretches that have robbed you of your wife."

Ravensford groaned, and was unable to make any reply.

"Have you, then, sir," asked Rattleton, " received any information which has given you cause to entertain such an opinion?"

" A man was brought before me, only this morning," replied Mr. Williamson, " who states, that, on the day when the son of his lordship was stolen, he saw a boat put off from the shore, containing two men, and a woman with a child in her arms; and that it made towards the strange vessel which had been lying at anchor for some days."

" Ah !" ejaculated Ravensford, eagerly, "and did he describe the men and the woman ?"

" He did," answered Mr. Williamson, " the men, he says, were dressed alike, and had all the appearance of common seamen, and the woman seemed to be old, and was dressed very shabbily."

" Doubtless it was the same woman whom Janet had seen lurking about in the neighbourhood," observed Rattleton.

" But the vessel ?" quickly demanded his lordship.

" Quickly afterwards it weighed anchor, and soon disappeared," replied the magistrate.

" Good God !" cried Ravensford, striking his forehead with his clenched fist, in the agony of his mind; ' that was undoubtedly m poor boy, and he is borne far enough away, and to a place of security before this time!—Perhaps his innocent blood has been shed to satiate the vengeance of my implacable enemy!"

"Nay, my lord," said Mr. Wilmott, "you suffer your apprehensions to gain too much an ascendancy over you. Had the intention of the villains been to take his life, they could have done so without removing him from the cottage."

"Certainly," coincided Mr. Williamson, "that idea is too reasonable to doubt."

"And has the true character of the vessel been ascertained?" inquired Rattleton.

"From what I have heard since, sir," answered Mr. Williamson, "there can be no doubt but that she was a smuggler!"

"Ah!" ejaculated Rattleton, "you astonish me, sir; and is it possible that a smuggling vessel should have been lying at anchor, as you state, for several days, and so near land, without any suspicion of her real character being excited, or an inquiry having been made into it?"

"There certainly was neglect in that respect," returned Mr. Williamson, "but there was no trouble taken in the business, and if there was any suspicion of her excited, I never heard any person express it."

"What course can we now pursue, after hearing this?" said Ravensford. "All hopes of recovering my son are destroyed; no doubt the smugglers, by the instructions of Adder, have seized him with an intention to bring him up to a life of crime, and I shall never see him again, or, seeing him, shall not know him."

This idea seemed so probable, that no one endeavoured to contravert it.

"And what course did the smuggler take?' asked Rattleton.

' I have not been able to learn," answered Mr. Williamson; "but a vessel has been sent out according to my directions, to go to the parts which the smugglers are known chiefly to resort to, and I entertain great hopes that they may be successful in overtaking her."

"I cannot sufficiently express my gratitude to you, sir, for your unexampled kindness," said Lord Ravensford, addressing himself to Mr. Williamson; "but, alas! I am fearful that your hopes are by far too sanguine. This is a heavy blow to me, sir, and following so soon after the disappearance of my wife, is one from which I shall never recover. I may too well reproach myself with being the indirect cause of the abduction of my son, for had I suffered him to remain at Holly Hall, he would now, in all probability, have been in safety."

"You know not that," observed Rattleton, "for it would have mattered little where the child was, in my opinion; as the villains who have got him in their power were determined to have him."

"To be sure it would not have made any difference where the child had been," said Mr.

Williamson;—"they could as well have taken him from one place as another, I should think."

"Oh, no; at Holly Hall they would have had no such opportunity," returned Lord Ravensford; "he would have been too strictly watched, and the ruffians would not have been able to gain access to the nursery."

"They would have found plenty of opportunities, no doubt," said Mr. Williamson; "they would not have kept the child entirely confined to the nursery, and would they not have had the same chance of seizing it some day, when it was being taken for an airing with the servant?"

"And what would you advise me to do?" asked Lord Ravensford.

"Nothing more can be done at present than that which I have ordered," replied the magistrate; "and we must wait, or endeavour to wait with patience, until the return of the officers that I have dispatched in search of the villains, and we are made acquainted with the results of their inquiries. In the meantime, I would offer a liberal reward for any person who can furnish us with any information which might lead to the destruction of the wretches, and might induce one of the smugglers to betray them."

"If money could restore him to my arms," cried Ravensford, "willingly would I sacrifice the whole of my fortune, or ten fortunes to do so!—Your suggestion, my dear sir, meets with my entire approbation, and I will leave it entirely to you to offer whatever reward you may think proper."

"Very well, then," answered Mr. Williamson, "that point is settled, and I will immediately give instructions for the printing and issuing of bills. But do you intend to leave this neighbourhood for the present?"

"Oh, no, decidedly not," replied Lord Ravensford; "I cannot think of quitting this spot until I have heard something from the persons whom you have despatched in different parts of the country. My two friends will, I dare say, be anxious to return to Holly Hall, to see how they get on there, and to endeavour to console them under this additional calamity."

"I wish I could persuade you to return with us," said Rattleton, "for you can do no good by staying here; and Mr. Williamson would, no doubt, send all the information he could, as soon as he obtained it, to the hall."

"Certainly," returned Mr. Williamson, "you may rest assured that I will lose no time in doing so."

"No, no," observed Lord Ravensford; "I will remain here for the present; my mind is too much distracted to visit the hall just yet; where the melancholy situation of Mr. Montalbert would but add to the poignancy of my grief, and make me truly wretched. Alas!—I fear that this accumulation of misfortunes will drive me also to madness."

"Be calm, be calm, my lord," remonstrated Rattleton; "giving way to any violent paroxysms of grief will but impair your constitution, without forwarding our wishes the least in the world. While you are here, I hope you will have the benefit of this gentleman's excellent counsel and consolation, and I am sure you will profit by them."

"His lordship may depend upon having all the assistance in my power," answered Mr. Williamson; "and I must request that, while he remains here, he will do me the honour to become my guest."

Lord Ravensford gave expression to his full sense of the kindness of Mr. Williamson, and with pleasure accepted the invitation which he had given him. And Rattleton and Wilmott, being highly pleased at this arrangement, also complimented the worthy magistrate warmly upon his kindness, and hoped that this interview would only be the prelude to a lasting friendship towards each other, a wish to which Mr. Williamson most cordially responded. The three gentlemen then took their leave, Lord Ravensford promising to return to the magistrate's house to avail himself of his invitation on the following day, when Rattleton and Mr. Wilmott would have taken their departure for Holly Hall.

By the joint exertions of his two friends, Lord Ravensford became more calm, and some-

MR. GOODMAN AND RATTLETON CONSULT ABOUT DISCOVERING ROSABELLE.

times a ray of hope would find its way to his mind, but it was only transient, and then he would suddenly sink into a state of despair and despondency from which it was found to be a very difficult matter to arouse him. He continued to entertain the opinion that the little Alfred had been seized by the smugglers, by the orders of the villain Adder, and that it was their intention to bring him up to a life of crime and depravity, and both Rattleton and Wilmott could not help being of the same opinion, although they endeavoured to calm the violent agitation which the thought engendered in his bosom, and inspire him with a hope that some-thing would transpire to foil the designs of the wretches, and restore both Rosabelle and the child to his arms; but he shook his head, and his looks sufficiently testified how little he partook of those hopes that they appeared to indulge in.

"What a fiendish heart must that wretch Adder possess, to have been guilty of two such inhuman crimes as those of which we suspect him, and of which, no doubt, he is the author," exclaimed Ravensford; "and yet this man for years was my companion, my confidant, my adviser; and the more schemes of vice that he could suggest to me, the better did I admire him!—Oh, what bitter anguish, what feelings of remorse does a retrospective review of my past conduct occasion me! My present punishment is a just although a severe retribution for the many offences against Heaven of which I have been guilty."

"You reproach yourself too severely, Ravensford," observed Rattleton, "and should endeavour to drive such thoughts from your mind. There are few of us but what have committed youthful indiscretions."

"Indiscretions! oh, no! that is too mild a term for the crimes of which I have been guilty." said Ravensford.

"Come, come, banish such thoughts as these from your mind, Ravensford," said Rattleton, "and endeavour to look forward with hope to the future."

"Hope!" eagerly cried Lord Ravensford; "yes, the hope of vengeance; vengeance on the heads of the accursed villain Adder, and the idiot, and unprincipled booby, Saunter. Oh, would that I could ascertain where they are; were it even to the remotest part of the world, I would pursue them, and never rest until I had satiated my revenge in their heart's blood. Oh, Rosabelle! hapless, wretched Rosabelle! how greatly have you been wronged; and what a fool—a villain I must be to have suspected your truth!—not to have seen through the whole of this nefarious plot before, then might I have thwarted their designs, and both you and my poor child would not have been torn from my bosom. Alas! alas! never, never shall I pardon myself."

Rattleton and Wilmott again sought to compose and tranquillise his feelings, but in vain; and at length they thought it would be better to allow him to give free indulgence to the violence of his grief, trusting that he would ultimately exhaust it, and become more calm.

"On, God!" continued he, "when I think upon the terrible fate which she may already have suffered, or be enduring, my heart shudders with horror, and I feel as if a hundred demons were worrying at my brain. But the miscreant Adder;—surely, base as he is, he would not dare to——Dare!—oh, what is there he would not dare to do to gratify his revenge, and to indulge his libidinous passions?—The thought is madness!—Oh, Heaven! let death be her fate, rather than to be exposed to such horrible degredation and shame."

The miserable Ravensford beat his breast as he spoke, and walked hastily across the room. His anguish was truly pitiable to behold, and both Rattleton and Wilmott were deeply affected. He continued at intervals to soliloquize in the manner we have described, then he would drop into a deep lethargy, from which neither of his friends offered to disturb him, and seemed to be brooding calmly over the heavy calamities by which he was visited.

In this manner the day passed over, and towards night, the feelings of Lord Ravensford became more tranquil, and he talked with more composure upon his affairs, and placing every confidence in the friendly exertions of Mr. Williamson, he even appeared to indulge a latent hope that he should be enabled to gain some intelligence of the little Alfred.

The next morning, after having accompanied Lord Ravensford to the house of Mr. Williamson, and promising to correspond with that gentleman, Rattleton and Wilmott took their departure for Holly Hall, where they arrived in the evening of the same day.

They found Mr. Goodman and Emily in a state of much consternation at the intelligence they had received of the mysterious disappearance of the child, and they put innumerable and eager questions to the two friends upon the subject, which they answered as briefly but explicitly as they could, and after hearing the particulars as we have already detailed them to the reader, Mr. Goodman and his daughter could only come to the same conclusion which Ravensford and they had done, namely, that the little Alfred had been seized by the smugglers, by the orders of Adder, and that it was their intention to bring him up, probably making him the means at some future period of extorting money.

"What a miscreant must this Adder be," observed Mr. Goodman; "one would scarcely believe that there could be such a wretch in existence."

"He must be a complete fiend in human shape," added Mrs. Rattleton. "Alas! poor Rosabelle, if she is in his power, how much have we cause to dread the worst from his cruel treatment towards her. Sooner would I hear of her death, than that she should be left at the disposal of such a monster as Adder."

"But this latter blow," ejaculated Mr. Goodman, "it is a most severe one, and I only wonder how Ravensford retains his senses under such heavy afflictions."

"It is, indeed, surprising," said Rattleton, "and I am afraid, if he does not shortly hear something of his wife or son, that the most serious consequences may be apprehended; for it has taken a deep and serious effect upon him, and we regretted having to leave him behind us, only that he is with so excellent a gentleman as Mr. Williamson, who I have lately been describing to you. However, I am not without a strong hope that the reward which has been offered will induce some one who is in the plot to betray his companions, and by that means, not only the child, but also Lady Ravensford may be speedily restored to us, and Adder and his associates be brought to punishment."

"I never heard of a plot of villany more systematically or successfully accomplished than this has been," remarked Mr. Goodman, "and when we come to reflect upon it, it appears almost incredible."

"It does," observed Mrs. Rattleton, "and what is equally mysterious and surprising is, that notwithstanding the strict search which has been made for them, and the certainty that they must have resided in the immediate vicinity of the hall, during part of the progress of the plot, we have never been able to discover them."

"It is most extraordinary," said her husband; "Adder must be a most crafty and ingenious fellow, to a certainty."

"There is no doubt but he was the writer of all those letters that were sent at different times," said Wilmott, "and also of those that Lord Saunter had received, and which he, the ready dupe, imagined to have come from Lady Ravensford."

"Unquestionably he was," returned Rattleton; "and a more consummate scoundrel there could not be."

'And you say that Ravensford succeeded in tracing Lord Saunter to Ireland?" said Mr. Goodman.

"Yes," answered Rattleton, "but ere he knew it, and could obtain an interview with him, he had abruptly departed, and he has not been enabled to gain any clue to him since."

"No doubt, terror, for 1 understand he is a most pitiful coward, has driven him abroad," remarked Mr. Goodman; "and there I would let him remain in peace; he is an enemy not worth pursuing or contending with, and I cannot help thinking that he is more to be pitied than anything else, as he possesses but a weak head, and has, doubtless, been made the dupe of the wretch, Adder."

"I agree with you in that opinion," said Rattleton, "and probably the booby lord may suffer quite a sufficient punishment from the constant state of alarm which he must be in. It seems that he is even afraid to correspond with his servants, or else they are cautioned not to know anything about the matter; for, although every inquiry has been made at his different establishments, no intelligence has been obtained of him."

"Why, it is not likely that he would fail to caution them," returned Mr. Goodman; "so I do not see anything remarkable in that."

"Certainly not; no more do I," coincided his daughter; "but I must away to my patient; alas! it is a mercy to the unfortunate gentleman that he is unconscious of this fresh calamity, or it would add to the violence of his frenzy."

As Mrs. Rattleton spoke, she retired to the chamber of Mr. Montalbert, the violence of whose paroxysms had much abated, and who had become comparatively calm, seldom raving out in the wild manner he had at first done, and obeying implicitly the wishes of Emily, to whom he was much attached, and unhappy when she was not with him.

"You are so good, so gentle, and so pretty, he would sometimes say to her; "ah! I once had a child—like you—no, no, not like you; for she was so surpassingly beautiful, that nothing could equal it. She is an angel now! yes, an angel all brightness and glory; it would dazzle your eyes to look at her; but I often see her! I often see her! And she talks to me, and calls me father. Father! why do I venture to give utterance to that word?—I am not a father now! No, no; she is dead!—she is dead! I followed her to the grave myself! And yet, liars as they were, they tried to persuade me that she still lived—that she had fled! Fled from me, her fond, fond father! The miscreants! —the knaves! I did not believe them! No; I did not credit their base calumny! The wretches! Were they here, I would make them pay dearly for seeking to make a father curse his only child! I would trample them beneath my feet, so, so, so!"

Then the unfortunate Montalbert would stamp his foot with vehemence, his eyes would become unusually wild, and fearing that he might become violent, she would endeavour to draw his thoughts to something else, and it was seldom that she failed to succeed.

Montalbert, however, who had shown in his madness the most unbounded affection for the little Alfred, quickly missed him, after Ravensford had taken him away from the hall, and it was some time ere they could manage by any means to pacify him. He thought that the child belonged to Mrs. Rattleton; he would join with him at times in his innocent gambols, with all the simplicity of a child of his own age. At other times he would take him on his knee, and when the little Alfred got playing with the poor old man's gray locks, he would laugh immoderately, and appear to enjoy it vastly. At such moments, the affectionate and susceptible Emily could not restrain her tears, and when she thought upon what the sufferings of Rosabelle would be, did she but know that her father was again a maniac, she felt the most intense anguish.

In all other respects, the malady of Mr. Montalbert remained precisely the same, and the medical attendants gave not the least hopes of his ever being restored to his senses, unless it was by some sudden and extraordinary shock, such as the restoration of his daughter to him, and then it might be attended by the most fatal consequences, seeing that his constitution was completely unhinged by the sufferings he had undergone.

It was a lucky job for the unfortunate Mr. Montalbert, that he had such disinterested and devoted friends as Mr. Goodman, his daughter, and the others, or exposed again to the horrors of the asylum, of which he had such a dread, he must soon have fallen a victim, and died.

Mr. Goodman managed his affairs admirabl

and was prepared at any time to render to Lady Ravensford or her husband, a satisfactory account of everything, and he thought nothing of the trouble and the anxiety which it cost him, so that he could be the means of serving them, and the preserving that property, which otherwise, under the circumstances in which Montalbert was placed, might have been ruined.

The fresh calamity which had befallen Lord Ravensford gained the commiseration of all who heard of it, and they were determined to use every means in their power to assist the inhabitants of the hall, in endeavouring to find out the villains Adder and Saunter, who they believed were the authors of all the mischief which had taken place; but the circumstance of the child having been taken aboard a ship, and no person being found who could inform them whither the vessel appeared to steer her course, made it a task not only of a most difficult but almost hopeless description.

CHAPTER XXI.

THE SECRET ASSASSIN.

LORD RAVENSFORD, beneath the roof of Mr. Williamson, notwithstanding the good advice of that gentleman, and his unremitting attention to him, experienced but little abatement of his anguish, more especially as day after day elapsed, and still they received no intelligence of the child or Lady Ravensford, although an immense reward had been offered to any one who could furnish them with satisfactory information.

"I shall never hear anything more of them," he exclaimed, in despair; "my wife, my child, are lost to me for ever! Oh, misery most insupportable! But am I thus to suffer without having revenge? No, by Heaven! I will not. I will go in search of the villains, and rest not until I have got upon their track."

"Whither would you go?" inquired Mr. Williamson.

"Something strikes me that they are secreted in some part of France," replied Ravensford, "and thither I am resolved to direct my course. Paris shall be the first place of my destination."

"And of all others, my dear sir," returned the worthy magistrate, "where it is the least likely that you will meet with them, in my opinion. Does it appear at all probable that they would go to a city where they would stand equally as much chance of speedily being detected as if they had gone to London?"

Lord Ravensford paused for a few moments, and traversed the room.

"I cannot divest my mind, at any rate, of the impression that I shall there meet with them, or gain some intelligence respecting them," said he, "and, therefore, I am determined to go."

"Well, I should be sorry to persuade you not to do anything which might afterwards prove to be well advised," replied Mr. Williamson; "but, at any rate, you will defer your departure until the return of the persons whom I have sent in search, I presume?"

"Why, no," answered his lordship, "and yet I would much rather not delay my departure; could you not send any information you might obtain to me?"

"Why, it is uncertain where a letter would find you, you know," said Mr. Williamson, "as I suppose you would not remain long in one place; or, at least, no longer than you had prosecuted your inquiries."

"Paris is a city that I could not search over in a day or two, my dear sir," said Lord Ravensford, "and no doubt a letter would find me there. However, as I do not suppose that it would be long before the persons will return from what I am afraid will prove a fruitless errand, I will remain with you."

"That is a wise determination on your lordship's part," remarked Mr. Williamson; "for their report must direct our future conduct, and, perhaps, there may be no necessity for you to go to Paris."

"I hope there may not, sir," said Ravensford; "but I cannot be so sanguine upon the matter as you appear to be."

A week more elapsed, and at the end of that time the men who had been despatched in search, came back, and without having succeeded in gaining the least clue to the wretches who had stolen the child. Ravensford was not disappointed, as he had never entertained but very slight hopes that they would gain any satisfactory intelligence; and he, therefore, made up his mind, after having expressed in the warmest manner possible his sense of the kindness, the disinterested attention and commiseration, he had experienced from Mr. Williamson, to depart immediately for France. He wrote to Holly Hall, to make them acquainted with his intention; and, having had everything in readiness for his journey for some time, he resolved to leave the residence of the magistrate the following day.

Mr. Williamson expressed his regret that they were so soon to separate, for he had imbibed a strong friendship for his lordship, which he hoped would be renewed at the earliest opportunity, when he trusted that they might meet under very different and far happier circumstances.

Lord Ravensford thanked him heartily for his good wishes, and for the interest and trouble he had taken in his affairs, and at the same time assured him that nothing could give him greater pleasure than enjoying the friendship of a gentleman who had proved himself to be so well worthy of his esteem, and he reciprocated Mr. Williamson's wish that they might meet before long under very different circumstances.

Mr. Williamson also promised to continue to be unremitting in his endeavours to detect the ruffians who had been guilty of so diabolical a crime, and likewise to obtain the restoration of his son, which promise Ravensford felt certain he would not fail to fulfil.

The evening before the day on which Lord Ravensford had determined to depart from the place where he was then residing, he walked forward to the cottage of Christopher Goldham and his wife, to give them some necessary instructions, and was detained rather later than he had intended; but the distance from Goldham's cottage was so short that he thought nothing of it, and accordingly took his departure.

The night was very dark, and the road he had to pursue was particularly dismal, and report gave it a very indifferent character, However, Ravensford, who was a stranger to fear, pushed on his way, and had just turned round the base of an acclivity, when suddenly the figure of a man, enveloped in a roquelaure, the folds of which he held before his face, crossed his path, and before he had time to speak to him, or to prevent him, he presented a pistol towards him, and fired. Ravensford felt himself shot, and sunk to the ground bleeding profusely. The place where this occurred was not many yards from the house of Mr. Williamson, and the inhabitants of the house could hear the report of the pistol; two servants immediately hastened to the spot from whence the report seemed to proceed, and there beheld the bleeding form of Lord Ravensford, prostrate upon the earth. They raised him in their arms, and with all possible care instantly bore him to the house, his lordship having in the meantime fainted through loss of blood.

Mr. Williamson, as may be expected, was very much astonished and alarmed when he saw Lord Ravensford brought back to the house, wounded and insensible, in the manner described, but immediately sent for medical assistance, and then despatched persons in pursuit of the villain who perpetrated the deed.

On the arrival of the medical gentlemen, and on examining the wound, Mr. Williamson was very happy to hear them pronounce an opinion that it was not mortal; and shortly afterwards, Ravensford being restored to sensibility, gave an account of the circumstance as it had taken place, and expressed his firm belief that the crime had not been committed by a robber, as he had immediately fled after he had fired, and did not offer to take anything from him. In this opinion, Mr. Williamson,

under the circumstances, could not but coincide; but yet, he felt at a loss to conceive what motive any person in that neighbourhoood should have in seeking his lordship's life.

"I have my opinion upon the subject," said Ravensford; "and the only one which appears probable to me, and that is that the ruffian who has done this has been employed by my bitter enemy, and who, having learnt where I am biding, has sent him to watch an opportunity to perpetrate the crime. This is the second attempt which has been made against me, and I know no one else who can harbour a design against my life."

"If that idea should prove to be correct," said Mr. Williamson, "I should imagine that the villain Adder is not far off; and yet I cannot think it is probable. However, I will see that a strict search is made in the neighbourhood."

Fearful of distressing his lordship by conversing with him, Mr. Williamson now departed to give the necessary instructions for the search to be made, and left Ravensford in the care of his attendants. He also immediately forwarded a letter to Holly Hall, to acquaint Mr. Goodman and the other friends of his lordship with what had happened.

Lord Ravensford suffered even more mental than bodily anguish at this fresh disaster, owing to the manner in which his intentions to depart for France had been frustrated, and he soon became so much excited, that the medical gentlemen began to entertain the most serious apprehensions for the consequences, and ordered him to be kept as quiet as possible. All that night, his senses left him, and he raved incessantly of his unfortunate wife and child, called himself their murderer, and could with difficulty be kept in bed. Towards morning, however, he became more composed, but reiterated his firm belief, that the assassin was employed by Adder, and that the ruffian would not cease until he had fully accomplished his wicked designs. He now regretted that he had taken the advice of Mr. Williamson, and remained at his house till after the return of the men, for notwithstanding the recent attempt which had been made upon his life, he still entertained the impression upon his mind, that he should find his enemies somewhere in France, and Mr. Williamson could not convince him of the improbability of such a supposition.

In the meantime, strict search had been made all over the neighbourhood for the assassin, but no person answering the description which Lord Ravensford had given of the man who had shot him, could be found nor even heard of, and there did not seem to be the least chance of his being detected. In spite of the remonstrances of the worthy magistrate, Ravensford still persisted in his determination to go to France, as soon as he was sufficiently recovered, and the time he was confined to his bed seemed to him doubly tedious. Two days after Mr. Williamson had despatched the letter to Holly Hall, Mr. Rattleton arrived, and was immediately introduced to the chamber of his wounded friend. He expressed the utmost sorrow at the occurrence, but was of a different opinion to that of Mr. Williamson and Ravensford, as to the fellow being employed by Adder, but, on the contrary, thought that the ruffian had mistaken his lordship for some other person, and that he was not the party he had intended to have assassinated.

"After the stir that has been made, and the large rewards that have been offered for the detection of the scoundrels who were guilty of the abduction of the child," observed Rattleton, "it is not likely that Adder would venture to make any attempt of the kind. He is, no doubt, far enough away by this time."

"He himself may be," said Ravensford, "but he may have his emissaries to perpetrate his diabolical work."

"But how do you suppose that he could have ascertained that you were staying in this neighbourhood?" asked Rattleton.

"Oh, very easy," answered his lordship; "doubtless he has his spies about, who will quickly give him all the information he may require."

"My opinion is still unaltered, that the ruffian who has attempted your life, and Adder, are unconnected with each other," said Rattleton;—"depend upon it, it is as I say, the attempted murderer has mistaken you for some other person, and that you were not his intended victim."

"Time perhaps may unravel the mystery," observed Lord Ravensford; "but I think that my surmises will some time or the other prove to be correct. But oh, Rattleton, feel for me; —I am sure you must, thus falling the victim to calamity after calamity, so quick in succession. To be thus confined, when every moment of delay is adding to the triumph, and ensuring the success of my enemies. My poor child! my unfortunate Rosabelle,—you then have not been able to learn anything of them?"

"We have not," replied Rattleton, "but pray compose yourself, or you know not what may be the consequences in your present situation."

"And why should I care about the consequences?" despairingly demanded his lordship; "have I not been basely robbed of all that can render life valuable to me?"

"Then it behoves you, Ravensford," remarked Rattleton, "to bear up as well as you can, seeing that you may be able yet to rescue your unfortunate wife and child from the danger by which they are now, in all probability, surrounded."

"Ah! it is well to advise, it is an easy task," sighed Ravensford; "but place yourself in my situation, Rattleton, and see if you could bear it with more patience and fortitude than I do."

"By thus fatiguing yourself, my dear sir," said Mr. Williamson, "you are only retarding your recovery, and thus procrastinating your resuming inquiries after those so dear to you. Rest assured, that in the meantime your friends will be indefatigable in their endeavours to discover the retreat of your enemies and in obtaining the restoration of your wife and child to your arms."

"I know they will, my dear, kind sir," said Ravensford; "but pray bear with me; I am sure you will, when you take into consideration my painful situation."

"All that can be done towards your prompt recovery, I need not tell you, shall be done," observed Mr. Williamson, "but that depends principally upon yourself. Keep yourself quiet, and endeavour to tranquillise your feelings. You have already talked too much. We will retire and consult upon the best means it will be for us to pursue, and in the meantime, you endeavour to compose yourself to sleep, which you will find will much refresh you."

"Alas!" exclaimed Ravensford, "sleep and I have long been strangers. But believe me, my dear friends, I thank you from the bottom of my heart for your kind solicitude, and will try to comply with your wishes. Do not let it be long before I see you again."

"We will visit you again, in a couple of hours," returned Mr. Williamson, and, taking the arm of Rattleton, they quitted the chamber of the patient together.

"This is an unfortunate circumstance," said Mr. Williamson to Rattleton, when they were alone, "and it is involved in so much mystery, that it completely bewilders a person in endeavouring to unravel it. What think you of it, my dear sir?"

"I scarcely know what to think, sir," answered Rattleton, "but it is as you say, a most unfortunate and alarming circumstance, and I am fearful that Lord Ravensford will never be able to support so many, and such a rapid succession of misfortunes—the loss of his wife and child, and then the last event. All these things are enough to try even stronger constitutions than that which his lordship possesses."

"Very true, sir," returned Mr. Williamson, "but we must endeavour all that we can to arouse him from despondency. After all, I do not really believe that Lord Ravensford was the intended victim of the assassin."

"What then is your opinion, my dear sir?" inquired Rattleton.

"Why, that the ruffian mistook his lordship

for some other individual," answered Mr. Williamson.

"And a very reasonable idea too," returned Rattleton.

"If Adder is really the villain who has got both Lady Ravensford and her child in his power," continued Mr. Williamson, "it does not appear to me to be at all probable that he would run the risk of coming hither for the purpose of wreaking farther vengeance upon Lord Ravensford.

"Why, my dear sir," replied Rattleton, "as for that matter, if, as we have every reason to suspect, Adder has any connection with the smugglers, he would have no occasion to come here himself to perpetrate such a deed, and would, most likely, employ one of the lawless crew to do it."

"But there is no vessel, but fair traders near the coast," observed Mr. Williamson, "and, therefore——"

"I know what you would say, sir," interrupted Rattleton, "but when the child was borne away from this neighbourhood, is it not possible that he, anticipating that his lordship, when he heard of the abduction, would be sure to come hither, left one of the smuggler crew, or more, behind him for the purpose of executing his diabolical wishes?"

"Why," answered the worthy magistrate, "that indeed is very probable; but there has been and is now, a most strict and indefatigable search made in every part of the neighbourhood, and for many miles around it, and no person upon whom suspicion could possibly alight has been apprehended."

"There is nothing surprising in that, my dear sir," returned Rattleton, "for it is not likely that the attempted assassin would remain anywhere near the place where his crime had been perpetrated; besides, according to the statement of Ravensford, he was muffled up in the roquelaure which he wore, and the act was so instantaneous, that there would be no possibility of his recognising him again."

"True," observed Mr. Williamson, "and, consequently, any search after the villain, will be entirely fruitless."

"I am afraid so."

"We must endeavour all we can," said the magistrate, "to impress upon his mind, the opinion which I have expressed, namely, that the accident which has befallen him, was the result of mistake. Should he continue to think that Adder is really the savage offender, it would only irritate his feelings, and most likely retard his recovery."

"I agree with your suggestion, sir," answered Rattleton, "and will do all I can to bring Ravensford to the same opinion; but any belief he may form, is not easily shaken, and I am fearful that, in this respect, our endeavours will not meet with much success, if

any. Oh, my dear sir, you cannot form any idea of the utter misery and desolation these dreadful events have occasioned. Could you but see poor Mr. Montalbert, with his still mild and benevolent countenance, but his eye wild and wandering; and listen to his melancholy and insane expressions, I am confident it would touch your humane heart to the core."

"Believe me, my good sir," returned Mr. Williamson, "I can imagine all you have described to me, and sincerely do I sympathise in the afflictions that have fallen upon this unfortunate family. Such daring outrages, and committed, as we have every reason to suppose, by one individual, we may say are almost unprecedented; and he surely cannot long escape the hands of justice."

"I am afraid that if ever he is apprehended, it will not be until after he has completed his hellish purpose," replied Rattleton; "in which case it would be a mercy to the much-injured Lady Rosabelle if death were to close her sufferings; degraded—dishonoured—broken-hearted as she would be."

"Alas, poor lady! But do you think it at all likely that Adder or Lord Saunter are in Paris, as Lord Ravensford has an idea they are?" asked Mr. Williamson.

"Certainly not," answered Rattleton; "such an idea is completely preposterous. Adder would be mad to go to such a place as Paris, where he must be certain that his detection would quickly take place;—he is in some obscure part of the continent, I have no doubt, but I am sadly afraid it will be a difficult matter to find where. The wretch is too crafty and cautious, and his plans have evidently been too well concerted for that."

"I am afraid so too," remarked Mr. Williamson; "but Lord Ravensford's idea does not appear likely to be easily shaken, and there is no doubt but that as soon as he has recovered, he will persist in taking his departure for France."

"No doubt of it," coincided Mr. Rattleton, "unless something should happen in the interim to render such a proceeding unnecessary."

"But you will not suffer him to go alone?"

"Decidedly not," answered Rattleton; "he will much need a confiding friend to guide and counsel him, and I have made up my mind to insist upon accompanying him."

"I am very glad to hear that, sir," said Mr. Williamson; "and I am certain that, with a friend like you by his side, he will not run into any of these dangers into which his impetuosity might otherwise plunge him."

Mr. Rattleton bowed to the magistrate for the compliment thus bestowed upon him.

"I feel highly flattered and obliged to you, my dear sir," he said, "for the good opinion you entertain of me; and at the same time I cannot sufficiently express the full sense I entertain of the sympathy you feel in the misfortunes of others, who are yet entire strangers to you."

"Had I been the friend of Mr. Montalbert and his cruelly-persecuted daughter, and also her husband, for any number of years, I could not feel a deeper interest in their misfortunes than I now do," returned Mr. Williamson; "and I sincerely hope that I may prove myself to be worthy of their warmest esteem, and, at no very distant period, we may all meet together in happiness—the husband re-united to the wife —the wife uninjured—the fond father restored to reason—and the base author or authors of these diabolical offences brought to a just retribution."

"Heaven send that the picture you have thus happily sketched, may be realised, my dear sir." exclaimed Rattleton, in energetic accents.

"And something seems to whisper me that it will be so," said Mr. Williamson.

"Alas, sir!" said Rattleton, "although my disposition is diametrically opposite to the melancholy or despairing mood, I cannot, on this occasion, allow myself to be too sanguine, or disappointment will come the heavier. At present, the prospect before us is as dismal and as hopeless as it can be. Lady Ravensford and her child both torn away, and without the least clue having been yet discovered as to the place where they are concealed, or, in fact, whether they still live—and Mr. Montalbert a raving maniac, without the least hopes, so his medical attendants have informed us, of his recovery."

"Dreary and cheerless indeed, I cannot but admit, are the prospects of those unfortunate persons," returned Mr. Williamson; "but still you must not despair, any of ye, or it will weaken your energies in endeavouring to bring about the happy results which I have sought to pourtray. How fortunate is it, my dear sir, that Mr. Montalbert and Lord Ravensford should have such friends as yourself, Mr. Goodman and Mrs. Rattleton."

"Believe me, sir," returned Rattleton, "I feel your compliments to myself and my dear friends the more powerfully, because I am convinced they are sincere."

"Not more sincere than they are deserved," said the magistrate; "and I am anxious for the time to come when I shall have the honour of being received as the friend of so many amiable individuals."

"And I can answer for my wife and her father, that their pleasure will be as great as any you can possibly experience," observed Rattleton.

"After all," remarked Mr. Williamson, after a short pause, "after all, I do not think that that foolish young nobleman as you describe him to be,—Lord Saunter—is so much to blame in this business. The fault appears to me to rest more with his head than his heart, and he has

evidently been made the tool of that most consummate scoundrel, Adder."

"I am of the same opinion, sir," replied Rattleton; "and although his vanity and ignorance have been the cause of so much misery, he is a being too contemptible for the resentment of Lord Ravensford."

"But still," added Mr. Williamson, "he must not be permitted to escape all punishment."

"I think the punishment he is, no doubt, at present enduring, from the fear he entertains of Ravensford encountering him, poor wretch, is almost severe enough," said Rattleton. "I would leave him to the contempt and detestation of the world, and the reproaches of his own conscience, when reason has brought him to reflect."

"You do not imagine that Saunter is with the villain Adder then?" interrogated Mr. Williamson.

"Certainly not; the information we obtained from Lord Saunter's former associates, Mowbray and Sir Harry Spangle, convinced us that he was not," replied Rattleton.

"But, think you, you ought to have placed any reliance upon them?" asked the magistrate; "might they not have deceived you?"

"They could have no motives for doing so, that I can see," returned Rattleton; "they were themselves inveterate against Saunter, because he had deceived them, and deluded them; besides, I have every reason to believe that they were sincere. They readily gave us all the information they could, and from them we learnt quite sufficient to exonerate the unfortunate Lady Rosabelle from all blame in being a willing party in the plot, and removed from the mind of Ravensford the dark suspicions that had before haunted it, and almost driven him to distraction. Besides, did not Ravensford visit the house where Saunter had been staying during the time he had been in Ireland, and ascertain, beyond a doubt, that it was him?"

"Well, it is very remarkable that he should be able so well to elude discovery," said Mr. Williamson, "and that the servants engaged at his different establishments should also be ignorant of what has become of him."

"That is not a matter of astonishment to me, by any means," answered Rattleton; "for, no doubt they have received strict injunctions and been well paid to evade any questions that might be put to them on the subject. But had we not better return to the bed-room of the invalid? The time we promised him that we would visit him again, is almost expired, and he will become impatient."

Mr. Williamson was of the same opinion, and, they, therefore, hastened to the chamber of Lord Ravensford, whom they found in a tranquil sleep, but he shortly afterwards awoke and expressed himself much pleased to find them there. He was better, and the wound he had received was doing well, and they were glad to find him in a more composed state than he had been for some time before, as they entertained strong hopes, if he could but be kept in the same spirits, that his recovery would be speedy. They endeavoured to divert his thoughts as much as possible from his own immediate sorrows, and to lead him into a conversation upon other subjects; and although it was not often they succeeded, when they did, it had a wonderful effect in abating the agony of his mind, and in advancing his progress towards convalescence.

Still they were unable to gain any intelligence which was calculated to raise their hopes in the least degree, notwithstanding their searches had been made with increased indefatigability. Additional rewards had been offered, the country had been scoured in all directions, but still all was to no purpose whatever, and the melancholy circumstances remained in the same state of impenetrable mystery in which they had all along been involved.

Day after day passed on in the same hopeless and tedious manner, and yet they had not obtained any knowledge of Adder, or the place in which he had secreted his victims; and the imagination was racked in vain to seek to form any conjecture as to what had become of them.

RAVENSFORD ENCOUNTERS SAUNTER AT THE HOTEL IN PARIS

Sometimes Lord Ravensford, in the deep horror of his despair, imagined they were no more. It seemed to him impossible that Rosabelle could long survive her awful and painful situation; and as for the little Alfred, it appeared to him not at all improbable that he had fallen a victim to the murderer's knife, as soon as he had fallen into the power of his bitter enemy.

Mr. Williamson and Rattleton tried all they could to banish these ideas from his mind, but they found it a more difficult task than they had probably imagined, and they frequently had a very hard matter to keep the unfortunate nobleman anything like within the bounds of reason.

However, in spite of this, he rapidly approached to convalescence, and was, in a short time, able to leave his couch, although he re- mained very weak for some time. He now began to repeat his determination to go to France, for the impression was still as strong as ever upon his mind that he should there find the miscreants he was so anxious to see. At first, both Mr. Williamson and Rattleton endeavoured to dissuade him from pursuing such a course, but it was all to no purpose; he had made up his mind to go, and nothing could alter his resolution. Rattleton well knew that, and he, therefore, desisted from the attempt. He now took him upon another point, which was that he should not go alone, and upon that they had a long argument, Lord Ravensford wishing to go unaccompanied; but Rattleton, well knowing the danger of permitting him to do so, in his present excited state, and when his feeling were likely to be exposed to still greater agony persisted, and aided by the arguments of Mr. Williamson, Rattleton at length drew from him a reluctant assent that he should be his companion. Rattleton then immediately wrote off to Holly Hall, to make his wife and father-in-law acquainted with his intention, which he knew they would approve of, and afterwards, at the earnest request of the impatient Ravensford, he set about making the necessary preparations for their departure with as much expedition as he possibly could. These did not take long in completing, and in the course of two or three days, Ravensford and his friend Rattleton, after a most friendly parting with Mr. Williamson, from whom they had experienced so much disinterested kindness and attention, and promising to communicate with him upon every opportunity, and let him know how they get on, they took their departure, and were shortly afterwards on board a vessel bound for Calais, from whence they purposed proceeding to Paris.

Their voyage was a short and a pleasant one, so far as the weather was concerned, but the mind of Lord Ravensford was continually tormented by alternate hopes and fears, and Rattleton had frequently a very difficult task to keep him anything like within the bounds of reason, and sometimes he would rave about his wife and his poor child, in a manner which frequently induced Rattleton to fear that his senses were leaving him. It was not always that the remonstrances of Rattleton would prevail, and he dreaded the disappointment which he anticipated Ravensford would meet with in the expectations he had formed, lest the shock should drive him at once to insanity; but, perhaps, his fears in that respect were greater than there was any occasion for. So great was the commiseration which Rattleton felt for his friend, that there was scarcely any sacrifice which he would not willingly have made, could he but have been the means of restoring him to happiness, and his wife and child once more to his arms; and there were times when he almost ventured to indulge a hope that their present journey would not be unattended with some portion of success, and that they might be able to obtain some clue to those they were in search of; but that hope was too pleasing to last long.

Although he, of course, sought all he could to raise the spirits of his distressed friend, he never ventured to encourage his hopes that their expedition would be attended with any favourable results to any great extent, knowing full well what would naturally be the effects of disappointment upon a mind already so much impaired by care and anxiety; and Ravensford would sometimes become quite impatient and testy because he did not enter into the same sanguine feelings as himself, upon the painful subject.

From Calais they took their departure in the heavy, lumbering diligence to Paris, where, after a tedious journey, they arrived, and put up at an English hotel. Now that their journey was completed, the mind of Lord Ravensford became a great deal more composed, and he submitted to the advice of Rattleton, that they should remain quiet for a day or two, to recruit his strength, and to enable them to concert measures that would be the most likely to cause them to prosecute their inquiries with greater facility. Immediately on their arrival, Rattleton despatched letters to Holly Hall, and to Mr. Williamson, to inform them of the circumstance, and to make them acquainted where to direct their letters to them, which they instructed them to do under fictitious names, Ravensford having assumed that of Mr. Anderson, and Rattleton that of Meredith. This was a very prudent precaution, and Lord Ravensford was perfectly satisfied with it, and again his hopes became more sanguine, and he was glad to think that Rattleton had accompanied him, as he had no doubt but that he should profit much by his counsel and suggestions, and two persons could certainly better prosecute their search than one individual.

They had not been at Paris more than a day or two, when Lord Ravensford's spirits became much more elated, and his health was considerably improved, although Rattleton and himself had left the house very seldom, and then in the dusk of the evening.

"Oh, Rattleton," exclaimed his lordship, on the third morning after their arrival in Paris, "I don't know how it is, but since my arrival here, I feel quite another man; my spirits are exhilarated, and something seems to whisper me that it will not be many days ere we shall gain some satisfactory intelligence of my wife and my poor child. I have acted, depend upon it, with judgment, in having persisted in coming to this place, notwithstanding you tried all you possibly could to dissuade me from so doing."

"I shall be most happy to acknowledge my folly, Ravensford, should your hopes be realised," returned Rattleton; "but I must still admit that I am not——"

"Not so sanguine as I am, you would say, Rattleton, I know," interrupted Ravensford, impatiently; "you are so very doubtful."

"No, it is not so exactly," said Rattleton; "but then I would by no means advise you to encourage too freely the surmises you have given utterance to, for should they not be realised, how much more bitterly would you feel the disappointment."

Lord Ravensford's countenance suddenly became more sad, and he paced the apartment for a few minutes without speaking. His thoughts were evidently of the most painful nature, and Rattleton almost repented having said anything to damp his hopes, and to effect such a change in his feelings; but still, he had not the slightest doubt that it would be all the better for him that he had done so, ultimately.

"To be sure," at length said Ravensford, with a deep sigh, and partly talking to himself, "the time which has elapsed is all against me; that confounded accident! Oh, had it not been for that, and I had started hither at the time I first wanted, there might have been some chance; but now, even should I discover my poor Rosabelle, may not the miscreant Adder have accomplished his base, his brutal wishes, and——Madness! a thousand demons seem worrying at my brain at that thought! The villain! but no——no——wretch as he is, he cannot, surely he cannot be guilty of so hellish a deed as that! I could more freely pardon him were he to take away her life! But then ——what dreadful ideas begin to haunt my imagination! My brain seems to be on fire! Rosabelle, my wife!——My child!——Oh, God! oh, God!"

He threw himself into a chair in an agony of mind almost indescribable, covered his face with his hands, and groaned aloud; and Rattleton, although he was deeply hurt at the anguish of his friend, and was anxious to offer him all the consolation in his power, did not seek to interrupt him, knowing full well that he would be better after he had given free indulgence to his feelings.

"Come——come, Ravensford," at last said Rattleton, "I must not suffer you thus to give way to such violent grief, as it will incapacitate you from exerting yourself in this painful affair; although I cannot go the length which your hopes are leading you to, I am still almost persuaded that something will transpire which will be the cause of the restoration of your wife and son to your arms, and that the scoundrel Adder, will be completely foiled in his designs, improbable as it may appear, after the time which has elapsed since he has had her in his power."

"Ah! do you think so?" demanded Ravensford, eagerly, and the paleness of his countenance had given place to a deep flush. "Repeat those words again, my dear Rattleton, they cheer my heart to listen to them!"

"I cannot believe," returned Rattleton, "I cannot believe that Providence will ever suffer a wretch to triumph in his attempt to commit so diabolical an act as that. The power of Lady Rosabelle's virtues——the dignity of her resentment, will awe and abash him, and prevent his advances, and——"

"They will—— they will!" hastily interrupted Lord Ravensford; "thank you, my dear friend, for these surmises; they inspire my bosom with renewed hope."

"Then pray become calm," expostulated Rattleton, "and let us coolly deliberate upon the best course to proceed. Remember, that all the time spent in useless conversation like this, is worse than wasted, for it not only procrastinates our endeavours, but also unfits us to proceed with that coolness and judgment which can alone offer any chance of success."

"You are right, Rattleton," returned Ravensford, with an air and tone of composure; ' and, henceforth, I will endeavour to conform with your wishes, knowing that they are prompted only by such feelings as would suggest themselves to the mind of a brother."

"Believe me, Ravensford," said Rattleton, "you no more than do me justice, and never shall you find me act otherwise than the most affectionate brother would do."

Lord Ravensford fervently pressed his hand, and his looks sufficiently explained his feelings, and the conversation, for the present, dropped.

They commenced making their inquiries in the most cautious manner on the following day, disguising themselves in such a manner that they might not be known, which they assumed at the residence of a poor man in an obscure part of the city, whom they well rewarded for any trouble or inconvenience they might put him to, and thus the suspicions of the *Maitre d'Hote*, where they were stopping, were not excited; and he saw nothing more particular in their conduct than in that of his ordinary frequenters, unless it was that when they were at home, they kept themselves most sedulously apart from all soceity, which for young and evidently fashionable men in that gay city, he certainly thought was rather singular; but then, it was no business of his, and consequently he did not trouble himself to think anything more about it.

They had now been in Paris more than fortnight, during which time they had been most indefatigable in their endeavours to find out anything which might lead them to imagine that the suspicions of Lord Ravensford were correct; but entirely without meeting with any success; and Lord Ravensford now began to give way as violently to despair, as he had before encouraged hope. Rattleton was not at all disappointed, for he had from the first considered it a most absurb idea to think that Adder would select such a place as Paris to take his victim to; and, as we have shown, he endeavoured all that he could to impress Ravensford with the same opinion, but all to no purpose, for when his lordship fixed his mind upon one idea, he would most obstinately adhere to it, and however ridiculous it might be, he would not be convinced that he was wrong, until the most glaring facts convinced him that he was so.

They had received letters from England, which afforded them no information upon the subject; although every one had been most unremitting in their endeavours, they had not been able to learn anything satisfactory, and the place to which the wretch Adder had conveyed Lady Rosabelle, was still involved in the greatest mystery as it had been at first. Mr. Goodman and his daughter both coincided in the opinion of Rattleton, namely, that it was a foolish idea to go to Paris in quest of them, as it was not by any means probable that Adder would act with an imprudence which would be sure to bring about his detection in a very short time, and not only frustrate all his plans, but bring him to punishment for the heinous offence of which he had been guilty. Those opinions—added to that which Rattleton had so frequently expressed—made at length some impression upon Lord Ravensford, and he began to think that he really had suffered his hopes to mislead him, and was ready to quit Paris whenever Rattleton might think proper, and they had fixed upon the route they should next pursue. This, however, Rattleton proposed should not take place for a day or two, so that they might take sufficient time to deliberate upon what it would be best to do, and not to act with too much precipitation. To this Lord Ravensford acceded, and, in fact, he determined, in future, to be guided entirely by the advice of Rattleton, who possessed by far more coolness and judgment than himself.

It was on the evening after they had received these letters, that Ravensford and Rattleton, as they were seated in their own apartment, heard an unusual noise from below, which drew their attention particularly. It was a noise proceeding from the uproarious mirth apparently of several individuals, who seemed to be in an uncommon state of hilarity. Glasses jingled—tables were hammered—songs were sung—toasts given—vociferously cheered —and there was every other symptom of its being a Bacchanalian revel, upon the most liberal principles. From the words that would occasionally reach their ears, they were satisfied that the gentlemen, if such they were, were English; but the circumstance would not have excited any notice from them, had not the hotel been generally so very quiet. Ravensford, however, though for what reason he could not imagine, felt a strange sensation stealing over him as he listened to the sounds, and Rattleton observed the change in his countenance, with no small portion of astonishment.

"It is only a few friends met together to celebrate some joyous event, the anniversary of a birth day, or something of that sort, I dare say," remarked Rattleton; "the hotel is generally very quiet, and, therefore, we have no cause to complain at being a little disturbed for once in a way."

"I do not complain," returned Lord Ravensford; "but—I should like to see the party."

"Nonsense! you would not wish to intrude upon strangers?"

"I know not that they are strangers," returned Lord Ravensford; "and there is something in the tones of their voices that I cannot listen to without emotion."

"Psha!" ejaculated Rattleton, "what a strange fellow you are, Ravensford; such singular ideas get possession of your reason."

"I don't care what you say, Rattleton," observed Lord Ravensford, who had advanced to the door and opened it; "I cannot help thinking that something more will occur from this circumstance than you imagine."

"How absurd!" laughed Rattleton.

"It may be, in your opinion," replied Ravensford, "but—ah!—hark!—Do you not hear that voice?"

Rattleton did listen, and heard some person speaking in a very loud tone, and whose voice certainly seemed familiar to his ears.

"By Heavens, I could swear that was the voice of the villain Saunter!" exclaimed Ravensford, and, as he spoke, he became dreadfully agitated; his lips were compressed; he clenched his fist, and his whole demeanour betokened the most ungovernable passion and general excitement. He laid his hand upon the door, and seemed almost determined to hasten down the stairs, when Rattleton, laying his hand upon his arm, arrested his purpose.

"How ridiculous," he said; "are there not plenty of voices alike, think you? Surely, you would not be guilty of such a breach of good manners as to obtrude yourself into the company of strangers?"

"Think you I have lost my senses, Rattleton," demanded Ravensford, "or that I would, through any idea of etiquette, suffer that villain to escape my vengeance? Oh, that it should be him!—I——But, listen—there again!"

Ravensford and Rattleton both listened attentively, and then heard the same voice singing a song, the words of which they were enabled to make out without much difficulty, and were as follows:—

"Hurrah! for woman's rosy lip,
　Hurrah for the man, whose only bliss
Dwells in that nectar gods might sip,
　The balm of beauty, love's warm kiss!

'Tis a transport! 'tis a pleasure,
　Worth an age of pain to know;
'Tis, oh, 'tis a heavenly treasure,
　Stol'n to make man blest below.

Hey! for the light of woman's eye,
　Whose weakest rays, whose mildest beam,
Rivals the blue and tranquil sky,
　Or Sol's rays, when they brightest gleam,

'Tis a starlight, shooting, dancing
　Holding o'er his soul its sway
'Tis a halo—soft—entrancing,
　Chasing sorrow's clouds away

> Then—hurrah ! for woman's rosy lip,
> Hurrah ! for the man, whose only bliss
> Lies in that nectar, gods might sip,
> The balm of beauty, love's warm kiss !"

"By my soul's welfare !" cried Ravensford, when the song was concluded, "I will swear that that is the voice of Saunter !"

"Bah ! are you going mad, Ravensford ?" interrogated Rattleton, again laying hold of his arm, and detaining him. "The voice, I am willing to admit, is like that of Saunter, but that would offer no excuse for your breaking in upon the harmony of a private party. There, now, pray be calm; seat yourself, and I will ring for Mr. Harding, and make some inquiries."

Ravensford was very reluctantly prevailed upon to do as Rattleton requested him, but his agitation every moment increased, and he trembled violently.

Rattleton rang the bell, and the *Maitre d'Hote*, Mr. Harding, who was an Englishman, quickly made his appearance. Rattleton, after apologising for the apparent boldness of the question, inquired who the gentlemen were, who seemed to be enjoying themselves so well below.

"There are five of them," answered Mr. Harding, "and they appear to me to be most of them Englishmen, but I never remember to have seen any of them before. The gentleman who cuts the most conspicuous figure amongst them is called Sir Waldegrave Weston, of whom I have heard much talk before; but I have been given to understand, by persons who seem to know him, that he is some young nobleman, who, for particular reasons, has thought proper to take up this incognito."

"Ah !" exclaimed Lord Ravensford, springing hastily from his seat, "give me a description of this man. Quick, quick ! I have particular reasons for asking it."

"He is about four-and-twenty," answered Mr. Harding, with some surprise,

"Complexion ?"

"Fair."

"Tall ?"

"Yes."

"And did you notice a scar upon his left cheek ?"

"I did."

"Ha ! ha ! ha !" hysterically laughed Lord Ravensford, hastily rushing towards the door; "by Heavens ! my suspicions are confirmed; it is he—it is the villain, Lord Saunter !"

And pushing Mr. Harding aside, Ravensford rushed precipitately down the stairs, followed by Rattleton.

CHAPTER XXII.

THE MEETING.

LORD SAUNTER, under the assumed name of Sir Waldegrave Weston, was not long, as we have stated in a previous chapter, in finding plenty of profligate companions, who, while they made him their ready dupe, laughed at him in their sleeves for an idiot, and thoroughly despised him. But Saunter had wealth, and he was superabundantly good-natured and easy, and, therefore, the dissipated young men of Paris found him a most useful associate; for whenever they wanted cash, and it was very seldom that they did not, he was always willing to accommodate them. Saunter was seldom sober, and, consequently, he did not trouble himself to think much about the past : but when he was, he was in a terrible state of apprehension lest Lord Ravensford should discover him, and wreak upon him his vengeance, and he did not fail to invoke curses upon the head of Adder for having so deceived him, and for his own folly in suffering himself to be so easily duped, and to be led into a dilemma from which he would find it rather difficult to extricate himself. He would have been very happy to have heard of the death of Lord Ravensford, for then his fears would be at an end, and he could return boldly to England, and, at most, only run the risk of an action from his friends, which he cared nothing about, having plenty of money.

He was very glad to think that he had got away from Captain Mowbray and Sir Harry Spangle, whose raillery had become very annoying to him, and he firmly hoped that he should not again encounter them.

Although he was known as Sir Waldegrave Weston in the giddy circles in which he mixed, with his usual imprudence, when he was inebriated, he had given his companions a pretty broad hint that that was not his real cognomen, and had, upon more than one occasion, said almost enough to divulge his real rank and title ; and had he given it a moment's serious reflection, he must have been convinced that he was in equally as much danger of discovery where he was as if he had remained in England ; but he went on in his own thoughtless career, until he was found out in the manner we are about to describe.

He saw, from the accounts in the English papers, that Lady Ravensford was not yet discovered; the effect it had had upon the unfortunate Mr. Montalbert; the abduction of the child, and the attempt which had been made upon Lord Ravensford; which two latter circumstances, he had no doubt, within his own mind, were the works of Adder. He was greatly disappointed when he found the assassin had failed in his purpose, and that Lord Ravensford was in a fair way of recovery, for he was in hopes that he should have got rid of the only person whom he had any actual cause to fear in the world.

In the continued round of wild dissipation, however, which he pursued, he forgot all about this circumstance, and gave himself up entirely to the follies and extravagances of his unprincipled associates. He became the complete lion, or rather the monkey, of the giddy circles of Paris, and the ready victim of all those who chose to humour his vanity.

On the occasion when Lord Ravensford and Rattleton met with him in so unexpected a manner, himself and a few of his dissipated companions had been led to the hotel entirely by accident, having been out on the ramble, and after having partaken too freely of the contents of the bottle, being in the immediate locality of the house, they did not feel inclined to proceed further for the present, and accordingly engaged a room to themselves, and continued the debauch they had been carrying on all day with the same avidity and recklessness as when they had first begun. Bottle atter bottle was despatched, and the unprincipled companions of the simple lord took good care that he should drink deeply, that they might the more easily dupe him afterwards at play; and it now appeared to have become a regular understood thing that they were never to pay for anything, his lordship was so "liberal," and so highly esteemed their "friendship."

From what we have already described, the reader will pretty well understand the scene which was enacted, and Lord Saunter at length attained that pitch which his wild associates had wished he should, and was ready to do anything they proposed, or to grant whatever they might think proper to request. As usual, when in that condition, he was unguarded enough to reveal everything he should have been most careful to conceal, and his real name and title, and the manner in which he had been duped by the crafty Adder, in his expected amour with Lady Ravensford, were divulged, and afforded his companions much food for amusement when they were by themselves. They had long been aware of his real title, but they were too prudent to let him know that he had disclosed anything of the kind when he was sober, lest they should lose so valuable a companion, and he had no suspicion of what he had really been saying when he was *compos mentes*.

On the present occasion, as we have before mentioned, he was particularly communicative, and told the whole of the shameful affair from beginning to end. In spite of all their efforts to the contrary, they found it impossible to repress their laughter when his lordship detailed in the most melancholy manner the various tricks which Adder had played him, and the clever manner in which he had at last got possession of our heroine, and borne her away; but at the same time that they pretended such warm friendship for him, like Captain Mowbray, Sir Harry Spangle, and the other individuals with whom he lately associated, they thoroughly despised him in their hearts for his cowardice, and they felt a pleasure in artfully contriving, by some apparently accidental observations, to arouse his fears, and to animadvert on the fame which Lord Ravensford had acquired in affairs of honour, not failing to exaggerate upon any anecdotes they might have heard of that unfortunate nobleman's duelling fame, when he was the victim rather than the votary of folly, vice, and dissipation.

"It must have been demmed provoking, Saunter, to have been cajoled out of the envied prize in that manner," observed Mr. Skeffington, who aped the manners of a complete exquisite, and was about the most unprincipled of any of them.

"Oh, abominably provoking," coincided another of the party, and with considerable difficulty concealing a smile, "abominably provoking; I wonder how his lordship could endure it with the patience and forbearance that he has done."

"And then to be duped, cajoled by a demmed reskel of a menial—a common valet! Peh !—horrible !"

"Did not your lordship feel terribly enraged against the fellow?" inquired a certain Mr. Brandon, in a sneering tone.

"Enraged !" stammered out Lord Saunter, endeavouring to look very desperate and courageous, and knocking his clenched fist heavily upon the table; "damme, I was furious—a perfect wild tiger."

"I dare say, demme," ironically remarked Mr. Skeffington.

"It was a devilish lucky thing for this Mr. Adder, as you call him," said Mr. Brandon, "that he managed to get clear off, for if you had encountered him—"

"If I had encountered him," interrupted Lord Saunter, making another desperate effort to look ferocious things—"if I had encountered him, the meeting would have been terrible—awful—for him !"

"Your lordship would have punished him," said Brandon.

"Dissected him !"

"Exterminated him !"

"Annihilated him !"

"Demme, cut him into mincemeat, the demmed reskel !" added Mr. Skeffington.

"I would ! I would !" replied Saunter; and he dealt the table another violent blow with his clenched fist to give force to his assertion.

"How demmed lucky for the reskel it was, that he escaped the awful eruption of the volcano of your lordship's wrath," exclaimed Mr. Skeffington; and there was a half laugh amongst the gentlemen, which Saunter took no notice of.

"It was, indeed," returned Lord Saunter; "but let him tremble."

"Ah!" said Mr. Brandon, "although he has escaped your lordship for the present, the time may not be far distant when you may discover him, and he will have to meet the full weight of your terrible and powerful resentment."

"It may; and then——"

Lord Saunter did not finish the sentence, and he sought by his looks to make his companions believe that his determination was too fearful and desperate for utterance.

"And yet he must be a demmed clever reskel," observed Mr. Skeffington, "to be able to dupe so many demmed individuals, and get the lady of his former master in his power."

"Very clever!" coincided the other gentlemen.

"The infernal scoundrel!" cried Saunter, gnashing his teeth.

"Oh, most abominable! but demmed clever," said Skeffington.

"And the Lady Rosabelle, if report speaks the truth, was a most beautiful woman," remarked Brandon.

"Oh, angelic!" exclaimed Saunter.

"Young?"

"Not more than twenty-four."

"A demmed beautiful age," ejaculated Skeffington, in a tone of rhapsody—"Dark?"

"Fair aa Hebe!"

"Tall?"

"Graceful and elegant."

"What a lovely creature," said Skeffington; "and to become the prize of a demmed reskel of a valet!"

"The thought maddens me!" said Saunter.

"Come, gentlemen, charge—charge again," said Mr. Brandon; "we must drink the Lady Rosabelle Ravensford's health, and better success to his lordship in his future amours."

The glasses were charged—the toast was drunk with all the noisy acclamation we have described; and it was after that, that Lord Saunter sang the song which we have quoted in these pages, and which was overheard by Ravensford and Rattleton, and was received, of course, with the utmost tumultuous applause by his base associates.

"An excellent song!" remarked one of the party, when Saunter had concluded.

"Superlatively, demmed excellent!" added Mr. Skeffington.

"Beautiful!" observed Mr. Brandon.

"And so demmed exquisitely sung by his lordship!" said Skeffington.

"Admirably executed," coincided Brandon.

"You really flatter me," observed Saunter, looking as silly as the effects of wine and nature could make him.

"Not a demmed morsel," returned Mr. Skeffington.

"Not a bit," added Brandon. "But I cannot help thinking of this beauteous Lady Rosabelle. Why, Lord Ravensford must actually be distracted at her loss!"

"Raving demmed mad!" said Skeffington; "I wonder the poor demmed fellow doesn't shoot himself, or cut his throat!"

Lord Saunter heartily wished that he would; and at the bare mention of Ravensford's name, he could not help turning remarkably pale, and trembled; but he endeavoured to conceal it as much as he could from the observation of his base companions; notwithstanding, they did notice it, but would not suffer him to see that they had.

"And if he has discovered the part that your lordship has played in this affair," said Brandon, "no doubt he is greatly exasperated against you; and when he can find you, will seek satisfaction."

"Most indubitably demmed true," added Skeffington; "and Lord Ravensford is, I understand, a regular infallible, kill-devil demmed fellow in a duel."

"Oh, he must be a most extraordinary shot, according to report," remarked Brandon.

"Which, of course, Lord Saunter would like all the better," said another of the gentleman—"the more danger, the more glory."

"Exactly so—just like the very demmed thing," uttered Skeffington.

"I dare say Lord Saunter only wishes he could meet with him," observed Brandon.

Saunter endeavoured to make a most courageous reply, but he failed, and for it substituted what was meant to be an approving smile, but which was converted into a ghastly grin.

"No doubt his lordship is exceedingly demmed anxious to give this Ravensford every satisfaction," said Skeffington, in a tone of bitter sarcasm, which was almost too pointed to escape the observation of Saunter—"of course he did not leave England to avoid him, but merely for his own pleasure."

"Certainly," agreed Brandon; "neither did he assume the name of Sir Waldegrave Weston to prevent his lordship from finding him out. It is very amusing, and not at all unfashionable, to preserve an incognito when travelling."

"Not at all," returned Skeffington, "and it is exceedingly demmed convenient sometimes, and to some persons. But, no doubt, Saunter will have the satisfaction of meeting this desperate demmed lord before long, and then it will not take them long to settle their differences."

Saunter turned still more pale than before, at the allusion which Skeffington had made to a particular kind of settlement, and he could not help thinking that he himself would most assuredly be soon settled if ever such a meeting took place. He, however, mustered up all the little courage he possessed, and putting on as bold a front as possible, he managed to make a reply to his companions, assuring them of his anxiety to deal destruction on the head of Adder, and to encounter Lord Ravensford in mortal combat.

"Villain! take then your wish!" exclaimed a voice which made them all start; in an instant the room-door was burst open, and Ravensford and Rattleton rushed into the place.

The cowardly Saunter had just taken up a glass of wine, and was about to propose a toast, but the glass immediately fell from his hand; his cheeks became ghastly pale; his limbs trembled, and he fixed his eyes upon the countenance of Lord Ravensford with a vacant and almost incredulous stare; then an involuntary exclamation of terror escaped his bosom, and he covered his face with his hands. Never was pitiable cowardice more strongly exemplified, and Lord Saunter, who was sobered in a minute, felt at that moment more degraded than a criminal at the bar.

Skeffington and the others needed no person to tell them who the intruder was, and, in fact, they richly enjoyed the confusion and agony of Saunter, and anticipated what they considered good sport in a short time.

Lord Ravensford stood in the doorway for a moment or two, and gazed upon the trembling being before him with a mingled expression of indignation, pity, and contempt; then advancing towards him, he seized him roughly by the collar, and grasping him tightly, exclaimed:—

"Wretch! miscreant!—at last, then, we have met!—Ah! coward, well may you tremble with conscious guilt and apprehension; our meeting must be a mortal one to one or both of us! Death alone shall again part us!— Look up, dastardly villain, and meet the gaze of that man you have so deeply, so irreparably injured!"

"Demmed fortunate," exclaimed Skeffington, "the very identical, demmed individual we wanted to see."

The wretched Saunter trembled beneath the grasp of the enfuriated Ravensford more violently than he had before done, and the looks of terror that he fixed upon the man whom he had injured so greatly, were painfully manifested.

"Speak, dastard, villain!" continued Ravensford, and his eyes flashed with the fury of his indignation, "what have you to say for yourself?—Acknowledge your guilt, and pray for mercy, or I will press the life out of you!"

"Spare me! spare me, Ravensford!" cried the poor terrified wretch; "I do acknowledge my guilty participation in the plot which has been the occasion of so much uneasiness to you. —I was wrong, very wrong; but I was made the dupe of Adder, and—"

"Base miscreant!" ejaculated Ravensford, dragging Saunter to his knees, while the companions of the latter, instead of offering to interfere, stood looking on, and it was evident from the expression of their countenances, that they enjoyed the scene vastly; "what reparation can you make me for the sorrows which you have caused me?—Pleading for mercy is useless;—I must have revenge, a terrible and mortal revenge!"

"Demmed boldly said, and exceedingly demmed manfully resented," observed Skeffington; and he and his vile associates exchanged looks of the bitterest sarcasm. Ravensford and Rattleton, however, glanced sternly upon them, and they seemed to be abashed.

In the meantime the unhappy Saunter remained in the most abject posture, and several times tried ineffectually, before he could give utterance to a syllable, while his lips quivered, and his looks plainly showed the agony which was passing in his breast.

"Lord Ravensford," at last he ejaculated, "again I implore your forbearance, and will make you all the atonement in my power; but spare me! spare me! I have long dreaded this meeting."

"Exquisitely demmed valiant!" remarked Skeffington.

"The courage of a lion!" added Branden.

"Cowardly wretch!" Rattleton could not help exclaiming, as he gazed on the hapless Lord Saunter, who still knelt with all the humble air of a boy expecting correction from his schoolmaster. Ravensford's pity and contempt almost superseded his rage, and he was half inclined to inflict summary punishment upon the booby nobleman, and let him go.

"Where is your base accomplice? Where is the detested villain, Adder?" he demanded, in fierce accents, and he did not relax his hold as he spoke.

"By Heaven I know not, Ravensford!"

"Attempt not to deceive me!"

"By all my hopes of mercy, I am not seeking to do so. I know not what has become of Adder since he was last seen by me in the neighbourhood of Holly Hall, and I have not the least idea of the place of his retreat!"

"And if you knew it, would you reveal it to me?"

"I would, indeed I would; once more I beg your forbearance, Ravensford."

"'Pshaw!—Follow me!"

"Wither?"

"To a convenient spot."

"For what purpose?" faltered out Lord Saunter, and getting paler and paler.

"Ask your own conscience," replied Ravensford, "and you will know what for. Come— I will not brook any delay: this moment I demand satisfaction."

"And will no apology—will no atonement suffice?" asked the alarmed nobleman, and he looked one of the veriest cowards that ever trembled in shoes; "Mr. Rattleton, you possess much influence over his lordship; pray——"

"Coward—contemptible coward!" interrupted Rattleton, frowning, and scarcely knowing whether or not to laugh at the really ludicrous position in which the unfortunate Saunter stood, who was now swinging backwards and forwards in his chair, in a state of the most intense agony imaginable, groaning and supplicating at intervals.

"Superlatively demmed amusing!" exclaimed Skeffington.

"Oh, capital!" added Brandon, with a bitter sneer: "how admirably Saunter plays his part."

"Excellent!" said another of the gentlemen, and then there was a general giggle.

The patience of Ravensford was completely exhausted, and he was half inclined to correct Saunter upon the spot.

"I will no longer wait," he observed; "are any of you gentlemen prepared to attend your friend?"

"Oh, ye-es," answered Skeffington, "that is most positively demmed certain. We will attend him; come—come, my lord, you have played this demmed farce quite long enough, so let us to demmed business now. You know how anxiously you wished you might encounter Lord Ravensford, not many minutes ago, and—"

THE DUEL BETWEEN RAVENSFORD AND SAUNTER.

"Oh, Ravensford," supplicated the dastard, clasping his hands, and looking with the most piteous expression in the countenance of his lordship, 'once more I entreat that you will not act with a rashness which you may afterwards sorely repent."

"Consummate coward!" cried Ravensford, and he struck Saunter a violent blow, which immediately felled him; and he remained prostrate upon the floor, absolutely crouching at the feet of his enraged enemy, until Brandon and the others, who could no longer forbear laughing outright at the awkward situation in which he was placed, and the agonising terrors he must be enduring, lifted him on his feet again.

"Come—come, Saunter," observed Skeffington, "this is all very exquisite, demmed fine, but it is going a leetle too far. You positively must give his lordship the demmed satisfaction he demands."

Saunter groaned.

"What!" demanded Brandon, "submit to a blow? Oh, no, I'm certain your lordship can never do so. My lord, we are ready to attend you to any fitting place where the duel between you and Lord Saunter can be managed without interruption. Have you pistols?"

"I will procure them," answered Ravensford. "Follow me if you please."

"Ravensford," gasped forth the trembling Saunter, and he seemed as though he were actually upon the point of fainting, "you would not, surely, deliberately murder me?"

"I give you a fair chance; I would act only as honour dictates," returned Ravensford, "but even were I to murder you, it would be no more than your just fate. Have you not been principally instrumental in murdering my peace of mind, as well as that of my unfortunate wife, for ever?"

"I will make every atonement."

"You cannot."

"I will use every endeavour to find out where Lady Ravensford is concealed, and restore her to your arms."

"Bah! are you ready to attend me?"

"I will submit to any degradation."

"You cannot be more degraded than you are at present."

"Will nothing serve to prevail upon you?"

"Nothing. This night one or both of us must die."

Ravensford uttered this declaration in a tone of determination which fell like a dead weight upon the heart of Saunter, and again he groaned in the agony of despair. At that moment he would gladly have resigned fortune, rank, title, everything he possessed, could he by so doing have gained the forgiveness of Ravensford. But he saw that all his entreaties were in vain, and he then turned his earnest looks alternately upon his companions and Rattleton, imploring them to intercede for him; but he met with nothing to console him from them. Although there was not one among the former but who was as great a coward as himself, no scene could have afforded them more enjoyment and amusement than this did; and had Ravensford, indeed, been inclined to relent, they would have been sure to have urged him, in an indirect manner, to persist, even though the consequences to them both should prove fatal. Cowardly ruffians take a delight in witnessing deeds of blood, although they have the greatest terror in mingling in them themselves.

"Well, positively, there must not be any more delay," observed Skeffington; "this is really demmed tiresome, and I did not think your lordship could have acted so, to delay sport so long. Come, come, let us begone, and no doubt we shall very soon be able to settle this business to both your lordships' satisfaction."

"Oh, yes, no doubt of it," added Brandon; "and nothing can be more opportune than the time. There is a bright moon, and you can see each other at fifty paces as distinctly as if it were broad daylight."

Lord Ravensford waved his hand in a commanding manner towards Saunter and his companions, and then without saying a word, left the apartment, attended by Rattleton. As he was about to ascend the stairs to his apartment, to provide himself with pistols from his travelling trunk, he met the *Maitre d'Hote*, Mr.

Harding, who had guessed, from the words which Ravensford had uttered, and his irritated manner, that something of a violent nature was about to take place, and who ventured to remonstrate with his lordship, and persuade him to forbear; but Ravensford returned him some abrupt answer, and hurrying into the room, procured the deadly weapons and hastened from the house, a short distance from which he saw Saunter and his friends, the latter having at length succeeded, almost by main force, in getting him from the house, but he was walking with a faultering air between Skeffington and Brandon, and his eye, when it rested on Ravensford, expressed the most indescribable mental anguish and despair.

Ravensford and Rattleton nodded slightly to the base associates of Saunter, but scarcely deigned to look at him; and then they walked on hastily, and left them to follow.

Several times the unhappy Saunter appeared almost ready to drop, and it is not at all improbable that he would not have been able to have sustained his trembling limbs, had it not been that he was supported by his two profligate companions.

Ravensford and Rattleton walked on, they scarcely knew in what direction; but at length they arrived at what appeared to them to be a most convenient spot.

It was an open field, upon which the moon shone most brilliantly, and every object could be seen as distinctly as if it had been daylight. Here Ravensford and Rattleton stopped, and the latter, seeing the deplorable situation of Saunter, who was being led very slowly by Skeffington and Branden towards the spot, ventured to expostulate with his lordship.

"Indeed, Ravensford," he said, "I think this has proceeded quite far enough; and the shame and mental agony which the contemptible wretch has been enduring for the last half hour has been a fearful punishment to him, and has likewise taught him a lesson that he will probably not easily forget. Be satisfied with that and by bringing him to an account for his nefarious transactions in a court of justice."

"Rattleton," answered his lordship, "you ought to know me too well to imagine for a moment, when my mind is made up, that anything can move me from it. Contemptible as I will allow the scoundrel to be, for the last time I repeat, that nothing but his life will satisfy me."

"Remember, Ravensford," said his friend, "what the consequences may be to yourself should you slay Lord Saunter. The trouble you will bring upon yourself."

"I have considered everything, and am prepared to meet it," answered Ravensford. "But come, no more of this, my dear Rattleton; you perceive that my mind is made up. There is one thing, however, that I must request of you, although from the devoted friendship you have ever evinced towards me, it is almost unnecessary to make it."

' What is it, my lord? You know you can command me in anything," said Rattleton.

"Should I fall in this duel," observed Ravensford, in a solemn tone of voice, " you must promise me that you will not relax in your endeavours to find out the retreat of my unfortunate Rosabelle and my poor child. That you will not rest until you have suceeeded in finding out that monstrous villain, Adder, and wreaked an ample vengeance upon his head. Will you, Rattleton— but I know you will—promise me this ?"

"You know I will, Ravensford," replied the former ; " and faithfully keep my word."

"Enough—enough," returned his lordship. hastily, and pressing Rattleton's hand fervently; " thank you, thank you; I am satisfied, and prepared for tho worst."

Saunter and his companions had now arrived upon the spot; the former looking for all the world like some unhappy wretch going to execution, and the pale moonbeams that fell upon his face, added greatly to its ghastly appearance. By dint, however, of the arguments, taunts, and remonstrances of Skeffington, Brandon, and the others, he somewhat rallied, and prompted by the desperation of despair, he became more firm ; but still he looked towards Ravensford with an air of the most earnest supplication, and attempted to speak, but his voice failed him; and the sternness of the countenance of Lord Ravensford, left him not the slightest room to hope.

It was a terrible moment to the cowardly libertine, while Rattleton proceeded to measure the ground. He could not but consider himself on the brink of eternity; and in a moment, all the vices and the crimes of which he had been guilty, rushed with distracting force to his brain, and he shuddered with horror at the fearful change he was most probably about to undergo. A prayer was on the guilty man's lips, but he could not, he dared not, give utterance to it. His head became giddy; he staggered, and would have fallen, had not Skeffington caught him. His associates aroused him ; and after a violent struggle with his feelings, he received the pistol from the hand of his second, and took up his position with much more firmness than could have been anticipated. He probably, however, at the moment, had no very clear idea of what he was doing, for despair had fixed itself upon his brain.

The fatal moment arrived ; the seconds having retired, not an instant elapsed. The report of the pistols was heard, and was followed by a loud cry of agony, like the exclamation of an infuriated maniac, and the ill-fated Lord Saunter, who, not an hour before, was engaged in debauchery and riotous mirth, was stretched upon the earth, no longer a thing of life.

CHAPTER XXIII.

THE SMUGGLERS.—THE PLOT.

" Oh, a jovial one is the smuggler's life,
　Free as the air he ploughs the deep ;
With mirth and joy he e'er is rife,
　O'er the billows as free as the wind they
　　sweep.
A foe to taxation, no duty he pays,
　Unless 'tis his duty to captain and lass.
Then ' a smuggler's life,' your voices now
　raise,
　And merrily, cheerily let the toast pass !"

SUCH was the rude chorus that was being sung, or rather shouted, by several coarse and desperate-looking men, who were seated around a table in a back room of a very low public-house, and which was never visited only by the most depraved persons who resided in, or resorted to the neighbourhood. They were smugglers, and if anything could be judged from their countenances, they were capable of doing the most desperate deeds. The table was covered with measures, bowls, and glasses, containing spirits, and of which they had all been evidently partaking very freely, and they were smoking as hard as they were able.

There was a large wood fire upon the hearth, and the red glare it cast upon their features gave them almost a supernatural appearance, and altogether the scene was as effective as one of those that are often represented in a melodrama. Obscene jokes and songs had been freely indulged in, and it did not seem as if they were inclined to leave off for some time. It was night, and the wind blew boisterously without; but the smugglers were making such a riot, that they heeded it not; and they were evidently determined to enjoy themselves to the most unlimited extent.

"Drink away, my lads," said Michael Hernwood, raising the glass to his lips as he spoke; " drink away ; we ought to be merry, for Fortune never smiled more brightly upon us than she has done for some time past."

" Ay, you say right, Michael," observed a tall, dark whiskered man, whom the smuggler's called Joe Deverell; " but leave the little crew of the Water Witch alone for doing business, and for availing themselves of Fortune's favours when they are to be obtained. Captain, a toast!"

" Ay, ay, a toast; a toast !" responded the others.

The smuggler captain raised a large glass, filled to the brim in his hand, and said :—

"Well, my lads, I will give you a toast, and that shall be, Success to the dare-devil crew of the saucy little Water Witch !"

" Bravo ! bravo !" shouted the smugglers. " Here's to the dare-devil crew of the saucy little Water Witch !"

"A capital toast, captain," said Michael Hernwood ; " and well responded to. With your leave, I will propose another."

"Ay, ay, a toast from Michael Hernwood!" shouted two or three of the smugglers, amongst whom he was a particular favourite: "a toast from Michael Hernwood."

"Fill your glasses, then, my lads," said Michael; "bumpers! bumpers!"

The smugglers needed no second invitation to do as Michael Hernwood desired, and the glasses were very quickly replenished.

"Here's confusion to the land sharks!" was Michael's toast; and it was followed by loud shouts from every one in the room; the landlord of the house at that moment entering, and joining loudly in acclamation of it.

"Ah!" observed Joe Deverell;—"the land sharks have found us rather troublesome customers to deal with, and will again, if they should venture to attack us."

"I don't think there is much fear of that," returned the captain: "for we keep too well out of their clutches, and have met with such a career of success, that we may set them at defiance!"

"Ay, ay," answered Michael Hernwood; "and may we always be able to do so; and all those daring fellows, who will run any risk to defend an unjust impost!"

"Well said, Michael," remarked the captain, "it is an unjust tax, and d—n the fellow, I say, who would not do all that is in his power to prevent it's being paid.'

"So I say," answered Joe Deverell. "Ah! little to the d—d swabs imagine that there is a subterranean passage underneath this house, which leads to the residence of Gordon."

"Nor that the vaults that open into it are so amply stored with booty," replied the captain.

"But captain," asked Michael, "do you not think it was a very foolish thing for us to lose so much time in effecting the accomplishment of this plot of Adder's?"

"Certainly not," returned the captain; "Adder has well rewarded us, and it will ultimately pay us much better than a trip would have done."

"How?" demanded Michael.

"Why, Adder must continue to do the thing that's liberal, or else his game will be up," replied the captain. "The lady is in our power, and we must continue to keep her so; if Adder does not come to our terms, why, Lord Ravensford, no doubt, will, and, therefore, we are sure of a reward one way or the other."

"Yes, the gallows!" observed one of the smugglers, who had been sitting apart from the rest, and, smoking his pipe heartily, did not seem to feel any particular interest in what was passing.

"There's Ben Ellwood at his croaking again," said Michael; "he seems to take a delight in——"

"Speaking the truth," added Ben, in a quiet, but satirical tone; "it is very unpleasant to hear it sometimes."

"Psaw! don't make yourself a fool, Ben," exclaimed the captain; "any one would suppose, to hear you talk, that you had become tired of a smuggler's life. But what think ye of my determination, my lads?"

"It is a famous one," answered Michael Hernwood, "and cannot fail to work us good."

"It must add much to our coffers one way or another," resumed the captain; "and I take no small credit to myself for the thought; besides, you know that we have the fellow Adder entirely in our power; that murder which——"

"Right, right," interrupted Michael; "if that were made known, it would not be long before Mr. Adder would swing upon a gallows."

"Indeed it would not," returned the captain; "and he knows that, and dreads us. The lady is a beautiful woman, and I almost envy him his prize; but something may yet happen to place her in my possession instead of his, and I do not know whether I should be over nice about availing myself of such an opportunity."

At this moment, between the pauses of the blast, they heard a loud knocking at the door, and they looked at each other suspiciously, and starting involuntarily to their feet, placed their hands upon their pistols, and prepared for action, in case they should be surprised.

"Who's there?" demanded the landlord.

"It's only I—Adder," was the answer, and being satisfied that it was his voice, the door was cautiously opened, and the villain entered. He greeted them all heartily, and then, by the invitation of the captain, having taken his seat at the table, the mirth of the smugglers was resumed, and carried on with increased spirit, Adder joining in with as much freedom as if he had been one of the crew.

"Well, Mr. Adder," asked the captain, "and don't you think I managed this business very well for you?"

"Ay, captain," returned Adder, "you did everything that I could wish; but think you she will be safe where she is?"

"Safe!" repeated the captain; "as safe as if she were buried deep in the bowels of the earth. Gordon is just the man who will take care of her.'

"That is well," replied Adder: "but it is not unlikely that I shall not have any occasion to trouble him long."

"Why, you would never be such a fool as to attempt to remove her from a place of security?" demanded the captain.

"Circumstances may compel me so to do."

"I understand you; but we must see about the best means of preventing all chance of that," said the captain; "you have been a lucky fellow, Adder, to get the lady of your former master in your power, and at your mercy; it is glorious revenge."

"It is, it is!" answered Adder; "but not sufficient to gratify me."

"No?"

"No!"

"What would you, then?"

"I would have the life of Ravensford."

"Ah! would you, then, again commit murder?"

"Hold! Monckton!" said Adder; "mention not my former crime; I cannot think of it without horror."

"And yet you can contemplate another deed equally as sanguinary?"

"Yes, the death of the detested Ravensford I can contemplate, coolly contemplate; and I shall never rest satisfied until it is accomplished."

"And would you dare to perpetrate it yourself?" asked Monckton, the captain.

"I dare," answered Adder, "were he to cross my path; but were I to follow him to England, or wherever he may be, I should in all probability be discovered, and taken prisoner, and then all my schemes would at once be frustrated. If any one would undertake to commit the crime, I would not fail to reward them handsomely."

"I see," said the captain; "you would have me or one of my men perpetrate the deed of blood!"

"I care not who it is, so that it is a man on whom I can depend."

"And the reward?"

"One hundred guineas!"

"It shall be done."

"Ah! say you so?—when?"

"Come, come, you are in too much of a hurry; and there is never anything done well where so much precipitation is used. We must first ascertain where Lord Ravensford is."

"And that we may have some difficulty at present in finding out," said Adder; "for, doubtless, he has gone in search of Lady Rosabelle. My heart throbs impatiently for the accomplishment of the deed, and I shall not rest until I have ascertained that Ravensford is no more."

"On your promise of the reward you have mentioned, the deed shall, by some means or another, be despatched," replied Monckton; "but you must wait with patience, and we will not lose any time or opportunity to discover where his lordship is, and to put our designs into execution."

"This assurance gratifies me, and I am satisfied that you will not deceive me!"

"You have had no reason to doubt me hitherto," returned Monckton; "and, therefore, there is no occasion for you to do so now."

"But have you any idea how to proceed?" asked Adder.

"In the first place," returned the captain, "it will be the best plan to despatch one of the crew to the neighbourhood of Holly Hall, in disguise, where he may be able to learn the proceedings of the family, and probably ascertain where to find Ravensford."

"I agree with your plan," said Adder, in reply; "and should it meet with success, I shall not be very particular about giving a few additional guineas to the sum already promised. But Rosabelle, for whom I have run such a risk, still remains obstinately opposed to my suit; and I do not think I shall be able to conquer her aversion in a hurry."

"And of what consequence will that be?" demanded Monckton; "since, as she is in your power, she must yield to your wishes, or else you can gain the gratification of your desires by using force."

"Force? but I would rather that my powers of persuasion would prevail; as, notwithstanding the warmth of my passion, I cannot bear the idea of using any violence towards her."

"Why, true, it would be much better if it were avoided," observed Monckton; "but, come, drink!"

"Here's success to all our future undertakings!" said Adder, and he quaffed off the contents of the glass.

"Success to all our future undertakings!" responded the smugglers, and the toast was drunk tumultuously.

"You have been a fortunate fellow, Adder, throughout your whole career," said the smuggler captain; "and have, no doubt, accumulated plenty of money."

"Why," returned Adder, with a self-satisfied grin, "I have not much cause to grumble. But then I have had to depend upon my own wit and ingenuity."

"I have no doubt you have," said the captain; "and if I am not mistaken, they have done you good service. Ravensford has had to pay you rather dearly for your services."

"He has, and I rejoice to think that I have made him so ready and so easy a dupe," answered Adder, and a disagreeable grin of exultation passed over his features.

"Well, certainly, Adder, you are a most perfect villain."

"I believe I may lay some slight claim to the character."

"Not a very slight one either," remarked the smuggler captain.

"You pay me a very high compliment."

"Ha! ha! ha!"

"But who among your crew will undertake the murder?"

The smuggler captain looked round upon his fellows, but in not one of their countenances, reckless and determined as they were, did he notice any signs of a desire to undertake the sanguinary deed.

"Who among ye is willing to earn this reward?" he asked.

There was no answer. Adder became impatient.

"What! are ye all silent?" asked the captain. No one offered to speak.

"What say you, Michael Hernwood?"

"I like not the shedding of human blood when it can be avoided," he answered; "if, however, captain, you order me to perpetrate this crime, although it is against my inclination, I will obey you; if I am permitted to use my own free will, I say I will not commit the crime. Will that answer suffice?"

"It will," said the captain; "but, Joe Deverell, you will not refuse the hundred guineas?"

"I would not stain my hands with innocent blood for twenty times one hundred guineas, unless it was by your command," was the answer.

"And Ben Ellwood, what say you?"

"I am a smuggler, ready to defend myself and my comrades from an attack; but I am not a cold-blooded deliberate murderer," replied Ben Ellwood.

"Damnation!" cried Adder, fiercely; and he arose from his seat and hastily traversed the room.

"Be patient," said Monckton; "this matter will be arranged, perhaps, quicker than you expect. You see, Adder, although they are desperate men, the crew of the Saucy Water Witch are not quite such astrocious monsters as the they have been thought by many."

"They are cowards if they shrink from the——"

Before he could finish the sentence, the smugglers were all upon their feet, and by their menacing looks, threatened vengeance.

"Hold!" cried Monckton, and they all immediately resumed their seats, although it was very evident that the observations of Adder had greatly enraged them; and there were many scowling brows, which convinced the villain that he had proceeded almost too far.

"Adder," continued Monckton, after a pause; "you should be more cautious in what you say; my men are not used to hearing such terms applied to them, nor do they merit it. If Jack Monckton thought he had a coward amongst his crew, he would hang him up to the first tree he came to."

"I was wrong—I was wrong," hastily apologised Adder; "and I hope the crew will pardon me."

"That is enough," observed Monckton, then turning again towards his men, he demanded—

"And, so you all refuse to do this deed?"

"We do!" was the answer from them all; "we shed not human blood only in our defence."

"One amongst ye shall do the deed, since I have promised this man, and I will not recall my word," said the smuggler captain, peremptorily.

There was a discontented murmuring arose from among the smugglers.

"What means this murmuring?" demanded the captain, and his eyes glanced fiercely upon them; "is there one among ye who would dare to disobey my commands?"

"I will answer for all my comrades, and say, no," said Ben Ellwood; "but we would avoid an unnecessary deed of blood, and especially under the circumstances."

"I have given my word, and it shall be kept," said Monckton, firmly; "you must cast lots!"

The smugglers still looked dissatisfied at this determination, and glanced significantly at each other, but they did not say a word. They scowled upon Adder, who, however, did not take much heed of them, certain as he was, that while the captain was on his side, he had nothing to fear from any act of violence they might otherwise contemplate towards him.

Reluctantly they were about to prepare to cast lots, when there was the well known signal heard at the room door, which being opened, Gordon was admitted.

"Ah!" exclaimed Monckton, "you have just come in time, Gordon; I have a proposition to make to you."

"Name it, captain," answered the ruffian. Monckton repeated the question he had put to the others. Gordon appeared to catch at the idea, and the smugglers eagerly awaited his reply, anxious to be released from the perpetration of the crime, from which they all revolted.

Gordon did not make any immediate answer, and he appeared to be meditating upon the proposal.

"Do you also hesitate, Gordon?" inquired the captain; "you were not always so particular."

"I do not hesitate, only for one reason," returned the miscreant.

"Name it!" said Monckton.

"Let Adder give two hundred guineas, and the deed shall be accomplished," was the villain's answer.

"It shall be yours," ejaculated Adder.

"Enough," said Gordon. "I have your word that the money shall be paid, and Monckton, no doubt, will be answerable that you do not fly from your agreement?"

"I will," returned the captain.

"There is no occasion for it," observed Adder; "if you do not deceive me I will not deceive you."

"You had better not," said Gordon, with a sinister look.

"You have good security for my keeping my promise," added Adder; "let the deed be done, and the money shall immediately be yours."

"But if I should fail?"

"If you do not wilfully fail, then one half the money shall be your reward for your trouble," said Adder.

"Enough," replied Gordon; "then the bargain is sealed; I will undertake the hazardous deed."

"Thanks—thanks!" said the blood-thirsty Adder; "perform your task well, and you will have my eternal gratitude."

"Pshaw!" cried the ruffian, with a sardonic grin; "of what use is gratitude to me? It is not a marketable commodity. But what about the care of Rosabelle?"

"Adder will reside in the house during your absence, and I will leave Joe Deverell to assist him in his charge," replied the captain.

"That arrangement will do," said Gordon, after a pause.

"When will you start on your expedition?" inquired Adder.

"Immediately. There is no necessity for delay," answered Gordon.

"'Tis well," observed Adder; "but you will go disguised?"

"Oh, leave me alone for that," returned Gordon. "I have more reasons than one not to wish to be known; or the first news that you heard of me would, in all probability, be that I was the inmate of a prison. I will so disguise myself, that it must be a penetrating eye, indeed, which could recognise me."

"To-morrow, then?"

"I quit this place, and make my way for Holly Hall!" rejoined Gordon.

"True; and to meet with success, I trust."

"It shall not be my fault, if I do not."

"You will forward us intelligence when you arrive there; for I shall be all impatience till I hear from you," said Adder.

"I will," replied Gordon, "unless I see that there would be danger in so doing."

"Certainly."

"And now that this business is settled," observed Monckton, "let us proceed to enjoy ourselves;—come, my lads, replenish your glasses."

The smugglers obeyed this order with hilarity, and the villain Adder, being satisfied with the inhuman design he had formed, and the atrocious wretch who had undertaken to accomplish it, joined heartily with them in their revelry, which they kept up for more than an hour afterwards, when Adder, Gordon, and Joe Deverell, returned to the house, and the captain and the rest of the smugglers hastened on board their vessel, they being bound for another trip that night.

Adder felt a savage sensation of delight fill his bosom, at the prospect of the full consummation of his most diabolical hatred and revenge against Lord Ravensford; and he entertained the most sanguine anticipations of the success of his plot. Gordon was a deep, designing, and determined villain, and he had no doubt but that the reward which he had promised him, would induce him to exert himself to the uttermost.

"Yes," he soliloquised, when he was alone in his chamber, after parting with Gordon and Joe Deverell for the night; "I feel confident that Gordon will not fail, and, that ere many weeks have elapsed, my hated foe will be no more. Oh, this will be goodly revenge for the insult he offered me, and which no time nor distance has since effaced from my memory. Rosabelle, too, will then be securely mine, and nothing will release her from my power!"

The wretch paced his chamber as he thus spoke, and his eyes sparkled with exultation. He pictured to himself in imagination, the unbounded bliss that was in store for him in the gratification of his sensual and disgusting passions, and he determined that but a short time should elapse, ere he would have the full accomplishment of all his wishes. He slept but little that night, for thinking upon his villanous stratagems; and when he reflected that he was beneath the same roof with the unfortunate Rosabelle, and had it in his power to force her to an immediate compliance with his desires, he could with difficulty keep his ecstasy within the bounds of reason.

In the morning, Gordon, after having so disguised himself that no person could by any possibility recognise him, and having received some fresh instructions and injunctions from Adder, took his departure on his inhuman errand, and Adder and Joe Deverell, with Cicely, the old woman, were left alone in the house, in charge of Lady Ravensford.

We need not inform the reader of the distracting hours of misery Rosabelle had undergone since her incarceration in the house. Her sufferings were almost too powerful for human endurance, and it was wonderful how she could retain her senses. Her agonising thoughts were divided between her own situation and that of her father, husband, and child; and her disordered imagination pictured them, if possible, more dreadful than they actually were.

"I shall never behold them again," she sighed, and scalding tears chased each other down her pale cheeks; "alas! I am torn from them for ever. Or, if we should be again destined to meet, under what circumstances may it not be? Myself, perhaps, dishonoured—heartbroken; my poor father a raving maniac; my husband——my child! Oh, Heaven! the picture that arises upon my imagination is too horrible for contemplation. The letter, too, which Phœbe promised to get forwarded to the Hall could never have reached there, or it is not improbable that I should not any longer be a prisoner, and that the heartless miscreant who has been the cause of all this unparalleled misery would have been brought to that punishment which he so justly merits."

She wrung her hands, and traversed her gloomy chamber with trembling steps.

"To be beneath the same roof with a murderer, too," she added, as the recollection of Gordon darted across her brain, "and that, too, a murderer of the blackest dye! Oh, God! have I not good reason to be distracted? That terrible night when I overheard the wretches conversing upon the monstrous crime of which they had been guilty—when I saw them inter the mangled body of the poor white-haired old man, their unfortunate victim, comes fresh upon my memory, as if it had only been just enacted. My heart seems chilled to ice; oh, surely the misfortunes that have since attended me have been a curse upon me for not having given such information of the circumstance as might have led to the apprehension of the assassins. The unfortunate old man's bones moulder in unhallowed ground, and his blood calls aloud to Heaven for retribution."

She trembled violently, and almost imagined that she heard a melancholy sigh breathed close to her ear. She staggered to a chair and leant upon it for support, fearing to look around her, lest she should encounter the ghastly and blood-stained face of the murdered man.

All was profoundly still in the house, and the miscreants who inhabited it seemed to be locked in the arms of sleep. Sleep! how could wretches whose consciences were burthend with such a heavy weight of crime, sleep?

The light in the lamp burnt dim, and imparted a still more gloomy appearance to the chamber; and the wind howled dismally without, increasing the horrors of that solemn hour. Rosabelle seated herself by the side of her bed, and, after a pause, did once more venture to look around the room, but nothing, but of an ordinary description, met her observation.

"What dreadful crimes may there not have been perpetrated in this house! in this very chamber!" she once more reflected, and again her terrors rose to a pitch almost insupportable.

The light in her lamp, which had for some time only been faintly glimmering, now suddenly died away, and our heroine was left in utter darkness. How she longed for the morning, and that she had some female companion near her in that dismal place, if it were only the repulsive old woman, Cicely; some to whom she could speak; but silent and dreary as everything was around her, it was like being confined in a tomb. She had kept the embers of the fire together as long as she could, but that had also become extinguished, and the room felt as cold as it was dismal and cheerless.

At length she crept into bed with her clothes on, and covered her head with the counterpane, filled with a sensation of terror, she found it utterly impossible to conquer. She endeavoured to sleep; but her mind was too much distressed to suffer her to succeed, and she tossed to and fro in a state of agitation, which no one, but those who have been placed in a similar situation, can form an adequate idea of. The interview she had had with Adder, rushed upon her memory, and she recollected every word that he had spoken, and which had given her every reason to apprehend the worst consequences from his determination. Even the sight of that inhuman man inspired her with a feeling of horror no language can do justice to, and she dreaded a second meeting with as much fear as she would have done the most fearful calamity which could have befallen her.

"But I will be firm," she reflected; "I will muster up all my woman's fortitude, strong in the defence of her honour, to meet him, and oppose his importunities in a manner that shall deter him from proceeding to violence. Providence surely will not forsake me in this moment of bitter trial, but will throw its protecting shield over me, and defeat the brutal designs of the libertine and miscreat! Yes, I will put my trust in Heaven, and prepare to meet my heavy trials with a firmness and resolution becoming me!"

These thoughts somewhat composed her spirits, and after a short time spent in further rumination, she did at last sink into a disturbed slumber, in which she remained until the sun had risen in the eastern horizon.

She arose, not in the least refreshed, and had not been up many minutes, when she heard the key turning in the lock, and soon afterwards Cicely entered with the breakfast things.

She placed them on the table, and then fixed upon our heroine a scrutinising look, and shook her head.

"Hey day," she said, in her usual disagreeable tones; "pale cheeks and red eyes; no sleep again, I suppose; well, it puzzles me how you young women can live without rest! When I was your age, nothing could ever prevent my sleeping."

"When the mind is oppressed with such unprecedented and heavy sorrows as those that disturb mine," answered Rosabelle; "if it be not entirely insensible, sleep may be courted in vain."

"Heigho! how very melancholy and dismal you do look, to be sure," answered Cicely; "any one would imagine that you had experienced all the troubles in the world; but stop till you become my age, and then you may have cause to complain."

"Some persons troubles," returned Rosabelle, "are brought on them by themselves; by their own vices, and——"

"Ah!" interrupted the old woman, snappishly, "no doubt you think that a very pointed and sarcastic observation, but, as the cap don't happen to fit me, I shall not wear it. Mr. Adder will pay you a visit presently, and perhaps you may deem it prudent to behave a little more civil to him."

Rosabelle shuddered.

"Oh, tell me," she said; "is he in the house?"

"Oh, yes, to be sure he is," answered Cicely; "for he has taken up his quarters here altogether now, and, therefore, you will have plenty of his company."

"Living in the same house!" muttered our heroine to herself, and she trembled more violently than before; "alas! what will become of me?"

"Oh, no doubt he will take plenty of care of you, young lady," answered Cicely, with a bitter sneer.

"He shall find," said Rosabelle, mustering up sudden firmness, and speaking in a tone which astonished and abashed the old woman, "he shall find that I have both the spirit and the virtue to resist his importunities, and Heaven will aid me to defeat his design. The guilty wretch! surely for his many crimes a terrible retribution must be impending o'er his head."

ROSABELLE AT PRAYERS IN THE SMUGGLER'S RETREAT.

"The spirit you boast of, young lady," said the old woman, "I have no doubt, will be very quickly tamed, or Mr. Adder is not half so accomplished as I take him to be."

Rosabelle darted upon her a look of disgust and indignation, but she could not make her any reply, and after making two or three observations of a similar description, Cicely quitted the room.

We need not attempt to describe the feelings of our heroine when the old woman was gone; the disgusting observations of Cicely, and the fearful prospects which was before her, filled her bosom with the utmost consternation, and although she tried very hard to rally her spirits, and prepare to meet Adder with becoming fortitude, it was some considerable time before she had it in her power to succeed. To know that Adder was the inmate of the same house with her, was sufficient of itself to excite the greatest agony in her bosom; and when she reflected that it was not probable that he would longer be able to control his wild, unbridled passions, and that any resistance on her part would be completely futile, she became almost distracted. Alas! she thought, how much more preferable would death have been to the state of agony in which she was thus continually kept. It was only for the sake of her husband and her child, whom she could not entirely despair of not beholding again, that she clung to life; and had she not had them to occupy her thoughts, and her heart's warmest affections, she would have met death with fortitude, nay, even pleasure. What had been the last few years of her life, but a round of perpetual misery? All mankind had seemed arrayed in enmity against her, and few indeed were the real friends she had found. Her tears flowed fast at these thoughts, and they gave relief to her overcharged bosom.

At length she struggled with her emotions, and so far regained her composure, that she was enabled to partake of the repast which Cicely had brought her, and to prepare to meet Adder, whom she had no doubt, and indeed the old woman had said he would, visit her in a short time.

She had but just risen from her knees, having implored the protection of the Most High, when she heard footsteps ascending the stairs, and directly afterwards, her room-door was unlocked, and the object of her fears and detestation entered.

He stood in the doorway for a minute or two, and it was hard to perceive whether he was awed and abashed by the calm dignity and firmness of her demeanour, or lost in admiration of her superlative beauty—still most exquisite, although her once blooming cheeks were pale and wan with heavy care.

Rosabelle had mustered up uncommon fortitude, and, as Adder entered, she fixed upon him a look which was sufficient to penetrate the most insensible breast. It was one of the most cutting reproach, while resentment, and a firm reliance upon the strength of her own virtue, and the protection of the Almighty, shone predominant in the general expression of her countenance.

Adder hesitated, and it was very evident that he had not been prepared to meet with such a reception; but he soon recovered himself when he thought of his own power, and how entirely useless was her indignation or her resistance, and, approaching her with a look of admiration which could create no other sentiment than one of hatred in her breast, he attempted to take her hand and press it to his lips; but she hastily withdrew it, and spurning him scornfully away from her, exclaimed—

"Begone, sir; your presence is disgusting to me. Dare not thus to insult the victim of your guilt—the injured wife of that nobleman in whom you ever found a kind and generous master."

"And who's the master now, fair Rosabelle?" demanded the villain, and a look of exultation overspread his features; "who triumphs now? —Ha! ha! ha!—Master!—He was always a weak fool—my dupe; and although I was subservient to him, it was only until I could sufficiently serve myself. In my heart I despised—abhorred him; and when he added to my hatred by the insult he offered to me—by a

blow—I vowed vengeance! I have not broken my vow—I triumph, and——"

"Oh, villain—heartless villain!" cried Lady Ravensford, her bosom swelling with agony, "can you stand there and talk to me thus? Are you not afraid that the vengeance of the Almighty will immediately descend upon your head, and render you powerless to do further harm?"

"I scorn it."

Rosabelle shuddered with horror at the words of the wretch; who, however, presently altered his tone, and once more endeavouring to take her hand, which she successfully resisted, he assumed an insinuating smile, and, in a voice of gentle persuasion, said—

"Pray pardon me, beauteous Rosabelle, if I have been led into the expression of words that have caused anguish to your feelings; but the injuries I have received from Lord Ravensford——"

"'Tis false!" scornfully replied our heroine, and her brilliant eyes appeared to flash fire; "Lord Ravensford never injured you, but you were ever the serpent in his bosom, waiting an opportunity to destroy his peace, and you have yourself, but a few minutes since, acknowledged the same, and expressed your inhuman exultation at the misery which you have caused him."

"Well," returned Adder, with the utmost coolness, and the boldness of his manner increasing, "I will not deny it, because there is no necessity for my so doing, as the power is now mine. I have already had a terrible revenge, but still it is not complete, and never will I rest until it is wholly accomplished."

"Oh, Adder!" ejaculated Rosabelle, her fortitude failing her when she saw the villain's recklessness and determination, and reflected that she was entirely in his power, and left solely to his mercy, or the interposition of Providence, "will nothing induce you to relent in your cruelty?"

"Nothing," answered Adder, "until I have gained the full gratification of my wishes, and the consummation of all my hopes. Then only shall I be satisfied."

"What mean you?"

"You will behold your husband no more."

"Oh, God!" ejaculated Rosabelle, and her heart throbbed heavily against her side, her cheeks turned ashy pale, and her limbs trembled violently, as a dread of something terrible about to take place, through the guilty machinations of the wretch who stood before her, darted upon her brain; "cruel as you are, surely you would not seek his life?"

A grim and sardonic smile passed over the features of Adder as she gave utterance to these words, but he returned her no answer; his looks spoke more than words, and had a thunderbolt at that moment descended upon her head, Rosabelle could not have felt more paralyzed and awe-struck than she did at that time. With distended eye-lids, she fixed upon him a look which was sufficient to have penetrated even the most obdurate heart, and to carry awe to the guilty soul: her features became stern and fixed ; her lips parted, but she uttered no sound, and, suddenly approaching the astonished Adder, she grasped his arm vehemently, and looked full upon him. Adder could not help, in spite of all his hardihood, shuddering beneath her gaze, and the singularity of her behaviour ; but he was not a minute before he completely recovered himself, and, looking coolly and indifferently upon her, awaited what she had got to say without first offering any observation of his own.

" Adder," at length exclaimed our heroine, in a solemn voice, and her brilliant and expressive eyes still fixed with the same earnestness of expression upon his countenance, " Adder, in the name of that Almighty power who guides all our actions, and before whose dread tribunal you must some time or the other appear, however much at present you may despise His name—by all your hopes of forgiveness for the many and heinous crimes you have committed, I charge you tell me—solemnly tell me, what are your wicked designs ?"

" Psha !" cried Adder, and a fearful smile again overspread his countenance.

" Nay, I command you, in the name of the Most High, to set my horrible doubts at rest, and tell me," demanded Rosabelle, and her heart throbbed more violently than ever, and her whole soul seemed to be wrapped up in the answer which Adder would return to her ; and she appeared as if if she would drag the secret from his heart with her eyes.

" Enough of this," at last said Adder, " I came not here to talk upon a subject like this, and——"

" Heartless miscreant !" interrupted Rosabelle, " too well can I read in your dark and portentious looks the base designs you have in contemplation. But Heaven will interpose to prevent the execution of your infamous intentions, and to save my dear husband from your monstrous machinations."

" We shall see," returned Adder, with the same consummate coolness he had before evinced ; " we shall see. But hear me, Rosabelle——"

" I will not listen to you, until you have answered my question," observed Rosabelle ; " your very words are as poison to my soul."

" But you must and shall hear me," exclaimed the other with a determined air, and once more endeavouring to take our heroine's hand ; " you are securely in my power, and think not that I will be frightened from my purpose by an obstinate woman's heroics. I come to offer you my love ; you reject it, but

that shall not avail you, for force shall make you comply with my wishes. As for Ravensford, I tell you once again you will see him no more."

The courage of Rosabelle completely failed her, tears gushed to her eyes, and, sinking upon her knees, with clasped hands, she supplicated the ruffian's forbearance : but she pleaded to a heart callous to every sense of feeling ; he gazed upon her emotion with indifference, and he secretly exulted at the manner in which he had subdued her spirit, and flattered himself that in time she would be entirely conquered, and made to yield subserviently to his will. However, he endeavoured to disguise his real faelings, and, assuming as mild an expression as he could, he raised Rosabelle from the posture in which she had been kneeling, and affected to smile kindly upon her. For the moment she was deceived by his looks, and hope suddenly darted upon her mind.

" You will relent," she ejaculated, " that smile assures me that you will. You cannot, surely, be so cruel as to seek the life of my unfortunate husband ? Has not the anguish you have already caused him, and the miseries he is at present undergoing, through you, been the means of sufficiently appeasing your vengeance ? Oh, Adder ! repent ere it be too late, and restore me to my friends, and again I promise you that you shall receive my pardon and that of those who are dear to me, although the injury you have inflicted upon me and them is almost irreparable. Come, come ; if there be one spark of humanity in your breast, if there be the smallest portion of that feeling remaining in your heart towards that sex who claim protection from every man, I shall not supplicate in vain ; you will accede to my request, and once more open to me the doors of liberty ; and suffer me to fly once more to the arms of my husband—my child—my poor bereaved parent !"

" Beauteous Rosabelle," returned the wretch ; " this is madness, and a silly waste of time. Think you, then, that after all the trouble I have taken, the risks I have run, and the plans I have laid down to get you in my power, that I will now quietly resign you ? Think you that I would place myself at the mercy of my enemies ? No—no ! you must give up all idea of such a thing, and, henceforth, look upon me in the same light as your husband, for you and I must not again easily separate ! You must yield to my wishes, and that speedily ; I would have you do so of your own free will ; but if, after a given time, you still remain foolishly obstinate, then must I, however much it may be against my wishes, use force. Resistance, you perceive, will be vain, and, therefore, I advise you to make up your mind to assent without it ; then shall you receive every attention from me, and I will behave to you in a manner that shall leave you no cause to regret your separation from your husband."

"Fiend in human shape," ejaculated Rosabelle, shrinking from him with the greatest horror depicted in her countenance, "leave me! My soul freezes with horror as I listen to you! But I will not entirely despair, although you have bid me do so; Heaven will interpose to prevent the execution of your base threats."

"Did Heaven interpose to prevent my getting you in my power?" inquired Adder, with a sardonic grin. "Once more I tell you, you shall be mine, and nothing shall save you!"

"Never, villain!" cried Rosabelle.

"Be cautious what you say, lady, lest you exasperate me," returned Adder, with a threatening frown, which made our heroine tremble; "you forget that I could this day— this very moment—force you to a compliance with my wishes, and where is there one near at hand who could come to save you?"

"By Heavens I would die first!"

"Bah!" sneered Adder; "but I am tired of this useless contest of words; you know my determination, and rest assured that I will only await a very few days for your answer, and, then, if you do not consent, you know the consequences."

"Once more I pray your mercy," said the distracted Lady Ravensford, with clasped hands, and looks of earnest supplication: "beware, oh, beware! ere you proceed to extremities."

"You have it in your power to move me to pity and to love, fair Rosabelle," returned Adder; "one smile from you, one word of affection from those ruby lips, would act with the influence of magic upon me, and make me quite a different man. Adder would then live alone for love and you; and there should not be a pleasure which it should not be my constant endeavour to procure you."

Rosabelle turned from the villain with a look of the utmost disgust, and she groaned aloud in the intensity of her anguished feelings. Adder advanced nearer to her, and sought to put his arms around her waist, but the action immediately aroused her, and retreating to the farther end of the room, she fixed upon him such a look as awed him into immediate forbearance.

"Still madly obstinate!" he exclaimed; "but time must alter this, proud beauty, and you must yield to the desires of Adder, however repugnant it may be to your feelings. At present I leave you, but you will shortly behold me again, and then I trust that you will see the policy of giving me a more favourable reception than you have done this morning."

As he spoke, Adder fixed one glance of expressive meaning, and then quitting the room, he securely fastened the door after him.

"The perverse woman!" he soliloquised, as he walked away; "but she must be subdued— she must be subdued; Adder cannot much longer endure her resistance. Oh, did she but know the plot I have formed against the life of her husband—but I said quite enough to arouse her fears, although I now wish that I had not done so, as it would be sure not to promote my wishes. I wish not to have to use violence, or I could do so directly; no, my greater triumph would be to prevail upon her to give her own free consent, and that would add to the gratification of my revenge! Adder, if you fail in this, it will be the first time that you have failed in any of their undertakings."

The villain walked away, and after giving strict injunctions to Joe Deverell to keep safe watch over his charge, he bent his footsteps towards the public-house, at which he and the smugglers had been the night before carousing, and where, in a back private room, he could commune with his own thoughts, without fear of interruption.

CHAPTER XXIV.

THE CRITICAL MOMENT.—THE ATTEMPTED ESCAPE.—THE ALARM.

WHEN Adder had retired from the room, our heroine gave free vent to the painful feelings which her interview with him had excited in her bosom; and hope seemed to have faded entirely away from her mind; for if the villain remained obstinately resolved to put his diabolical threats into execution, what means had she of resisting him? None! Then again the hints he had given regarding Lord Ravensford, convinced her that he had some base design against him, and she trembled for the life of her husband, and probably also that of her child.

She was aroused from these reflections by the entrance of Cicely, who had come to do something in her apartment, and whose disagreeable looks assured our heroine that she took a pleasure in tormenting her, and saying anything which she thought might excite her feelings, and Rosabelle, therefore, determined to avoid conversing with her, as much as she possibly could. The old woman, however, appeared to be determined that she should not escape so easily; for the words she had so pointedly directed to her in the morning, remained in her memory; and after having eyed her with an insolent glance for a second or two, she ejaculated, in her usual harsh and querulous tones—

"I hope your ladyship feels happier after the interview you have had with your lover, and that the observations he has addressed to you, have met with your approbation. Oh, he is a very nice gentleman, although I am told he was only your gentleman's gentleman a short time ago. He! he! he!"

And the disgusting old woman croaked forth a laugh, which could scarcely have been imagined to have been uttered by anything but a witch; and appeared to think that she had spoken very wittily and sarcastically. But Rosabelle did not deign to condescend her any answer, and she averted her eyes, for there was something so remarkably disagreeable in the physiognomy of Cicely, that she could not bear to look upon it.

The old woman saw plainly enough that her observations annoyed Rosabelle, and although she felt rather vexed and disappointed that she did not answer her, she determined to follow them up.

"It seems that you have lost your tongue since your interview with Mr. Adder," she said; "but that is of very little consequence; I can talk enough for you and me too; and as Gordon as left the house, you will in all probability have a little more of my company than you otherwise would have done."

"Gordon left the house?" repeated our heroine eagerly; "thank Heaven!"

"Indeed!" said Cicely; "then, if his absence affords you pleasure, I can tell you that it will not be of long duration;—he is only gone some distance on a secret mission, for which he is to receive a handsome reward from Mr. Adder!"

"Ah!" cried our heroine, turning very pale, and a feeling of horror coming over her; "on a secret mission for Adder? In what fresh plot of villany is he engaged?"

"Oh, that I do not know," answered Cicely; "and if I did, it is not likely that I should inform you. It is something of importance, I dare say, or else Gordon would not have been employed; and no doubt concerns you."

Rosabelle felt her horror increase, and she trembled so that she could scarcely stand. Cicely observed her emotion with much satisfaction, and a savage grin overspread her features.

"Something that concerns me!" she exclaimed, and her terrible forebodings convinced her that the old woman did not make use of the observation without good reason.

"Oh, my poor husband!" she added, as she recalled to her memory the dark hints which Adder had given utterance to, and covering her face with her hands, she sobbed hysterically. "Oh, my unfortunate husband," she continued, "I tremble for you; surely this is some dark plot against you. Heaven protect you, and avert the evil fate destined to you by your implacable enemy!"

"If Adder only plays his cards as successfully as he has hitherto done, I do not think there is much chance of your seeing your *poor*

unfortunate husband again," said Cicely with a sneer, and a look which was perfectly hideous.

Poor Rosabelle gazed upon the unnatural old beldame with a look of horror and disgust.

"Inhuman woman," she ejaculated, "thus to take pleasure in torturing one of your own sex, who has never offended you, and whose misfortunes and oppressions ought to excite your pity and sympathy."

"Pity and sympathy," repeated Cicely, with bitter sarcasm; "they are qualities that none but fools would retain possession of; I never experienced them from any person yet, and I have banished mine from my breast many years since."

"I do believe you," sighed Rosabelle; "but I can sincerely pity *you*, for there will a time come when you will be brought to a terrible sense of your iniquities, and awful will then be the punishment you will have to undergo.'

"Hey day!" exclaimed Cicely; "I declare your ladyship is quite an adept at preaching a sermon; but its beauties are entirely lost upon me, and I do not think you will find Mr. Adder any more ready to approve of them than I am."

"Leave the room," said Rosabelle, in a tone of resentment, "and let me alone to my reflections; your language is brutal, and I will not listen to it."

"But I am afraid you will have to listen to it very frequently," returned the old woman, "as disagreeable as it may be. As for leaving the room, you will please to recollect that you are not mistress here, consequently I shall not attend to your orders until it pleases me."

Rosabelle walked away, and throwing herself into a chair, once more covered her face with her hands, determined not to pay any future attention to what the old harridan might say. The latter laughed sneeringly, and after muttering a few spiteful remarks that our heroine did not hear, she applied herself more assiduously to the task she had to perform in the room, and at the same time hummed, in discordant tones, snatches from different vulgar songs, which fell listlessly upon the ear of Rosabelle, who was too deeply engaged by her own melancholy thoughts to pay any attention to them.

At length having, much to the satisfaction of our heroine, completed her domestic duties in the room, old Cicely fixed upon Rosabelle a spiteful look, and then retired from the apartment. When she had gone, our heroine immediately sunk upon her knees, and, with upraised hands, she implored the mercy of the Supreme Being, and that He would protect her husband and all her dear friends from any danger by which they might be threatened. She arose more composed and confident, and endeavoured to hope that, after all, the wicked designs of Adder might be foiled, and that something would yet transpire to release her from her present incarceration and the future persecution of the villain Adder, for whom no punishment seemed adequate for the different crimes he had been guilty of.

Frequently did her thoughts revert to Mrs. Rattleton, her affectionate Emily, and she could well imagine the grief she must experience at her mysterious disappearance, for she knew that no sister could love her with more fervour than she did. But with the anguish which these reflections caused her, was mingled a feeling of satisfaction, when she remembered the melancholy situation of her father, and that in Emily he would find the same affectionate attention as if she had been with him herself. The idea of the deplorable condition of Mr. Montalbert was maddening, nay, perhaps he was no more, and she had not been present to receive his last sigh, or to enfold him in a dying embrace. The thought was almost past endurance, and it was a fortunate thing for our heroine that a torrent of tears came to the relief of her overcharged heart.

Three weeks elapsed without any material change taking place in the situation or prospects of Rosabelle. Adder visited her every day, and she was annoyed by his disgusting importunities; and frequently was the miscreant so worked up by the opposition which she offered to him, that he was half tempted to proceed to violence; but a secret power appeared to restrain him, and to watch over his unfortunate victim.

Adder was in a state of considerable anxiety and suspense, for he had not yet heard anything from Gordon, and sometimes he was apprehensive that he had been detected and was in custody; but again he thought, if he had been so, he should have seen some account of it in the newspapers, and he, therefore, at last endeavoured to conclude that Gordon thought it prudent not to write to him, and that he was in a fair way of being ultimately successful in his blood-thirsty designs.

The smugglers had made several successful trips, since the departure of Gordon, and they were not less anxious than Adder was to know what had become of him, and whether he was safe, for Gordon was acquainted with many circumstances that might greatly endanger them, should he be tempted to divulge them. Such is the doubt and suspicion that ever exist between the guilty!

At length, however, after another fortnight, a letter arrived at the house of Gordon, which was from him, and it may very well be imagined with what eager haste Adder broke the seal, and glanced his eye over the contents. They afforded him the most unbounded satisfaction. By some means or the other, but with which we are not acquainted, Gordon had ascertained all the particulars of the place where Ravensford had left the child, although he knew not then wither the former had gone;

and he suggested to Adder in the letter, that it would be a great addition to the gratification of his revenge if he were to get the young Alfred in his power. This, he added, might be easily accomplished, as it was left all day in the care of a woman, who might be soon overpowered, and the child taken away from her.

"Ah! by the infernal host! this is a capital suggestion," exclaimed Adder, when he had concluded perusing the letter; "it shall be done! The infant son of Ravensford in my power as well as his fair bride, my vengeance will be all but complete; and I have no doubt that Gordon will shortly be able to discover Ravensford, and to accomplish the deed for which my soul pants. Besides, when Rosabelle knows that her child is in my possession, and that her only chance of having him restored to her will be by a compliance with my desires, she must and will become an easy conquest."

He immediately sought out Monckton, who was at his usual place of resort when he was not on his smuggling expeditions, and showed him the letter from Gordon. The smuggler captain perused it with satisfaction, and his apprehensions were now at rest.

"What think you of the suggestion which Gordon has made?" asked Adder, when Monckton had finished reading the letter.

"Why, that it is a very excellent one," answered the smuggler captain; "for the possession of this child might be turned to account two or three different ways."

"True," coincided Adder.

"You will avail yourself of it, then?"

"Why, think you not I should be foolish to miss such an opportunity?"

"I do."

"Gordon deserves an extra reward for this."

"He is a shrewd fellow."

"And one who does not stand particular about trifles."

"No; crime and he are familiar. But how would you accomplish this design?"

"I have not yet had time to consider it properly," answered Adder; "can you give me any advice, captain?"

"Gordon I do not think can do it without assistance."

"Probably not."

"If I and my crew run the risk of going in our vessel to the place, and bring the child away, of course you will reward us?"

"Certainly; but that course will be attended with much danger, for should the real character of your vessel be known—"

"Oh, I can manage it so, that there will be no danger of a discovery being made," replied Monckton.

"Ah!—then be it so, and we will not fall out about the reward."

"Agreed!" answered the captain of the

smugglers; "an answer must, therefore, be despatched to the place where Gordon is staying, acquainting him with our intentions, so that he may make the necessary preparations for putting our designs into execution "

"It shall be done immediately. But think you that success is at all likely?"

"It is all but certain."

"And had the child better be brought to the house where the lady is confined?"

"That you can use your own pleasure in," replied Monckton.

Adder reflected for a few minutes.

"No," he at last said, "it shall not be so at present; I think it would be as well not to let Lady Ravensford know anything about it for a short time."

"Why so?"

"Why," returned Adder, "in the first place the sudden shock might be attended with fatal consequences to her; and in the next, I think it would be better to break it out to her by degrees, and make the circumstance subservient to my designs upon her."

"That is my opinion," remarked Monckton; "but you are a fool, Adder, to delay the indulgence of your desires so long, when you have it in your power to gratify them immediately. If you wait until you prevail upon the lady to consent, I think you will be likely to have to tarry a long while."

"That is your opinion?"

"It is."

"Mine is a different one."

"You must have a very high opinion of your powers of captivation, if that is really your belief," returned Monckton.

"Perhaps so," said Adder; "but time will show; and now that I have the prospect of getting this brat in my power, I am the more disposed to wait patiently and give my plans a fair trial."

"And wait until Lord Ravensford or his friends discover the retreat of the lady, force her from your power, and bring you to punishment," rejoined Monckton.

"If Gordon is successful, there will be no fear of that."

"May be so; but you remember the old proverb,—'a bird in the hand is worth two in the bush.'"

"At any rate, I have made up my mind to run the chance of it."

"Well, of course, you are at liberty to do as you think proper," observed the captain; "but if we succeed in getting this youngster in our power, where do you think of placing him?"

"Know you of any female that can be trusted with him?"

"I do."

"And does she reside far from this place?"

"Close upon the spot."

"Is the place obscure?"

"It is little frequented."

"And who is she?"

"The wife of one of my crew; you may depend upon her."

"'Tis well; and you think she will accept of the charge?"

"I am certain of it; she would do so gladly."

"Perhaps you will see her and make the proposal to her; it would come better from your lips than mine."

"I will do so."

"You have my thanks, captain."

"'Pshaw! I don't want them. But, mark now, she must be well paid for her trouble, and keeping the secret."

"I have no objection to that."

"This will be an expensive job for you."

"Were it to cost me twenty times as much, I would not begrudge it for my revenge."

"You are a most implacable foe."

"So my enemies have good reason to say."

"But come, there is no necessity for delay; let the letter be written and forwarded to Gordon as quickly as possible."

"It shall be done."

"In the meantime I will go down to Bet Kitson, and make the proposal to her."

"Ay, do; and do not be afraid to promise her a most liberal remuneration."

"I will do so, depend upon it."

"And when do you purpose starting on this expedition?"

"By the night after to-morrow, at the latest."

"Your promptitude pleases me."

"Delay is dangerous; that is always my motto."

"And a very good one; I will adopt it on this occasion; farewell."

"Good night; although I shall probably see you again."

"Well do, if you can, for I shall be anxious to know whether or not this Bet Kitson, as you call her, will undertake this charge."

"Oh, there is very little doubt but that she will do so."

Having arrived at the conclusion of this brief colloquy, the two worthies separated, and Adder bent his way to the house, to write the letter to Gordon; elated at the prospect of the success of his diabolical stratagems, and determined at any expense or danger to prosecute them.

"In the epistle, he gave Gordon all the information he could require, and highly praised his indefatigability, at the same time encouraging him to further exertions, by the promise of rewarding him accordingly.

This letter was immediately forwarded to the proper quarter, and Adder had not long done so, when Monckton returned.

"Well, captain, how have you succeeded?" asked Adder.

"As I anticipated."

"Then the woman is willing to take the child?"

"She is."

"And think you we may depend upon her secrecy?"

"There is no fear of that!"

"Did you not bind her by an oath?"

"There was no necessity for that! Bet Kitson's word is her bond, or she would not do to be the wife of a smuggler."

"And did you make her acquainted with the particulars?"

"I was compelled to do so to enable her to be more upon her guard."

"Ay, true! And you mentioned the reward?"

"It is not so much as I anticipated."

"What is it?"

"She demands twenty guineas."

"It shall be her's freely, immediately the child is placed in her care, and twenty more to that, if she well performs her task, and keeps the secret inviolable."

"I tell you again, there is no fear of her not doing that."

"Then all, so far, is well," observed Adder; "but may not the child being seen with this woman excite some curiosity?"

"Undoubtedly it would, if she were to let it be seen," answered Monckton; "but there is no necessity for her doing that; and it must be our principal care that it is not seen by any person in the neighbourhood."

"It shall be so; and now, Monckton, we will have a glass or two together, to drink success to this undertaking."

"With all my heart," replied the smuggler captain: and taking his seat, bottles were immediately placed upon the table, and they proceeded to drink with much alacrity, toast after toast following each other in rapid succession, while the deep potations which they quaffed, took but a trifling effect upon them, so accustomed were they to habits of intemperance.

We shall not trouble the readers by detailing the particulars of the manner in which the villain's proceeded, and the success they met with, as they are already made acquainted with them, also of the attempt which was made upon Ravensford's life by Gordon. The child was safely conveyed to Jersey, where he was placed in the care of the woman who had undertaken to take charge of him, and the ecstasy of the inhuman Adder knew no bounds.

Gordon, who imagined that he had actually killed Lord Ravensford, had also returned, and Adder loaded him with presents for the villanous part he had acted in the transactions.

Nothing could equal the exultation of Adder, for now he made sure that his triumph was complete; and that his success with the unfortunate Lady Ravensford was certain; but he was very much disappointed when, from the newspapers, he learnt that Lord Ravensford was not killed, neither was the wound mortal, and that he was in a very fair way of recovery.

"Curses light upon him," he exclaimed one day, when in company with Monckton; "this is an unfortunate failure, although it is not the fault of Gordon."

"And yet the torture of mind which Lord Ravensford must endure, in consequence of the loss of his child, ought, I think, sufficiently to satisfy your revenge," said Monckton.

"Yes, he must indeed be suffering most severe mental agony," said Adder, "and that is a great source of exultation to me;—but if he recovers, I shall still be in fear of his discovering all that it has cost me so much to concoct."

"Pshaw!" cried the smuggler captain, "your fears are groundless. He would never think of seeking for you here."

"Perhaps not," returned Adder; "still it would have been much more satisfactory had Gordon succeeded in dispatching him."

"I like not the unnecessary shedding of human blood."

"Then you have never felt the sentiments that I do."

"You know not that; but, smuggler as I am, and have been from a boy, I never yet shed the blood of my fellow man, unless it was in a combat, and in self-defence."

"And yet you would have insisted upon one of your crew committing murder, had not Gordon undertaken to do it."

"Because I had pledged my word to you that it should be done, and nothing would have induced me to break it."

"Ha! ha! ha!" laughed Adder;—"there's honour for you, in the captain of a desperate crew of smugglers."

"Ay, you may mock me, if you think proper, but I have spoken the truth."

Adder made no further observation, but walked away, and Monckton rejoined his companions at their rendezvous.

In the meantime, Rosabelle was just as helpless as ever, and Adder daily continued to annoy her with importunities. After the abduction of the little Alfred, he became much more bold and confident in his manners towards her, and she noticed it, and could not help thinking that something had happened to occasion this alteration in his behaviour, and at times her mind felt some severe misgivings, which she found it impossible to comprehend. Adder had not, however, yet mentioned anything about the child, and, therefore, she could not entertain any suspicion of that circumstance.

So well secured was every place, that our heroine had long since given up all idea of escaping, an i rested her only hope of deliverance upon her friends discovering the place of her confinement; but a circumstance a short time after this happened, which gave her some reason to hope.

Notwithstanding the utter disgust which our heroine ever evinced in the company of old Cicely, that disagreeable woman obtruded her society upon her at ever opportunity, and, as we have before stated, it was very evident that s he felt a pleasure in making Rosabelle uncomfortable. Guilt is always envious of the virtues it never possessed, and feels a delight in evincing its hatred of the possessor in every possible manner, and thus it was with Cicely. Although Rosabelle had never done anything to offend her, from the first moment she beheld her, she felt the greatest detestation towards her, and was determined to annoy her in every possible way. This, however, she concealed from Adder, well aware that he would not approve of it, and Rosabelle thought it too contemptible to take any notice of it, and it she had, she would not have troubled herself to mention it to her prosecutor, who might feel little disposed to trouble himself in the matter.

Cicely would make any excuse to be in the same room with our heroine, and when she was

ROSABELLE ENTREATS THE COMPASSION OF ADDER.

tired of talking to her, Rosabelle seldom condescending her a reply, she would sing portions of vulgar songs, in a manner which would have done honour to St. Giles's. Rosabelle's mind, however, was so fully occupied with her own thoughts that she seldom paid any attention to her, and not unfrequently was she almost entirely unconscious of her presence.

It was one evening, a short time after the events that we have been recording had taken place, that Cicely paid our heroine her accustomed and unwelcome visit, and, as soon as she entered the room, Rosabelle could perceive that she had been drinking and was quite inintoxicated.

This circumstance rather alarmed her, for she was afraid that the old woman being thus excited, might be guilty of some excesses; but still she reflected, she had nothing to apprehend from her, as the persons who were in the house would be sure to come to her aid, and thus she was in safety. But to be alone, and in the power of wretches who cared not what crime they committed, was sufficient of itself to fill her mind with terror, and she had great difficulty in supporting her feelings.

The old woman staggered to a seat, for she could scarcely stand, and having dropped into it, she raised her blood-shot eyes towards the countenance of our heroine, and fixed upon her a look expressive of her usual malevolence.

Rosabelle averted her head, and taking up a

book, pretended to be reading; but the old woman was not to be diverted that way, and after several ineffectual attempts to speak, she stammered out—

"They are all gone out but Gordon, and he has fallen fast asleep in the chair by the fire-place, and so I thought I would come up stairs and keep you company: you are fond of my company, I know.

> 'Come all ye prigs and hoof-padders,
>   And listen to my song,
> I'm going to sing 'bout what took place
>   The morn Jack Rawn was hung!' "

This speech, and the exquisite lines that we have quoted above, was accompanied by sundry hiccups, and the disgusting old woman rolled about in the chair apparently in the most uncomfortable manner. Rosabelle trembled, but she endeavoured to conceal her fears as much as possible, and pretended to be continuing to read the book she held in her hand, and did not make any reply.

"Mr. Adder is a very foolish man," continued the old woman, after he had indulged in innumerable fal lal la's, by way of embellishment to the song; "he is a foolish man, or he would not stand *shilly-shallying* and *dilly-dallying* with you, my fine lady, in the manner he has. Such squeamish minxes, indeed; poh!

> 'From north to south, from east to west,
>   The news like lightning run,
> And half of London was resolved
>   That day to see the fun;
> For he was the last of highwawmen,
>   And a daring fellow he,
> And thousands flocked to see him swing
>   Upon the gallows tree !' "

We need not attempt to describe the feelings of our heroine, while the old woman was thus proceeding; she endeavoured to close her ears to the words she was giving utterance to, but in vain, and the disgust which she felt was most unbounded.

"Why don't you answer me?" demanded Cicely, in a surly tone; "I suppose you think yourself above me, don't you? But I can tell you you are not. You are a prisoner, but I am not, and—

> 'The rope was round his wizen placed,
>   He looked up at the beam;
> A smile was on his daring brow,
>   And he quite pleased did seem.
> Game as could be resolved to die——' "

A very long yawn stopped the old woman's harmony, and her head dropped upon the table. She muttered two or three incoherent words, and shortly afterwards her loud snoring convinced our heroine that the effects of the liquor she had been drinking had overpowered her, and that she had fallen off to sleep.

Rosabelle laid down her book; a sudden thought darted across her mind, and her heart palpitated with emotion. She remembered what Cicely had said about there being no one in the house but Gordon, and that he was asleep below. The room door was open—the old woman slept soundly, and she was not likely to be awakened easily—a famous opportunity presented itself for her to attempt to make her escape. The chance was worth encountering any danger in making the effort, and she determined to avail herself of it.

Hastily putting on her bonnet and cloak, Rosabelle mentally invoked the assistance of Heaven, and then, with noiseless footsteps, approached the chair on which the old woman was sitting, to make sure that she was not assuming drunkenness and sleep, and she was soon convinced that she was not. She now lightly stepped on to the landing, and closing the door gently upon the unconscious old woman, locked it after her, and thus left her a secure prisoner. She then leant her head over the banisters, and listened attentively, but hearing no noise below, she was in hopes that all was right, and ventured to begin to descend the stairs.

Having passed down one flight, she once more paused, and listened most attentively, but all remained as still as death, and her hopes became more sanguine.

At length she reached the door of the parlour which was closed, and Rosabelle hesitated, and her heart beat so vehemently against her side that she could scarcely support herself.

"Courage—courage !" she whispered to herself, "this is the critical moment. Let me be firm, and I may escape."

Her trembling and hesitation decreased as these thoughts crossed her mind, and she laid her hand on the handle of the door. It opened with a creaking noise, which again excited her fear, lest it should arouse Gordon; but her alarm was, fortunately, groundless. A light was burning on the table, and the fire also cast forth a cheerful blaze, and by their light our heroine beheld the ruffian Gordon, as Cicely had described him, seated in the chair, his arms folded across his chest, and fast asleep.

Rosabelle's heart bounded, and hope was strengthened tenfold. The near prospect of liberty excited in her breast a feeling of ecstasy which may be conceived, but cannot be described. The moon shone brightly in at the window, and its silvery beams seemed to smile encouragement upon her. Another moment, she reflected, and she might inhale the pure air, and be as free. The thought nerved her on; and knowing that every moment was fraught with danger, she determined to act with promptitude. But Gordon was so seated that she could not gain the door without passing him closely, and then she must act with the greatest caution, or she might arouse him. She advanced one step, but hastily retreated again, hearing Gordon yawn, and he seemed as if he were about to awaken. She stood in trembling suspense, but it was not for long; Gordon having stretched out his arms, and yawned two or three times, sunk back on his chair again, and his loud snoring soon convinced her that he was again asleep.

She now once more commended herself to the protection of Heaven, and again advanced towards the door. She had passed the sleeping ruffian—the door was in her hand, and liberty was just before her; when there was a loud noise, like that of some heavy weight falling, from the room above; and Rosabelle was so alarmed that she had not the power of moving one way or the other, but stood at the door trembling violently.

The noise immediately aroused the sleeping ruffian, and hastily starting to his feet, he rubbed his eyes, and stared eagerly around the room. They instantly rested on our unfortunate heroine, and giving utterance to a dreadful oath, he rushed towards her, and seizing her fiercely by the arm, dragged her back. Rosabelle sunk upon her knees, and in terrified accents exclaimed—

"Oh, mercy—mercy! spare me—save me, for the love of Heaven, save me!"

"Ah! would you escape?" exclaimed Gordon; "speak, answer me—how did you contrive to leave the apartment in which you have been confined?"

The ruffian looked ferociously upon her while he spoke, and Rosabelle trembled more violently than before when she gazed upon the frightful features of the murderer, and remembered the awful adventure in *The Lover's Resting Place*. Her lips quivered, and in vain did she endeavour to articulate a syllable.

"Speak, I tell you again!" demanded the villain; "how came you hither? By what means did you contrive to leave the room?"

"The door was left unfastened," faultered out Rosabelle; "oh, do not harm me."

"The door left unfastened!" repeated Gordon; "who left it so?"

"Cicely."

"Ah! the old hag!—if she has done this she shall answer for it. But where is she?"

"In the room I have just quitted, and asleep," replied Rosabelle.

"Ah! I see how it is; myself and Cicely have been indulging ourselves rather too freely, and both are to blame; we must be more cautious for the future. Come, my lady, you must allow me to escort you to your old quarters, and depend upon it, you will not have such another opportunity as this. Come!"

"Oh, Gordon," supplicated our heroine, not thinking in the despair of the moment, of the uselessness of appealing to the flinty heart of the murderer, "do not consign me, I beseech you, to that dismal apartment again, but take pity upon me, a deeply injured woman as I am, and suffer me to escape. Believe me, you shall be amply rewarded for such an inestimable service."

"Oh, no," returned the ruffian, and a malignant grin overspread his features; "it won't do; I'm not to be caught in that way; I can very well understand what my reward would be; but they must catch me before they give it me. Ha—ha—ha! Come—come, you must come with me, or I must use force, that's all about it."

Poor Rosabelle clasped her hands in the intensity of her agony, and finding that it would be useless to entreat any further, with a despairing heart, she slowly retraced her footsteps to the chamber from which she had so recently escaped, followed by the wretch, Gordon.

On opening the door, they found the old woman stretched at full length upon the floor; and it was evident that it was from her that the noise had proceeded, which so unfortunately aroused Gordon, and prevented her escape, at the very moment when the chance was before her.

It was some time before Gordon could arouse the old woman to sensibility, and when he did so, he commanded her sternly to follow him.

"Hey day!" cried Cicely, rubbing her eyes, and looking with stupified amazement at our heroine, who had sunk despairingly in a chair, and leaning her elbow upon the table, and her head upon her hand, she was weeping bitterly; "what's the matter now?"

"What's the matter!" reiterated Gordon; "why, that through your infernal stupidity, the bird had nearly flown."

"Ah! what, do you mean to say that she had nearly escaped?" croaked forth the old woman, and she looked more savagely than ever at Rosabelle.

"Yes, I mean to say that she would have escaped," replied Gordon, and a very pretty hobble we should then both have got in."

"Why, where was I at the time?"

"Fast asleep, and a safe prisoner in this room; locked in."

"Locked in!" ejaculated Cicely; "oh, I see it all now; that confounded Hollands got the better of me, and you, too, I think, Gordon; and, therefore, one is as much to blame as the other. We ought to thank our lucky stars that it has turned out as it has. But the artful jade, to lock me in, to—to——"

"There, that's enough," interrupted Gordon; "you would stand talking there all night. We will leave the lady to her own reflections, which, doubtless, will not be very pleasant. Mr. Adder will be home very shortly, I expect, and, should he find us together, he might suspect something wrong. Good night, my lady, and when you next try to escape, you had better use a little more expedition with your caution. Come, Cicely, we must see and arrange this business somehow or another."

The old woman fixed upon Rosabelle one more malicious look, and appeared to exult in the agony she was undergoing at having been thwarted in her attempt, and then following the wretch Gordon, they both quitted the room together, and secured the door after them.

They both congratulated themselves when they had got below, that Rosabelle had not been successful, and were determined to be more cautious in future. Another moment, and our heroine would have been at liberty, and they trembled when they reflected upon the consequences that would have been certain to have followed her escape. They both, however, considered that it would be better for them not to mention anything about it to Adder or the others, as it would only excite his suspicious that all was not right, and probably deprive them of his confidence and friendship; which as he was very liberal, was not to be treated lightly. Thus the affair was amicably arranged between the two worthies, and old Cicely determined to annoy our unfortunate heroine more than ever, for the "audacious" (as she termed it) attempt she had made to escape, and, moreover, for her unparalleled presumption and atrocity, in having actually made her a prisoner in the very place where she had been herself confined.

As for poor Rosabelle, she was completely overwhelmed with the intensity of her anguish and disappointment, and for some time after Gordon and the old woman had left her, she remained in a state of almost unconsciousness.

"Alas!" she at last ejaculated, beating her breast; "fate has conspired against me, and I am doomed to perpetual misery. Am I never to escape from the power of these wretches? Has the Omnipotent Being entirely forsaken me? Oh, God! let me die rather than live to endure this succession of miseries and disappointments."

She clasped her burning temples, and arising from her chair, traversed the room in the greatest possible agony. If Adder should become acquainted with the circumstance, she could not help thinking that he would be induced to adopt even more stringent measures towards her; but then she consoled herself with the reflection that it was not likely that Gordon or the old woman would let him know anything about it, as they would be blamed for neglect, and Adder might deem it prudent to remove her to some other place of confinement. She passed two or three hours in the greatest state of agitation, and could not venture to retire to rest, but listened to the slightest sound which proceeded from below, fearing to hear the villain Adder return home.

At length all was still in the house, and tired out with thinking, Rosabelle committed herself to the care of providence, and undressing herself, hastened into bed, and, in spite of the state of her mind, after the painful event which we have been detailing, she was so weary, that it was not long ere she sunk to sleep.

CHAPTER XXV.

THE INTERVIEW.—THE MOTHER AND HER CHILD.

MRS. KITSON, the woman to whom the child was entrusted, although ignorant and vulgar, did not possess a heart entirely depraved, and she behaved towards the little Alfred with much kindness, as she had been enjoined to do by Adder himself. She had not long before lost by death a child of her own, on whom she had doated, and she could not but view the poor boy who had been placed in her charge under such remarkable circumstances with the deepest sympathy. Albeit not used to the melting mood, and accustomed to scenes of vice, there were times when the better feelings of Mrs. Kitson would triumph, and this event was one that called them forth.

"What a lovely boy," she observed, when he was first presented to her, and the child as if conscious of the compliment paid him, smiled sweetly, and entwined his little fingers in her hair, playfully. Mrs. Kitson hugged him to her boson, and kissed his rosy cheeks several times.

"To be sure," said she, "his is a cruel fate, to be so early introduced to sorrow, although he is unconscious of it, poor dear."

"Bah!" ejaculated Adder, impatiently; "although I would not have you behave unkind to the brat, you must not be too chicken-hearted, or it might work harm to my plot."

"I have given you my word, sir," answered Mrs. Kitson, "I have given you my word, that my conduct in this affair shall never give you cause to complain, and you will find that I can be depended upon. Poor little dear, how he smiles; ah! he little thinks the dreadful anguish his parents are now enduring on his account."

"No more of this," cried Adder, and again frowning, he paced the room backwards and forwards, apparently in no very pleasant mood from the observations which Mrs. Kitson had made; "one of his parents will, ere long, behold him again, and will have him restored to her, if she is not mad enough to reject my propositions to her; his father shall see him no more."

"Poor gentleman!"

"Ah!—Monckton has deceived me, I am afraid," remarked Adder, with a look of astonishment.

"Monckton has not deceived you, sir," replied Mrs. Kitson; "the captain, I believe told you that I could be entrusted with a secret, and that you may depend upon my performing the agreement I have entered into with you faithfully; and he has spoken nothing but the truth."

"And nothing will ever induce you to divulge the particulars with which you have been made acquainted?" demanded Adder.

"Nothing!"

"You are ready to swear that?"

"No;—of what use is an oath?—I value not an oath at all, and, therefore, it would only be madness administering one to me. I have, I repeat, pledged my word, and nothing whatever will tempt me to swerve from the promise I have made."

"I will be satisfied."

"If you are not, entrust some other person with the child, and you will still find me faithful."

"On that depends the reward you will receive," said Adder.

"I have named the price of the remuneration I expect to receive," returned Mrs. Kitson; "and I require no more;—that I will take good care shall be mine."

"Humph!" returned Adder, looking at the smuggler's wife with some surprise; "you are plain spoken, at any rate."

"Probably so," she answered; "and what is more, I mean what I say."

"Well, your candour does not displease me; and let me see;—the agreement was, I believe, that you should receive the money the moment the child was entrusted to your care?"

"It was."

"Here, then, it is."

"Nay, I do not want it; I will not take it, until you are satisfied that my attention to your instructions merits it; if you think afterwards that it does not, I will not take from you a single coin."

"You are a strange woman."

"So many have called me before you. The smuggler's wife, perhaps, is not quite the vulgar and ignorant woman that she has been represented."

"From the short acquaintance that I have had with you," said Adder, "I can answer for it that she is not."

"But you will not keep the poor child from its mother?"

"I have before told you that that depends upon the latter."

"Restore it to her, and gratitude for that action may induce her sooner than anything else to yield to your wishes."

"I shall see."

"And I hope you will avail yourself of my simple suggestion. In the meantime, once more, I assure you, that you may depend upon my paying the child every attention. I have been a mother myself, and a parent—"

"There, there," interrupted Adder, impatiently, for he was tired of the conference; "I know what you would say, and do not wish to hear it. What I principally request of you is, that you will keep the child confined to your own place, until I may fetch him away from you."

"You may trust me."

"I hope I may."

"I have given you no cause to doubt me."

"True. Do you have many visitors?"

"None, but my husband and some of the crew, who are all, of course, acquainted with the secret; and, therefore, if you have any confidence in them, you have nothing to apprehend."

"'Tis well," answered Adder; "I am satisfied, and shall not question you any more, unless I see something to excite my suspicions."

"Which you never will."

"I hope not."

"What interest could I have in deceiving you?"

"None, that I am aware of."

"Then why question me at all?"

"Perhaps I was wrong; but the importance of the trust must plead my excuse."

"I have promised the captain, and my husband, as well as myself, is involved in my fidelity."

"Well, well; there let the matter rest. Good-day; I shall call to see you every morning."

"Good-day, sir," responded Mrs. Kitson, and Adder quitted the cottage of the smuggler's wife.

Although he was at first doubtful of the fidelity of Mrs. Kitson, her answers, which were so candidly spoken, perfectly satisfied him, and he returned to the house, very well pleased to think that Captain Monckton had recommended him to a female in whom he could evidently place the strictest confidence.

Mrs. Kitson well performed the task entrusted to her, and no person in the neighbourhood had the least idea of the child being in her care. She behaved with the utmost kindness to him, and at times she felt keenly for the suffering of the unhappy parents who had been so cruelly and unjustly deprived of their offspring; and would have been much happier had she got it in her power to restore it to them, instead of having entered into the nefarious plot of Adder and his infamous colleagues.

Adder called daily, as he had promised, upon her, and as he beheld the increasing likeness which the little Alfred bore to his father, his hatred for it increased, and he was at times almost determined to sacrifice it to his diabolical spirit of revenge; but an inscrutable power withheld his arm, and preserved the poor innocent child for another, and ultimately more fortunate fate.

He had not even hinted in a remote manner to Rosabelle, that the child was in his power, although his conduct, as we have before observed, was sufficiently altered to convince her that something particular had occurred, although what that was, she had not the most remote means of conjecturing; and he was at a loss in what manner to bring about the scheme which he had in contemplation, fearful that if he were to announce the fact in too abrupt a manner to her, it might be productive of the most fatal consequences, and that he should thus be deprived of the gratification which it cost him so much trouble, care, anxiety, and danger, to obtain. He wanted to hit upon some new idea, which would render the advantage he had obtained, by the abduction of the child, subservient to his wishes, and it was not long ere his prolific invention in any schemes of villany afforded him the opportunity and the means he sought.

The child had been five weeks in the care of Mrs. Kitson, when he determined upon a trial of his plot, and the manner in which he succeeded, will be seen by the sequel.

The same evening on which the villain came to this determination, Captain Monckton and his companions having once more returned from another successful expedition, Adder, as usual, joined them at their usual rendezvous in the evening, they always preferring that to the house of Gordon, as there were so many secret and subterranean outlets, by which they could baffle the revenue officers, if they should think fit to surprise them, without receiving in return any particular injury themselves.

It was a very remarkable circumstance, that, although the place of their resort, and most of their haunts, were perfectly well known to the authorities, they had never but once ventured to attack them, and ever since then, so signally were they defeated, that the smugglers were permitted to carry on their contraband trade with impunity; nor did the officers even venture to annoy old Davey Grampus, which was the name of the landlord of the house they frequented; but, it was very evident that some of the old officers, who were smarting under the defeat they had experienced in the before-mentioned affray, had not forgotten it; so far from it, indeed, that they only waited and longed for an opportunity of retaliating upon them. There was, however, but little chance of that, for at the time of which we are writing, most of the inhabitants of the island were smugglers, and those who were not engaged in such pursuits, were fully prepared to take their part, should the former require their assistance.

"The Caboose," as the haunt of the smugglers was called, was a very old, but substantial building, built almost entirely of stone, and before it fell into the occupation of Davey Grampus, had remained empty for some time, and like most old fabrics of the same description, in all parts of the country, superstition had attached many most extravagant and improbable stories to it, and no one felt inclined to take it, although it was offered upon most advantageous terms, until Davey Grampus made his appearance in that part of the country. He had formerly been a wrecker, and was at that time connected with several bands of smugglers, and a most shrewd, designing, and daring ruffian.

Here, then, did Davey Grampus take up his residence, and hence the acquaintance of Monckton and the others with him. We have already hinted at the manner in which the Miscreant Adder and Monckton, the smuggler-captain, had been introduced to each other, and we shall more fully explain ourselves at some future period. Adder entertained a great dread of Monckton, for he well knew that his word could bring him at once to an ignominious end; and he was, therefore, anxious to conciliate his friendship, and that of his companions who were in the secret, as much as possible; consequently, while he remained in the neighbourhood, and whenever the smuggler-captain and his daring crew returned from a trip, he always remained in their society as much as he conveniently could, and was most liberal in his conduct. It required no gentle hint to loosen his purse-strings; fear ever caused his purse to open, and, from what has already been shown, he was ever most liberal and lavish in his hospitality. In company of any description, man of the world as he was, Adder also knew the way to make himself agreeable, from the most vulgar to the most highly polished. The smugglers always viewed him as a most welcome guest, and they were not at all displeased with him, although they were not all acquainted with the exact nature of that which had done so.

On the evening to which we have alluded, Adder felt particularly exhilarated, after having formed the resolution which he had done, and he, therefore, met Monckton and his dissipated associates, with much pleasure.

"Well, Adder, my lad," said the smuggler-captain, familiarly, "we are right glad to see you; we just wanted you company to add to the mirth of the evening; for wherever you are, dull care never ventures to show its face. Sit down, my Trojan, and let the grog pass merrily round; we will always have a cheerful night of it when we meet together."

"Ay, to be sure we will, Monckton," replied Adder; "and, in truth I am in an excellent humour for you this evening, and never felt in better spirits."

"Why," returned Michael Hernwood, "if a man who has got so pretty a woman at his service as you have is not happy, I don't know who should be."

"Ay," observed Monckton; "how is the little stubborn one, Adder?"

"Exquisitely lovely, as usual, but most devilishly obstinate," answered Adder.

"Which is entirely your own fault," returned the smuggler captain. "You have her securely in your power, and what is to prevent you from making her yield, if you think proper?"

"True," said the villain to whom the above speech was addressed; "but the fact of it is, Monckton, that, reckless as I own I am, and have proved myself to be, in other respects, I cannot—confound me if I can!—make up my mind to use violence towards her. There is something in the expression of her handsome countenance which would always restrain my fierce desires, even whilst they were at their highest pitch."

"Such childish ideas may deter you from the accomplishment of your wishes," said Michael; "but, were I situated as you are, they should not stand in my way."

"Nor in mine," coincided Monckton.

"I would force her to my will," exclaimed Michael Hernwood, with a scowl of ferocity.

"I thought so once," replied Adder; "but since I have been brought into contact with Rosabelle, I have found how erroneous were my opinions; and I who have hitherto hesitated at no deed of guilt—who have stopped at no crime, stand in her presence awed and abashed by the power of virtue and innocence."

"Very pretty and sentimental," said Michael Hernwood, with a half sneering laugh; "but I question much if you would find another man with the same advantage as that which you hold—at least, not one in a hundred who would entertain the same nicety of feeling."

"Perhaps not," said Adder; "and I do not know that I should have done so at one time."

"I am sure you would not," remarked Hernwood, "at the period our acquaintance commenced. You would not then have hesitated at bolder deeds than the subjugation of the whims of a snivelling woman."

"You are right, Michael," said Monckton, "and it strikes me that our friend Adder will alter his opinion before long."

"I think you will find yourself mistaken, captain," observed Adder; "I am rather more delicate in my amours than you seem inclined to give me credit for. I would not conquer the fair one who hath enslaved my heart with the brute force of the Indian savage. No, I would induce her to love me, by—"

"Love!—Ha! ha! ha!" laughed Monckton; "love, indeed! and have you the presumption to think that you can ever impress the heart of that woman with such a sentiment,

when, although you may rail against violence, and all that, you have forcibly torn her from the arms of her husband, father, child, friends, and placed her in a confinement which, under any circumstances, must be far from pleasant? If that's the way you estimate women's hearts and affections, Adder, you must have a very indifferent opinion of the sex."

Adder made no answer to this, but walked backwards across the room for a few seconds. He seemed to feel the force of Monckton's observations (who, though an unpolished man, was by no means an ignorant one), and he already began to perceive that the manner of triumphing over Rosabelle, which he had designed for himself, was not so easy of accomplishment as he had at first imagined.

"Well, Adder," said the smuggler captain, at last, who had been watching the former narrowly, "my observations do not appear to have very well satisfied you."

"There you are wrong, captain," replied Adder with a forced smile, "for they have perfectly satisfied me upon one point, namely, that that you are quite correct, and I am decidedly wrong. Persuasion will not effect the attainment of my wishes; but I have another scheme which may make her be glad to yield."

"And what is that, pray?" demanded Monckton.

"The child."

"Ah! that was a fortunate idea of Gordon's," observed Monckton.

"It was," coincided Adder, "and to you and all your crew I am equally indebted for the manner in which you executed the plot."

"Ay," said one of the smugglers, emitting a large volume of smoke from his mouth as he spoke; "I don't think that anything could be much better managed than that was."

"Well, and this child," remarked the smuggler captain, "how do you mean to act respecting him? Bet Kitson has made a capital nurse to it, I think."

"She has," replied Adder, "and, luckily for the brat, a very affectionate one."

"Ay, ay," observed Sam Kitson, the husband of the female alluded to, who was present, "you wont find her equal for many a good mile, I'll warrant, although she is the wife of a smuggler. My Bet is one of the best of women as ever stood in two shoes, and those who say a word to the contrary must answer for it to your humble servant."

"Well said, Sam," returned Michael Hernwood; "I always like to hear every man speak well of his wife; and as soon as ever I hear a fellow do the contrary, why, I sets him down for a damned swab, and the woman he is speaking against, as some poor unfortunate creature, who deserves to be tied to something better."

"But you have not yet told me your plan

concerning the child, Adder," said the smuggler captain.

"Why," replied the former; "to-morrow I mean to introduce them to each other."

"Ah!"

"Yes."

"But you will not do so abruptly, of course," remarked the captain; "for the sudden shock might take a very different effect to that which you might wish it to have."

"Oh, no, I will manage that, never fear me," returned Adder; "I have planned it all out; I will work upon her feelings, and when I see an advantage, take it. The restoration of her child to her arms, must be the price of her compliance with my desires."

"In that case," observed Monckton; "the power of a mother's feelings may tempt her to yield."

"And if it does not," said Adder; "I then know my only course, and shall not longer hesitate to adopt it. But come, how stand the glasses?"

"Ay, lads, charge!" cried Monckton.

The smugglers obeyed with their usual hilarity.

"A toast, my lads!" observed the captain, rising; "Here's to the free of the free and open sea!"

Tumultuous shouts followed this toast, which was responded to by all present most heartily, Davey Grampus making his appearance to add *eclat* to the riotous applause.

Again the glasses were replenished, and this time Adder arose upon his feet, and addressing himself to the captain and his associates, he said:—

"After sincerely responding to your toast, captain, allow me to propose one!"

"Ay, ay," shouted several smugglers in a breath; "a toast from Adder! A toast from Adder!"

"My toast, then, is simply, 'Woman!'" cried the unprincipled wretch, and he prided himself upon having said a very pretty and gallant thing; and forgetting or affecting to forget, that he had been one of woman's most cruel and heartless oppressors. Many of the coarse individuals present, had by far more delicate notions of the fair sex than himself, and would have scorned to have acted in the diabolical manner in which he had done, to gain possession of our unfortunate heroine.

Adder having given the toast, was not satisfied with that, and being also flushed with several glasses of brandy which he had quaffed, he insisted upon favouring the rude guests assembled with a song in embellishment of the toast he had given them, and Monckton, who was ever ready to encourage him in his festivity, knowing that, as his hilarity increased, so did his liberality with it, urged him on, so that at last, Adder, who had really an excellent voice, and sang with much effect, and which, although not apparently in the style which seemed at all likely to please them, was listened to by the smugglers with much delight :—

"Woman, since I have first known thee,
It has been my pride to own thee
Empress of my hopes and cares,
Of all my pleasures, all my fears!
In thy smile I've lived delighted,
By thy smile I've been requited,
My thoughts and dreams of ecstacy,
Woman! have ever been of thee!

"Woman, thou'rt my destiny,
I thy slave must ever be;
Bound by chains of bliss and love,
Who my taste can e'er reprove?
Brilliant eyes, bewitching grace,
Sparkling wit, enchanting face;
Bliss the greatest that can be,
Woman! is centred all in thee!"

"Bravo, Adder," exclaimed Monckton, when the libertine had concluded; "by Jupiter, you make a most eloquent advocate in the cause of beauty, and yet you have been one of its most troublesome customers."

"I may have been," returned the villain Adder, and his brow lowered as he spoke. "When the persons upon whom I had fixed my thoughts were obstinately opposed to my wishes, and ——"

"Was that the case with her, who——"

"Hush!" interrupted Adder, turning ghastly pale, and looking fearfully around him, while he trembled in every limb;—"not a word upon that dreadful subject;—not a word; —I have often cautioned you before, Monckton, and I am surprised that——"

"Well, well, I was wrong, certainly, to say such a thing," said the smuggler captain; "but it slipped out without a thought;—come, come, suppose we change the subject? To-morrow morning, then, it is your intention to make the Lady Ravensford acquainted with the child being in your power?"

"That depends upon circumstances," replied the villain to whom the question was addressed; "I shall first hear how she receives the hints upon the subject which I shall throw out, and act accordingly."

"Ay, ay, I see," observed Monckton, "slow and cautious as usual. But, as I before observed, there is nothing but the idea of being restored to the arms of her child which, in my opinion, will ever tempt her to yield to your desires; and that will not be obtained without considerable difficulty, and craftiness of persuasion; but of that, you do not require any addition to the stock which you already possess, Adder."

Adder smiled at what he took to be a very high compliment.

"In that, I can answer for it," said he, "that you do me no more than justice. My abilities must prevail; the lady must yield, or she and her child do not see each other again."

"And after all," remarked Monckton, after a pause, "I no not see any difference to her yielding to it in that manner, or being forced by violence to it."

"Perhaps not, in your opinion," said Adder; "but the other happens to be mine, and, consequently, that makes the difference."

"Bet Kitson will not feel very well pleased at losing her young charge," said Monckton; "for, from what I have seen of her behaviour to it, she loves it almost as well as if it had been one of her own."

"Ay, you may say that, captain," said Sam Kitson; "the poor lass is indeed fond of it; and, somehow or other, I can't say but that I have taken a fancy to it myself. It is such a funny little fellow, and has such engaging ways with him too. Any one who didn't know it, might take an oath that he was a nobleman's child; he has such a look, such an eye, and——"

"Ha! ha! ha!" interrupted the principal portion of the smugglers, with a laugh of derision, which disconcerted Sam Kitson in pursuing his eulogiums on the little Alfred, and he looked rather stupid, as, from the latter part of his speech, any person would imagine he would be likely to look.

ADDER CAROUSING WITH THE SMUGGLERS.

"Why, Sam," remarked Monckton, the captain, when the laughter had in some measure subsided, "and pray, how long is it since you have been able to discover the wonderful difference between the brat of a nobleman and that of a poor man? Pshaw! let us hear no more of this, or myself and my comrades may not be inclined to let you off very easily. The fact of the matter is, it is a fine child, and I dare say both you and your wife are very fond of it; but it seems you are likely to lose it soon, and, therefore, must make up your minds to it."

"As I before stated," remarked Adder, "it is not certain whether the lady will yet win the protection of her child by her behaviour; and if she does not, until such time as she accedes, the child will still remain under the care of yourself and wife."

The rough smuggler, who, like his wife, beneath a coarse covering concealed a kind heart, felt very well pleased at this intimation, and returned an answer accordingly; and then the mirth of the evening was resumed in all that tumultuous manner in which the smugglers were in the habit of keeping their carousals. The brandy, Hollands, and other smuggled liquors went freely round, and there was not one among them who was not very well capable of playing a liberal character in such a scene; and it may, therefore, be easily conceived what a scene of drunkenness prevailed.

Adder, exhilarated with what he had partaken of, laughed, sung, joked, and swore by turns, in which he was most lustily joined by Monckton, who, although he was perfectly sober—at least, as perfectly sober as he usually was, and that was, to know everything that was passing about him, and to be considerably more sagacious than on ordinary occasions—thought it at all times prudent to act the same part as Adder did, by which means he could always arrive the readier at his purse. Strange as it may appear, Monckton acted the same part towards Adder as the latter did towards Saunter—Adder was his dupe; and although he knew it, for he was too much a man of the world not to do so, he was compelled, through terror, not to do otherwise than submit. A thousand and a thousand times did he curse the unfortunate accident which had put Monckton in the possession of that dreadful secret upon which his life depended, and longed for something or another to occur to rid him of a man whom he had so much cause to live in dread of. Could he not contrive by any means to get rid of him, was a thought which had frequently occurred to him, but he generally rejected it as soon as it crossed his mind, and something seemed to him that any attempt of the kind would be certain to bring upon his own head the most fearful consequences.

But, situated as he was, he was entirely in the power of the smuggler captain, who, if he thought proper to impeach against him, could undoubtedly bring him to the gallows, without running any risk himself.

He once or twice regretted that he had employed the smugglers in aiding him to bear away Lady Ravensford, and the subsequent nefarious transactions, by which he had involved himself still further in their power. But then, what others could he have got better to assist him, or in whom he could with so much safety confide? If he had employed strangers, he would have been placed equally the same in their power; and, consequently, he could not see that he had had any other alternative than to act in the manner he had done.

He had no fear Monckton would betray him, while he did not offend him. He had already kept the secret for many years; and, therefore, he had no reason to doubt him now. To be sure, he liked to be well rewarded, and very frequently, and that was what particularly perplexed the villain Adder, who did not like to part with his ill-gotten gold, although he now possessed such an abundance of it. But it was useless for him to repine; he was in Monckton's power, and he must submit, even though he should extort from him the last coin he had in the world; that would be better than dying an ignominious death upon the scaffold.

Before the smuggler captain and Adder separated that night, the latter was very much inebriated, and the former had contrived to get from him a goodly sum in gold, as a further security against his divulging the fearful secret of former days. Adder staggered home to the house of Gordon, and Monckton laughed heartily in his sleeve at the success he had met with, and the profitable victim he had got. He saw plainly that he had him entirely in his power; that Adder dreaded him almost as much as he did the hangman; and he resolved to take every advantage of it. He well knew the nefarious way in which Adder had accumulated his wealth, and he, therefore, felt not the least repugnance in fleecing him out of it all, if possible, and was determined that it should not be his fault if he did not.

Adder staggered home to the house of Gordon, where he immediately retired to his chamber, and was soon snoring most loudly, with the effects of the deep potations he had been taking.

Rosabelle, after her interview with Cicely, who usually contrived to so favour her morning, noon, and night, and two or three times in the course of the day, felt, as usual, in a most uneasy and depressed state of mind, and sat in the apartment in which she was held a prisoner, the very picture of despair. For the last day or two, her heart had foreboded something of an extraordinary description which was about to happen to her; and in spite of all her efforts to the contrary, she found it utterly impossible to divest the impression from her thoughts. Although, as we have observed, Adder had not directly told her that her child was in his possession, there was something in his behaviour, and the mysterious hints he had thrown out to her, in the last interview they had had together, which convinced her that he had something in contemplation, and that he possessed more in his power than he chose at that time to divulge.

She was positive that at the next interview she would be made acquainted with something that she had a foreboding was most deeply connected with herself.

On the evening which we have been describing, when Adder and his friends caroused at "The Caboose," Rosabelle had been particularly miserable, and, seated in her chamber, with her elbow leaning upon the window-sill, and her head upon her hand, she gazed vacantly upon the cheerless prospect which she could observe from the casement. Sobs heaved her bosom; and tears alternately chased each other down the poor persecuted one's pale cheeks; and it was very evident that she felt more than usually depressed even than she had done for some time, even under all the many afflicting circumstances under which she had been so frequently placed. Still, there was a melancholy beauty in the appearance of Lady Ravensford, which must have deeply interested the beholder; and it was rendered doubly impressive by the peculiar circumstances under which she was placed.

The afternoon had passed drearily away; the sun had sunk in the western horizon; twilight had succeeded; and the pale moon had taken her silvery throne in the Heavens; but so deeply involved in the thoughts that occupied her mind, Rosabelle had suffered all these changes to take place, and had not heeded them, or scarcely so; and hour after hour had passed away without her undergoing any change;—she sat like a statue, whose heavy breathing alone denoted that she was a thing of life; and, as the beams of Luna reflected upon her beauteous countenance, a sculptor would have been delighted to have had such an exquisite model for his chisel.

The scene upon which the fair mourner's eyes rested, was as uninteresting a one as could well be imagined, and was by no means calculated to dispel the sorrowful thoughts that crowded upon the imagination of Rosabelle. It was a wild moor at the back of the house, and, as far as the eye could stretch, she could not see a single object to break the dull monotony of the scene, until the lofty rocks in the distance enclosed the dark perspective.

There was not a house on that side of the building for several miles, and the place was a very fitting one for the nefarious transactions that were carried on in it, and the dark deeds that had doubtless been perpetrated in it. The keen wind from the bosom of the ocean whistled around the house, and added to the horrors of the place.

Several hours before, Lady Ravensford had been released from the society of the hateful old woman, Cicely, who had been more than usually sarcastic, and because she saw that our heroine was more than commonly sorrowful, the infamous old harridan determined to take advantage of it, and set all her diabolical ingenuity to work to wound the distracted feelings of Lady Rosabelle to the very utmost. She commenced in her usual way, but her harsh and grating tones fell listlessly upon our heroine's ear. She had become so used to the splenetic observations of the old beldame, that she paid little or no attention to them, and treated them, as they deserved, with the most ineffable disdain. At length, completely tired of conversing without receiving any answer, Cicely, having given utterance to some coarse invectives by way of a finale, took her departure from the room, and left Lady Ravensford to herself, much to the relief of the latter, who was now enabled to give the most unrestrained indulgence to her sorrows.

The whole of the morning, as we have before mentioned, her mind had been occupied by the most dismal forebodings, yet with them at the same time was mingled a certain feeling of joy, for which she was at a loss to account; and with every hour those feelings had increased, until they had become almost insupportable. Adder, on their last meeting, in spite of all his precaution to the contrary, had let out sufficient to give her to understand that he had something of importance in his mind, on which, in all probability, her fate depended; and she could not help imagining that something was shortly about to occur on which her future happiness or perpetual misery rested.

She had listened for some time, but had not heard any person but old Cicely stirring in the house, and she was at last tempted to believe that Gordon had gone out, the old woman having informed her that Adder had quitted the house at an early hour in the morning.

She felt her mind somewhat relieved at this reflection, for while the villain from whom she had so much to dread was in the house, she was kept in a continual state of excitement, which, notwithstanding her efforts, she found it impossible to conquer. And she feared his return, as of some evil genii that haunted her path.

Again she looked across the wild moor, as far as the moon's pale beams would permit her, but she saw no object to attract her attention. Her mind became more and more depressed, and she could not divest it of an impression that the crisis of her fate was at hand. Nor, although this at any other time would have afforded her more satisfaction than otherwise, as any fate would be preferable to the state of anxiety and tormenting suspense in which she was kept, now that it seemed to be approaching, she could not contemplate it without a feeling of the most unbounded horror, and she trembled violently in every limb. She thought upon her husband, father, child, and the idea of being about to quit the world without again seeing them racked her breast to distraction, and caused her tears to flow most copiously.

At length she somewhat aroused herself, as the absurdity of the supposition became apparent to her. Alas! she feared that a fate far more terrible than dead awaited her; it was not probable that Adder, after the risk and trouble he had been at, and the most consummate acts he had made use of to get possession of her, would long suffer his disgusting passion to go ungratified; and then, indeed, would she be a poor, lost, fallen, degraded being. But could she survive such infamy, such brutality? Oh, no, the bare thought was madness! Her heart must sink beneath it; human nature could not possibly endure such an accumulation of horrors.

Ever and anon she could hear the shriek of the wild sea-mew, which served but to add to the terrors under which her mind laboured; and all being now quite still in the house, she had no doubt that old Cicely had fallen asleep. She looked at the door of her apartment, and then at the iron-barred casement, and their evident security increased her despair. Then she remembered her former adventure, when she was frustrated in her attempt to make an escape, and the agony, suspense, and disappointment she underwent on that night, came fresh upon her memory, and increased her emotion. The failure of that attempt, at the very moment when it seemed most likely to be accomplished, quite disheartened her from making any future attempt; and then the fearful looks and threats of that man of blood, Gordon, struck a deadly chill to her heart as she thought upon them. And yet, why should she fear death? What prospect had she before her but the most brutal shame and misery? and surely any death, however cruel it might be, would be preferable to that!

She was interrupted in these reflections by hearing a loud knock at the outer door, and soon afterwards Cicely opened it, and our heroine heard the voice of Gordon, so that she was convinced that her first surmises were correct; namely, that he had been out, and that she and Cicely had been left in the house by themselves.

Gorden, as usual, was evidently inebriated, and Rosabelle could hear him staggering about, and occasionally saluting her with some coarse and vulgar epithet, in the utterance and choice of which, like all fellows of his stamp, he was a perfect adept.

Delicate and sensitive as were the nerves of Lady Ravensford, she had become almost familiarized with this brutal and disgusting language, and what would at any other time have excited her utmost disgust and horror, now fell, as it were, listlessly upon her ear.

A short time afterwards, Rosabelle heard the old woman retire to her chamber, muttering and grumbling all the way she proceeded, and as she passed by the door of Rosabelle's appartment, for she slept in the room immediately above her.

Gorden was thus left to himself, and seemed in no inclination to go to sleep, for, at intervals, Rosabelle could hear him dancing, and accompanying himself with a shrill whistle; then he would pause for a short time, and afterwards commence singing in a most stentorian voice.

Rosabelle felt tired, weary, but still never once thought of retiring to rest. No! while Gordon was up and in such a state, the most terrible apprehensions constantly came over her, and the torments of perdition could not more dreadfully have agonized her mind.

She still remained in the same position as at first at the casement, and looked with a vacant gaze across the wild moor. Suddenly she beheld some indistinct object moving in the distance, and which, in a few minutes, she recognised as a human form, which seemed to be performing sundry various pantomimic actions, which Lady Ravensford was at a loss to understand.

It was the miscreant Adder, who, after having quitted Monckton and his associates, was so inebriated that he would not enter the house from any of the secret passages leading from the "Caboose," but would leave the house altogether. The consequence was, that he missed his way, and had been wandering about the moor for a considerable time. How he at last got into the right direction for the house, we are at a loss to form any conjecture of; but so he had, and he had not proceeded many more yards, when our heroine recognised him. He was describing several circles, and semi-circles, as he proceeded, and it it was very evident that he had had considerably more than what the drunkard would technically call "a skinful," and occasionally he was bawling with all his strength of lung, the song we have before quoted, namely :—

"Woman, since I first have known thee,
    It has been my pride to own thee
    Empress of my hopes and cares,
    Of all my pleasures, all my fears!
    In thy smile I've lived delighted,
    By thy smile I've been requited;
    My thoughts and dreams of ecstasy,
    Woman! have ever been of thee!

"Woman, thou'rt my destiny,
    I thy slave must ever be;
    Bound by drains of bliss and love,
    Who my taste can e'er reprove?
    Brilliant eyes! bewitching grace,
    Sparkling wit; enchanting face,
    Bliss, the greatest that can be,
    Woman! is centred all in thee!"

To these stanzas, after a pause, the libertine added the following :—

"Woman, in the hour of woe
    Thou'rt man's comfort here below;
    And the solace by thee giv'n,
    Falls just like the balm of Heav'n!
    Woman, thou'rt the star of life,
    Whether as widow, maid, or wife!—
    And though whate'er my lot may be,
    Woman must be my Deity!"

"What a pollution of the name of woman, from lips such as his," exclaimed Rosabelle, when Adder had concluded; "base, unmanly hypocrite, what regard can you have for that weak and defenceless sex, whom you affect to praise? Must you not delight in their misery? You must; or never could you have adopted the villanous, and systematic course you did to get me in your power, and also to prejudice the mind of my unfortunate husband against me; and now to hold me in your power! Oh, God! I wonder that a wretch like you are, are not afraid of the avenging wrath of the Almighty overtaking you."

Adder continued to sing the song as he came towards the house, embellished with innumerable hiccups, and at length reaching the house, gave several loud knocks at the door, which, Gordon having fallen off to sleep, were at first unheeded; but at length Gordon was aroused, and Rosabelle heard him stagger to the door and admit him.

Gordon greeted Adder most unceremoniously, but they shortly appeared to have settled down into a friendly, though drunken, chit-chat, and they appeared to be upon very good terms together. This was a moment of considerable dread and suspense to our heroine, and she trembled every time they moved, lest Adder should be induced to obtrude himself upon her; but at length she became somewhat more calm, especially after she had offered up her prayers to the Most High.

At last Rosabelle heard the two villains bid each other good-night, and make a movement as if they were about to separate. She was quickly convinced that her surmises were correct, and that they had both retired to their chambers; for the house was quickly involved in all the stillness of the tomb. Some time longer Rosabelle continued to sit up, until at length, wearied completely out, she hastened to her couch, and sleep happily descended upon her eye-lids.

Visions of the most terrific nature haunted her imagination, and rendered sleep anything but refreshing to her. At one moment she fancied herself struggling in the loathsome embraces of the detested and unprincipled miscreant, Adder, who pressed licentious kisses upon her lips, and polluted her with his hateful caresses. Again the scene changed, and she beheld the corpse of her husband stretched upon a bed; his countenance black and distorted, as if he had died a violent death; while Adder was standing over him, with looks of fiendish triumph and exultation stamped upon his countenance. With horror she awoke, but quickly to fall asleep again, and once more her busy and disordered fancy was at work to torment her.

She now fancied herself in the same apartment in which she was confined at the house of Gordon; when suddenly her attention was drawn to a noise outside the door, and immediately after the door was thrown back on its hinges, and Adder entered, leading the child Alfred by the hand. Frantically the fond mother imagined that she rushed forth to embrace her offspring, when Adder raised his hand and arrested her purpose.

"No," she imagined he said, in a determined tone of voice, and with his usual stern expression of countenance; "never again shall you embrace this brat until you have yielded a willing compliance with my desires! Will you consent?"

"Never!" in her frenzy, Lady Ravensford fancied she replied; and as she gave utterance to the words, the eyes of the villain Adder became bloodshot with the most diabolical and ungovernable rage; his whole frame was convulsed with emotion, and his countenance so changed with the power of his guilty passions, that it was quite hideous to look upon. Rosabelle imagined that she trembled violently, but had not the power to speak, her faculties seemed charmed and bound up in horror, and she was unable to move a step towards rescuing her child from the wretch's grasp, although, at the same time, she felt all the innate fury of the aroused tigress, and a mother's feelings seemed to rise so powerfully within her breast, that she felt herself capable of perpetrating any desperate deed to rescue her offspring from the dreaded power which held it. Adder, she imagined in her frightful dream, stood contemplating, with looks of the most savage determination, herself and the little Alfred alternately, who, on beholding his mother, whom he appeared to recognise immediately, stretched forth his little hands, and cried to go to her. Adder, however, was callous to the cries innocence; his whole soul was wrapped up in the gratification of his libidinous wishes, and them he appeared determined to satiate at all hazards.

"My child! my child!" Rosabelle imagined she shrieked frantically, and stretching forth her arms to receive him. But Adder drew him back, and with an expression of demoniacal eagerness, exclaimed—

"Will you yield to my desires?"

"Never!" answered our heroine.

"Then you have sealed his doom," she fancied in her dream she heard the villain ejaculate; and raising the little innocent in his arms, while his whole countenance glowed with the most barbarous resolution, he drew forth a long knife, and prepared to plunge it in the child's breast. Rosabelle was transfixed with horror, and had not the power to move or to offer to save her offspring. She saw the upraised hand which held the fatal knife, and gradually descended. It was within an inch of his breast, when human nature could endure no more—she screamed and awoke!

It was several minutes after she had awoke ere Rosabelle could sufficiently collect her senses, to come to any satisfactory conclusion whether it was imagination or reality. She rubbed her eyes, and looked fearfully and vacantly around her, almost expecting to see the dark horrors of her vision realized. The place was buried in profound darkness, for the light had long died away before our heroine retired to rest, and everything around wore an aspect of the most impressive gloom. Rosabelle could not hear the least sound stirring in the house, and she was, therefore, at last convinced that she had only been dreaming. But oh, what horrible dreams! They harrowed up her soul when she recalled them to her memory; and then they accorded so well with the dismal forebodings and terrors that had for the last few days distracted her mind.

She started from her couch, for she could not think of lying longer, fearing sleep might again close her eye-lids, and that her imagination would again be haunted by similar terrific dreams to those which had before alarmed it. Shivering with a sensation of cold, she hastily dressed herself, and then approached the room door and tried it; but it was quite secure. She threw herself into a seat, and covering her face with her hands, she gave herself up for some time to all the terrors of the most agonizing description, which her situation, and the dreams that had so alarmed her, had naturally engendered in her bosom. Suddenly she started up, as a racking thought darted across her brain.

"Ah!" she cried, "my infant is in his power! He has gained possession of my poor child, and will make him the means of furthering his atrocious designs against me! A dreadful foreboding tells me that it is so, and thus is one part of my terrible vision explained. It was to accomplish this infamous deed that the wretch Gordon was despatched from hence lately. My God!—my God!—where will the villanies of the miscreant Adder cease!"

Her tears flowed copiously as she gave expression to these lamentations, and she wrung her hands in all the poignancy of despair. The impression had stamped itself upon her mind, and she found that it would be utterly impossible for her to efface it.

She once more took her place at the casement at which she had been seated for so many hours the night before. The moon, however, had now disappeared, and beyond and around her, all was now buried in profound darkness, which the gloominess of her own thoughts rendered doubly dismal. But Rosabelle had become used to gloom, and it had but little effect upon her. Still did she sit ruminating upon the dreams that had haunted her imagination, and heeded not anything around.

It was very cold and cheerless, but Rosabelle felt it not, and she sat in a complete state of apathy, until at last the gray mists of night disappeared, and, gradually, a faint streak of light, the first appearance of day, traced its outline on the eastern horizon. Gradually it expanded, until the eastern sky was clad in one mantle of ensanguine hue, and then the bright orb of day mounted his golden chariot in the Heavens. It was a lovely morn, presenting a great contrast to the preceding night. The mild morn, illumined by the radiant beams of the sun, had quite a cheerful aspect.

Rosabelle continued to sit at the casement, but her eyes fell listlessly upon all around her, and her whole thoughts were entirely concentrated in the dismal thoughts which the frightful visions her imagination had conjured up had naturally engendered in her bosom. She was at last interrupted from this reverie by hearing a footstep ascending the stairs, and, fearing that it might be Adder, she endeavoured to collect her thoughts and her firmness, and to be prepared to meet her oppressor with a demeanour which might render his triumph less secure.

She was, however, agreeably disappointed, for on the door being opened, old Cicely entered, singing that exquisite production giving an account of the last dying moments of that celebrated knight of the post, Jack Rawn, and with which she had favoured the unfortunate Lady Ravensford on a former occasion.

Rosabelle, as usual, took no notice of her, for she always expected the sort of salute she would receive from her, and, on this occasion, she was not doomed to be disappointed.

"Hoity, toity," said the disagreeable old beldame, fixing a sardonic look upon our heroine; "moping, mumping, and sullen as usual! Ah! well, it is all the fruits of a crabbed sour temper."

Rosabelle only sighed.

"Heigho!" said the old woman, mockingly, "the sentimental fools of females are all sighs now-a-days, like a pair of blacksmith's bellows! All sham and affectation: no substantial feeling about 'em. Now, for my part, I never let anything trouble me, for what's the use of it?"

"Old woman!" exclaimed Rosabelle, unable longer to contain herself.

"Old woman!" repeated the disgusting creature, tossing her head, and looking spitefully at our heroine; "old woman, too," she repeated; "come, I like that."

"'Tis well," said Rosabelle, with a look of the most bitter sarcasm, and in a tone which could not fail to have its due effect upon the wretch to whom it was addressed; "'tis well that you are ashamed of old age, for age is disgraced by you."

"I should advise you to be a little more cautious in the language you use towards me," said Cicely, in a harsh, querulous tone; "I would advise you to be a little more circumspect, young lady; I have the means of rendering your situation wretched, insupportable, and those who once offend Cicely, are sure to have to encounter her vengeance in some shape or the other."

"I have no doubt of it," answered our heroine, firmly; "for I have experienced it ever since I have been here; but I defy your malice, and treat your observations with becoming contempt."

"You may not always do so!"

"I trust that Providence will always give me the power to do so."

"You talk a good deal about Providence, young lady."

"It is in Him that I put my trust. He never yet deserted the innocent and oppressed; neither will he fail to bring the guilty to punishment."

"Humph!"

"You may affect to despise it; but you cannot in your heart."

"Bah!"

"The reply of every fool!"

The old woman coloured up with rage.

"Beware!" she said.

"I have before told you that I scorn your threats."

"You had better not."

"My determination is fixed."

"You know not my power."

"Neither do I care for it. Providence—"

"Providence, again!" interrupted the hateful old woman, with a sarcastic grin;—"why does not this same Providence of whom you talk so much about, and who, you would make it appear, is such a particular friend of yours, rescue you from your present situation?"

"In His own wise time I have no doubt He will," ejaculated Rosabelle, confidentially.

"Ha! ha! ha!" laughed the old woman. "He must break through a good many locks, bolts, and bars, and hoodwink Gordon, Mr. Adder, and myself, before he does that, and I think this same Providence will be puzzled to do that."

Rosabelle looked at the old woman with an expression of countenance which we need not attempt to describe.

"Shock not my ears with your horrible blasphemy, old woman," she observed; "I must not, I will not listen to it."

"But indeed you shall listen to just as much as I think proper to favour you with," said the unnatural and disgusting old Cicely; "it so happens, you see, that what you do not like to hear, I feel a pleasure in treating you with."

"Unnatural woman!"

"Oh, I don't mind your compliments; I am by no means partial to flattery."

"Almighty God!" cried Rosabelle, in a tone of the utmost horror and disgust; "can this be a woman, and so callous to every feeling which ought to characterise the sex?"

"Yourself an amiable sample of the qualities I presume!" returned Cicely, with a bitter sneer.

"Will you leave me to myself?"

"When it suits me!"

"I feel horror-struck and disgusted in your presence."

"Which is one of the principal things that induces me to remain."

"I will not listen to you."

"Then you must become very deaf, indeed, for I will speak loud enough to make you hear."

Rosabelle raised her hands and eyes towards Heaven, in agony, and Cicely appeared to exult in the feeling she experienced, and to prolong the interview to the utmost. A pause ensued, for the strength of our heroine's feelings was almost overpowered, and in the interim the old woman seemed to be enjoying her anguish greatly. Although she pretended not to care anything about the epithets and observations which the unfortunate Lady Ravensford applied to her, she was, in reality, greatly chagrined at them, and secretly determined, even though she should have to hazard everything by the attempt, to have her ample share of revenge for the same, and to tantalize her at every opportunity.

Lady Ravensford could not help feeling a mingled sensation of sorrow and pity, at the unhappy and guilty disposition of old Cicely, and when she recalled to her memory the different observations she had made use of, she shuddered with horror.

"But think not," remarked our heroine, with a look of the most ineffable disgust, indignation, and pity; "think not that I will tamely submit to your insolence."

"And how are you to help yourself?" demanded Cicely, with a spiteful grin.

"At any rate, the fellow who holds me here in his power," returned Rosabelle, "wretch as he is, will not permit a creature merely in his pay to assume the tyrant over me."

"Creature, indeed!" exclaimed the old woman, malignantly; "as I before told you, you had better be a little more choice in your language towards me; not that I care a straw about the names you are pleased to call me; for such slang does not effect me the least in the world; but it might induce me to add a little to the method by which it is evident I know so well how to teaze you. As for the fellow, as you call him, who holds you in his power, I care no more for him than I do for you; he is more in my power than I am in his, and he knows much better than to offend me."

"Why should your malice be directed towards me?"

"Because it is my whim."

"I never offended you."

"I know it."

"Why, then, should you take a pleasure in endeavouring to increase my misery?"

"Because I detest, despise the whole of my sex."

"Surely you cannot be a woman?"

"Curses on the power that made me one."

"Oh, what should make you feel such an unnatural hatred towards your own sex?"

" I know not, nor care not. But so it is, and none more greatly shares my hatred than yourself."

"Strange, unaccountable malignity," said our heroine ; "and yet would I willingly act with kindness and forbearance towards you, notwithstanding the painfulness of my situation."

" No doubt you would," maliciously said the old woman; "but you see I do not think proper to accept of any reconciliation on your part. The 'creature,' and the 'unnatual old woman,' will follow her own designs, and which, she has no doubt, will prove very gratifying to you."

" Unfortunate woman," said our heroine, " I pity you for your ignorance, and——"

" Ignorance !" repeated old Cicely, in a harsh croaking tone; "ignorance indeed. Well, I can't say you have exhibited any superior sense since you have been here—or you would prefer living a life of liberty and luxury with a man worthy of you, to that of remaining a prisoner, caged up in this dismal old house, and where you seem to think your companions so very *agreeable* to you !"

Rosabelle once more raised her hands and eyes towards Heaven, completely disgusted with the wicked old woman's observations. She would have been very glad if she would have quitted the room, and left her to herself, but she knew it was no use endeavouring by persuasion to prevail upon the old harridan to do so, and she, therefore, remained silent.

" I suppose you want some breakfast ?" said Cicely, at last ;—" I don't suppose you are so terribly afflicted that you cannot eat, as well as other people."

Lady Ravensford shook her head mournfully.

" I do not care for anything this morning," she answered, for she dreaded the protracted presence of old Cicely, whose observations, and general disgusting behaviour, had already quite unnerved her.

" Oh, that's all nonsense," replied the old woman, who appeared to read her thoughts; " mere affectation ! I shall bring it whether or no."

It was perfectly useless for our heroine attempting to offer any further opposition, as the old woman had made up her mind, and seeing that it was against the former's inclinations, was the more likely to persevere in doing so, for the purpose of tormenting her. Cicely, therefore, having indulged in another malicious grin, left the room for the purpose of putting her intentions into execution, and Rosabelle had a temporary respite from the misery of her society.

When she had quitted the apartment, our heroine threw herself on her knees, and, with streaming eyes, again implored the interposition of the Almighty to save her from the dreadful fate with which she was threatened, and to rescue her from the wretched, the deplorable, and agonising situation in which she was at present placed.

She arose from her knees rather more composed, and walked towards the casement. She had not long stood there, when she heard a slight bustle in the house, which she at first attributed to old Cicely returning with the breakfast things; but she was shortly convinced to the contrary, for the outer-door was opened, and Adder issued forth, our heroine observing him as he emerged from underneath the portal. He looked up at the casement of the room in which she was confined, and observing her, waved his hand. Her cheeks glowing with disgust and indignation, however, she hastily withdrew from the casement, and shortly afterwards old Cicely made her appearance, bringing in the breakfast things.

" There, now we shall see whether you will eat," said Cicely ; " though, perhaps, you will do so with a better appetite when you learn that your oppressor, as you call him, has gone out."

" Thank Heaven !" exclaimed Lady Ravensford, clasping her hands.

"Indeed," returned Cicely ; "perhaps you have not so much occasion to thank Heaven ; Mr. Adder will see you in the course of the day, I know."

Rosabelle's heart sank.

" Oh, Cicely," she eagerly cried, as an unaccountable idea darted across her brain, " whither has he gone, and for what purpose: tell me, I entreat."

" Not I, indeed," said the old woman, in her usual disagreeable accents ; " it is not my place to tell the secrets of those that employ me. You, will find out, I dare say, quite soon enough ; and it strikes me that the interview you will have with Mr. Adder by and by, will be of a very different description to any that you have hitherto had."

" What mean you ?" interrogated our heroine, shuddering, as the frightful visions that had haunted her imagination on the previous night returned to her memory.

" What mean I ?" answered the old woman; " oh, that you must find out; I shall not explain any further. I can only tell you this much, young lady, that it is quite useless for you to show any of your fine obstinate airs; for Mr. Adder has all the power on his own side, and he is a fool if he does not exercise it ; that's all I have got to say in the matter."

" Good God !" cried Rosabelle, unable to restrain her emotion, " what will become of me ? What fresh calamity is in store for me?"

" Calamity, you call it, do you," said Cicely, " to have the offer of a very nice young man, who will behave to you as well as if you were his wife ? Pshaw ! some persons do not know when they have a good chance put in their way. However, like it or like it not, it strikes me very forcibly that you will be compelled to make it agreeable to yourself; for Mr. Adder is not the man to be trifled with, and, for my part, if I had been in his place, I would not have waited so long and so patiently when I had the game in my power."

Rosabelle could only fix upon the detestable old woman a look of the most ineffable contempt, disgust, and indignation; but the latter observed it, and grinning most maliciously, she said—

"Oh, I care not a pin's point for your looks; I know very well what you mean. Your opinion and mine do not coincide, but, nevertheless, it is one which I shall always maintain. Mr. Adder will, I dare say, be able to bring you to your senses before long, or else I am most egregiously mistaken."

"Adder is a wretch, unworthy the name of man," exclaimed our heroine, firmly, "and I will not degrade myself by appealing to his mercy. No, I will rely upon the protection of Providence—"

"Providence once more!" interrupted Cicely, with a bitter grin; "you are remarkably fond of appealing to that power, and seem

MRS KITSON REBUKES ADDER FOR HIS EVIL PASSIONS.

to rely greatly on its assistance, yet it seems very tardy in rendering you any."

"Let me hear no more of your blasphemy," said Rosabelle, "it shocks mine ears."

"Dear me, then it is a pity your sense of hearing is so delicate," returned the old woman, in a satirical tone; "perhaps in the course of a few hours you may not be quite so sensitive."

"Neither time nor circumstance can alter my sentiments and determination," replied Lady Ravensford, mustering up all the firmness she could assume.

"Many bolder spirits than yours have said the same thing," remarked Cicely, "and yet,

when the moment of trial has come, they have been glad enough to yield; that will be the case with you."

"Wicked old woman, whose greatest pleasure is in the sorrows and afflictions of your fellow-creatures, especially those of your own sex, I will no longer talk to you."

"That is a matter of very little consequence to me," retorted the aggravating old beldame; 'as I have only to amuse myself by talking the more to you."

Rosabelle averted her head, but could not repress a deep sigh, and all this added to the unnatural exultation of Cicely.

"Oh, there will be a most remakable change,

I have no doubt, when Mr. Adder returns," she remarked, after a pause ; " there will be a most remarkable change."

' And why should there be so ?" our heroine eagerly interrogated, forgetting, in the curiosity which the dark hints of Cicely had excited in her bosom, the assertion she had only a few minutes before made, to remain silent with the old woman.

"Ha! ha! ha!" laughed Cicely, sardonically, " how soon the firm lady can break her vows! How soon her affectation is made apparent. I thought you were not a going to degrade yourself by talking to me again? Ha! ha! ha! Beat old Cicely, and you have only another to conquer."

Rosabelle once more wrung her hands in an agony of grief, and mentally prayed that Cicely would leave the room ; but the latter gave no symptoms of doing so ; but, on the contrary, found something to do in the room, and because she saw that it evidently annoyed and disgusted our heroine, she once more sung that blackguard song which has already appeared in the pages of this narrative.

How long she would have remained there was uncertain ; but probably it would have been until the return of the villain Adder, the misery and anguish of Lady Ravensford being amusement to her ; but suddenly the voice of Gordon was heard calling her from below, and he seemed to be impatient at the length of her absence ; and Cicely growling several curses against him, and fixing a look of the utmost hatred upon the unfortunate prisoner, prepared, although very reluctantly, to obey his summons.

She retired from the apartment, and our heroine, overcome by the taunts and insults she had received from her, and that, in the first instance, without any provocation on her part, burst into a paroxysm of sobs and tears, in which she indulged for several minutes.

Her mind was distracted by a variety of the most perplexing thoughts, and the dark hints that the old woman had given utterance to relating to Adder, created in her bosom a number of the most tormenting doubts and apprehensions, which it was in vain for her, under the present painful circumstances, to banish from her mind. She could not help thinking that that day would be productive of something extraordinary and astonishing to her, and she awaited, in the utmost state of suspense and dread, the return of the wretch who held her in his power. Then the frightful visions which we have described in some of our former pages, recurred to her memory, in all their horror, and she could not divest herself of the thought that they would be found to have some connection with the calamitous events, which she apprehended were impending over her. She scarcely dared to think, and yet what could drive thought from her mind ? When the hu-

man heart is troubled with any sorrow, the slightest trouble falls upon it with double the weight that it would do at any other time, and in vain may the poor sufferer struggle to release itself from its destructive influence. So was it with our heroine ; care-worn as she was from a long series of almost unprecedented sorrows and oppressions ; spirit-broken and despairing from long confinement, and the fearful prospects which were before her ; the most trivial circumstance, notwithstanding the struggle to appear firm, had a most powerful effect upon her, and she almost sank beneath, what at any other time she would, in all probability, look upon as trifling.

She felt, however, greatly relieved when Cicely had quitted the room, for nothing could equal the detestation, almost amounting to terror, with which she viewed that wretched sample of humanity ; and such was the opinion she formed of the fiendish disposition of that diabolical old woman, that she had not the least doubt, if she had not feared Adder and Gordon, she would not have hesitated to have inflicted some personal violence against her. Had it not been for her own personal observation, she could not have believed that such a monster, especially in the female form, could exist.

Weary of thinking, and hoping that she should not be again troubled with the presence of Cicely for the present, Lady Ravensford threw herself upon the couch, and covering her face with her hands, endeavoured to banish thought. This was no easy task, and her head ached, and her eyes burned with the violence of her emotions. As for the morning repast which the old woman had brought up, it remained on the table untouched ; Rosabelle had no appetite, and the very sight of the breakfast made her feel sick. At length, completely exhausted, although the sun was shining brightly in at the casement of her chamber, Lady Ravensford fell into a more tranquil sleep than might have been anticipated, and in which she remained for several hours, Cicely not troubling her again, as she was obliged to leave the house upon some particular business.

We will now return to the villain Adder, who having slept off the effects of the deep potations he had partaken of at the previous night's debauch, arose at an early hour, and departed from the house to make his way to Mrs. Kitson. We have before stated, that in emerging from the portal of the building, he raised his eyes towards the casement of the apartment in which his victim was confined, and there beheld her standing, and waved his hand towards her. His keen and penetrating eye discovered in a moment the look of abhorrence which she fixed upon him, and the air of disdain with which she turned away from the casement ; and, as he walked on, he soliloquised :—

"Proud, scornful beauty! thou mayest affect to despise me; thou mayest look upon me with hatred and scorn, and think to shame me from my purpose; but, by all the infernal host, thou shalt not; a few hours only shall make thee alter thy tone and haughty demeanour, or the feelings of a mother are banished from thy bosom; and all the affection thou hast pretended for thy child has been but a mockery! Yes, a few hours only, and Rosabelle, perhaps thy severest hour of trial will have come."

The wretch felt a sensation of the most powerful and unnatural exultation as he spoke, and his eyes gleamed brightly. He hurried on his way, heedless of the beauty of the morning, for his mind was too much occupied with his own nefarious projects to notice anything else, and it was not long ere he arrived at the cottage of Bet Kitson, as she was familiarly called by the smugglers.

The woman was surprised to see him there so early, although she had been up, as she was accustomed to be, for several hours; she, however, guessed that he had some particular reason for his visit, and she feared that it was something relating to the child, to whom she had now become so much attached, that she could not bear the idea of parting with it.

The child reposed in a clean little cot, and Mrs. Kitson, on the entrance of Adder, was watching as tenderly by it as if it had been her own offspring. Adder walked unceremoniously up to the cot, and fixed his eyes upon the young Alfred, without speaking a word to his nurse. Its extreme beauty could not but interest him, and he could not have harmed that little innocent, guilty and heartless as he was, even had he have known that his reward for so doing would have been a princely diadem. Mrs. Kitson did not offer to interrupt him, for she could scarcely guess from the expression of his countenance the feelings that were passing in his bosom, and the thoughts he at that moment was indulging in; but at length, appearing to recollect himself, he turned away from the child, and addressing the smuggler's wife, said,—

"Good morning, Mother Kitson."

"Good morning, Mr. Adder," she responded.

"I dare say you did not expect to see me here so early?"

"I did not."

"It is not at all unlikely that I shall release you from your charge to-day."

"Ah!—I am sorry to hear that!"

"Why so?"

"Simply because I am become as fond of the youngster as if it were my own child, and I would willingly bring him up as such."

"I think you would soon be tired of your bargain," observed Adder.

"Indeed I should not," answered Mrs. Kitson; "it is a sweet child, so innocent—so beautiful."

"Pshaw!—what a parcel of nonsense women always say of every brat," returned Adder; "but I suspect that the deep interest you appear to take in this child is excited by other motives than any particular attachment which you have towards this boy."

"What mean you?"

"Why," replied Adder, "probably you would like to keep him in your possession until you could find an opportunity of restoring him to his father, in the hope of getting handsomely rewarded."

Mrs. Kitson frowned indignantly, as Adder thus expressed his suspicions.

"If that is the opinion you entertain of me," she ejaculated, "why did you ever trust me?"

"Well, well, perhaps I have wronged you."

"That indeed you have," answered the woman; "such insinuations as these were never before uttered against Bet Kitson, and had my husband been present and heard them, he might not have taken them in very good part."

"Ah! I see," returned Adder; "I was too hasty, and apologise."

"It is not the first time you have been so hasty, Mr. Adder."

"True; but I promise you that it shall not occur again. I am so fearful that the possession of the child should be found out, that it makes me more suspicious, and causes me to use harsher terms than I otherwise would."

"I wish I had not had anything to do with the affair," observed Mrs. Kitson.

"And why do you repent?"

"Because I shall feel as much the loss of the boy as if he were my own," answered Mrs. Kitson.

"But I am going to introduce him to his mother," said Adder.

"Ah!" eagerly exclaimed Mrs. Kitson, "restore him to his mother! Then, indeed, I do not regret his loss! Poor thing, how——"

"Nay," interrupted Adder, "you misunderstand me! I said not that I should restore him to his mother."

"Oh, it would be the height of brutality to keep the poor little innocent from her fostering arms," returned Mrs. Kitson; and the many good feelings that really inhabited the poor woman's bosom, rose to her heart in a moment, and she looked appealingly in the countenance of Adder.

"It will depend entirely upon her own conduct," answered the latter.

"How so?"

"If she freely consents to my wishes, the child shall be restored to her; if not, it shall still be kept away from her."

"Oh, that would be too cruel, too unnatural," ejaculated Mrs. Kitson.

"At any rate," replied Adder, "if your assertions, as far as regards your attachment for the child, be sincere, you would have no cause to regret such a result."

"For what reason?"

"Why, the brat would still remain in your charge."

"And I should feel myself a party to the anguish of the unhappy parent, and be rendered truly miserable," remarked Mrs. Kitson.

"You are too tender-hearted, by far," said Adder.

"I may be, in your opinion, sir," replied Mrs. Kitson; "but such is my feeling, and I don't think I shall easily banish it from my breast."

"The brat's mother must be an absolute fool, if she remains obstinate," said the villain.

Mrs. Kitson shook her head disapprovingly.

"She must be callous to all the upright feelings of her sex or affection for her husband, if she would not suffer death rather than yield a compliance with your wishes," said Mrs. Kitson.

"Ah!" exclaimed Adder, with astonishment, "such nice feelings in a smuggler's wife?"

"They are feelings that I believe I have no occasion to be ashamed of," replied Mrs. Kitson.

"Humph!" ejaculated Adder; "you seem to be quite an adept at preaching a sermon."

"Sermon or not," returned the woman, "I can sympathize in the misery the poor lady must endure."

"It is a pity," said Adder, "since your feelings are so very sensitive on this point, that you ever became acquainted with scenes of vice."

"Would to Heaven I had not!" replied Mrs. Kitson, fervently; "I should now have been far happier than I am."

"You are rather too old in sin to repent now; so what's the use of regretting that which cannot be recalled?" said Adder.

"Alas!" cied Mrs. Kitson, "I fear it is too late to repent, or——"

"I suppose," added the villain, in a harsh tone of voice, and fixing a piercing look upon the countenance of the woman; "or I suppose you would become so penitent that you would confess all of which you have been guilty; this secret of the abduction of the child amongst the rest?"

Mrs. Kitson fixed upon him an expressive look, but she made him no answer. Adder, however, understood her, and he thought it prudent to alter his tone.

"Again, I must ask you to excuse me, Mother Kitson," he observed; "but I am so fearful of this brat being discovered, as I have before stated, that it renders me suspicious where I am afterwards convinced I have no occasion. But enough of this. And so you think that the lady will not yield to my desires?"

"If what I have heard of her character be true, and she really possesses those virtues which I believe her to do, most certainly she will consider any fate preferable to such a one as that," answered Mrs. Kitson.

"What, not to get her offspring in her power?" demanded Adder.

"No," replied Mrs. Kitson, "the feelings of the parent, the wife, all would be sacrificed by such a degradation, and she would suffer death first."

"Degradation!" muttered Adder, and he bit his lips; "degradation!"

"Ay, sir, degradation!" reiterated Mrs. Kitson; "what other term can you apply to it?"

"You might have found one less harsh when speaking of it to me," said Adder, in reply.

"Why, sir," returned Mrs. Kitson, "the fact of the matter is, that I am a very unpolished, plain-spoken woman, and apt to speak plainly what I mean, without endeavouring to embellish it."

"Well," observed Adder, after a pause, "I like you none the worse for that; for I can understand you all the better."

"True, you may, if you like, for I seek no disguise," added the woman; "and yet you have several times thrown out the most unjust suspicions of me."

"I have," admitted Adder, "but I have apologised sufficiently for them, I think; I was too hasty."

"But there are many that would not have been so ready to accept of an apology as I have been," returned Mrs. Kitson.

"And what think you they would have done?" asked Adder.

"That of which you had suspected them," replied Mrs. Kitson; "they would have sought the earliest opportunity of betraying you.'

"But they would have found that no easy task," returned Adder; "my suspicions being aroused, I should have watched them with too vigilant an eye."

"Probably you might, and yet have been deceived," observed Mrs. Kitson: "but about this child?"

"What of him?"

"You will not take him away by yourself?" interrogated Mrs. Kitson.

"Certainly not," answered Adder;—"you must accompany me to the house. You still have charge of him, and should the mother remain obstinate, he will continue to remain with you."

Mrs. Kitson's countenance brightened for a moment, and then became sad again.

"You will think better of this, Mr. Adder," she said; "you cannot be so cruel, so unnatural as to keep the child from its parent?"

"'Psha! stuff!" hastily exclaimed the villain, "I want to hear no more of this. I have told you my determination, which, when once made up, is not easily to be shaken. But we are wasting time here; your husband is from home?"

"You know he is with his associates," answered Mrs. Kitson.

"Are you ready to accompany me?"

"I am."

"The child still sleeps."

"Lovely innocent! unconscious of the misery of his unhappy parent! How beautiful he looks!—Oh, who could have the heart to harm that little one?"

"Well—well!"

"And see, now he smiles!—Oh, nothing could be more interesting than that sweet boy!"

"Bah!"

"Ah! well, I cannot help expressing my sentiments, although they may appear weak and ridiculous to you."

"They are useless."

"They may be so."

"They are out of place at present. Come, I grow impatient of the delay; will you get ready to attend me?"

"I will."

"Be quick, then; we have already tarried too long."

"You will have time enough to accomplish all you wish; the poor lady cannot run away," answered Mrs. Kitson.

"That is true," returned Adder; "yet am I anxious to see what effect my scheme will have upon her. See, the boy wakes."

The little Alfred, who had been wrapt in a cherub slumber, now opened his eyes, and not seeing any one near him, he began to cry, but when he beheld Mrs. Kitson, he ceased, smiled, and stretched forth his little arms to go to her; and when she took him up, he rested his innocent head in her bosom, the same as if she she had been his mother.

"There, there," said Adder, impatiently, "there is quite enough of this nonsense; we shall not get away to day."

The child hearing the harsh voice of the villain, removed its head from the bosom of Mrs. Kitson, and no sooner saw Adder, than he burst out crying violently, and Mrs. Kitson found it a most difficult matter to pacify him. Adder frowned, and traversed the apartment for a few minutes in silence, but it was very evident that the most violent and malignant passions raged within his breast.

"Come," he said at length, turning hastily to Mrs. Kitson, "do not let us any longer delay; dress the brat directly, and let us begone; I am tired of waiting here, and it is only an idle waste of time."

"I cannot help it," returned Adder, "and

I am a fool to have been standing talking here so long, about subjects of no importance to the furtherance of my designs."

"Well, I will not keep you long," said Mrs. Kitson; and she prepared to dress the child.

"I will proceed at once towards the house," said Adder, "you can follow me as speedily as possible with the child."

"Very well."

"But be cautious;—conceal the child from observation, or all might be lost," said Adder.

"Oh, you need not fear me," replied Mrs. Kitson; "I will use every necessary precaution, and be at the house of Gordon Desborough, nearly as soon as you are. The distance from hence is no great deal."

"It is not; and you know the most unfrequented way."

"I do."

"Adieu then, for the present; and I shall expect that it will not be long ere we shall meet again."

"It will not."

"Beware!"

"Oh, you have no occasion to warn me."

"Enough; I will then depart."

"Good morning."

"Good morning, till we meet again."

With these words Adder wrapped his cloak around him, and quitted the cottage, leaving Mrs. Kitson dressing the child; and he hastened on his way back to the house of Gordon Desborough.

On his way thither, he soliloquised—

"I am almost afraid that this Mrs. Kitson is too tender-hearted, and might be —— But no—Monckton would not have deceived me!—I ought not to doubt him. And then there is something in the manners of the woman which bespeaks sincerity. I will not doubt her. Now, Rosabelle, the hour of your trial approaches; and I long to see the effect which my announcement will have upon you."

As he thus spoke, he redoubled his speed, and soon arrived at the house of Gordon.

———

CHAPTER XXVI.

A MOTHER'S TRIALS.

In the meantime Mrs. Kitson proceeded with the dressing of the child, and as she did so, she felt a sensation of melancholy and compunction gradually steal over her, which she had seldom experienced before. The idea of the anguish to which the unfortunate parent would be subjected by the cruel designs of Adder, made her shudder, and again she felt the deepest regret that she had had anything to do with the plot; but still she had nothing to upbraid herself with in the treatment she had bestowed upon the child, and she reflected that, had it fallen into other hands, it might not have been so fortunate. Sincerely did she hope that something would occur to frustrate the wicked and diabolical intentions of Adder, and restore the mother and child to each other, and both to their distracted friends.

Many grave offences had Mrs. Kitson looked upon formerly with a feeling approaching to indifference, but there was something so uncommon in the systematic villany of Adder, that she could not even reflect upon them without a sensation of the utmost disgust and terror.

Adder had quitted the cottage of Mrs. Kitson full half an hour, before she thought of starting, and then she did so very reluctantly; but at length wrapping the child up in a shawl, and concealing him beneath her cloak, she issued from the cottage, and fastened the door after her.

She took the more circuitous and less frequented path which led to the house of Gordon; but although she endeavoured to increase her speed, in order that she might keep her faith with Adder, some inscrutable power appeared to arrest her footsteps, and to retard her progress. To add to her difficulty, ere she had preceeded far, the sky became overcast, the thunder pealed in the distance, and everything betokened a coming storm.

Mrs. Kitson looked around her for some place of shelter, but it was some minutes ere she could perceive any, and at last a hollow in a lofty cliff, which overhung the ocean, offered her the accommodation she wanted.

She hastened towards it, but before she could reach it, the rain began to descend in a perfect deluge, and the thunder rolled in heavy and terrific peals.

She huddled the child closer to her breast to shield him from the tempest, for almost in an instant she herself was nearly wet through, and made her way with rapid strides to the cliff, which she at length reached, and found a secure shelter, in which she seemed likely to be obliged to remain for some time.

The child, which had fallen asleep in her arms, was awakened by the noise of the storm, and the roaring of the thunder, and naturally alarmed, began to cry most piteously, and Mrs. Kitson found it a most difficult matter, indeed, to pacify him.

It certainly turned out to be a most awful morning, and Mrs. Kitson pictured to herself the terror and suspense which the wretch Adder would be labouring under, at the length of their absence from the house, and the perfect ignorance he would be under at the way they had taken. But so far from feeling any regret at the anguish it would cause him, the torture which she was certain he was enduring gave her the greatest satisfaction, and she would

have enjoyed his misery, doubts, and apprehensions, could she have seen him.

For more than an hour Mrs. Kitson and her tender charge remained in this situation, and still the storm did not offer the least signs of abatement; the thunder roared just as loudly as it had done before, and the rain continued to descend in the same overwhelming torrent; the earth sending up volumes of steam from its fury.

Mrs. Kitson had at last succeeded in composing the little Alfred, and he nestled closer in her bosom.

In this manner another dreary half-hour passed away, when the storm somewhat abated, and the thunder ceased; the heavens were not quite so black, but still the rain descended rapidly, and Mrs. Kitson saw it was no use to attempt to issue forth at present. She, however, waited very patiently under the circumstances, and knowing that every moment of delay would be agony to Adder, she felt more satisfied than otherwise.

At last the storm entirely ceased, and Mrs. Kitson having no further excuse for delay, quitted the hollow in the cliff, and took the path which led to the house of Gordon.

When she came within sight of it, she saw Adder and Gordon running about in a state of the utmost trepidation, and the former no sooner beheld her than he rushed towards her with an air of delirious delight.

"The child!—the boy!" he exclaimed, breathlessly. "Speak—quick!"

"He is quite safe," answered Mrs. Kitson.

"Ah! that is all right!" he added, joyfully; "I had thought some accident had happened from the length of your absence."

"Why, you could not expect me to come through all the fury of the storm?" said Mrs. Kitson.

"True; but to me every moment of procrastination appeared an age."

"I dare say it did."

"Well, in, in to the house; I am easy now."

"It is well for you that you can be so."

"There now, let's have no more preaching," uttered Adder, impatiently, and frowning, "we have had enough of that already,"

"Ay, ay, let's have no nonsense, Mother Kitson," observed the ruffian Gordon, in a disagreeable voice; "you know it's all mockery."

"Your opinion was not asked, black whiskers," retorted Mrs. Kitson,—"and I should thank you to keep your observations to yourself: I was talking to your master."

"Master!" repeated the ruffian, with a frown, "I have none, and you had better mind that you do not offend me."

"Oh, I do not care for your black looks, nor your threats," returned Mrs. Kitson, with a look of scorn. "Sam Kitson is as good a man as the villain Gordon Desborough, and would not fail to retaliate for any insult you might offer me."

"Sam Kitson! ha! ha! ha!" laughed Gordon, scornfully.

"Hold!" cried Adder, in a commanding tone, "let's have no squabbling here. Mother Kitson, never mind what he says; it's only wind."

"You may treat my words lightly, Mr. Adder," said Gordon Desborough, with a scowl; "but it is not every one that would, and you may not do so always."

"Come, come, Gordon, are you mad?" demanded Adder; "we have no occasion to quarrel."

"I don't want to quarrel."

"Well then, let the business drop."

"Oh, I'm agreeable, but d—n me if I like to hear a woman prate."

"Then why did you trouble yourself with that woman in the first instance?" asked Mrs. Kitson, fixing upon Gordon a look of the utmost contempt and detestation.

"There, no more talk about the matter," said Adder, impatiently; "let us into the house; I have waited long enough, and cannot brook of any further delay."

"It is no fault of mine," returned Mrs. Kitson, with the utmost coolness and indifference; "you will have plenty of time to put the schemes you have in contemplation into effect; that is, if you triumph so easily as you seem to anticipate."

"Mother Kitson, you are too bold," said Adder.

"I know it not, then."

"Come, into the house."

Gordon Desborough having fixed upon Mrs. Kitson an evil look, led the way into the house, and Adder and Mrs. Kitson, with the child, followed. The boy still slept; but soon after their entrance into the parlour, it awoke, and once more fixing its little eyes upon Adder, burst into a loud cry of terror, and Mrs. Kitson used her utmost endeavours, in vain, for some time, to quiet it.

It would be impossible to describe as it ought to be the state of agony, suspense, and consternation under which the guilty villain, Adder, laboured, during the interval which elasped from the time of his leaving Mrs. Kitson's cottage until her arrival with the child at the house of Gordon Desborough. Although the fury of the storm ought to have been sufficient to account for the delay, such was the strength of his constant apprehensions, that he could not help fearing that some accident had occurred to them, or that Mrs. Kitson had deceived him, and he blamed himself for having ventured to leave the cottage without being accompanied by her and the child.

To Gordon he imparted his fears; but he treated them with indifference, and endeavoured to persuade Adder to rest himself contented until the storm had ceased, when he had no doubt but that he would quickly see the objects of his anxiety. Adder could not, however, be so easily quieted, and he insisted upon going from the house, attended by Gordon, to ascertain whether they could see anything of them coming. But although Gordon knew pretty well every inch of the ground for miles around, he could not hit upon the way which Mrs. Kitson had taken, and they returned to the house, Adder in a greater state of agitation than before.

Still he could not settle in the house, and accompanied by Gordon, he had just returned from searching in another direction, when Mrs. Kitson appeared in sight, as we have described.

"Confound that brat's noise," exclaimed Adder, pacing the room with much trepidation;—"it will reach the ears of the mother, and spoil the scheme I have in contemplation. Stifle it! stifle it by some means or the other."

"How am I to do so?" asked Mrs. Kitson.

"Curse the child, it no sooner beholds me, than it commences its d—d croaking," added the villain; "and yet I know not that I am so confounded ugly. At least the fair sex have not always said so, or thought so, if I may judge by the conquests I have made."

"You do well to have a good opinion of yourself," said Gordon, with a grin. Mrs. Kitson fixed upon Adder a look of the utmost contempt, and endeavoured to pacify the child, who still cried loudly.

"Take it from the house for a few minutes," said Adder, "and perhaps it will then cease its d—d noise."

"And if the crying of the child should reach Lady Ravensford's ears," observed Mrs. Kitson, "of what consequence can it be? She cannot have any idea that it is her offspring."

"True," replied Adder; "but it is as well to avoid any suspicion, if possible."

Mrs. Kitson now quitted the house, and walked a short distance from it, to endeavour to quiet the child; but Adder followed to the door of the house, and seemed fearful of her being out of sight.

We left our heroine in a calm slumber, into which she had sunk after the fatigue of thinking and the anguish of her mind. She continued in it until the storm arose, which awoke her, and jumping up in the bed, she scarcely knew where she was. Confused thoughts darted across her perturbed imagination, and she had in an instant a foreboding, a presentiment, that something particular was about to occur to her. She heard no one but old Cicely moving below, for at that time Adder and Gordan were away from the house, looking for Mrs. Kitson and her tender charge, and recollecting that she had seen Adder quit the house at an early hour in the morning, she thought it was probable that he had not yet returned, and she became rather more composed. Then, however, she remembered the dark hints which the hateful old woman Cicely had thrown out to her in the morning, and again were her utmost apprehensions of some fresh misery excited. Some time she continued in this manner, when she heard a confusion of voices from below, among which she distinguished that of a female, and Adder's, but she could not understand a single word that they gave utterance to. She was, however, certain that the voice was not that of Cicely, and she was lost in a chaos of conjecture as to who it could be.

The cries of a child suddenly startled her, and she jumped involuntarily to her feet: her heart palpitated, and her whole frame trembled so voilently, that she could with difficulty prevent herself from sinking. An instinctive feeling came over her. And yet why should the crying of a child astonish and alarm her? It probably belonged to the woman whose voice she had heard, and why should she feel any interest in it? But yet the very sound of an infant's voice, under her present deplorable circumstances, was quite sufficient to create a feeling of the deepest anguish in her breast. She listened with breathless attention, and as she did so her emotions increased to an almost insupportable degree. At length she heard the outer door opened and shut again, and the cries of the child no longer reached her ears.

She now endeavoured to calm her feelings, and to prepare for the meeting which, she had no doubt, would shortly take place between her and Adder, who she was resolved to meet with all the fortitude she could possibly muster. She knelt down, and supplicated the aid of the Almighty; and implored that He would frustrate the designs of the wicked, and not suffer her to fall a victim to the diabolical stratagems of the miscreant who at present held her in his power.

As is ever the case, when the sincere heart breathes its prayers to Heaven, our heroine felt almost immediately more tranquil and prepared to meet her oppressor, and she arose from her knees with a determination to support herself with an air of fortitude, which should abash rather than encourage the villain's nefarious hopes.

She had not long come to this resolution, when she heard a footstep ascendin the stairs, and shortly afterwards the door of her apartment was unbolted, and the object of her hatred and her fears presented himself before her. She met his looks firmly, and with an air of becoming dignity, and it was evident, although he endeavoured to disguise it, that something of more importance than usual occupied his thoughts.

He stood for a second or two in the doorway, and seemed anxious to address her, yet at a loss how to begin. Then he seemed abashed at the calm dignity of Rosabelle's manner, and at the same time lost in admiration of her extreme beauty, which, although much impaired by the ravages of time, was still most superlative.

Notwithstanding the firmness which she assumed, Rosabelle felt a trembling apprehension of the interview, and had much difficulty in conquering her feelings.

At length, Adder advanced nearer to our heroine, closing the door after him, and after several ineffectual attempts to speak, he observed, in as insinuating a tone as he could assume—

"Beauteous Rosabelle, after a temporary absence from your presence, which has appeared an age to me, I again come to bask in the sunshine of your beauty—again to solicit a return of that passion which I so ardently feel for you."

"Villain!" ejaculated Rosabelle, "receive my answer in the utter contempt, disgust, and abhorrence I feel for you: and rest assured that no other feeling can ever inhabit my breast towards a wretch who has proved himself destitute of every feeling of humanity."

"This violence is useless, Rosabelle," returned Adder; "I have given you plenty of time to consider; this day I come hither to decide: I have waited patiently long enough."

"Monster!" cried the distracted lady, and her eyes at the same time beamed an expression which seemed as if it would penetrate to his soul; "where is my husband?—Where is my child?—Where my poor father, from whom you have so mercilessly torn me? Can you recollect the guilty, the unparalleled act of cruelty you have been guilty of, and yet stand there and talk to me, the bride of another, and a mother, about love?"

"To all these passionate expressions I pay little or no attention; for they affect me not," returned the hardened villain. "It is enough that I have fixed my mind on you; I have laboured hard, and risked much, to get possession of you—you are now in my power; and mine, in spite of all entreaties and tears, you shall be!"

"Oh, heartless miscreant!"

"Nay, think not that I would willingly resort to violence," observed Adder, in a milder tone of voice; "no, I would win you by my actions; by my love;—I would be to you the most ardent and affectionate companion that woman can desire; I——"

"Cease!" interrupted Rosabelle, in a commanding tone of voice, which seemed to enforce immediate obedience; "I will not listen to your guilty language, it disgusts me. Your presence makes me feel as if a fiend, instead of a human being, were standing before me;

begone! and leave me to the solitude of my unjust confinement."

"Not yet, fair Rosabelle," returned Adder, with a supercilious smile; "you and I must not part until we understand each other."

"I perfectly understand you, sir," said Lady Ravensford, "and depend upon it, all that you can say will but add to the utter abhorrence which I bear towards you."

"But you must yield!"

"Never!"

"How can you save yourself? Are you not in my power?"

"True; but I have a friend in Providence, who will not suffer me to fall a victim to the nefarious designs of a diabolical villain like you."

"Upon my word you are very liberal with your compliments," said Adder, with a half-sneering laugh, although it was very plain to be seen that he was very much chagrined at the manner in which our heroine addressed him.

"Is there any epithet strong enough that I can apply to a man like you?" demanded Rosabelle. "Has not your conduct proved you to be a miscreant, too——"

"Come, come," interrupted Adder—and a slight scowl passed over his brows—"I do not mind a little flattery; but when it proceeds to extremes, I must acknowledge that I have no

ROSABELLE RESCUES ALFRED FROM ADDER.

stomach to take it. Any epithet that you may apply to me, you must be aware cannot have any other effect than that of exasperating me to that which I might afterwards be sorry for. But how can you be so foolish as to remain thus obstinately opposed to the wishes of a man who would make it his unceasing study to render you happy?"

"Happy!" exclaimed Rosabelle; "and dare you talk to me of happiness, when I am torn from all that renders life desirable? Wretch, unnatural monster you must think me, to be capable of listening to the licentious vows of a man who has been the author of all my miseries!—Talk to me of happiness, and keep me confined in this awful house, sur-rounded only by the votaries of guilt, who would not hesitate to dye their hands in my blood."

"They dare not; they act alone by my orders," answered Adder. "But why thus delay the time in conversing on matters of no immediate interest? Again, Rosabelle, I solicit your love. Say that you will be mine, all but that which the idle ceremony of wedlock can make you, and there is not a pleasure which money can purchase, or this world can supply, which you shall not have at your command. We will hasten far from hence, and in a place where we are unknown, forget that there are any others than ourselves in existence."

No. 29.

Lady Ravensford shuddered with horror at the coolness and effrontery with which the libertine uttered these expressions, and she could scarcely believe that she was standing in the presence of a human being.

"Oh! how my heart revolts at the idea of your nefarious propositions," she at last ejaculated; "for mercy's sake leave me, and no longer torture and herrify me with your disgusting and diabolical language."

"Oh, no," replied Adder, "think not that I can be induced to leave you so soon this day, at any rate. Upon your determined answer your fate depends."

"You have already had my answer," returned Lady Ravensford.

"Will nothing persuade you to alter it?"

"Nothing, by heaven!"

"Beware! Take not an oath!"

"I can with safety, for nothing could induce me to swerve from it."

"You had better bethink yourself."

"I have thought sufficiently, and am decided."

"Recollect that, if you refuse, I shall be compelled to resort to force."

"I will die first."

"You will not have the means."

"Almighty God surely will never suffer so black a deed!"

"Bah!—this is all idle cant. Think, too, that if you refuse, you will still be kept here a prisoner, deprived of every comfort, and yet subservient to my wishes."

"Oh, horror! You surely cannot be such a monster!"

"I would not willingly, but you would drive me to."

"Oh, repent! repent!"

"Pshaw! Will that gratify my desires?"

"It will afford you a far greater gratification."

"I shall not try it."

"Alas! you, you are indeed a guilty miscreant!"

"Thank you again for your compliment; I have pointed out to you the horrors that will attend your refusal; say, shall I point out to you the happiness that will attend you, if you comply with my wishes?"

"I want not to hear them, they cannot make any alteration in my determination," answered our heroine, covering her face with her handkerchief, and sobbing aloud with her disgusted and wounded feelings.

"Still must I think that you will change your mind," returned Adder, with the same guilty expression of countenance in which his features were almost constantly clad; "remember the sweets of liberty will then be your's."

"And of what use would liberty be to me, when it would be purchased by a life of infamy?" demanded Rosabelle; "could anything ever reconcile it to my conscience, to become the base paramour of a guilty being like you? The bare idea fills me with a sensation of the utmost dread, and death in its most horrible form would be preferable to such a course of life."

"But is there nothing that could prevail upon you?"

"Nothing," answered Rosabelle, with a look of the greatest disgust and horror.

"Think again!"

"I have nothing more to say upon the detested subject."

"If, by so doing, you could purchase the restoration of your child to your arms ——"

"Ah!" gasped forth Rosabelle, turning deadly pale, and clutching the arm of Adder, and with distended eye-lids;—"what mean you? Speak! speak!—I knew you have something of a particular nature to impart to me! Reveal it! I beseech you, and keep me not in suspense!—Oh, Adder, if you have, indeed, any regard for my feelings, tell me, what of my child?"

"Calm your feelings!"

"You rack me!"

"Compose yourself!"

"Talk not to me of composure!" shrieked Rosabelle;—"my child! my child!"

"He is in my power!"

Lady Ravensford tried to speak, but she could not; she was transfixed to the spot, and gazed upon Adder with a look in which the greatest astonishment and horror were depicted! The announcement of Adder came like a thunderbolt upon her, and her faculties seemed to be bound up in the suddenness and unexpectedness of the circumstance.

"If you are not a monster of the blackest dye," exclaimed Rosabelle, at length, "you will not delight in agonizing a mother's feelings! but tell me, have you indeed said that which is true?"

"I have," answered Adder;—"the child, your offspring, is now in my power!"

"Gracious Heaven! Where?—where?" ejaculated our heroine.

"In this house!"

"Oh, let me behold him! Let me once more enfold my darling child in my arms!" cried Lady Ravensford.

"Be calm!"

"Are you bent to drive me mad?" exclaimed the frenzied Rosabelle, as with clasped hands, she gazed vehemently and supplicatingly in the countenance of her oppressor.

"No, no! I would restore you to happiness," replied Adder.

"Happiness!" groaned Lady Ravensford; "oh, cruel mockery to talk to me thus; and to continue to keep me in this state of agony and suspense. Oh, give me my child! A mother's heart will burst its tenement, and leap towards him! My child!—my child!—my Alfred!—you dare not keep him from me!"

"Compose yourself," again remonstrated Adder, in a gentler tone than he had before spoken, and at the same time venturing to approach her closer; "compose yourself, and I will immediately comply with your wishes."

"I will be calm; I will be calm!" sobbed forth our heroine; "but have mercy; if you have spoken the truth, keep not my child longer from my arms."

Adder stamped three times with his foot upon the floor, and at the third signal, the room-door was thrown open, and Mrs. Kitson, bearing the little innocent in her arms, entered the room.

The little Alfred, as if he knew his unfortunate mother, no sooner beheld her than he stretched forth his arms, and a heavenly smile irradiated his beauteous features. With a delirious air, and a wild and frantic cry, our heroine rushed forward, and snatching her boy from the arms of Mrs. Kitson, and pressing him closely to her breast, she devoured him with kisses, until her feelings overpowered her, and she sunk insensible upon the floor.

CHAPTER XXVII.

THE IMPEACHMENT.

IT was not until the lapse of several hours, and Mrs. Kitson and Adder had promised faithfully that the former should remain in the house with the child, that the unfortunate heroine of these pages could be restored to anything like a degree of composure; but the sudden surprise had had such a violent effect upon her nerves, that she was compelled to be put to bed immediately, and Mrs. Kitson, who was rather skilled in the use of herbs, was left to attend upon her.

This latter circumstance was a source of much vexation to old Cicely, and she felt not a little jealousy towards the smuggler's wife. But she had no one to whom she could express her thoughts, and she was, therefore, compelled to mutter her spleen to herself, which she did not fail to do most liberally, as she moved about the house.

The absence of Cicely was a great relief to Lady Ravensford, and she was prepossessed greatly in favour of Mrs. Kitson, for there was an expression of kindness in her features which no one could fail to understand at first sight. Mrs. Kitson, too, who really sympathised in the misfortunes of Lady Ravensford, was very pleased to think she had been deputed to attend upon her, and she determined to impart to her all the consolation which was within her simple power.

She had been duly cautioned by the wary Adder, as to the conduct she was to pursue towards Lady Ravensford, and above all, to keep all knowledge of the proceedings with which she was acquainted from her, and which, according to the engagement she had entered into with Adder, she felt herself bound to do. But she now, more than ever, regretted that she had in that respect made herself indirectly a party in the guilty plot.

The whole of that afternoon and evening, Lady Rosabelle was only sensible at intervals; and towards night, she was in a high fever.

Adder, who felt very much alarmed lest the shock should prove too violent, sent frequently to inquire how she was, and was really in a state of great anxiety. He now plainly perceived what Mrs. Kitson and others had frequently hinted to him, namely, that he had acted with great imprudence in making so sudden a disclosure to Lady Ravensford, whose spirits, weakened as they were by long anguish of mind and incarceration, were not in a fit state to endure it; but it was too late to repent now, and he had only to see to the readiest means of promoting her recovery. But this was a task not so easy as might have been imagined, placed in the awkward situation in which they were. He could not call in the aid of a medical man, for if he had done so, a discovery of the truth would of necessity follow, and thus at once all his plans be rendered abortive. It was a fortunate job for him, that Mrs. Kitson was so far skilled in surgery as to be able to prescribe for Rosabelle as she at present was, but should she be taken any worse, it was not likely that she could undertake to administer to her relief, however anxious and attentive she might be.

The little Alfred having once beheld his unfortunate mother, with the instinct natural to most children, would not suffer himself to be removed from her sight again, and every attempt which was made to do so, only made him scream the more violently; so that Mrs. Kitson was at last obliged to endeavour to pacify him, and she could not entirely succeed in doing so until she had placed him in the same bed as his mother, close to whose bosom he nestled, and quickly went to sleep, unconscious of the anguish that racked that fond mother's bosom.

Lady Ravensford was only at times conscious that her child was with her, although she raved all night incessantly of him, and frequently hugged him to her bosom with a wild fervour which alarmed Mrs. Kitson, who was afraid that she would, unknowingly, inflict some injury on the child.

Adder slept little that night, for the thoughts of the illness of Rosabelle kept him waking, and her cries frequently reached his ears. Sometimes she called upon the name of her husband, and accused him (Adder) of being his murderer; then she would laugh hysterically, and rave of her child, which she said no earthly power should keep from her arms. He perceived that so far from forwarding his base designs, he had only procrastinated them, for Lady Ravensford had now possession of her offspring, and should he persist in forcing it away from her, he had not the least doubt, from the power of her feelings, that it would be the cause of her death, or a most serious illness to her, which would, in all probability, be the means of betraying his diabolical schemes, and put at once an end to his intentions.

It was a late hour before Adder thought of retiring to rest, and he sat up in the front parlour of the house, the villain Gordon being his companion.

"Well, this seems to be a failure of your's, master," said the latter.

"I am afraid it is," laconically replied Adder.

"I never had much of an opinion of it," added Gordon.

"Hadn't you?" returned Adder, sullenly.

"No," said Gordon.

"For what reason?"

"Because it seemed to be preposterous."

"Indeed?"

"Yes."

"You pride yourself on your sagacity, then?"

"A little, sometimes; it was something of that sort, I believe, which made me discover Lord Ravensford, and also where this brat was."

"Well, well."

"But I do not like so much delay. You had the lady in your power, and why not at once gratify the passion which had prompted you to run such risks to obtain possession of her?"

"I have stated my reasons often enough. I wished to gain her consent, and not to use violence."

"Psha!—that is only what some love-sick youth of eighteen would say."

"It would have added tenfold to my triumph."

"I do not perceive it."

"Probably not."

"It is my belief that you will play with the mouse until you lose it."

"Why do you think so?"

"While you are thus procrastinating, something may transpire to let her friends know where she is, and she will be rescued from your power."

"Nonsense! I have no such dread."

"Perhaps you may flatter yourself too much on your security."

"What chance have her friends of ascertaining where she is?"

"I can't say; but such chances often occur when we least expect them."

"Which is not likely to happen in this instance," said Adder, "unless one of the smugglers, or some of those who are acquainted with the secret, should betray me."

"And, of course you do not suspect any of them?"

"I have hitherto had no occasion."

"And I do not think it is likely that you will have."

"Should her illness last?"

"Ay, that is a very awkward job; for you cannot send for a doctor, and it is not to be supposed that Mother Kitson can know sufficient to prescribe for her, if she does not get any better," said Gordon.

"True," coincided Adder, and he paced the room with hasty and disordered steps. "Something must be done."

"And speedily; but I know not what. I do not see how you can act in such a situation."

"After all, it may not turn out so bad as we apprehend," observed Adder, after a pause. "When she has recovered from the sudden shock which the unexpected meeting with her child has occasioned her, she may quickly be restored to convalescence, and nothing more occur to disturb me."

"But what will you do with the child?"

"It must remain with her, I suppose," answered Adder, biting his lips; "I am fearful, that if I were to attempt to force it away, the worst consequences would be the result."

"Decidedly so," said Gordon, "and thus you see at once the failure of your scheme."

"I do."

"You have been at all this trouble, merely to add to the comfort of the lady," muttered Gordon.

"Well, it is too late to repine, now."

"I do not blame you for endeavouring to bear your disappointment with patience," remarked Gordon.

"Besides," said Adder, "at any rate, I have gratified my revenge, by racking the mind of Ravensford, who will be in such a dreadful state of anxiety at the uncertainty of the fate of both his wife and offspring."

"Why, that is true; but I think your vengeance ought to be pretty well satiated by this time."

"Satiated!" said the villain, and his eyes gleamed like balls of fire: "by hell, there is nothing that could fully satiate the deadly hatred I feel against that man. Methinks I could wade through oceans of blood to rack and torture him."

"And yet, from what you have stated, I do not see that he gave you such bitter cause for hatred."

"Did he not strike me?"

"Why not resent it at the time?"

"No; I was determined to have a more deliberate, a more deadly revenge."

"Had I been placed in your situation," observed Gordon, "I should have proceeded very differently; I should have acted on the impulse of the moment, and the life's blood of one or both of us must have at that time stained the earth."

"And so did my feelings prompt me; but I had other designs, and I arrested my arm, and subdued my rage."

"But you afterwards sought his life?" inquired Gordon.

"I did, twice."

"And failed!"

"Of course; you know that."

"Ay, ay, I knew not what I said."

"I often regret that your arm failed, in the recent attempt you made."

"It was no fault of mine."

"I do not say it was."

"My aim was sure, though it proved not mortal"

"True."

"But the torment you are at present inflicting on him, must be worse than death."

"It must; and, therefore, am I content that he shall live," answered Adder, with a look of the most savage and unnatural exultation. "But, do you think that Mrs. Kitson can be trusted?—I ought not to ask you though, as you and her are not upon very good terms together."

"Oh, you may ask me with safety," answered Gordon Desborough; "for although I and mother Kitson do not agree upon several things, I will not say anything unjustly to her prejudice; not I."

"You think she may be trusted then?"

"I do."

"That is fortunate," observed Adder, "especially as she will have to remain here to look after the child and Lady Ravensford."

"You may depend upon her—she has been tried often enough."

"Then, if such is the case, and you are all faithful to me, I cannot conceive what occasion I have to entertain the apprehension you suggested a short time since."

"What was that?"

"Why, that the place of Lady Ravensford's confinement and that of her child, should be discovered by her friends," replied Adder.

"Well, perhaps not; only it is always best to be cautious."

"Ay, we cannot be too cautious, particularly in so peculiar an affair as this."

"To be sure not; for sometimes discoveries are made by the most simple means."

"Have you long held possession of this house?" demanded Adder.

"About four years."

"And of whom do you rent it?"

"No one."

"Ah! how's that?"

"I found it uninhabited when I came hither, and as there was no claimant, I thought I might take possession of it as anybody else."

"And you have held it ever since without interruption?"

"I have; and now that I am so closely connected with Monckton and his comrades, I do not think they would find it a very easy task to get rid of me."

"And what made you come hither?"

"That matters not," replied Gordon, changing countenance; "you may be certain that it was none of my good deeds that caused me to come hither."

"That I'll be bound it was not," returned Adder.

"We will not speak upon that subject, if you please."

"Very well, I have no interest in wishing to urge it. Are not Monckton and his companions gone longer this time than usual?"

"They are," answered Gordon, "but there is no accounting for that; they may not be far off, but unable to run their cargo for the present."

"And some accident may have befallen them," suggested Adder; "they may have encountered their enemies."

"Why, they might, to be sure," said Gordon, in reply; "but I have not much fear of that: and if they should have done so, I do not fear the consequences, The smugglers will sooner die than yield."

"I believe it. But it is getting late, and Lady Ravensford appears to be getting more calm. I will retire to rest. Good night."

"Good night," returned Gordon, lighting another lamp, Adder having taken up one. "I am devilish sleepy, and, therefore, do not care how soon I am in bed. Old Cicely has been snoring away these two hours."

The two villains now separated, but before Adder sought his bed, he knocked at the chamber-door of our heroine, and inquired how the patient was. Mrs. Kitson replied that she was in a high fever, at which Adder expressed his alarm, and retired to his bedroom.

When he had reached his apartment, he traversed it for some time in a state of the greatest agitation. He cursed his folly a hundred times in having acted with so little caution as he had done, so as to cause such a sudden shock to the feelings of Rosabelle, and he was in a state of the most violent alarm, lest her malady should increase, in which event he was perfectly at a loss in what manner he should act. He saw too late that all that Gordon had in the recent interview said to him, and the observations of Captain Monckton and Mrs. Kitson upon the subject, were perfectly correct; and he could not imagine how he could have been so blindly obstinate as not to have been convinced of it before. He continued to traverse his room for some time after he had retired to it, in a state of extreme emotion, and it was not till the clock had tolled the midnight hour, before he thought of retiring to bed.

When he did so, he was far from being inclined to sleep, and he lay tossing about, and revolving the circumstances in his mind, without being able to come to any satisfactory conclusion as to the course he should pursue. When he did fall to sleep, troublesome dreams haunted his imagination, and he frequently started from it, in a state of great consternation, and looked fearfully around him, imagining that his retreat had been discovered, Rosabelle and her child rescued, and himself consigned to a prison. So forcible were these fearful imaginations, that he had some difficulty in effacing the impression from his mind; and so restless and perturbed was his sleep, that he looked anxiously for the dawn.

Frequently, notwithstanding he slept in an opposite wing to the building, the indistinct cries of Lady Ravensford in her delirious ravings would reach his ears, and we need not seek to describe the torture it caused him. He began to fear that he had completely ruined his plot, and looked u on the past with regret, and upon the future with the greatest apprehension. But he was determined that the restoration of Rosabelle to her friends should never take place, and that even if he was compelled to adopt the most cruel and desperate measures, he would do so, rather than his enemies should triumph. Yes, the inhuman monster was resolved that, should he be driven to so horrible an extremity, the blood of our unfortunate heroine should be shed, sooner than she should be restored alive to her friends.

In the meantime, Mrs. Kitson continued to attend upon the much injured patient with the greatest assiduity, and no person could have had a more attentive or skilful nurse. She applied all those little remedies, with which she was so well acquainted, and which had often before proved most efficacious; but for the whole of the night, Rosabelle underwent very little change, raving incessantly of her child, her husband and her father, and drawing the most alarming pictures of their situation.

Mrs. Kitson most deeply sympathized with her unprecedented fate, and heartily wished that it was in her power to restore her to liberty and to her friends. Upon Adder, who had wrought such unpardonable misery, and who was a miscreant of the blackest dye, she could not help looking without a feeling of the most unbounded disgust and horror, and was fully determined not to touch a coin of the money he had offered her for taking charge of the child. Ill-gotten, she had no doubt it was, and besides, she shrunk with horror from the bare idea of making herself a paid accomplice of such a notorious and unnatural villain as Adder. She knew that her husband, rough as he was, would not upbraid her for the feeling, and whether he did or not, he mind was made up.

Notwithstanding the ravings of its unhappy parent, the child slept soundly, and instinctively Rosabelle, although unconscious of what she did, took the greatest care of it, and never disturbed it.

Towards the morning our heroine became more calm, and at length dropped into a refreshing slumber, in which she continued two or three hours, Mrs. Kitson watching her with the utmost solicitude. Suddenly she awoke, and looked vacantly around her for a second or two; then, raising herself on her elbow in the bed, she exclaimed, pressing her hand across her forehead—

"Where am I?—where have I been? Methought my child—my own innocent Alfred —was restored to my arms. But I suppose it was all a dream. But no—what sleeping cherub is this? Ah! I cannot mistake his angelic features! It was no delusion, but bright and blissful reality! My boy! my child! my Alfred! Thy mother presses the again to her heart, from whence no earthly power shall again tear thee!"

As the unfortunate mother thus spoke, she hugged the child still closer to her breast, and devoured its rosy cheeks with kisses. The child had awakened, and sweet and innocent smiles beamed in its countenance.

Mrs. Kitson watched the scene for some time without offering to interrupt Lady Ravensford, and without being observed; but at length, fearing that the power of Rosabelle's emotions would occasion a relapse, she approached nearer to the bedside, and in a voice of gentleness, ejaculated—

"My dearest lady, let me beseech you to be calm, lest, in your present weak state, you might——

"And who are you?" interrupted Lady Ravensford, turning her penetrating eyes hastily upon Mrs. Kitson; "ah, I see I am in the same horrible place! But tell me, woman, who are you?"

"I am deputed to attend upon you, my lady," replied Mrs. Kitson.

"Ah!" hastily ejaculated our heroine, "you, then, are one of the accomplices of the villain Adder?"

"Nay, my dear madam," said Mrs. Kitson, "do not judge me too harshly. It is true I am employed by Adder; but you shall find that I will behave to you with care and kindness."

"And that hateful old woman—where is she?"

"She will not be suffered to come near you whilst I am with you, my lady," answered Mrs. Kitson.

"Oh, that, indeed, will be a relief," cried

Lady Ravensford. "And you seem kind—far kinder than any I have yet seen here."

"I am sorry for your misfortunes, my lady," said Mrs. Kitson; "and anything that my humble means will allow me to do towards alleviating your distresses, I am sure I shall feel a pleasure in doing."

Lady Ravensford's eyes brightened, and turning gratefully to Mrs. Kitson, she said, in her usual gentle tones—

Oh, thanks—thanks for this! This is, indeed, a kindness which I never expected to meet with here. But my child? Say—he will not be torn from my arms again?"

"Adder can never be so cruel as to attempt it," replied Mrs. Kitson.

Oh, talk not to me of Adder," cried Lady Ravensford: "he has barbarity enough for anything, the villain—the miscreant! If it be left entirely to him, then, indeed, there is little hope. But I will die ere he shall again tear my little one away from me."

"Pray compose yourself, my lady," said Mrs. Kitson. "I have very good reason to believe that Adder will not attempt it."

"Your words speak comfort to me, my good woman," observed Lady Ravensford. "Pray who are you, and how came you to be connected with the guilty wretch, Adder?"

"I have known him but a short time, my lady," answered Mrs. Kitson; "as to who I am, I wish I could answer more satisfactorily. I am the wife of one of the smugglers; but yet, indeed, believe me, I have a heart that is not intirely insensible to the feelings of humanity."

"I believe you," answered our heroine; "but tell me, by what means did Adder get my child in his power?"

"Pardon me, my lady, but a binding promise precludes me from being enabled to answer that question," replied Mrs. Kitson.

"But you can tell me how long he has had him in his possession, I presume?" interrogated Lady Ravensford.

"About two months, my lady," answered Mrs. Kitson.

"And who, during that time, has been his nurse?" inquired our heroine, eagerly.

"That task has devolved on me, my lady," replied Mrs. Kitson, "and God knows, had he been my own child, I could not have bestowed upon him more attention."

"Heaven bless you for that!" cried Rosabelle, fervently; "I do believe you, for your words speak candour and truth. Heaven bless and reward you, I again say."

"Oh, my lady," returned Mrs. Kitson, "what greater reward ought I to wish for, than the satisfaction of having done my duty? I must, indeed, have been a monster, unworthy the name of woman, could I have acted any otherwise than with affection and attention to-wards that little innocent; his manners were so engaging, too. Ah! I lost one of my own but a short time since, and, excuse me, my lady, but this little one used so to remind me of him, that I used to love him as if he had really been my own."

"You have an excellent heart, I see," observed Lady Ravensford, with more composure in her manner and the expression of her countenance than had been apparent for some time; "you have an excellent heart, and I sincerely regret that fate has placed you in a situation of life where your merits are so unlikely to shine. But tell me, is the villain, Adder, still in the house?"

"He is; but will not venture to intrude upon you while you are so ill, my lady."

"It was only the sudden surprise, the shock," observed Rosabelle; "I shall soon be better now, and with my dear, dear boy near me."

"I trust that you will, my lady," returned Mrs. Kitson; and if there is anything I can do to add to your comfort, you have but to mention it, and I am sure I shall feel a pleasure in complying with your wishes."

Thanks—thanks!" replied Rosabelle; "I know you will; already I can read your thoughts, as if they were exhibited in a mirror before me. And you say that you are deputed to attend upon me?"

"Yes, my lady."

"And that unnatural and hateful old woman, Cicely, will not be suffered to come near me?"

"Certainly not, while I am with you, my lady," answered Mrs. Kitson.

"Oh, that is, indeed, happy news," said our heroine; a more wicked or detestable woman than she is could not be. If you did but know half the taunts, the sarcasms, the insults I have had to endure from her, you would, indeed, pity me."

Believe me, my lady," returned Mrs. Kitson, "I can as it is; for well do I know the odious character of that woman, Cicely. I do not believe that there is scarcely a crime of which she has not been guilty."

"The very sight of her makes me shudder," said Lady Ravensford; "and yet she will persist in forcing her hateful presence and society upon me."

"But, my lady," remarked Mrs. Kitson, "base as Adder certainly is, I do not believe that he would sanction such conduct, were he acquainted with it. I will take good care to let him know of it, and if Providence does not release you from your present unjust incarceration, depend upon it you will cease to be annoyed by her."

"Again I thank you, my good woman," said Rosabelle, "for your consideration and kindness."

"Oh, do not mention it, my lady," replied Mrs. Kitson; "it is more than I deserve. But you have had a terrible night, and must be quite exhausted. Endeavour to compose yourself to sleep for an hour or two."

"I do, indeed, feel fatigued," said Lady Ravensford, "and will try to do as you say. But you will not leave my bedside, will you?"

"Certainly not, my lady," answered Mrs. Kitson; "and whilst I am with you, you may consider yourself as perfectly safe."

"God bless you!" gratefully ejaculated our heroine, and once more kissing the rosy cheeks of her child, she hugged him closer to her bosom, and gradually sunk into a calm and refreshing sleep.

Mrs. Kitson felt truly thankful that her patient had so far recovered, and sat by her bedside, watching her and her child with the most anxious solicitude.

She had not been seated long thus, when she heard a loud knock at the chamber-door, and en going to it, she found it was Adder, who had come to inquire how Lady Ravensford was.

Mrs. Kitson informed him that she seemed a little better, but that she needed quiet and repose, for, that the least thing which might occur to disturb her, would be sure to cause in her a relapse, and the most fatal results might then, unquestionably, be anticipated.

Adder could not conceal his pleasure at the information which Mrs. Kitson had given him, and acknowledging the justice of her observations, requested her to pay her every attention, and promised to adhere closely to the advice she had given him. He then retired from the door, and once more hastened below.

We have already described the great state of apprehension and uneasiness he was in, and that had increased every moment, until it became almost insupportable. He several times ascended the stairs and listened at the door, but something withheld him from knocking; but as all remained quiet, he at last endeavoured to console himself by imagining that Rosabelle was better. But this state of doubt, uncertainty, and suspense, was more than he could at length endure—and he knocked at the chamber-door of his much injured prisoner, as we have described.

He was quite pleased with the answer of Mrs. Kitson, and the violent apprehensions he had just before entertained, were almost entirely dismissed from his mind.

Gordon Desborough had left the house at an early hour that morning, and, therefore, Adder was left entirely alone to his own reflections, without any fear of interruption. The nature of his thoughts need no particular description from us, for they were strictly devoted to our heroine, and in endeavouring to form a conjecture of the course it would be best for him in future to pursue. He now saw plainly enough that it would be madness for him to attempt to take away the child again from Rosabelle, and that thus one of his principal schemes was foiled, and our heroine had reaped the advantage of that which had cost him so much trouble, and expense, and danger to obtain. He also saw that there was no other chance of gaining the gratification of his unlawful and licentious desires, without resorting to force, and from the bare idea of that, even his heart somehow revolted. Notwithstanding all that he had been guilty of to get his unfortunate victim in his power, and the strength of his passions, and the determinations he had so frequently formed, there was something in the looks and dignified manner of Lady Ravensford which awed him, and made him recoil from the idea of using violence at the very moment when his passions were most painful.

He resolved to let matters rest as they were for the present, and not to endanger the health of Rosabelle by being too premature in his advances. Still he was fearful of the delay, which might be the means of frustrating his designs altogether, and finally restoring Rosabelle and her child to their friends, without his having succeeded in completing his scheme of vengeance. Let, moreover, whatever might be the consequences, he saw no other alternative, and was, therefore, compelled to adopt it, let whatever might prove the results.

There were times, too, when Adder felt rather uneasy at the prolonged absence of the smugglers; for should any accident have happened to them, he apprehended some danger to himself. It was to ascertain, if possible, what had become of them, that Gordon Desborough left the house so early that morning; and Adder, therefore, awaited his return with some impatience and anxiety, not doubting that he would bring some intelligence of them, to satisfy his doubts one way or the other.

The morning passed away, however, and Gordon returned not; and Adder sought to divert his thoughts to some other subject, and, therefore, walked from the house for a short time. He took his way towards the rocks, almost unconscious whither he wandered, and was so deeply wrapped in meditation that he was reckless as to where he went.

It was now the afternoon, and a fine one it was. The sun was shining brilliantly, and the scenery upon which his beams shone, although wild, had an appearance of much beauty.

Adder at length looking up, perceived the direction he was wandering in, and turned from the path into that which led to the rendezvous of the smugglers.

He had not proceeded far when he heard some one singing a rude song, and, looking up, he beheld Gordon Desborough approaching him.

Adder was very well pleased upon recognising him, and immediately hastened towards him.

"It's all right," said the ruffian, when Adder had got up to him.

"Are they all safe?" eagerly demanded Adder.

"Perfectly safe, and as merry as good grog and cheerful society can make them," replied Gordon.

"I am glad to hear that."

"I dare say you are."

"But where are they?"

"At the 'Caboose.'"

"And is Monckton with them?"

"When I left, he was not; he had gone somewhere upon business."

"I will hasten to them."

"Ay—ay, they will be glad of your company. I have no doubt."

"Will you not return with me?"

"No, I cannot; I have a little business to transact; but I will join ye by and by."

"Then farewell, for the present."

"Oh, good by."

"Do not do anything to annoy or disturb Lady Ravensford while I am gone."

"Why should I want to annoy her?"

"Well—well, you understand me.   But be

MRS. KITSON SHELTERING FROM THE STORM.

sure not to let old Cicely go near her; her very looks are enough to frighten her."

"I will take care of that. Cicely is certainly a crabbed old devil; it is her nature to make herself disagreeable to every one, especially those of her own sex. But it is no use standing talking here; I shall see you again in the evening."

"Very well, good-by."

Gordon once more responded to the latter, and hurried on his way to the house, whilst Adder bent his footsteps, very well pleased at the intelligence he had received, towards the 'Caboose,' at which Gordon had informed him the smugglers had assembled.

Having given the well-known signal among the smugglers, Adder was admitted, and as soon as he had reached the long passage which led to the back place in which the smugglers assembled, he heard them singing most vociferously, and evidently in high glee. This was no unwelcome sound to him, for it assured him that all was right, and that there had been no necessity for the apprehensions which he had previously entertained. Adder admired their rough joviality; and he could not resist the temptation of listening to what they were singing. The words of the solo, which were sung very well by Michael Hernwood, were as follows, and the smugglers joined in chorus in the rather boisterous burthen of the song :—

"Oh, give me the wide and billowy tide,
  That noble deep, the dark blue seas ;
With a vessel smart, swift as a dart,
  And gallant hearts and a fav'ring breeze !
Away we sail 'midst wind and gale,
  Saving the duty fools only pay.
We know no fear but when danger's near ;
  We spread our sails, and away ! away !
Down with the landsharks ! we're the boys,
Then hurrah for the sea, and a smuggler's joys !"

Adder having waited outside the door, until this song and chorus was finished, entered, and was greeted in the most cordial manner by the crew. He took his seat among them, and made himself as much at home as if he had been one of their companions. The grog passed freely round, and old Davey Grampus had already a face as red as a fire-bucket.

"Well," said Michael Hernwood, addressing himself to Adder, "I suppose you thought we were never going to return again."

"Why, I certainly did begin to be apprehensive that something had happened to ye," answered Adder ; "when did ye arrive ?"

"This morning," returned Hernwood ; "and ye lost nothing by our delay."

"I am glad to hear it."

"We have a rare cargo this morning ; and safe enough it is stowed away, in the subterranean vaults beneath this building," said the smuggler.

"And is your captain quite well ?"

"Well, ay, and as cheerful and bold as ever."

"He is a daring fellow."

"Ah ! so you would say, had you seen him in some of the squabbles we have encountered."

"He appears to be quite reckless of danger," observed Adder.

"Danger !" exclaimed Hernwood, with a look of scorn ; "why, the word is quite a foreigner to him."

"I wonder he is not among you now."

"Business must be attended to, you know," said Michael Hernwood, "and the captain having some to transact, was away this morning before daylight ; but there is no fear but that he will be with us anon. In the meantime, all that we have to do is to make ourselves merry. Of course, you will make one of us ?"

"Oh, certainly ; but where is Sam Kitson ?"

"Here am I, yer honour," said the smuggler, who had been blowing a stiff cloud in the chimney corner ; —"and how's my old woman ?"

"She is very well, Sam," replied Adder ; "but away from home."

"Away from home ! What do you mean ?"

"Necessity compels her for the present to be at the house of Gordon Desborough, with the child," returned Adder ; "but I suppose you do not mind that ?"

"Why, yer honour," said Sam, scratching his head, "yer see it is rather awkward ; but I suppose it can't be helped, and that no harm will come to her ; so I must be content."

"Oh, you have no occasion to fear but that she is safe enough," answered Adder ; "she is so fond of her charge, that I cannot spare her a moment from it. Besides the lady is ill, and your wife is an excellent nurse."

The grog now passed freely round, and the smugglers were as jovial as possibly could be. Adder entered into the festivities of the smugglers with much freedom, and felt himself more contented than he had done for some time. The influence of the liquor always worked an extraordinary change in the mind of Adder, and if he had ever so much care in his thoughts, he was sure to become quite happy and indifferent to everything.

Two or three hours passed away in this manner, and the smugglers continued their revelry with unabated spirit, and Gordon Desborough rejoined them. He was greeted heartily by the smugglers, and was very ready to join them in the festivity, for where there was plenty of eating, drinking, and carousing, none were more ready to make one of the party than Gordon Desborough.

"Our captain tarries," said Michael Hernwood.

"Yes, he does," said Gordon ; "but doubtless he is detained by business ; for leave him alone for being among ye, especially upon an occasion like this."

"Oh, he will be here presently, I dare say," said Sam Kitson ; "and we shall have a jovial night of it."

"Ay, Ay," said Davey Grampus ; "I like to see people jolly ; and smugglers are the last fellows in the world to encourage care."

"That's true," observed Michael Hernwood ; "and of what use is it being melancholy ? It only gives a person the cholic, and renders them unfit for society."

"Why, that's true enough, Michael," observed Sam Kitson ; "and for my part I never was on good terms with it. Now, Mr. Adder ought to be a very happy man, with such a beauteous lady with him, and—"

"There, there," interrupted Hernwood ; "you are rather too bold, Sam ; his honour may not like such liberties taken with him."

"Oh, I mind it not," said Adder, though in fact he was rather displeased with the freedom of Sam Kitson's speech ; "jokes are at liberty to go free here ; and I do not see that Sam has any cause to grumble about his partner ; for I seldom have seen a more domestic or homely woman in my life."

"Why, yes, yer honour," returned Sam ; "I

have had her these fifteen years, and so I have had plenty of opportunities of knowing her disposition and her worth. A better woman, although I say it, never trod in two shoes."

"Well said, Sam," observed Michael Hernwood; "I like to hear you speak well of your wife, because I know she deserves it."

"Yes, you may say that, Michael," said Sam; "and not flatter her neither."

At this moment the captain's whistle was heard outside, and the door was immediately opened, and Monckton entered. He seemed very much ruffled in his temper, and cast his eyes eagerly round upon the persons present.

"Ah! Adder," he hastily exclaimed; "you are here then? I greet you! I am vexed—agitated—and——"

"What is the matter, captain?" asked several of the smugglers in a breath, and looking very much alarmed at the agitation of his manner; "has anything happened?"

"What has thus vexed you?" cried Adder, who partook largely of the apprehensions of the smugglers.

"Oh, I scarcely know," replied Monckton; "I am afraid we have a traitor amongst us."

"A traitor!" cried the smugglers in a breath, jumping to their feet, and placing their hands on their swords and pistols. "A traitor! where?"

"Where is Bill Eldon?" demanded the smuggler captain, again looking fiercely round the room.

"Ah!" cried Michael Hernwood; "I never once thought of him. I have not seen him since our arrival this morning."

"D——n! the infernal scoundrel!—it is then as I suspected!" ejaculated the captain, and his countenance evinced the utmost indignation. "The villain, out of revenge, has gone to impeach against us."

"Death to the traitor!" cried the smugglers.

"But why do you suspect this Bill Eldon?" interrogated Adder, who was as much alarmed as the smugglers.

"The fellow and I had a quarrel on our recent trip," answered Monckton, "and I suppose that he has done this out of revenge."

"But did he threaten you?"

"He dared not," replied Monckton, "for the rascal knew that his doom would have been the ocean. Curses light upon him! We must shift our quarters directly."

"Directly?" repeated Adder.

"Ay, we must begone this very night," answered Monckton, "or the Philistines will be down upon us, and will doubtless bring a force that we shall be unable to compete with."

"We will conquer them or die!" cried the smugglers fiercely.

"I know your bravery, my lads," said Monckton; "but we had better not run the risk of losing our booty. We must immediately set to work, and stow our property where the d——d land-sharks cannot find it."

"And what am I to do?" asked Adder; "whither am I to go?"

"To the same destination that I have fixed upon, if you like," replied Monckton; "or you can remain behind and chance it."

"I am lost!" returned Adder; "Lady Ravensford is so ill, that to attempt to remove her would be attended with death."

"Ill!" exclaimed Monckton; "ah! that is, indeed, unfortunate. But I suppose you have been guilty of some imprudent action or the other to occasion this?—Where is the child?"

"With the mother."

"Ah! I see it plain enough," returned the smuggler captain, "you have made her ill by the suddenness of the shock; I guessed how it would be. But you would not be counselled by me. Now I will tell you that you will stand a chance of losing her altogether."

Adder turned very pale.

"It is useless to upbraid me now," said Adder; "I see my folly and regret it; but I cannot help it, and must put up with the consequences. As for leaving the house of Gordon, and taking Rosabelle with me, in her present condition, it would be impossible."

"I do not see so much cause for fear as you appear to apprehend, captain," said Gordon Desborough; "and I shall not budge from the house, but chance it. I do not fear but that I shall be able to elude the vigilance of the Philistines, and learn them a trick, if they should come down upon me."

"Well you can do as you like," said Monckton; "but I must not suffer the property of my comrades to become the prize of the fellows; so, come, my lads, let us to work without more delay."

"We are ready to obey you, captain," cried the smugglers.

"But what do you say, Sam Kitson?" demanded Adder of the smuggler; "will you be afraid to trust your wife behind you under the circumstances?"

"Why," ejaculated the smuggler, slowly, "I did not like to leave the old woman behind, but still I do not think that any harm will come to her; and as your honour, no doubt, will soon be able to join us, why I will e'en make up my mind to let her remain with you."

"You shall not go unrewarded for it," said Adder, "and I trust that the captain's fares will prove groundless; and as soon as Lady Ravensford is sufficiently recovered, I will rejoin you, if nothing happens in the meantime."

"Come, my lads, let us lose no more time," cried Monckton. "I never liked the sly disposition of that Bill Eldon, and ought to have been more cautious with him."

The smugglers now arose simultaneously, and prepared to attend Monckton in removing the contraband property from the place where it had been so long concealed, and to hide it in different cavaties of the rock, where the revenue officers would have no suspicion of it, while Davey Grampus exhausted all the oaths in his vocabulary, which was a pretty long list.

It is wonderful the expedition which the smugglers used; bales of goods, casks of spirits, and other articles were stowed away with a celerity which Adder could scarcely credit; who sat there in the most gloomy rumination, and in a state of fear and suspense which may be readily imagined. That Rosabelle should be taken ill at such a time as that was most unfortunate, but he had no alternative left; he must leave everything to chance, for he could not think of removing her from the house at present, which, from her weak state, would be certain to cause her sudden death. Should the worst fears of Monckton be realised, all the risk and labour he had run would have been of no avail; Rosabelle and her child would be again restored to liberty, and probably he might be taken into the custody of his enemies, and brought to punishment for the unprecedented crimes of which he had been guilty.

"But no," he reflected, "by hell, that should never be; the dogs should not take me alive, to triumph over me, and taunt and execrate me. My own hands should end my fate, and I would show them that I had the courage to die rather than fall into their hands. And even then I should not die unavenged; the torment I have already inflicted upon him whom I so mortally detest, has been sufficient for the insult Ravensford offered me; and I shall die with the satisfaction of having broken the peace of mind of my enemy, probably, for ever."

Thus soliloquised the guilty villain, notwithstanding the danger in which he was at present placed, and, as he did so, his determination became more fixed.

In less than three hours the smugglers had stowed away as much of their booty as they could in the rocks, and the rest they had got safely on board their own craft, and Monckton impatiently waited for dark that they might depart from the place.

Monckton described minutely to Adder the place where they were going to, so that he might rejoin them as soon as the health of Lady Ravensford would permit, if nothing else occurred to prevent him, and he then again sat down with his companions, and the grog passed merrily round; old Davey Grampus expressing his regret at the circumstance which had deprived him of such good customers, and hoping that it would not be long before they would be enabled to return to their old quarters again.

As soon as night had thrown its gray mantle over the face of nature, Monckton and his companions were on the stir, and, after very few preliminaries, and a few more cautions to Adder, they left the house, and making their way to the sea-beach, were quickly aboard their own vessel, and away to their place of destination.

Adder and Gordon did not remain long afterwards at the 'Caboose,' and made their way to their house.

"This is an unfortunate job," said the former: "a very unfortunate job."

"Oh, you must not begin to fear yet," said Gordon; "for probably there may be no occasion for it. This Bill Eldon is a strange character, but still I do not think he would be guilty of that which Monckton and the other smugglers suspect him."

"But you hear that he and the captain have had a quarrel," returned Adder.

"And what of that?"

"Why, is it not likely enough that he may have been induced by revenge to betray them?"

"He may do so; but I do not think it."

"But does not his abandoning his former companions look suspicious?"

"It does; but he may only have done that to alarm them."

"After all, I do not think you ought to treat the matter so lightly."

"Perhaps not; but I am still of opinion that I ought not to treat it more seriously, nor do I think that anything will accrue from it."

"I hope your surmises may prove correct; but I cannot help saying as I said before, that it is an unfortunate job!"

"Why, yes," returned Gordon Desborough, "should it turn out as Monckton and the smugglers suspect, situated as you are, it would be; but should the land-sharks offer to interrupt us, we may have the means of eluding them."

"How so?"

"By taking refuge in the subterranean apartments under the path leading from my house to the 'Caboose,'" replied Gordon.

"But this Bill Eldon, as you call him," remarked Adder, "being thoroughly acquainted with those secret places as well as yourself, it is not likely he would fail to let the fellows become acquainted with them."

"And if he did, we could secure ourselves in such a manner in some of the inner ones, so as to defy their endeavours to get at us, and there we could remain, until we found an opportunity to escape. Besides, when they found that the smugglers had abandoned the place, I do not think it is likely they would trouble themselves about us."

"Perhaps not," said Adder, "but the fellows, thinking to get well-rewarded, might be induced to hasten to the friends of Lady Ravensford, and to make them acquainted with where she is, and thus all my schemes would be frustrated."

"Well," said Gordon Desborough, "I do see the utility of alarming ourselves with what, after all, may turn out to be fruitless apprehensions; the best way is to be prepared for the worst, and, by acting with coolness and decision, we may the better be enabled to defeat the designs of our enemies."

Adder could not contradict the justness of these observations, and seeing the firmness of Gordon, he really became more composed, and determined to abide entirely by his advice.

It was a very dark night, and the wind blew keen, and the two worthies, therefore, walked at a rapid pace, and it was not long ere they reached the house, in the parlour of which they found old Cicely, who had been rather surprised at their long absence, and exhibited no great pleasure at the restrictions under which she had been placed, and was, in fact, in one of her surliest moods. Adder took no notice of the old beldame, but impatient to know how his prisoner was, he hurried up stairs, and gently tapping at the room-door, Mrs. Kitson speedily answered it. The villain inquired eagerly after Lady Ravensford, and was very happy to hear that she was considerably better than she had been in the morning. In fact, our heroine, beneath the assiduous care of Mrs. Kitson, sympathy being a stranger to her since she had been in the power of Adder, and having her child restored to her, soon tended to alleviate her anguish, and to recover her from the shock which her feelings had sustained by the sudden and unexpected surprise of the restoration of the little Alfred. During the day, released from the visits of Adder, and the company of the detestable old woman Cicely, she had become wonderfully composed to what might have been expected in so short a space of time, and she listened with much pleasure and satisfaction to the conversation of Mrs. Kitson, who did her utmost to ameliorate her grief, and endeavour to buoy her mind up with hopes that she was not destined to fall a victim to the sinful passions of Adder, and that if she firmly resisted him, something, she had no doubt, would ere long take place, which would bring about her restoration to her friends, and to punish the villain who had been to her so bitter an enemy.

"Heaven knows," continued Mrs. Kitson, "sinful woman as I have been, no one would be more sincerely glad if such an event were to take place than I should; no one would hail with greater pleasure than myself, your restoration to your friends."

"I do believe you, my good woman," returned our heroine, with one of her most gracious smiles; "but alas! perhaps ere this I have no friends to receive me!"

"Oh, say not so, my lady," kindly observed Mrs. Kitson; "your anticipations are by far too gloomy."

"Alas! my poor father!" ejaculated Lady Rosabelle, and sobs almost choked her utterance; "he never could survive so many dreadful calamities! My husband too! Oh, does he still live? I fear not; and thoughtless as I am, the very circumstance which affords me such rapture, may have proved a death-blow to him! Surely the loss of his child, as well as his wife, will break his heart!"

For some moments the anguish of our heroine was so violent that she could scarcely support herself, and was unable to utter a syllable, but wept and sobbed hysterically. Mrs. Kitson feared to interrupt her; in fact, she knew not what to offer by way of consolation, and thought that by allowing her to give free indulgence to her sorrow, it would enable her to obtain relief for her heavily afflicted mind.

Mrs. Kitson felt rather surprised that both Gordon and Adder should be absent from the house so long together, but she had no idea whither they had gone. Nearly the whole of the day the house was left in charge of old Cicely, who frequently came up to the door with some idle excuse, and endeavoured to wheedle herself into the room; but Mrs. Kitson was a fair match for her, and most peremptorily refused her admittance, and the old woman, therefore, always went away in a great rage, consigning Mrs. Kitson, Lady Ravensford, and Adder, all to the devil, and growling the most awful oaths and maledictions she could turn her tongue to.

Adder having, on his return, as we have before mentioned, ascertained the state of the patient, requested to speak a few words to Mrs. Kitson, who, having followed him to the parlour, wondering what he had got to impart to her, he informed her of the disappearance of Bill Eldon, the suspicions of Monckton, the precautions he had used, and the departure of himself and his comrades from the place.

Mrs. Kitson was astonished to hear this account, but she evinced no alarm, as the smugglers had made good their retreat; and as to themselves, she did not consider that they had much cause to apprehend.

Adder was more composed upon hearing her opinion than he had been before, and immediately dispatched her to the chamber of her patient again, whither Mrs. Kitson was very glad to depart.

As the villain had not enjoined her to secrecy upon this occasion, she immediately made Lady Ravensford acquainted with the whole circumstance on her return to the chamber. Rosabelle listened attentively, and when she had concluded, a ray of hope suddenly irradiated her features, and she exclaimed:—

"Ah! this circumstance inspires me with hope!—Should the officers examine this place, they will discover me, and, upon my explaining who I am, that surely would be the means of restoring me to liberty, and to those who are dear to me!"

"I coincide in your opinion, my lady," remarked Mrs. Kitson, who had been entertaining similar ideas; "and, therefore, what your oppressor considers a source of apprehension, may prove to you the production of happiness. Heaven grant that your most sanguine anticipations may be realised."

"Oh, how can I sufficiently thank you for your sympathy and kindness?" cried Lady Ravensford.

"If you would not make me feel uncomfortable, my lady," returned Mrs. Kitson, "you will not make use of such words. You have nothing at all to thank me for; for I must be a wretch indeed if I could not sympathise in and pity the misfortunes of one of my own sex especially."

"Alas!" cried Lady Ravensford, "there are few in the world like you, Mrs. Kitson, especially placed in the situation in which you are. But I wonder that Gordon, whom I know to be a man of crime, should be bold enough to remain here, when he is so threatened with danger."

"You know him to be a man of crime, my lady!" repeated Mrs. Kitson, with astonishment.

"Yes, Mrs. Kitson," replied our heroine, "I know him to be a man of crime; you can keep a secret, I know, and, therefore, I do not mind divulging it to you."

"It will be as safe deposited in my bosom, my lady, as if you had never divulged it," answered Mrs. Kitson, whose curiosity was evidently excited.

"Be sure that no one is listening," said Lady Ravensford, looking towards the door, "for should any one of them overhear me, there is no knowing what might be the consequences to us both."

Mrs. Kitson stepped cautiously to the door and opened it, but she did not observe any one, so Rosabelle proceeded without any further hesitation to detail to her all the horrible particulars of the awful adventure she had met with in the "Lover's resting place," when she had seen Gordon and his companion bury the body of their murdered victim, and had been so nearly discovered by them herself.

Mrs. Kitson listened to our heroine with feelings of the utmost horror and astonishment, and when she had concluded, she remained for some moments silent, looking at Rosabelle with an expression of surprise and almost incredulity.

"Oh, my lady," she at length said, "what a dreadful tale is this you have been relating. I shudder with horror when I think of it."

"And well you may," remarked Lady Ravensford; "I have scarcely ever had the scene from my eyes, since I witnessed it."

"I do not wonder at it," said Mrs. Kitson;

"it must have been a most awful one; I would not have witnessed it for all the world."

"Would to Heaven that I had not," said Lady Ravensford, "for the dreadful spectacle has never been absent from my sight since I witnessed it."

"And did you actually see the corpse, my lady?" asked Mrs. Kitson.

"I did, indeed," replied our heroine, "and, oh! it looked so ghastly. The eyes were wide open, as if staring into the faces of his murderers; and there was the poor old man's gray hair clotted together with blood."

"Oh, horrible!"

"It was a sight which I shall never forget," observed Lady Ravensford.

"And what a providential thing it was, my lady," said Mrs. Kitson, "that they did not discover you. No doubt they would have murdered both you and your dear child if they had."

"That they would have been certain to have done to have prevented detection," replied Rosabelle.

"Certainly," observed Mrs. Kitson; "but are you confident, my lady, that Gordon is one of the wretches?"

"Oh, yes, I am quite positive," replied our heroine; "I had a clear view of his features, and once beheld, they must be stamped upon the memory for ever."

"And do you think you should know his blood-thirsty companion, if you were to see him again?" asked Mrs. Kitson.

"Oh, yes," replied Lady Ravensford; "I should know him from amongst a thousand."

They remained silent for a second or two, when Rosabelle inquired—

"And did you reside in this neighbourhood when Gordon Desborough first made his appearance in it?"

"I did, my lady."

"And did he come here alone?"

"No; there was another man with him," answered Mrs. Kitson; "but they only remained together for a day or two, and then separated, and he has not been seen near this spot since."

"Do you know what description of man it was who accompanied Gordon?" asked Lady Ravensford.

"I never saw him myself, but I have heard my husband describe him as a tall, raw-boned man, with large black whiskers, and a slight cast in one of his eyes," replied Mrs. Kitson.

"That was the other assassin," said Rosabelle, "and probably they only stayed together to share their ill-gotten booty, when the other miscreant took the course which he thought best."

"That is very likely, my lady," returned Mrs. Kitson, "and no doubt he has gone to some foreign land, if he has not paid the penalty on the scaffold, for some other crime which he has perpetrated. Oh, dear me, I looked upon

Gordon Desborough with feelings of disgust and abhorrence before, but now I shall never be able to gaze upon his countenance without imagining the pale bloody features of the murdered man, as you have described them, are upon me."

"Frequently, Mrs. Kitson," observed our heroine, "has the awful scene recurred to me in my dreams since, and inspired my mind with the most indescribable horror."

"Oh, I dare say it has, my lady," remarked Mrs. Kitson; "and I do not wonder at it; I am sure such an adventure, and under such circumstances as those in which you were placed, would have frightened me to death. I wonder who the poor murdered man could be? Did you never hear, my lady?"

Rosabelle replied in the negative.

"And did you not make known to the justices what you had seen?"

"Alas! no," answered Rosabelle; "and I have ever since regretted it, and attributed the misfortunes that have constantly pursued me to that unfortunate neglect."

"It is, indeed, a pity that you neglected to do so, my dear lady," observed Mrs. Kitson, "for then the assassins might probably have been apprehended before they had quitted the country, and justice rendered to the poor old man's fate."

"I should have done so," said Lady Ravensford; "but the severity of my own troubles, and the lamentable circumstances in which I was placed, entirely occupied my distracted mind, and drove everything else, however important, from my thoughts."

"But, my lady," said Mrs. Kitson, "one of the murderers is living, and should Providence rescue you from the power which now holds you, it will not be too late to perform an act of justice, and bring one of the villains, at any rate, to punishment."

"It will not, indeed," uttered Lady Ravensford; "and, believe me, I will not rest until I have done so."

"Providence will aid you in so worthy a design; and I firmly believe that this affair, which has induced Monckton and his companions so suddenly to shift their quarters, will ultimately be the cause of restoring you and your offspring to liberty."

"Oh, say you so?" said Rosabelle, her eyes brightening as she spoke, elated with hope; "oh, how thankful ought I to feel for the circumstance which has brought you near me, to enliven with hope those hours that were once so cheerless and so dismal. And do you, indeed, think it is likely to occur as you have said?"

"Yes," replied Mrs. Kitson, "indeed I do; for, should the officers visit the house, they can have no business with you, and some of them may be prevailed upon by feelings of humanity, either to rescue you, or to make your friends acquainted where you are, and in whose power."

"But unless they at once deliver me," said our heroine, "their good intentions will be rendered useless; for if they were to make known to my friends where I was concealed, before they could fly to my rescue, the villain Adder would take good care to remove me to another place, where it would baffle all their endeavours to find me out."

"Why, that is true," answered Mrs. Kitson; "but surely some among them would attend to your supplications, and force you from the power of the villain who now holds you in his thraldom."

"Surely they will," observed Lady Ravensford; "and I will not, therefore, give way to despair. But Adder, will he not, when he finds that I am getting better, endeavour to force my child from me?"

"No," replied Mrs. Kitson, "I do not believe that he will; for he is fearful that by so doing, he might give your feelings such a shock, as would be productive of the most fatal consequences. Besides, I have greater reason to believe that he will not, from the conversation he had with me, and the principal portion of which I repeated to you. But I am afraid that you will fatigue yourself with conversing so much, after the severe illness which you had last night."

"Oh, no," returned Rosabelle, "I shall not; on the contrary, it relieves my mind."

"But it is now getting late," said Mrs. Kitson, "and you had better endeavoured to gain some repose."

"I am indebted to you for your kind solicitude and attention," said Lady Ravensford; "and will endeavour to do as you desire."

"That's right, my lady," returned her companion; "a little sleep will much refresh you. I will sit up for a short time longer, and watch by your bed side; when I will retire to rest also."

"And do you think that Adder and Gordon Desborough have retired to bed?" inquired Lady Ravensford.

"All is quite still in the house," answered Mrs. Kitson, "and I have, therefore, no doubt that they have."

"Then I feel safe," said Rosabelle.

"You are perfectly safe, while I am with you, my lady," said Mrs. Kitson, "and I will take good care to secure the door, so as to prevent any intrusion, should Adder dare to make such an attempt, which I do not believe he would; so rest your mind contented, lady."

"Your gentle manners would comfort any one," said Lady Ravensford, with a look of gratitude; "with my child by my side in safety, I will place my reliance in Omnipotence, whose goodness, notwithstanding the many trials and vicissitudes to which I have been subjected, has been so largely extended to me, and endeavour to rest content."

"Do you feel yourself better, my lady?" asked her kind attendant.

"Oh, yes," replied Lady Ravensford; "I am much better—much better. It was only the sudden surprise and the shock which overcame me. But I feel as if I could rest; good night, Mrs. Kitson, and Heaven bless you for your sympathy and attention."

"Good night, my dear lady," responded Mrs. Kitson, "and may all good angels watch over and protect you and your offspring."

"And those dear friends, husband, father, from whom we have been so cruelly forced," added Rosabelle, with a deep sigh.

Mrs. Kitson reciprocated her prayer, and soon afterwards, pressing he child closely to her heart, the affectionate mother sank into a calm and refreshing sleep.

Mrs. Kitson sat up for about an hour longer, and watched by the couch of Lady Ravensford, when finding that Rosabelle slept soundly, and from the stillness which reigned in the house, that Adder and the others had gone to their separate chambers, she saw to the security of the door, and then retired to her own bed, which was placed in the same apartment as that of our heroine.

Adder having learned that Lady Ravensford was so much better, felt more contented, and determined not to press his suit until she had completely recovered her strength, and the result of the adventure of the smugglers was known. He, however, upon more mature reflection, did not feel satisfied to remain at the house any longer than her strength would permit of her removal; for, in spite of what Gordon had said, he could not help imagining that there was more danger in staying there than the ruffian appeared to think; for, even should they not interfere with them, (which it was most probable that they would, knowing that they were associates of the smugglers,) they would discover Rosabelle, and that would be almost certain to lead to her restoration to her friends and to the decided frustration of his hopes. He was, therefore, determined to rejoin Monckton and his companions, as soon as ever the situation of Lady Ravensford would permit.

The smuggler captain, as we have before said, had furnished him with every particular about the place where they had retired to, and he had furthermore promised him, that whenever he made him acquainted with his desire to join them, he would take care for making arrangements for conveying him and his fair charge to them, from the island. Upon this point, therefore, Adder felt perfectly satisfied.

"Well," said Gordon, when he made him acquainted with his resolution in the morning, "you can do as you think proper, of course; but for my part, I shall keep to the determination I at first formed, and remain here, let whatever may be the consequences. It will not be such as this said Bill Eldon, that shall triumph over me."

"Well," returned Adder, "of course I do not wish to persuade you, and I have probably more to risk than you have."

"You know not that," replied Gordon. "It can tell you, I have no particular wish to fall into the fangs of the law; for a few unpleasant truths might chance to come out, that would place me in rather an awkward predicament."

"Well, well; with that I have nothing to do," said Adder; "my mind is also made up. If the Lady Ravensford should be seen, all the expense, trouble, care, and anxiety, to which I have been, might be rendered useless, and Rosabelle and her child might be again restored to my detested enemy."

"And for that fear," said Gordon, "I do not see even the most trivial cause."

"Why not?" demanded Adder.

"For one very good reason," returned Desborough; "because, before they could gain admittance to the house, as I have told you before, we could make our retreat by the vaults, and underground passages."

"But Bill Eldon, I repeat," said Adder, "being as well acquainted with them as yourself, would be sure to apprise them of them; and the means you speak of would thus be rendered futile."

"Well, I see that nothing will serve to quiet your apprehensions," remarked Gordon, carelessly, "so e'en take your own course, and I wish you success in it."

"I am satisfied that it will be the most secure," said Adder; "and, therefore, if they do not come down upon us before, as soon as the strength of Lady Rosabelle will admit of her being removed, I shall adopt it."

"Then you had better send word to Monckton, informing him of your resolution, without delay, so that he may make the necessary arrangements for the accomplishment of it," said Gordon.

"I thank you for the suggestion," said Adder, "and will immediately attend to it."

"Monckton will run some risk in aiding you," observed Gordon, "and you ought to feel much indebted to him for it."

"I dare say he will not go unrewarded," said Adder; "I believe that you have had pretty substantial proof before now that I am not unmindful of any services that are rendered me."

"Why, that is true," replied Gordon, "and I did not mean to insinuate that you were not."

"You, at any rate, have had no reason."

"I did not say that I had. But enough of this; I did not mean to offend you. I only wish I could persuade you to remain where you are; it would save you a great deal of trouble and expense too, and I do not believe that it would be fraught with the least danger."

"No; I should be in a state of doubt, fear, and suspense all the time," said Adder.

"Well, you know best," returned Gordon Desborough; "and, of course, neither I nor anybody else has any right to dictate to you. I only know this, and mind what I say—you will be glad to return here again by-and-by."

"Probably I may," answered Adder, "but it must be when I am perfectly satisfied that all the danger is past."

"That of course," said Gordon Desborough;

"but I must say that you have had trouble enough for this fair one, and, whether you have won her or not, at any rate ought to wear her. You have acted, too, according to my thinking, rather a wild and imprudent part towards her, and you must possess an abundant share of patience, or you could not have done so."

"What do you mean?"

"Why, when the prize was in your hands," replied Gordon, "to let it remain idle so long upon some niceties and notions that nobody understands but yourself."

"Upon that point we have argued before," said Adder, "and as we could not agree upon

THE ATTACK ON THE SMUGGLERS' RETREAT.

it, I think it is quite useless for us to converse upon it now."

"Oh, very well," said Gordon Desborough, with a half satirical smile; "that is only my simple opinion; but I hope no offence. Time will show which of us is correct."

"True," coincided Adder, "and till then, say no more about it. Who comes here? Some one is ascending the steps that lead to the trap-door."

Gordon, who also heard the footsteps, but did not feel any alarm, as the person, whoever it was, could not raise the trap unless some one assisted him from above, stooped down to the secret trap, which, to a person unacquainted with the secret, was imperceptible in the boards, and demanded who was there.

"Why it is I, to be sure," replied a gruff voice; "who the devil do you think it is?"

"Oh," said Gordon — "Davey. Davey Grampus, is that you?"

"To be sure it is," answered Grampus; "and pray how much longer are you going to keep me here under hatches?"

"Not a minute," answered Gordon; and, touching the secret spring, with the assistance of the person underneath, he raised the trap, and the head of Davey Grampus, surmounted as usual with a woollen cap, and his jaws embellished with a short pipe, protruded from the aperture.

"What the devil were you afraid of?" asked Davey, unceremoniously taking his seat in the chimney-corner, and emitting dense clouds of smoke from his pipe and mouth; "you kept me long enough."

"Why," answered Gordon, "you know, Davey, since this affair of Bill Eldon's, it makes one cautious; and how was I to know, until I heard your voice, whether you were friend or foe?"

"Bah!" ejaculated Grampus; "I wonder that Monckton should be so qualmish; for my own part, I do not see any cause for such apprehension."

"So I say, Davey," returned Desborough; "and that's the very thing I have been endeavouring to persuade Mr. Adder here to."

"Why, your honour," said Grampus, "you are not so foolish as to entertain any alarm, are you?"

"I think there is very good reason to be so," answered Adder; "and it is always best to be cautious."

"Why, yes," replied Davey, emitting an extra cloud of smoke, like that coming from the small funnel of a steam-packet, "I agree with your honour that it is always best to be cautious, but I am not of the same opinion, namely, that there is much to fear in this case, if anything."

"But why should you think so?" demanded Adder; "is not the quarrel between Eldon and the captain, and the sudden disappearance of the former, quite sufficient to excite suspicion?"

"It may be, in some persons' opinion," answered Davey Grampus, "but it is not, in mine, because, yer see, I happen to know a little more about these matters. As for Eldon, I think he is a different sort of a fellow to do anything of the kind, notwithstanding he has had a quarrel with Monckton."

"And so do I, Davey," coincided Gordon Desborough, "but, you see, Mr. Adder is of a different opinion, and is fearful if he remains here, he will get into a mess, and lose his lady and all, into the bargain."

"Pshaw!" ejaculated Grampus, "and a very foolish idea too, and I do not mind making bold to tell his honour so, too. Why, she could not be safer than she would be here, for you could convey her privately by the secret passages to my place, and catch them meddling with old Davey Grampus! Ha! ha! They would have all the inhabitants of the place about their ears."

"That is just the very thing that I have been endeavouring to persuade Mr. Adder to," remarked Gordon.

"And very proper too," said Grampus; "but I suppose the gentleman could not be satisfied upon that point?"

"True."

"Well, then, I am sorry for him to think he should give himself so much unnecessary trouble," observed Davey Grampus; "and where does your honour intend to go with the lady?"

"Why," answered Adder, "it is my intention to join Monckton, and his companions, where they have gone to."

"Plague take their fears," ejaculated Grampus; "now they have gone, I am not only deprived of companions, but something more substantial."

"Never mind, Davey," said Gordon, "take my word for it, it will not be for long."

"There I believe you are right, Gordon," said Grampus, "they will not easily find a place where they are so secure as they are here, and they will soon return; and then if Mr. Adder comes back with them, see what a deal of trouble and expense he will have put himself to, which he might have avoided if he had remained here."

"Oh, as for the expense, I care nothing," said Adder; "any expense would be better than running the risk of losing that which has cost me so much pains and ingenuity to obtain."

"Well," returned Grampus, "that your honour knows best about; but I know this, if I was situated as you are, it would not be all the land-sharks in the world that should frighten me to budge an inch. I tell you, under the protection of old Davey Grampus, you are as safe as if you were in a palace. There is not a man, woman, or boy in this neighbourhood but what knows me, and who would not be ready to rush out to my assistance if I needed them. Monckton knew that very well, and I wonder, therefore, that he is so easily alarmed, for what with his own men, and those persons I have mentioned, we might bid defiance to all the force they could send against us. He was not wont to be so qualmish, and I don't know what has come to him."

"He was not," said Gordon, "and I am no less surprised than yourself; but perhaps he has more reasons for his conduct than he has thought proper to make us acquainted with, you know."

"Why, there may be something in that," coincided Grampus; "but we shall soon have him amongst us again."

"If the landsharks do not steal a march upon him, where he has gone to," added Gordon.

"Ay, ay, there are more unlikely things than that," observed Davey; "but I do not think that Bill Eldon will be the cause of it."

"Neither do I."

"The fact is," continued Grampus, "it is my opinion that Bill Eldon has long been tired of the life of a smuggler, and has only been waiting for an opportunity decently to escape from it. This quarrel with Monckton has formed a sufficient excuse; but, as for betraying the captain, and his former companions, I do not think he had ever any idea of it."

"To be sure he had not," returned Grampus, "and no one shall ever make me believe to the contrary. But we shall soon see who is correct in his surmises."

"Yes, we shall," observed Gordon; "but if it does not turn out as you say, I will forfeit my life."

"You may venture to say that, with safety," said Davey Grampus, "it is very seldom that I am wrong, especially in matters of this kind. But as for Mr. Adder, he will think better of his resolution, I should imagine, and remain where he is perfectly safe, I will undertake to answer for."

"He cannot put his intention into execution yet," observed Gordon, "for the lady's health is in that condition that it will not permit her to be removed."

"Well, then, if he can venture to remain here for a day or two, he may contentedly stop altogether, for the Philistines will be down upon us soon, or not at all."

"We shall see what happens in the meantime," said Adder; "but I must still be of the same opinion, as regards the danger of remaining here, and shall be uneasy until I am able to remove."

"What useless fears," said Grampus in a tone of impatience.

"Completely!" coincided Gordon.

"His honour has never yet seen the underground apartments, and the secret communication to my 'Caboose,' has he?" inquired Grampus.

"He has not," answered Gordon.

"We had better show them to him," continued Grampus, "and I think it is not at all unlikely that he will then alter his opinion. Perhaps, sir, you will accompany me and Desborough to my house, and you will not regret the time spent."

"But Lady Ravensford," observed Adder, "it would not be prudent to leave her and the two females in the house by themselves."

"Oh, fear not," answered Grampus; "they will be safe enough; but should any danger threaten, old Cicely knows the secret of the trap as well as we do, and would soon be able to communicate with us."

"She would," said Gordon, "but for my part, I do not see that there is the slightest cause for fear."

"You appear to treat the matter very lightly, both of you; but I cannot do so," said Adder; "however, I will venture to comply with the wish of Grampus, after I have made inquiries after Lady Ravensford."

Adder now quitted Grampus and Desborough, who laughed at his fears, and made his way up-stairs to the chamber-door of Rosabelle. at which he gently knocked, and, upon Mrs. Kitson opening it, he inquired eagerly after the health of her patient.

Mrs. Kitson, who was fearful that, if she gave too favourable an answer, Adder would again want to have an interview with Lady Ravensford, was guilty of telling a falsehood, and informed him that Rosabelle had past an indifferent night, and was not quite so well as she had been the evening before. Adder was very much agitated to hear this; and his alarm lest he should not be able to remove her before the officers should arrive at the house, increased. Telling Mrs. Kitson to take every care of her, he descended to the parlour below, in which Davey Grampus and Gordon Desborough were waiting for him; and, after giving old Cicely strict injunctions to apprize them immediately, should she see any cause for apprehension, he prepared to accompany his two companions on their subterranean journey.

Gordon and Grampus raised the trap, and having first lighted a dark lanthorn, they prepared to descend the steps, desiring Adder to follow them. He did so, and with much caution began to descend the steps, Gordon telling him to close the trap, which he let fall heavily after him, and it closed securely with a spring, no one being able to open it from the outside, unless the persons inside thought proper.

It was very dark and gloomy; the stairs were remarkably steep, and Adder not being able to ascertain the depth, from the faint light Gordon Desborough carried, stepped with the utmost caution.

At length they reached the bottom, and looking up, Adder beheld that they were in a long narrow passage, dug out of the earth, and securely bricked. Along this they proceeded, and, at the extremity of it, they turned to the right into another, much lower, and not of such a length. Having reached the end of this, they came to another flight of steps, which they descended, and then found themselves in a wide open space, paved with stone. From this place to the right and left, vaults of extensive dimensions branched off, and in which the smugglers deposited their booty. These were all secured with strong iron-barred doors, keys to the locks of which Gordon Desborough and Davey Grampus possessed.

These vaults his companions particularly pointed out to his notice, and he was surprised at their extent and construction. They then passed through the range to the right, many of them being fitted up in a manner approaching to comfort, and at length entered upon another long and lofty passage, the arch rising as they proceeded, until suddenly Adder was startled by a strong flood of light, which streamed in from an aperture or chasm in the wall.

"This passage goes through one of the locks," said Davey Grampus, noticing his astonishment, " in which that is a small opening."

Adder listened, and was soon convinced of the truth of what Grampus said, for he could hear the roar of the waves that washed its base.

" Certainly," said he, " this is a remarkable place, and could not have been excavated by human hands."

" In that I agree with you," observed Grampus, " although human hands have done much towards it."

" And are these places exactly in the state in which you found them, when you first became acquainted with them?" interrogated Adder, of Davey and Gordon.

" Exactly," answered the former; " they are very old, and so is my house, and the house in which Gordon resides."

" I cannot conceive the use to which they have been formerly put," said Adder.

" Nor I," replied Grampus; " but that is of very little consequence; they have done Monckton good service, and he ought never to have removed his booty from them. It could not have been more safe than it was here. What say you, Gordon?"

" Why," answered Desborough, " you know, Davey, that, upon that point, you and I agree. I disapprove of the manner in which he has acted altogether."

" And so do I," said Grampus; " and it strikes me that Monckton himself regrets, by this time, having been so hasty."

" He is so confoundedly obstinate and determined, when he takes anything into his head," said Gordon.

" Yes, he is," observed Grampus; " and nothing could persuade him to alter his resolution. However, he will find that there is no place like his old quarters, after all."

" That you may depend upon it he will," coincided Gordon; " but come, we are delaying, and I can see that Mr. Adder is becoming impatient."

" It is very cold here," said the latter, " and these subterranean vaults are none of the most cheerful or agreeable places."

" They have been worth a palace to me and Monckton," said Grampus.

" I have no doubt they have," observed Adder.

They now again proceeded on their way, Adder closely following Grampus and Gordon, for the light in the lanthorn only threw a faint ray across their path, and he was afraid of stumbling, not knowing what there might be in the way to impede his progress.

The passage led them into a low arched vault, in which was an iron door, which Grampus unlocked, from a large bunch of keys, and they then found another flight of steps, which ascended to a landing above, but so low that they could with difficulty stand upright.

Grampus and Gordon placed their hands above their heads, and appeared to be pressing against something in the boarding over them with all their might.

Adder was not long kept in suspense, for at length a large portion of the boards gave way, and revealed to him the little back room in which the smugglers had been accustomed to hold their meetings and carousals. Grampus and Gordon leaped up into the room above with much agility, and let down a ladder to Adder, for him to ascend by. Having done so, the trap was immediately let down again, and not the least signs of it could be traced from the rest of the boarding.

Adder was really astonished at what he had seen, and could not have imagined that there were such places underground, had he not had occular demonstration; and he certainly could not help thinking that Monckton had acted by no means prudently, in having removed the property from such a place of unquestionable security.

" Well," said Grampus, when Adder had taken a seat, " what do you think of what you have seen?"

" I am astonished," answered Adder.

" I thought you would be," said Grampus; " now, do you think Monckton could have a more secure or compact retreat?"

" I do not."

" He will not find such another," remarked Gordon, " let him search the country through, I know."

" I am certain he cannot," returned Grampus; then turning to Adder, he continued,— " Now, sir, after we have shown you all these secret places, and the ready means that are provided for eluding danger, what do you think of the apprehensions you have so strongly expressed? Do you not waver in your determination?"

' No," replied Adder; " I must still be of the same opinion as I was before."

" And you are yet resolved to join Monckton and the others, as soon as circumstances will permit you?" interrogated Desborough.

" I am," answered Adder; " and I cannot get rid of the impression that it is the safest plan."

" Well, I cannot conceive how you can think so," said Davey Grampus, lighting his pipe; " but of course, the business has nothing to do with either me or Gordon, and I only hope that you may not have any cause to repent of your determination."

" I hope so to," said Gordon, " but I cannot see that there would be any more danger in remaining here, than in venturing to rejoin the captain."

" That is your opinion: but I have my own," said Adder, impatiently.

" Undoubtedly," retorted Gordon; " and I

have no right to interfere with it. But I must make bold enough to say, that I think you will ultimately find that it is a very foolish one."

"You do not flatter me."

"I never learnt the art."

"But should any inquiries be made here, after I am gone, about me or Lady Ravensford, may I depend upon your secrecy, and that of Grampus?"

"Why do you ask the question?" demanded Gordon; "have I ever given you cause to doubt me?"

"Or I?" demanded Grampus;—"no, no—leave Davey alone. Though a person's opinion and mine may not agree, when I have once given them my word to keep a secret, I will do so inviolable. No, you need not apprehend any danger from me, your honour; and I am certain I can say the same of Gordon."

"Ay, that you may, and safely too, Davey," remarked Gordon; "but I am surprised that Mr. Adder should have made use of such an observation."

"Well, well," replied Adder; "I said it unthinkingly, so I hope that you and Grampus will excuse me. The peculiar circumstances under which I am placed, will be sufficient to apologise for me. But it is useless to talk to me further upon the subject, as my mind is entirely made up."

"Well, as it is so," said Grampus, "it is, as you say, no use our endeavouring to dissuade you from your purpose; and you have an undoubted right to do as you think proper. But we only did so from good motives, and from an impression that we were advising you for the best."

"I am certain of that," replied Adder, "and I am much obliged to you both for the trouble and interest you have taken in the affair. Let us have a friendly glass or two, Davey, for we must shortly separate, although I do not know how long it may be for."

"And do you think of returning hither?" asked Grampus.

"When Monckton thinks it is safe to do so, I shall undoubtedly," replied Adder; "unless something happens in the meantime to render such a plan imprudent."

"Ay, this is the place, after all, your honour," said Grampus; "and so you will find, or I am much mistaken."

"Yes," added Gordon Desborough, "and take my word for it, that the time will soon come, when Monckton, Mr. Adder, and all our associates will be seated here again together, carousing; and they will then be ready to admit, or else I am much mistaken, how groundless were their apprehensions."

"I shall be very happy if your surmises prove correct," said Adder; "and will not mind standing a handsome supper on the occasion."

"Then I have not the least doubt but that

we shall have to tax your liberality," said Gordon. "But come, Davey, fetch the grog! Some of the right sort. But I have no occasion to tell you."

"Of course you have not," returned Grampus; "Davey Grampus never does keep anything but the right sort in his casks."

Thus speaking, Davey Grampus hastened away to fetch the grog, and was not long before he returned, with a good stiff jorum, of which himself and Gordon were very eager to partake; but Adder felt too uneasy about Rosabelle to partake of it with any pleasure, neither could he join in the conversation which was passing between Gordon and Grampus, and which was of anything but an interesting description to him; and he, therefore, made an excuse to get away and return to the house as soon as he possibly could, fearful that something of an unpleasant nature might happen during his absence.

"Will you not stay till I return?" asked Gordon.

"No," replied Adder, "I would much rather be at home."

"More fears," exclaimed Gordon, with a half laugh of derision; "trust me, Mr. Adder, in spite of all your apprehensions, you will find the lady safe enough when you return, or my name is not Gordon Desborough. This is all through that terrible fellow, Bill Eldon."

Adder frowned at the boldness of Gordon, and bit his lips, but he said nothing; and after the lapse of another quarter of an hour, he arose from his seat to go. He did not intend to return by the secret way, which he could not have done, indeed, without a conductor, and, therefore, bidding Grampus good day, and desiring Gordon not to be late home, he quitted the house.

He revolved in his mind, as he proceeded, all that he had seen, and all that Gordon and Grampus had said to dissuade him from his purpose; but he saw nothing to shake his resolution, or remove the apprehensions he entertained. He felt very uneasy to think that Rosabelle was worse than she had been on the previous evening, for every hour of delay was, in his opinion, fraught with danger; and such was his eagerness to remove her from the house of Gordon, that he could not rest, night or day, until he should have it in his power to do so.

He was not long in reaching the house, and was much relieved when he found that all was safe, and that nothing had occurred during his absence. He once more anxiously inquired after the health of Rosabelle, and received an answer from Mrs. Kitson, that "she was much the same," which, as may be expected, did not tend in the least to abate his uneasiness. He had, however, made up his mind, and that was, to write immediately to Monckton, to inform him of his wish to join him as soon as possible; and he was determined, in spite of the consequences that might follow, to convey Lady Ravensford on shipboard, and bear her away. He did not see so much danger in this resolution as he had done at first, and his mind was now firmly made up to take the chance of the result.

The first thing he did after he had returned home, was to write the letter to Monckton, which he forwarded in the way he had directed him; and that done, he felt somewhat more at ease. He then set about making the necessary arrangements for their departure, so that they might be in readiness at a moment's notice, and he had entirely completed them before the evening set in.

He was most anxious for an interview with Lady Ravensford; but of course he knew, in her present situation, that was impossible, and it would be almost indelicate in him to urge it.

Although he would not appear to be of that opinion before Gordon, Monckton, and the others who had rallied him upon the subject, he now was convinced that he had acted very foolishly in not having at once forced Rosabelle to a compliance with his nefarious designs, instead of waiting for that which was preposterous in the very idea; and there were moments when he feared that he had suffered the opportunity, which he had hazarded so much to obtain, to slip by, and that something would occur to remove our heroine from his power, and to restore her to her friends; and thus he would be laughed at for an idiot by all those who were acquainted with the circumstances, and would ever have occasion to reproach himself for having been that egregious fools as to suffer his schemes to be frustrated, when he had every means of accomplishing them without the least fear of interruption or discovery. He would, in fact, have duped himself as much as he had done Lord Saunter, upon whom he now seldom, if ever, condescended a thought. He was, however, determined, if he escaped the danger that threatened him, and Lady Ravensford recovered from her illness, not to suffer any more such foolish ideas to withhold him from his purpose, but to complete his designs on Rosabelle, even though his own life should the next moment have to pay the penalty of his doing so. Having formed these villanous resolutions, the miscreant Adder became more contented.

Wishing to make Mrs. Kitson acquainted with his intentions, in order that she might be in a condition to prepare Lady Ravensford for the change in her situation, which she was shortly to undergo, he sent for her, and that good woman shortly attended, wondering what it was that Adder could want with her, but fully prepared to answer him, let it be whatever it might.

"Be seated, Mrs. Kitson," he said, on her entrance. Mrs. Kitson took a chair, and did as he desired her.

"I wish to speak to you, Mrs. Kitson," he continued, "upon one or two things of importance."

"Very well, sir," said the woman, "I attend your pleasure, and am ready to hear you."

"In the first place, what is the exact state of your patient's health?"

"Why do you ask the question, sir?"

"Why, you must be aware how anxious I must be to know."

"I informed you not half an hour since," returned Mrs. Kitson, "and why, therefore, should you again ask the question? You seem to doubt my word."

"No, no," hastily ejaculated Adder, "do not misunderstand me; I do not doubt your word, but I have particular reasons for desiring you earnestly to answer me without equivocation."

"I am not in the habit of equivocating, sir," retorted Mrs. Kitson, seriously; "those who really are, are the more apt to suspect it in others."

"There, now, Mrs. Kitson," observed Adder, in an insinuating tone, "I am surprised at you; you will not still understand me right. I meant not to offend you. I only wish to know whether Lady Ravensford is in such a condition as to render it likely that she will be compelled to keep herself confined to her bed long?"

"I cannot say," answered Mrs. Kitson; "she is at present in a very weak condition."

"And you think that it would be attended with danger to attempt to remove her?" interrogated Adder.

"To attempt to remove her?" repeated Mrs. Kitson, in a tone of surprise—"bless my soul! Poor lady—why her immediate death must follow!"

"D——n!" growled Adder, between his teeth; and he hastily arose, and paced the room backwards and forwards in a state of the most violent agitation. Mrs. Kitson remarked him with some astonishment, but partly guessed what he was going to talk to her about, and was prepared to answer him.

"Mrs. Kitson," he at length said, "I have made you acquainted with all the particulars of the situation in which we are now placed; the cause of Monckton and his associates' hasty retreat, and the danger which threatens us while we remain here."

"You have, sir,"

"I cannot rest a minute while we remain in this house," said Adder; "I shall not be easy until we have joined Monckton and the others at the place where they have gone to."

"But dear me, sir," said Mrs. Kitson, "you cannot think of removing Lady Ravensford while she is in her present condition?"

"I have just written off to Monckton to inform him of my resolution," said Adder, "and it must be so."

"Why, poor dear lady, it will be the death of her."

"Nonsense!" replied Adder, "it will not be so bad as you apprehend. Besides, we shall only have to remove her from hence to the sea-beach, where a vessel will be waiting for us, and once on ship-board, she will suffer no more than as if she were in her own chamber here."

"Oh, sir," said Mrs. Kitson, "you can little imagine the weak state the poor dear lady is in, or you would not say so."

"You are mistaken, Mrs. Kitson," answered Adder; "I can fully appreciate what Lady Ravensford suffers, and regret that necessity compels me to adopt such a course; but it cannot be avoided. If we remain here, she would, in all probability, be discoverd, and thus all the plans I have formed would be crushed, and the trouble I have been at, will have been thrown away."

"Oh, sir," said Mrs. Kitson, "and why, if you really pity her, as you say you do, why not repent and restore her to liberty, to her friends? —Surely it is most brutal to detain the mother and child from ——"

"Silence, woman!" fiercely interrupted Adder; "you are becoming too bold to speak to me upon such a subject. My will is my own, and I will not have it questioned. I tell you, Lady Ravensford must be removed from this place, and that before three days have elapsed."

"But, really, sir," said Mrs. Kitson, in a different tone of voice; "really, I do not see that you have any cause to fear."

"There, there," impatiently ejaculated Adder, "I have had enough of that. Grampus and Gordon have been endeavouring to persuade me to that, but I have my own opinion, and nothing can alter it; but I will act accordingly."

"But it is now two days since Monckton and the other smugglers departed," observed Mrs. Kitson, "and nothing has happened to create our alarm, and if we remain here three days longer, and we still receive no interruption, what, then, shall we have to fear?"

"It matters not," said Adder, who was deaf to all reason upon the subject; "I have formed my own plans, and they must be put into execution."

"If it be your will and determination," said Mrs. Kitson, "of course it is no use in arguing with you, or endeavouring to dissuade you from it. But I am fearful that the poor lady will never be able to survive the exertion of being removed."

"Pshaw!" ejaculated Adder; "you think too seriously upon this subject. Lady Ravensford is only suffering from excitement, at the sudden restoration of her child, and a few hours will probably restore her to strength."

"I wish your surmises might prove correct, sir," said Mrs. Kitson, "though much I fear there is but little chance of their doing so. I wish that any persuasion of mine might urge you, out of pity to the poor lady, to alter your resolution."

"I have before said it is useless your endeavouring to do so," replied Adder; "for my mind is made up, and when once my resolution is formed, nothing can alter it."

"Poor Lady Ravensford, she will be shocked when she hears it," said Mrs. Kitson.

"You must break it to her in the best manner you can," observed Adder,—"and endeavour to induce her to prepare for the removal; assuring her that every comfort and attendance that can be procured, she and her child shall receive."

"I much fear that all I can say will be of little avail," said Mrs. Kitson, in reply; "but I will do my best."

"That is all I require of you," said Adder; "and if you do that, I shall be satisfied. Of course, you will be her companion."

"And Gordon and Cicely?" interrogated Mrs. Kitson.

"They will remain here; but if they did not, you would have nothing to apprehend from them; they would not dare to insult you or Lady Ravensford, when they know that you are acting by my orders. Now, hasten to your patient, who will, perhaps, be surprised and uneasy at the length of your absence, and be sure that you bear in mind what I have told you."

Mrs. Kitson merely nodded her head, and quitting the room, hastened to the apartment of Lady Ravensford, to make her acquainted with what had just transpired at her interview with her cruel oppressor.

Adder, notwithstanding all that Mrs. Kitson had said, was determined to put his designs into execution, and he was half inclined to believe that she exaggerated in her account of the state of our heroine's health, for the purpose of inducing him to abandon his resolution not to remain at the house of Gordon Desborough, or in the neighbourhood; and in that imagination, as, no doubt, the reader has suspected, he was decidedly correct. Lady Ravensford was, in fact, able to sit up, and felt but little from the effects of the late excitement she had experienced. Happy in the society of her darling child, whose innocent prattle now began to amuse her, and temporarily released from the hateful and dreaded presence of Adder, and the scarcely less to be dreaded society of old Cicely, she felt more tranquil than she had done for some time before, more especially as in Mrs. Kitson she had now one who could kindly sympathise in her sufferings, and who exerted herself to the utmost to alleviate the violence of them.

Rosabelle felt surprised, and rather uneasy, when the message from Adder came, demanding Mrs. Kitson to attend him, and she awaited with much impatience and anxiety her return. The time appeared to be double the length that she was absent from her, and she paced her chamber, frequently going to the room-door and listening, with the greatest uneasiness.

At length Mrs. Kitson did make her appearance, and it needed no one to inform her, from the expression in her countenance, that she had been compelled to listen to something of a most unpleasant nature during her absence.

The maternal fears of Lady Ravensford at first suggested to her that Adder had come to the determination of depriving her again of the little Alfred, and that he had sent for Mrs. Kitson for the purpose of informing her of his intention; but if it should indeed be as she apprehended, she was resolved to lose her own life rather than part with her offspring.

Mrs. Kitson, however, soon put her out of her suspense, and detailed to her the whole papticulars of the interview, exactly as they had taken place.

Lady Ravensford did not evince so much agitation as Mrs. Kitson had feared she would have done. She listened attentively to her, and when she had concluded, she said—

The villain entertains the same ideas that we do, it is evident; he imagines that if we were to remain here, and the officers should by any chance visit the place, that if they did not or could not release me then, they would make known my situation to my friends, and that his plans would be rendered abortive."

"From the observations which he made to me," answered Mrs. Kitson, "that is precisely what I think is his opinion."

"And he said that my child should remain with me?" eagerly interrogated Rosabelle.

"He did," replied Mrs. Kitson.

"And that you should attend me?"

Mrs. Kitson replied in the affirmative.

"Then," exclaimed Lady Ravensford, firmly, "I do not care for the change. Where we are going to, the same Providence will watch over and protect me and my poor boy, and when we least expect it, bring about my restoration to my friends."

"True, my lady," said Mrs. Kitson; "and I am happy to see that you do not give yourself up entirely to despair."

"Despair?—no!" cried Rosabelle, energetically, "I will not despair. The Almighty has already been very good to me in protecting me from falling a victim to the sinful desires of my cruel persecutor, and while I put my trust in Him, He will not desert me. I will, with fortitude, resign myself to the will of fate."

Mrs Kitson could not help gazing upon our heroine (as she raised her hands and eyes piously and solemnly towards Heaven) with the most fervent admiration, and for a moment or two she remained silent.

"Most happy, my lady," she said at last, "most happy am I to find you in such a state of mind. But, thinking to dissuade Adder from his purpose, I represented you to be much worse than you are; and told him that I was fearful that your removal in your present condition would be attended with the most serious consequences."

"You acted for the best, Mrs. Kitson, I know," said our heroine, "and I am obliged to you for it. But when you speak to him again, do not misrepresent the case. I would rather the truth be spoken, let the result be whatever it may."

"I will attend to what you request, my lady," said Mrs Kitson; "but I am sure you will do me the justice to believe that I acted in the way that I have told you I did from the purest motives, only?"

"I have already assured you of that, my dear Mrs. Kitson," said Lady Ravensford: "and I am sure I should indeed be doing you an injustice did I believe that you could act otherwise—especially towards me—after what I have already experienced."

"Your ladyship, I fear, entertains too high an opinion of me," said Mrs. Kitson.

"Oh, no, I am confident I do not," returned our heroine; "but when did you say that Adder informed you I must prepare for my removal?"

"In three days, at the latest, my lady," answered her attendant.

"It is well," said Rosabelle, "I shall be fully prepared for it; for something seems to tell me that the change will be productive of some benefit to me."

"Heaven send that your hopes may be realised, madam!" said Mrs. Kitson, in a tone which bespoke her sincerity.

"Besides, in the interim, something may occur to prevent the resolution of Adder from being put into execution," added our heroine, "and to release me from his power."

"True, my lady," answered Mrs. Kitson: "for instance, the officers might come down to the house, in which case I have not the least doubt but that you would be released, and Adder delivered into the hands of justice."

"The villain!—richly does he merit the severest punishment," said Rosabelle, "for the unparalleled and systematic cruelty of which he has been guilty towards me and my unfortunate family."

"He does, indeed, my lady," coincided Mrs. Kitson. "I never heard of such a miscreant, and it seems almost incredible that any human being should have the base mind to invent, or the cruelty to execute, such a villanous plot. But he certainly will not escape the vengeance of Heaven !"

"He cannot—he cannot," energetically cried our heroine; "and already do I believe the wrath of the Almighty is impending over his head. At any rate, I do firmly believe that his career is nearly at a close."

"Sincerely do I hope that it may be as you premise, my lady," observed her companion; "and I am happy to think that you can look upon the removal with resignation."

"Why, as for that, Mrs. Kitson," observed Lady Ravensford, "it matters little whither I am taken while I remain in the power of my bitter enemy, and I cannot be worse treated than I am here."

"Adder, no doubt, will behave to you better than he has done, madam," observed Mrs. Kitson, "for fear that you should suffer a relapse of the illness you are recovering from. In fact, he told me to assure you that every comfort that you could wish for, for yourself and child, you should receive."

"I am satisfied," said Lady Ravensford, and here the conversation dropped; and our heroine, feeling rather exhausted from remaining up too long in her present weak state, retired to her couch for awhile, to rest herself,

THE FLIGHT FROM THE SMUGGLERS' RETREAT.

while Mrs. Kitson busied herself about in making such arrangements for their departure as Rosabelle had instructed her in doing.

Adder, in the course of the afternoon, again made inquiries after the health of our heroine, and was most agreeably surprised to be informed that she was again better, and appeared likely to continue so.

"The change," said he, looking ironically at Mrs. Kitson, "is most marvellously sudden, is it not?"

Mrs. Kitson exhibited some confusion, and returned no answer.

"Well," continued Adder, "I am very glad to hear that Lady Ravensford is so much better, and, therefore, if she continues so, there can be no doubt of our being able to depart at the time I have fixed upon."

Mrs. Kitson replied in the affirmative, and then quitted the parlour, and returned to the chamber of our heroine.

Adder was indeed pleased to hear that Rosabelle was so much better, as it would prevent any fear of danger from the removal; and his apprehensions were almost at an end, unless anything should occur in the interim.

Gordon Desborough did not return until late in the evening, but he then forbore to converse with Adder further upon the subject of his departure, as he had tried all his force of argument without any success, and he knew it would be useless to say any more upon the subject. Adder was too much immersed in his own thoughts, too, to feel inclined to enter into conversation, and he retired to his chamber at an early hour.

The following day, Adder expected an answer from Monckton to his letter, and he was not disappointed, for towards the evening one was brought him, in which the smuggler-captain hastily informed him of his having arrived safe at the place where he had destined to conceal himself and his men for a while, and that they had not hitherto met with anything to excite their suspicions. He expressed some surprise that they had heard nothing, and received no interruption from where they were staying, but at the same time gave it as his opinion that Bill Eldon was only delaying it for a few days, the better to forward his plans, and by lulling them into fancied security, render the gratification of his revenge, and the success of the officers, the more certain and complete. He applauded the resolution of Adder, and bade him be ready before daylight in the morning, when a boat would be ready on the beach to take him and the lady to the vessel which he would send to convey them away.

Adder was very well satisfied with the prompt manner in which Monckton had answered his note, and also with all the arrangements he had made, and as his prepara-tions, which were few, were ready, he had nothing to do but to order Mrs. Kitson to tell Rosabelle to hold herself in readiness to depart the following morning. This, he was glad to hear, she was ready to do, as she was much better; and thus, everything appearing to go favourable to his wishes, the villain was more at ease than he had been ever since he had heard of the suspected impeachment of Bill Eldon, and when he was once away from the house of Gordon Desborough, would consider himself in perfect security.

CHAPTER XXVIII.

THE VOYAGE.—THE SMUGGLERS ATTACKED. THE BATTLE.—THE ESCAPE.

So elate were the hopes of our heroine that something would result from the change in her situation to restore her to liberty, that she looked forward to the following morning with a feeling of impatience; and Mrs. Kitson, who was naturally anxious to behold her husband, was glad to see her so composed, and did not attempt to discourage her in the hopes she had formed; in fact, so far from having any wish to do so, she largely shared in the ideas herself, and was not sorry for the change which was about to take place, and for being about to be removed from a house, beneath the roof of which dwelt such a wretch as Gordon Des-borough, whom the account which Lady Ravensford had given of him, made her

look upon him with the most inconceivable terror and dread.

Lady Rosabelle's preparations were soon made, and before she and Mrs. Kitson retired to rest that night, they had everything in readiness. Knowing how soon they would have to rise in the morning, they retired to rest at an early hour, and Rosabelle, having felt in better spirits than she had done for some time before, soon sunk off to repose, and slept soundly, no alarming dreams flitting before her imagination to disturb her.

Long before daylight the following morning, they were awakened by a loud knocking at the ante-room door, and they immediately started up in bed, and inquired who was there?

It was Adder, who requested them imme-diately so prepare to hasten to the boat which was waiting to receive them, as it was past three o'clock, and they had no time to lose.

Mrs. Kitson, by the direction of Lady Ravensford, informed him that they would be ready to attend him in a few minutes, and he once more hastened below.

Our heroine and her companion were not long in dressing themselves and the child, (who seemed greatly amused by all the proceedings, and several times asked his mother where they were going,) and then Mrs. Kitson having waited until Rosabelle had fervently invoked the protection of Heaven, unfastened the room-door, and they descended the stairs.

It was some time since Lady Ravensford had quitted her chamber, indeed, never since the time when she attempted, and was so near making her escape from the house altogether, and her heart beat quick with hope and expec-tation.

They found Adder and Gordon Desborough awaiting them in the parlour. The former ad-vanced towards our heroine, and would have spoken, but she repulsed him with a look of the deepest hatred and reproach; and, abashed, he turned away, and addressing himself to Gordon, said,—

"Well, Gordon, have you made up your mind to accompany us to the beach?"

"To be sure I have," answered the ruffian; "did I not tell you so?"

"Well, then, let us be going," said Adder, "for I dare say the men are already tired of waiting for us."

"I am ready to attend you," said Gordon, and Adder, once more venturing to turn to Lady Ravensford, had the audacity to offer her his arm, but she rejected it with a look of the most ineffable disgust, and taking the arm of Mrs. Kitson, who held the little Alfred by the hand, they followed the two villains from the house.

Adder and his companion, however, did not suffer them to walk alone, when they had got into the open air, although there was no danger of their escaping, but kept close by their sides;

and Adder seemed to be in a state of great uneasiness until they reached the beach.

The moon was shining very brilliantly, and Rosabelle gazed upon the broad expanse of the ocean, a short distance from them, and which was perfectly calm. The air revived her, and she felt better from that temporary relief from confinement, as though new life had been instilled into her.

They were not long in gaining the beach, where they found a long boat and a couple of men waiting to receive them.

Rosabelle and Mrs. Kitson, with the child, stepped into the boat without assistance, and then Adder, looking cautiously around them to see that the coast was clear, turned to Gordon Desborough, and said,—

"Well, now, Gordon, we must part; good-by, and remember to keep everything secret."

"Oh, you need not entertain any doubts of me, as I have before told you," answered Gordon; "farewell, and I wish you success; but it will not be long before we shall meet again."

"Probably not," returned Adder; "but it must be when all danger is entirely at an end."

"And it is because I firmly believe that there is not the least danger to apprehend, that I think you are putting yourself to unnecessary trouble," returned Gordon.

"There, there, that is enough," impatiently observed Adder; "you know, upon that point, you and I cannot agree."

"Well, I suppose you know best," replied Gordon: "but every person has a right to enjoy their own opinion. Farewell; good-by, my lady; a pleasant and safe voyage to you."

"Thank you," said Adder, answering for them all, as our heroine and Mrs. Kitson averted their faces in disgust and horror.

The men in the boat having now given expression to their impatience, Adder waved his hand significantly to Gordon, who hurried from the beach, and the boat was then pushed away, and was soon scudding over the deep bosom of the ocean, upon whose surface the moon shone with a silvery light, and added to the beauty and serenity of the scene.

Adder entered into conversation with the men in the boat, not venturing scarcely to look towards our heroine, whose glances, so full of calm dignity and offended virtue, had completely abashed him, and made him feel not only his guilt but his own insignificance.

Each dash of the oars in the water, and which was the means of hastening them further from the shore, added to his easiness, and he eyed the light vessel which was waiting for them in the distance, with welcome and eager looks.

As for Rosabelle, she was perfectly composed, and resigned to her fate, whatever it might be; but she could not help hoping that Providence

had in store for her some speedy amelioration of her sufferings and alteration in her circumstances, and she looked forward to the change in her situation rather with pleasure than otherwise.

Lady Ravensford and Mrs. Kitson did not hold any conversation together while they were in the boat, for they could not do so without the other persons overhearing them, and they both had quite sufficient to occupy their thoughts without.

Soon the boat reached the vessel, and they were received on board by Michael Hernwood, who had been deputed by Monckton to fetch them. Mrs. Kitson there also beheld her husband, which afforded her much pleasure, for his presence was a guarantee for their being secure from any insult which might otherwise have been offered them by the boldness of some of the crew.

They were shown to one of the best cabins, which had been prepared for their reception, and the vessel having weighed anchor, glided quickly over the depth of waters, with a favouring breeze, and all signs of the shore were quickly hidden from the sight.

The voyage was a short one, and the first red glow of the rising sun had only tinged the horizon, when the vessel was run into a small inlet; and they cast anchor off what appeared to be a small island. The vessel was hid from observation by lofty rocks; and the boat being hauled over, Adder and the females were rowed ashore first.

On the beach a man, enveloped in a large mantle, was standing, whose appearance at first alarmed Adder; but the smugglers, by their looks, assured him that he had nothing to fear, and they shortly afterwards landed in safety.

The man in the mantle immediately advanced towards them, and, lifting up his hat, which had been slouched down and concealed his features, they recognised Monckton.

"You have reached here in safety, then," said he. "That is fortunate: follow me."

Lady Rosabelle took the arm of Mrs. Kitson; and Adder, walking by the side of Monckton, accompanied by the smugglers, they followed at a quick pace.

It was not long ere they reached a stone house, of much the same appearance as that of Gordon Desborough's, only much larger, where Monckton approached a low and obscure door, and gave three distinct and peculiar knocks with his knuckles. It was immediately opened by one of the smugglers, and they were all admitted into a parlour, in which was a dense cloud of smoke, proceeding from the extravagant manner in which the different persons there assembled were smoking.

"Apartments have been prepared, as comfortable as circumstances would permit, for the females, up-stairs," said Monckton; "which,

I think, I had better conduct them to at once; and there some refreshment after the voyage will probably be acceptable to them."

Rosabelle and her companion could not help thanking the smuggler captain, by their looks, for his consideration; and being anxious to escape from the presence of Adder and the smugglers, they arose on his making the observation, and, by their manners, showed how ready they were to avail themselves of his suggestion.

Monckton arose from his chair, and, proceeding towards a back door, motioned our heroine and Mrs. Kitson to follow him. They needed no second invitation, and Adder, without speaking, but with significant looks, suffered them to attend him without offering any objection.

Mrs. Kitson led the child by the hand, and Monckton having opened the door, they ascended several flights of stairs, for the building was very lofty and spacious, until at length he stopped at the door of an apartment, which he unlocked, and desired them to enter.

It consisted of a suite of three rooms, opening one into the other, and furnished with a degree of comfort which showed that it had formerly been occupied by very different tenants to the smuggler crew.

There was a cheerful fire blazing in the front room, and, as Monckton had said, it was evident that the apartments had been prepared expressly for their reception.

"I will send you some refreshments speedily," he observed, "and you will then receive no further interruption, but rest yourselves satisfied, for no harm shall come to you here."

As Monckton spoke these words, he withdrew, and fastened the door after him.

He had uttered the last words with an emphasis, and there was something so peculiar in his manner altogether, that it had most forcibly struck Lady Ravensford and Mrs. Kitson, and they sat for some time conversing upon it after he had gone.

In about a quarter of an hour one of the smugglers made his appearance with a plenteous and even delicate repast; and both our heroine and Mrs. Kitson being very hungry, partook of it most heartily.

We will now return to the parlour, in which Monckton, Adder, and the smugglers were assembled.

"Well, Adder," said the former, "you have arrived here in safety."

"Yes," replied Adder, "thanks to your ready compliance with my wishes, and the trouble you have taken, for which I must feel for ever indebted."

"Oh, don't mention that," said the smuggler-captain; "you ought to know that Monckton never promises anything but he is sure to keep his word."

"I do know it, Monckton," replied Adder, "for I have often experienced it, and you know that I am not ungrateful for it."

"Well, what do you think of our present retreat, Adder?" demanded the smuggler-captain; "is it not a snug place, and quite remote from the landsharks?"

"It appears to be so," answered Adder.

"And it is so," added Monckton. "Here I defy the cunning of Bill Eldon or his bull-dogs to find us."

"But do you still think that you have anything to apprehend from him?" interrogated Adder.

"Yes," replied Monckton.

"There has, as I have informed you, nothing occurred to sanction such an idea, at the place from which I have just come," said Adder.

"That may be," returned Monckton; "but, in my opinion, we have none the less to apprehend for that. Bill Eldon is a most crafty fellow, and is only waiting, in all probability, until he imagines that our apprehensions may be quieted, when he can put his treacherous designs into execution with the greatest prospect of security."

"Old Davey Grampus and Gordon Desborough deride such fears altogether," remarked Adder; "and their opinion——"

"I do not value a straw," interrupted Monckton. "I am certain that I have acted with the greatest caution and prudence, whatever they may say. But what think you upon the subject?"

"Why," answered Adder, "there is no necessity for such a question. You may be certain that I think exactly as you do, or I should not have taken the step I have."

"And so, Gordon Desborough remained so strong in his belief that there was no danger, that he would not accompany you?" inquired the smuggler-captain.

Adder answered in the affirmative.

"Then, I consider him an obstinate fool," said Monckton.

"So also do I," returned Adder. "But do you think that, if anything should happen, and the officers should visit his house, and that he and Davey Grampus were to get into trouble, that they may be depended upon? Do you feel convinced that they would not betray whither we have gone, and the particulars of Lady Ravensford being in my power?"

"Pshaw! why do you entertain any doubt of their fidelity?" demanded Monckton, impatiently; "I am convinced that they would sooner lose their lives than they would betray us."

"Well, you know them better than I do."

"I know that they may be depended upon."

"This island appears to be an unfrequented place."

"There are but few inhabitants upon it,"

answered Monckton, "and they are principally wreckers, and others favourable to our proceedings; so that, you see, I could not have chosen a place of greater security."

"True," replied Adder; "and the Lady Ravensford will also be perfectly safe here?"

Monckton frowned.

"Why do you doubt?" he interrogated.

"The same house in which she is placed," returned Adder, with some confusion, "will also be inhabited by your crew. What I meant to inquire was, whether she would be secure from their intrusion, or——"

"Bah!" interrupted the smuggler-captain, "why do you entertain such an opinion of my men? Have they ever given you any cause for doing so?"

Adder found that he had proceeded almost too far, for the black looks of the smugglers plainly indicated that they liked not his insinuations and suspicions; he scarcely knew how to answer, or what excuse to make.

"No, no," he at last said; "I did not mean to say that they had, but——"

"Your honour's lady is perfectly safe," observed Michael Hernwood; "we have most of us got wives of our own, and we are content not to go astray."

Upon this the smugglers all laughed, and Adder felt himself placed, by his own folly, in a very ridiculous position, and would fain have recalled his words. The mirth of the smugglers, however, having subsided, no further notice was taken of the matter.

"And how did the lady bear the thoughts of removal?" asked Monckton.

"Remarkably well," answered Adder; "far better than I expected, after her illness."

"She is a beautiful woman; but she looks very ill."

"And how can it be expected that she can look otherwise," observed Adder, "under the circumstances in which she is placed? Torn from her husband, and with the probable reflection continually haunting her mind, that her father is again a raving maniac."

"And has he ever before lost his reason?" demanded Monckton.

"Yes," replied Adder, "but I thought I had informed you of the particulars."

"No, you did not," returned the smuggler-captain; "you must indeed possess a most callous heart, Adder, to know yourself the guilty author of so much misery, and yet to treat it with indifference."

"It comes well from you, Monckton," said Adder, "to preach of feeling."

"Well, well, so you may think," replied the former; "but a man may be a smuggler without being entirely destitute of all the feelings of humanity."

"That's true."

"Especially when a young and beautiful woman's in the case," added the smuggler-captain.

Adder frowned and fixed a penetrating look upon Monckton, but he said nothing.

"And you have never told me the name of Lady Ravensford's father," said Monckton.

"His name is Montalbert, and——"

"Montalbert!" interrupted the smuggler-captain, starting; "Montalbert, say you?"

"Yes," replied Adder, with a look of surprise; "but why do you betray such emotion?"

"Mr. Montalbert, of the town of B——," hastily demanded Monckton; "formerly merchant, and——"

"The same," answered Adder; "but why do you ask?"

"No matter!" returned the smuggler-captain; "and you say that Lady Ravensford is the daughter of this unfortunate gentleman?"

"She is."

"Strange that it should thus be brought about," observed Monckton.

"What is it that agitates you?" interrogated Adder, and he trembled with some secret apprehension; "you appear to know this Mr. Montalbert?"

"Know him!" repeated Monckton; "indeed I do; and I wish that I had been aware that it had been him before."

"Why?" eagerly asked Adder.

"You will probably have good reason to know, ere long," replied the smuggler-captain, with a sinister look, which made the former individual feel far from comfortable.

"Monckton," observed he, seriously, "I do not understand you."

"But it is not at all unlikely that you will do so anon," answered Monckton. "Adder, you must follow me into another apartment; we must have some conversation alone."

"I am ready to attend you," said Adder, looking searchingly in the smuggler-captain's countenance, and trembling.

"This way then," added Monckton, opening a door which led to a small passage, and beckoning Adder to follow him.

The smugglers all looked amazed, but not one of them offered an observation, and Adder, rising from his seat, followed Monckton, who ascended one flight of stairs, and entered a small room to the right.

"Be seated," said he, pointing to a chair; Adder obeyed, and Monckton closed the door again. Adder, in spite of his endeavours to the contrary, could not avoid trembling with a secret dread, and waiting very impatiently to hear what it was he wanted him for, and what he had to impart to him.

Monckton paused for a few seconds, and fixed an earnest look upon his companion, while he appeared to undergo considerable emotion.

"Adder," at length he said; "do you remember what this day is the anniversary of?"

"No," replied the former.

"Indeed," returned Monckton; "it is well for you that your conscience is so accommodating. Do you not remember a circumstance which happened this day sixteen years; when a poor, poisoned, dying female, was, by your instructions, brought on board my ship?"

Adder turned ghastly pale—his lips quivered—and he glanced his eyes wildly around the room, as though he were fearful of encountering some dreadful object.

"Oh, Monckton," he ejaculated; "spare me! spare me! Why recur to that dreadful circumstance? It was not I that murdered her!"

"But you did," replied Monckton, "and the infant that was in her womb!"

"Oh, be silent! be silent! It was herself that took the poison."

"Yes, by your persuasions," returned the smuggler-captain; "under the impression that you were about to follow her terrible example. But I will recall the particulars to your memory. Listen to me!"

"Oh, no, no, no!" groaned forth the wretched, guilty man; "not for the world! What are your motives for thus torturing me?"

"No matter," replied Monckton, coolly; "I am just in the vein, and you must hear me. There was a certain maiden of many charms, called Rose Allerton, who resided with her parents, humble, but honest people, in a certain little village not far from the ancient city of Chester, and was their only pride, and the admiration of all who knew her."

"No more! no more!" gasped forth Adder; "in mercy do not rack me!"

"Nay, nay, do not interrupt me," said the smuggler-captain; "I have but just commenced my story."

Adder groaned aloud with mental agony, and covered his face with his hands; but his anguish appeared to afford Monckton pleasure rather than to excite his pity, and after a brief pause, he continued,—

"Happily dwelt poor Rose Allerton with her parents for several years, and might long, nay, for ever while they lived, have remained the pride of their hearts; the prop, the charm, the blessing of their declining days, but a dark insidious fiend was at hand, to lay waste this prospect of felicity."

"Monckton!" exclaimed Adder, "can this be you?—I can scarcely believe the evidence of my senses."

"As your memory is so bad," said Monckton, "I think it is necessary that I should refresh it. But do not interrupt me; I must proceed with my narrative. The name of this villain, was Adder, and he went to reside with his master in the neighbourhood where he en-countered poor Rose, and became, (or mistook brutal desire for love,) enamoured of her. He took plenty of opportunities of meeting her, and at last, an intimacy sprang up between them; and so well did the hypocrite play his part, that he won the affections of his victim. She believed him sincere, and——"

"Cease! cease! or I shall go mad."

"Months elapsed, and he succeeded, by the promise of marriage, in triumphing over her virtue;—Rose Allerton fell a victim to the seducer's art. Too late she was awakened to a full sense of her degraded situation, and then, with looks of distraction, implored the man who had robbed her of her virtue to fulfil his promise, and make her his wife, ere her shame should become known: for she was *enciente.* He promised that he would do so, but for months evaded her repeated solicitations, until it was no longer in her power to conceal her situation from the prying eye of idle curiosity. He then, under a pretext of putting his promise into execution, as his master was about to go to another part of the country, persuaded her to elope with him. This she did; forsaking parents, home, everything for his sake."

"Again I implore you to spare me!" cried the agonised Adder.

"The tale is not yet finished," continued Monckton, in the same tone of indifference. "When they had reached the place of their destination, Rose Allerton fully expected that her seducer was going to keep his word; but that had ever been the most remote from his thoughts. After the delay of two or three days, he informed the unfortunate girl that peculiar circumstances would not permit him to marry her, and that he was determined not to live without her. He informed her that it was his resolution to take poison, and endeavoured to persuade her to follow his example, that, as they had loved each other, so they might die together; as he could not endure the thought of her becoming the wife of another. Driven to madness, although in the last stage of pregnancy, the wretched victim complied; her seducer pretended to drink poison, but she took the fatal draught in reality, which had been procured by his hands."

Here Adder became so agitated that he could scarcely retain his senses, but Monckton seemed to exult in his suffering, and continued—

"It happened, unfortunately, (and never since it happened have I forgot the dreadful circumstance, or the part which I enacted in the cruel tragedy,) that I was lying off that coast, and encountered Adder, whom I had formerly known. By the offer of a reward, I was prevailed upon to receive the murdered girl on board my craft, where she shortly afterwards died, in the greatest agony, and her body was consigned to the deep. Oh, never shall I forget, if I live for a century longer, the horror of her last moments——"

"Monckton! Monckton!" again groaned Adder, with blood-shot eyes, "I shall go mad! Spare me! spare me!"

"Oh, then," said the smuggler captain, "you do not like the tale? I thought you would not. But you cannot deny its truth?"

"Alas! no!" gasped Adder, and he rocked backwards and forwards in his chair, with the most intense agony imaginable.

"Monckton," at length he said, "why have you repeated this painful tale? What strange and sudden idea has taken possession of your mind?"

"It matters not," said the smuggler-captain; "you know that which I have spoken to be the truth, do you not?"

"I do! I do! would that it had never happened!"

"It is too late to repent now, the bloody crime is done, and depend upon it, one time or another, retribution will most assuredly overtake you" said Monckton.

"What would you with me?"

"You know the power I possess?"

"Alas, I do."

"One word of mine would consign you to the scaffold!"

"And did you not participate in the deed?"

"Never mind; upon that point, I must take my own chance."

"You would not forget the promise you made me, and kept so long?" asked Adder, with quivering lips; "you would not betray me?"

"That depends upon yourself. Upon certain conditions I will promise you that I will not; refuse to assent to them, and your life is not worth a farthing!"

"I did not expect it would come to this," observed Adder.

"I dare say you did not," returned Monckton; "but circumstances have materially altered my ideas within the last hour."

"What conditions do you exact for your secrecy?" inquired Adder.

"That you attempt not to harm the Lady Ravensford," replied Monckton; "that you abandon your base designs against her, for the present, at any rate."

"How!" uttered Adder, with astonishment.

"Nay, these are the conditions I exact," returned Monckton; "and on no other will I agree to spare your life."

"I can scarcely believe my ears, Monckton."

"Ay, it is me," returned the smuggler-captain, "and I repeat what I have said."

"What can have been the cause of this sudden and remarkable resolution?" exclaimed Adder.

"The knowledge that you have imparted to me, that Lady Ravensford is the daughter of the unfortunate Mr. Montalbert," replied Monckton; "let that suffice."

"I will no longer intrude upon you," said Adder, trembling; "I will, with the lady, seek a retreat elsewhere."

"Oh, no, you will not though," returned Monckton; "you and I will not part so easily as all that. It is not my intention to lose sight of you yet."

"Monckton," ejaculated Adder, "you do not mean to play me false, do you?"

"You have heard my determination," answered the smuggler-captain, "and you must either abide by it, or take the consequences that will most certainly follow."

"The conditions are very severe," observed Adder, despairingly.

"They are the only ones that I will agree to," returned Monckton.

"But is Rosabelle still to remain my prisoner?" inquired Adder.

"Yes," answered the smuggler-captain; "but you must not attempt any violence against her; you have so long foreborne from doing so, for your own pleasure, when you had the power so to do, and you must now do so for mine."

Adder traversed the room for a few moments with hasty strides, and in silence, and knew not in which way to act. Monckton watched him with eager looks, and he evidently felt a secret gratification at the mental torture he was undergoing.

"Do you consent?" he demanded at last.

Adder hesitated but for a minute, and then, in a hoarse voice replied:—

"I am unfortunately in your power; therefore, I do"

"Mind," added Monckton; "if I find that you have deceived me the least in the world, I will lose no time, but immediately be the means of delivering you into the hands of justice."

Adder turned away from him with a groan.

"You have consented, and wisely so," said Monckton, "therefore our interview is at an end. Let us rejoin my companions."

The smuggler-captain led the way towards the door as he spoke, and with a heavy and a foreboding heart, Adder followed.

The smugglers were all enjoying themselves on their return, and Monckton joined them with his accustomed hilarity, and there was not the least sign in his countenance or general demeanour of anything unusual having happened, for he was as cheerful as he had been before Adder's arrival.

The latter, however, was in no state of mind to join in their mirth, and after having sparingly partaken of their morning meal, he excused himself, and retired to the apartments that were allotted to him while he remained there.

Language must fail to do justice to the state

of his mind after the interview he had with the smuggler-captain; for a short time he was in a state of complete distraction. Whatever could be Monckton's motives for his extraordinary conduct, he was at a perfect loss to conjecture, but he saw enough that he was not safe a moment from being betrayed, and having all his plans frustrated; indeed, after the promise that the smuggler-captain had extorted from him, he could scarcely see the use of retaining Rosabelle in his power.

A thousand times did he curse the accident which had made Monckton acquainted with the name of Lady Ravensford's father; and he racked his brain to no purpose to endeavour to conceive what could be his reasons for being so violently agitated when he heard it, and which had caused him to come to so sudden and singular a determination.

Again he cursed himself for not having been prevailed upon by Gordon Desborough or Davey Grampus, to remain behind in the other place, then this unpleasant affair might not have taken place. But he exhausted his curses in vain, he knew himself to be thoroughly in the power of Monckton, and he did not know how to escape from it; and he was also aware that, if he did not strictly comply with the injunctions of Monckton, he would be sure not to fail to put his threats into execution.

The dreadful facts which the smuggler-captain had taken such pains to recal to his memory, harrowed up his feelings with horror when he reflected upon them, and the shade of the unfortunate murdered Rose Allerton, appeared to stand before his eyes. In his hours of the utmost gaiety, he had never been able to drive that ill-fated girl from his thoughts, and although he endeavoured to find oblivion in the wine-cup, it would rush in still vivid characters upon his memory and render him miserable. He was in constant dread that something would occur to make his guilt known, and to bring him to that punishment which was his due, and thus his days and nights were generally those of wretchedness.

The disappearance of poor Rose Allerton had caused much excitement at the time, and Adder was examined minutely about it. The body of a female, very much resembling Rose, and pregnant also, was found about a week after her disappearance, in a state of partial decomposition, in a pond close by the residence of her unfortunate parents. A coroner's inquest sat upon the body of Rose Allerton, and, after a minute and patient investigation, they returned a verdict of "found drowned," and it was generally believed that she had committed suicide. Her parents' hearts were broken, and only a few months after the death of their daughter, they were consigned to the silent tomb.

Still, in spite of the injunction of Monckton, Adder was not without hopes that something would occur to place him and our heroine beyond the power of the smugglers; and after mature deliberation, he determined to adhere to the rules which Monckton had exacted, with as much calmness and indifference as he possibly could.

The day passed away without anything particular occurring to Lady Rosabelle and Mrs. Kitson worthy of recording. They were much more comfortable in the apartments that were now appropriated to their use than they had been in the house of Gordon Desborough, and they had not forgotten the kindness with which Monckton had behaved to them in the morning. Had our heroine been made acquainted with what had passed between Monckton and Adder, and the motives that had stimulated the conduct of the former, she would indeed have been elated with hope; but it was not long ere she was destined to be informed of every particular in connexion with it.

"There is something in the appearance and manners of Monckton," said our heroine, "that convinces me he has not always moved in the situation in which he is now placed."

"I have often thought so too, my lady," replied Mrs. Kitson; "but the captain has always been very close about his former history, and I do not think that anybody but himself is acquainted with it."

"There was something so very kind, too, in his manners towards us this morning," added Rosabelle, "that I have not forgotten it since."

"There was, indeed," answered Mrs. Kitson, "and something whispers to me that he already sympathises in your misfortunes, my lady, and may, ere long, be induced to serve you."

"That hope is almost too sanguine for me to encourage it," said Rosabelle; "but still I cannot help thinking that he does indeed pity me."

"I am certain he does, my lady," returned her companion; "his looks fully convinced me of that; and as Adder is, I know, entirely in his power, if it be his wish to serve you, you have everything to hope."

"Still will I put my trust in Omnipotence," calmly ejaculated our heroine, "and will not entirely give way to despair."

"Despair, my lady!" repeated Mrs. Kitson; "oh, dear, no, I am sure there is no necessity for that, for I am certain your prospects begin to brighten."

"I cannot help being of the same opinion," said our heroine; "and I trust that the time is now fast approaching when I shall be released from the danger with which I have been so long threatened."

"I trust that your ideas may be realised," said Mrs. Kitson, "and I am sure no one would be more thankful than I should be myself to Providence for its mercy."

In conversation similar to this the day passed away, and Rosabelle was not intruded upon by Adder. Their refreshments had been brought to them regularly by Sam Kitson, who also showed by his manner that he was not insensible to the injuries that had been inflicted, and were still so unjustly inflicted upon Lady Ravensford. Although an illiterate man, he was far from being indifferent or insensible to the feelings of humanity and kindness.

They retired at an early hour to rest, and they felt in perfect security, as they had the means of fastening the doors on the inside, so that it was impossible for any individual from without to effect an entrance. The noisy revelry of the smugglers frequently reached their ears, and kept them waking; but at length that ceased, and they fell off to sleep.

Nothing occurred in the night to disturb them, and they awoke in the morning much refreshed, and Lady Rosabelle still more sanguine than ever with hope.

In the meantime Adder's agitation was unabated, although Monckton had resumed his former behaviour, and acted as if nothing of the kind which we have been describing had happened. Adder knew that he watched him with an eye of suspicion, and he was as much a prisoner, in fact, as Lady Ravensford herself. He had no other alternative than to submit

ADDER'S FIRST MEETING WITH ROSE ALLERTON.

to his will, for should he attempt, with our heroine, to escape, he would be sure not to lose any time in making known his former crime, and he would quickly be pursued and brought to justice. Fearful of exciting the suspicions of the smuggler-captain, anxious as he was, he did not seek an interview with Lady Rosabelle, and the latter was thus left undisturbed.

Our heroine and Mrs. Kitson saw nothing of Monckton on the second day of their being at the house, neither were they visited by any other person, except Sam Kitson, who brought them their provisions, so that they were left entirely to the free indulgence of their own thoughts and conversation, and the second day elapsed in the same manner as the first, without anything taking place which is worthy of notice in these pages. Night came, and after hearing that all was still in the house, and judging that the smugglers had retired to rest, they became easy, and also went to repose.

How long they had slept they had no idea, but they were suddenly aroused by a strange confused noise from below. They started up alarmed, and looked around them. The moon was shining brightly in at the window, and the room was as light as noon-day. They listened with breathless attention, and the sounds grew louder. It was a confused sound of swearing, clashing of swords, and other sounds that betokened a scuffle.

"Something has happened,' exclaimed our heroine, as she hastily arose, and slipped on her clothes, following the example of Mrs. Kitson; "the smugglers are attacked."

"I fear they are," exclaimed Mrs. Kitson; "Heaven protect my husband!"

The confusion from below now increased, and the clashing of swords, and the exclamations of different voices became more distinct. It was now very evident that the smugglers were attacked, and the report of pistols quickly followed.

"What will become of us?" exclaimed our heroine; "the smugglers are certainly attacked."

"We have nothing to fear, my lady," said Mrs. Kitson, "so compose yourself; they will not harm us."

"Hark!" cried our heroine; "there is the captain's voice."

They now listened attentively, and the voice of Monckton plainly reached their ears, giving utterance to the following words,—

"D—d villain! traitor! You, at any rate, shall not escape without your due reward!"

The report of a pistol quickly followed, and then a heavy burthen falling upon the floor.

"It is Eldon," ejaculated Mrs. Kitson, "whom the captain has slain, and it is very evident that the attack proceeds from the revenue officers."

"Hark!" gasped forth Lady Ravensford, "some persons are ascending the stairs."

"Courage! courage! my lady!" said Mrs. Kitson; "this may be the long looked-for moment of rescue."

She had scarcely given utterance to the words, when they heard two or three persons stop at the door, but, finding they could not open it, they requested that the females would admit them.

"Who's there?" demanded Mrs. Kitson, in a firm tone.

"Friends," answered the man; "fear not, but open the door."

Our heroine, who was encouraged by the words of the man, motioned to her companion to obey, and they had no sooner entered the place, than they discovered that their surmises were quite correct, and that they were revenue officers.

"Fear not, ladies," said the foremost of the men, "you will be perfectly safe under our protection. Will you attend us below?"

"Oh, where is my husband?" said Mrs. Kitson, with alarm; "alas! should he have fallen."

"If Bill Eldon is your husband, poor fellow," said the officer, "he has fallen sure enough, by the hands of the captain, who is fighting with the desperate courage of an aroused tiger."

With throbbing hearts did Rosabelle and Mrs. Kitson attend the officers below, but they had scarcely reached the bottom of the stairs, when they were met by a party of the smugglers, and it was very evident, from their loud shouts of exultation, that victory was in their favour.

"Ah! my husband!" exclaimed Mrs. Kitson, as she recognised him, and, in the confusion of the moment, she rushed with the child in her hand towards him, and was quickly led by him and two or three more of the smugglers from the house, in spite of the shrieks of our heroine, who, finding herself thus deprived of her child, uttered a loud cry of agony, and fainted.

On recovering her senses she found herself in the open air, near the sea beach, and in the arms of Adder, who was supporting her, and endeavouring to bear her towards a boat which was waiting within sight, as Rosabelle could distinguish, for the moon was shining brilliantly.

"Where am I? where is my child? Oh, villain! unhand me!" frantically screamed our heroine, endeavouring to release herself from his hold.

"Nay," ejaculated Adder, "you have nothing to fear; no harm shall come to you; as for your child and Mrs. Kitson, they are both safe, and I am conveying you to them."

"You would deceive me," cried Rosabelle, still struggling as violently as her limited strength would permit her; "let me go! let me go."

"It is useless struggling," exclaimed Adder, "besides, there is no occasion for it, no harm is intended you."

He looked back as he spoke, and uttered an exclamation of fear.

"Ah!" he cried, "they are close upon me; my situation is desperate; and thus——"

The shouts of a couple of men prevented his finishing the sentence, and Rosabelle, looking back, beheld two of the revenue officers within a few yards of them. Her heart palpitated for a moment with the hope of liberty; but where was her child?—and it sunk again.

Adder put forward the whole of his strength to reach the boat, and called to the men in it, who, at last seeing his danger, quitted it, all but one, and flew to his assistance, just as the officers came up, and attacked him fiercely.

Adder was armed, and fought well; besides, the combat was an unequal one, as there were only two of the officers; consequently, although the latter were brave fellows, and did their best, they were overpowered, and were at last compelled to take to flight, and Adder and the smugglers speedily conveyed Rosabelle to the boat, which was pushed off from the shore, and beneath a bright moon was quickly gliding over the deep towards the smugglers' vessel, which was waiting for them in the distance.

They soon reached it, and were received on board by Monckton, who immediately shouted to the men, in a voice of thunder—

"Stretch every stitch of canvas! The wind is in our favour, and we may quickly give the Philistines the go by, should they venture to pursue us."

"Ay, ay, captain," said Michael Hernwood, "but they know better than to do that. We have taught them a pretty tidy lesson this morning, I think."

"Conduct the lady below," said Monckton, turning to the smugglers who had borne her and Adder from the shore; he then added, in gentle and impressive accents—"Fear not, Lady Ravensford—no harm shall come to you; you are under the protection of Archibald Monckton, and have nothing to fear."

Adder bit his lips.

"Oh, where is my child?—Do not take me from my boy!" exclaimed our heroine, with great emotion, and appealing affectionately to the smuggler-captain.

"Your child, my lady, is quite safe, and you will see him below," said Monckton, in the same voice of gentleness which he had previously assumed.

"Oh, thanks, thanks!" cried the fond mother, in a transport of the most unbounded joy; "oh, let me fly to him!" and she hastily followed the smugglers to the cabin below, where she beheld Mrs. Kitson, and once more embraced her child.

Adder remained for awhile on deck, and watched eagerly the manners of the smuggler-captain.

"Whither are you going?" he at last ventured to inquire.

"To the house of Gordon Desborough," replied Monckton; "I now perceive that he was right, and that it was very ill-advised our leaving there at all. We could not have been in a place of greater security than the secret vaults underground, which would have afforded us every facility to escape, if we had been overpowered by numbers."

"But will they not be sure to pursue us thither?" interrogated Adder.

"No," answered Monckton; "they have had such a severe dressing in this affair, that I do not think they will be inclined to make an attack on us again in a hurry."

"But how do you imagine that Eldon found out where you had gone to?" asked Adder, with some curiosity.

"Oh," returned Monckton, "the fellow is so crafty, that there is no doubt he soon became aware of our intentions, and was close upon our heels directly. But he has paid for his treachery with his life."

"He has—but we have had a narrow escape with Lady Rosabelle," said Adder; "although after the restrictions you have placed upon my conduct towards her, she might as well have escaped as not, seeing that I have no power over her."

"There is enough of that for the present," observed Monckton, hastily; "we will talk further upon it anon. You know my determination, and I have ample reasons for my conduct."

Adder turned sullenly away, muttering his dissatisfaction, and Monckton proceeded to another part of the vessel, which was proceeding with the lightness of a feather over the deep blue waters, and was far away in a very short space of time from the scene where the late desperate encounter had taken place.

CHAPTER XXIX.

THE SECRET MURDER.—THE SMUGGLER AND THE ASSASSIN.

DAYLIGHT had not dawned more than hour when the smugglers' vessel was run into the usual place, and the crew, and our heroine and Mrs. Kitson, protected by Monckton and Adder, and Sam Kitson and Michael Hernwood, quickly landed, and proceeded at once to the house of Gordon Desborough.

Gordon had arisen, but expressed very little astonishment at their return. They walked into the parlour, and Lady Rosabelle and Mrs. Kitson were immediately suffered to retire to the apartments which they had formerly occupied.

"I told you that you would not be long ere you returned, captain," said Gordon.

"You did, Gordon," returned Monckton, "and it seems that your predictions are verified."

"And what hath brought you back again so soon?" inquired the former.

"The land-sharks have been down upon us!" answered Monckton.

"Ah!" exclaimed Gordon Desborough, with astonishment; "so quick? And were they brought down by the party you suspected?"

"They were; and he had even the audacity to lead them on," replied the smuggler-captain.

"The traitor! I did not think him capable of it."

"I know you did not; but you see you were deceived."

"And were you and your companions successful as usual?"

"We were; and we dusted their jackets well."

"And what became of Bill Eldon?"

"A shot from my pistol stretched him dead as soon as I beheld him," answered Monckton; "may such be the fate of every traitor."

"Ay, so I say, captain," ejaculated Gordon;

"and I know every one here will respond to such a wish."

"Ay, ay, death to every traitor!" cried the smugglers, simultaneously.

"And so you thought you could not find a place of better security than your old one?" said Gordon Desborough.

"You're right, Gordon," returned Monckton; "and I am sorry that we went to the trouble to leave it. But it's over now, and I do not think it is likely that the officers will trouble us for one while again, at any rate."

"They will have no idea, I should think," observed Gordon, "that you would return direct to your old quarters. But I am glad you have come back, and I know old Davey Grampus will be equally so."

"I dare say he will," said Monckton; "but come, now we have met again, let us be a little merry on the occasion of our triumph over the d——d Philistines. Come, Adder, why do you look so sad? You're as dull as if you had met with some terrible misfortune, instead of having escaped triumphantly from so critical a situation as that we were all of us placed in."

"To tell the truth, Monckton," replied Adder, "I am rather low-spirited this morning, and——"

"Psha!" hastily interrupted Monckton, "send the blue devils adrift! They and I always are upon the worst of terms. Michael Hernwood, just go and let old Davey Grampus know that we are here, and we shall not be many minutes without his company, I'll be bound for it, and something good to cheer our spirits, in the bargain."

Michael Hernwood needed no second order, but immediately bent his way to the "caboose," to apprize Davey Grampus of the return of the smugglers.

Adder would fain have excused himself, but he knew it would have been of no use his attempting to do so, and he retained his seat with a very bad grace, and listened with impatience to the coarse jokes that were bandied about by the smugglers. After the dreadful tale which Monckton had taken such pains so minutely to recall to his memory, it was not likely that that he could quickly recover his wonted spirits, notwithstanding the callousness and recklessness of his nature, and he now looked upon him as if he were a slave in his power, and dreaded him as the man in whose hands his own fate and that of our heroine rested. It was evident that there was something of an important nature which had connected him with Mr. Montalbert, and which had so suddenly changed his feelings towards Rosabelle the moment he heard that she was the daughter of that unfortunate gentleman; but what the nature of it was he was unable to form even the most remote idea.

Davey Grampus was not long in making his appearance, and his jolly red face gave full indication of the pleasure he felt at the return of his old associates. Himself and Michael Hernwood were both loaded with the good things with which Monckton and his companions had resolved to enjoy themselves.

"Welcome, captain, again to your old quarters," exclaimed Davey Grampus, advancing towards the captain, and extending to him his hand, which Monckton struck heartily; "no one can feel greater pleasure than I do that you have come back again. So I hear you have given it to the d——d swabs again."

"Ay, Davey," answered Monckton, "we have indeed given them another taste of our quality."

"What an infernal turncoat that Bill Eldon must have been," said Grampus; "damme, if I shouldn't have liked the flogging of him. But, however, it has cost him his life, and that's as much as any person can forfeit for his conduct, to be sure."

"Right, Davey," returned the smuggler-captain.

"If you had taken my advice, and that of Gordon Desborough, captain," said Grampus, "though, to be sure, you had no right to do that unless you liked, you would not have moved from here at all, nor given yourself the least trouble. What if the land-sharks had come down upon us, do you not think they would have found as warm work of it here as they did at the place where you have come from?"

Monckton nodded his assent.

"To be sure they would," continued Davey; "and you would not have been at the trouble to have removed your property."

"Well, that's very true, Davey," coincided Monckton; "and I see my folly now, although I acted for the best. But now I have come back again, let whatever may be the consequences, nothing shall induce me again to quit the place."

"Hurrah! that's right, captain," cried Davey Grampus, in accents of delight; "a wise resolution, and I am glad to hear you say so. We will be merry this day, at any rate. I see his honour has come back with you, and I hear that the lady is quite safe, and in her old quarters. But what's the matter with Mr. Adder?—He looks as dull as——"

"Oh, he will soon cheer up," hastily interrupted Monckton, anxious to put an end to the inquisitiveness of Davey: "some trifle or the other, has ruffled his temper, I suppose, but this is the sort of stuff, is it not Davey, to revive the spirits?"

"Ah! you may say that, captain," replied Davey Grumpus; "it is the finest antidote I can find, and I ought to be a bit of a judge, I imagine, seeing that I take it morning, noon, and night—

" Let fools at good spirits rail,
    To patronise them I'll ne'er fail;
    It's the stuff to banish care,
    And to the devil send despair !
                    Fal de ra !

" When I'm dead and in my grave,
    No costly monument I'd have—
    Let my grave be snug and neat,
    With a glass of grog at my head and feet !
                    Fal de ra !

" This, my epitaph should be,
    Here lies one who ne'er, d'ye see,
    Refused to moisten well his clay,
    And drank his life and care away !
                    Fal de ra !"

"That's my favourite song, you know, captain," continued Grampus, after bawling the above talented production forth, with stentorian lungs ; " and that's better, in my opinion, than all the sorrows which the stupid professors of sobriety can preach."

"It's a very excellent song, no doubt, Davey," said Monckton, with a smile. " But come, Adder," he continued, turning to the latter individual, who was still seated in a corner, with his head resting on his hand, and his elbow leaning upon a table, and filled with the most gloomy ideas :—" Come, come ; what the devil's the use of moping in this manner ? Drink, and endeavour to be merry; you will have time enough to be sad at another period. Besides, you don't know what may be the result of what you are thinking about yet. Come, drink ! Nay, I insist upon it; I will have no sad faces here. We have had plenty of cause to rejoice, rather, in the triumph which we have been enabled to obtain over those d—d swabs !"

Adder felt confused, for the eyes of all the smugglers were fixed inquisitively and rudely upon him; but he endeavoured to conquer his feelings, and even feigned a smile as he looked up at Monckton, and said—

" I—I—am not dull, but——"

" But your physiognomy is the best imitation of dulness that I ever saw," said Monckton, with a sarcastic grin; " but taste deeply of this, and if it does not quickly revive you, say that my name's not Monckton."

The smuggler-captain pushed round a stiff glass of grog to Adder as he spoke, who took it with much reluctance, and fixed upon the former a look which he well understood, but of which he did not take any notice ; and raising it to his lips, was compelled to drink. He had seldom felt more uncomfortably situated in his life, and he was burning with indignation against Monckton, who had got him so completely in his power, and who appeared to exult in his knowledge of the same. He could not see the least prospect of escaping from his trammels, for if he should attempt to do so, and to bear Lady Ravensford away,

Monckton would be certain to fulfil the threats that he had held out to him—namely, that he would make known to the officers of justice the dreadful crime he had formerly perpetrated, and the unfortunate fate of the hapless Rose Allerton; in the event of which, nothing, he was convinced, could save him from the ignominious fate which he had incurred by his cruel deed.

Thus he at once saw, that unless something occurred to thwart the designs of Monckton, all the trouble, danger, and expense he had been at to get Rosabelle in his power had been entirely thrown away, and that, moreover, he should only be exposed to the ridicule of all who were acquainted with the circumstances.

He regretted beyond measure that he had not taken Rosabelle away in another direction, and where it would not be known to his former associates, at the time when Monckton and the smugglers left the house of Gordon Desborough. But it was no use repining now, and all that he had to do, all that he could hope for was an opportunity to present itself when he might foil the designs of Monckton, and convey his victim to some place of security where there would be no discovering them. This, after some time spent in reflection, he did not entirely despair of being enabled to put in practice, and he determined, after all, to make the attempt, even at any risk.

He would have been very well pleased, if he could, by any means, have excused himself from the company he was at present in, but he was convinced that it was no use attempting it; for Monckton seemed to take a delight in the uneasiness he felt, and would be sure to oppose such a wish; and he was, therefore, constrained to remain where he was.

He in vain racked his brain to imagine what could have been the reason for such a remarkable alteration in his conduct, as regarded Lady Ravensford, when he had been informed of the name of her father, and he did not see any chance of his being enabled to arrive at the truth, for the present, at any rate.

We will now return to the passage from which we have thus slightly digressed.

Adder having partaken of the grog, endeavoured to appear more at his ease, but he succeeded very indifferently, and the looks of the smugglers plainly evinced that they could well guess the state of his mind.

" Well," said Davey Grampus, after Adder had drunk, " that looks better; on, never fear, your honour will soon be cheerful enough, if you only adopt my plan, which is—

" Drink while you can, be it port, ale, or sherry,
    There is nothing like drinking to make a man
        merry.
    Send care to the devil, only master the proge,
    And your sorrows quickly drown in a glass of
        good grog !"

"Bravo, Davey," said Monckton; "you are always merry!"

"Merry, captain," replied Grampus, after having taken another hearty swig of the grog; "to be sure, I am; what's the use of being sad? I never found any benefit from it; and, therefore, I am a sworn enemy of it."

The grog continued to be passed briskly round, and the smugglers were not long before they became uproariously noisy, and Adder felt more and more uncomfortable, and anxious to get away, but it was no use his attempting such a thing, for Monckton watched him narrowly, and was ready in a moment to oppose his wishes.

After two or three hours passed at the house of Gordon, Davey Grampus proposed, as was his usual custom, that they should adjourn to the "caboose," to which Monckton and the others assented. Here Adder again sought to excuse himself, but to no purpose: the smuggler-captain would insist that he should accompany them, and he was, therefore, reluctantly compelled to obey. They proceeded by the subterranean way to the house of Davey Grampus, where they remained drinking and carousing in the same manner which they had done while they were at the house of Gordon Desborough, till the evening, when Monckton ordered his men to see about replacing the booty where it had formerly been deposited, and Adder was at length permitted to depart.

He slowly retraced his way to the house of Gordon Desborough, revolving in his mind the circumstances that had recently taken place, and the awkward position in which he was placed, and he was at a perfect loss in which way he should proceed. It was late when he reached the house, and he learned, on inquiry of Mrs. Kitson, that Lady Ravensford had retired to rest, and even if she had not, he would have felt afraid to have sought an interview with her.

Mrs. Kitson, however, had not told the truth, for she and our heroine had been too deeply engaged in conversation to feel any inclination to do so. The change again in their situation, and the singular alteration in the behaviour of Monckton, afforded them plenty of subject for discourse and speculation, and they were unable to come to any other than the most favourable conclusion.

"Rest assured, my dear lady," observed Mrs. Kitson, "that the captain's feelings towards you have undergone a material change. I noticed particularly the kindness of his behaviour the last time we saw him, and that, depend upon it, augurs some good."

"Your thoughts and mine, Mrs. Kitson," said Lady Ravensford, "perfectly agree; and I cannot help surmising that some good may result from it."

"Besides, my lady," said Mrs. Kitson; "I observed a particular expression in his countenance when he addressed himself to you, and depend upon it, there is more in it than we at present imagine."

"There is another circumstance, also," said our heroine, "which has inspired me with hope, and that is, that Adder has not annoyed us with his presence, and he appears to entertain a fear and deference for Monckton, which shows plainly that he is in his power, and is fearful of offending him."

"I have heard, my lady," said Mrs. Kitson, "that Adder has, indeed, good reasons to fear Captain Monckton, who is acquainted with some crime which the former has committed, and which, if he should divulge, would be sure to bring him to an ignominious end."

"If that be the case," remarked Rosabelle, "I wonder that Adder should ever have employed Monckton in the stratagem against me."

"It is remarkable," observed Mrs. Kitson; "but, perhaps, he did so, thinking to bind him to greater secrecy."

"It might be so," said our heroine; "but I cannot help thinking that Monckton is interested in my favour. The kindness with which he behaved to me at the place from whence we have just came, and also his behaviour when I was taken on board the vessel which conveyed us hither, all serve to strengthen that idea; and it is most forcibly impressed upon my mind that it will not be long that I shall remain a prisoner of the hateful and consummate villain, Adder."

"In that belief I coincide, my lady," said Mrs. Kitson; "and I trust that our hopes are not doomed to be disappointed."

"Oh, my husband!" exclaimed Rosabelle, with the most intense emotion, and clasping her hands vehemently together, "and are you, indeed, still living? and do you believe me innocent?—Oh, what unspeakable rapture would it be for me to be again clasped in your arms, and to listen to your asseverations of affection!—My dear, dear, unfortunate father, too—oh, I cannot think upon you without a shudder of dread! If you are once more a wretched maniac, better would it be—far more contented should I feel to hear that the silent tomb had closed over your sorrows and misfortunes!—Alas! alas! and can this unparalleled train of calamities and horrors have been inflicted by offended Heaven for the first error of which I was guilty, and into which I was led by the strength of my love and inexperience? Bitterly, indeed, have I been doomed to suffer since, and all the unfortunate beings connected with me!"

"My dearest lady," ejaculated her companion, "you accuse yourself too severely. Ample has been the atonement you have made for the indiscretion into which you were led, and Heaven will most assuredly soon ameliorate the severity of your sufferings, and punish the guilty wretch who has inflicted them upon you."

Lady Ravensford wept, and the little Alfred, who had been seated upon her knee, looked up innocently in her face, and, in a voice which went to her heart, lisped forth—

"Mamma cry—Alfred do not like to see mamma cry. He will be a good boy, and not make poor mamma weep."

"Darling child—sweet prattler!" cried the fond mother, snatching her offspring to her bosom, and covering his rosy cheeks with kisses. Mrs. Kitson was also affected to tears, and turned away to conceal her emotion.

A short pause ensued, after which the latter endeavoured to impart consolation to Rosabelle, in which she happily succeeded, and our heroine became more tranquil.

The noise made by the smugglers below frequently reached their ears in the course of the day, and often interrupted their conversation; but after the behaviour of Monckton, and the assurances which he had given Lady Ravensford, they entertained no fear of any intrusion from them. But at length all became quiet, and they were then satisfied that they had quitted the house.

They continued to converse upon different subjects, but principally upon that one which almost entirely engrossed their thoughts, until Adder returned from the "caboose," when he made the inquiry which we have mentioned of Mrs. Kitson, and shortly afterwards, being tired with thinking, and also of the vexatious events of the day, he retired to his chamber. Not long afterwards, Rosabelle and Mrs. Kitson sought repose, and Gordon Desborough having come home, leaving Monckton and his companions at the "caboose," the house was buried in profound silence, and every door was secured to prevent the possibility of any persons intruding from without. The property of the smugglers had all been safely returned to its old quarters, and Monckton and his associates had banished from their minds all apprehension of being again interrupted.

It is needless to say that Adder restlessly pressed his pillow; his thoughts were in a complete state of ferment, and there were moments when he was half tempted to set the threats and the power of the smuggler-captain at defiance, and to force Lady Ravensford from the house in the course of the night; but then, such an idea was little better than madness, for what could he do singly, and where was he, in that strange place, where he knew no one but the smugglers, to obtain assistance? He was, indeed, placed in a dilemma from which he knew not how to extricate himself, and he cursed and raved violently, his feelings almost overpowering his

reason. He who had so often prided himself, and had been so successful in duping others, who had imagined that his cunning surpassed that of any human being, to be thus triumphed over, and held in actual subjection and terror by the smuggler-captain, was more than he had patience to endure, and he gave himself up to the most violent rage.

Deeply did he now regret that the revenue officers had not been more successful against Monckton, or that they had not slain him, then he would have been rid of one whom he had so much constant fear of, and his designs against Rosabelle might have proceeded without any fear of interruption.

"He has made me promise that I will not force my presence upon Lady Ravesford," soliloquised Adder; "and does he think that I will keep my word? No, by hell! I will only wait until he shall, with his associates, have quitted this spot, and then, whatever may be the consequences, Rosabelle shall again see me, and hear my determination from my own lips!"

Adder felt a kind of savage satisfaction as he formed this resolution, and after some more reflections of a similar description, he fell asleep.

The next morning his determination remained unaltered, and the consequence was, that he was enabled to meet Monckton and his companions, when they came to the house, with considerable more composure than he had done before. This was not a little increased, when, in the course of conversation, the former informed him that, the next morning, it was his intention to depart upon another trip, which he expected would be a longer one than usual, and Adder could scarcely conceal his pleasure at the intelligence when he reflected upon the opportunity he should thus have of putting his resolution into effect. He did not, however, suffer the smuggler-captain to observe the change in the expression of his countenance, and he affected to treat the information with the utmost indifference.

The day passed away in a similar manner to the previous one, and was entirely destitute of any incident of interest sufficient to find a place in these pages. Sam Kitson, as he had before done, brought Lady Ravensford and his wife their provisions, and informed them of all that took place, and of the intention of Monckton to depart on the following morning.

Our heroine felt far from satisfied at this intelligence, for since the alteration in the behaviour of Monckton, she looked upon him as a protector, and when he was gone, she was fearful that she should again be exposed to the importunities of Adder, who, it was most probable, would take advantage of the absence of Monckton and his associates, to press his guilty suit.

Mrs. Kitson endeavoured to combat her fears, lest she should not be able to meet the advances of Adder with fortitude, should her apprehension be realized.

"I am convinced, my lady," she observed, "as I before informed you, that Adder being held in terror by Monckton being acquainted with his former crime, he will be fearful of doing as you surmise, lest he should encounter the wrath and vengeance of the captain, who, it is evident, is, from some motive or the other, now deeply interested in your favour."

"Why, that supposition might appear reasonable," answered Lady Rosabelle; "but experience has convinced me that Adder is so daring and reckless a villain that no terror will prevent him from persisting in any evil designs he may have fixed his mind upon."

Mrs. Kitson was not prepared to return any immediate answer to this, for it was too probable; nevertheless, she endeavoured, all that was in her power, to console Lady Ravensford, and in which she ultimately succeeded better than she at first anticipated.

Adder, as we have before said, felt highly pleased when he was informed by Monckton of his determination, and it was not without the greatest difficulty that he could prevent his satisfaction from being noticed by the smuggler-captain. The resolution he had formed, with regard to our heroine, was unaltered, and all fear of the consequences was destroyed in the hope of triumph which he entertained. Monckton had told him also, that he expected his intended trip would be a longer one than usual, and that would afford him time to execute his purpose, and perhaps afford him an opportunity of conveying away the lady altogether. Could he by any means contrive to get over to France with our heroine, he flattered himself that he should be enabled to find some place of security, where neither the friends of Rosabelle, nor Monckton would be able to discover him. But that would be a task of such difficulty, that he almost looked upon the idea as hopeless. To ensure success to such a project, it would be indispensably necessary that he should get the assistance of Gordon Desborough, and so firmly was that ruffian attached to Monckton and his crew, that he was doubtful whether the offer of a reward, however large, would tempt him to act a part so contrary to the smuggler-captain's wishes, nay, commands; for, although Adder was not aware of that Monckton had sought a private interview with Gordon, almost immediately after his return, and having made him acquainted with his designs, cautioned him as to his behaviour, and commanded him to keep a strict watch over the conduct of Adder at any time when he (Monckton) might be away, and to be sure to report to him all that might transpire. This Gordon promised faithfully to obey, and there was not the least doubt but that he would keep his word.

In spite of the doubts that occurred to his mind, however, the miscreant Adder determined while Monckton was away, to make a bold attempt to put his designs into practice, and he had fully made up his mind, that, if ever he should fail in pursuading Gordon Desborough to assist him in quitting the place, with the victim of his persecution, he would forcibly gratify those disgusting and nefarious passions, which he had so long postponed the indulgence of, notwithstanding our heroine had been entirely in his power. Never, however, did it once occur to the mind of the villain that Providence watched over the innocent object of his cruelty, and that he had himself determined upon the likeliest means of rendering his vile schemes abortive, and of bringing shame and confusion upon himself.

On the evening when Monckton made the announcement of his intended departure on the following morning, after some time passed among his companions, he significantly motioned Adder to follow him out. The latter reluctantly obeyed, for he dreaded that something of an unpleasant nature was about to take place, or that the smuggler captain had something else to say to him to torture his feelings, and to arouse him afresh to all the horrors of a guilty conscience.

Monckton telling the smugglers that he should not be long before he rejoined them, led the way from the house, and Adder attended him. They neither of them spoke a word as they proceeded, and Monckton bent his footsteps towards the chain of rocks, at a short distance only from the house of Gordon Desborough.

It was moonlight, and the tall figure of the smuggler-captain, which cast a long shadow before it on the earth, was peculiarly striking, and looked like one of those characters that are often represented with such effect in a melodrama.

Adder, in spite of his efforts to the contrary, could not help feeling a sensation of mingled awe and dread while in his presence, and he could not but acknowledge to himself the power which he held over him. Great, indeed, was the change which only a day or two had wrought in him; then he had been his willing accessary; but now he knew him not only the acknowledged enemy of his designs, but the determined frustrator of the same, and of his power to do so, he could not entertain but very little doubt, in fact, none—the only chance of his failing being some extraordinary event.

Having reached a retired and gloomy spot among the rocks, Monckton paused, and after looking at Adder for some moments with a scrutinising expression, and as if he would penetrate to his utmost thoughts, he laid his hand vehemently on his arm, and, in impressive accents, said—

"To-morrow morning, as I have told you, I and my companions quit this place for some time; do you remember the interview we had before our return hither?"

"I do," answered Adder, sullenly; "I think you gave me reason enough to remember it. Why should you recall it to my memory now?"

"I have my reasons for doing so," was Monckton's reply; and he appeared to feel a pleasure in the uneasiness which the former evidently endured; "you have not then, since you boast of your memory being so good, forgotten the injunctions which I then imposed upon you?"

"I have not."

"I would caution you, then, to retain them in your memory," said Monckton, "during my absence, and to obey them, if you would save your neck from the halter."

Adder frowned, but he returned no answer. To pretend to oppose the will of Monckton, he knew, would be madness, and he was, therefore, constrained to submit.

"But," continued the smuggler-captain, after a pause, "I have something with me, which, I think, will secure your compliance

THE BETRAYAL OF ROSE ALLERTON BY ADDER.

more readily than any threats which I can hold out. Come hither."

As Monckton spoke, he laid hold of the arm of Adder, and, with gentle force, drew him forward into the moonlight. He then produced from his pocket a piece of paper, which he unfolded and revealed to the eyes of Adder, beneath the pale rays of the moon. He pointed significantly at the paper, on which were inscribed a few lines, in a delicate handwriting, and then, with a look of exultation, demanded of his companion:—

"Do you know these characters?"

Adder turned ghastly pale as his eyes fell upon them, and he trembled violently. Monckton repeated the question.

"I do! I do!" gasped forth the trembling guilty man; "but do not rack me!"

"Whose hand-writing is it?" interrogated the smuggler-captain, noticing the horror of Adder with gratification; "whose hand-writing is it, I demand?" he repeated.

"Rose Allerton's," answered Adder, in hollow tones, and he covered his face with his hands, and groaned. "Oh, what is the meaning of this?—Spare me, Monckton; your conduct to me is inexplicable."

"Is it?" said the latter, with a sarcastic grin; "perhaps it may be explained sooner than you will like. Yes, you have guessed right; these characters were traced by the hand of your unfortunate murdered victim.

They were written by her in her dying moments, and confided to my care. Read them."

"No—no; I—"

"Read them, I say, and satisfy yourself," demanded Monckton, placing the paper still nearer to the gaze of Adder, whose agony we need not describe. "Read them," he once more repeated.

Adder just fearfully glanced towards the paper, and then averted his gaze.

"I cannot,—I cannot peruse them," he ejaculated; "there is a mist before my eyes."

Monckton smiled triumphantly.

"I dare say there is," he said; "but since you cannot, I will read them for you."

"No—no—I want not to hear them."

"Pshaw!—it will be more satisfactory for you to do so," returned Monckton. "Listen!"

"Monckton," exclaimed Adder, "why should you thus take so savage a delight in agonizing me?—Let me begone."

"Not till you have heard the dying acknowledgment of Rose Allerton," cried Monckton, detaining him. "Hear me. Thus writes the murdered victim:—

"' With my latest breath I declare that it was Adder who purchased the poison, and persuaded me to take it. I pardon him, and may Heaven do so likewise.

(Signed,) 'ROSE ALLERTON.

(Witnesses) { "ARCHIBALD MONCKTON.
    "MICHAEL HERNWOOD,
    "SAMUEL KITSON.

"On board the smuggling vessel, 'DESPERADO,'—June 4th, 1784.'"

Monckton paused for a short time, after perusing these lines, to notice the effect which they had upon Adder, who was groaning intensely, and covering his face with his hands, was totally incapable of giving utterance to a syllable.

"What think you of that document?" the smuggler-captain at length inquired. "Do you not think that would go a long way in corroborating any statements I might deem it necessary to make?"

"Oh, Monckton," supplicated Adder, in a humble voice. and shuddering; "I do, indeed, acknowledge myself entirely in your power; but have some mercy; in pity do!"

"Ha! ha! ha! excuse my laughing," said Monckton, ironically; "but I cannot help it, when I hear the desperate and ever sagacious Adder, he who prides himself so much upon duping others, suing to me for mercy. Ha! ha! ha!"

"This is unbearable!" cried Adder, walking backwards and forwards with hasty and disordered steps; "fool that I was to seek your aid again."

"Ay," returned Monckton, sarcastically, "that was rather short-sighted of you, I must confess. But it's too late to repent now; and

you must submit to my commands, or you know the consequences."

"Monckton," said Adder, with an anxious look; "what reason have I given you for this change in your conduct towards me?"

"It matters not; I do not think proper to satisfy you upon that point," replied the former. "Little did I imagine who the Lady Ravensford was, or you would never have had my aid in your nefarious designs. But your life depends upon your behaviour to her whilst I am away; and you had, therefore, better see to it."

Adder would have made some reply, but Monckton waved his hand impatiently, and moved away from the spot to return to the house, looking back at Adder to see that he followed him.

Language could not do justice to the rage of the latter, as he walked slowly behind the smuggler-captain; he felt himself, in fact, scarcely better than a slave to Monckton, so entirely in subjection did he now hold him. How heartily did he wish that something might happen to him on his forthcoming trip, to prevent his returning; that he might be attacked again by the officers, and fall in the affray, then should he be released from the principal cause of his terror. Still there was enough cause for his fear in the fact of Michael Hernwood and Samuel Kitson having been witnesses to the dying affirmation of the murderer Rose Allerton, and while they lived, he felt sure enough that he should not be out of danger.

Monckton returned to the house of Gordon, but soon afterwards he and his associates took their departure for the "caboose," where they slept, (with the exception of those who had to look after the vessel,) being anxious to retire to rest, as they would have to be up at such an early hour in the morning, to depart on their voyage.

Adder was very glad when they quitted the place, for he felt uncomfortable in the presence of that man whom he knew to be his bitter enemy, and who was probably at that very time contemplating his destruction; and he almost immediately afterwards retired to his chamber, where he revelled in his mind all that had transpired in the evening; the lines which the ill-fated Rose Allerton had written in her dying moments, seemed to be impressed upon his brain in characters of fire, and the agony of remorse which he endured, almost superseded every other feeling. Still, in spite of the threats of Monckton, and the certainty which he felt that he would not fail to put them into effect, he could not forego the resolution he had formed to prosecute his designs against Lady Ravensford, and he looked forward to the departure of the smugglers in the morning, with the utmost impatience.

He hastened to bed and endeavoured to sleep, but his thoughts were too busily engaged to allow him to do so, and he lay tossing about on the bed, until the old clock in the house chimed the hour of two, at which time he had understood from Monckton, it was their intention to depart. Soon after this he heard Gordon stirring in the house, and he, therefore, arose, having made up his mind to accompany Desborough to the " caboose" to witness the departure of the smugglers.

On their arrival at the latter place they learnt that the smugglers had already quitted for the sea-beach, and they, therefore, hastened after them as quick as they could.

The light splashing of the waves against the rocks was all that disturbed the tranquillity of the scene, and the air came upon the senses refreshing and salubrious. When they were some distance from them they saw the smugglers bustling about on the beach, and the dark shadow of the ship, as she rested on the bosom of the ocean waiting for them, met their gaze. There were no other objects to be seen stirring but the smugglers, and they looked like the supernatural masters of all around them.

Adder and Gordon hastened forward, and Monckton, seeing them approach, motioned to the men who had got into the boat, to wait.

"Well, Gordon," said Monckton, when they had got up to them, " so you have come to see us depart?"

"Ay, captain," answered the former, "and to wish you success on your trip."

"Thank you," said Monckton; " I have no doubt that our usual good fortune will attend us. Good by, Gordon; you will not forget the instructions I have given you."

Adder caught at these words, and he looked suspiciously at Monckton and Gordon Desborough; they, however, exchanged glances with one another, and appeared to take but little or no notice of him.

"You know you may depend upon me, captain," said Gordon, in reply to Monckton; " I will attend to them to the very letter; the——"

"Hush!" interrupted Monckton; " I know what you would say, but you have no occasion to repeat it here; besides, it would not be politic. I can depend upon you."

"Ay, to be sure you can," answered Gordon; " good-by, and I trust it will not be long before we shall see you all again, with an increase of booty, and bringing additional confusion to the land swabs."

"Thanks for your good wishes," remarked Monckton. Then turning to Adder, he said—

"You, also, will do well to bear in mind what has passed between us at our different interviews; and, if you are wise, you will not attempt to oppose my will."

" I thought enough had been said upon that subject," remarked Adder, surlily; "I need not to be reminded of it so often."

"It will be better for you if you do not," returned Monckton; "farewell till we meet again."

Adder bit his lips, but was unable to return any answer, and Monckton having addressed a few observations to Gordon, in an under tone, jumped into the boat, waved his hand to them both, and the men applying themselves to the oars, the boat was soon scudding swiftly over the ocean to the smugglers' vessel. Adder and Gordon watched it as long as they could discern it, when they turned away, and retraced their steps towards the house of the latter.

They proceeded for some distance in silence, when Adder, being unable longer to restrain his curiosity, said—

"Monckton appears to have left some very important instructions behind him with you, and, if I am not mistaken, I am not an uninterested party in the same."

"What makes you imagine so?" demanded Gordon.

"Oh, I have my reasons," answered Adder, " and——"

"Probably you have," answered Gordon, interrupting him hastily, "and so have I for keeping a still tongue in my head, and, therefore, you need not trouble yourself to put any more questions to me."

"You are rather bold and abrupt," said Adder, in a tone of the deepest chagrin.

"Well," returned Desborough, with the greatest nonchalance, "if you think so, you are at perfect liberty to enjoy your opinion."

"And I can use my own pleasure how far I may put up with your insolence."

"Indeed!—Perhaps you may find that you have not so much liberty as you appear to suppose. You remember the caution which Monckton gave you not many minutes since?"

"D——n! this is too much!" cried Adder, unable to restrain his indignation. "Gordon Desborough, what do you mean by this conduct?"

"Nay," replied Gordon, with perfect coolness, "it is too much trouble, and rather inconvenient to enter into an explanation now; besides, there is no necessity for us to quarrel, and, therefore, we may as well drop the subject."

"I like not the behaviour of either yourself or Monckton," said Adder; "but secure as you may both think yourselves, whatever designs you may have against me, may be thwarted when you least expect."

"Well, well," said Gordon, with a disagreeable grin, "you are at liberty to entertain that opinion; we will not fall out about it; time will show."

They neither of them appeared disposed to converse further, and they soon afterwards reached the house, Gordon opening the door with his own private key.

Early as it was, neither Gordon nor Adder felt inclined to return to their chambers, and the former having kindled a fire, filled his pipe, seated himself in the chimney corner, and blew a stiff cloud, and seemed wrapped in his own thoughts, and fully immersed in the enjoyment of the tobacco in his pipe. Adder took his seat on the opposite side of the fire-place, and was for some time too much agitated by the observations of Gordon Desborough and Monckton, to offer any remark. At length, however, after revolving in his mind the readiest means of inducing Gordon to become favourable to his wishes and designs—

"Gordon Desborough," he said, turning to him, and fixing upon him a penetrating and persuasive look; "since we have known each other, you have, I think, never had cause to complain of my liberality in rewarding you for any services I may have required of you."

"True," replied Desborough, carelessly, taking his pipe from his mouth, and emitting a thick cloud of smoke; "and you have always found me execute any business you may have employed me in with fidelity and skill."

"That is also true," observed Adder; "then why should you and I become enemies?"

"Whenever did you know two rogues agree?" demanded Gordon, with an ironical grin, and resuming his pipe, with the same air of indifference as had characterised him before.

Adder looked at him for a moment in astonishment, and frowned.

"Well, well," at length said Adder, "you might be a little less abrupt in your observations; but it matters not. We shall probably understand one another better shortly."

"What is it you wish to talk about?" asked Gordon, drawing away at his pipe.

"You would not object to receive a rich reward, I dare say," remarked Adder, looking at the ruffian keenly.

"Why, no," replied Gordon; "not if I could do so honourably."

"Honourably!" repeated Adder, affecting to laugh; "that observation comes well from your lips."

"Doubtless you may think so," returned Gordon; "but that is not to the purpose; what is it you are hinting at? Be a little more explicit, and then I shall understand you."

"I would once more purchase your assistance, then," replied Adder; "to speak plainly; and for it I will reward you more handsomely, by ten-fold, than I have hitherto done."

"What would you have me do?"

"I feel confident that you are set as a spy over my actions."

"There are more unlikely things than that."

"Monckton has deceived me!"

"And what has that to do with me?"

"Nay, nay, not so hasty; hear me out. He has himself imbibed a passion, or something of the kind, I suspect, for Lady Ravensford, whom I have been at so much risk and expense to get in my power, and would frustrate my designs."

Gordon Desbourough here looked up, and for a moment taking the pipe from his lips, grinned ironically.

"Knowing this, I do not consider either her or myself safe," continued Adder, "while he knows where we are, and has us in his power."

"And so you would have me aid you to convey the lady from hence?" added Gordon.

"Exactly so," replied the villain, "you have just guessed it; and, of course, for a handsome sum of money, you will not refuse me?"

"There you are decidedly mistaken," returned Gordon Desborough, with a provoking grin; "for I shall do nothing of the kind."

"You will not?"

"I *will* not!"

"But what if I persist in conveying Lady Ravensford away myself?"

"Why," coolly replied Gordon Desborough; "then I must prevent you, I suppose; that's all about it."

"How!" exclaimed Adder, starting to his feet, with the utmost resentment depicted in his countenance.

"Nay!" cried Gordon, never offering to move from his seat, and still smoking his pipe with the greatest possible indifference; "you need not put yourself in a rage, Mr. Adder: I mean what I say."

"And think you I will submit to your will?" demanded Adder. "Am I to be treated as a nonentity?"

"You will find that 'you have no other alternative than submission," replied Gordon; "I am not without the means to enforce it."

Adder bit his lips, and nearly bursting with rage, he traversed the room, in the most agitated manner.

"By hell!" he at length exclaimed; "I have been regularly deceived, duped, trepanned!"

"Well, you may have been so," returned Gordon, "but that has nothing to do with me; and if it is as you say, it is no more than you have served others; so you know it is all tit-for-tat!"

"Gordon Desborough!" ejaculated Adder, his cheeks pale and his lips livid with the excess of his rage; "do not try my patience too far, or you may repent it."

"Ha! ha! ha!" laughed the ruffian, scornfully, "and think you by your threats to intimidate Gordon Desborough? His temper must be strangely altered before he can be so easily alarmed. But you may as well spare your anger, as I told you before; it will do you no good, and I heed it not near so much as I do this whiff of tobacco smoke."

As Gordon Desborough thus spoke, he once more emitted a dense volume of smoke from his mouth, leaned his elbows on his knees, and puffed away with the greatest coolness imaginable. As for Adder, he scarcely knew what to do. To threaten was only a waste of breath, to expostulate would be equally useless; and yet, to be treated with actual contempt and derision by the very wretch whom he had been wont to look upon as his creature, required more than ordinary patience to endure. He continued for some time longer to pace the apartment with folded arms, but without speaking, during which interval Gordon took no more notice of him than as if he had not been present. At last, he subdued his resentment sufficiently to observe,—

"Gordon, I would not that we should be foes. Will nothing prevail upon you to accede to my wishes?"

"Nothing!" replied Gordon, resolutely.

"And why not?"

"Because I have given my word to Monckton, and I would not break it for fifty times the sum you have offered me."

"Consider."

"It requires no consideration; my mind is made up."

"But you cannot prevent my having an interview with Lady Ravensford."

"We shall see."

"By all the infernal host, you shall find it no easy task to prevent me."

"It strikes me that you will be disappointed in that supposition."

"This is not to be borne."

"But you must bear it."

"Gordon Desborough, before you proceed to extremities, I once more caution you to bethink yourself."

"And allow me also to advice you, Mr. Adder, to say no more about it, as it is only a waste of time. I am bound to do the bidding of Monckton, and, depend upon it, I will not fail to do my duty!"

"Infernal scoundrel!" was upon the lips of Adder; but he noticed the determined and reckless looks of Gordon, and well knowing his desperate character, fear, or a feeling very much resembling it, prevented him, and he returned no answer.

A pause ensued, during which, Gordon continued to smoke his pipe with increased relish, and Adder having resumed his seat, rocked himself backwards and forwards upon it, evidently in a very uncomfortable state of mind. He, however, endeavoured to conquer his resentment, for he saw clearly that no end could be gained by it, and that no passionate observations that he could make use of, could have any other effect upon Gordon than that of exciting his utmost derision and contempt, and that the only chance he had of winning him to his purposes was by diametrically opposite conduct.

"Well," he observed, at length, "it is, as you say, useless for us to quarrel upon the subject. You will, perhaps, think better of it."

"I shall not think otherwise than I do at present, that you may depend upon," answered Gordon.

"I will not believe you," said Adder, in a conciliatory tone.

"You may," replied the ruffian.

"I will not still believe you," replied Adder; "but for the present we will drop the subject."

With these words, he bade Gordon good morning, and retired to his own room, to meditate upon what had passed.

We will not try the patience of our readers by detailing the reflections that distracted his mind, for they can be easily conjectured. He saw himself placed in a dilemma, from which, he was confident, it would be no easy task for him to extricate himself; and as for our heroine, unless he could hit upon some desperate stratagem, she was evidently lost to him for ever. He was, nevertheless, determined to risk everything, nay, even life itself, rather than Monckton should triumph over him. From the observations which Gordon Desborough had made, it was very clear he was not left without assistance, should such be required, and it was, therefore, evident that the smuggler-captain had used every precaution that was necessary to render the success of his plans secure, and to prevent his being foiled by the crafty persecutor of Lady Ravensford.

What bewildered the mind of Adder more than all, was, to account for the resolution which Monckton had so suddenly formed with regard to Rosabelle, and the interest which he took in her fate. At one time he was half inclined to think that Monckton had imbibed a similar sentiment towards her which inhabited his (Adder's) breast; but that idea was quickly banished from his mind, when he remembered that it was not until he had heard that Mr. Montalbert was her father, that the change in his conduct took place, and it was very evident from his observations, that it was only owing to his being connected by some event or the other with that gentleman, that he was so suddenly, and so unfortunately for Adder, to become her friend and protector. That he would ultimately restore her to her friends, unless he could adopt some means of preventing him, he felt convinced of; and, therefore, which ever way he looked, he saw the greatest cause to fear him.

Had he not have gained Gordon Desborough over to enter into his plans, Adder would not so much have cared, for then there would have been a better prospect of his being able to frustrate the intentions of Monckton; but situated as he now was, without any one whom he could trust, or who could assist him, there was indeed little left for him but despair and disappointment.

Tired at length of thinking, Adder threw himself upon the bed, as it was not then more than four o'clock in the morning, and gradually fell off to sleep, in which he continued till daylight.

CHAPTER XXX.

ADDER'S INTERVIEW WITH ROSABELLE.— HER DETERMINED RESISTANCE.

THREE days elapsed after the departure of Monckton and the rest of the smugglers, without anything of consequence occurring. Gordon Desborough remained constantly at home, and Adder had not yet found an oppotunity of seeking the interview with our heroine which he was so anxious for. But still he had not given up the determination which he had formed; and the better to ensure success, he had contrived to secure a key which would open the room door, and he, therefore, imagined that there was no doubt of his being enabled to ensure free access to the apartments that were appropriated to Rosabelle, whenever he thought proper, or when Gordon Desborough was out of the way. Gordon continued to behave in the same morose and careless manner as he had done before, and Adder, therefore, was restrained from talking to him further upon the subject of Rosabelle, seeing that it would be entirely useless endeavouring to persuade him to abandon the designs of Monckton, and to aid him in effecting his own and our heroine's escape from the smuggler-captain's power. In order that the suspicions of Gordon might not be excited, but that he might, on the contrary, be induced to imagine that he had given up his designs against Lady Ravensford in despair, Adder materially altered his behaviour, and appeared upon the same friendly and sociable terms with the ruffian as usual. But he calculated very wrong if he thought to deceive Gordon, for that villain was by far too sagacious, and, notwithstanding Adder talked to him with freedom upon topics quite foreign to that which wholly engrossed his thoughts, and did not betray the least confusion or emotion in his manner, Gordon could clearly read his thoughts, and kept a most vigilant eye upon his actions.

Davey Grampus daily visited the house, and once or twice he was accompanied by two or three rough-looking men, whom Adder imagined that he had seen among the smugglers, although he could not be positive, and whether or not such was the fact, he had not the least doubt but that they were employed by Monckton to assist Gordon in protecting our heroine, and preventing him (Adder) from attempting to convey her away during the absence of the smugglers.

In the meantime, Gordon Desborough constantly took Rosabelle and Mrs. Kitson their provisions, old Cicely, who had become more crabbed and sour, not being permitted to go near them, and the remarkable change in his manners also, could not escape their observation. When in the presence of Rosabelle, he entirely divested himself of the coarse and brutal manners that had formerly characterised him, and behaved with a civility, which no one who had known his character could have thought it possible he could have assumed.

Rosabelle and her companion were greatly astonished at this change, but still, in spite of the alteration in the ruffian's manners, when they remembered the horrible crime of which they knew him to be guilty, they could not help shuddering with terror when they beheld him, and could not make any reply to any observation which he might make to them, without feeling that disgust which the knowledge of the character of the miscreant had engendered in their breasts.

"What can be the meaning of this?" said Lady Rosabelle, on the second day after the departure of Monckton and his companions; "why is this remarkable alteration in the conduct of Gordon Desborough, as well as Monckton?—I feel myself entirely at a loss to account for it."

"And I, my lady," observed Mrs. Kitson, "can augur from it nothing but good. Gordon, no doubt, acts according to the orders of the captain, and, therefore, it is evident that you have nothing to fear from him."

"And, apparently, not from Adder, either," added our heroine, in better spirits, "for, although we are well aware that he is still an inmate of the house, he has not intruded himself upon me since our return to this place; by which it seems as if he were held under restraint."

"I am decidedly of your opinion, my lady," returned Mrs. Kitson; "and that strengthens my belief that Monckton is interested in your favour, and is determined to save you from his power."

"But then," remarked Rosabelle, after a pause, "if that were really the case, why should it have been so long ere that change was wrought in his sentiments, or what can have produced such a change? And why, again, did he not at once release me if it were his intention so to do?"

"It is impossible for us to guess exactly the reasons for Monckton's actions," replied

Mrs. Kitson; "but that my opinion of his ultimate intentions is, I feel, almost correct; and so, I trust, it will be proved ere long."

"Alas!" remarked Lady Ravensford, after a minute or two spent in meditation; "perhaps I have as much reason to dread the captain's feeling interested about me, as I have the persecution of the guilty wretch to whom I owe nearly all my misfortunes. Perhaps his real designs may be equally as base."

"Oh, no, my lady," uttered Mrs. Kitson; "I feel certain that you wrong Monckton by such an opinion; lawless as his course of life is, I have reason to believe that he is not destitute of honourable and honest feelings, and he would hate himself if he thought he could act the part of a villain towards one of the fair sex."

"You seem to possess an excellent opinion of the smuggler-captain."

"My husband being one of the crew, I have had plenty of opportunities of learning his character, and I do not think I have done him more than justice."

"I shall be most happy if experience convinces me that you have not," replied Rosabelle; "he told me, also, that he was my friend."

"And having said so, you may rest assured, my lady, that you are secure from your enemy," observed Mrs. Kitson; "Monckton's word is his bond at all times, and there is no danger he would fear to encounter to accomplish his wishes, especially when it was to serve one to whom he had promised his protection."

"The character you give of Monckton," said our heroine, "is noble."

"It is no more than he deserves," was Mrs. Kitson's reply.

"It is a great pity he is not moving in another station of society."

"He would not exchange the roving life of liberty he is at present leading," remarked Mrs. Kitson, "for one of the greatest luxury and splendour. He is a complete son of the ocean, and a sworn enemy to all tyrannical and oppressive imposts."

"Know you anything of his early history?" interrogated Lady Ravensford.

Mrs. Kitson answered in the negative,

"Then you do not know whether he was ever married, I suppose?" said Rosabelle; "I confess, after what you have said about this smuggler-captain, my curiosity is excited."

"Yes, my lady," replied Mrs. Kitson, "I have heard that he was married, before he took to his present course of life; but it is supposed that it was productive of sorrow to him, for such a thing is never hinted without his betraying the greatest emotion."

"But after all that you have said about the captain, and in his praise," remarked our heroine, after a short interval of silence, "there is

one circumstance which makes me entertain some prejudice against him."

"And pray what is that, my lady?" inquired Mrs. Kitson.

"Why, you have informed me that he is acquainted with some deed of blood which Adder has perpetrated at a former period; and if he his so, is he not equally as bad as that villain for concealing it, and suffering such a wretch to escape the punishment which is his due?"

"Why," replied Mrs. Kitson, "his conduct in that respect does, I confess, surprise me; but we know not what powerful motives he may have for his behaviour."

"There can be no innocent motives for shielding a murderer from justice," returned Rosabelle, "and for conniving with him in hiding his crime; nay more, for afterwards associating with that murderer, and aiding him in his base designs against that very sex, towards whom you have asserted that it was impossible he could act the villain."

"There certainly is some mystery in his conduct, in that respect," said Mrs. Kitson; "but, in all probability, everything will be explained satisfactorily before long."

"When I reflect upon those circumstances," continued Lady Ravensford, "it lessons the good opinion I had begun to form of Monckton, and makes me fearful that I have given encouragement to hopes that are only destined to be destroyed by disappointment."

"You must not again give way to despair, my lady," remonstrated Mrs. Kitson; "and I must request of you to reserve your decided opinion of Monckton until a future period, and when you may have a better opportunity of judging."

"Well, well; I will do so," replied our heroine, "although I am afraid that I shall not have any reason to discard the surmises which that you have told me has created in my bosom."

"At any rate, my lady," observed her companion, "Mr. Monckton has told you that he was your friend, and you should, therefore, in justice to him, I humbly sugggest, wait until you have seen whether or not he keeps his word. His former vices and his present ones may be great; but, although you may regret them, should he act as a friend towards you, by rescuing you from the villain Adder, and restoring you to your friends, you will have an undoubted right to feel grateful to him. But, pray excuse me, my lady. I am fearful that you will consider the words I have addressed to you too bold."

"By no means, Mrs. Kitson," answered Rosabelle, with her usual urbanity: "observations that are founded in truth can never be too boldly spoken. I perfectly agree with what you have just said, and shall act according to your suggestion."

"Oh, my lady, you do me too much honour for my simple advice," said the poor woman; "but still I hope that you will do as you say, for I am convinced that it will relieve the anguish of your mind. Something strikes me very forcibly that the present absence of Monckton is not altogether unconnected with you, and that he will make your friends acquainted with your situation, and where you are, and——"

"Oh, do you, indeed, think so?" eagerly interrupted our heroine: her eyes sparkling with renewed hope; "but," she added, after a brief pause, and her countenance changed; "alas! no; there is nothing reasonable in such a supposition; it would be preposterous to entertain such an idea."

"Why so?" hastily enquired her companion.

"Why," answered Lady Ravensfored, "if it were indeed Monckton's intentions to restore me to my friends, had he not the power to do so at once, and to bear me away from hence, without leaving me here a prisoner until he had made them aware of my situation?"

Mrs. Kitson was at a loss to answer this query, and she, therefore, remained silent for a short time, but at length she said——

"Doubtless, the captain, if he has made up his mind to serve you, my lady, which I am still firmly of opinion he has, has arranged his plans, and until they are put in practice, his conduct must appear ambiguous and inexplicable to us. But I do think that, on his return to this place, we shall soon be made acquainted with the truth of his intentions; and that this tedious and painful affair will be speedily brought to a termination one way or the other."

"There is one thing, at any rate," observed Lady Ravensford, "for which I ought to feel grateful to Captain Monckton."

"And what is that, pray, my lady?" asked Mrs. Kitson.

"Why, for having been the means, through commending you to Adder to take charge of my dear child, of introducing you to me," answered our heroine. "I am certain that had that detestable and heartless old woman, Cicely, have been suffered to attend me much longer, my spirits must have sunk beneath her continual annoyances, and it is not at all unlikely that I should have been, ere this, no more."

"Cicely is, indeed, as you say, my lady," coincided Mrs. Kitson, "a most detestable old woman, and actually delights in the miseries of her fellow-creatures, especially those of her own sex. But I wonder that you never spoke to Adder about her conduct; he surely would not have suffered it if you had."

"Oh, you need not wonder that I did not do so," observed Lady Ravensford, "when you think upon the disgust with which I must have viewed that villain, and the repugnance I must feel in speaking to him at all. Besides, it is not likely that I could imagine she acted any otherwise than by the orders and authority of Adder."

"Well, my lady," said Mrs. Kitson, "that unpleasantness is at an end now, and you need not apprehend that you will be annoyed by her again."

Thus alternately wavering between hope, doubt, and fear, the hours passed away; Mrs. Kitson, with a most praiseworthy zeal, always endeavouring to keep up the spirits of Lady Rosabelle, by inspiring her with hope, and being prepared with some argument to combat her fears, and, through her exertions, the former generally predominated in our heroine's mind.

Monckton and his companions had now been gone a week, and hitherto, although Adder had watched most eagerly and impatiently, he had not seen the slightest chance of putting his wishes into effect; Gordon never, even for a short time, leaving the house, and being most careful that he should not have any opportunity of seeing or speaking to Lady Ravensford or her companion. There were times when, notwithstanding his endeavours to do so, Adder could scarcely retain his rage within bounds, and when he was half-tempted to lay violent hands on Gordon, and, by a desperate effort, to enforce the accomplishment of his wishes; but there was something in the looks and manners of the ruffian that withheld him, and kept him in a state of dread; and thus he saw day after day wane away without any prospect of an alteration, or of the realisation of his desires, and he almost sunk into a state of complete despair.

At length, on the seventh day, while he was seated in company with Gordon, in the parlour of his house, Cicely hastily entered with a note in her hand, which she presented to the ruffian, who hastily unfolded it, and glanced over the contents. They evidently occasioned him much emotion, and after he had perused them, he jumped up hurriedly, and putting on his hat, without taking any notice of Adder, he addressed himself to Cicely, and said——

"Mind and do as I have told you; I shall not be back, I dare say, before the evening."

Cicely muttered an obedience to his orders, and he then immediately quitted the house.

What it was that Cicely had promised to do, Adder was ignorant of, but Gordon Desborough had not been gone many minutes, when she retired to her own little closet, where she always had a bottle or two of the best, and was very soon in a fair way to enjoy herself, and to become entirely unconscious of all that was taking place; and Adder hailing the so long-looked-for opportunity with pleasure, he ascended the stairs on tip-toe, and having reached the door which opened upon the suite of rooms appropriated to the use of Lady Ravensford, he knocked.

Mrs. Kitson, probably thinking it was Gordon Desborough, quickly opened the door, but started back with no little amazement, agitation, and confusion, when she beheld the villain Adder. He immediately stepped into the room, and Rosabelle having heard the exclamation which Mrs. Kitson had given utterance to, came from her chamber, but on seeing Adder, she turned very pale, and trembled so violently that she could scarcely prevent herself from sinking on the floor.

The stern and forbidding features of Adder relaxed into a smile, which he meant to be one of kindness, but he could not conceal his exultation, and the guilty passions that raged like a tempest within his bosom, and turning to Mrs. Kitson, he exclaimed in an authoritative tone—

"Leave the room, woman!"

Mrs. Kitson hesitated, and looked at our heroine.

"Do you hear?" demanded Adder, in a

THE QUARREL BETWEEN ADDER AND THE SMUGGLERS.

louder tone; "begone, I have something to say to Lady Ravensford, which must not meet your prying inquisitive ear."

"You should have nothing to say to me, sir," said our heroine, regaining her firmness, "which should be kept a secret from a second person. Mrs. Kitson, I desire you to remain where you are; Mr. Adder can have no authority for obtruding his hateful presence upon one whom he has already so deeply, so irreparably injured. Do not offer to depart, Mrs. Kitson—I desire, nay, command you."

"These mandates are of no avail," cried Adder; "I have long sought this interview, and I will not now be foiled. Begone, I say!"

"I shall remain where I am, sir, while it is the wish of Lady Ravensford," returned Mrs. Kitson, boldly.

"Ah!" exclaimed Adder, his eyes sparkling with rage, "dare you?—then you must e'en go by force."

Immediately seizing Mrs. Kitson, as he spoke, by the shoulders, he pushed her violently from the room, and closing the door, locked it, preventing her entrance. He then advanced towards Lady Rosabelle, who, upon the impulse of the moment, was in the act of retreating to her chamber, and fastening herself in, when the villain sprang quickly forward, and seizing her vehemently by the arm, he drew her back.

The little Alfred clung to his mother's

knees, and looking up anxiously and imploringly in the face of Adder, he cried aloud, sobbing that,—"The naughty man should not hurt his poor mamma."

"Unmanly ruffian!" cried Rosabelle, "unhand me, or my cries shall reach the ears of those who will punish you for your boldness and cruelty!—What is the meaning of this savage outrage?"

"It means, fair Rosabelle," replied Adder, forcibly throwing his arm around her waist, and drawing her towards him, "that, finding I have too long been a weak forbearing fool, when I had you securely in my power, I am determined that I will no longer wait for the gratification of my burning desires. I have condescended to sue to you, where I might long since have enforced your compliance; I have made you every reasonable proposal, and have submitted patiently to your scorn, and contemptuous rejection of my suit; but I am now aroused to a full sense of my folly, and am determined at all hazards, that your person shall be mine!"

"Brutal monster!" exclaimed Rosabelle, struggling violently, although the expressions of Adder, and his determined demeanour, filled her with terror; "are you not satisfied with probably having murdered my unfortunate husband and father, and inflicted upon me a series of miseries almost unparalleled in the annals of humanity, but that you would now add to your barbarity by so atrocious a crime as that you threaten?—Oh, help! help!—Just Heaven, I call upon thee for thy protection!—Oh, save me! save me!"

As the distracted and terrified lady thus screamed, she struggled violently to extricate herself from the embraces of the ruffian Adder, but her efforts were for some time entirely ineffectual, and with every endeavour she made, the passions of Adder increased, and his cheeks glowed and his eyes flashed with the guilty desires that raged within his breast. He sought, however, to stifle her cries, but in vain.

"Nay," he cried, "you scream for help in vain; there is no one at hand to interpose to save you! The triumph so long protracted, now is mine! This hour—this very moment gives you to my arms!"

"Almighty God! protect me! save me!" again shrieked our heroine, in the most frantic accents, and, with a desperate effort, she released herself from Adder's hold, and retreated to the farther end of the apartment, where on a table was a knife. Scarcely knowing what she did, she snatched it up, and, as Adder approached towards her, she flourished it menacingly, and exclaimed—

"Villain! advance but one inch towards me, and this knife shall stretch me a bleeding corpse at your feet!"

Adder was completely staggered by the determined air which Rosabelle assumed, and he was transfixed to the spot whereon he stood, not knowing what course to pursue.

Our heroine still flourished the knife menacingly, and holding her child with one hand, kept the villain at bay.

"You see I am resolute," she cried; "and, by Heaven, sooner than I will be dishonoured, I will put my threat into execution! Death is preferable to the dreadful, the disgusting fate with which you have threatened me. Nay, nothing can move me from my purpose! Quit the room, miscreant, unless you would have my death to answer for, in addition to your other numerous crimes!"

"Rosabelle," ejaculated Adder, offering to approach her; "hear me!"

"Not a word," firmly replied Rosabelle; "nothing whatever can shake my resolution; begone!"

At that moment a loud noise was heard at the chamber-door, and immediately afterwards the voices of several persons, and that of Mrs. Kitson above the rest.

Adder turned pale and trembled.

"Ah!" he ejaculated; "fool that I was not to secure her. The woman Kitson has betrayed me!"

"Open the door, or it will be worse for you!" now demanded the voice of Gordon Desborough.

"Never!" cried Adder, desperately, and placing his back against it as he spoke.

"Then we must use force," returned Gordon; "now, lads, your aid."

In an instant the door was burst open, and Gordon, followed by three rough-looking men, the same that Adder had before seen at the house, entered the room.

"Seize him, my lads; and bear him hence!" cried Gordon, and in a moment the men rushed upon Adder, who made a desperate resistance, but was quickly overpowered, and was conveyed, struggling, swearing, and foaming at the mouth from the room, and being dragged to one of the dark vaults underground, was, by the orders of Gordon, locked in, and left to his own reflections, the nature of which may be readily conjectured, but cannot be properly described.

Mrs. Kitson, immediately on being thrust out of the room by Adder, had hastened below, where, ascertaining that Gordon was from home, although it was very reluctantly that old Cicely furnished her with the information, she made the best of her way to the "caboose," where she fortunately found him, in company with the men before mentioned, and having informed him of the perilous situation of our heroine, he left the place, and, as has been shown, arrived just at the critical juncture, to save her from destruction.

CHAPTER XXXI.

MONCKTON'S EXPLANATION TO ROSABELLE.— THE VILLAIN DEFEATED.

ADDER had no sooner been forced away from the room, than our heroine, overpowered by her feelings, and the unusual excitement she had undergone, fainted, and Mrs. Kitson was once more left alone with her, and immediately set about the means of restoring her to sensibility.

It would be impossible to portray correctly the disappointment and ungovernable rage of Adder, when he found himself not only foiled in his diabolical attempt, but made a prisoner in that gloomy vault. He raved; he stormed; he cursed, and swore, and breathed the most fearful maledictions against Mrs. Kitson, Gordon, and Monckton. Then he made the place re-echo again, with his cries to be released, but the hollow revereberations of that subterranean place, were the only answeres he received, and he traversed the limited space in which he was confined, in a state bordering upon madness. He now at once saw that he was caught, trepanned, defeated, and all his well-laid schemes rendered abortive, and himself left entirely at the mercy of Monckton and his associates; and when he recollected the threats which the former had held out to him, if he should make any attempt against the peace of Rosabelle, during his absence, he felt that he had every reason to apprehend the most terrible consequences through his mad impetuosity. All the horrors of an ignominious death rushed upon his mind, and his anguish was so great, that he completely sunk under it. He crouched down in one corner of his cell, and became the image of despair. It appeared as though his career of guilt were fast drawing to a close, and that fate had destined that every attempt he should in future make, should be frustrated.

In this state he remained for more than two hours, without any one appearing to interrupt him, when he heard some one unbolting the door of his cell, and immediately afterwards it was thrown back on its hinges, and Gordon Desborough, accompanied by one of the men who had been his companions in the seizure, entered.

He brought with him a stone pitcher, containing water, and a loaf, which he placed on the ground, and then eyed Adder with a look of the most malignant exultation.

Adder sprang to his feet, fury gleaming in his eyes, and advancing towards Gordon, he cried, in a hoarse voice—

"Dastard knave! why am I thus seized and made a prisoner of in this dismal place?"

"Recollect your recent conduct, and the warning of Monckton," said Gordon, coolly, "and you are answered."

"And what authority has either he or you for detaining me?" demanded Adder.

"Upon that point I dare say you will be satisfied at a future time," returned Gordon, in the same deliberate and careless tones.

"But you will not dare detain me?"

"That has to be proved."

"Villain! you will have to answer dearly for this," said Adder.

"Previous to which," retorted Gordon, ironically, "you will probably be called to a slight account for the abduction and unlawful detention of Lady Ravensford, also for a certain crime perpetrated about sixteen years since, and——"

"Confusion!" interrupted Adder; "am I then placed in the power of every wretch? Oh, Monckton!—Monckton! for this, my heaviest malediction light upon you head."

"Trusting that you may soon fell at home in your new apartment," said Gordon, with a most provoking grin, "I will now leave you to the enjoyment of it. Come on, Ned."

And thus saying, before Adder could give utterance to another syllable, although his looks evinced the torturing feelings of chagrin, disappointment, and resentment he was undergoing, Gordon Desborough and his companion quitted the cell, and slammed and bolted the door after them, leaving Adder involved in utter darkness, for they had not supplied him with a lamp.

Adder threw himself on the hard ground, and he groaned aloud with the agony of his feelings, but his present suffering was nothing compared with the horrors of anticipation, and he dreaded the return of Monkton, fearing that the terrible result would be that which he had promised him.

Three days and nights passed away in this manner, and Adder was still kept a prisoner in the subterranean vault, and was daily visited by Gordon Desborough, who came to bring him his scanty allowance of provisions, and to taunt him with his degraded and altered situation. The unhappy wretch was at length completely subdued in spirit, and was incapable of answering the ruffian, and he was at last so humbled as to entreat Gordon's mercy, and to pray that he would release him from his present place of confinement to one less dismal. This request, however, Gordon only treated with scorn and derision; so true it is that none feel greater pleasure than the guilty in torturing one another. Although Adder had never given the ruffian the least cause for offence, but, on the contrary, according to his own admission, had liberally rewarded him for the nefarious transactions in which he had employed him, he now felt the most savage delight in adding to his misery as much as possible; and the more he saw him suffer, and the more humbled he was, the greater did he exult. He had no doubt he should receive great praise, and something more substantial from Monckton for the manner in which he had acted, and he anticipated his return with much impatience. He was not made thoroughly acquainted with Monckton's intention as regarded Rosabelle, but, he had not the least doubt it was to restore her to her friends, and he imagined that he would ensure from them a rich reward, in which he also expected to become a sharer to no small amount, for the services he had rendered. How far his expectations were realised, will be seen anon.

When our heroine had quite recovered from the shock which she had received from the behaviour of the villain Adder, she returned the most heartfelt thanks to the Almighty for her preservation, and for the fortitude with which she had been imbued to resist him. She then expressed her warmest acknowledgments to Mrs. Kitson, to whose presence of mind in hastening for the aid of Gordon Desborough, she might, in a great measure, attribute her preservation. The conduct of Gordon, who, there could not be the least doubt, acted entirely by the orders of Monckton, left her no longer any room to doubt but that the latter was really the friend and protector he had told her he was; and now that Adder was thrust into confinement, from which they were assured he would not be released until the return of the smuggler-captain, our heroine felt that she was safe.

"What ready means guilt often unthinkingly takes to defeat its own designs," observed Mrs. Kitson. "Adder thrusting me out of the room, was the very cause of bringing about his own confusion, and frustrating his evil intentions; for, had he placed me in another room, and confined me therein, he might easily have silenced old Cicely, had she been inclined to oppose him, and thus he would have been almost certain to have obtained his object."

"Oh, no," returned Rosabelle, "my mind was fully made up; never did I feel more determined, and he perceived it. I would have plunged the knife to my heart, sooner than he should have triumphed in his disgusting and diabolical purpose!"

"Oh, my lady," said Mrs. Kitson, "the idea of that makes me shudder with horror! Heaven be praised, that preserved you from such a dreadful and untimely end. But the wretch will no doubt be amply punished for his crimes, and for all the sufferings that he has inflicted upon you."

"And how think you that Monckton will dispose of him?" interrogated Rosabelle.

"Deliver him up to the hands of justice," replied Mr. Kitson.

"How can he do so without getting himself into trouble?"

"Oh, there is no doubt but that he will readily hit upon a plan," said Mrs. Kitson;

"I dare say he has already arranged that, without knowing anything of the late circumstance. Cheer up, my lady, for, depend upon it, your troubles are fast drawing to a close, and not many days will elapse ere you will be again restored to your friends."

"Alas!" ejaculated Lady Ravensford, tears gushing to her eyes, "perhaps I have no dear friends to receive me! Oh, how my poor heart chills at the thought!"

"Pray, my dear lady," said Mrs. Kitson, "do not encourage fears, which, after all, may prove unfounded. Great, no doubt, as has been the sufferings of Lord Ravensford and your father, I firmly believe that they are still living, or Monckton and the others would have been certain to have heard it."

"My unhappy husband may have been enabled to withstand the severity of his accumulated and unparalleled calamities," observed Lady Ravensford, "but my poor father—oh, well am I convinced that his mind must have again become a wreck, in which case, it would be a mercy if the Almighty should be pleased to take him to Himself. Poor grey-haired old man, fondest of fathers, best of human beings! shall I ever again be enfolded to thy paternal bosom, with the conviction that thou art conscious it is thy poor persecuted daughter thou dost embrace?—Alas! I fear never."

"Oh, yes, my lady, you will," ejaculated Mrs. Kitson, energetically. "Heaven in its infinite mercy will not deny you such a blessing after the many afflictions you have so undeservedly undergone. Have you not every reason to place the firmest reliance upon its goodness, after the manner in which you have ever been preserved in the moment of the most imminent danger?"

"Yes, my good woman," replied our heroine, drying her tears; "indeed I have, and it is ungrateful in me thus to give way to despair. But my mind is so continually tormented, that I scarcely know what I am saying."

"At any rate, my lady," observed her companion, "now that Adder is made a prisoner, you may rest yourself secure, and Monckton, I dare say, will not be long before he returns, when you will speedily be made acquainted with his intentions, which, as I have all along predicted, depend upon it, will be all in your favour."

The ideas of Mrs. Kitson were too reasonable to be rejected by Rosabelle, and she looked forward to the return of the smuggler-captain with the greatest anxiety.

A fortnight had now waned away, and still Monckton and his companions did not return; and Gordon, who did not expect that they would be gone so long, was fearful lest some accident should have befallen them. He still kept the wretched Adder confined in the same place, and he now became the complete victim of despair. His form had wasted away, and his countenance betrayed the deep, the intense agony which perpetually tortured his mind. How dreary were the days and nights passed in that dark cell, where he had nothing to commune with but his own dreadful thoughts, and where the horrors of his own guilty conscience constantly brought to his imagination the many crimes he had committed, but above all, the murder of the unfortunate Rose Allerton, whose ghastly form was continually before his eyes, and ringing in his ears were the curses of offended Heaven. Conjecture cannot form but a weak picture of the mental sufferings of that man of crime. Oh, who would be guilty, did they but think upon the horrors that must sooner or later overtake them?—For the gratification of some moment of sensual pleasure; for the transitory indulgence of some ambitious wish, the unhappy wretch falls into crime, to pay for it by years of mental suffering, and ignominious death, and an eternity of torment!—Oh, how fearful the price, would but erring mortals pause and think!

It was on a stormy midnight, and nearly three weeks had elapsed since the smugglers had left on their adventurous trip, when Davey Grampus, who was smoking away as usual, in company with Gordon Desborough, in the little back room, and although it was so late, they had neither of them thought of separating, when they were suddenly aroused by hearing a shrill whistle. The pipes were removed from their lips in an instant, and they both jumped hastily to their feet.

"Monckton's signal by all that's fortunate;" exclaimed Davey Grampus, taking up the lamp, and followed by Gordon, advancing towards the door; "they have come back at last, and all safe, I hope!"

"Quick! quick! Davey; "you are not quite so active as you were, methinks," exclaimed a well-known voice.

"Hurrah!" cried Grampus, joyfully; "there's the captain, safe and sound, at any rate. Coming, my trojan!"

Gordon now eagerly assisted Grampus to remove the massive chains that secured the door, and immediately, to their satisfaction, Monckton, Michael Hernwood, and Sam Kitson entered, and snatching their hands, shook them heartily.

"You have come back then, captain," said Davey Grampus; "and is all safe?"

"Everything, my hearties," answered Monckton, who appeared to be in unusual spirits, "and as prosperous as we could wish."

"Are the lads all returned?" asked Grampus.

"All of them," was the reply, "and they will be here, when they have finished stowing away the cargo."

"This has, indeed, been a long trip, cap-

tain," said Gordon Desborough, "and I had began to fear that you were never going to return."

"Better late than never," answered Monckton. "But how is all at the house?"

"Quite safe, captain," replied Desborough, with a peculiar grin; "the lady in her own apartments with her companion, Mrs. Kitson, and that arrant scoundrel, Adder, confined in one of the vaults underground, where he has been ever since two or three days after your departure."

"Ah!" exclaimed the smuggler-captain; "has he then dared to scorn the warning I gave him?"

Gordon briefly related what had taken place between Adder and our heroine.

"Why, the damned shark!" cried Monckton, passionately; "after the strict injunctions which I laid upon him, and knowing that he was placed entirely at my mercy. But he shall pay dearly for it; his doom is sealed."

"I did not know whether you would approve of the lodging I had given the fellow?" said Gordon.

"You have acted perfectly right," said Monckton; "and I commend you for what you have done. Adder shall quickly have another berth, and his career he may reckon at an end. And is the lady quite well?"

Gordon answered in the affirmative.

"I am happy to hear that," said Monckton, "she shall not much longer remain in the position she is now placed in. Poor lady, I shall for ever regret having been instrumental, in any way, towards her unhappiness; but I knew not who she was, or the villain, Adder, should not long have retained possession of her. However, his time of shame is fast approaching, and bitterly will he have to pay for all."

"It is, then, your intention to restore the lady to liberty?" asked Gordon.

"Certainly," answered Monckton, "and to her friends."

"But you will run a great risk in so doing, will you not, captain?"

"No—leave me alone for that; I have arranged everything in my own mind," said Monckton.

"I was only thinking, captain," observed Gordon, "that after the death of Bill Eldon—which you say was by your hand—that the d——d land-swabs would keep a sharper look out for you than they had before done."

"Pshaw!" ejaculated Monckton; "I defy them all; and while my brave fellows only remain true to me, I think I have good reason to do so."

"Ay, ay, that's correct," said Davey Grampus, "and no more than they deserve; and I know they will fight like devils, through fire and water, to serve you, captain."

"They are gallant fellows," said Monckton, "and I love them all as if they were my brothers."

"But how do you intend to dispose of Adder?" interrogated Gordon.

"I have not exactly made up my mind, although I did threaten him with death," answered Monckton. "To-morrow night, or the next, I shall convey the lubber on board ship, and far away from hence."

"You would not deprive him of life?" asked Desborough.

"No," replied Monckton, "not by my own hands; besides it would be a pity to deprive the hangman of a job."

Gordon did not return any answer to this, for when he recollected the crimes of which he had himself been guilty, he thought that it was not at all unlikely that he should himself afford employment for that functionary, sooner or later.

The rest of the smugglers now joined them, and, after sitting for about an hour longer, carousing, Gordon Desborough arose to leave them, and Monckton and his companions retired to rest.

In the morning early, the smuggler-captain was traversing his way from the "caboose," along the vaulted passages that communicated with that place and the house of Gordon Desborough, and at length stopped at the door of the vault in which Adder was confined. There he paused and listened, for he could hear him uttering exclamations of anguish, and he could not help feeling that he was only justly punished for the part he had played towards the unfortunate Lady Ravensford and her friends, independant of the monstrous crime he had committed by murdering Rose Allerton and her unborn infant.

At length he withdrew the bolts, and entered the cell. The dim light which was emitted by the lamp which Monckton carried, could but faintly penetrate the gloom of the miserable place, so that Adder did not at first perceive who it was that had entered, and, no doubt, did not think that it was any one else than Gordon; and the smuggler stood contemplating him for a minute or two in silence, but resentment was strongly pourtrayed in his countenance.

"So, villain," he at length said, "you have dared to brave my threats, to disobey my injunctions, and have again offered to ——"

He was interrupted by a loud exclamation from Adder, who, upon recognising his voice, sprang forward, and in the most abject manner knelt at Monckton's feet, and looked up in his face with the most earnest supplication.

"Oh, Monckton," he cried, in the most impressive tones, "spare me—pity me—pardon me! I will own my guilt—I will acknowledge I was wrong; but let the agony I have for the last fortnight in this place satisfy you, and do not—oh, do not proceed to extremities."

Monckton fixed upon him a look of the utmost contempt, as he replied—

"And have you, then, the effrontery to crave pardon, after setting all my injunctions at defiance?—I gave you sufficient warning of what the consequences would be, did you not obey me; you have scorned it, and those consequences you must abide by."

"No, no," groaned the poor, terrified wretch, still remaining on his knees to the smuggler-captain, and looking the very picture of death, with the excess of his fears; "you surely will not do as you say?—You will not deliver me up to justice?—Consign me to an ignominious and violent death!—Pause ere you do so!—My death will avail you nothing. Suffer me therefore to live to repent, and I promise you that Lady Ravensford or her friends shall not receive any further annoyance from me!"

"I will take especial care that they do not," returned Monckton, with a sarcastic grin.

"My life will at any time be in your hands," added the poor, trembling coward; "should I again break my word, Monckton, I beg of you, I supplicate to you in the most humble manner, do not doom me yet to death!"

"Despicable scoundrel!" ejaculated Monckton; "so callous to the sufferings of others, and yet so fearful of suffering himself. Wretch! you deserve to die the death of a dog, and you will do so."

Adder groaned and covered his face with his hands.

"Prepare yourself to depart from hence in my custody to-morrow night," said Monckton, as he moved towards the door of the cell.

"Whither, Monckton, and for what purpose? Oh, tell me—tell me!" intreated Adder, his whole frame violently convulsed with the power of his emotions. Monckton looked at him for a moment, in silence, and then replied—

"You will know anon; at present I shall leave you to form your own conjectures, and to ask your conscience what ought to be your destiny."

"Stay, Monckton, I beseech you!" cried the unfortunate prisoner, in delirious accents; but the smuggler-captain had immediately quitted the cell, and securing the door, was quickly far out of hearing.

"Inquire whether Lady Ravensford will do me the favour to grant me an interview," said Monckton, addressing himself to Gordon Desborough, soon after he had entered the parlour, after quitting the place in which Adder was confined.

Gordon, without offering any observation, hastened to do as he was bid, and quickly returned with an answer in the affirmative. Monckton then hurried up-stairs, and knocking at the door, was ushered into the presence of Lady Ravensford.

He paused at the door, and bowed to our

heroine with an air of the utmost respect, and he was altogether lost in the admiration of Rosabelle's beauty. Her cheeks had become flushed immediately on her hearing the message from Monckton, and her heart palpitated violently against her side with rekindled hopes.

"Lady Ravensford," at last observed Monckton, in a respectful tone of voice; "I have no doubt that I have suffered much in your opinion, from the part which I at first unfortunately enacted in the plot against you by your enemy, Adder?"

Our heroine attempted to reply, but she was too much confused to do so, and Monckton continued—

"I am now, however, anxious to make all the reparation in my power, by restoring you to liberty and your friends!"

Rosablle uttered an exclamation of mingled delight and gratitude, and instantly sunk at the feet of Monckton, and while the tears gushed from her eyes, she sobbed—

"Oh, thanks! thanks! kind sir, for this—"

Monckton interrupted her, and gently raised her from her knees.

"Nay, my dear lady," he said, "I merit not your thanks; for, probably, had it not have been for a certain discovery I, by accident, made, I might still have taken no interest in your fate."

"A discovery!" repeated Rosabelle, with a look of astonishment.

"Ay," answered the smuggler-captain;— "that you are the daughter of the good, but unfortunate, Mr. Montalbert,"

"Ah!" ejaculated Rosabelle; "know you then poor, dear father?"

"Lady," answered the smuggler-captain, in peculiar accents, "I have reason to know him, to be unceasing in my gratitude towards him."

"Oh, say, does he still live?"

"He does!"

"Heaven receive my thanks!" cried our heroine, fervently, clasping her hands, and raising her eyes. "But his reason;—oh, does he still retain that?"

Monckton remained silent.

"Alas!" ejaculated Rosabelle, "your silence convinces me that his mind is again a wreck! Oh, what a curse have I, his wretched daughter, proved to him."

"Be calm, be calm, be calm, lady, I beg of you," said Monckton; "all may yet be well; your restoration to his arms may recall his scattered senses."

Lady Ravensford shook her head despairingly.

—"Lady Ravensford," continued Monckton; "I have not yet informed you why I have such reasons to feel grateful to your father, and to befriend his daughter. Listen:—Probably,

you may have heard your father mention a circumstance which I am now about to repeat to you. A young couple named Malcolm were his tenants, who had not been long married when he was killed by an accident. His wife, at the time, was pregnant, and would have been reduced to a state of the greatest distress, had it not been for the kindness and benevolence of Mr. Montalbert and your amiable mother. They took her into their house, and behaved to her with the same attention as if she had been their own relation. She, however, died in her confinement, but her child, a boy, lived. That child Mr. Montalbert adopted as his own, and he was brought up under his care, and educated in a superior manner, on the completion of which, his benefactor placed him in his counting-house, intending to bring him up to mercantile pursuits. The young man was very wild, and abused the kindness of his benefactor. He robbed him to a large amount and absconded. After squandering away his ill-gotten money in scenes of vice, he went to sea, and at last became connected with smugglers. Need I explain any further? In Archibald Monckton, the captain of the smugglers, who now stands before you, you behold that ungrateful object of your father's philanthrophy, Raymond Malcolm!'

Rosabelle, who had listened to the smuggler-captain with much attention, expressed her surprise. Monckton paused for a minute only, and then continued:—

"The moment that I heard that you were the daughter of Mr. Montalbert, I was determined to make all the atonement I could for the ingratitude with which I had behaved towards your father, by restoring you to liberty, and I will do so, even though my own life should be sacrificed."

Rosabelle again sunk on her knees to the smuggler-captain, and by her looks, (for she could not speak), expressed her unbounded gratitude. Monckton, however, again gently raised her, and said,—

"No more, lady, I have told you the reasons for my conduct, and I have done. For the present, farewell; in three days more I will fulfil my promise to you, and restore you to your friends; until which time, I beg of you to wait patiently, and to rest assured that I will not deceive you."

Having thus spoken, Monckton bowed most respectfully to our heroine, and, before she could make use of another observation, he quitted the apartment.

We shall not seek to describe the feelings of delight which our heroine and Mrs. Kitson experienced when Monckton was gone; but the first thing which Lady Ravensford did, was to sink on her knees and to return thanks to Heaven for its goodness to her, in which her kind companion most heartily joined.

All the hopes and expectations of the latter were thus realised, and she a thousand times expressed her delight at the speedy deliverance from long and painful confinement, which Lady Rosabelle was promised by Monckton that she should experience. The tale which the smuggler-captain had imparted to our heroine, had created her deepest interest and surprise, and she well remembered that her father had made frequent mention of the circumstance, and referred to young Archibald's delinquency, with the deepest regret.

"There is only one circumstance which I shall regret," observed Mrs. Kitson, "and that is, that we shall be so soon separated, and the probability that I may never behold you again, my lady."

"Oh, but surely that may be avoided," said Lady Ravensford; "could your husband be persuaded to abandon his present course of life, I know that Lord Ravensford would establish him in some situation, and then you could, if you liked, remain near my person."

"Oh, most glad should I be if I were able to persuade my husband to do so," observed Mrs. Kitson; "but I know he is so attached to Captain Monckton and his other associates, that nothing would induce him to leave them."

"At any rate, he would not object to your visiting me sometimes," said Rosabelle.

"Oh, no, he would not do that, my lady, I am certain," replied Mrs. Kitson; and most happy should I be, would your ladyship grant me that honour."

"My good woman," remarked our heroine, "your visits will afford me as much pleasure as they can do yourself; for always must I entertain a most grateful sense of your kindness to me."

Mrs. Kitson returned her acknowledgments to Lady Ravensford for this condescension, and they then changed the topic of conversation, and discoursed upon the singular defeat which the villain, Adder, had so suddenly experienced, and the fortuitous circumstances that had brought about the restoration of our heroine to liberty.

After her interview with the smuggler-captain, Lady Ravensford had become, as it were, quite another being, and her past sufferings were almost forgotten in her anticipation of the future. She looked forward to the third day, when Monckton had promised to release her from her place of confinement with the utmost anxiety, although, after what he had said, she did not entertain the least idea that he would deceive her.

CHAPTER XXXII.

THE RESCUE.—THE DEFEATED VILLAIN.

ON the following evening, whilst Adder was pacing his narrow cell with disordered footsteps, and in a state of mind bordering upon frenzy, his cell door was thrown open, and two or three of the smugglers, followed by Monckton, entered.

"Seize him, my lads," cried the latter, "and convey him on board; we will soon find a way to dispose of the scoundrel."

"Monckton," said Adder, struggling despairingly in the grasp of the smugglers, "beware of what you do!"

"There, do not listen to his jargon, but away with him!" commanded Monckton.

Adder was immediately gagged, and forced away from the place, hurried along to the beach, where a boat was waiting for them, into which he was forced, Monckton and the others following, and making their way towards the ship which awaited for them.

And now terror and despair was upon that villain's heart, who erst had been so hardened and reckless, and whose greatest delight had appeared to be in the miseries of others. The poor, guilty malefactor, standing upon the verge of eternity, into which he is about to be plunged by a violent and shameful death, could not feel greater tortures than he experienced at that moment; indeed, he felt himself placed in a similar situation, for his fears made him anticipate the worst, and he did not doubt but that Monckton was about to put the threats he had made to him into execution, and that ere long he should be the inmate of a gaol, awaiting a painful and ignominious trial, with all the prospects of conviction before his eyes, and at last an awful death upon the public scaffold. How those individuals whom he had so cruelly persecuted would exult at his downfall—his disgraceful situation—Lord Ravensford, his wife—all—all! The torture of madness seized upon his brain when he reflected that the latter was now most certainly lost to him for ever, and the fool he had been, after having so long had her in his power, to suffer the opportunity of gratifying his disgusting passions to go by; and then he again cursed the folly which had induced him to trust to Monckton in the affair at all. But yet, had he not entrusted him with a far more important secret, and he had not betrayed him, and, therefore, had he not every reason to place confidence in him on that occasion? Never could he have been persuaded that he would have acted as he had done, and he could scarcely credit his senses, or convince himself that he was not labouring under the influence of some remarkable dream. Alas! the stern reality was too soon to break upon him.

All these thoughts passed through the

miscreant Adder's mind with the rapidity of the whirlwind, and with the same destructive effect, as the smugglers conveyed him from the "caboose" to the sea-beach, and he looked with an expression of supplication upon Monckton; but the stern glance which met his, convinced him that he had nothing to hope there, and groaning aloud with mental agony, he was constrained to submit to his fate, terrible as he had every reason to fear it would be.

"I have changed my mind, my lads," said the smuggler-captain, as they proceeded, "I will e'en accompany ye, for, perhaps, my presence may be required in the disposal of this lubber."

'Well, as you like, captain," said one of the smugglers; "we shall be very glad of your company, although you need not fear but that we should have disposed of the gentleman well enough, and in a manner that would have given you every satisfaction."

'I have no doubt you would, Ned Mayling," observed Monckton, "and am much obliged to you for your good intentions; but, as the *gentleman* and I are very old acquaintances, it would show a very great want of etiquette on my part were I to separate from him so unceremoniously."

Monckton laughed as he thus spoke, in bitter irony, and every word that he uttered went to the heart of Adder, while the look

ADDER MAKES AN ATTEMPT UPON THE LIFE OF MONCKTON.

which the former fixed upon him was one which made him feel his shame and humiliation more than all.

Monckton noticed the violent workings of Adder's countenance, which plainly showed the deep mental anguish he must be enduring, with looks of exultation, and Adder, perceiving that, made a desperate effort to conquer his emotions, and to assume a different air; the attempt, however, was a most miserable failure, and the smuggler-captain's triumph was rather increased than dimished by observing it, and he laughed aloud in bitter scorn.

They had now reached the boat, into which Monckton and his companions stepped, and into it Adder was dragged like a dog, where

his arms and his legs were pinioned, to prevent his endeavouring to make his escape, by plunging into the sea, and he was placed at the bottom of the boat. Despair had now completely overpowered him, and had they not have secured him, he would have remained passive as an infant. He cast his eyes up towards the black clouds above his head, his senses reeled, and he became unconscious of what was passing, or how the smugglers were disposing of him.

When he was restored to sensibility, he found himself in a little miserable, confined cabin, where there was scarcely room enough for him to move about, and which was involved in total darkness. The cords had been removed, but his limbs were sore and aching where they had been placed, from the unfeeling manner in which the smugglers had bound him. The motion of the vessel was violent, the waves dashed with a hollow, monotonous sound against its sides, and it seemed to blow a stiff gale. Adder listened, and could distinctly hear the heavy tread of the persons who kept watch upon deck. His mind was still racked with the most torturing thoughts, and his brain was hot and feverish. The crisis of his fate, he knew full well, was rapidly approaching, but what that fate would be, he could not form any other conjecture than that Monckton would find some means of delivering him up to the hands of justice, and accusing him of the murder of the unfortunate and ill-fated Rose Allerton, yet how he could do so without involving himself in danger, he was at a loss to imagine. He was suddenly aroused from these reflections by hearing the sounds of revelry and mirth, which seemed to proceed from a part of the vessel contiguous to the cabin in which he was confined; and paying stricter attention, he was enabled to make out the following words, which were sung by the smugglers in their usual style of course glee,—

"The landsman joy can never know,
Like those who o'er the ocean go,
    With a good stiff breeze,
    O'er the dark blue seas,
The white spray kissing the vessel's sides.
    Oh, what can compare
    To the life so rare,
    When the grog we quaff,
    And at danger laugh,
As our gallant barque o'er the billows glides?
    Oh, this is a life of liberty,
    And none so happy as smugglers be!

"The storm may rage, and the waves may rise,
Their white crests mounting towards the skies;
    But we laugh at fear,
    And when danger's near,
Each heart his threatening form derides.
    Stiff blows the gale,
    Yet no fears assail,
    But the grog we quaff,
    And at danger scoff,
As our gallant barque o'er the billows glides.
    Oh, this is a life of liberty,
    And none so happy as smuggler's be!"

With what different feelings to those that the smugglers evidently experienced did the guilty Adder listen to their rude mirth, and which seemed to be exhibited in mockery to his sufferings. He knew himself to be a doomed man—one who was at that time most likely on the way to death, and he smote his breast, and groaned in all the hopeless horrors of his destiny. How dearly had he purchased the unlicensed pleasures his guilt had led him to indulge in; how dreadful was the penalty he was then paying in the agony of anticipa-

tion he was then undergoing! Could he but have recalled the past, and have reflected upon the shame and torture which never fail to await upon crime, how different would his life have been! All the numerous villanies of which he had been guilty now passed before his mind's eye in fearful array, and retrospection was clothed in such dark horrors, that the poor wretch trembled to be alone. There was something so awful to him in the roaring of the waves; the voice of offended Heaven seemed to thunder despair to his guilty soul through it. Never was the cowardice of defeated villany more powerfully exemplified than in this miserable man. He crouched down on a bench in one corner of the cabin, and became lost to everything but the horror of his own thoughts.

An hour passed away in this manner, when he was aroused by a light suddenly streaming across his eyes, and looking up, he beheld Monckton standing before him, and contemplating him with looks of triumph.

"Well, Adder," he said, at length, "you now see the consequences of disobeying my injunctions—you are properly punished for your daring. Your thoughts do not appear to be of the most agreeable nature."

"Monckton," ejaculated Adder, in a melancholy tone of voice, "whatever can have caused this change in your conduct towards me? Why should you take a delight in my sufferings?"

"Because it is some satisfaction to see one who has taken such delight in the miseries of others suffer himself," answered Monckton. "You are only justly punished for your crimes."

"What hypocrisy is this!" exclaimed Adder, in a firmer tone; "have you not yourself shared in my vices?—have you not aided me in many of those crimes you now affect to decry?"

"I am ashamed to acknowledge that I have," replied Monckton; "but I am determined now to make all the atonement I can to outraged justice. And think not that, althought I lent you my assistance, I looked upon you as a friend. No! What friendship was ever known to exist between villains? From the first I hated and despised you, and I have been many times half tempted to deliver you up to the punishment which by your guilt you had incurred, and which your crimes so richly merited; but I know not what infernal power withheld me from doing so, and which, had I done so, would have been the cause of saving so many persons from misery. However, it is not too late."

"But you will not, surely, do as you have threatened?" gasped forth Adder.

"You will see."

"Oh, no, you will think better of it," cried the wretched man; "you will pity me; have mercy on me. Be contented with the punishment you have already inflicted upon me, by foiling me in my designs."

"Look for pity and mercy from those you have so deeply injured, and not from me," said Monckton, sternly.

"Nay, you cannot be in earnest," exclaimed Adder, trembling more violently than ever in every limb.

"Well," said Monckton, with a look of scorn, "if you think I am joking, I hope you will enjoy the sequel of it."

"Where are you conveying me?"

"A few hours will answer your question."

"And can nothing induce you to relent?"

"Nothing."

"Name your own price in gold, for your forbearance, and it shall be yours."

"No sum that you could mention, and that you have obtained by such base means—nay, not even all that you possess, can alter my decision."

"I would repent."

"Then make the best use of the time you have to do so."

"Is there then, indeed no hope?"

"None, for a wretch like you, either here or hereafter," replied Monckton.

Adder again groaned, and paced the cabin with hasty strides.

"I dreamt not it would come to this," he muttered.

"I daresay you did not," remarked the smuggler-captain; "and methinks you will not find it any vision now, either."

"Again, Monckton, I implore you not to decide too hastily."

"I have decided already."

"You may repent having done so."

"I rather think I shall not," returned the smuggler; "however, that I must leave to chance, as I do most other things in my hazardous life."

"But Rosabelle?"

"Ah! you would know of her?"

"What are your designs towards her?"

"Those of a friend—a protector!"

"A friend!—a protector!" repeated Adder, contemptuously, and biting his lips; "the title assumed by the libertine and seducer towards his victim!"

"Which none should be better acquainted with than yourself," retorted Monckton, sarcastically; "but hark you, Adder, you are at liberty to put what construction you please upon my conduct; it is sufficient for me to know that Lady Ravensford will have nothing to dread from you in future; that she will be removed far from where you might, perchance, have the power of doing her further injury."

"Where will you remove her to?"

"Before the sun has three times run his daily course, she will be restored to liberty, and on her way to the arms of her friends,"

answered Monckton. "But I waste time in talking to you. I will leave you in this pleasant place to your own reflections; when we see each other again, it will be for the settlement of business."

"Stay, Monckton," cried Adder, starting forward as the latter was about to retire, and clinging to him with all the desperation of a drowning man; "you must not leave me thus!—you shall not go until——"

"Bah!" interrupted the smuggler-captain, with a look of scorn; "this cowardice is sickening. I have already told you my mind. You appeal in vain."

Fresh courage rushed to the heart of Adder, and in a voice of firmness, he exclaimed:—

"Audacious scoundrel!—felon of the seas!—lawless wretch as you are, by what authority do you thus act? And think you that you will be suffered to escape, or to set for ever the laws of your country at defiance?—No; your carcase shall swing upon as high a jibbet as that of Adder's, if my hand now fail to inflict that vengeance upon you, which your infernal treachery merits!"

The eye of the villain had rested upon a knife which Monckton carried in his belt, and, as he uttered the last words, thinking to take the smuggler-captain off his guard, he suddenly sprang upon him, and attempted to snatch the deadly weapon from him. But the keen eye of Monckton had watched the expression of his countenance, and read his thoughts in a moment, and with the most astonishing coolness and ease, he seized Adder by the throat, and dashing him to the floor, he placed his foot upon his chest.

"Fool!" he cried, and he laughed contemptuously upon his prostrate enemy, "and did you think Monckton would suffer himself to be caught by such a scurvy knave of a land-lubber as you?—This instant I could take your life; but I would not defile my hands with your blood. However, you will gain nothing by your daring. What ho! my lads!"

As Monckton spoke he stamped his foot loudly upon the floor, and Ned Mayling, as he had called him, and another man entered.

"What now, captain?" interrogated Ned; "is there mutiny on board?"

"It is only this infernal swab," replied the former; "who has just had the audacity to attempt my life."

"Ah!" cried the smugglers in a breath, and looking fiercely upon Adder, whom Monckton had now suffered to rise; "death to the lubber!—death to the mutineer!"

"Nay, nay, not so," returned Monckton; "it is better not to do that for nothing which Jack Ketch will be paid for doing. Just clap him in irons; they will perhaps serve to amuse him in his confinement, for the few hours he will be aboard."

"Ay, ay, captain," said Ned Mayling, and Monckton having fixed upon Adder a parting look of derision, abruptly quitted the cabin, leaving the men to execute his orders.

He rejoined Michael Hernwood and the rest of the smugglers, whom he had left a short time before, to whom he related what had just taken place.

"The daring rascal!" said Michael Hernwood, "I did not think he had so much pluck in him. But what is it your intention to do with him?—Do you mean to deliver him over to the law?"

"D——n the law!" replied Monckton, "I like to have as little to do with that as possible, and no doubt it will overtake him quick enough without my help. Besides, I do not think that such a course would be prudent on my part, considering that I have not myself been altogether immaculate; and especially after the late encounter with the land-sharks, and the death of Bill Eldon."

"True, it would not," coincided Michael.

"Besides, Lady Ravensford will be restored to her friends," added Monckton, "and his power of harming her or them will be at an end; and in her restoration all my designs will be answered."

"Perfectly correct, captain," said Michael; "but, have you made up your mind in what manner you will dispose of the scoundrel?"

"I have," replied Monckton; "when we reach the place of our destination, I will turn him adrift, and let him go where he likes. Fear, no doubt, will induce him to quit the country, and I dare say we shall hear no more of him until we hear of his execution."

"I don't know that," observed Michael Hernwood, doubtfully; "are you not afraid that he may turn the tables upon us, and, like Bill Eldon, lead the officers to our retreat?"

"Pshaw! no!" returned Monckton; "he would not have the courage to do that. The evidence I have of his guilt in the murder of Rose Allerton, he knows full well, would be sufficient to place his neck in the noose."

"Why, to be sure," said Michael; "that would be rather an awkward piece of business for him to get over. I did not think of that. And the poor lady; how grateful will she feel to you for her deliverance. I'm sure, captain, I don't know how it is, but I am certain it would be worth while running any risk for the satisfaction a person must feel at having done such a deed."

"You are right, Michael," said the smuggler-captain, "and I commend you for your opinion. No action that I have ever performed in the course of my life, has, I am confident, afforded me half the gratification that the restoration of that unfortunate lady to liberty and her friends will do."

"Her husband must have suffered much during her absence," observed Michael Hernwood.

"He must indeed," returned Monckton; "and I shall ever regret having countenanced the cruel and infamous design which Adder had against his life."

"But you took no part in the plot," said Michael.

"I accepted a reward for keeping it a secret," said the captain; "at the same time that I should, on the contrary, have opposed the abominable plot all that was in my power, and have scouted the villain for having made a proposition to me, or any of my men."

"Well, well, captain," said Michael, "it is no use reproaching yourself; it can't be helped now, and you ought to feel glad that the bloody plot did not entirely succeed."

"Indeed I am," answered Monckton; "for, since I have discovered who Lady Ravensford is, especially, I should never have forgiven myself, had her husband fallen beneath the hand of the assassin."

"Gordon Desborough must be a most hardened, reckless, and blood-thirsty villain to have undertaken to perpetrate such a dreadful deed," remarked Michael Hernwood.

"He is a wretch familiar with every crime," returned the captain, "and it would not have been the first deed of blood he has committed. But he, like Adder, will only have his day, and no doubt, is doomed for the gallows. There's one thing I can say of him, if that may be considered anything in his favour, which is, that he is a most faithful villain; and in whatever he may engage to perform, he will remain faithful to his employer, and I do not think that anything would induce him to abandon him, not even if he were offered ten times the amount as a reward, by another party."

"Well, after all," said Michael Hernwood, "save me from any worse temptation than that of cheating the revenue. There's no sin, that I can see, in opposing a tyrannical impost, commonly called a duty. I mean to say that it is the *duty* of every person to stand clear of the *duty*, if they possibly can."

"Ay, ay, Michael," said Monckton, smiling, "there you and I perfectly agree; and I think we have done our share towards that *duty*, at any rate, and have paid ourselves pretty well for our pains."

"And so we ought," observed Michael, "and every brave fellow who has the courage to run the risks that we do."

"Risks, Michael?" ejaculated Mockton; "we have long ceased to recognise that word. What the land-lubber might call risk, is to us nothing but amusement."

"True again, captain," coincided the smuggler; "as the song we have not long since been singing, says—

'Oh, what can compare
To the life so rare?
When the grog we quaff,
And at danger we laugh,
As our gallant barque o'er the billows glides.
Oh, this is a life of liberty,
And none so happy as smugglers be.'"

"Bravo, Michael," cried the captain; "you are always merry."

"Merry!" reiterated Hernwood; "ay, to be sure; so we all are, ain't we? And what's the use of being sad? By what time do you expect we shall reach the place of our destination, captain?"

"By sunrise, at the latest," answered Monckton. "But come, we will push the grog about. I have a toast to propose, to which I expect you will all heartily respond. Come, my lads, charge, charge!"

The smugglers very quickly and willingly obeyed.

"Now, my lads," said the captain, "here's the health of Lady Ravensford, and confusion to her enemies."

"Bravo!" simultaneously shouted the smugglers. "Lady Ravensford's health, and confusion to her enemies!"

Toast after toast was proposed, and the smugglers were, as usual, in high glee; in which pleasurable condition we will for the present leave them, and return to Adder.

How different was the state of mind of that guilty and humiliated wretch, to that of the reckless but happy beings we have just quitted! Heavy fetters now loaded his limbs, and he was totally incapable of moving, and that, added to the bitter agony of his thoughts, almost drove him to madness!—Alternately he complained of the severity of his fate, and cursed and swore in the most dreadful manner; invoking the most terrific maledictions upon the head of Monckton, and raving against the destiny which had thus placed him entirely in the smuggler's power, and made him the subject of his scorn and derision. Again, when the horrors of the fate which seemed inevitably to await him, rushed upon his brain, in the most horrible form that his disordered imagination could picture, he trembled with fear, and shrunk appalled within himself, groaning and weeping by turns, with all the weakness of a child. To die the death of a dog, after his long successful career of villany, amid the execrations of an exulting multitude! Oh, it was more than he had even the fortitude to contemplate. What would he not have given, had he the power to transport himself to some distant clime, far from the power of those stern laws he had offended, and where he might be suffered still to live, unmolested and unknown, how differently did he think he would pass his days for the future. He would become another

being; abandon crime, and live in repentance of the past! But there was no hope for him! —Black despair enclosed him on every side; and a voice of thunder shouting—"Retribution! retribution!"—seemed to reverberate in his ears!—He feared to trust his eyes into the darkness of his narrow place of confinement, lest they should encounter the ghastly shade of the victim of his cruelty, the unfortunate Rose Allerton; and, wound up to a pitch of the greatest excitement, large drops of perspiration stood upon his forehead, and his limbs trembled as if he were suffering with a fit of the ague.

He cursed his folly in having been led by the fury of his rage to behave in the manner he had done to Monckton, at their recent interview, which he was well convinced could have no other effect than that of exasperating the smuggler to go to the full extent of that which he had threatened, when he might otherwise have been ultimately prevailed upon to shew him some mercy, although at the meeting he had supplicated him apparently in vain.

As the vessel dashed on its way, the terrors of the guilty man increased, for it seemed that he approached the nearer to the consummation of his fate. How thankful would he have been, could he have slept, and gained a transitory forgetfulness of his miseries; but had not his mental anguish entirely have precluded every chance of that wish being gratified, the pain of his limbs, galled by the fetters that loaded them, would have been sufficient to have rendered sleep impossible. Stretched upon the hard boards, he writhed in bodily and mental torture.

Dismally passed the hours away, until, at length, as near as he was capable of judging, it must have been near the morning, when he was aroused by hearing an unusual bustle upon deck, and, raising himself with difficulty upon his elbow, he listened with fearful expectancy. The vessel did not appear to be moving, and he, therefore, concluded that they had cast anchor, and that their voyage was at an end. And with that thought came an increase of the unhappy man's terrors, and he sunk back again upon the floor, unable to support himself.

He was not long kept in suspense. He heard footsteps descending the companion ladder, and directly afterwards the door of the cabin was thrown open, and Michael Hernwood, Ned Mayling, and another man entered, and approaching him, prepared to release him from his irons.

Adder trembled, and looked inquiringly in the swarthy countenances of the smugglers, but, for a short time, he was unable to articulate a syllable. At length, gazing earnestly at Michael Hernwood, he asked what they were going to do with him.

"Oh," answered Michael Hernwood, "I

have neither time nor inclination to answer your interrogatories, but you will soon know when we get you on deck."

Adder still trembled, and looked very pale, but seeing it was useless to ask any more questions, he remained silent, and the men having removed his fetters, raised him on his feet.

"The crisis of my fate," thought the poor dastard wretch, "is now at hand. How shall I find fortitude to meet it?"

The culprit going to the place of execution could not have endured greater agony than he did at that moment; but brief was the time given him for thought; he was hurried upon deck, where he found Monckton and most of the other smugglers assembled. He hastily cast his eyes towards the former, in whose countenance he expected to read his fate. It was stern, and he was standing near the mast with his arms folded, and giving some instructions to one of the men, in an under tone. A ray of hope darted upon the soul of Adder, but it was very faint, and was almost as quickly banished as it had been indulged in.

Two or three of the smugglers were busy, as well as the dim light would permit Adder to distinguish, for the morn was only just beginning to dawn, in getting the long-boat overboard, and this again excited the worst apprehensions of the guilty Adder. He was not kept long in suspense. Monckton motioned to Michael Hernwood and his companions to bring their prisoner forward, and he was immediately placed before the captain, who had not relaxed any of the stern expression of his countenance, and he fixed upon Adder a searching glance, while at the same time, the curl of his lip was contemptuous.

"Is all ready?" he demanded of the smugglers who were seeing after the boat, at length.

"Ay, ay, captain," replied one of the men, "the boat is alongside, and we are only waiting for your orders."

"Which you shall have in a trice," said Monckton; then turning once more to Adder, he thus addressed him—

"The time is now come when you and I must part company, and I must let you know your fate."

"Oh, Monckton," implored Adder, in accents of the most piteous supplication, "once more I implore you to have mercy on me."

"Mercy!" reiterated the captain; "what right have you to expect it of me, after your late behaviour, especially?"

'I own I was wrong, Monckton," replied Adder; "but forgive me, and make some allowances for my excited feelings."

"Hark you, Adder," observed Monckton; in a few minutes I could place you in gaol, and your fate would quickly be decided; but

it would cost me more trouble than I can now well afford to encounter for such a thing as you."

"You will spare me, then?" exclaimed the poor wretch, eagerly. "Oh, thanks! thanks!"

"Bah!" cried the captain, impatiently; "it is seldom that I am worse than my word, but after exacting from you certain promises, I am induced to do so on the present occasion, and to save the hangman a job until some future time."

"Tell me," ejaculated Adder, "what would you have me promise?"

"That which you will not only willingly agree to, but be faithful to it, if you would have the gibbet wait for you for a year or two longer."

"I will abide by anything you decree; name it."

"On your agreeing to quit the country for ever, and never more seeking to annoy those you have already so deeply injured, my men will convey you ashore, and set you at liberty."

"Oh, this is more than I expected," cried the astonished Adder; "I will readily promise, nay, swear, to comply with your demands, and will never cease to remember your forbearance with gratitude."

"Gratitude from you?—ha! ha! ha!" laughed Monckton, scornfully; "however, you know the power I possess of destroying you, the knowledge I have, the evidence I hold, and, mark me—the moment I hear that you have returned to England, I will take effectual means of ending your career at once. Remember the murdered Rose Allerton; and, if you value your neck, be faithful to your promise."

"I will, I will!" cried Adder, and so overcome was he by this unexpected issue, that he sunk in the most abject manner at the feet of the smuggler-captain, and endeavoured to give utterance to his thoughts, but he could not speak. Monckton turned away from him with a look of hatred and contempt.

"Now, my lads," he exclaimed, speaking to the smugglers, "away with the fellow as quick as possible, and do as I have instructed you."

"Ay, ay, captain," said the smugglers, and laying hold of Adder, they unceremoniously let him down the side of the vessel into the boat, followed themselves, and were soon quickly making their way towards the opposite shore, Monckton watching their progress, until veering round a lofty rock, which stretched itself into the ocean, they were hidden from the view.

"There, Michael," said Monckton, turning to the smuggler, "I think I have disposed of that lubber safely enough for one while,"

"You know best, captain," replied Michael,

"but, for my part, I do not think he will be got rid of so easily."

"Psha!" returned Monckton; "he knows what the consequences would be of his disobedience, and will not be bold or foolish enough to brave them."

"So you might have thought before, captain," observed Michael Hernwood, "when you left him with such strict injunctions at the house of Gordon Desborough, and after the threats that you had held out to him."

"And think you now that he knows perfectly well that Lady Ravensford will be placed far beyond his power of molesting her again, and that the vengeance of her friends would be sure to pursue him to the very utmost, he would venture to come to England?" asked Monckton.

"The villain may all be very fair at present, captain," replied Michael; "but I do believe that his mind is so prone to evil and mischief, that he will not rest long without seeking some means of revenge for the chagrin, humiliation, disappointment, and defeat which he has experienced."

"And what think you he will do?" interrogated Monckton.

"Give information to the officers when, how, and where we may be surprised," answered Michael Hernwood; "he can do that without appearing himself in the affair, and afterwards leaving the country, will be perfectly secure from any danger that might follow his treachery."

"And if he were to do so," said Monckton, "I should not care; any attempt which the landsharks might make upon us, would meet with the same defeat as the late affray at which Bill Eldon was at the head. We are too watchful and wary to let the swabs get over us so easily. But you are not afraid, are you, Michael?"

"Afraid, captain?" replied Hernwood, reproachfully; "how have I merited this? You never asked me such a question before, and I knew not that I had given you any reason to do so. Michael Hernwood is not so easily alarmed, I can tell you; if you think he is, he is unworthy to be one of your bold crew."

"Nay, nay, Michael, my lad," observed Monckton, "you have mistaken me; or perhaps I did not express myself as I ought to have done. I did not mean to doubt your bravery, of which I have had many years' proof; but I thought that perhaps your zeal for the safety of myself rendered you fearful that I had acted imprudently in giving the fellow Adder his liberty."

"Come, come, captain," said Michael, "prithee belay there; there needs no apology, I'm sure, and perhaps I was too hasty. But you know that yourself, and the whole of the crew are so jealous of their bravery being called into question, that——"

"Enough," interrupted Monckton; "I know very well what you would say, and perfectly agree with your sentiments. However, I think it is very improbable that we shall hear from Adder again in a hurry, unless it is an account of his public execution."

"And a very good riddance there would be to the world of one of the greatest scoundrels that ever existed," said Michael Hernwood. "I never felt honoured by his company from the time I first became acquainted with him; for you know, captain, although we are smugglers, we do not prey upon our fellow creatures; we only are opposed to injustice, and whenever we are engaged in any affray, we only act in self defence. If the landswabs did not trouble themselves about us, I warrant we should not interfere with them."

"Very true, Michael," coincided the captain, "and I feel proud to be the commander of such a bold set of fellows, who always act in unison with one another, and are ready to stand by me while they have a drop of blood left in their veins."

"Well said, captain," returned Hernwood, "you only pay us a compliment, which I myself can answer for, it is no more than justly our due; and I trust that we shall always be found to merit it."

"Which I have no doubt you will," returned Monckton, "and if I thought to the contrary, we would part company in very quick time."

"We shall never part company, captain, I trust," said Hernwood, "until death pops us under hatches. But see, our comrades return; they have landed their cargo, and a worse lot never came under their hands, I'll be bound."

The boat soon came alongside, and the smugglers jumped aboard.

"Well," said Monckton, addressing himself to the foremost of them, "have you landed the fellow?"

"Ay, captain," answered the man, "and at no very inviting part of the shore, either."

"And how did he behave?"

"Oh, he said not a word while he was in the boat, and when we put him on shore, he scampered off like a wild fellow, or a boy just broke loose from school for the holidays. He was out of sight, like a flash of lightning."

"And bad luck be close to his heels, wherever he shapes his course, say I," observed the captain.

"It is sure to attend him," said Michael Hernwood; "how can such a scoundrel expect anything else?"

"And yet he has for many years been most successful in his villany," said Monckton, "and might have continued to be so, had I not become his enemy."

The anchor was now quickly weighed, and soon the smuggler's vessel was gliding swiftly away over the deep, on its return to the place from whence it had come. Monckton felt more satisfied with what he had done, than any action which he had performed for many a day, and he felt confident in his own mind that the scoundrel Adder was now got rid of for ever, and he believed that justice would shortly overtake him, and punish him for the numerous and heinous crimes of which he had been guilty. He was most anxious to get back to the house of Gordon, so that he might fulfil the promise he had made to Lady Ravensford, and who he was certain would be waiting, in the greatest suspense, his return. The discovery which Monckton, or rather Archibald Malcolm, had made of Rosabelle's being the daughter of his former benefactor, Mr. Montalbert, had rekindled feelings in his bosom which he had not experienced for many years before, and the retrospect caused him the most poignant anguish and regret. The part he had acted towards Mr. Montalbert, who had been to him a parent, and would have continued to be so, was that of a most ungrateful villain, and he felt that he could not sufficiently atone for it. How different, in all probability, would now have been his situation had he acted properly!

He might have been moving in an honourable and elevated station of society, respected by all who knew him, and rendered doubly happy by being looked upon by our heroine with the same affection as if she had been his sister! When the smuggler thus ruminated he could not but feel regret and dissatisfaction; but he quickly banished the thoughts from his mind, and resolved no more to recall them to his memory. His future fortunes were now bound up with those of his bold and faithful companions, and he determined that henceforth he would suffer no painful regrets to disturb his mind.

CHAPTER XXXIII.

ROSABELLE'S RESTORATION TO LIBERTY.— THE STORM.—THE ADVENTURE.

ANXIOUSLY indeed did both Lady Ravensford and Mrs. Kitson look forward to the return of the smugglers, but the hopes of the latter were not unmingled with regret; she would be separated from our heroine and the little Alfred, and it was quite uncertain when or whether she ever would behold them again. The amiable manners of Rosabelle; the kindness she had shown towards her; and the sportive innocence of her child, had so fondly attached her to them, that she could not think of being parted, even for a short time from them, without the utmost pain.

"We shall meet again, and that soon, Mrs. Kitson, never fear," said our heroine, in consolitary accents.

"Oh, no, my lady," said Mrs. Kitson, in a melancholy voice; "I fear that, when restored to your friends, and far away from this place, you will have too many other and more important subjects to occupy your mind, to suffer you to bestow a thought upon so humble an individual as myself. Indeed, I ought not to be so presumptuous to expect it."

"Mrs. Kitson," replied our heroine, with a look of reproach, "you do me an injustice by such a supposition; were I capable of acting in the manner you anticipate, I should despise myself, and should consider that I had but ill-requited the kindness and attention you have ever paid to me and my child, since first we were introduced to each other."

"Pardon me, my lady," observed Mrs. Kitson; "I have been too bold; I ought to have known that your unexampled goodness, and——"

"There, now, my good woman," interrupted Rosabelle, smiling at the manner of her honest but simple companion; "I want no flattery, it is sufficient that you remove all doubts from your mind, and rest assured, if Providence permit, that we shall most certainly meet again, and it is to be hoped under happier circumstances than we have hitherto been placed in together. Your husband will, I have no doubt, permit you to visit me, when he knows that it is my request, and I am certain that Lord Ravensford, and my dear friends, will heartily welcome one who has done so much to alleviate my distress, in the horrors of my unjust captivity."

Mrs. Kitson was completely overwhelmed by the manner in which our heroine spoke to her; tears came to her eyes, and she could not give utterance to a word, although she was eager to express her due sense of Rosabelle's urbanity.

Mrs. Kitson was not without a share of vanity, and she felt herself not a little honoured by being thus kindly addressed by one so much above her. But above all, she was most anxious to see our heroine once more in the bosom of her family, and restored to that happiness from which she had been so long estranged.

"Heaven send," ejaculated Lady Ravensford, fervently; "Heaven send that no accident may befal Monckton, or that he may not change his mind, or all my high-raised hopes will be annihilated, and my prospects will probably be as dismal and cheerless as ever."

"I trust that Monckton will return safe, my lady," observed Mrs. Kitson; "as for changing his mind, I am sure he will not do that, and you ought to be the last to apprehend such a thing, after what you have told me of the account he gave you of the anxiety he felt to make some atonement for the ingratitude with which he had behaved towards your father."

"You are right, Mrs. Kitson," replied Rosabelle. "I will not believe him capable of acting so cruel a part, as his deceiving me would now be ; besides, what good would it do him to sport with my feelings in this manner?"

"Very true, my lady," said Mrs. Kitson ; " he could have no possible interest in doing so. Besides, his behaviour towards the villain Adder, ought to convince you of the honour of his intentions towards you."

"I will no longer doubt him," observed Lady Ravensford ; "and I ought never to have done so. The time is now short when every fear will be set at rest."

"Yes, my lady," answered Mrs. Kitson, " Monckton is a man of his word, and I have not the least doubt, if the weather will permit him, and no accident happens to him, that he will be here at the time he has promised. But do you think the tale he has told you is true?"

"Certainly," answered Lady Ravensford ; "I have often heard my father speak of him."

"What a pity that he should so have committed himself, my lady, after your amiable father behaving so kindly towards him," said Mrs. Kitson.

ROSABELLE'S RESTORATION TO HER FRIENDS.

"It is, indeed," coincided our heroine ; "and I much regret it, for Monckton evidently possesses talents that would have rendered him an ornament to society. I wonder how he has disposed of the scoundrel, Adder?"

"Doubtless in such a manner, my lady," answered Mrs. Kitson, " as will prevent him from having any chance of annoying you again."

Thus, in conversation, Lady Ravensford and her companion passed the time away during the absence of Monckton and the smugglers, and at length the third day from the time when the smugglers had departed, dawned, and the hopes and expectations of Rosabelle and Mrs. Kitson became more elated. The hours appeared to pass unusually slow, and they listened anxiously to every noise that proceeded from below, in the hope that Monckton and his companions had returned.

The day waned slowly away, and evening set in, but still nothing occurred to gratify their wishes and expectations. Seven, eight, nine o'clock tolled forth from a neighbouring church, but still all remained quiet in the house. Rosabelle became uneasy, and when ten o'clock struck, her suspense became so great that she could scarcely support it with any degree of patience.

"He will not come to-night," she said, " I fear that I have encouraged hopes that are doomed to be disappointed, and that some accident has befallen him, or——"

"Hark, my lady," suddenly interrupted Mrs. Kitson, advancing towards the room-door; "there is a great noise below, do you not hear it?"

Our heroine listened with eager, and breathless attention, and soon the voices of several men reached her ears.

"It is they," ejaculated Mrs. Kitson, joyfully, "I can plainly distinguish the voice of Monckton."

Lady Ravensford listened in a state of anxiety which needs no description, and, from among the voices of several men, who appeared to be highly elated at something, she plainly recognised the voice of the smuggler-captain. Her heart throbbed violently against her side with hope and expectation, and she involuntarily raised her hands and eyes towards Heaven, and mentally uttered a prayer of thanks.

"It is, indeed, he," exclaimed Rosabelle, addressing her companion; "Providence, in its infinite goodness, has heard my prayers, and preserved him who has promised to rescue me from danger! Hark! Mrs. Kitson; the mirthful tone of the smugglers assures me that their brief voyage has been attended with their usual success."

"Yes, my lady," returned Mrs. Kitson; "I am convinced it has; Heaven be thanked for it. It is no more than my sanguine expectations anticipated, and I have always told you so, my lady; depend upon it, your troubles are fast drawing to a termination, and ere many hours have elapsed, you will be restored to liberty."

"Liberty!" repeated our heroine, with emphasis, "how blessed is the sound! And shall I then again experience its blessings? All merciful Father, raise not my hopes but to be disappointed; for the sake of my husband, my poor parent!"

"Oh, no, my lady," said her kind attendant; "I am confident this time that you will not be disappointed. Monckton cannot have any motive for sporting with your feelings by breaking his word: and I well know that nothing whatever would induce him to do so under any circumstances."

"And yet," observed Lady Ravensford, "do you not think that he pledged his word to Adder to assist him in his plot, and has he not broken that?"

"I do not believe, my lady," answered her companion, "that Monckton ever pledged his word to the villain you have mentioned; and if he even had, surely the character of the man, and the reason which has induced him to break it, would offer every reasonable and sufficient excuse."

"Why, that is true," coincided our heroine, after a moment's hesitation; "but hark! some one is ascending the stairs. It is he of whom we speak, no doubt."

"Calm your agitation," I beseech you, my lady;" said Mrs. Kitson; "he is, doubtless, only coming to apprize you of his intentions, which, I will stake my life, are in strict accordance with the promises he has made to you."

The person, whoever it was, had now reached the door, and having knocked, Mrs. Kitson, at the request of Lady Rosabelle, hastened to open it, and when she had done so, she gave admittance to her husband.

"Well, my lass," exclaimed Sam Kitson, "you see we have returned once more, safe and sound, and I can see by the sparkling of your twinklers, that you are glad of it. Give us a kiss, and——"

Mrs. Kitson blushed and looked ashamed, while the simple, but honest fellow threw his arms round her neck, without any ceremony, and did as he desired.

"Excuse me, my lady," said Sam, scraping a bow to our heroine, who could not forbear a smile; "I forgot that you were present. But, after all, there is no harm in kissing those we love, especially one's own wife, and, therefore, I do not see that it needs any apology, and, so that's all about it."

"Well, but, Sam," impatiently ejaculated his wife, "what of the captain?"

"Oh, yes," returned the former, "I am fully aware of what you and her ladyship are anxious to know. The captain is all right—and by peep o' day, my lady, if no accident occurs to-night, you will be as free as a whisp of straw in a gale of wind."

Rosabelle clasped her hands, and pleasure illumined the good-natured countenance of her companion.

"Thank Heaven!" fervently exclaimed Rosabelle; "Monckton will not then prove unfaithful to his promise?"

"Unfaithful to his promise, my lady!" repeated Sam Kitson, with honest emphasis; "unfaithful to his promise! Who could ever suspect our captain to be capable of such a thing—especially when it is made to a female? He should not have Sam Kitson for one of his crew, if I thought he could do so."

Mrs. Kitson smiled approvingly upon her husband, and our heroine could not but admire the honest bluntness of his manner.

"Monckton, then, has spoken of his intentions towards her ladyship during the time you have been gone?" asked the former.

"To be sure he has," replied Sam, "and was all anxiety until he returned, so that nothing might occur to prevent him fulfilling his promise. I can assure her ladyship, from what I have myself observed, that there is not a person who entertains more sincere respect for her than Captain Monckton, or who is more heartily sorry that he should ever be made a party in any plot against her happiness."

"Oh," cried Lady Ravensford, "if he does, indeed, do as he said he will, my gratitude will be for ever due to him!"

"As for that, my lady," returned Sam "the captain, I am certain, does not consider that which it is his intention to perform any more than an act of duty—and I have heard him say as much. He would himself have come to see you to-night, but he has been obliged to go out upon a little business; however, he desired me to request that your ladyship would hold yourself in readiness to leave this place at an early hour in the morning."

Our heroine's countenance again became brighter than before, and she desired Sam Kitson to inform his captain that she would not fail to attend to his wishes.

"And now, my lady," said Sam, "I have a question to ask you, if you please"

"And what is that, Mr. Kitson?" asked Rosabelle, smiling blandly.

"Why, my lady,' observed Sam, "I do not know that there is any necessity for my putting the question, because I am convinced in my own mind what the answer will be; hows'ever, here goes—I wants to know then, my lady, if you please, whether my wife here has given you satisfaction since she has had the honour to attend upon you?"

Our heroine fervently and kindly replied in the affirmative, and the smuggler having given utterance to an expression of satisfaction, once more threw his arms arms around his wife's neck and kissed her two or three times, much to the discomfiture of the latter, who was fearful that the freedom of his manners might give offence to her ladyship. Rosabelle, however, only smiled at the simple but honest affection of the man; and once more assured him of the kindness and attention she had experienced from Mrs. Kitson; the gratitude she felt, and should ever feel for the same, and her deep regret that circumstances should compel them to part so soon.

"Oh, my lady, madam," cried Sam, scraping half a dozen bows in rapid succession, and his swarthy countenance animated with an expression of pride and pleasure; "I am afraid you o my Nell too much honour; but I am glad she has given your ladyship satisfaction; and should be very glad if your ladyship would think her worthy of—but then my situation in life prevents all chance of that, and——"

"And why not change your situation in life, Mr. Kitson?" demanded our heroine; "you and your wife might live comfortably together, and you should never want a friend whilst I or Lord Ravensford exist."

"What!" exclaimed Sam Kitson, warmly, and his cheeks glowing; "desert my captain after weathering with him the calm and the storm for so many years; no, damme, if I would to be made an emperor! But I beg pardon, your ladyship. I am much obliged to you for your goodness I'm sure; and so is Nell, I know; but—but—I was a going to say—

only perhaps your ladyship might think me too bold. I was about to say—to——"

"To what, my good man?" interrupted our heroine, smiling encouragingly upon him; "do not be afraid of me, but speak at once what you wish."

"Your ladyship is very kind, dam—but I ax your ladyship's pardon; I forget that I am not on board now," observed Sam; "well then, since you have given me leave to speak, I will; and know my Nell guesses what I am going to say, for her eyes sparkle so. You see, your ladyship, that my wife has, I am aware, formed a great attachment to you and the little boy, bless his little heart; I never look upon him but I think I sees my young Sam afore me; and I was bold enough to think that, when your ladyship was restored to your friends, you would not perhaps object to my Nell calling sometimes, and just inquiring after your ladyship and your noble son!"

Mrs. Kitson by her looks expressed her thanks to her husband, and then gazed at our heroine with an expressive glance.

'And would you permit her, Mr. Kitson, to visit me? Would you not mind the distance she would probably have to come?" asked Lady Rosabelle.

"Permit her, your ladyship," repeated the smuggler: "mind the distance! Oh, I feel too proud by the honour which your ladyship would do me and my wife. But what says Nell? Oh, I see, I have no occasion to ax the question, her looks are a sufficient answer to me. But will your ladyship grant my request?"

"Most certainly," returned our heroine; "myself and Mrs. Kitson have been talking upon the subject, and we only required your assent to settle everything satisfactorily. But whenever your wife visits me, remember, you must not object to her remaining with me for a few weeks."

'Why, your ladyship,' replied Sam Kitson, 'I believe my Nell needs no telling that I am fond of her, and that I do not like to be out of her company any more than I can help, but when she is with your ladyship, knowing as I shall, that she will be perfectly safe and comfortable, I shall not care much whether she stays with you six days or six months. And perhaps if we happen to put in at that port, if I disguise myself, you will not object to my dropping anchor for a short time, just to see how she is getting on; no one will know me, and if they did, I do not know but that they might meet with many a worse acquaintance than Sam Kitson, although he is a smuggler!"

Our heroine assured him that she should at any time be most happy to see him, and thus was the business, which for the last few days had occupied and disturbed the mind of Mrs. Kitson, settled to the satisfaction of all, and the poor woman felt extremely happy and thankful to her husband for having so thoughtfully entered into her views and wishes.

"And did anything particular occur to you on the voyage from which you have just returned?" asked our heroine.

"Nothing at all, my lady," answered Sam.

"And what did you with Mr. Adder?" eagerly interrogated Lady Ravensford.

"Oh, the d——d swab," exclaimed the smuggler, warmly, in reply; "we disposed of him; but he may thank his lucky stars that he was not left to my mercy, or he would not have got off so easily as he has done."

"Monckton then spared his life?" said Rosabelle.

"Spared his life!" reiterated Sam; "the captain would not have stained his hands with the blood of such a fellow. It would have been a downright robbery upon that portion of the laws of the country which we respect, to have suffered such an arrant scoundrel to escape the gallows. But if I had had my will, I would have taken good care that he should not have escaped the hands of justice."

"Then what did you do with him?" inquired Mrs. Kitson.

"Why," answered her husband, "we merely took him to the place of our destination, where upon his promising the captain to transport himself to a foreign land, and never more to make his appearance in England, or anywhere where he could annoy your ladyship, or your friends, we turned him adrift, and left him to take his own course."

"And do you believe that the villain will keep his promise?" asked Lady Ravensford.

"Why, as to that, my lady," answered Sam Kitson, "I scarcely know what to think. I can only say that if Adder breaks his word, he is a greater fool than I take him to be, seeing that the captain is possessed of such knowledge and witnesses as would be certain to consign him to the gallows."

"Then I am glad that Monckton has acted in the way he has done," ejaculated our heroine; "should the unhung wretch be awakened to a sense of remorse and repentance, his mental anguish will be far greater to him for the crimes he has committed than any punishment which the hands of men could inflict."

"Why, that is very true, I dare say, your ladyship," observed Sam Kitson; "and I sincerely hope it may turn out as you say, for a more arrant rascal never remained unhung, and it would be a pity if he did not receive a severe punishment for the many offences of which he has been guilty, in some way or other. But good-night, your ladyship, good-night, Nell; I must return to my companions, and I dare say that you and Lady Ravensford have something to talk over, which would be of no interest to me. Good-night."

"Good-night," responded Rosabelle; and

the smuggler having once more kissed his wife, (of whom he was very fond, and to whom he had ever behaved in the most exemplary manner) quitted the room, and left Mrs. Kitson and our heroine to themselves.

When he had gone, our heroine and Mrs. Kitson both gave vent to their grateful feelings at the realization of their hopes which seemed certain now to take place, and the pleasure of the former at the flattering prospect of speedy deliverance from her long and painful incarceration, found vent in a copious flood of tears; after which she fervently returned her thanks to the Almighty, and prayed that nothing might transpire to prevent her restoration to her friends, at the same time she most earnestly hoped that she might find her husband and father in a less distracted condition than her fears were too ready to anticipate. She pressed her child to her bosom, and covered his rosy cheeks with kisses, and a tide of joy rushed to her heart, which she had not experienced before for many a day.

Mrs. Kitson gazed at her with feelings of the most unfeigned delight, and no one could look forward with more joy to the happy momens of Rosabelle's restoration to liberty than did that honest, kind-hearted woman.

"Oh, my lady," said the worthy creature, "I never felt so joyful at any circumstance in my life, as I do at this moment. I knew that Captain Monckton would not deceive you. May Heaven's blessing light upon him for it."

Lady Ravensford fervently responded to the wishes of Mrs. Kitson.

"And most assuredly will he meet with his reward," she added. "Would that he would enable me more sensibly to mark my gratitude for the inestimable service he is about to render me, by abandoning his present course of life. But my unfortunate husband—my poor father; how shall I meet them? Perhaps both upon the verge of the grave, and my restoration to their arms may but be the prelude to my separation from them for ever, until we meet again in eternity!"

"Nay, my dear lady," said her companion, "do not, I beg of you, give way to such gloomy apprehensions; indulge in hope. Providence is good, and will not, I trust, visit with such heavy calamities one who has already endured so much."

"But how can I do otherwise than anticipate the worst," demanded our heroine, "after what has taken place? How can I expect that my husband or my father can have been able to support my unfortunate less, or that of my child? Black despair must have preyed upon their vitals, and——"

"Oh, my lady," interrupted Mrs. Kitson, "let me again beg of you to alleviate the agony of your fears, and to await the result with fortitude, which a few short days must now bring about. Something tells me that everything will terminate hapily, and that you and Lord Ravensford, with you unfortunate father, and your dear friends, will yet live to enjoy many years of uninterrupted felicity, a just reward for the cruel sufferings to which you have all been so long subjected."

"Thanks, Mrs. Kitson, for your kind advice and wishes," observed our heroine. "I should, indeed, endeavour to act as you advise. I ought not to despair, after the goodness which the Almighty has shown towards me, in preserving me from the shame and degradation with which I was threatened by my villanous oppressor, and when despair seemed to have enclosed around me. To-morrow, then, I quit these hated walls, I hope, for ever."

"Amen!" responded Mrs. Kitson, emphatically; "and ere many hours have elapsed, I trust you and your child will once more be enfolded to the heart of your husband and parent. Oh, how anxious I shall be to hear from you, my lady."

"Depend upon it, my good friend," replied Lady Ravensford, in her usual accents of benevolence, "that I will not fail to make you acquainted with every particular of that adventure with the termination of which you will be in such suspense to learn; and I hope that it will not be long ere, under very different circumstances to those I am now placed in, we shall meet again, and when I shall have the pleasure of evincing to you my acknowledgments for the kindness I have experienced from you, since it was my good fortune to be introduced to you."

"Spare me, my dear lady," said Mrs. Kitson; "surely I deserve not so many thanks for that which my duty to my fellow-creatures rendered imperative on me."

"You entertain too indifferent an opinion of your own merits, my good Mrs. Kitson," said our heroine; "had it not been for you, I should have sunk beneath the weight of despair, and the detestable conduct of that despicable woman, old Cicely. Your consolation and sympathy in my misfortunes raised me to hope, when I should otherwise, most probably, have been reduced to all the anguish of cheerless grief, and I shall ever feel myself indebted to you."

Mrs. Kitson could not refrain from tears at the manner in which Lady Ravensford expressed herself towards her, and she was unable to speak. A short pause ensued, during which both our heroine and the former were enabled to compose their feelings, and they then set about making the few trifling arrangements that were necessary for Rosabelle's departure in the morning.

Mrs. Kitson regretted that she could not accompany our heroine on her journey, but she had been given to understand by her husband that Monckton, for reasons which he did not think proper to explain, would not give his assent to that, and she was, therefore, compelled to content herself with the alternative, well convinced, in her own mind, that the smuggler-captain would not leave her ladyship until she was perfectly safe from every danger. Besides, she had little danger to apprehend, now that her great enemy, Adder, was so securely disposed of.

The smugglers had now departed as usual to the "caboose," and the house was buried in profound silence. Rosabelle felt now quite tranquil, and with the assistance of her companion, packed up the few things of which her wardrobe consisted, and once more sat down quite composed to converse for the last time in the present place upon her future hopes and prospects. It was twelve o'clock before either of them thought of retiring to repose, and never had our heroine enjoyed more refreshing sleep than she did on that occasion; dreams of the most pleasing description floated before her imagination, and she awoke at the first blush of dawn in the morning, refreshed and prepared for all that might take place.

Mrs. Kitson had already risen, and when our heroine awoke, she was seated at the table with her head leaning on her hand, and was giving vent to the melancholy feelings which her speedy separation from Lady Ravensford, whose misfortunes and amiable manners had engendered so much esteem in her bosom, naturally produced.

Rosobelle endeavoured to compose her, and promised that she would write to her with all possible despatch, to let her know in what manner her journey from the house of Gordon Desborough had terminated, and also that she would, at the very first opportunity, send her an invitation to visit her.

"Oh, my lady," said Mrs. Kitson, "you are so very amiable and kind, that I ought to feel convinced you will not lose the earliest opportunity to fulfil your promise. Heaven send that you may safely reach your friends, and be restored to all that happiness which your virtues deserve."

Rosabelle, with the assistance of Mrs. Kitson, had soon performed the duties of her toilette, and soon after she had done so, they heard a bustle in the rooms below, which convinced them that Monckton had arrived.

And now the momentous period approached, and they heard footsteps ascending the stairs.

Rosabelle's heart palpitated violently, and Mrs. Kitson's agitation was scarcely less than her own.

In another moment, there was a knock at the room door, and a voice inquired whether they had arisen.

"It is my husband," said Mrs. Kitson; and

she immediately opened the door and admitted him.

"The captain sent me to inquire, my lady," said he, bowing respectfully to our heroine; "whether you were ready to admit him to your presence."

Lady Ravensford answered in the affirmative in a faint and tremulous voice, and Mrs. Kitson looked at her with an expression of emotion, which plainly evinced the pain she felt at their approaching separation, while, at the same time, she so heartily and sincerely rejoiced at her restoration to liberty.

"I should have been most glad, my lady," said Sam Kitson, "if my wife could have attended you on your journey; for I dare say, after your having been so long together, you would have been glad of her company. But the captain objects to it, and he most likely has some reason for doing so which he does not think proper to explain."

"I feel obliged to you for your kind consideration," observed our heroine; "and, if fortune favours me, shall, most likely, shortly have to appeal further to it for permission for your wife to visit me at Holly Hall."

"Sincerely do I hope, my lady, that you may," returned the smuggler; and most happy shall I feel in complying with the request with which you may be pleased to honour myself and my Nell, immediately. Come, come, Nell, my lass, do not look so dull; I dare say it will not be long before you and her ladyship will meet again."

Mrs. Kitson could not speak, she was so overpowered by her emotions; but Rosabelle looked at her most kindly, and pressed her hand vehemently, and her bland manners reassured and tranquillised her feelings.

"The captain will become impatient, my lady," at length observed Sam, "and I know that there is not any time to lose."

"Very true," replied Lady Ravensford; "pray tell Mr. Monckton that I am waiting to receive him."

"Ay, ay, my lady," returned Sam Kitson, and he bowed himself out of the room.

"And now, my dear friend," said our heroine, turning kindly to Mrs. Kitson, who was still in tears; "the moment so long hoped for and anticipated has arrived; and if there is one circumstance which excites my regret on leaving this place, where, until you became my companion, I was subjected to such insupportable misery, believe me, it is the necessity which Monckton appears to think for our separation."

"The poor humble individual whom you have been pleased to honour with your favour, my dear lady, is unworthy of so much consideration," said Mrs. Kitson, sobbing. "I am acting very wrong, indeed, I know I am; for, at this very moment I ought rather to rejoice at the prospect of your speedy deliverance from confinement; but one cannot help one's feelings, my lady, and——"

"I know well what you would say, my kind creature," interrupted Lady Rosabelle, deeply affected. "Well do I appreciate your honest feelings; but let me entreat that you will endeavour to conquer your emotions, and let this be our brief parting, with the assurance that we shall see each other again ere long."

"I will do as you desire, my lady," said Mrs. Kitson, drying up her tears; "it would be unseemly to betray this agitation before the captain. Farewell, then, my lady—farewell, and may Heaven's choicest blessings pursue you, and be showered in abundance upon your head. Farewell!"

"Adieu, my dearest friend," exclaimed our heroine, embracing her; "again rest assured that I will write to you at the earliest opportunity, and furnish you with every particular. Adieu, until, with the blessing of Heaven, we may meet again under happier circumstances than we have hitherto known each other."

Mrs. Kitson could not speak, but her manners and the expression of her countenance sufficiently evinced the feelings that overflowed her heart. She made an effort, however, and conquered her emtions, as they heard the footsteps of the captain on the stairs, and, by the time he knocked at the door, both her and Lady Ravensford were completely tranquil, and Mrs. Kitson remained in the back chamber during the time time the latter's interview with Monckton was taking place.

The smuggler-captain entered with a most respectful air, and stood for a second or two at the door, apparently absorbed in admiration of Lady Ravensford, who had advanced gracefully to meet him. His countenance seemed characterised by something more deeply interesting than usual, and it was easily to be perceived that the innate satisfaction he felt at the action he was about to perform, more than adequately rewarded him for any trouble he might be at, or any danger he might run.

"Lady Ravensford," at length he said, in accents of the utmost respect; "I know not whether you placed any confidence in the honesty of the promises which I made you; but I am now happy to inform you that it is in my power to remove every doubt from your mind, and that the moment has arrived when I can restore you to that liberty of which you have been so long and so unjustly deprived. Your bitter enemy will no more trouble you, and I trust that your restoration to those so dear to you will be the forerunner of every happiness to you."

"Mr. Malcolm," replied Lady Rosabelle, at the same time that her brilliant eyes sparkled with gratitude; "for your goodness

I shall owe you a debt of gratitude, it will never be in my power sufficiently to repay, and—"

"Hold, Lady Ravensford, I beg of you," interrupted Monckton; "for any service which it is in my power to render you, you owe me nothing. Nothing that I can now do, can ever sufficiently repay the debt of gratitude I owe to your father, or make atonement for the crime of which I was guilty towards him. Would that it had never taken place. But it is too late to regret now, and—excuse me, Lady Ravensford, but we have no time for procrastination—the vessel waits, and time wanes apace; it would be advisable for us to get clear of this coast before the people of the neighbourhood are stirring."

"I am ready to attend you, sir," answered our heroine, and her heart palpitated more powerfully than ever. She looked towards the room in which Mrs. Kitson was standing in trembling suspense, and beckoned her to come forward. The good woman obeyed with a melancholy air, notwithstanding she endeavoured to appear to the contrary, and Rosabelle looked kindly and encouragingly upon her.

"I am sorry that, for particular reasons, I cannot allow Mrs. Kitson to accompany you, my lady," observed Monckton; "but you may rest your mind contented that you shall receive the utmost respect and attention while you are under my care and protection; Mrs. Kitson, I think, if she does me justice, will answer for that."

"It would be ungenerous of me to doubt you, sir," replied our heroine; "you cannot have any motives for deceiving me."

"You do me no more than justice by that supposition, Lady Ravensford," said Monckton "but I trust you will pardon me for having taken any share in the base plot of the scoundrel, Adder, against you."

Rosabelle assured him by her looks that she was ready enough to comply with his wishes, and after a pause, she once more turned to Mrs. Kitson, and they having fervently embraced, Rosabelle gave her arm to the smuggler-captain (whose demeanour was that of the most polished gentleman), and they quitted the room together, and descended the stairs. In the parlour they found several of the smugglers waiting, and on seeing our heroine, they doffed their hats, and bowed most respectfully, as her and the captain passed in between them.

Mrs. Kitson followed them to the door, and once more her eyes, and those of Lady Ravensford met, and there was an expression in the glances of the latter so encouragingly, that it immediately seemed to have the effect of tranquillizing the poor woman's feelings. Her husband was close at hand, and having kissed her, and whispered a few words of affection and consolation in her ear, they also separated, and he attended the other smugglers who were making their way to the vessel.

And now our heroine once more crossed the threshold of that house in which she had been so long a prisoner, she hoped for the last time. Her feelings overpowered her, and had it not been for the support of Monckton, she must have sunk to the earth. The balmy freshness of the air, however, shortly revived her, and with a light and bounding heart, as hope suddenly shed its bright influence upon her mind, she smiled her thanks to the smuggler-captain, felt the strictest confidence in the honour of his intentions, and with a firm step accompanied him to the beach. In a few minutes more, Rosabelle was on board that vessel which was destined to convey her far from the scene of her sorrows, and, as she hoped, soon to bear her to the arms of those from whom she had been so long and so cruelly torn.

Here, in the most energetic manner, unable to restrain her feelings, she sunk upon her knees at the feet of the smuggler-captain, and poured forth her thanks to him in the most impressive language. Monckton raised her gently from her position, and it was very evident that he was affected by the earnestness of her manner. He turned away his head for a moment, and seemed incapable of speaking, then, in accents of the greatest respect, he observed—

"Lady Ravensford, this posture, to me I cannot, I will not permit; I feel myself totally unworthy of so much condescension; and for the service which I am happy to think it is in my power to render you I am more than amply repaid in the satisfaction arising from the reflection that I have done my duty. I beg your ladyship to be calm, and to look forward with sanguine hopes to brighter prospects."

"Indeed, sir," returned Rosabelle, "you greatly underrate your own goodness in thus having rescued me from misery, shame, and despair. Oh, with what feelings of unbounded gratitude will Lord Ravensford greet the preserver of his unfortunate Rosabelle and child; how will my poor father's heart (if he still retains his senses) overflow with thankfulness to that man who has rescued his daughter from a fate even worse than death."

Monckton remained silent for an instant, and gazed with admiration in the handsome countenance of Lady Ravensford, now animated with hope and joy.

"I regret, my lady," he said at last, "that circumstances will not permit me to convey you any further than G———m, and that I, therefore, cannot avail myself of the honour you speak of; but the time may not be far distant when I may have the pleasure of meeting your friends and relations, and of expressing my sorrow to your father for the ungrateful conduct of which I was guilty towards him, and to seek from his own lips an assurance of his forgiveness."

"Which," rejoined our heroine, "I am confident he would be most happy to grant, and to established you once more in his friendship."

"No, my lady," returned Monckton, "that must not be. Mr. Montalbert's forgiveness I may seek and receive, but my conduct hath for ever precluded me from his friendship. I ought not to expect it."

"Great as your offence, sir, I must admit to have been," remarked Rosabelle, "I cannot but think that you visit it on yourself with too much severity, and——"

"Excuse me, lady Ravensford," interrupted the captain, "upon that subject you must permit me to retain my own opinion, which nothing can alter. But we will not converse further upon it. As I said before, I am very sorry that I shall not be able to accompany you any further than G——m; but you will then be enabled to meet the mail, which will convey you and your child to the immediate neighbourhood of Holly Hall."

Rosabelle again expressed her thanks, and then the captain called to him a decent-looking female, who was standing upon the deck, apparently awaiting the orders of the former.

"Conduct Lady Ravensford to the cabin prepared for her reception, Margaret," said Monckton; "and remember my instructions."

Margaret curtseyed very politely to the captain, and looked respectfully upon our heroine, who, after exchanging a few more words with Monckton, followed the female whither he had directed her to conduct her.

The cabin was fitted up with ever attention to comfort, and was the same which Rosabelle had occupied during their brief voyage from the house of Gordon Desborough to the place in which the revenue officers had made the attack upon the smugglers.

Margaret had already prepared coffee and other refreshments, which she respectfully invited Lady Ravensford to partake of, and the mind of the latter being relieved from a mountain of care, readily assented, and made a heartier meal than she had done for some time before.

The little Alfred seemed to partake of his mother's hopes and happiness, for his beauteous countenance was more rosy and animated than usual, caused, no doubt, by her fond caresses, and the powerful change in her manners altogether.

Margaret appeared to be a quiet, simple girl, and she was most sedulous in paying our heroine every attention, which the latter repaid by her thanks, feeling a due sense, at the same time, of the consideration of Monck-

ton, in having provided her with so civil an attendant in the place of Mrs. Kitson.

Margaret, however, was called to the performance of other duties in another part of the vessel, and Rosabelle was left alone in the cabin with her offspring.

Her heart overflowing with the feelings of delight which the prospects that now opened upon her naturally engendered, Rosabelle, as soon as Margaret had retired, sunk upon her knees, and poured forth in energetic tones her thanks to the Almighty for her preservation, and implored a continuance of His merciful protection, and that she might also find her husband and father in far different circumstances to those her fears would, in spite of her efforts to the contrary, depicture.

After the performance of this pious duty, Rosabelle felt completely tranquil, and listened with feelings there is no necessity for us to describe, to the dashing of the waves against the vessel's sides, and to the whistling of the gale, whose voice seemed to whisper to her approaching happiness.

Monckton was for some time occupied in giving orders about the ship, but at length, after first inquiring of Margaret whether Lady Ravensford was at leisure, he rejoined her in the cabin, where in conversation upon a variety of topics, he served to pass away the time, which might otherwise have hung tediously upon the mind of Rosabelle.

To natural talents, which pre-eminently qualified him to shine in a far different sphere of society, Monckton, or Malcolm, had experienced all the advantages which the liberal education bestowed upon him by Mr. Montalbert had enabled him to receive, and divesting himself of that style of conversation in which he was under the necessity of addressing himself to the limited comprehensions of his associates, Rosabelle found him accomplished and well informed, and while she was pleased with his society, she could not help feeling a sensation of regret that he should have been driven, by the indiscretions of youth, to adopt the present course of life he was pursuing. Mingled with these feelings, however, when Rosabelle recalled to her memory what Mrs Kitson had told her respecting his having a guilty knowledge of some dreadful crime which Adder had formerly perpetrated, she could not help looking upon him with a sensation of dread, although she was unwilling to believe him really guilty unless she had some more substantial proof than mere rumour and suspicion.

"And is it far from hence where you are about to convey me?" she inquired of the smuggler-captain.

"We shall reach there, I expect, by the evening," replied Monckton; "I am sorry that I am compelled to part from you before I have seen you safe under the protection of your friends; but no doubt you will meet the mail soon after your arrival there, and that you will be enabled to reach Holly Hall, without any fear of molestation. There is one favour, however, I would request of your ladyship."

"Name it, sir," said our heroine; "and if it is in my power, I shall feel a pleasure in complying with it."

"And yet, my lady," continued Monckton, "such is the opinion I am certain I do but justly form of your character, that probably I may act wrong, and with unnecessary precaution in making it. I would merely ask your ladyship to avoid mentioning to any person any of the particulars connected with myself and my associates, and such facts concerning our retreat as may have come to your knowledge during your residence at the house of Gordon Desborough."

"You may depend upon me, Mr. Monckton," said our heroine; "I should but ill-requite the inestimable service rendered me by my preserver were I to do otherwise."

"Thanks—thanks, my lady," said Monckton; "I must again solicit your forgiveness for having made a request for which there was no absolute necessity. There is, however, another favour which I would ask you, and which I can do with more confidence."

Lady Ravensford again desired that he would speak his wishes.

"Probably, my lady," answered the smug-

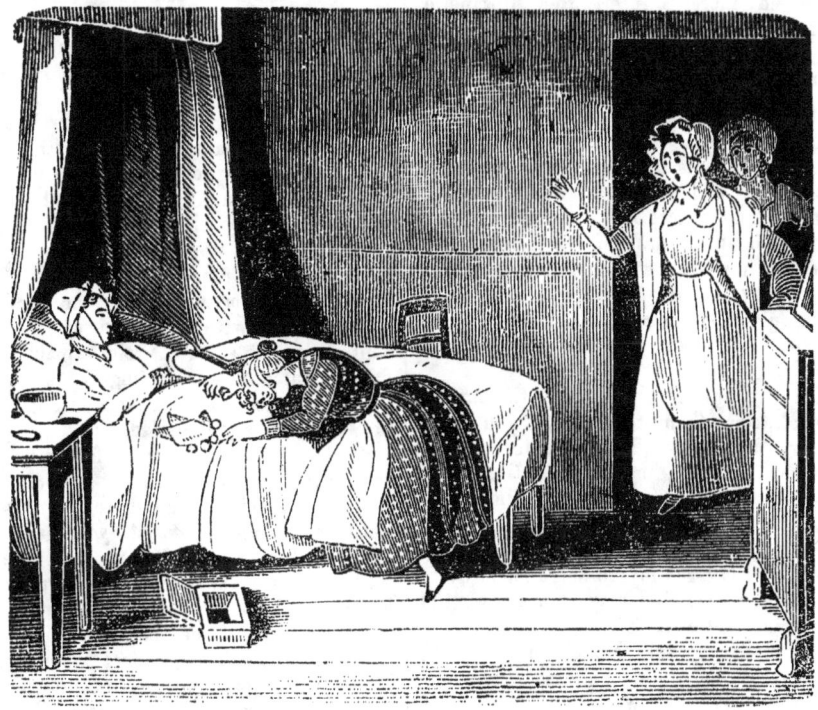

THE DEATH-BED OF THE MOTHER OF MRS. BELGRAVE.

gler-captain, "there is no necessity for me to assure you that, feeling as I now do so deep an interest in your welfare, I shall be most anxious to be made acquainted with your safe arrival at the hall. Will you oblige me by forwarding to the house of Gordon, as soon as convenient, a letter addressed to me, and just merely informing me of your safe restoration to the arms of your friends?"

"Certainly, sir," answered Rosabelle, "you may depend upon my not losing any time in doing so."

"This is very kind and condescending of your ladyship," observed Monckton, apparently much pleased, "and nothing will afford me greater satisfaction than to hear that you have reached the place of your destination without the recurrence of any fresh calamity; and that your return may be the cause of quickly restoring the minds of your husband and father, and all those friends who are dear to you, to tranquillity and peace."

Rosabelle sighed; for, at the mention of the names of her husband and father, particularly the latter, a gloomy presentiment crossed her mind, which she found it would be a difficult task for her to endeavour to banish.

"But you have heard of my father, latterly, Mr. Malcolm," she said, with a searching and melancholy glance; "indeed, I am certain that you have, by some observations that you made to me a short time since, and your manners on the present occasion. Oh, tell me, have you not so?"

"It is useless to deny, your ladyship, that I have," answered Monckton, with evident reluctance; "but do not let your apprehensions become too powerful, for, after all, report may greatly have exaggerated the facts."

"Ah!" exclaimed Rosabelle, with the utmost agitation depicted in her countenance; "and what, then, says report? My worst surmises, no doubt, are realised; my unfortunate parent's mind is again a wreck!"

Monckton hesitated, but seeing that it would be useless attempting to deceive her, he said—

"I have, indeed, heard, my lady, that Mr. Montalbert has suffered a relapse, but ——"

"Say no more," interrupted Rosabelle, wringing her hands; "my mind forebodes the worst. My poor father! Alas! never, never can you survive this second attack! Oh, God! how vain my hopes of restoration to peace!"

"Again, my dear Lady Ravensford," said Monckton, in accents of sympathy and kindness, "again let me beg of you not to give way to despair. Circumstances may not turn out near so bad as it is but natural for you to anticipate. Your return may work wonders, and your presence may have the happy and speedy effect of restoring Mr. Montalbert to his senses."

Our heroine shook her head gloomily and hopelessly.

"Had you but seen him during the time of his mental attack," she remarked, "you would think very differently. I feel convinced that neither my presence, nor any attention I may bestow upon him, will ever restore him to his senses, now that his reason has again fled. Alas! alas! of what value will liberty be to me, when I shall see myself surrounded by so much misery, of which I may accuse myself of being the indirect cause?"

"Nay, my lady," said Monckton, "say not so; I cannot see how you can reasonably blame yourself the least in the world. Say, rather, it is the work of that abominable scoundrel, Adder; may eternal curses light upon him!"

"Terrible indeed may have been the effects of that guilty man's persecution of me," said our heroine; "but for myself, had I been the only sufferer, I could have been content, and have forgiven him, now that I am released from his power. But when I think upon the distracted brain of my poor father—and perhaps the broken heart of my husband, my soul shudders with horror at the weight of his enormities, and I cannot help praying for that retribution upon his head, which, sooner or later, is sure to overtake him."

"You are right, Lady Ravensford," returned the smuggler captain; "depend upon it he will not long escape that punishment to which I at first thought of consigning him, on removing him from the vaults under the house of Gordon Desborough."

"And do you not think he will disregard your injunctions, Mr. Malcolm?" inquired Rosabelle, "and either not retire from England at all; or speedily return to it?"

"No, my lady," answered Monckton; "the wretch is fully aware that that would be the very way to expedite his ignominious end, and he is too great a coward to run the risk of that; take my word for it. Your ladyship may rest your mind quite contented; you have nothing more to apprehend from him. But, my lady, as the present is, perhaps, the only opportunity I may have of speaking to you, previous to our arrival at G——m, there is something else I would ask you. May I make so bold as to intrude upon your kindness and attention?"

"Most certainly, sir," answered Rosabelle; —"I have before assured you of my readiness to grant you any request which I can reasonably and honourably comply with."

"Lady Ravensford will perhaps do the smuggler-captain the justice to believe him incapable of proposing anything dishonourable to her," said Monckton, emphatically, and a slight flush for a moment suffused his cheeks. Rosabelle returned no answer, but she awaited with some suspense what the captain might say. A slight pause ensued, during which he was feeling for something in his coat-pocket, and at length produced a small brown paper packet, sealed.

"Should your unfortunate father be restored to health," he at last said, "I would request of your ladyship to deliver to him this packet, with an account of what you have seen of me, and that which I have told you. He will know the hand-writing, and perhaps may be induced to forgive the writer, whom he once loved as if he had been his own son, and who must ever reflect with the most bitter and agonizing remorse upon the ungrateful, the villanous conduct of which he was guilty towards him. Besides letters, the packet contains a certain sum of money, the amount of which I plundered my benefactor in the days of my youth; that and my sincere penitence is the only atonement I have to offer,

Lady Ravensford took the packet, and was moved by the earnestness of Monckton's manner. She would have spoken, but the smuggler seeing her intention, prevented her.

"Will your ladyship promise me to do as I desire?" he eagerly interrogated.

Rosabelle immediately answered in the affirmative.

"And if my poor, unfortunate parent should never be in a condition to receive it?" she asked, with a heavy sigh.

"Then are the contents of the packet yours,

my lady," answered Monckton; "I obtained the money surreptitiously from your father's coffers, and it must return to them, or go to those who have a claim upon his property after his decease. Your ladyship has given your consent?"

"Undoubtedly," answered Rosabelle.

"Thanks, thanks! Heaven bless you!" cried the smuggler-captain, vehemently; "I am more than repaid for all that I have done."

Having spoken thus, before our heroine could make any observation in reply, Monckton hastily arose from his seat, and abruptly quitted the cabin.

Rosabelle had felt deeply interested in the behaviour of the smuggler-captain; but her thoughts were soon diverted into the painful channel into which they had formerly wandered, and she thought upon the mental sufferings which in all probability awaited her at Holly Hall, with the most poignant and unconquerable anguish.

She was not long left alone, for Margaret returned to the cabin, and being very loquacious, she contrived to estrange for awhile the thoughts of our heroine from the painful subjects that had before engrossed them, and in order to pass the time away, Rosabelle did not discourage her; but, on the contrary, smiled affably, and enjoyed the simple observations which Margaret made use of.

Rosabelle saw no more of Monckton for several hours, and the vessel proceeded so swiftly, that the termination of their voyage promised quickly to arrive. Our heroine did not look forward to the time of their reaching G——m so impatiently as she would otherwise have done, were she not there to have been deprived of her protector; but, after her long incarceration, {and the troubles to which she had been subjected, she could not help looking forward to the journey to the Hall with apprehension, knowing that, in a stage coach, an unprotected female was often exposed to insult, and that it was likewise the case, that others who should rather stand forward to prevent it, too frequently were not only ready to abet the outrage, but enjoyed it as a very rich joke, and suffered the offender to proceed with impunity.

She, however, could easily account for Monckton's behaviour, as regarded his leaving her at G——m, and was satisfied, although she regretted the necessity which compelled him to do so.

The afternoon had far advanced, when Monckton rejoined our heroine, and she had by that time become a ° more composed than when he quitted he   morning. He was evidently pleased t   and expressed himself accordingly.

"In two hours, at the furthest," he observed,

"our voyage will be over, and we shall have reached G——m."

Rosabelle expressed her satisfaction at this intelligence.

"There your ladyship and I part company," added the smuggler-captain, with a smile, "and it is uncertain when, if ever, we shall cast anchor alongside of each other again."

"I trust, sir," replied Rosabelle, "that we may see each other again, and that when we do, we may both be very differently situated to what we are at present."

Monckton looked his thanks. He then invited our heroine to walk upon deck, to inhale the purity of the sea breeze, and view the beauties of the setting sun; an offer of which she gladly availed herself, and left the cabin in his company.

Upon reaching the deck of the vessel, the sight which burst upon her observation was one of the most impressive grandeur, and her whole attention quickly became absorbed in the contemplation of it. The whole of the western ocean appeared to be one liquid mass of gold, as the monarch of the day sunk in radiant majesty to rest from his diurnal course. A gentle and refreshing breeze just appeared to move the waves, over which the light vessel glided as graceful as a fine skiff. In the distance Rosabelle beheld the lofty chain of rocks that bounded the coast of G——m, and upon whose summits the last golden streaks of declining day rested. Here and there was to be seen a fisherman's boat, and sometimes the simple song of the fisherman as he pursued his wearisome and uncertain toil, was conveyed by the wind to the ear.

There was but one or two of the smugglers upon the deck, so that Rosabelle was not interrupted in her contemplation of the sublime grandeur of Nature; and both her body and her mind felt refreshed.

She remained upon deck until the last rays of the sun set in the western horizon, and darkness began to spread itself upon the ocean, when feeling cold, she returned to the cabin, and awaited anxiously for the termination of the voyage, which, she was now aware, was fast drawing to a close.

Another half hour passed away, when the cessation of the vessel convinced Rosabelle that they had cast anchor, and the voyage was over. She pressed the little Alfred to her heart, once more implored the protection of omnipotence, and then felt firmly prepared for whatever might take place.

She was not long kept in suspense. Monckton entered the cabin, and advancing hastily towards her, he said—

"The voyage is over; we are not more than half a mile from G——m, and the boat is waiting to convey you ashore. Will your ladyship attend me?"

Lady Ravensford felt a sudden faintness come over her, and an apprehension of she scarcely knew what; but she arose, and giving her hand to the smuggler-captain, she suffered him to lead her and her child from the cabin in silence.

When they had reached the deck, she found Sam Kitson and two others of the smugglers waiting to receive her and her child in the boat, and here she paused, and looked at Monckton, who, after having given her some instructions as to the way she was to proceed when she reached the shore, placed a purse in her hand, saying—

"You will, I am sure, my lady, receive this as it is meant, as a trifle merely to defray the expenses of your journey. And now we must part; I beseech you to remember the favours I have asked of you, and which you have been pleased to promise to comply with. Farewell, daughter of my benefactor, and sometimes in your prayers do not forget Archibald Malcolm the smuggler."

Lady Ravensford looked more than she could have expressed in words, and graciously extending her fair hand to Monckton to kiss, and which he raised vehemently, but respectfully to his lips, she fervently uttered "Farewell," and suffered him to hand her and Alfred into the boat. Sam Kitson and his companions then followed, and swiftly rowed towards the shore, the smuggler-captain remaining upon the deck, and watching their progress, until the boat was hidden from the view in the obscurity of the darkness.

The mingled feelings of joy and anxiety which filled the bosom of our heroine now found vent in a copious flood of tears, and it was not until the boat had reached the shore that she was aroused from the consciousness of anything but her own thoughts.

Hope and courage suddenly animated her breast, and she was handed on shore by Sam, and she raised her eyes towards Heaven, with a firm reliance upon its protection.

"Yonder pathway, my lady," said Sam, "will bring you to the road which leads to the town. I wish I could conduct you there, for it is a dark night. Good-by, my lady; Heaven preserve you on your journey, and bring you happier times. Has your ladyship any message to send to my wife?"

"Tell her, Mr. Kitson," answered our heroine, fervently, "that I shall never cease to remember her with esteem and friendship, and that I will not fail to write to her at the very earliest opportunity. Give her also this ring, which I request she will accept in remembrance of me!"

Thus saying, Rosabelle took a handsome ring from her finger, and placed it in the hand of Sam.

"Oh, my lady," said the smuggler; "this kindness and——"

Rosabelle waited not to hear the finish of the sentance, but bidding Sam adieu, she took her child in her arms, wrapped her cloak around him, for the evening air blew keen, and hurried along the path which he had pointed out.

The evening had set in dark and threatening, and ere our heroine had proceeded far, large drops of rain began to descend, and gave notice of a violent storm. Rosabelle felt alarmed and dispirited, for she had been given to understand that it was some considerable distance from the town, and if she did not proceed thither with all possible despatch, the mail would have left, and she would then be placed in the dilemma of having to remain in a strange place till the morning.

Urged on by these apprehensions, Lady Ravensford pushed on her way as fast as she could, but the weight of her child, who had fallen asleep, retarded her progress, and he was almost more than her strength could carry.

And now heavy peals of thunder rolled above, and flashes of lightning blazed along the sky. The rain also began to descend in torrents, and the heart of our heroine sunk with despair. As far as her eyes could stretch through the deep gloom, she could not perceive the least signs of a human habitation. She therefore turned off towards the rocks that bounded her right, thinking she might find a shelter amongst them until the storm had subsided; and she prayed to Heaven for assistance in her present dismal situation. Surely, she thought, Monckton might have contrived some safer and readier means of restoring her to her friends, for now she was surrounded by dangers that made her tremble to contemplate.

The rain descended so heavily that she was already nearly drenched to the skin, and, in a strange place, and on such a night, her feelings may be readily conceived.

She had now reached the rocks, when suddenly a vivid flash of lightning revealed to her a large cavity in one of them, which offered her a secure shelter from the pelting storm. She hailed the place with pleasure, although the place was dismal in the extreme, and at another time she would have avoided it with alarm. But now she hastened towards it, and treading cautiously into its deepest recesses, seated herself, exhausted, upon a projection of the rock.

Flash after flash of the blue forked-lightning darted along the sky, preceding heavy peals of thunder, which reverberated awfully among the rocks, and nothing could be more hopeless or alarming than the situation of our heroine. Oh, how she wished herself again on board the smuggler's vessel, and the cheering idea of liberty was banished from her thoughts. The storm seemed likely, too, to last for some time, and altogether nothing could be more dismal than our heroine's prospects.

CHAPTER XXXIV.

A STRANGE ADVENTURE.

HALF an hour elapsed in this manner; one of the most gloomy half hours Rosabelle ever remembered to have experienced. The storm still raged as violently as ever, and she saw no prospect of proceeding on her journey. It was now also getting late, and Rosabelle was fearful that she would lose all chance of getting a place in the mail that night.

Suddenly Rosabelle started with amazement and alarm from the place where she had been seated, for she was almost certain that she saw a flash of light, as if proceeding from a lamp or lanthorn, streaming along the ground. She was confident it was not the lightning; but it was gone in an instant, and the place was again involved in impenetrable darkness. Rosabelle trembled and pressed her child closer to her breast; she was certain it was no delusion, yet what could it be, and from whence could it proceed? She was fixed immovable to the spot, and, although her fears urged her to it, it would have been complete madness for her to have quitted the place, while the storm still raged so violently.

A few minutes elapsed, and Rosabelle, in a state of trepidation, and pressing her child closely to her heart, kept her eyes fixed upon the spot from whence she was almost certain she had seen the light issue, which had so much surprised and alarmed her. And now again a flood of light, broader than the other, glowed upon the rocky wall, proceeding from the extreme end of the place, and it was followed by a rustling sound of some person or persons moving to and fro.

Rosabelle was so astonished and terrified, that she still remained fixed to the spot on which she was standing like a statue, and with her eyes rivetted upon the spot where she had seen the light.

"Surely," she thought, "there must be another cavern beyond this, and which is inhabited; or whence that light! My God! should it be by robbers!"

Her slumbering energies were aroused at this thought, and, in spite of the storm, she was moving from the spot, when her footsteps were arrested by the tones of a human voice vibrating in her ear, and which evidently proceeded from the same place as the light had issued.

The voice was that of a female, and was one of much sweetness and flexibility. The melody which it sung with great taste, was one of simple beauty, and could not fail to interest the hearer.

Rosabelle listened with the most profound attention, and heard the following words of the

SONG.

" The orb of day was brightly gleaming,
  From a blue and cloudless sky,
Over hill and valley breathing,
  And fragrant breathed the zephyr's sigh.
From his humble couch to labour,
  The lowly peasant hastes away ;
But, why sounds the pipe and tabour ?—
  This is Helen's bridal day.

" To the village church repairing,
  Now is seen the bridal train ;
Seldom's seen a sight so cheering,
  As came bounding o'er the plain.
Rustic hearts devoid of sorrow,
  Simple beings light and gay ;
Thought not of the coming morrow,—
  It was Helen's bridal day.

" Helen was the village beauty,
  Helen was the village pride ;
Many bow'd to her in duty,
  Many sought her for a bride.
But Edwin, by her loved—and loving,
  To her charms did homage pay ;
And their parents, all approving,—
  This is Helen's bridal day.

" And now the old church-porch surrounding,
  A joyous throng waits patiently ;
Every heart with pleasure bounding,
  But the bridegroom—where is he ?
Edwin he was false and changing,
  And for wealth did her betray :
To a distant part now raging,
  Broken's Helen's heart to-day.

" The roses now her cheeks are flying,
  No more is seen that healthful bloom ;
Helen falls,—she's pale—she's dying,
  Dismal is the maiden's doom.
Looking calmly up to Heaven,
  Helen now is heard to pray ;
Edwin false, by her 's forgiven,
  Death closed Helen's fate that day !"

Rosabelle listened with the deepest interest and astonishment to the words of the simple ballad, to which the invisible vocalist imparted a double charm by the sweetness of the style in which she sang it, and she never for an instant removed her eyes from the spot on which they had become rivetted. She was not long kept in suspense after the conclusion of the song ; the light again issued from the back of the cavern, and immediately afterwards, a heavy stone which concealed an aperture sufficiently large for a person to pass through, was thrown down, and a tall figure in white, carrying a lighted lamp in her hand, stepped from it into the cavern, which our heroine no sooner beheld than, overpowered by her fears that were naturally excited by the singularity of the adventure, she uttered an exclamation of terror, and fainte .

On recovering her senses she was completely bewildered and astonished on beholding the change in her situation. She was placed in a handsome bed, in an elegant chamber; her child reposed by her side, and hanging over the couch was a middle-aged female, extremely handsome, and whose dress and figure convinced her it was the same she had seen in the rocky cavity. There was an expression of solicitude in her face and demeanour, and, altogether, she was a being who could not fail to create esteem and confidence at first sight.

On beholding our heroine open her eyes, the lady uttered an exclamation of pleasure, and immediately rang a bell to summon the attendance of a female domestic.

Rosabelle raised herself in the bed, and looking with eager astonishment, first upon the lady, and then around the apartment, she exclaimed—

"Where am I? How came I hither? And what is the meaning of this?"

"Do not alarm yourself, my dear madam," said the lady, "you are in the house of one who has neither the will nor the power to harm you, I regret that my sudden appearance to you in the cavern should so have terrified you; but, of course, I was not aware that you were there."

"Then I am not wrong in the supposition I entertained, madam," said our heroine; "you are the same individual who appeared to me in so mysterious a manner while I was seeking shelter from the fury of the storm?"

"I am," answered the lady; "there is a secret communication from this, my house, to that place, which is known only to myself and one faithful servant. I was taking one of my melancholy strolls, when I so unexpectedly met you; and when you became insensible, I had you, and your sweet child, conveyed to my house, to which you are heartily welcome. After all, it strikes me that it is a fortunate job I saw you, as the storm has not in the least abated, and at any rate you will be much more comfortable beneath this roof, than you would have been in that dismal cavern."

"And to whom am I indebted for this kindness?" asked Rosabelle.

"To one who has drunk deeply of the cup of sorrow," answered the lady, with a deep sigh; "but that is no matter. You are now beneath the roof of Mrs. Belgrave, madam, who has the honour of now addressing you. And may I be so bold as to inquire whom I have the honour to have as a guest?"

Our heroine informed her without hesita-

tion. Mrs. Belgrave started on hearing her name, and her looks expressed astonishment and pleasure.

"And have I, indeed, the pleasure of seeing the much-injured Lady Ravensford," she ejaculated, "her who, as well as her child, has been so long torn from the arms of her friends, and for whom search has been made in vain?"

"You have, indeed, madam," replied Rosabelle; "but a few hours only have I been set at liberty, and I was on my way to the town of G——m, in the hope of meeting the coach, when I was overtaken by the storm, and sought shelter in the place where you found me."

"Wonderful!" exclaimed Mrs. Belgrave. "Oh, Lady Ravensford, how delighted I am to see you, and to find that you have at last escaped from your enemies. What transport will your restoration to your friends impart to their agonised hearts."

"And do you know my friends, my dear madam?" interrogated Rosabelle.

"I have frequently had the honour of seeing Lord Ravensford, some few years since, at his father's," replied Mrs. Belgrave; "and when I heard of his heavy misfortunes, and your unaccountable disappearance, I could not help feeling regret and sympathy in his troubles, and the severity of your ladyship's fate. But I am so surprised and pleased at our extraordinary meeting, that I can scarcely believe the evidence of my senses. Here, then, my lady, you are welcome to remain as long as you may think proper to honour me, but not doubting that you will be anxious to pursue your journey in the morning, when a post chaise can be procured from the town as early as you like."

"Many thanks, my dearest madam, for your kindness," said our heroine; "and glad I am that the circumstance took place which has thus introduced me to the house of so amiable a lady as Mrs. Belgrave. But tell me, I beg of you, have you heard anything of the present situation of my husband,—my father? Oh, tell me!"

Mrs. Belgrave shook her head, and replied in the negative.

"The last which I heard of Lord Ravensford," replied Mrs. Belgrave, "was the account which I read in the newspapers of the villanous attempt upon his life."

"Ah!" exclaimed our heroine, her heart shuddering with horror; "how implacable has been the enemy by whom we have been persecuted. My poor husband! Doubtless the wretch who made this atrocious attempt, was employed by that most inhuman of scoundrels, Adder. And now I think of it, this indeed fully accounts for the departure of Gordon Desborough from his house, and explains the dark insinuations of Cicely. Are you acquainted, my dear madam, with the particulars of that event ?"

"I have the newspaper by me with the account in," answered Mrs. Belgrave. "I will hasten and bring it to you; and, in the meantime, if you feel disposed, probably you will arise to supper."

Rosabelle nodded her assent, and Mrs. Belgrave quitted the room. She then arose and awaited her return with some degree of impatience.

She was not at all displeased at the adventure which had thus introduced her to Mrs. Belgrave, whose manners, and a reciprocity of sentiment, she admired, she having also, according to her account, suffered deeply in the school of adversity. She considered it very fortunate that her footsteps had accidentally been guided to the cavity in the rock, as the storm had never abated in the least, and situated as she was in a strange place, and where she would have been compelled to remain the whole of the night, and amongst strangers, from whom she might receive some insult.

The villanous attempt upon the life of her husband, filled her breast with the utmost terror, and she could not help believing that Adder was the wretch who had been the cause of the atrocious attempt. But how grateful did she feel to the Almighty who had foiled the purpose of the assassin. She raised her hands towards Heaven, and gave utterance to her thanks in the most fervent and glowing language,

Mrs. Belgrave quickly returned with the newspaper she had mentioned, and the reader may be well aware with what interest and agony Rosabelle perused the paragraph.

"The miscreant!" exclaimed our heroine, when she had finished reading the account; "how bitter has been his enmity towards my unfortunate husband; how heavy the sorrows he has been the means of inflicting upon us."

"And do you then really believe, my lady, that the wretch who made the attempt upon Lord Ravensford's life was employed by Adder?" asked Mrs. Belgrave.

"Oh, yes," replied Rosabelle; "who else can I judge? My husband has not another enemy in the world that I know of besides him."

"If it is, indeed, as you suspect, my lady," observed Mrs. Belgrave; "this Adder must be one of the most cruel and blood-thirsty scoundrels that ever I heard of. Oh! how great must have been your sufferings, placed as you were, in the power of such a man."

"Alas! few persons can form any idea of the extent of them," returned Lady Ravensford; "if you will not deem the melancholy particulars tedious, my dear madam, or have

time to devote from your couch, I will detail them to you after supper."

"Most anxious am I, my dear lady, to hear them," returned Mrs. Belgrave; "but I am fearful that the task will be troublesome and painful to you."

"Oh, no, madam," observed our heroine; "on the contrary, it will be a relief to my mind, confident as I am that I am talking to one that can sympathise in my misfortunes."

"You do me no more than justice by that supposition, Lady Ravensford," said Mrs. Belgrave; "few indeed have suffered more vicissitudes than I have, and in many instances, from what I have heard of your history, your fate and mine have been by no means dissimilar."

"Sorry, my dear madam," said Lady Rosabelle, "am I to hear you say so; alas! that villany should so often triumph in its nefarious practices. But you must be very lonely in this place, provided as it is with every comfort, notwithstanding."

"No, my lady," answered Mrs. Belgrave; "solitude and retirement now suit me best; for I have seen enough of the world to embitter my mind against it."

Mrs. Belgrave sighed, and our heroine already felt the deepest sympathy towards her, and a curiosity to be made acquainted with her history.

The servant now brought in the supper-things, and Rosabelle having partaken of the repast, with a better appetite than she had done for many months before, and the cloth being cleared, she related, as briefly as possible, all that had happened to her from the time of her abduction, Mrs. Belgrave frequently interrupting her to give expression to her feelings of sorrow and regret for the many sufferings to which the narrator had been subjected, and her disgust and abhorrence of the villany of her infamous persecutor.

When our heroine had concluded, Mrs. Belgrave observed—

"Fearful and almost unprecedented have been your sorrows, my dear Lady Ravensford; but never sufficiently grateful can you be to the mercy of Providence, who has shielded you from the more terrible fate to which the wretch Adder had destined you, and for the miraculous manner in which it raised you a preserver in one whom you had so little cause to expect would prove your friend."

"Most true are your observations, my dear madam," returned Rosabelle, "and believe me, most constantly shall my thankful prayers be raised to that Almighty power from whom I have experienced so much mercy."

"A pity it is that a man who had so excellent an opportunity of raising himself to honour and esteem in the world, as Archibald Malcolm, should have been tempted in youth so to have committed himself, and blighted his prospects for the future," remarked Mrs. Belgrave.

"It is, indeed, madam," said our heroine, "and after the inestimable service he has rendered me, and certain, as I am that he possesses talents and other intrinsic qualities so admirably calculated to make him a worthy member of society, no one can regret his vices and indiscretions more than I do."

"Much as I have experienced of the cruelty and villany of mankind," added Mrs. Belgrave, "this Adder is certainly the basest scoundrel I ever heard of. I am only fearful that Monckton, as he calls himself, has shown him too much leniency, and that, while he remains at large, he will be tempted to try some other means to annoy you and your husband in future."

"The inevitable consequences of his doing so will surely prevent him," replied Lady Ravensford; "and being constantly on our guard, we may devise some means of rendering his plans futile, and of bringing upon him that speedy retribution which his crimes so richly merit; but which, by obeying the injunctions of Mockton, he may for awhile retard."

"I trust that your hopes may not be disappointed, Lady Ravensford," replied Mrs. Belgrave. "But it is now getting late, and I daresay you want to retire to rest. I will see about procuring you a post-chaise in the morning, and may Heaven speed you safe to your friends, and that you may find their misery far less than your fears anticipate."

"Many thanks to you, madam, for your kind wishes," said our heroine, pressing fervently the hand which Mrs. Belgrave extended towards her. "Most happy, too, shall I be if this accidental meeting should prove the prelude to a long and lasting friendship between us."

The countenance of Mrs. Belgrave brightened, and a gentle smile played around her lips as she answered—

"Oh, how happy shall I feel to be honoured by the friendship of the amiable Lady Ravensford—of one who, like myself, has endured so many sorrows, and can, therefore, sympathise with me. At some future period, should Fate destine us ever to meet again, I will make you acquainted with my melancholy history, trusting that while you condemn my follies and indiscretions, you will acknowledge that I have been adequately punished for them. Alas! could we but think upon the numerous miseries that almost invariably follow one single act of indiscretion, how guarded should we be against the many snares that are too frequently laid to entrap the unwary youth."

Rosabelle sighed deeply, and tears involuntarily started to her eyes, for how sadly—how fearfully had she experienced the truth of Mrs. Belgrave's observations. Alas! perhaps even at that time her unfortunate parent was the victim of that dreadful malady, which, in the first instance, was brought upon him by the fatal errors of her youth. Mrs. Belgrave appeared to read her thoughts, and pressing her hand affectionately, she said—

"We will drop this subject for the present, which seems to be too painful to us both. To-morrow morning I hope to find you refreshed from your night's rest; and, although I shall regret losing your society so soon, it is mitigated by my anxiety that you should be restored to your friends with the least possible delay. Good night, my dear Lady Ravensford, and may all good angels guard your rest."

Sincerely did our heroine reciprocate the wishes of that kind and benevolent lady, of whose house she had so singularly become an inmate, and Mrs. Belgrave retired, sending Amy, one of her domestics, to Rosabelle to assist her in preparing for her couch.

Happy in the security of her situation, our heroine quickly fell into a refreshing slumber, but her thoughts being fixed upon that home, and those dear friends from whom she had been so long separated, dreams of mingled pleasure and pain flitted before her busy imagination, and she awoke in the morning with mingled feelings of hope and fear inhabiting her bosom.

On descending to the breakfast room, which was furnished with a degree of elegance which showed the taste of the fair owner of the house, she found Mrs. Belgrave already there, and awaiting her arrival. She greeted her with the same kindness and familiarity as if they had been acquainted for years, and made many anxious inquiries after her health, and the manner in which she had rested, to which our heroine promptly replied.

"I am compelled, my dear Lady Ravensford," said Mrs. Belgrave, after a pause, "I am afraid that I shall cause you some regret by the information I have to give you."

Rosabelle's countenance changed, and she looked alarmed. Mrs. Belgrave smiled.

"Nay, my lady," she observed, "do not alarm yourself; what I have to tell you is not of that serious nature which you seem to apprehend. There is only one post-chaise to let out on hire in this remote town, and that will not be here until to-morrow morning, and the mail that would convey you to the neighbourhood of Holly Hall will not depart until six o'clock in the evening; consequently, your journey must unavoidably be deferred for several hours, if you think proper to go by the coach, although, if I might advise you, it would be that you should postpone your journey until you can go by the chaise in the morning, which will be much more safe and pleasant travelling."

"Although every minute's procrastination, you must be aware, Mrs. Belgrave, causes me the greatest uneasiness, anxious as I am to reach Holly Hall." returned Lady Ravensford, "I will be guided by your advice, and e'en delay my departure from hence until to morrow morning."

Mrs. Belgrave seemed pleased at her decision, and the breakfast passed over very pleasantly. When it was concluded, and after a short time spent in conversation upon different subjects, our heroine reminded the former of the promise she had made her, to make her acquainted with her history, and Mrs. Belgrave agreed to gratify her curiosity. After the lapse of a few minutes, during which, Mrs. Belgrave was occupied in collecting her thoughts, she commenced her eventful narrative in the following words :—

CHAPTER XXXV.

MRS. BELGRAVE'S TALE.

"AMIDST all the errors of my past life, few individuals who were thoroughly acquainted with me, would ever deny me the credit of candour and truth; I will, therefore, in my present recital, not seek to gloss over my own faults, nor garble events to hide my errors, but relate them as they took place exactly, however unfavourable the impression may be which they might cause in your ladyship's mind towards me.

"My father, Mr. Claremont, was in early

MRS. BELGRAVE, THROUGH WANT, COMMITS A THEFT.

life the inheritor of a handsome fortune, while his younger brother, who, notwithstanding he was said to be the favourite of his widowed mother, was kept in a most dependant state, which, I am sorry to have to state, was principally occasioned by the jealous and covetous disposition of my father, who had said everything to his prejudice, and consequently his mother was made to believe him a wild, dissipated, and hopeless young man, and he had constantly to endure the reproaches of his mother and elder brother, until, at length, he was driven from his paternal roof, and purchasing a commission in a regiment which was going on foreign service, no more was heard of him for many years afterwards.

"But the estrangement from his friends was the least of my uncle's afflictions ; his heart had been devoted to Adeline Beaumont, and she returning his affection, they were betrothed to each other, with every prospect of their union taking place, when just before his departure from England, the poisoned breath of calumny prejudiced Adeline against him; she was led to believe that he was faithless to her, and the match was broken off for ever.

"I am now speaking of my mother, for she soon after became my father's wife; but although she ever most sacredly performed the duties of an affectionate wife and mother, the penetrating eye might discover that she still warmly cherished in her bosom the germs of that ardent passion which the object of her first love had inspired.

"Dear sainted mother!—May this heart cease to beat for ever, when my memory shall cease to retain the recollection of your numerous virtues—your mild, your gentle disposition; the cares, the affections, the anxieties you bestowed upon your poor unfortunate child!—Would that Heaven had not deprived me of you at so early a period, then should I probably never have been guilty of the errors I afterwards was, nor have known the many miseries it was my fate to experience. But let me not murmur at the all-wise decrees of Providence.

"I was the only child of my parents, and at the time this narrative may be said to commence, we resided in the family mansion, my grandmother living with us. Every affectionate care and attention were bestowed upon me, and the days of my childhood passed happily away; but alas! misfortune, at an early period, was destined to select me for one of its numerous victims.

"My father was naturally extravagant, and addicted to the ruinous dice, although he had taken such precautions that he imagined his mother and his wife were entirely ignorant of his unfortunate propensities.

"Several years passed away, and I had just attained my tenth year, when my father unluckily formed an acquaintance with the Marquis Montveillers, a French nobleman, and from that period the change in his behaviour was so marked that it could not escape the observation of my mother. Notwithstanding his addiction to the vice of gambling, he had almost invariably been accustomed to spend his evenings at home, but now they were usually devoted to the company of the marquis, and it often occurred that he did not return home till daylight, when he would be in a state of inebriation and excitement, and would hasten to his chamber, without deigning to account to my mother for so alarming an alteration in his behaviour and habits towards her.

"Almost heart-broken at this neglect, and entertaining the most painful apprehensions as to the cause of his conduct, my poor mother passed many a wretched day and night; yet did she forbear to reproach him, but at length, unable any longer to confine her agonising thoughts and feelings to her own bosom, she questioned my grandmother upon the subject, and asked her if she had not also noticed the extraordinary change in my father's conduct.

"'Alas! Adeline,' replied the old lady, 'too long have I been sensible to that alarming alteration, and many are the pangs it has secretly cost me. I tremble for the consequences of his increasing intimacy with the marquis, who I am certain is an unprincipled profligate. Had it not been for you, and my

dear, dear Constance, I should long since have reproached Valentine for his conduct, and have reprobated his connection with Montveillers. But, depend upon it, I shall take an opportunity of mildly, yet firmly reprimanding him for his conduct, and of pointing out to him the ruin, which, I fear, will ensue to himself, if he does not break off the intimacy with that man.'

"My mother felt more tranquil after her interview with my grandmother, and the promises which the latter had made to her; but, alas! the hour of painful trial was fast approaching.

"The nocturnal absences of my father from home became more frequent, and in his sober moments, his manners were so altered, that no person would scarcely have believed that he had been the same man. He avoided conversing with my mother as much as possible, and constant care seemed to be seated upon his brow.

"At length, alarmed at the evident inroads care was making upon the naturally delicate constitution of my mother, my grandmother would delay her resolution no longer, and, therefore, sought an interview with my father, one morning after he had spent the night away in the usual manner.

"Her son affected to be surprised at the nature of her accusations, but his now care-worn, pale, and haggard countenance, was a sufficient confirmation of the justice of her reproaches, and he seemed at a loss to reply; traversing the apartment with hasty steps, and frequently turning to speak, without having the power to do so.

"'Alas! Valentine!' exclaimed the poor old lady, in impressive and melancholy accents; 'you stand upon the brink of a fearful precipice. Pause, ere you plunge yourself into the dreadful abyss. Be warned ere it is too late; it is your mother who speaks to you, who would reclaim you, and save you from destruction! Oh, scorn not her voice! Well do I know the vices to which you have been addicted since your acquaintance with that bad man. Be not, then, senseless to shame, to repentance. Remember, Valentine, that you are my son, that you were the favourite of your father, and the inheritor of nearly all the large fortune he had accumulated by industry and perseverance. What is the use you are now making of that fortune? Are you not dissipating it in profligacy, heedless of the sorrowing hearts of your affectionate wife, and your unfortunate mother, and the future prospects of your child? Answer me, son, and that truly, have I not drawn a correct picture of the destructive and disgraceful course you are now pursuing?'

"Unprepared as my father was for these severe reproaches, he was completely, as it were, thunderstruck; he groaned, and stood trembling before his mother, as if he had been guilty of some heinous crime against the laws of his country. He knew himself guilty—he knew the justice of his mother's observations, and he had not a word to offer in extenuation of his conduct.

"The countenance of the old lady had become remarkably stern, and her eyes were fixed upon him with a look which seemed as if it would penetrate to his soul.

"'Oh, my mother,' he at length groaned, 'be merciful! Torture me not thus severely. Too well indeed do I merit it all; but oh, in pity spare me! You have demanded the truth, and by all my hopes here and hereafter, I will not attempt to deceive you in the most trival circumstance! Think me not entirely lost; deem me not quite callous to the voice of virtue; and yet alas! mother, I am a ruined, wretched man! Oh, curses light upon the infernal dice, my mother, to which your unhappy son has become a victim. Hear me patiently, while I tell the brief but painful history. Caught within the meshes of that damned vice, I lost large sums of money, and then borrowed money to retrieve those losses. The spell of the fiend of darkness was upon me; my unlucky star was in the ascendant. Again I lost, and again I sought the too ready means of supplying my wants. Dark and insidious was the plot laid to ensnare me, and the base concocter of it succeeded but too well; he was not satisfied until he had accomplished my ruin! Our family mansion is mortgaged, and so relentless is my villanous creditor, that ere long it must be sold to satisfy his demands. I am a beggar! We have nothing left but my child's invested property; thus, mother, have I told you the whole dreadful truth, and trembling, I kneel at your feet to solicit your pardon!'

"Although I was very young at the time, I have frequently heard my father describe emphatically to my mother this scene, and it is stamped indelibly upon my memory. Mrs. Claremont was a woman of the strongest passions, and you, my lady, may, therefore, well imagine the effect this information from the lips of her misguided son, must have had upon her. They stood alone together in the saloon of the hall, where his breakfast had long been waiting for him, but remained untouched. She had listened to him with the most profound and awful attention, and for some minutes after he had ceased, she stood fixed in the same attitude, her eyes gleaming upon him with the looks of the wildest despair; while her heavily heaving bosom plainly told the deep mental and maternal anguish she was enduring. But not a tear behewed her eyelids, nor did she seem to be in the least degree affected by his agitation; on the contrary, she appeared to swell with indignation, and as my unfortunate father knelt beside her, and with clasped hands, gazed into her face with the most vehement and energetic

supplication, she spurned him from her, and vociferated in accents made fierce by the violence of her resentment—

"'Rise, hateful, cruel wretch!—Rise, and listen to the reproaches of her who brought you into the world, to disgrace her name, abuse her maternal care, and break the hearts of those that should be dearer to thee than thine own life; but whose happiness—whose hopes—whose prospects, thou hast now blasted for ever. Was it for this infamy I pressed thee to my maternal bosom, and cradled thee with such motherly care and fondness?—Was it to work this ruin, that thy father left thy younger brother a beggar, to have to battle with the vicissitudes of the world; that he might bestow upon thee the whole of his wealth? Left thee the sole representative of his ancient and honourable house? Oh, monster! villain! was it not for this thy brother was driven an outcast from his home, whilst thou wert suffered to remain behind basking in all the luxury and happiness that fortune can bestow? And now what are thou?—A beggar!—A wretch like one of those poor abject beings whom yesterday thou wouldst probably have despised! What hast thou made of thy poor wife and innocent child? Beggars—beggars! Yes, and so wouldst thou reduce the poor aged, enfeebled woman who bore thee in her womb, but that thou hast not the power; thou canst not touch a fraction of that which I inherit. No—no, barbarian as thou art, there art thou thwarted! Thy scarilegious hands shall never touch a single coin! It is my grandchild's—my own sweet innocent's! Nay, implore not to me; supplicate not to mercy to her who is now dead to thy sufferings! Thou kneelest in vain! I mock—I exult in thine anguish; thou deservest it all, and oh, how much more, after the misery which thou hast wrought. Kneel and sue for mercy of an offended God! Seek it of thy much injured wife, and her innocent offspring; to me all thy supplications are useless! Hope not for forgiveness from me; away, detested recreant to a fond mother's affection!'

"Dreadful, indeed, it must have been to have witnessed that painful interview between mother and son; to have heard the fierce ejaculations and reproaches of the former, and to notice the wild despair and agony of my father! But the aged woman had now completely exhausted herself; her mental agony had long laboured for vent, and covering her face with her hands, she burst into a paroxysm of tears, and her bosom heaved with convulsive sobs. But the powerful effect of her reproaches upon her distracted son, who seemed to be nearly driven to madness, recalled her to reason, and, in spite of her assertions, drew her whole maternal attention towards him.

"He had heard her bitter invectives, and listened to her refusal to forgive him!—His form trembled; he clenched his fists so tight, in the vehemence of his emotion, that his finger nails penetrated the palms of his hands, and the blood flowed freely. His countenance assumed the livid hue of death; his eyes glared vacantly and terrfically, while his tongue refused to give utterance to a syllable; a pause ensued; it was an awful interval, although brief; but at length, wrought up to all the fury and desperation of despair, my unfortunate father rushed into an ante-room, and bringing forth a loaded pistol, holding it towards his head, he again stood before his mother, with an air of wild determination, and after the lapse of only a few seconds, he cried in a voice which plainly evinced his resolution to put his threat into execution,—

" ' Mother, mother, I will sue to thee no more! Thou hast closed thine heart against me, and bade me seek for mercy only of the Most High! I obey thee, and will in a few minutes appear before His awful tribunal, there to answer for all my faults! This moment will I die before thee, and thus at once end that career of vice thou hast so severely censured. Mother, farewell! in this world we part for ever!'

" As my father thus spoke, he was about to do as he had threatened, when his deadly purpose was arrested by the piercing screams of Mrs. Claremont, who rushed hastily upon him, and with a strength which no person would have believed from her age she could have possessed, she forced the murderous weapon from him, and dashing it way, cried in delirious tones:—

" ' Hold! hold! Valentine, my son! oh, forbear to rush thus guiltily into the presence of thine offended Maker! Oh, my son, my son, do not do that which will blast the happiness to thy poor bereaved parent for ever!'

" ' Mother, mother!' cried her son, still gazing wildly at the pistol which my grandmother had thrown upon the floor, ' tell me, have I thy pardon? My fate rests upon thy lips!'

" ' Then live! oh, live! my dearest Valentine!' exclaimed the poor old woman, pressing him frantically to her heart; ' live to repent; I do, indeed, forgive thee! Abandon thy follies; turn from the ruinous path into which thou hast been so villanously seduced, and all that has taken place shall be buried in oblivion. Oh, Valentine! doubt me not! let this, thy fond mother's kiss, so oft imprinted upon thy cheek, assure thee of my sincerity and thy forgiveness!'

My mother,' exclaimed her son, completely overpowered by his feelings; ' this is more than my misconduct has merited; much more than my vices have deserved. But I will indeed do as thou hast said; live that I may repent of them, and to make reparation to thee and my deeply-injured Adeline. But I have

yet another request to make of thee, mother, which is, that thou wilt not reveal to Adeline the particulars of this fatal interview, and I hope the time is not far distant when we shall all be once more restored to our former happiness.'

" ' Act as thou sayest, my son,' returned Mrs. Claremont, ' and calm thy present agitation, and I promise that it shall be no fault of mine, if we are not indeed happy.'

" The poor old lady was in a state of great agitation and fear, for the wild looks of her son left her cause to fear that he had not entirely abandoned his terrible purpose; and she was, therefore, compelled to use all the mild persuasions and arguments she could think of, to induce him to leave the room, and to accede to her wishes. It was some time ere she was satisfied that she had succeeded, when she linked her arm firmly in his, assumed as much composure as possible, and they walked from the saloon. After a short time she persuaded him to retire to bed, where he soon dropped into a sound sleep, and did not awaken for some time after the return of my mother and myself from our customary walk before breakfast, and being very much refreshed, there was nothing unsound in his manner or looks to excite a'arm.

" My grandmother concealed, as she had promised, the particulars of what had taken place between her and her son at their meeting, from my mother, although she was afterwards made acquainted with them by her erring husband himself; but she did not deny that an interview had taken place between them, that they had quarrelled, and that some severe language had been exchanged; but she assured my mother her husband's mind was filled with compunction for his past indiscretions, and that having promised he would alter his conduct, she had pardoned him, and had every reason to believe he would make a more dutiful and affectionate husband in future.

My gentle and affectionate mother made but few observations in reply to what Mrs. Claremont had stated, although she had her suspicions that the interview between the latter and my father had been of a far more stormy description than the old lady had thought proper to acknowledge; but seeing, in spite of Mrs. Claremont's efforts to the contrary, the violence of her agitation, she forebore to give utterance to her thoughts, lest she should cause her additional uneasiness; and although she plainly saw that ruin was about to descend upon us, she stifled her feelings, and anticipated the impending blow with all that gentle patience and fortitude, which so distinguished her character.

" And too soon, alas! were her worst fears doomed to be realised; the secret which my father had so long trembled to divulge, he could conceal no longer; his rapacious creditor pressed too heavily upon him, and the inevitable change which had to take place in our circumstances, at length compelled my unfortunate father to confess that his own improvidence, and the cursed gambling table, had brought him to ruin. With many scalding tears he implored her to forgive him; nor were his supplications for a moment unheeded by that amiable being to whom he sued. She repined not at the dissipation of that wealth which she brought him when they were united, though deeply did she regret that it had not been put to another purpose than that of glutting the mercenary designing vices of a heartless scoundrel. Her pangs were not for herself, but for me, her child, whose sunny prospects were thus o'erclouded altogether. But she forebore to reproach her unhappy and penitent husband, and extending her hand to him, she breathed her fervent forgiveness on his bosom. These assurances were couched in language that convinced him she was sincere, and although we had now only the bare wreck of our former fortune to live upon, and circumscribed most woefully, in comparison, were our means, she submitted without a murmur, and never made any inquiries of him in future as to the manner in which he proceeded with his painful and deeply enthralled circumstances, confident as she was, now that he was truly awakened to compunction, he would do the best that fate would permit him.

"But patient and resigned as was my gentle mother, it was very different with Mrs. Claremont. The barbed arrow had gone to her heart; and while grieved for the miseries of her daughter in-law, she secretly wept many a distracted hour away over the ruin of her son, and mourned for me, for far dearer was I to that poor old lady than her heart's blood.

"I am now about to describe a scene, which, although thirty years have nearly vanished since it took place, is as fresh in my memory as if it had only been the occurrence of yesterday.

"The lively season of spring had just set in, and Nature was redolent of fragrance and early flowers, that had just begun to expand their blooming beauties to the sight. I was very fond of the poor old lady, and considering the unbounded affection she ever evinced towards me, it is only natural that I should be. Could I win from her a smile, and a kiss of approbation, or any little childish attention I might have paid her, the ultimation of my wishes was gratified, and I was the happiest little thing alive.

Still do I think that I behold that aged relative, with her mild and placid features, and her thin, silvery hair, as, seated in her easy chair, she would instil into my youthful mind some useful lesson, and when I had accomplished my task, a kiss and a kiss again was my reward. And oh, how ample did that reward appear to me then! Yes, I valued it more then than I should a coronet now, and I was the happiest child in the universe. But I fear, my dear Lady Ravensford, that you will think I am becoming tedious. I will return to that part of my story from which I have thus digressed.

"As I have before said, it was a lovely morning—a morning which makes the heart bound with pleasure, and when the bosom is elate with all the best and most cheerful feelings of our nature.

"I had walked forth, soon after quitting my couch, into the garden, and gathering the sweetest flowers I could find, I hastened with a light step, a laughing eye, and eager haste to the room in which my grandmother was seated, and presented my simple, but fragrant offering to her; her cheek was pale, but her eyes were bright, and they sparkled with more than their usual brilliancy when she saw me, and the little present I had brought her.

"She snatched me to her bosom, and pressed fervent kisses on my lips, while I ejaculated, in accents of pleasure and simplicity—

"'Is it not pretty, dear grandmother? is it not a sweet nosegay, and all from my own little garden, gathered fresh this morning for you; I know you will accept them, will you not, dear grandmamma?'

"'Accept them, my darling,' cried Mrs. Claremont, energetically; 'yes, my sweet child, as the choicest offering which could be made to me.'

"'Oh, thank you, dearest grandmamma,' I exclaimed, and my little heart bounded with rapture, 'that is so very kind of you. But you are so good to your poor little Constance, that she knows not in what manner to make to you a sufficient return.'

"Again the poor old lady pressed me fervently to her bosom, and her tears fell upon my cheek, but she could not speak.

"'Are they not beautiful, dear grandmama?' I said again, and pointing at some honeysuckles and violets that were in the nosegay; 'such bright colours, and then they smell so sweet; oh, nothing can be half so lovely, I am sure.'

"'Oh yes, there can,' hastily returned my grandmother; 'they are not half so beautiful, in all their fragrance, as thou art, my sweetest. And yet, how evanescent is their beauty—how transient their bloom; like thee and I, my child, they must quickly fade, and leave scarcely the least remembrance of their loveliness and fragrance behind. Constance, dear Constance, our lives are but a few fleeting years, but the sweet flowers which thou so much admirest, when spring shall again unfold its vernal sweets, will bloom once more in all their pristine loveliness. Alas! to joy there is no renewal of summer, and when once we perish, our sublunary career is ended for ever, never again shall we resume our former shape and beauty.'

"'Oh, yes, grandmamma,' I cried, fixing my eyes intently on the venerable and mild countenance of the poor old lady, 'we do resume our former shape, but in another and a happier world! Do we not, if we are good, become angelic spirits? and brighter and fairer than all the flowers that ever blossomed, or that mortal can conceive, are the angels of Heaven!'

"'Darling child!' ejaculated my grandmamma, holding me still closer to her heart, and parting the hair from my temples, which she kissed vehemently, 'my such be thy happy fate, the bright reward of virtue and innocence.'

"The solemn tone in which my poor grandmother spoke, drew my attention closer towards her, and fixing my eyes more earnestly upon her countenance than I had before done, I could perceive that, independent of her being deeply affected, she was not so well as she had been, although her health had for some time been impaired. On me she had placed her utmost love, from the first hour which gave me to life, and the peculiar tone in which I had spoken made a deeper impression upon her mind at that time than it would, in all probability, have done at any other. On me had she settled all her property, leaving me independent of parents, kindred, or the world, and having done this, and seen her son and his wife likely to be restored to peace, although their pecuniary affairs were so changed, she had scarcely any other wish remaining than that she might breathe her last in the halls of her ancestors before that ancient seat had passed into the sacrilegious hands of the mercenary villain who had ruined my misguided father, and so blighted his future prospects.

"While I still looked in my aged relative's face, she sighed, and tears trembled in her eyes.

"'Dearest grandmamma,' I exclaimed, throwing my little arms around her neck, and looking with the deepest concern in her venerable countenance, 'you are ill this morning—I am convinced that you are. Is there anything that you wish for? and I am sure you know that your Constance will fly to get it for you. Or my mamma—oh, had I not better tell her to come to you?''

"'No—no, my sweetest,' replied Mrs. Claremont, 'thou hast no occasion to do so yet. Open the windows, Constance, that I may once more inhale the fragrance of the flowers as they exhale their sweets from their rich and variegated parterres, and view unimpeded the glorious progress of the rich orb of day, as in his chariot of gold he steers magnificently through the heavens.'

"I hastened to do as she desired, and she drew her chair closer to the window, and seemed to enjoy the balmy freshness of the air.

"'Oh, that is reviving,' she said; "thank thee—thank thee, my darling, I breathe more free again. There, there—that is enough—I am better—I feel refreshed now.'

"Notwithstanding the words of the old lady were very encouraging, the faintness of her voice, and the alteration in her accents, convinced me that she was very, very ill, and as her strength appeared to become more exhausted, and her cheeks to assume a paler hue, my fears increased, and rushing from her arms, in spite of what she had said, I violently pulled the bell, and then hastened to support the head of the poor old lady, which had now sunk against the back of the chair. Her eyes were closed—I just heard her sigh, but it was so low that it was scarcely audible, and I thought she was merely fainting through weakness. Never had I witnessed a scene like it before, and, therefore, my feelings, child as I was, may be better imagined by you, Lady Ravensford, than any force of language of mine could describe them. My limbs trembled, and again and again I placed my ears to her lips, to ascertain whether she was breathing, and then I tore myself from her, and once more pulled more violently at the bell than I had done before. While I was thus employed, my father and mother both entered the room, and rushing towards them, I sobbed forth in tones of the greatest emotion—

"'Oh, help! help!—my poor grandmamma will die! Save her—help her!'

"My father and mother hastened to the chair in which Mrs. Claremont was seated, and gently raising her, whispered a few words in her ear, while their countenances sufficiently evinced the power of their grief and the apprehensions under which they laboured. With the most intense anxiety did I watch them, and the now ghastly countenance of my aged relative, and for a moment my hopes revived when I beheld her open her eyes; her lips separated, and she endeavoured to give utterance to something, but her efforts were ineffectual. She was supported in my father's arms, while my mother stood with clasped hands, eagerly watching at the other side of her. Suddenly the head of the old lady sunk upon his bosom—one gentle sigh only escaped her lips, and her spirit had winged its flight to the realms of bliss.

CHAPTER XXXVI.

MRS. BELGRAVE'S NARRATIVE CONTINUED.

"I AM fearful," continued Mrs. Belgrave, after a pause to recover herself from the emotion which the dismal retrospection of the past had created in her bosom; "I am fearful, Lady Ravensford, that the melancholy circumstances I have to relate, will sound extremely prolix and uninteresting to you; but, alas! there are but few sunny spots in my history—few the moments of happiness I have to record. From an early period, my life may be said to have been as a dreary waste; a cheerless blank; upon which the rays of peace have but seldom dawned. But let me proceed.

"I need not describe to you the violence of the grief which this melancholy and unexpected calamity caused in our family. My father was for some time inconsolable, and argument and persuasion failed alike to assuage the vehemence of my anguish.

"Daily were my childish prayers offered up to Heaven for the repose of her soul, and to implore the protection of her spirit.

"But more bitter were the emotions my unfortunate father was doomed to suffer, than any which could be experienced by me and my mother. He had been most doatingly fond of his aged mother, and his mind was agonised by the most powerful feelings of self-reproach, when he reflected that his conduct had in all probability not only embittered her latter days, but prematurely ended her mortal career. Besides, he was deprived of her counsel and advice, at a time when the critical situation of his affairs, and the daily prospect of actual beggary before him, rendered him most in need of them; and when he reflected upon the dismal prospect before him, and the ruin he had brought upon himself and his amiable partner, his fortitude almost entirely forsook him.

"In those moments of trial, he was supported by the advice and consolation of that wife he had by his folly so irreparably injured. Hers were the gentle accents of hope that whispered in his ear, and breathed the balm of comfort upon his heart, when despair had almost entirely usurped it, and slowly he became more resigned to the will of Heaven, which erring mortals too frequently question and decry.

"But his mind was, unfortunately, soon more actively employed in the settlement of the difficulties by which he was encompassed on every side, and his thoughts were almost entirely occupied in the arrangement of his affairs, and prevented from gloomily meditating upon that which would otherwise have held such paramount sway over his mind.

"Weeks passed away, and still the poignancy of my grief was but little, if any, abated. No wonder that my feelings were so powerfully affected by the death of that aged and fond relative. It was the first severe blow they had ever experienced, and it came like the withering blast upon my young heart. Alas! little did I then think that to me it was but the prelude of so many, and such heavy misfortunes!—But, notwithstanding the violence of my sorrows, I took the most sedulous pains to control my feelings when I was in the presence of my parents. Well did I know that they had already enough to distract their minds, and I felt it to be my duty to appear composed and happy, that they might from that supposition, derive some portion of consolation. And most heavily did their misfortunes press upon them. The heartless wretch who had effected this wreck in the fortunes of my family, was inexorable. Like Shylock, he would have his full pound of flesh; and, at length, finding that all further endeavours at anything like an arrangement were hopeless, my father suffered the climax of his destiny to arrive, and in less than six months after the demise of my grandmother, we bade adieu to the noble home, the princely abode of our forefathers, for ever. The miscreant who had lured my father to vice, and afterwards triumphed over his duplicity, became its possessor, and the humble shelter of a small but convenient cottage, several miles away from the place, received us.

"Not far from the spot where we now resided, was the handsome house of Mr. Wilmington and his family, with whom my father had formerly been on the most intimate terms, and who was most willing and happy to renew that intimacy, more especially as misfortune had now alighted upon us. A more sincere friend than Mr. Wilmington could not be; never were more amiable beings in existence than his wife and two lovely daughters. What powerful reasons have I for remembering them with the fondest affection! What an ungrateful being should I be, could I ever efface from my recollection that virtuous family from whom I experienced so much kindness.

"Mrs. Wilmington loved me as fondly as if I had been her own child, and her two beauteous daughters behaved with as much affection towards me, as if I had been their sister.

"The wreck of my father's fortune was barely enough to support us with anything like independence; but the gentle soothings of my mother, and the ardent friendship of Mr. Wilmington, gradually reconciled him to it, and he was restored to comparative tranquillity. Alas! it was not fated to last long. A blow heavier even than any we had yet experienced, was about to descend upon our heads.

"My poor mother, although she had never murmured at the reverse of fortune, and had struggled to appear resigned in the presence of her husband, had mentally suffered most severely. The blow had fallen upon her heart, and preying secretly upon her vitals, hastened that calamity both myself and my father had cause to look upon as the heaviest which could possibly befal us. Her delicate constitution was unable to endure such a weight of constant care, and at length it became but too apparent to us, that she was gradually sinking, and that the silent tomb would shortly enclose her cold but sacred remains. But the close of her earthly sorrows was to be more speedily brought about than we had anticipated, by a melancholy and fatal circumstance.

"Among the list of the killed in some great battle that had taken place, my mother read the name of my uncle, and, although she struggled hard to conquer and conceal her feelings, it was very evident that the annihilating blow had been struck; that the barbed arrow had entered too deeply into her already severely lacerated heart; and that the fate of that man who had won her heart's first fond affections, was but the melancholy prelude to her own approaching dissolution. At that time, however, I was unable fully to understand or appreciate the feelings of my mother; for my parents and my grandmother had never made me acquainted that I had so dear a relation living, and, of course, I was, therefore, entirely ignorant of all the circumstances connected with him. I cannot question their prudence in keeping this a secret from me, but I afterwards became acquainted with every particular, as I have described it to you, my dear Lady Ravensford, and many were the hours of anguish which I passed in ruminating upon them.

" Daily did I watch the fragile form of my dying mother, as it became more and more attenuated, and the hue of her cheeks and lips more pale and livid, and remembering the death of my grandmother, I anticipated her speedy dissolution with feelings of agony I found it impossible to control. Oh, what could ever repair that dreadful loss which her death would occasion? Where could I look for one so kind, so affectionate, so gentle? Oh, no! nothing could ever supply her loss in my heart; nothing could ever have sufficient power to fill up that dismal vacuum her death would occasion. I could not bear to reflect upon it with any degree of fortitude and patience, in spite of the unremitting attentions and excellent advice of Mrs. Wilmington and her daughters; and my own anxiety to calm the violence of my agitation before my mother, lest it might serve to increase her own sufferings.

"But still more violent was the agony of my father, and it was very evident that he contemplated the approaching and inevitable demise of his wife, with a feeling bordering upon horror. And, oh, in the moments of her greatest suffering, when the anguish of her disorder was almost too excruciating for human endurance, how did she endeavour to impart consolation to his breast, and to persuade him to look with calmness and resignation upon that event there was no avoiding;

and urged him to firmness for the sake of that child, of whom he would then be left the only protector.

"My poor father endeavoured to obey her; but none except those who have experienced the heavy trial can form any idea of how arduous was that task. Death is awful at any time, and under any circumstances, but when it comes to one in whom is concentrated every gentle, amiable, and virtuous feeling, who is the only hope to which a fond partner has to cling, how much greater are its terrors! How doubly severe appears to be the visitation of Heaven! My father anticipated his heavy affliction, as the weary traveller views the coming tempest, without the least prospect of a shelter from its fury; and his manly fortitude shrunk appalled at the contemplation. Remorse and compunction increased his misery, for he could not but accuse himself of being the primary cause of hastening my mother's death; her sensibility having, he was certain, notwithstanding she upbraided him not, received a severe shock by the change in their circumstances, a change that his own mad folly and improvidence had entirely brought about.

"Let me pass over an event, which retrospection brings to my mind, with all the poignancy of former years, and which time has served to ameliorate, as quickly as possible. The dreary months of winter set in, and soon its chilling and fatal influence had its effect upon my poor mother's debilitated frame. Her death was as calm as an infant's slumber; so gentle was the emotion with which her spotless soul quitted its mortal tenement, that the last struggle was imperceptible, and I knew not that she was no more, until the deep and uncontrolable sobs of my father too fully convinced me of the awful event. I fixed but one intense look upon the pale face of that fond parent, whose lips I was never more to hear pronounce a blessing; I saw the heavenly smile upon her features, and immediately afterwards became insensible.

"I will not tire your patience, Lady Ravensford, by minutely detailing all the weeks and months of anguish which I suffered after the death of my dear mother. For some time I was entirely deaf to the voice of consolation, although reason told me that I was acting sinfully in thus repining at the decrees of an all-wise Providence, however severe they may appear to be, and my most melancholy pleasure was in visiting my mother's grave, and giving free indulgence to my grief while kneeling upon the daisy-speckled sod which covered it.

"My father had yielded to the solicitations of Mr. Wilmington, and, after the death of my mother, we abandoned the cottage to the care of an aged female servant, and took up our residence at the hospitable mansion, in which we had ever experienced the warmest friendship. But the rapid succession of calamity after calamity preyed upon the mind of my father; his pride had received a shock he could not surmount in the ruin of his fortunes, and although he tried, for my sake, to bear up against the effects of his misfortunes, it was very clear that his constitution was almost entirely destroyed, and that I should in a very short time be left an orphan, without a relation that I knew of in the world, and dependant upon the protection of those upon whom I had no other claim than that feeling of humanity and Christian charity, which should be common with us all towards each other. But at that time I did not know the extent of my misfortunes; I did not know that my unfortunate father, who had full control over the few hundreds which my grandmother had bequeathed to me, had been driven by stern necessity to make use of them in litigation, in which he was unsuccessful, and that the knowledge that I should be left in absolute beggary, added to the cankerworm which was preying upon his heart, was hastening his progress to the tomb. I knew not this, and my hapless parent shrunk from the task of making me acquainted with it, while Mr. Wilmington, in a spirit of mercy and benevolence which I can never cease to remember, also withheld the painful and overwhelming secret from me, and endeavoured to soothe the poignancy of my father's anguish

THE DEATH OF MRS. CLAREMONT.

and self-reproach, by assuring him that he would protect and provide for me the same as if I had been one of his own children. Greatly as my father appreciated the noble philanthropy of Mr. Wilmington, and confident that that excellent man would faithfully adhere to what he promised, his pride revolted with a feeling of the most insurmountable shame from the idea of leaving his only child in so dependant a state, when had it not been for his unfortunate folly and extravagance, she would have been left a wealthy heiress, with every prospect of happiness before her.

"Mr. Wilmington well knew and appreciated his sentiments, but he endeavoured to combat them by every means in his power. But only partially, indeed, was he successful, and the constitution of my father daily became more weakened, under the influence of corroding care.

"I saw plainly the heavy blow that was impending over me, and that but a short time could elapse before I should be left an orphan; and need I tell your ladyship what my sufferings were? I am certain I need not. All that consolation and advice could do, was tried by my kind friends to prepare my mind to meet the affliction with fortitude, but, young as I was, it would have been a matter of surprise had they entirely succeeded. Six months only after the death of my mother, my father breathed his last, and I was left without fortune or prospects upon the bounty of Mr. Wilmington. But fortunate was I to fall into the hands of such a friend, alas! that my evil destiny should have led me to abuse that friendship! But how weak is reason, prudence, and every worthy sentiment, too often, when opposed to the strength of our passions. One moment of irresolution, one moment of unhappy thoughtlessness, too often proves our ruin, and virtue and rectitude are made to succumb to that which they had previously shrunk from even the contemplating with horror! Let no weak mortal place too much confidence in its own strength of virtue, or mock at and too severely reproach the fall of its fellow creatures: in one unguarded moment, the noblest structure may be razed to the ground!

"Time, and the indefatigable exertions of the Wilmington family, ameliorated the violence of my grief, and the natural buoyancy of youth gradually prevailed over the power of those afflictions with which I had been visited at so early a period of my life. By the dint of great exertion, I regained my spirits, and a brilliant summer seemed likely to succeed the dreary winter of sorrow it had been my lot to experience.

"Flora and Selina Wilmington were two lovely girls, several years my seniors, and uniting all the graces that can enrich the human mind, to the elegances of person and manners. They had ever looked upon me as their little pet and adopted sister, and they needed no encouragement from their excellent parents to induce them to behave to me with unvaried kindness and affection. They were ever studious to devise every scheme which their amiable dispositions could suggest, for the promotion of my happiness, and they were never so joyous themselves as when they saw me cheerful; the hours not devoted to our studies were passed in rambling over the delightful grounds attached to Wilmington Abbey, and it was seldom that we strolled or had a wish beyond them.

"Mr. and Mrs. Wilmington saw but little company, and their greatest pleasure was in the enjoyment of the happiness of their own domestic circle. The abbey was indeed the abode of content and peace; the domestics lived in uninterrupted amity with each other, and revered those benevolent people in whose service it was their good fortune to be.

"Five years passed away with little or no change in my circumstances, with the exception of the marriage of both the Miss Wilmingtons, by which I was deprived of their constant society; but they were frequently visiting at the abbey, and I as often was their guest, so that I had little to regret, especially when I found that they were united to gentlemen who were every way worthy of them.

"I was now seventeen, and, if I am to believe all the flattering things that were said of me, although they had but little effect upon my vanity, I was not without many personal attractions; to speak lightly of my intrinsic recommendations, would be to pass a bad compliment to the virtuous attentions of one of the best of mothers, and the most virtuous of friends.

"My time was passed in one uninterrupted calm; I had no wish unindulged, no care, no anxiety to cause me the slightest pang.

"Days of innocence and bliss, would that I could recal ye, and erase from the dark page of my history, the errors that afterwards beset me! But alas! how vain is the wish, unless it be to strengthen regret and the anguish of remorse.

"I am now coming to the guilty part of my eventful life, and I must claim your ladyship's indulgence and clemency."

Our heroine sighed deeply, and pressed the hand of the narrator in silence.

Mrs. Belgrave paused for a short time, and then proceeded with her interesting recital.

"I was staying with Lady Flora, the eldest of the daughters of my guardians, who had married Lord Calverly, when they were visited by the son and daughter of Sir George Freeland, with whom the family of Lord Calverly had been on terms of intimacy for a number of years. That fatal visit! little did I then imagine that it would ultimately prove the forerunner to the destruction of my happiness!

"Herbert Fleeland was at the time I was so unfortunately introduced to him, not more than nineteen, and nature never formed a more elegant person or handsome countenance; manly, graceful, and dignified. To accomplishments of mind was added an amiableness and candour of manner that endeared him to every one, and made an immediate impression upon those whose minds were not entirely unsusceptible to the most prepossessing attractions of human nature. Would to Heaven that I had been less sensible to the power of those dangerous accomplishments that afterwards proved my ruin! Herbert Freeland, from the very first moment I beheld him, stamped his image upon my heart; my thoughts, my wishes, my self-will, all became enslaved, and truckled in helpless imbecility to the power of the passion with which he had inspired me!

"From that time I have become, as it were, another being; a sentiment held predominant sway over my bosom, which was entirely new to me; but coupling with it the image of Herbert, nature quickly assured me it was love! Fain would I have persuaded myself that I was the victim of some strange delusion, and endeavoured to banish Herbert Freeland from my thoughts, but the sentiment only gained strength by the attempt, and the being who had created it, held greater power over my mind than ever.

"Night and day this feeling constantly pursued me, and the more I formed the resolution to avoid the presence of Herbert as much as possible, the greater did my anxiety to be in his society increase. One moment I wished that his visit to Calverly Castle would be a brief one, and the next, I anticipated his departure, and the chance of my not beholding him again, with a trembling sensation of dread I found it impossible to conquer. I longed to impart my feelings to the ear of Lady Flora, and yet dreaded the idea of confiding to her bosom, from which I had hitherto had no secrets, the sentiments and thoughts that now harassed and tormented my mind.

"But, powerful as was the impression which Herbert Freeland had made upon me, to judge from the marked description of his behaviour towards me, I had excited an equal interest in his breast. Whenever his eyes met mine, they sparkled with more than their usual lustre, and his countenance became strongly flushed. He seemed to hang with profound attention and silent rapture upon every word which escaped my lips, and if he addressed me, his voice was tremulous, and there was an air of confusion in his manner which spoke more than a verbal acknowledgment could have had the power to do. What could this mean? Could it be love? The thought imparted a secret feeling of indescribable rapture to my bosom, and yet I felt as if I were culpable for indulging it.

"What an alteration had a few short days effected in my mind; and yet I scarcely knew whether I should rejoice at or regret the change! If the object that had inspired that passion were worthy of my love; if he reciprocated my sentiments, why should I fear to acknowledge to myself their power? But then in a moment another thought flashed across my brain, and overclouded all my hopes! Herbert Freeland was the heir to large wealth; the son of a baronet, and no doubt, possessing all the pride attendant upon rank and fortune! What was I? A poor portionless girl; a humble dependant upon the friendship and benevolence of those upon whom I had not the slightest claims by the ties of consanguinity! How then could I dare to raise my presumptuous thoughts towards one of fortune and station? My tears flowed fast at this thought, and never had I felt my dependant condition so severely as I did at that time! But no murmur of regret or reproach escaped my lips for the fault of my father, which had been the means of reducing me to that condition. It may be imagined that, with my mind thus occupied, it would have been an impossibility for me to maintain the same composure

of behaviour that I had hitherto done, although I exerted myself to the very utmost to do so; but, fortunately, Lady Flora did not appear to notice the change, and I was thus spared the pain of making any excuse, or to act the part of the hypocrite, from the bare idea of which I always shrunk with abhorrence.

"Herbert Freeland and his sister stayed a month at the castle, and the morning of their departure was one of the greatest anguish to me I had experienced for many a day. It was with extreme difficulty that I could sufficiently conquer my feelings so as to prevent myself from betraying the real character of my thoughts; and when Herbert, in a faint and tremulous voice, bade me adieu, and expressed a hope that he might have the pleasure of seeing me again, such deep blushes suffused my cheeks, and my form trembled so violently, that I wonder how my agitation could possibly escape the observation of Lady Flora. What answer I faultered out I know not, but I felt Herbert's hand press mine vehemently, and notwithstanding I retained my sensibility, I was conscious of nothing more than the rumbling noise of the wheels of the carriage which bore Herbert and his sister away, until I found myself in the drawing-room, and in the society of Lord and Lady Calverly.

"You may guess, Lady Ravensford, what I suffered in endeavouring to conceal my feelings from the observation of my friends; and how I succeeded so well as I did, has often been to me since a subject for astonishment. Lady Flora did, however, notice that I was not in such good spirits as usual, and asked if I were unwell. I was glad of the suggestion, and availed myself of it with avidity, complaining of a head-ache, and requesting to retire for a short time to my chamber. That request, of course, was complied with, and quitting the society of Lady Flora and her husband, I hastened to my own apartment, where, unrestrained, I gave indulgence to my feelings, which found vent in a copious flood of tears.

"'And shall I never behold him again?' I soliloquised; 'will not fate ordain that we shall ever see each other more? Oh, I dare not encourage such a thought, or despair would quite unnerve me! But why this powerful feeling? Whence these hopes and fears? Oh, Constance! thy fluttering heart too readily returns an answer. Herbert Freeland, why did we ever meet, since I fear it will be the forerunner of unhappiness to us both? To us both? Presumptuous, vain girl, to suppose that the poor dependant can ever create any interest in the bosom of the son of the proud and wealthy Sir George Freeland!'

"I checked myself, for something seemed to whisper to me, that I did Herbert an injustice. I remembered his every look, his every word, his every action, when we had been in each other's company; his agitation and confusion at our parting; the emotion with which he had pressed my hand, his tone and looks, when he bade me adieu, and I was more convinced than ever that I had made an impression on him, and the thought imparted to me a feeling that I had never before known. Little did I then imagine the contrary sentiment I should have entertained; little did I deem that it should have caused in me a feeling of regret and pain.

"'And will he ever think of me while absent?' I reflected; 'will he ever bestow one thought, one care upon the poor girl over whose affections she feels that he has gained so powerful an ascendancy, that neither time nor circumstance, she is convinced, can alter? There is presumption, perhaps sin, in the thought, and yet to discourage it, would be to make herself truly wretched. Better would it be, Constance, to die, than to know herself to be an object of indifference to Herbert Freeland.'

"Such was the nature and subject of my meditations, and although they occasioned me a mixture of pleasure and of pain, I could not bring my mind to think I was wrong in indulging them.

"Before, however, I rejoined Lord and Lady Calverly, I had so far gained the command over my feelings, as to be able to conceal my emotions from their observations; and what little agitation I evinced, they naturally attributed to the effect of the indisposition I had complained of.

"From that time, Herbert Freeland was never absent from my thoughts, and whenever I heard his name mentioned, my heart would palpitate so violently against my side, that I could scarcely contain myself, and my cheeks would become so suffused with blushes, that it is surprising to me that the suspicions of Lady Flora or her husband were never excited.

"A fortnight after the departure of Herbert Freeland and his sister, I left Calverly Castle, and returned to Wilmington Abbey; but a very different being to what I was previous to my leaving it. I was restless and unhappy, and those pleasures I had before there enjoyed, had now lost their power to charm me.

"What a revolution does love cause in the human mind! That which before possessed every fascination in my eyes, now appeared dull and insipid to me. The gardens seemed to be divested of all their beauty; the flowers to have lost their fragrance; the fountains, as they still played as fantastically as they had used to do, to my imagination now murmured forth melancholy sounds and tones of despair. My usual walks were lonely and cheerless; the birds' soft notes no more sounded sweet and mellifluous to my ears. In short, every former enjoyment now to me bore a new character, and had lost their power to please. Still, so new and strange was the passion to me, that I could scarcely persuade myself that I really loved.

"My kind friends could not but notice the alteration in my conduct, for I who was formerly all life and volatility, mirth and vivacity, was now serious, often decidedly melancholy, reserved and taciturn. This change of course caused them much uneasiness, while to me it was only a source of the deepest regret and perplexity. In vain they inquired whether I was unwell, if anything had occurred to wound my mind, and if I had any reason to complain of their conduct towards me? I sedulously evaded their questions, and they never could elicit from me an unequivocal answer.

"But when alone most severely did I reproach myself for my conduct towards those who had behaved to me with such unexampled friendship, such more than parental affection; and there were times when I half determined to unburthen my thoughts to them, and no longer keep from them a secret upon which I so much needed their counsel and advice, and which if I were left to the direction of my own impetuous passions, might ultimately be the means of bringing me to so much misery and disgrace. But still I shrunk from the task with a timidity which I vainly endeavoured to conquer, and kept the secret of my unfortunate love confined entirely to my own bosom.

"Oh, how often have I since had reason to curse the mad infatuation which guided my conduct. Would that I had availed myself of the excellent advice of these amiable people, then should I not have had reason to look back upon my past conduct with shame and remorse. But it is too late to repent now.

"I exerted myself to the very utmost to appear composed and possessed of a portion of my former spirits, and I so far succeeded, as to deceive Mr. and Mrs. Wilmington, and they expressed the pleasure they felt at the rapid progress which I was making towards recovering my former gaiety and happiness; and were studious to increase my tranquillity by every means in their power, and attributed my recent depression of spirits to indisposition.

"'You were never in London, my love, I believe?' said Mrs. Wilmington.

"I answered in the negative, and added—

"'And although I have heard much of its gaieties, and sights, and wonders, I have also heard so much of its follies, allurements, and vices, that I must confess I feel very little inclination to visit it.'

"'True, my dear Constance,' observed Mr.

Wilmington, 'London is a dangerous place for the wild, the young, the giddy, the thoughtless, and the unprotected; but to those who are armed against its temptations, and protected from the destructive vortex in which many fall, it possesses pleasures that few know truly how to enjoy, and of which the inexperienced cannot form the most remote conception. Few persons are more attached to a country life of rural simplicity than I am; but, after all, London for a change, with its ever-changing variety of scene and character.'

"'Your picture of the gay metropolis, as I have heard it usually designated, my dear sir,' I observed, 'has, I declare, given me quite a different opinion of it, and I should really like to see it for once, if it were only to test the merits of the pleasures of which you have just spoken.'

"'I have no doubt but that you will have an opportunity of doing so 'ere long, my dear Constance,' said Mrs. Wilmington; 'Sir George Freeland has a very elegant mansion in town, and he has often invited us to visit him there, so that 'with the consent of Mr. Wilmington, we will avail ourselves of the opportunity in the summer.'

"I know I must have changed colour several times at the mention of the name of Sir George Freeland, the father of that young gentleman who had made so powerful an impression upon my heart, and I was unable to make any remark, notwithstanding I felt a degree of ecstasy at the bare idea of the probability of my thus having a chance of meeting Herbert again, which I am confident I have no occasion to describe to you, my lady. Neither Mr. or Mrs. Wilmington, however, noticed my emotion, and the former having expressed his readiness to comply with the request of his wife, the conversation upon that topic was dropped, and I retired from the room.

"How I now longed for the time to arrive when our projected visit to the gay metropolis should take place; and I was so elated with the prospect it afforded me of once more beholding Herbert Freeland, that my countenance became clad in its former smiles, and my heart felt lighter than it had done since the departure of Herbert from Calverly Castle.

"Several weeks passed away without anything taking place worthy of being mentioned, and with little or no change in my circumstances or conduct; but an event was about to take place, which was fated to set my doubts at rest, and to effect another and powerful change in my mind.

"I had been to the neighbouring village, as was my custom two or three times a week, and was returning to the abbey, when just as I got within sight of it, I saw a man walking backwards and forwards beneath the garden-wall, as if he were watching for some person. He was dressed in livery, and it struck me that I had seen the livery before, and when I approached him nearer, you may imagine my surprise and agitation, when I discovered that it was that of the Freeland family.

"My heart palpitated violently, and my emotion was, in other respects, so great, that I had the greatest difficulty imaginable to prevent myself from sinking to the earth. A variety of thoughts in a moment darted through my mind. Surely Sir George or his son could not be at the abbey?—No, if that had been his intention, he would certainly have made Mr. Wilmington acquainted with it beforehand, and the hope that I had thus hastily suffered to enter my mind, was in a moment destroyed.

"I conquered my agitation as well as I possibly could, and walked on towards Wilmington Abbey. The man, who had been looking in a contrary direction, now observed me, and he no sooner did so, than he hurried towards me with an air of much satisfaction, and when he had 'come up to me, he made his obeisance in the most respectful manner, and without speaking, took a letter from his pocket, which he placed hastily in my hand, and not waiting an instant, he flew from the spot, and was quickly out of sight.

"I stood transfixed to the spot with astonishment and agitation, like a statue, and holding the letter almost unconsciously in my hand, gazed after the retreating servant in mute amazement. The event was so singular, so sudden and unexpected, that it appeared more like a dream than anything else; but at length, partially recovering myself, I fixed my eyes upon the superscription of the letter with eager curiosity, and my heart throbbed more violently than before.

"It was in the handwriting of Herbert Freeland, which I had seen before, and was addressed to 'Miss Claremont.'

"My hand shook as I held the letter, and I hesitated, although at the same time my bosom was filled with the most anxious curiosity. What could be his motives for writing to me in so clandestine a manner, and would it be right or prudent for me to peruse a letter sent to me under such circumstances? For a moment or two I was undecided how to act, but, at length, I hastily placed the letter in my bosom, and entering the abbey, made my way directly to my own apartment, where I threw myself into a chair, and for a short time gave way to a variety of conflicting and perplexing thoughts.

"I took the letter from my bosom, and continued for awhile to gaze at the superscription, without having the courage to break the seal. Prudence told me that I should not read it, and yet a secret and irresistible impulse urged me to do so, and at last, with a trembling hand, and a palpitating heart, I broke the seal, unfolded the letter, and fixed my eyes upon the contents. A mist seemed to float before me, and, for a short time, I could not distinguish a syllable. With much exertion, however, I at last gained more firmness and resolution, and commenced reading it. The first words upon which my eyes fell, filled my bosom with mingled feelings of astonishment, hope, and delight. In language tender, eloquent, and graceful, Herbert Freeland acknowledged an ardent passion for me; declared that he had not had a moment's peace of mind since he had first beheld me, and that his only hopes of future happiness depended upon my returning his love, which he vowed, nor time, nor circumstance could ever change: He begged me to forgive him for having adopted such a plan for making known his sentiments to me, declaring that he had not the courage to do so personally while at Calverly Casle, but that he could no longer keep the secret in his breast, and live; and declared, in language the most forcible, that unless I returned his love, there was nothing in the world which could longer attach him to life. He dared to hope, from what he had observed in my behaviour while in was at the castle, that I was not entirely insensible to a reciprocal sentiment; and entreated me to answer his letter, which Richard, his servant, would call for, at a place mentioned, the day after I had received his letter;—or, by remaining silent, to leave him to despair and misery.

"How shall I endeavour to pourtray my feelings on perusing this epistle?—Oh, who but those who have experienced it, can imagine the rapture of that moment which assures you you are beloved by that dear object upon whom you have fixed your warmest affections?—It is a moment of bliss, such as no after pleasure can equal!—It is a foretaste of the bliss of Heaven!

" I could scarcely believe the evidence of my senses: the happiness seemed too great to be real. An irresistible charm fixed my eyes to the glowing sentences written by Herbert: again and again did I peruse the contents of the letter, and hung with transport upon every word. It was no dream—it was no illusion! —Herbert, dear Herbert Freeland confessed that he loved me; that in me, all his hopes of happiness, his every wish, was centred, and every word was stamped with sincerity! —Involuntarily, I pressed the *billet doux* to my lips, and tears of transport coursed each other down my cheeks. Fatal passion!—Airy-formed hopes!—Little did I imagine the misery, the shame, the many hours of self-reproach, the encouragement of them was fated to cause me!

" But how should I act?—How proceed?—

Could I act the hypocrite by denying the passion with which he had inspired me?—refuse to answer his eloquent appeal to my heart, and leave him to the misery and despair he had described? I could not bear to think of such a course; as soon could I have laid violent hands upon myself. And yet, to assent to his wishes, and carry on a clandestine correspondence, was equally repugnant to my feelings, and contrary to my ideas of right and wrong. Was it not highly culpable, I reflected, for me any longer not to make my kind guardians acquainted with the secret of my love, and the sentiments of Herbert towards me, so that I might receive their counsel and advice? I felt convinced that it was. I had never yet withheld a thought from their knowledge, and yet, I now feared to reveal that upon which, in all probability, my future happiness or misery depended. Would that I had had the moral courage to have confided my feelings to the affectionate and sympathising bosom of Lady Flora, what bitter suffering would it afterwards have saved me!

" One moment I was half decided to write to Lady Calverly, and unburthen to her the whole of my mind, and the passion which Herbert had confessed for me; but the resolution was quickly destroyed; some fatal inscrutable power withheld me from doing that which prudence, propriety, and virtue dictated, and I was hurried on by the power of my passions to the extreme verge of that fearful precipice, down which I was finally destined to plunge into the dark gulph of shame and sorrow.

" I excused myself upon the plea of indisposition from the society of Mr. Wilmington, and passed the greater part of that memorable day in my own chamber, locking the door, to prevent the possibility of my being intruded upon, or interrupted.

" It was several hours before, after the most earnest reflection; I could come to any decision of the manner in which I should act; but love at last prevailed over all my other feelings, and I determined to answer the letter of Herbert—to reply to it as my heart prompted, and without any concealment of my sentiments. In a state of the utmost emotion I set about my arduous task, and arduous, indeed, did it prove to me. Sheet after sheet of paper did I fill, and each was as quickly destroyed as filled, ere I could write a reply to please me. One was too cold and formal, another too feeble and pointless. One was too free, another too affectedly prudish!—' Never,' I reflected, ' shall I be able to write with the eloquence and grace displayed in his letter.'

"And what could I write? And even doing so, should I not be guilty of a most unpardonable indiscretion? Never, in the whole course of my eventful life did I pass an afternoon of such pain, anxiety, doubt, and irresolution as on that occasion. Would that I had had the fortitude to have abandoned my determination! But it was not to be!—I was doomed to become the slave of my own passions, and nothing could rescue me from the chains in which they held me.

"At length, however, I did complete a letter which afforded me something like satisfaction, and I determined that there my task should end; I would be content to deem it accomplished.

"What I wrote in that fatal letter, I cannot now remember, and scarcely knew at the time. I perused it, notwithstanding, many times before I ventured to fold and seal it, and having done so, I knelt down, and implored the Almighty to guide me, and to prevent me from acting in any way which might afterwards cause me to repent. Alas! my prayers were not heard; I had already sinned, and fearful was the punishment which was allotted to me.

"And yet, after awhile, I felt my mind relieved from a heavy weight, after I had thus unburthened my thoughts to the object who created my love; and by the evening I had so far regained my composure, that I was enabled to join Mr. and Mrs. Wilmington at dinner.

"What sleep I had that night was disturbed by troublesome dreams, and I was glad when the morning arrived.

"After breakfast was over, going for my customary walk, I had an opportunity of putting my intentions into execution, and with trembling and hesitating footsteps, I made my way to the place at which Richard was to be waiting to receive the answer to his master's letter.

"Often did I look behind me, to see whether I was watched, and I felt as if I were a criminal who had committed some great offence, and was fearful of the pursuit of justice. Several times I paused also, and was half inclined to turn back, and abandon my resolution, but my evil genius always prevailed, and I hurried on.

"The place of appointment was in a little dell, beyond the village, and at some distance from Wilmington Abbey, but when I reached there, Richard had not arrived. I felt uneasy and impatient at his delay, and fearful lest my wandering about there might excite the surprise of some passenger who might know me; and I was walking away from the spot, thinking to return to it again in a short time, when I saw the servant of my lover approaching.

"Seeing me, he increased his speed, and on coming up to me, he apologised for being behind his time, having been, he said, detained by unforeseen business.

"I blushed and trembled in this man's presence, for I had no doubt he was the confidant of his master, and I could not help thinking that he must entertain no very great opinion of me for my conduct.

"I, however, hastily placed in his hands the letter, and without uttering a word, I was about to hurry from the spot, when Richard, respectfully touching his hat, said—

"'My young master ordered me to inform you, Miss, that in about a fortnight business will call him to this neighbourhood, when he will visit Wilmington Abbey.'

"A sensation of joy, which I need not describe, shot through my frame at this intelligence, and I am certain that my blushes, and the pleasure which was evinced in my face, must have made the man thoroughly aware of my feelings, if he had not guessed the same before. However, I made him no reply, and anxious to reach the Abbey, where I could in the privacy of my own chamber give free indulgence to my thoughts, and the effect which they were sure to have upon me, I left the spot, and hurried on as well as my agitation would permit me.

"Well, one difficult struggle was over; Herbert by that time was aware of the sentiments with which he had inspired me;—candidly, undisguisedly I had confessed them to him, and I felt more easy than I had done before. And why should I regret the love which raged within my bosom?—Was not Herbert every way worthy of my heart's warmest passions?—Was he not noble, virtuous, and good?—Had he not avowed a reciprocal attachment, and could I doubt his sincerity?—Oh, virtue itself must be base if Herbert could deceive!—His looks, his actions, and every sentence he had written in his letter to me were stamped with truth, and I must be ungenerous indeed could I doubt him.

"These reflections had their full effect upon me; but at the same time the thought would present itself to me, that, consequently, I should not hesitate or be ashamed to acknowledge to my friends the state of my mind, and consult them upon a subject so important to my future happiness. I felt that I was wrong, extremely wrong in neglecting so to do; but yet I could not make up my mind to act differently. What mad infatuation could have urged me to behave in that imprudent and fatal manner, I have often since been at a loss to conceive, and bitterly have I had cause to reflect on it since.

"But what feelings of delight had the few words that Richard had uttered, and which had informed me of the intention of Herbert Freeland so shortly to visit Wilmington Abbey, imparted to me! I could scarcely contain my joy, and yet, with a natural feeling of modesty, I trembled to meet him, and longed, yet dreaded, to hear the avowal from his lips which he had communicated in his letter to me. But would he keep his sentiments a secret from his father, or would his father, knowing my portionless state, sanction his love? Surely his pride and ambition would lead him to disapprove of it, and here again had I fresh cause for anguish. Hopeless as the idea of Sir George Freeland's approving of the passion of his only son and heir for a poor moneyless girl appeared to be, ought I to have given any encouragement to Herbert's vows? Ought I not, rather than have confessed myself the slave of that love he had created, to have endeavoured to stifle it in its infancy, and have taken the precaution to have avoided not only his presence for the future, but also holding any conversation with him?

"These questions appeared so reasonable, that I could not deny their power; still, love would assert its pre-eminence, and I had no power to act as reason and propriety suggested.

"All these ideas were completely over powered by one thought—'I shall see Herbert again;' and I looked forward to the event with as much impatience as if my life depended upon the certainty of its taking place.

"Then I reflected upon the probable effect which my answer to his letter was likely to have upon him; I pictured to myself the eager haste with which he would pursue it; the expression of joy which would animate his handsome countenance; the feelings of rapture that would float around his heart, and then I feared that I had not said half enough to satisfy him of the strength and sincerity of the mutual sentiments which he had created in my bosom.

"After having conquered the power of my emotions, I felt happier, during the time that intervened before the expected visit of Herbert Freeland to Wilmington Abbey, than I had done for a long time before; and as the day approached when, from a letter which Mr. and Mrs. Wilmington had received from him, I had become acquainted he would be at the abbey, I became more confident and tranquil, and felt myself fully prepared to meet him. Surely there could be no diffidence in acknowledging a sincere passion to the being who had inspired it; who was noble, virtuous, and generous, and who avowed a most ardent return. 'No,' I ruminated, 'I will not do Herbert the injustice to believe him capable of depreciating me for doing so, or suppose that he will take any advantage of the power which he will find he has gained over me.'

"These thoughts completely re-assured me, and I began to hope that the visit of Herbert to the abbey would be the prelude to the perfect establishment of my happiness; he would take upon himself the task of making known to my friends and protectors the sentiments that subsisted between us, and thus should I be saved the trouble of doing that from which I shrunk with the most strange, powerful and unaccountable repugnance.

"I was frequently thrown into a state of considerable confusion and difficulty by the observations made in my presence by Mr. and Mrs. Wilmington, after they had received the letter from Herbert Freeland, announcing to them the honour he intended to do himself by visiting them. They passed the highest encomiums upon his character, and two or three times asked my opinion of him, a question which I evaded as well as I could, lest by the warmth of my reply I should betray the nature of those feelings which I wished to conceal from them for the present.

"At length the long-expected day arrived, and, punctual to the time, Herbert Freeland came to Wilmington Abbey.

"How I met him I cannot say, but I felt as if I should sink to the earth, and my heart throbbed more violently than ever I had felt it to do before. Herbert, however, met me with an air of the most studied politeness, and it has often surprised me to think how he could so well command his feelings. Alas! I ought not to feel surprised at anything he could do, after his base conduct to me!

"There was, nevertheless, sufficient in the pressure of his hand to assure me of the actual state of his mind, and when his brilliant and intelligent eyes met mine, there was an expression in them which went immediately to my heart, and inspired me with courage and admiration.

"In my opinion, he looked handsomer than ever, and there was something in his manners altogether which seemed to say that Heaven had formed him for me. Foolish, weak girl!—too soon wert thou doomed to be awakened from that flattering dream!

"That day passed happily away, and in the society of him I so ardently loved, I felt as if I were another being. Herbert had an excellent flow of wit and general conversation, and his manners were so pleasing, that they could not fail to ingratiate him into the favour of young and old. With what rapture did I listen to every word which fell from his lips, and with what pleasure and satisfaction did I notice the looks of admiration which Mr. and Mrs. Wilmington fixed upon him.

"I could easily perceive that Herbert was most anxious of getting an opportunity of being alone with me, and I was no less eager for the interview, although I heartily wished it were over. But the day passed over without any chance presenting itself, and we separated for the night.

"At night I slept but little, for my thoughts were too busily occupied. I treasured in my memory every word which Herbert had spoken, and hung over them in meditation with feelings of the most supreme delight. To me Herbert appeared a being far superior to all the rest of mankind, or, at least, he greatly surpassed the notions I had hitherto formed of them ; and to possess the affections of such a man was, I considered, far greater than what my humble merits deserved. But let me not become tedious.

"The next day arrived—the day which I may reckon to have sealed my fate. Herbert expressed a wish, when he saw that Mr. and Mrs. Wilmington were engaged, to take a stroll in the gardens, and requested that he might be permitted the honour of Miss Clare-mont's company, to point out to him the different beauties that might otherwise escape his observation. Mr. Wilmington smiled, and having asked if I were agreeable, and received a timid answer in the affirmative, Herbert politely took my arm, and we walked together from the abbey.

"I will pass over what followed at that interview, for I know, my dear Lady Ravensford, that you can very well imagine it. A few minutes only and Herbert Freeland enfolded me to his heart, his acknowledged lover.

"When we had become more calm, I ventured to inquire of Herbert whether he entertained any hopes of gaining the consent of his father to our passion. He professed the utmost confidence in his approbation, but

THE APPREHENSION OF MRS. BELGRAVE FOR THE THEFT.

suggested the propriety of his keeping his sentiments a secret from him during his minority, and he likewise objected to making Mr. and Mrs. Wilmington acquainted with our love for the present.

"I must confess that his objections appeared to me at the time extremely weak and singular; but he combated my opinions too successfully, and I depended entirely upon his honour, and agreed, most willingly at last agreed to be guided alone by his advice. Fatal compliance—unfortunate confidence! But how could I imagine that he would ever be the villain to take advantage of them?

"From that time we had no thoughts apart from each other, and we agreed to keep up a constant correspondence with one another, when circumstances would not permit us to meet. Herbert determined to prolong his stay at the abbey as much as he could, and I looked upon the time when he would be compelled to depart with a feeling of grief which I need not seek to describe. Happy would it have been for me had we then separated never to meet again! But fate had ordained that it should be otherwise. I had commenced the path which was destined to lead me to ruin, and quickly did I traverse it to its fullest extent.

CHAPTER XXXVII.

MRS. BELGRAVE'S NARRATIVE CONCLUDED.

"How readily does villany too frequently find the means of accomplishing its nefarious designs; and fatally have I experienced this truth.

"I will not shock your ears, dear Lady Ravensford, by detailing minutely all the different well-laid schemes which Herbert Freeland had concocted to triumph over that unfortunate girl he had marked for his victim. It would rack my brain to madness to dwell upon them.

"Herbert only remained a fortnight at Wilmington Abbey, and nothing could be more affecting than our parting. Again and again he repeated his vows of love and constancy, and received my warmest and most sincere asseverations in return. He promised that nothing but death should prevent him from shortly meeting me again, and, in the meantime, promised constantly to correspond with me, we having fixed upon places to which we should direct each other's letters, in order to prevent suspicion or discovery.

"His anxiety for secrecy ought to have opened my eyes; but alas! I was blinded by the power of my love; I could not believe that anything which Herbert might do or purpose could be wrong, and dearly did I have to pay for my credulity.

"We parted, and after he was gone, I felt a vacuum in my heart which nothing could fill.

"Day after day elapsed, and week succeeded week, and every letter which I received from Herbert teemed with additional and more ardent vows of affection; but there was a tone of melancholy in them which deeply afflicted me. He animadverted on the length of time which must elapse ere we could hope to be united, and said that he had partly hinted to his father about his love, but the manner in which he had received it, left him but little room to hope that he would ever give his consent to our union. He also said that he was most anxious for the expiration of his minority, for then he would be master of his own actions, but he regretted the length of time. He declared that the delay was distraction to him, and he was afraid would ultimately affect his constitution, and at last he ventured to hint at a private marriage.

"From that idea I at first revolted with the greatest repugnance, but when I weighed in my mind all the arguments that Herbert had made use of in support of it, I found my resolution gradually yielding, and at length I could read the proposition not only calmly and patiently, but with a feeling of pleasure, which I neither could nor wished to banish. Yet my heart revolted at the thoughts of becoming the bride of Sir George Freeland's son and heir without the consent of the former, with a feeling of becoming pride; still was I ready to make any sacrifice of my feelings rather than I could endure the thoughts of losing that man, without whom life was of no value to me. He had said that he should be distracted if I did not consent; and could I bear to know him miserable? Could I live and know that Herbert, dear Herbert Freeland was unhappy? No, no; even though my destruction were the consequences I could not think upon that with any degree of patience.

"With feelings such as these inhabiting my breast, need it cause you any particular astonishment, Lady Ravensford, that Herbert found me so easy a victim to the snares which he had laid for my ruin? My letters to him quickly made him acquainted with the power he had gained over me, and too soon did he take advantage of it.

"Two months elapsed, when one afternoon while walking out, I met Richard, who placed a letter in my hand and immediately departed. It was from Herbert: he was in the neighbourhood of the abbey, but not wishing Mr. and Mrs. Wilmington to be made acquainted with it, as he had come there unknown to any one but his confidential servant, he had taken temporary lodgings in the vicinity, and requested me to meet him in the evening, as he had something particular to impart to me.

"I was so delighted at the thoughts of so quickly seeing my lover again, that I thought not of the singularity and impropriety of his conduct, neither did I shrink from the idea, as I ought to have done, of a secret assignation. I determined to comply with his wishes, and returned to the abbey, filled with hopes and expectations.

"At the hour which Herbert appointed to meet me, I secretly left the abbey, unseen by any person, and made my way to the dell. Herbert was already there and anxiously awaiting my arrival. We rushed rapturously into each other's arms, and for a few moments were unable to give utterance to a word, such was the power of our emotions.

"I cannot recount all that was said at that fatal meeting, all the arguments the crafty seducer made use of to win me to his purpose. He triumphed!—I returned no more to Wilmington Abbey; the same evening beheld me seated in a post-chaise, which was rapidly rolling on its way to a distant part of the country, where Herbert, who was seated by my side, had taken a commodious cottage for the present. I had consented to become his bride by a secret marriage.

"Let me hurriedly pass over my career of guilt, for by no milder term can I call it. Herbert imposed upon my credulity by a fictitious marriage, and I fell a victim to his villany. He was compelled to leave me in two or three days after my supposed union, and he did so with many tears of apparent regret. But he promised soon to return to me. He was absent from me only a month, when his father being from town, he said he should be able to remain with me for some time. And he did so, and blissfully passed away that period; great was then my happiness, but which I little expected was so soon to be succeeded by misery, shame, and despair. Herbert was all that my fondest hopes could wish him in his behaviour to me, and he seemed absolutely to adore me.

"But if I were to say that there were not moments when feelings of anguish would steal over me. I should be telling that which is not true; Mr. and Mrs. Wilmington and their two amiable daughters, would often dart upon my memory, accompanied by the most painful idea. What could they think of my conduct? Would they not deem me base, guilty, and ungrateful? Alas! what other conclusion could they come to? Would to Heaven that I could make them acquainted with my situation; but that wish Herbert most strenuously opposed, and was at no loss for arguments to persuade me that he was advising me for the best; that ere long a revelation could be made to all our friends, and everything satisfactorily arranged, and that we should all of us again be united. What could I say?—what could I do? He possessed supreme power over me, and in his fond endearments I became satisfied and content.

"And now I found myself in a situation which rendered my affection for my supposed husband doubly strong; and his love for me appeared to increse daily. The villain! at that very time he was contemplating the most cruel blow that a seducer could inflict upon his victim.

"He had been with me about a month, stolen from his father's society, when he, with many protestations of regret, told me that he should be compelled to leave me again for awhile, and, as it was uncertain what time he should be able to see me again, though I might rest assured he would seize upon the earliest opportunity, he left with me a hundred pounds, which I might want for my present use. We parted with more than our usual affection even, and I felt a weight at my heart and a dismal foreboding which I had never experienced before, and vainly endeavoured to conquer.

"That parting was our last!—I never beheld my seducer again!—A few days afterwards I received a cold, formal letter from him, which at once showed the misery of my situation, and disclosed the villanous part he had acted towards me. He informed me that we must never meet more! He begged me to forgive him for the manner in which he had been induced to deceive me by a fictitious marriage, and to which he was urged by the power of his passion; but that, as he could never hope to gain the consent of his father to our union, he had thought it was best to separate at once, although it was not without a great sacrifice to his feelings that he had been able to make up his mind to such a determination. He bade me many fond adieus, and concluded by hoping that I might meet with some man more worthy of me than himself, and who would make me happy. In a postscript he also informed me that by the time his letter reached me, he should, with his family, be on the way to the continent, where they intended in future to reside, and that it was not likely he should return to England for several years, if ever he did again, and by which time he trusted that I should have lost all remembrance of our unhappy connection!

"Judge the state of my mind, my dear Lady Ravensford, on the receipt of this cruel letter, for I cannot depicture it! An alarming illness was the consequence, which brought on premature labour. I was delivered of a girl. Better had it been for me had we both died!

"Many weeks elapsed ere I was able to leave my bed, and shortly afterwards, behold me in the coach on my way to London. Why I was going thither I scarcely knew; but any place was preferable to that in which I had resided with the betrayer of my innocence, and from the idea of seeking the presence of my former friends and protectors, I revolted with a feeling of horror! They could never forgive me, I thought; and I would not shock them by my presence!

"I arrived in London, and took up my abode in a humble lodging, where I hoped, by taking in needle-work, to be able to support myself and my child; for I had but little money now by me, and that, let me be ever so frugal, I reflected, must soon be exhausted.

"I will not dwell upon the many bitter hours of remorse and suffering I underwent; it was no more than I deserved, I felt, and I bore it all with patience. I soon learned that Herbert had spoken the truth; the family of Sir George Freeland had left town for the continent, and the mansion was sold to another family.

"At length my money was all spent, and I was unable to procure anything to do. And now the utmost misery, nay, even starvation for myself and child stared me in the face. The final blow came at last. I had not a farthing in the world!—I had no food for my child, and the landlady had told me that unless I could procure her some money, she could not permit me to lodge with her any longer! What was I to do?—I knew not!—I had no means of getting a penny! In this wretched state of mind, I pressed my poor child, who was very ill, to my heart, one cold winter's morning, and rushed into the street, totally regardless of he way I went, and unconscious of what I was going to do. To return to that house without money, however, I was determined I would not, and the plaintive cries of my infant, wound me up to a pitch of desperation!

"Long I wandered I knew not whither, and the wildness of my looks and demeanour, frequently arrested the attention and curiosity of the passengers.

"At length, feeling tired, I paused, and looked around me. I was standing close to a silversmith's shop, and the costliness of the different articles so profusely displayed in the shop-window, attracted my attention.

"I thought of my own wretched situation, and my starving child, and at that moment a fearful thought darted across my mind.

"While I thus stood, I beheld a gentleman standing before the counter, and apparently bargaining for a watch!—He took out his purse, it seemed heavy; he placed it carelessly by his, at that end of the counter which was nearest the door, and taking up the watch to examine it, turned his back towards the purse. The demon tempted me, and acting upon the impulse of the moment, I rushed with the speed of lightning into the shop, snatched up the purse, and thrusting it into my bosom, fled, but not before I was observed by the gentleman and the master of the shop, who pursued me with the cry of 'stop thief!' Terror and desperation lent redoubled speed to my feet, and I was enabled, as I thought, to outstrip them, and elude them altogether.

"I reached the house where I lodged in the most breathless trepidation, and rushing up stairs threw myself upon my humble bed, completely overpowered.

"Not long was I suffered thus to remain. There was a loud knocking at the street-door, and immediately afterwards, I heard persons ascending the stairs!—I cannot describe the horror of that moment!—I started from the bed, clasped my child frantically to my breast, and sunk upon my knees, the perfect image of despair! The room-door was pushed violently open, and my landlady, with the gentleman from whom I had stolen the purse, entered! I uttered a loud scream, and sunk senseless on the floor.

"When I recovered, I found the gentleman, who was a handsome-looking, middle-aged man, dressed in a military uniform, supporting me in his arms, and bathing my temples, while my landlady was endeavouring to pacify my poor child! She had told him as much as she knew of my melancholy history, and he pitied me!

"I clasped my hands together, and implored his mercy for the sake of my child. He begged that I would compose myself, and he would not harm me, and with this assurance,

and convinced by his benevolent looks that he was not deceiving me, I did indeed become more calm, and some gentle restorative having been administered to me, I revived and was able to talk more freely.

"There was something in the countenance of the stranger which went immediately to my heart, and his placid and benevolent features assured me that in him, in spite of the crime which misery and destitution, and the starving cries of my child, had urged me to commit, I should find a friend.

"'Oh, sir,' I cried, 'spare the poor miserable wretch, whom hunger alone goaded to the guilty deed I have committed. For my poor babe alone I ask; for myself, I care not, even though death be the punishment of my crime. Death hath no terrors to the unhappy Constance!'

"'My poor woman,' returned the gentleman, kindly, 'pray compose yourself; your landlady has giving me an appalling description of your distress, and not for mines of wealth would I harm you. But, (and believe me I ask it only from motives of pity and philanthropy,) if you will make me acquainted with the particulars of your melancholy story, you may find in me a friend whom——'

"I looked at the stranger for a minute with a searching glance; but his composed demeanour and florid features completely disarmed my suspicions, and inspired me with confidence; something urged me to comply with his request without hesitation, and I could not resist the impulse. He motioned Mrs. Simpson, my landlady, to retire, and then, with many interruptions, tears, and blushes of shame, I detailed to him as briefly as possible, my melancholy story.'

"He listened to me with the deepest attention, and I could frequently observe the tear of sympathy trembling on his manly cheek.

"When I had concluded, he paused for a few moments, and traversed the room, wrapt in thought: then suddenly turning to me, he hastily ejaculated—

"'But your name, poor injured one?'

"'Is Constance Claremont, sir,' I replied, with a deep sigh.

"He started, and the paleness of death was immediately on his countenance; he fixed his eyes intently upon me, and with quivering lips he exclaimed—

"'Repeat that name again. Let me be certain my ears do not deceive me.'

"'Constance Claremont,' I repeated in firm accents.

"'Claremont!' he cried, and his whole frame was convulsed with emotion; 'but the names of your parents?'

"'Were Valentine and Adeline Claremont,' I added.

" ' Gracious powers !' he cried, rushing quickly towards me, and enfolding me in his embraces; ' it is her—my poor niece—the child of my sainted Adeline !'

" Yes, it was indeed my uncle, whom report had reckoned among the slain on the battle-field ; he had returned with honour and fortune to his native land ; to encounter his unfortunate and only surviving relative in so remarkable and disgrace a manner !

" I have little more to add, ere I close my dismal narrative. My uncle deeply commis-erated my unfortunate fate, and execrated the villain who had betrayed me. He saw me safe beneath a comfortable house he had purchased in the country, near Wilmington Abbey, and I was once more restored to the affection of those dear friends who had ever possessed my warmest regard.

" My uncle having been disappointed in his hopes, had made a vow of celibacy, and now looked up to me as his only source of happiness.

" Having settled our more immediate pressing affairs, my uncle dispatched a letter to Sir George Freeland and his son, demanding satisfaction for the injury done to his niece, and the disgrace done to his name. The answer was laconic and impressive ; the misguided Herbert was removed beyond the reach of mortal vengeance ; a fever brought on by a cold, had terminated his existence, at the early age of twenty !

" This intelligence, you may be sure, greatly shocked me ; for, in spite of his cold-hearted and deliberate villany, Herbert Freeland still held a predominant sway o'er my soul's most ardent affections. Thus it is, that in spite of the voice of reason and prudence, we often cling to the cause of our sorrow, misery, and ruin, with a fondness most remarkable ; as the debauchee still perseveres in indulging in that baneful drink, which he knows is sapping his vitals, and hastening his progress to the grave.

" Many, many were the bitter tears I shed ; many the pangs that rent my bosom ; and my excellent uncle, although he endeavoured all in his power to console me, never reproached me for my sorrow ; he could well appreciate my feelings, and commiserate with my sufferings. He had himself felt bitterly the pangs of disap-pointed love ; a passion that had overcloaded his future prospects, and seared his heart ; and even now, when our conversation should happen to turn upon my poor mother, the violent agony he evinced showed how deeply her image was enshrined in his heart, and how severely that heart must have felt the dis-appointment to its hopes.

" My uncle, although he deprecated deeply the conduct of his brother, which had been productive of such ruinous consequences, I am convinced, freely forgave him ; but although he would have felt glad to have regained

possesion of the ancient seat of our ancestors, he considered that it would be much better to place the large sum of money which it would take to pay the mortgage at my command, should his death take place, so that myself and child might be amply provided for ; and he therefore suffered it to go from our family, and contented himself with the elegant villa which he had purchased for the future residence of himself and me.

" Nothing could exceed the happiness with which myself and my uncle lived together ; he adored the very ground I walked upon, and had he been my own father, I could not have loved him better than I did. Frequently would he gaze at me steadfastly a few minutes, then bursting into tears, unable to control his feelings, he would retire hastily to his own chamber, where he would remain for hours, before he would be in a fit condition to appear in my presence again.

" This vehement emotion was occasioned, as he has frequently declared, by the extraordinary likeness which I bore to my late mother.

" I had had frequent offers of marriage, from gentlemen of wealth and station, but I res-pectfully rejected them all, having determined, like my uncle, to live in future a life of celibacy. I had experienced enough of the cruelty and hypocrisy of mankind, to again embark my happiness in so great a risk ; and although I cannot defend the justice of my feelings, I must confess that I was deeply prejudiced against the whole of the masculine race. If one so every way noble and virtuous as Her-bert Freeland had appeared to be, could act the part of an hypocrite and a villain, I would not believe that honour could exist among mankind, and I looked upon them with a feel-ing of dread and repugnance, which, although I certainly endeavoured, yet I could not succeed in conquering.

" Thus passed away two years, when my child was attacked with the scarlet fever, and which soon exhibited such alarming symptoms, that not the least hopes were entertained of her recovery.

" This was another severe trial to me, for my little Constance had just become very en-gaging, and her innocent prattle, and playful gambols, were among the greatest of my own and my uncle's pleasures.

" But relentless death is no respecter to persons, ages, or pleasures ; he comes in the midst of our greatest enjoyments ; his awful dart is directed against his victims, perhaps in the moment of their greatest gaiety, and when the arrival is least expected.

" In spite of every care and attention, and the most eminent advice which could be ob-tained, my poor child died, and was placed in the same tomb which held the remains of my parents.

" It was some time ere I could recover from this affliction, and for a long while, in fact, I was completely inconsolable; but at length time mellowed my sorrow, and I became calm and resigned.

" I was frequently the guest of Mr. and Mrs. Wilmington, who behaved to me with the same affection that they had ever done, and never alluded, even in the most remote manner, to the events of my past life.

" Their youngest daughter was now happily married, and they had several beautiful grand-children to increase their happiness.

" But I was shortly to be deprived of the friendship of these excellent people. Mrs. Wilmington caught a malignant fever, which she communicated to her husband, and so powerful was its effects, that, only a few days after they were first attacked with it, they breathed their last, within a few minutes of each other.

" No one could possibly have regretted their loss more than I did, for I had looked upon them as my second parents; and certainly the manner in which they had behaved to me while I was under their protection, rendered them full deserving of that title.

" I shed many tears to their memory, and their names are engraven upon my heart in characters that nothing can efface, until that heart shall cease to beat for ever.

" Shortly after the death of their honoured parents, Lady Flora and her husband, and her sister and her husband, left England to reside on the Continent, and thus, I may say, that I was at once deprived of all my friends and acquaintances.

" I have never seen them but once since they have left England, when they returned for two or three months to settle some domestic affairs; but we still correspond together; and, if I may judge from their letters, I hold as firm a place in their friendship as ever.

" My uncle and myself might be said to lead almost a life of seclusion; a life which was now consonant with my feelings. I had seen enough of the world to hate and despise it, and I had not a wish beyond the affection of my amiable relative, and the comfortable and commodious place we inhabited.

" Our principal enjoyments were each other's society, reading, and cultivating the extensive garden attached to our residence; and in those we found that calm and genuine pleasure, which the worldling might well envy. How different were those simple pleasures we enjoyed, to the false-named and evanescent joys of fashionable life; how cheering were the reflections they left behind. Would to Heaven I had never known any other! what little cause should I have for self-reproach at present. But, short-sighted mortals as we are, we never can perceive what true happi-

ness is, until we purchase the knowledge by woeful experience. Although the truth is pointed out to us, we obstinately avoid it, and will pursue our own way, until we find, when it is too late, that it leads to ruin and all its following miseries.

" These, my dear Lady Ravensford, are my sentiments, and you must admit that I speak from experience, purchased in the school of adversity.'

Our heroine sighed.

" Alas !' she observed; " too well do I know and feel the truth of those remarks; too fatally have I cause, Mrs. Belgrave, to entertain a reciprocity of sentiment with you."

Mrs. Belgrave looked at her ladyship for a moment or two with an expression of the deepest compassion. She had heard of our heroine's early sorrows and errors, but Rosabelle had not stated anything about them in the narrative which she had given Mrs. Belgrave, and that lady had, of course, from motives of delicacy, forborne to allude to them in the slightest degree.

Mrs. Belgrave, however, made no answer to what Lady Rosabelle said, and after a pause, during which the latter was enabled to regain her composure, she resumed her story in the following words—

" But uninterrupted happiness was not fated to be my portion, and I was shortly doomed to experience the heaviest blow of any that it had been my lot to endure for many a day.

" My uncle left me at an early hour one morning to go upon business a few miles in the country, and did not expect that he would be able to get back till the evening.

" The evening arrived, and he came not. Hour after hour passed away, and still he was absent. I became uneasy, for he was a most punctual man, and I knew that he had a considerable sum of money about his person.

" It was now nine o'clock, and the night was very dark, for the autumn was for advanced, and my apprehensions increasing, I despatched two servants different ways, to ascertain whether they could see anything of him.

" They returned after two hours fruitless search, and you may then imagine in what a distracted state of mind I must have been.

" I felt confident that something must have happened to him, and, unable to endure the agonising suspense, I sent a trusty man servant off with all possible speed to the place whither my uncle had gone, to learn whether he was detained there by some unexpected business, or whether he had left there, and at what time.

" In the interval that elapsed while the man was gone, I endured some of the most painful moments of anxiety I ever remember to have suffered.

"Presentiments the most awful crowded upon my busy imagination, and at last I was worked up to such a pitch of agitation, that I was in a state bordering upon madness. The least sound which met my ears alarmed me, or filled me with hopes that were doomed immediately to be disappointed.

"I could with difficulty find patience sufficient to remain in the house, and ever and anon I went to the hall door, as fancied sounds smote my ears.

"In this manner the time slowly waned away, and at length I heard the hour of twelve chime from the village church.

"Still neither my uncle nor the servant whom I had despatched in search of him returned.

"I was worked up to a complete state of frenzy, and, scarcely knowing what I did, in spite of the remonstrances of my female attendant, I had put on my bonnet and scarf, and was about to quit the house, when I heard the noise of several voices outside, and presently afterwards there was a loud knocking at the outer door.

"I fled, rather than ran, followed by my waiting-maid, to the door, which had already been opened, and there my eyes encountered a sight which smote my heart with a sensation of the most indescribable horror.

"My poor unfortunate uncle—pale, bleeding, and insensible, was borne in the arms of several men, who had found him in a lonely spot, only a short distance from the village, stretched upon the earth, and bleeding copiously from two or three severe wounds which he had received on the head, apparently from a bludgeon, or some blunt implement.

"Overcome by horror at the dreadful sight, I gave utterance do a fearful shriek, and immediately fainted.

"I soon recovered, and hastened to the chamber of my uncle.

"He was sensible, and was able to speak, but was apparently in great pain, and I could soon ascertain from the looks of the medical gentlemen who had been called in to attend him, that they considered the wounds he had received to be mortal.

"My agony was most intense, but my uncle mustered all the strength he could gather, and endeavoured to console me. He, however, did not attempt to deceive me with false hopes, and admitted that he felt himself that his end was approaching.

"I endeavoured to appear more calm, but alas! how futile was the effort.

"My uncle, it appeared, had been detained at the place where he had gone to transact his business, longer than he had at first expected he should be, and it was late ere he started on his way to return home.

"He had reached the lonely moor where he had been found, when, by the faint light which the partially-obscured moon threw across his path, he thought he beheld the shadows of two or three human forms.

"Before he had time to turn round to see whether there were any persons near him, he received a violent blow, which instantly knocked him off his horse; and he was no sooner dismounted than he was attacked with bludgeons in the most ferocious manner, by three ruffians, who had the appearance of labourers.

"Unable to defend himself from their repeated blows, he became insensible, and remembered no more, until he found himself in his own chamber.

"The villains had plundered him of a large sum in gold, and had got clearly off, for it was so dark, and the attack was so sudden, that my uncle could not give a sufficient description of them to give the least hope of their being detected and apprehended.

"My ill-fated uncle lingered in great agony for four days, when he breathed his last on my bosom; that bosom which was now deprived of every happiness that could render life desirable.

"As I knelt by the side of the coffin, and pressed the cold hand of the corpse to my lips, how often and fervently did I pray that it would please the Almighty to take me from that world in which I was now left alone; without one friend to whom I could confide my thoughts, or who would sympathise with my sorrows.

"The remains of my last relative were consigned to the tomb, and my feelings, that had been stretched beyond the pitch of human endurance, took such an effect upon me, that I was seized with a fit of illness, from which it was never expected by the eminent professional gentlemen who attended me, I should recover.

"But youth, and a naturally strong constitution prevailed, and I was at length restored to convalescence, my sorrows having settled into a dead calm, which was not the less powerful than the most violent demonstrations of grief.

"Often when I took a retrospective view of the occurrences of the last few years of my life especially, I could not help thinking that fate had never destined me to mingle in the busy scenes of the world, and although my retirement from it latterly had been almost complete, I was half inclined to form a resolution to seclude myself from it altogether.

"On doing one thing I was determined, and that was, to quit the house in which I was at present residing as quickly as possible.

"While I remained there, every object upon which I fixed my eyes must remind me of my misfortunes, and my murdered uncle, whose irreparable loss I could never cease to deplore. There was not a single thing upon which I could gaze, but would bring him to my mind's eye, and make me perpetually miserable.

"The well-selected library, from whose ample store he had so often read to amuse and instruct me—the garden which had been partly cultivated by him—the flowers, that were planted by his hand—his favourite walks—even the most trifling thing, would be sure to bring him to my recollection in the most vivid colours, and keep my wounds for ever open.

"I instructed the person who had the management of my affairs, to look out for a convenient residence for me, in a retired part of the country, and where I might not expect to be intruded upon by society, and it was not long before he heard of the house which I at present inhabit.

"I was delighted with the situation, for it was as lonely and quiet as the greatest hater of the world could desire, and, apart from the busy, bustling scenes of life, would allow me plenty of opportunity for reflection, without the fear of intrusion. The inhabitants of the place were principally poor fishermen and others, and I could calculate upon retirement without entire seclusion, if I may make use of the observation, and, moreover, I could exercise my charitable inclinations towards my humble fellow-creatures with advantage to myself. That would prove one of the greatest solaces to my mind; for how truly and beautifully does the immortal bard speak the language of philosophy and truth, when he says that

"Charity falleth like the gentle dews of Heaven.
It is twice blessed. It blesses those who give,
    And they who receive.

I therefore authorised my agent to secure the house upon the terms offered, which I considered were far from exorbitant, and having quickly settled my arrangements, I removed hither with all possible despatch. Your ladyship will be able to judge whether my plan was a wise one, situated as I was; at any rate, I have had no cause to regret it, for since I have resided here I have passed more hours of real and tranquil enjoyment, than I have experienced since the fatal catastrophe which deprived me of my inestimable relative. Here have I formed a little world of my own, and have not a wish beyond it, till it shall please the Almighty to take me to those celestial regions, of which the truly penitent may hope to be partakers, and where the corroding pangs of care are unknown.

"The better to prevent suspicion, or idle curiosity, I assumed the name of Mrs. Belgrave, and am known here by no other title than the ' Good Widow;' but how far I have succeeded, of course, it is not for me to boast.

"Shortly after my residence here, in one of my rambles over the house, I accidently discovered the secret entrance to the rocky cavity, in which my sudden appearance to you yesterday evening caused you so much alarm; and being of a romantic turn of mind, I took great pains to make such alterations in it, as might render it a pleasant retreat, and a means of recreation. In that rocky grotto, Nature's most beauteous work, I pass many of my happiest hours, watching the sun as it rises or declines in the bosom of the deep, or the different vessels as they bound over its surface, like things of magic.

"Frequently have I felt the pleasure of being able to shelter and contribute to the comfort of the shipwrecked mariner; and, everything combined, I am far happier than I feel my errors have deserved.

"Thus, Lady Ravensford, do I close the melancholy recital of my past life, confident that you will make every allowance for those faults to which our sex are often tempted, although their principles may be based in rectitude and virtue.

"May there be few instances of future suffering and indiscretion, like those recounted by the unfortunate Constance Claremont."

———

CHAPTER XXXVIII.

THE DEPARTURE.—THE WOOD.

THUS did the nominal Mrs. Belgrave conclude her unfortunate and eventful history, to which, we need not say, our heroine had listened with the most absorbing interest and the deepest sympathy.

The principal chain of events were so similar to her own, that, while they excited her utmost commiseration, created in the bosom of Lady Rosabelle many emotions of the most powerful and painful description. A feeling, however, of shame and delicacy prevented her from alluding to the circumstances of her first meeting with Lord Ravensford, then Captain Beresford, and the subsequent errors, of which they had both so sincerely repented since, and she restrained her feelings as much as possible, so that they might not excite the curiosity and attention of Mrs. Belgrave.

" Yours has indeed been a life of sorrow, my dear Mrs. Belgrave," said our heroine, " and few can know so well how to appreciate your misfortunes as myself. I trust, however, that your future days may be those of tranquillity and happiness."

" That I am happy in the life I have chosen, Lady Ravensford," replied Mrs. Belgrave, " I have already told you; but painful reflection, bitter retrospection will, in spite of all my efforts, at times obtrude, and render me wretched. The being who has once strayed from the paths of virtue, alas! can never again be permanently happy."

Rosabelle felt keenly these observations, but she endeavoured to conquer her emotions, and succeeded much better than might have been expected.

"My dear, Mrs. Belgrave," she observed, after a pause, "I must still consider that you reproach yourself far too severely. There are many misguided mortals who have erred far greater than yourself, and have not been aroused to feelings of compunction and remorse, until it was too late. They are, indeed, the unfortunates whose fates are more keenly to be regretted, whose sufferings must be the more intense and lamentable."

"True," returned Mrs. Belgrave, "and perhaps I do wrong to repine against the mercy of Omnipotence who has so awakened me to a sense of remorse, and afforded me the opportunity of obtaining forgiveness by penitence. Few recent circumstances, my lady, have afforded me such sincere gratification as my singular introduction to you, and I am sanguine enough to hope that you may not deem me unworthy of your future friendship and esteem."

"Unworthy!" ejaculated our heroine, fervently; "few individuals, I am confident, can have a greater claim upon my friendship than the amiable Constance Claremont."

Mrs. Belgrave seized the hand of the fair

ROSABELLE'S PAINFUL INTERVIEW WITH HER MANIAC FATHER.

speaker with avidity, and while tears of gratitude sparkled in her still bright and expressive eyes, she pressed it vehemently to her lips.

"May this be but the prelude to many future meetings, dear Lady Ravensford," she exclaimed.

"Oh, yes, it will," said Rosabelle, with equal ardour; "depend upon it, I shall never again forget the Rock House, and its kind mistress; and should Providence permit, after the unfortunate circumstances that have so long unsettled me and my dear friends are arranged, I shall frequently do myself the infinite pleasure of becoming your guest."

"Oh, my dear Lady Ravensford," cried Mrs. Belgrave, her cheeks glowing with pleasure, "I can never express my due sense of this kindness."

"Believe me, Mrs. Belgrave," replied our heroine, "the pleasure will be equally great on my side. But I expect a return."

"I know what you would say," observed Mrs. Belgrave.

"I must request that you will sometimes be a visitor at Holly Hall."

Mrs. Belgrave paused.

"Nay," added Lady Ravensford, in a playful tone; "on that point I must be despotic. I have fixed my determination not to be refused. I will not except of any excuses;

there is not the least occasion for them, and I will not hear them."

Mrs. Belgrave faintly smiled.

"I must confess, Lady Ravensford," she said, "that if there is anything that could possibly induce me to break from this seclusion, it would be the temptation to comply with your kind invitation."

"And as I do not see that you have any reasonable cause to resist that temptation," remarked Rosabelle, "I shall conclude that point as settled."

"No, but——"

"No but—there, I will not hear any excuse; you will promise me, won't you?"

"After the promise I have exacted from you," replied Mrs. Belgrave, "I cannot refuse."

"Thanks, thanks," returned our heroine, cordially pressing her hand; "nothing will afford me a greater pleasure than to see you at Holly Hall; and I am confident that my husband, my poor father (if he is still blessed with the light of reason), and my dear friends, Mr. Goodman, and Mr. and Mrs. Rattle'on, will vie with each other in giving you a hearty welcome, and endeavouring to make you happy while you remain with us. Heaven send that such anticipated pleasures may not be far from realization."

"Amen!" fervently exclaimed Mrs. Belgrave.

"And now, my dear Lady Ravensford," she added, "as we have yet an hour to spare previous to dinner, if you are so disposed, and feel any curiosity, I will show you my secluded residence."

"Nothing would afford me greater pleasure," replied Lady Rosabelle; and taking Alfred by the hand, she followed Mrs. Belgrave from the room.

The Rock House was not large, but the apartments were very commodious. The exterior bore all the marks of age, from the style of architecture, and the ivy that thickly mounted its walls; but since Mrs. Belgrave had inhabited it, she had caused many improvements to be made, and kept it in thorough repair; and its appearance was, although unassuming, such as would be sure to attract the attention and admiration of those who loved retirement and gothic simplicity.

Its gable frontage, ancient porch, and small pointed casements, gave it an aspect of romantic interest, and often attracted the attention and curiosity of the traveller.

The interior was characterised by an air of simple elegance and comfort, that might have been expected from the taste and habits of the fair inhabitant; and the furniture was of the most chaste and handsome description.

There was a neat little library of well selected books by the best authors, and a gallery of paintings, amongst which were some of the choicest gems by the most eminent and modern masters.

On the right of the house was a garden, highly cultivated, and containing the most rare and fragrant exotics, and which sloped its way to within a very short distance of the beach, which was washed by the waters of the vast deep.

In this garden was a pleasant little summer-house, round which the honeysuckle richly climbed, and in this fragrant and calm retreat Mrs. Belgrave passed many of her happiest moments.

The secret passage which led to the cavity in the rock that adjoined the house, and from which it derived its name, Mrs. Belgrave had, with trouble and taste, formed into a kind of subterranean grotto, illuminated by Chinese lamps, that cast a mellow light upon the variegated shells with which the walls were encrusted.

This place no one was acquainted with but herself and her favourite attendant, and she took a romantic delight in wandering to it, and from the cavity watching the stately vessels as they glided over the dark green waves of the ocean.

Frequently the shipwrecked seaman had found relief beneath the hospitable roof of Mrs. Belgrave, and she could feel no greater pleasure than in being useful and charitable to her fellow-creatures.

The fortune her uncle had left her was ample, and allowed her free scope to the indulgence of her benevolence; and many were the humble individuals who had cause to bless and revere her name, and who, but for her, must have felt all the gnawing horrors of misery and destitution.

Few there are who possess the excellent heart of Mrs. Belgrave, or the distress which prevails among the humble and industrious classes would speedily be ameliorated, and poverty be but little known in this free and enlightened nation.

But avarice and selfishness are the prevailing passions of the wealthy, and they can squander fortunes in useless luxuries, while they close their ears to the cries of those who have a right to partake of those comforts and pleasures they so abundantly possess.

It must be a debased and contemptible mind that can boast of the thousands squandered upon the race-course, at a gaming-table, or in glittering gew-gaws, to flatter the pride of some favourite mistress, while those who have laboured hard, and their ancestors before them, to produce the wealth that is so lavishly wasted, are drawing out a wretched existence in misery and starvation.

But how proudly the haughty aristocrat can boast of his rights and privileges, and deem a state of abject pauperism too good for the very classes, upon whom they are, in fact, the most degraded paupers and detested locusts.

The patrician prides himself upon the wealth

and rank of his ancestors, and it is well that his narrow soul can find gratification in so doing, for it is seldom that they can boast of those intrinsic riches, nobility and virtue of mind.

The rich have the ambition to be great, forgetting the opportunity of being so is in every person's power. The secret of being great is everywhere the same; it is to be virtuous!

These reflections occurred to the mind of Lady Ravensford, as she walked over the beautiful retreat of Mrs. Belgrave, and thought upon the life that amiable lady led; and it was not too much to say that she envied her her happiness.

She was perfectly delighted with everything she saw, and hoped to be often able to revisit them, when fate should have brightened her prospects, and a summer's day should have succeeded to the long and dreary night of winter it had long been her destiny to endure.

Many were the encomiums which she passed upon the refined taste and judgment which Mrs. Belgrave had displayed in the arrangement of her secluded establishment, which proved so well how richly the well cultivated mind can provided for its own enjoyments under the most peculiar circumstances.

Mrs. Belgrave felt highly flattered by the compliments that were bestowed upon her by Lady Ravensford, and, as she observed, from that time, the Rock House would possess a double value in her estimation, and increase its superiority to the more ostentatious dwellings of the great.

By the time they had completed their examination of the house, and the attractions that surrounded it, the hour of dinner had arrived, and they returned to the house.

The dinner passed over in the most agreeable manner, and the subsequent time was spent in the most delightful conversation, during which our heroine felt happier than she had done for a considerable time before, and by the kind and sympathising efforts of Mrs. Belgrave, she began to hope more happiness for the future.

She was, however, most anxious to resume her journey, and awaited with impatience for the arrival of the next day.

The two friends were so pleased with each other's society that they did not think of retiring to rest until the night had far advanced, and then Mrs. Belgrave did so with particular regret, for but a few short hours must intervene ere Lady Rosabelle would depart, and she should again be left alone to that solitude which she should now feel somewhat painful after having briefly enjoyed the society of one whose misfortunes had been so similar to her own, and who possessed a heart which could so ardently and sincerely commiserate with her.

Rosabelle also regretted the necessity of their separating so soon, but she trusted that it would not be long ere they might meet again, and with that idea, and that it might be under happier circumstances than at present, she consoled herself.

The next morning Lady Ravensford rose at an early hour, and descended the stairs.

Mrs. Belgrave had been up since the first break of day, and our heroine learnt from her attendant that she was walking in the garden.

Rosabelle hastened thither to join her, and found her seated in the little summer-house, apparently more melancholy than she had been since our heroine had been an inmate of the house.

Rosabelle inquired the cause.

"Pardon me, dear Lady Ravensford," said Mrs. Belgrave, "but I cannot divest my mind of a selfish feeling. I cannot help feeling severely the loss I am so shortly to sustain in being deprived of your society. And yet humanity would prompt me to be as anxious as yourself for your departure to be restored to those friends from whom you have been so long separated."

Indeed, my dear Mrs. Belgrave, I sincerely reciprocate your feelings," said Lady Ravensford; but I entertain the most sanguine hopes that the time will be short, indeed, before we shall meet again, and when my mind will be in a far more fitting condition to render my society pleasing to you. Depend upon it, during my absence, Mrs. Belgrave and the Rock House will ever hold a prominent place in my thoughts.'

"I am certain, my dear lady," replied Mrs. Belgrave, "that you speak sincerely; and rest assured, that paramount in my esteem will be fixed the image of Lady Ravensford."

"It is yet very early," said Rosabelle, "what time do you expect the chaise to arrive at the Rock House, Mrs. Belgrave?"

"I ordered the servant to tell them to be sure not to make it later than nine o'clock," replied the latter.

"And if they are punctual, what time do you imagine I shall reach Holly Hall?" inquired our heroine.

"The neighbourhood of Holly Hall is a considerable distance from here," remarked Mrs. Belgrave, "and the roads are very bad to travel. I do not think you will possibly arrive at the end of your journey until a late hour at night."

"I hope the man will not disappoint me," said Rosabelle.

"There is not much fear of that, I think," returned Mrs. Belgrave, "for they are pretty punctual."

It was a beautiful morning, and Rosabelle much enjoyed the pure and fragrant breeze which she inhaled from the garden, and the broad expanse of the ocean.

Mrs. Belgrave and our heroine walked around the garden several times, and conversed upon different subjects, until a female servant made her appearance to inform them that the breakfast awaited them.

They then entered the elegantly-furnished parlour, which commanded a full view of the pleasures they had been enjoying, and by the time the meal had been despatch, it was nine o'clock.

But the post-chaise did not arrive, and another half hour passed away and still it came not.

Lady Rosabelle became impatient, and when she heard the hour of ten peal from the old church, she requested Mrs. Belgrave to despatch a domestic to the post-house to ascertain the cause of the delay.

The servant was not long before she returned and informed them that the master of the post-house was very sorry, but that the man had not yet come back from a journey, and it would be quite impossible to send the chaise till the afternoon.

Rosabelle was very much vexed at this disappointment and delay, but it could not be helped, and she was, therefore, compelled to content herself; but she was resolved, if they were not punctual in the afternoon, she would not procrastinate her journey any longer than the evening, when she would go by the mail.

Mrs. Belgrave did not attempt to dissuade her from this resolution, for she could well appreciate the anxiety and impatience Rosabelle must endure, after her long estrangement from her friends, and the many sufferings she had undergone.

It was four o'clock in the afternoon before the man arrived with the post-chaise, and our heroine, after a most affectionate parting with Mrs. Belgrave, and repeating her hope of their shortly meeting again, stepped into the vehicle with her child, and at length resumed her journey, with mingled feelings of hope and apprehension as to the probable result of it.

The vehicle proceeded at a rapid rate, but the man who drove it, in reply to questions put to him by our heroine, said he did not think it possible that they could arrive at their journey's end before the morning, even if she designed to travel all night, which he should advice her not to do, as the road was a bad one, and much infested by highwaymen.

Rosabelle, however, was so anxious to get to the end of the journey, that she conquered the fears which the information of the man was calculated to create in her bosom, and determined to continue travelling without stopping until she had reached the place of her destination, and the postilion, although he evidently did not at all approve of this job, could not, of course, offer any objection.

Nothing particular or worthy of recording took place, until night had set in, the postilion having twice stopped to change horses, and to enable our heroine to procure such necessary refreshment on the road as she might require; when they entered upon a wood so dark and gloomy, that scarcely a ray of light penetrated through the umbrageous foliage of the trees, which were clustered so thickly together, that it was not without considerable difficulty the vehicle could proceed.

Rosabelle now, for the first time, felt alarmed. She remembered what the postilion had said about the highwaymen, and certainly if there was any truth in what he had mentioned to her, a more fitting place for robbery and murder than the one they were travelling through there could not be.

The chaise, too, could only proceed at a very slow pace, and the wind, which blew keenly, rattled in at the carriage windows in powerful gusts, that made our heroine and her child, the latter especially, tremble with the cold.

From the manner in which the postilion conducted himself, Rosabelle was inclined to think that he knew very little of the way he was travelling, and her fears were soon confirmed, for he suddenly stopped, dismounted, and coming to the door of the vehicle, he, with many apologies and expressions of regret, informed her that, the darkness being so great, he had mistaken the way, and was quite at a loss how to proceed.

Here was another cause for vexation, and our heroine began to think that there was a spell upon her.

What was now to be done in this dilemma? Rosabelle was quite at a loss to form any conjecture, and the postilion did not appear to know any better than herself. To go forward it would be perfectly useless, and, indeed, the postilion was too much alarmed to make such an endeavour, even if it had been to any purpose, and it was now getting so late that it was necessary they should come to some decision, unless they should think fit to take up their lodgings for the night in the gloomy wood.

Rosabelle could not forbear giving expression to her vexation, and reprimanding the postilion for his carelessness in mistaking the road, and she now regretted that she had not done as she had first intended to do, namely, to prosecute her journey in the mail.

The man could not but admit that he had been rather neglectful, but he could not account for his neglect, as "he knew every inch of the ground, and had travelled that way hundreds of times. But it could not now be helped;" and he furthermore endeavoured to console our heroine with the hacknied observation that it would be advisable to make the best of a bad bargain, though how, or in which way they were to better the said bargain, he did not at first appear to have the slightest idea.

At length, after scratching his head for about five minutes, while Rosabelle was shivering all the time in the vehicle, until his patience was completely exhausted, he observed—

"The whole on it is, my lady, it is a bad job, and we must endeavour to make the best on it. We can't go forward, my lady, and if we could, we should be worse than mad to do so, for we should be certain to be stopped and plundered, and, mayhap, murdered by some of the terrible chaps as infest this wood. Why, it was only the other night, my lady, that—"

"Never mind what happened the other night, my good man," interrupted our heroine; "if you have any advice to offer to extricate us from our present dilemma, do so, I pray you, without any further delay.'

"Why, the fact on it is, my lady,' replied the postilion, 'the only alternative which I can see we have, is to return to the town we lately passed through, and put up' at the inn there for the night. I am sorry that this delay should occur to your ladyship, but, indeed, it is entirely accidental. I never was so out of my reckoning before in all my life. I and Joe Jervis what——"

Rosabelle interrupted the important information which the postilion was about to favour her with concerning the doings of himself and Joe Jervis, by requesting him to return to the town as speedily as possible, and remounting, he gave his whip a hearty crack, which resounded through the wood, and turning round, proceeded to retrace the way to the town they had quitted about an hour before, as quick as the intricacy of the way, and the imperviousness of the wood would permit him.

Throwing herself back in the vehicle, our heroine gave herself up to thoughts of not the most pleasant description. It appeared to her as though she was never destined to reach the end of her journey, and she could not divest her mind of the melancholy forebodings that crowded upon it.

Nothing could be more tedious than the delay she had met with since she had been released by Monckton from the power of the villain Adder; for every hour which procrastinated her return to Holly Hall appeared to her an age; and now another night and day must intervene before she could hope to be restored to those from whom she had been so long separated.

And in what a fearful state might she find them! Her husband, perhaps, absent from the hall in search of her, no one knew whither; her poor father a raving maniac!

The picture was too horrible for contemplation, and groaning with mental agony, she passed her hands across her eyes, as if she would shut it out from her gaze.

Her child had now fallen asleep on her lap, and she had nothing to divest her thoughts from wandering in the dismal channel they had hitherto pursued.

At length they emerged from the wood, much to the satisfaction of Lady Ravensford, and no less so to that of the postilion, and soon afterwards the lights proceeding from the town they were approaching, met their sight.

It was past ten o'clock when they arrived there, and they were only just in time to procure accommodation at the inn.

Desiring the man to be ready to resume their journey at an early hour in the morning, Lady Ravensford, after partaking of some slight refreshment with the host and hostess in their private parlour, retired with her child to the chamber allotted to them.

After having invoked the protection of Heaven, Rosabelle and the little Alfred hastened to bed, where, worn out with fatigue and vexatious thought, she quickly sank into a sound and refreshing sleep.

CHAPTER XXXIX.

THE REVELLERS.—THE UNEXPECTED MEETING.—THE INTERRUPTION.

THE scene we are now about to describe was the coffee-room of an inn; the time, five o'clock in the morning—the persons present were Captain Mowbray, Sir Harry Spangle, and two or three other noisy and dissipated revellers, whose flushed countenances, bloodshot eyes, and other equally striking symptoms, showed plainly enough that they had been "making a night of it."

Sir Harry Spangle and Captain Mowbray appeared to be the most sober of the company, not that their potations had been less deep or less frequent than their companions, but that constant practice had so inured them to the wine cup, that it was long ere they showed any ill-effects from it.

They certainly were particularly noisy and merry, and their companions lent their aid to the conviviality, by knocking down everything the aforesaid gentlemen said or did, in the most tumultuous manner.

One individual, in the classic tongue of the drunkard, was "quite done up," and was stretched at full length upon the floor, under one of the tables, with his hat for a pillow, and a portion of the carpet for a coverlid; and every now and then he added to the general tumult by a loud snore of the most hoggish description.

The proprietor of the inn had several times requested the party to break up, but as the said party threatened to break his head instead, if he interfered with them, he thought it was best to desist from his importunies, and after supplying them with enough wine for the night, he retired to his own chamber, and left them, very reluctantly, to the indulgence of their noisy revels.

At the time we have thought proper to open this scene, it was, as we have before stated, about five o'clock in the morning, and the landlord of the inn had arisen, and his servants also, and the usual bustle in such places prevailed, but still the debauchees continued their riotous mirth, and it appeared as if they had fully made up their minds to make another day of it at least.

"The song, Sir Harry, the song, the song! We will have no excuses!" shouted Captain Mowbary.

"Ay—ay, the song—the song, we will have no excuses!" chorussed three or four voices, and the gentleman under the table gave a loud snore.

"Ah, the song—ah! well I don't mind trying one, just to keep up the conviviality;" said Sir Harry Spangle, who was seated on rather a high chair, with his legs negligently deposited on one end of the table, and twiddling a fine-flavoured cigar in his finger and thumb. "The song—let me see—ah, what shall it be? Oh, I have it—very appropriate I think you will admit."

And then without any further ceremony, Sir Harry Spangle, who had really an excellent voice, and sound musical judgment, commenced singing the following words :—

SONG.

" While we have wine and wit beyond measure,
   While we have mirth and good humour galore,
Who shall proclaim there are bounds to our pleasure,
   Where is the fool who'd wish revelry o'er?
Fill, fill your glasses, the lasses, the lasses,
   Blue eyes, and black eyes, we'll ne'er make a fuss,
We'll care not a fig which hue surpasses,
   So long as they sparkle with love upon us!
      Then fill, fill your glasses, the lasses, the lasses,
         Whose soft beaming smiles speak of Heaven divine;
      The pleasure that's courted by all who're not asses,
         Are wit and good humour, fair woman and wine!

" Oh, woman and wine must our senses e'er capture,
   They are the antidotes ever of care;
Both were ordained a man's heart to enrapture,
   The older the wine, but the younger the fair!

Round with it, round with it, the room shall resound with it,
   The toast I propose, in our hearts we'll entwine;
And while we have those, we shall pleasure abound with it,
   The lasses, the lasses, young women, old wine!
      Then fill, fill your glasses, the lasses, the lasses,
         Whose soft beaming smiles speak of Heaven divine;
      The pleasure that's counted by all who're not asses,
         Are wit and good humour, fair woman and wine!"

The demonstrations of applause that greeted this bacchanalian display, were of the most uproarious kind, and by the time the companions of Sir Harry Spangle and Captain Mowbray had given full scope to the exuberance of their delight and approbation, they were one and all " done up," and one by one dropped off to sleep, leaving the two above-named gentlemen to the uninterrupted enjoyment of their own society.

"Ha! ha! ha!" laughed Spangle; " they are regularly floored; poor devils!"

"Completely finished and done up," coincided Mowbray ;—"ha! ha! ha!"

"They are not half fellows to be done up with one night's carouse, poor devils! ha! ha!" observed Spangle.

"Poor weak creatures, to be knocked down by a dozen or two of wine; ha! ha! ha!" again laughed Mowbray.

"Not like you and I, Mowbray!" added Spangle.

"Not a bit of it."

"No comparison."

"A farthing rushlight to the moon."

"Half a pint of table beer to a pipe of wine."

"They cannot stand anything!"

"Positively nothing!"

"They're twaddlers!"

"Drivellers!"

"Noodles!"

"Boobies!"

"Nincompoops!"

"Humbugs!"

It may be as well to observe here that these compliments were bestowed upon the party at large, who had been liberally carousing Sir Harry Spangle and Captain Mowbray, without expecting the latter to pay a farthing of the reckoning, and consequently they may be considered fully entitled to the elegant epithets that were lavishly bestowed upon them.

"You and I are the fellows to do it, Spangle," said Mowbray.

"Positively the very fellows," coincided his friend.

"We are no skulkers while there is plenty of good wine before us," added Mowbray.

" Never think of such a thing."

" It would ruin our reputation, if we were known to do such a thing."

" And that would be a most melancholy thing."

" Positively awful !"

" We will never let the enemy beat us."

" No, damme !" returned Mowbray ; " but down with it, down with it, and at it again !"

" At it again ! Ha ! ha ! ha !"

" We are wine proof !"

" Full proof !"

" Above proof, by Jupiter !"

" But talking about women," observed Mowbray, " that Adder was a devilish fortunate fellow."

" Cunning rogue !" replied Spangle ; " he managed his business famously, and has contrived admirably to elude the vigilance of Ravensford and his friends."

" They have not heard anything of them yet, I believe ?"

" Nothing !"

" Poor Ravensford."

" Yes, and poor Saunter, too."

" Ah ! the weak fool, he made a proper stupid job of it."

" Yes, and paid for it with his life."

" I wonder what has become of Ravensford ?"

" Oh, he is doubtless with his friend, Rattleton, still making every inquiry after his wife, and wisely keeping out of the way until that awkward affair of the duel is settled."

" It is, indeed, an awkward affair, but no more than I anticipated. The friends of Saunter are powerful."

" Yes; and it is only natural that they should exert that power to the uttermost, to avenge the death of their relative."

" Well, positively, I pity Ravensford."

" And so do I ; he is not a bad fellow."

" By no means."

" We have pledged our word to aid him in endeavouring to discover the retreat of Adder and his lady."

" And I, for one, am determined, to redeem that pledge."

" And so am I."

" And you mean to say that you would make one to rescue the lady from Adder's power, and deliver the latter into the hands of justice ?"

" Undoubtedly ; would not you ?"

" I would ; for after all I cannot help thinking that Adder has carried his villany rather too far."

" Besides, he is a plebeian."

" Ay, to be sure, and ought not to indulge in such luxuries."

" Decidedly not."

" When I think of the misery he has caused in that family, I really feel that I have something human in my composition yet. I must have another glass of wine after that, positively."

" I have a touch of the feeling about me, too, when I think of the sufferings of those at Holly Hall. Lady Rosabelle's father is in a deplorable state of insanity again."

" Ay, it's all up with the old gentleman. He will never live to see his daughter again, and, if he does, he will not know her."

" And it is my firm belief that Lady Ravensford will never live to see her father, her husband, or her friends again."

" I am of the same opinion ; a sensitive, high-minded woman like her will never be able to survive long the misery and degradation which Adder has heaped upon her."

" He positively must be a most arrant scoundrel."

" I never heard of one to equal him."

" Such a systematic way as he went to work to accomplish his villany."

" The ingenious and complicated plot he devised to bring about the gratification of his wishes."

" The artful manner in which he contrived to make the simpleton, Saunter, his dupe, too ; the ready tool to further his deep-laid stratagem."

" He must have had his education in the school of art and vice, certainly."

" Yes, and been a ready pupil, too."

" But is it not strange that every stratagem has failed to find the slightest clue to the place of his retreat ?"

" Wonderful !"

" And then the attempt upon Ravensford's life !"

" Doubtless by some ruffian employed by him."

" There cannot be a doubt of it."

" And the mysterious abduction of the child from the cottage in which Ravensford had placed it !"

" In all probability his work also."

" To be sure. Revenge has incited him to it."

" He is a dangerous fellow to offend."

" A very devil."

" At any rate, he does not fail to play the very devil with those who excite his enmity."

" True."

" But he must be defeated at last."

" Certainly ; there is not much prospect of it at present."

" Oh, no doubt he will be caught in some of his own snares by-and-by."

" And it is only fair that he should be."

" To be sure it is."

" But do you think he has murdered the boy ?"

" He is villain enough for anything."

" He must be a monster, indeed, if he

could perpetrate such a bloody crime as that. I must have another glass of wine."

"Do you think that he who did not hesitate to attempt the life of the father, and the violation of the mother, would shrink from the murder of the son?"

"But then its youth—its innocence!"

"Psha! he is a stranger to such feelings as they ought to inspire."

"Why, to be sure, from his general conduct, we have an undoubted right to suppose that he is."

"And yet I think that he has had some other motive for getting the child in his power; that he has found him necessary to advance his base schemes."

"Ay, and that the child still lives?"

"I hope so."

There was a pause ensued.

"Well, I declare I am getting quite sympathetic," at length said Captain Mowbray, in a tone half serious, half jocular.

"And positively so am I," remarked Sir Harry Spangle.

"But that Adder is really a most terrible fellow," added Mowbray.

"Oh! a most abominable rascal," rejoined his friend.

"But the scoundrel has talents."

"Of the first order."

"In the order of villany, you mean?"

"Exactly so."

"Ravensford ought to have thought him an invaluable fellow, before he did the matrimonial," remarked Mowbray.

"Oh, exquisite!"

"I do not wonder that he was generally so very successful in his amours."

"Not at all."

"It was all that demed Adder's doings," said Mowbray.

"Everything," coincided Spangle.

"He could not have done anything without him."

"Positively nothing at all."

"They must have been wise, indeed, who could escape the artifices of so crafty a villain as Adder."

"I believe you."

"Every stratagem, every scheme of rascality I do believe, that that rascal of rascals was up to."

"Positively every demed scheme," said Sir Harry Spangle; "but this is a dry subject, and as we are so sentimentally inclined, I must have another glass of wine."

"I feel to want one myself, too," observed Captain Mowbray, filling his glass from the decanter.—"Well, here's wishing that Adder may soon be taken."

"And Lady Ravensford restored to her husband and friends," exclaimed Sir Harry Spangle.

"Quite safe."

"Quite safe," repeated Spangle.

"And yet I am afraid there is not much chance of that."

"Nor I."

"Leave that consummate scoundrel, Adder, alone for that."

"Ay—ay."

"He would not fail to enforce his wishes."

"To be sure he would not."

"And what resistance could she make?"

"None at all."

"She is so completly in his power."

"Completely."

"Without a friend at hand to fly to her rescue."

"Not a friend; and, besides, no one knows, or can form the least conjecture whither he has taken her."

"Not the least shadow of an idea," said Mowbray.

"Any person would positively imagine that the fellow had some dealings in the black art," added Spangle, "and that she was conveyed away by magic, like Aladdin's palace."

"That they certainly would," observed Mowbray.

"I would not mind a cool hundred to know where the fellow is."

"Why, that would be rather awkward, I imagine, Spangle," returned Mowbray, with an expressive grin.

"Ha—ha!" laughed Spangle, clapping his hand significantly to his pocket: "finances rather queer, you think? Ha—ha—ha! I understand!"

"Exchequer low."

"Ha—ha—ha!"

"It is not a very laughable matter though."

"What's the use of being sad over it?" asked Spangle.

"None at all, certainly," replied Captain Mowbray; "but it is devilish unpleasant, though."

"Very unpleasant."

"To be straightened for a few hundreds."

"Very disagreeable."

"And people have no faith in the word and honour of gentlemen, now-a-days."

"Upon my word and honour, they have not," remarked Spangle.

"The unreasonable curmudgeons!"

"The unconscionable varlets."

"But we must do something to raise the wind."

"That's very evident."

"Quite certain."

"Quite."

"We must make good use of these boobies," said Mowbray.

"To be sure. Leave us alone for that," replied Spangle.

"They will be all right for a few hundreds," observed Mowbray.

"Oh, yes, I am certain of that."

"They are very easy."

"Poor devils!"

"Fit sport for us."

"Just the sort of game we like to hunt," returned Spangle.

"They have got a few thousands, which they seem bent upon wasting."

"And we might as well reap the benefit as any other persons."

"To be sure."

"And we will, too."

"Oh, there is not the least doubt of that. Ha! ha! ha!"

"By-the-by, we ought not to feel much obliged to Adder for depriving us of Saunter."

"No; that was a d——d bore."

"Remarkably unpleasant."

"A few hundreds out of our way."

"Yes."

"He was a good patient of ours."

"Excellent!"

"He used to bleed very well."

"Very free, indeed—very free;—the good-natured, conceited, stupid, d——d fool!"

"I am sorry for his fate, though."

"And so am I."

"It was paying rather too dear for his whim."

"A devilish high price."

ADDER, DISGUISED AS A BLACK, DEFENDS LORD RAVENSFORD FROM THE ROBBERS.

"I think Ravensford was rather too hasty and severe in that affair."

"Consider his excited feelings."

"True."

"The loss he has sustained."

"Ah! and the manner in which Saunter figured away in the plot."

"Yes, yes; it was enough to make a man desperate."

"But yet I don't know; it was not much better than murder to make a poor chicken-hearted devil like that fight."

"I don't think I could have done it."

"And I'm sure that I could not, especially after he had so humbly apologised."

"And on his knees begged for mercy."

"And crying like a child."

"Poor devil! It must have been a good joke at first."

"But the termination was much too serious."

"Oh, dear, yes."

"It was a most unfortunate thing, both for Ravensford and his victim."

"Very unfortunate."

"Now, if it had been Adder instead."

"Ah! then there would have been no cause to regret the circumstance at all."

"No, but to exult at it."

"Yes."

"Ravensford, I think, ought to have taken pity on the poor shallow-pated lord, when he might have been convinced that he was merely made the tool and the dupe of by Adder."

" Well, so I really think also."

" There is nothing to boast of in defeating a wretched creature like that."

"Nothing at all."

" But then we must make allowances for the distracted state which Ravensford's mind must have been in at the time."

" Yes, to be sure; he must have been in a complete state of frenzy. I know I should be at losing a beauteous wife."

" So should I, if she were good with it; if not, she might go to the devil for me."

" Oh, ah, that would materially alter the case "

" I believe he would not be persuaded but that Saunter knew where Adder and Lady Ravensford were concealed."

" So it appears ; although Saunter solemnly protested to the contrary ; and *we* knew well enough that he did not."

"Certainly."

" Well, I think that both Ravensford and his friend Rattleton are very silly to keep out of the way."

" So I think."

" They had much better surrender themselves and let the affair come to an issue at once."

" Undoubtedly they had."

" After all, I do not think that the jury would find a verdict of manslaughter against them on their trial, although the coroner's inquest that set upon the body, when it was removed from France to this country, was unanimous in coming to that decision."

" Oh, no ; under all the circumstances, I think they would be inclined to take a merciful view of it."

" Exactly so."

" I should surrender, if I were them."

" To be sure, and trust to fate."

" Ay, as we have done many a time."

" And probably shall have to do again."

" Most likely."

" Well, we are fully prepared for it."

" I should think so."

" We are not alarmed at trifles."

" What's the use ?"

" None at all."

" We have mingled in some strange scenes together."

" You may say that."

" We have been in luck together."

" Out of luck together."

" In debt together."

" In prison together."

" Damme! we have shared all the smiles and frowns of fortune together."

" And we will continue to do so, my boy."

" To be sure we will."

" Another glass of wine."

" I join you. Here's fortune !"

" Curse the jade, she is fickle."

" We have played her some sad tricks, you know."

" Why, that's true. So here's fortune, and may we soon be on more friendly terms with her than ever."

" Bravo !"

The two friends quaffed off glass after glass, with as much gusto as if they had only just commenced a night's carouse ; and then each crossing their legs in an indolent and careless manner, remained silent for a short time. The sleepers were snoring in concert, and did not seem likely to awake for some time, but to monopolise the coffee-room room for a chamber, for that day at least.

After the lapse of a short interval, Sir Harry Spangle looked up with an expression of countenance, half solemn, and half humorous, and, addressing himself to Mowbray, said—

" Mowbray, my boy !"

" Well, my dear fellow," said Mowbray.

" I have been thinking, Mowbray."

" And what have you been thinking ?" interrogated his dissipated companion.

" Why, that we have been a pair of d—d scoundrels !"

" Ha! ha! ha! What a discovery !—Why, I have known and felt that long ago, Sir Harry." returned Mowbray,

" We have taken that which did not belong to us," added Spangle, " and borrowed that which we never repaid."

" And never meant to repay," observed Captain Mowbray, with a laugh.

" We have diddled our tailor—broken the fortunes and the hearts of innumerable bootmakers, hatters, frizzeurs, laundresses, and other creditors."

" Very true," remarked Mowbray, " and we are likely enough to break the hearts of a great many more, if they are silly enough to trust us."

" Ah !" ejaculated Spangle, and he fetched a very deep sigh, reflectively.

" Ah !" mimicked Captain Mowbray ; " why, confound me, if you are not getting absolutely melancholy."

" I am becoming penitent," replied Sir Harry Spangle, in a tone still half serious ; " I am becoming penitent, Mowbray."

" Penitent !"

" Yes, downright compunctious."

" Ha! ha! ha!"

" Don't laugh ; I feel a touch of the serious," remarked Sir Harry Spangle. " I think it is high time that we began to think about a reformation, Mowbray."

" Well, positively !"

" Ah ! it may be well, positively," repeated Spangle ; " and, positively, I wish it to be well !"

"And what is your plan of reformation ?" inquired Mowbray.

"Why, matrimony."

"Matrimony ?"

"Ay, sober wedlock," answered Spangle ; "it would be advisable for us to do the steady and the amiable for some time, until we can meet with a favourable match ; a handsome sum in the shape of a wedding dowry, and a handsome wife, and then we may settle down into two worthy gentlemen, very patterns of domesticated virtue."

"Not a bad plan," said Mowbray, smiling ; "but it is almost too soon to think about that, yet."

"Not at all."

"That is only your opinion."

"And I have no doubt, as we have hitherto generally agreed, that it will be your opinion also."

"I cannot make up my mind to be shackled just yet, my dear fellow," replied Mowbray.

"Nonsense ! you may let the opportunity go by, and then you would repent it, take my word for it."

"Probably, I might," said Mowbray ; "but I shall e'en trust fortune a little while longer."

"But fortune will not trust to you ;—we owe her too large an account already," observed Sir Harry Spangle.

"But I am determined to jilt the jade still further, yet."

"Mind you do not deceive yourself."

"Leave me alone for that."

"After all, if a pretty girl, with a handsome portion, is thrown in your way, I do not fear but that I shall be able to make you a convert."

"Well, we'll leave that till the opportunity offers itself."

"Be it so."

"But are you really serious ?"

"Positively, quite serious."

"Ha, ha, ha ! we must have another glass of wine after that," laughed Mowbray. "Here's fortune and matrimony !"

"Fortune and matrimony !" responded Sir Harry Spangle, raising the glass to his lips, and then another pause of a few minutes took place.

"I have been thinking, Mowbray," at length Spangle broke silence, "that, after all, the whereabouts of Adder and Lady Rosabelle may not be so difficult to trace out as hitherto it has proved."

"Ah ! what makes you think so ?"

"Why," replied Spangle, "you know, that for a few days prior to the abduction of the child from the cottage, a strange vessel was seen off the place, which disappeared at the same time as the child."

"True."

"There is no doubt but that it was a smuggling vessel," continued Spangle, "and Mr. Williamson was very thoughtless that he did not make inquiries into the nature of the craft."

"So he was. And you think that the boy was taken away in that vessel ?"

"There can be but very little doubt of it. That is the general opinion."

"And do you think that Adder was on board of her ?"

"He might have been, to be sure," replied Spangle, "but I do not think it is probable that he would venture to be so ; although the smugglers were, I dare say, employed by him to accomplish the plot."

"Well, and what then ?"

"Why, have you never heard that Adder was in some way connected with the notorious smuggler, known by the name of Captain Monckton ?"

"I have heard something about it," answered Mowbray.

"Doubtless, then, that was one of Monckton's vessels," observed Spangle ; "and if this said smuggler could only be met with, he might be prevailed upon to divulge the whole truth, upon his receiving an ample reward for so doing."

"But do you suppose that Adder has ventured to make him an entire confidant, and that he is acquainted with his retreat ?" interrogated Mowbray.

"I think there is nothing more probable," replied Spangle ; "Adder could not act without emissaries, and I know of no one more likely to be employed by him than this Captain Monckton, as he designates himself."

"I am of a different opinion," observed Captain Mowbray ; "I do not think it likely that so shrewd a rascal as Adder would venture to entrust his secrets to the keeping of such a man as a smuggler-captain. It does not seem feasible."

"To me it does, perfectly so," returned Sir Harry Spangle ; "but, at any rate, there is no harm in the suggestion."

"Decidedly not."

"Could we meet with him, we might propose terms to him, in the name of Lord Ravensford, who, we may be certain, would be very glad to accede to any terms with him."

"Ah ! if we could meet with him," added Mowbray, significantly.

"I do not think it would be so difficult as you appear to imagine."

"The experiment would be fraught with some danger."

"Not at all."

"He might be inclined to suspect us of being spies upon his actions," said Mowbray, "and deal with us accordingly."

"Oh, no such thing," returned Spangle ; "if report speaks true, Monckton is a man of sense and education, and whose discernment would soon convince him that we meant nothing wrong."

"But you know the old axiom," observed Mowbray, "there is honour among thieves."

"Well, and admitting the force and truth of that adage," replied Spangle, "what has it to do with the subject I am speaking upon?"

"A great deal, I think."

"Explain yourself."

"That I can soon do."

"In what manner?"

"You shall hear. This smuggler-captain, if he be, as you suspect, the confident and emissary of Adder, has doubtless been bound to secrecy; consequently, if he professes the merits you have given him credit for, he will not divulge a syllable which might lead to a discovery of his employer."

Spangle paused.

"Why, that is a reasonable answer, truly," he remarked at last; "but still, money often does wonders, and there is no knowing what effect the offer of a larger reward than Adder could make him, might have upon him."

"I have no opinion of your suggestion, Spangle," said Mowbray; "but still, I should be very glad if we could see Ravensford, to talk the affair over with him."

"And so should I," answered Spangle; "but still we might consult with his friend, Mr. Goodman, upon the subject."

"Very true," said Captain Mowbray; "and if you like, when we have got rid of these fellows, we will lose no time in going to Holly Hall."

"Agreed!" answered Spangle; and at that moment the sound of the guard's horn announced the arrival of one of the mails.

"It is the Dover and London coach," said Spangle, looking from the window. "Well, certainly, this room does not appear to be exactly in order to show the passengers into, and I hear them coming this way,"

"Well, it can't be helped," replied Mowbray; "gentlemen must be accommodated. How do you feel, Spangle?"

"As sober as a judge."

"And so do I."

"Ha! ha! ha!" laughed Mowbray, tossing off another glass of wine, "we are the fellows to do it. But we have company coming, I hear.'

"This way, this way, gentlemen, if you please," said the landlord, without; "I hope you will excuse it, but——"

"There, there, no apologies, my dear fellow," interrupted a voice which made both Spangle and Mowbray start, and look towards the door, for its tones were quite familiar to their ears; "we have not long to stop, and it will do very well for us; I dare say we shall not disturb the gentlemen."

At that moment the door opened, and the landlord of the inn entered, escorting in two gentlemen, wrapped up in the ample folds of large roquelairs, in the fur collars of which their faces were so immersed, that their features were almost entirely concealed. But no sooner had they fixed their eyes upon Sir Harry Spangle and Captain Mowbray, than they uttered a mutual exclamation of surprise, and motioned the landlord, hurriedly, to retire from the room.

He obeyed, and the travellers having turned down the collars of their coats—

"Ravensford! Rattleton!" exclaimed the two exquisites, in a breath.

"Hush! be cautious!" whispered Rattleton; "you know"—placing his finger upon his lips.

Yes, it was Lord Ravensford and his devoted friend Rattleton, who had just alighted from the coach, and who had been guided to the very inn in which Mowbray and Spangle were staying.

But how greatly changed was the former from what he had once been! His countenance was pale and haggard with constant care, and his form was wasted with the anxiety and fatigue he had undergone for many months.

"Are these your friends?" he inquired, looking cautiously upon the different sleepers.

Spangle and Mowbray replied in the affirmative, the latter adding—

"I think we might trust them if they were even sensible to what is passing; but they are all completely done up, and you may speak without fear."

"This is an unexpected meeting," said Lord Ravensford, throwing himself into a chair.

"Unexpected, indeed!" repeated Spangle, "but most opportune; we were, not many minutes ago, talking about you."

"Of course you know the reason of our using this precaution?" said Rattleton.

"Certainly," was the laconic answer.

"We are on our way to Holly Hall," added Rattleton, "where we mean to surrender ourselves, and end at once the suspense and care we have been perpetually kept in."

"Ah, the wisest plan, as I was not long since observing no Mowbray," said Sir Harry Spangle. "But how glad I am that fortune should cause us to meet in this singular manner."

"You are still our friends?" hastily asked Ravensford, looking eagerly in the countenances of Spangle and Mowbray.

"Undoubtedly so," replied both of them, in a breath, and in a tone of seriousness, which was enough to convince the anxious questioner of their sincerity.

"And Adder and my poor wife—you have heard nothing of them?" cried Lord Ravensford.

"Nothing, nothing, Ravensford, we regret to say," answered Mowbray, "and by that question, we are apprehensive that you have been equally unsuccessful in your inquiries."

Ravensford groaned, but could not answer.

"Alas! 'tis too true," said Rattleton. "Vain, fruitless, has been our search; we have not been enabled to get the least clue to the retreat of the miscreant Adder, or the fates of the unfortunate Lady Ravensford and her offspring."

"Hope is at an end," groaned Ravensford, in a tone of the most impressive despair; "my poor wife—my beauteous boy—are lost to me for ever!"

"Nay, nay," remonstrated Spangle, in more serious accents than he had before been known to assume; "do not give way to despair; I cannot persuade myself but that you will have them restored to your arms."

"But how?" cried Lord Ravensford, wildly —"under what horrible circumstances? As the degraded victim of the brutality of that worse than savage? Oh, no! I shall never behold either of them again! My poor Rosabelle could never survive the shame. Oh, God! it is wonderful that I have so long retained my senses under this heavy, this unparalleled trial!"

He covered his face with his hands, and unable to control his feelings, he sobbed like a child, and was for some time completely deaf to the expostulations and remonstrances of Rattleton and the two others.

"Many, many weary miles have we traversed in vain," at length said Ravensford, in a tone of calm and settled despair; "sometimes elated with hopes that were fated never to be realised. No tidings have we been enabled to gain of them; and had it not been for my friend, my more than brother, Rattleton, I am certain I should, in the moments of my frenzy, long since have laid violent hands upon myself."

"But I trust, my lord, that you are reserved for a much happier fate," observed Spangle.

"Oh, yes," added Mowbray, "it is never too late to improve."

"And whither have you come from now?" inquired Spangle of Rattleton.

"From Dover," replied the latter. "After the unfortunate rencontre with the ill-fated and misguided Lord Saunier, the particulars of which you have, doubtless, heard, we left France with all possible despatch, and have since been travelling about in various parts of the Continent, with the hope of gaining some intelligence of Lady Ravensford and her child, and to avoid the myrmidons of the law. I need not repeat how unsuccessful have been our efforts, and that we are now on our return to Holly Hall. But have you also, my friends, according to your promises, persevered in your inquiries since our last meeting?"

"We have, indeed," replied Sir Harry Spangle; "we have been most indefatigable."

And so they really had.

"And your endeavours have all been futile?" asked Mr. Rattleton.

Spangle and Mowbray, with looks of regret, replied in the affirmative.

Lord Ravensford again groaned in the intense agony of his feelings.

"There is no hope," he cried; "alas! it is enough to make one arraign the mercy of the Almighty, who seems at times to further the ends of villany. Oh, Rosabelle!—oh, my poor child!"

"Courage, courage, Ravensford," ejaculated Rattleton; happiness may dawn upon you when least expected."

"Happiness!" cried Ravensford; "oh, what happiness can ever again be mine? Consider the months that my wife has been torn from me, and think you it is at all likely that the miscreant Adder would suffer such a time to elapse without enforcing the consummation of his diabolical designs?"

Rattleton and the others were unable to return any suitable reply to this, and Ravensford again indulged in the violence of his grief.

"And have you heard anything from the hall, lately?" asked Rattleton of Spangle and his friend.

"We have," replied Spangle, "but I am sorry to inform you that no change for the better has taken place. Mr. Montalbert remains in the same lamentable condition as at first, and they have alike been unsuccessful in their endeavours to gain intelligence of Lady Ravensford and her child."

"I thought so; my worst fears apprehended as much," sighed Lord Ravensford. "Oh, despair, despair!"

"But are you going so remain here?" inquired Rattleton.

"For two or three days," replied Mowbray, "at the furthest."

"When we had intended to go to Holly Hall," added Spangle.

"For what purpose?" eagerly asked Rattleton.

"To consult with Mr. Goodman."

"Oh! upon what subject?"

Spangle in a few words explained himself, and the ideas that had suggested themselves to his mind.

Ravensford and his friend appeared to catch at them with avidity, and for a moment an expression of hope passed over the countenance of the former, which, however quickly vanished.

"Ah! that Monckton," exclaimed his lordship; "I have heard of him. But are you certain that he and Adder are connected?"

"I am positive that they have been connected in former transactions," replied Spangle, "and it appears to me not at all improbable that he would employ him to assist him in the present stratagem, in preference to any other person."

"Certainly," coincided Rattleton; "nothing can appear more reasonable. We must see this smuggler-captain."

"But how—where?" demanded Lord Ravensford.

"That must be decided by after and more mature consideration," answered Rattleton; "but see him we must at all hazards."

Lord Ravensford shook his head, still despairingly.

"There is nothing to be done without perseverance," observed Rattleton, "and I myself will undertake to devise some means of obtaining an interview with Captain Monckton; and if his character is drawn correctly, although his calling is a lawless one, should he really possess the knowledge we suspect he does, I do not despair of being able to pursuade him to confide it to me. At any rate, trial shall be made."

Ravensford pressed the hand of his dearest friend in gratitude and silence, but his looks spoke more, far more than any language could possibly have done.

"But where is he to be found?" at length said Ravensford; "alas! what is the use of encouraging hopes of accomplishing that which appears to me to be entirely impracticable?"

"Not so," replied Spangle; "I think it is quite practicable, and I am only sorry that the thought did not suggest itself to me before. I knew one of the smuggler's crew, for he was formerly a domestic in my family, and from him I learned that Monckton's principal retreat was somewhere near the Island of Guernsey."

"Thither, then," cried Rattleton, eagerly, "I will repair without any further delay, after we have been to Holly Hall."

"And my friend and myself will rejoin you at the latter place, in a day or two," observed Spangle, "and, if it be agreeable, will accompany you. What say you, Mowbray?"

"Why," answered Captain Mowbray, "that I am as willing as yourself."

"Thanks—thanks, my friends," said Rattleton; "depend upon it your kindness will never be forgotten by either me or Lord Ravensford."

"I also must accompany you," said Ravensford; "on such an important errand, I must certainly be one of your party."

"Of course," said Rattleton, "I cannot compel your lordship not to do so; but as a friend, I would advise you to remain at the hall while we prosecute our inquiries."

"Oh, no," impatiently ejaculated his lordship.

"You require rest after the many fatigues you have for the last few months undergone," observed Rattleton.

"And think you I could rest, Rattleton, in so dreadful a state of suspense and mingled hope, uncertainty, and despair?" demanded Ravensford. "Oh, no—no, I am certain that I should go mad."

"Well—well, be it as you desire," observed Rattleton, "although I would much rather that you would yield to my advice."

"I thank you heartily all the same," said his lordship, "but my mind is already made up. And should we see this Monckton, and I feel convinced that he possesses some knowledge of the place where my poor wife and child are concealed, should he refuse to comply with our wishes, by Heaven, I will force the secret from his heart, even though I perish in the effort."

"Such desperate measures would, I am convinced, be useless, and I trust there will be no necessity for adopting them," remarked Spangle.

"A liberal reward would probably effect all that you wish," said Mowbray.

"Reward!" cried Ravensford; "by all my hopes of eternity, I would not think the sacrifice of all I possess too great a price to gain the restoration of my wife and child. Without them, of what value is fortune, life, anything to me?"

"In a short time, then," said Rattleton, speaking to Sir Harry Spangle, "we shall meet again at Holly Hall?"

"In three days at the latest," replied the latter.

"Do not delay it longer," added Rattleton, "for we shall be most anxious to depart."

"We shall be punctual," answered both Spangle and Mowbray together.

"But what about this affair of the duel?" asked the latter.

"We shall surrender to the magistrates immediately on our return to Holly Hall," answered Rattleton, "and put in bail for our future appearance to take our trial."

"Exactly," observed Sir Harry Spangle; "that is just what I imagined. You have no other course."

"None that I can see," rejoined Mowbray.

"And now," remarked Rattleton, rising, "we must part; for the coach is waiting to resume its journey. We preferred travelling by the mail, thinking we were not so likely to be suspected, and not wishing to be taken until after we had reached Holly Hall."

At this moment the guard entered the room to announce to the travellers that the coach was ready to start, and Rattleton having received a repetition of Mowbray and Spangle's promises to be with them punctually in three days at Holly Hall, the two former left the room.

Rattleton had already resumed his seat in the vehicle, and Ravensford was about to follow him, when he observed a post-chaise drawn up to the door of the inn, towards which his attention and curiosity were attracted, although from what motive he could not form the slightest conjecture.

Directly afterwards the postilion let down the steps of the vehicle, and a female, leading a child by the hand, issued from the inn, and approached the chaise, close to which Ravensford was standing.

The lady turned her head, and his eyes fell upon her countenance.

"Gracious Heaven!" he almost shrieked; "is this some beauteous vision got up to torture me to madness? Rosabelle—Rosabelle! My child—my cherub boy! Ha! ha! ha!"

A wild shriek answered him!—It was no delusion! He sprang forward with delirious speed, just time enough to clasp the fainting form of his long-lost wife in his arms.

———

CHAPTER XL.

THE JOURNEY COMPLETED.—ARRIVAL AT THE HALL.—THE MEETING OF FRIENDS.—THE MANIAC FATHER.

How shall our weak pen essay the task to describe the scene which followed this strange, this unexpected meeting? The very inn at which our heroine and her child had stopped, was the place to which her husband and Rattleton were led, and where the scene and the dialogue took place which we have described at such length in the previous chapter.

Insensible, Lady Rosabelle was re-conveyed to the apartment in the inn which she had just before quitted, whither her husband followed, and could not be persuaded to leave her sight for an instant.

Again and again he enfolded his wife and beauteous offspring in his arms; pressed warm kisses on their lips, their cheeks, their temples, and laughed and wept like a child, by turns. Then he threw himself upon his knees; clasped his hands vehemently together, and poured forth an eloquent prayer to the Most High.

Rattleton began to entertain a fear that the sudden surprise, and so powerful a shock as it must be to his feelings, would have a fatal effect upon his senses; and he did all that he possibly could to calm his emotions.

His efforts were, however, for some time unavailing, but at length he became more tranquillised, and resigning Rosabelle to the care of the persons who had been called in to attend her, he sank into a chair, and covering his face with his hands, gave full vent to the emotions that overflowed his heart, in a copious flood of tears.

Rattleton in this did not attempt to interrupt him, for he well knew what a relief it would be to him, and he turned his eyes from Ravensford to watch the progress which was being made towards the recovery of Lady Rosabelle.

His joy was scarcely less than that of Ravensford, although it did not exhibit itself in so violent a manner, and his heart teemed with gratitude to the Almighty, who had brought about their restoration to each other in so miraculous a manner.

It was not long before Lady Ravensford was restored to animation; and looking eagerly around her, she exclaimed—

"Where is he?—Was it a dream?—Oh, where is my husband?"

"He is here, my love—my long lost one—my only earthly hope!" cried Ravensford, and again they were enfolded to each other's hearts, while further utterance was denied them by the power of their emotions.

We must hastily draw a veil over that scene, which the imagination of our readers can depicture far better than any language of ours, however powerful, could describe it.

Those moments were a foretaste of Heaven, succeeding the torment of purgatory! Their ecstasy was so great, that they could scarcely believe the evidence of their senses. It was some time ere they could satisfy themselves that they spoke, they breathed, or that they were still inhabitants of this sublunary scene!

But when, by the joint efforts of Rattleton and Mowbray, and Spangle, (who, having heard of the extraordinary occurrence, had hastened to the apartment,) they became more tranquillised, the scene which followed was affecting in the extreme. The mother, father, and child were locked in one fond embrace, and mingled their tears and sighs of thanksgiving together.

The post-chaise was discharged for a few hours, as they would not yet be sufficiently composed to resume their journey to that home in which they had not together met for so long a period, and where they had never expected to meet again; and Rattleton and the others, after a short time, left them to themselves, to enter into that mutual explanation they were each so anxious to obtain.

With what feelings of horror, disgust, and indignation, did Lord Ravensford listen to the recital of his wife, but how did his heart overflow with gratitude, when he heard of the manner in which Rosabelle had been enabled to resist the diabolical attempts and importunities of the villain Adder; and as he pressed her to his heart, he again poured forth his thanks to the Almighty for her preservation from such accumulated and fearful dangers.

"The monster! the fiend!—for he cannot be anything human, although he bears the form of man," cried Ravensford, speaking of Adder;

"oh, how I regret that he has been suffered to escape my vengeance !"

"But he will not that of Heaven, my husband !" ejaculated Lady Ravensford ; oh, most assuredly that will ere long overtake him in its most terrible form, for the many, the almost unequalled crimes of which he has been guilty !"

"True, my love," returned her husband— and his eyes sparkled with rapture as he gazed upon that dear countenance he had never expected to behold again ; "and oh ! if ever atrocity deserved punishment, dreadful will be his doom. To concoct so infernal a plot, by which he not only tore you from my arms, and deprived me of my offspring, but actually to cause me to suspect your truth ! Oh, Rosabelle, you can never forgive me for entertaining that cruel suspicion !"

Rosabelle smiled beautifully through her tears, and throwing her fair arms around the neck of her husband, the kisses she so fervently pressed upon his lips convinced him more powerfully of her pardon than she could have conveyed to him in the most powerful language.

"Say no more upon that painful subject, my dearest Alfred," she ejaculated. "Let it from this joyful moment be for ever buried in oblivion."

"It shall—it shall, my sweetest," replied Ravensford. "But oh ! what a debt of gratitude do I owe to your generous preserver, Archibald Malcolm, or Captain Monckton, as he thinks proper to call himself. Would that I could see him, that I might to himself express the power of my feelings. Nothing can ever sufficiently reward that man for the inestimable service he has rendered me."

"I need not assure you, Alfred," rejoined Lady Rosabelle, "that I most warmly concur in your feelings ; and I trust that at some future period Monckton may be able to visit us, and receive the demonstrations of our mutual gratitude, and, moreover, be persuaded to quit the life he is at present leading, for that society of which he is formed, by intrinsic accomplishments, to become a bright ornament."

"Pity it is, that he should, by some cursed fatality urging him to crime, be driven from it," observed Ravensford, "but I dare say that his offences have never been so heinous as to exclude him from all hope of earthly pardon."

"No, I cannot believe that they have," replied Lady Ravensford ; "but he is so much attached to his present wild life of freedom, and his associates, that I am doubtful whether he will ever he induced to abandon them."

"My influence and exertions to induce him to do so, shall not be wanting," said Ravensford. "Still, I am sorry that he should have changed his first determination, namely to deliver the wretch Adder into the hands of justice. While I know that villain to be living, and still at large, my mind cannot be entirely at rest ; for however watchful and vigilant we may be, after what we have already so fearfully experienced from his villanous artifices, have we not reason to fear that he will devise some means of further annoying us, and gratifying his demoniacal revenge ?"

"Do not, I beg of you, my love," said our heroine, "harass your mind by groundless apprehensions. Adder is left entirely at the mercy of Monckton, my preserver ; his crimes have rendered his life forfeited to the offended laws of his country, and I, therefore, feel convinced that he will not venture to return to England again."

"Heaven grant that your surmises may prove correct, Rosabelle," observed Ravensford ; "but I candidly own that I cannot entirely divest my mind of the fears which I have described ; and should anything happen again to you, my love, or our lovely child, all my manly fortitude would entirely forsake me, and I should never be able to survive the shock !"

"Pray, Ravensford," urged Rosabelle, "if you would not make me miserable, endeavour, struggle to banish such gloomy thoughts from your bosom, and trust to the goodness of Providence, which has hitherto so mercifully preserved us, when the darkest snares of villany sought to ruin and destroy us."

"For your sake, my love, my Rosabelle," replied her husband, once more affectionately kissing her cheek, "I will endeavour to do so ; but still you surely will not blame me for not placing too much confidence in our security, which might prevent me from being watchful and wary to defeat any base plans that might be devised against our future peace ?"

"Oh, no, Alfred," returned our heroine, "in that you will only act with prudence and wisdom, although, I must repeat, that I sincerely trust there will not be found any necessity for that precaution. But my poor father— what of him ? How has he supported my loss ? You have not told me ! Ah, your silence—the alteration in your looks convince me that my worst fears are verified. But speak—speak— let me know every particular ! I am prepared to hear all—everything."

"Oh, my love," ejaculated Ravensford, "would that Heaven had spared me that painful task ; but pray be calm and hear the melancholy intelligence I have to give you with fortitude and resignation."

"Speak on, speak on, I am prepared for the worst," ejaculated our heroine ; "I know what you would say. My poor father !"

"Need I then say more ?" rejoined her husband ; "I see that you perfectly understand me, my beloved Rosabelle : he is all that your worst fears apprehend him to be."

"The poor grey-headed old man," cried

Rosabelle, with the most powerful emotion; "this—this indeed is a terrible affliction! Heaven save him, for much I fear that mortal d cannot !"

She was unable to conquer her feelings, and Lord Ravensford, knowing that it would relieve her heavily surcharged heart, did not attempt to interrupt her.

At length she became more tranquillised, and she then requested her husband to make her acquainted with the circumstances that had happened to him since they had last met, and by what singular event he was conducted by the will of Providence to the very inn at which she had only stopped through pure accident——

namely, through the postilion mistaking his way in the wood.

This was a task from which her husband shrunk with dread, for he well knew what anguish it would cause his wife to hear the different sufferings he had endured since their separation, and the awkward dilemma in which he was placed, through his fatal duel with the ill-fated Lord Saunter.

She noticed the reluctance with which he complied with her request, and that made her only the more urgent.

At length, after much hesitation, Lord Ravensford complied with the wishes of our heroine, passing over the troubles he had

MONCKTON RESCUES ROSABELLE FROM ADDER, DISGUISED AS A NEGRO.

undergone as lightly as possible. But when he came to the account of his meeting with the unfortunate Saunter, and the duel which had taken place between them, and in which that misguided young nobleman lost his life, the mental agony of Rosabelle evinced itself in the most powerful manner, and occasioned Ravensford considerable alarm.

It was some time before he could any way succeed in pacifying her, and even then she stifled the expression of her feelings because she would not add to his anguish.

"Oh, Alfred, Alfred !" at last she observed, "would to Heaven that you had been spared the perpetration of that crime !"

"Crime, Rosabelle !" repeated Ravensford, with a look of astonishment ; "call you that a crime to which I was urged in defence of your

honour, and the many injuries we had received ? Had I not a right to seek for satisfaction ?"

"Satisfaction !" reiterated Rosabelle; "oh, how I hate that word ! Alas ! Ravensford, I cannot see anything which can be offered in defence of duelling. After all, it is but another name for deliberate murder."

"Rosabelle ! Rosabelle !" exclaimed her agonized husband ; "you surely cannot know what you are saying. Your words will drive me to madness."

"Would to Heaven that you had not shed the blood of that unfortunate nobleman," sighed Lady Ravensford.

"Rosabelle," returned her husband, "and do you then blame me for doing that to which I was prompted by my affection for you ? Do you attempt to defend Saunter's conduct ?"

No. 4.

"Ravensford!" solemnly ejaculated our heroine, and she fixed a look of bitter reproach upon her husband; "surely my ears deceive me? I cannot—I cannot believe it was my husband who made use of that cruel, that unjust observation."

"Oh, forgive me—forgive me, Rosabelle!" implored her husband; "I know not scarcely what I am saying, my mind is so bewildered with the mingled feelings of joy and sorrow, hope and fear. Pardon my observations, I entreat you."

A fervent kiss sealed his pardon.

"But oh, Alfred,' exclaimed Rosabelle, in the most melancholy accents, "how do I tremble for the alarming situation in which yourself and your devoted friend, Mr. Rattleton, are placed. Should the jury on your trial——'

"For Heaven's sake, Rosabelle," interrupted Ravensford, "do not thus give way to despair and apprehension, or you will unman me. Indeed I do not fear the result of the trial, which, if the jury are impartial, must terminate in our favour."

Lady Ravensford clasped her hands together, and raised her eyes towards Heaven, as she fervently expressed a wish that the sanguine anticipations of her husband would be realised, and then a silence of a few moments succeeded.

"We will drop this painful subject for the present, my love," at length said Lord Ravensford; "let me beg of you to try to compose yourself, and to prepare for the melancholy meeting which will shortly take place between you and your unfortunate father."

Rosabelle hastily wiped away the tears that had trembled on her eyelids, and with an air of calmness which astonished her husband, she replied—

"I shall meet the poor old man with firmness; it is the will of the Almighty to visit him with this terrible affliction, and that will what erring mortal shall dare question?"

Ravensford pressed her to his bosom without making any reply, and for some time they gave full vent to their powerful emotions of ecstacy and gratitude in silence.

In this manner the morning passed away, and by the arrival of the afternoon, Lord and Lady Ravensford found themselves sufficiently composed to resume their journey, and, accompanied by Rattleton, they stepped into the post-chaise, after bidding Sir Harry Spangle and Captain Mowbray adieu, and inviting them to Holly Hall at the time they had previously promised to be there, and the vehicle was driven off.

After their departure, Spangle and Mowbray aroused their sleeping companions, and persuaded them to go to bed for a few hours to recover themselves, whilst they, in preference, took a stroll into the fields, not doubting but the fresh air would blow away, as it had always done before, all effects of their last night's debauch.

As the vehicle which was conveying them to Holly Hall proceeded on its way, Lord Ravensford and Rattleton exerted themselves to the utmost to compose the feelings of Lady Rosabelle, and to prepare her for the melancholy meeting with Mr. Montalbert, and she appeared to be pacified and calm, although, at the same time, her heart was nearly bursting when she thought of the awful situation of that good old man.

And not the least agonising to her feelings was the danger and trouble to which her husband and his attached friend, Rattleton, had exposed themselves by the fatal duel with the unfortunate Lord Saunter; and although she despised that thoughtless nobleman for his numerous vices, she must have suffered her gentle nature to lament his fate, if even it had been inflicted by any other hands than those of her husband.

Frequently she could not help fearing that the trial would not terminate with so favourable a result as they appeared to anticipate; and conflicting thoughts, doubts, and apprehensions would, in spite of her efforts to the contrary, and to conceal her emotions from the observation of Lord Ravensford and Rattleton, distract her mind, which was susceptible to the most tender feelings of pity, no matter who the persons were that excited it, or under what circumstances it was drawn forth.

Nothing worthy of particular notice occurred to the travellers until they had arrived within two stages of the termination of their journey, when they stopped at an hotel for a short time, Rosabelle feeling rather unwell, and having a wish to be left alone for about an hour, so that she might sufficiently collect her thoughts and tranquillise her feelings for the approaching interview.

Our heroine, with the little Alfred, were shown into a private room, and Lord Ravensford and Rattleton entered a parlour to refresh themselves during her temporary absence.

Lady Rosabelle had not long retired, and was absorbed in deep thought, when she was suddenly aroused by a noise which proceeded from below, and immediately afterwards, the voice of her husband and Rattleton, speaking in loud tones, met her ears.

A trembling sensation came over her directly and her ready forebodings anticipated that something particular and of a painful nature had happened.

With much anxiety, she took her child by the hand, and opening the chamber door, she listened for a second or so on the landing, in order that she might convince herself she was not mistaken.

She was quickly assured that what she had at first surmised was correct, and that it was

Lord Ravensford and his friend who were speaking, and that, from the loud accents in which they gave utterance to their observations, something of an unusual description had taken place to excite them.

She waited no more, but descended the stairs as precipitately as she could, and entered the parlour, the room door of which was standing wide open.

The worst fears she had entertained rushed more forcibly to her mind than before, when she beheld her husband and Rattleton standing between two men, the staves in whose hands quickly informed her that they were officers.

She no sooner saw them, then, uttering a loud cry of terror, she immediately sank upon the floor insensible.

Ravensford raised her in his arms and summoned assistance.

" I wish you had proceeded less abruptly about your errand," he observed, addressing himself to the men; " however, I must request that you will wait until Lady Ravensford has somewhat recovered from her alarm, when we will accompany you without any further delay."

" Oh, very well, my lord," replied one of the men civilly, " we are in no particular hurry, and, of course, neither you nor this gentleman will attempt to make any resistance. We are only doing our duty, and I am very sorry we happened to be near this spot, and to see you when you arrived at this hotel. But, in course, it cannot be helped now, my lord."

" Certainly not," replied Ravensford, " and we do not blame you; but I regret that you did see us, for it was our intention, after we had been to Holly Hall, to surrender ourselves to the magistrate."

It was some considerable time ere they could succeed in restoring Lady Ravensford to animation, and the men having in the mean time retired outside the door, she looked around, and then eagerly demanded—

" Ah! where are they? Have they gone? or was it only a dream?"

" Compose yourself, my love," said Ravensford, " there is not so much danger to apprehend as you imagine, believe me. You and Alfred remain here while I and Rattleton accompany the officers to the magistrate's, where, on our putting in bail, we shall, no doubt, be immediately liberated, and will return to you with all possible speed."

Lady Rosabelle, by a powerful effort, was enabled greatly to appease her agitation, and made answer—

" Be it so, Ravensford; but oh, do not, for Heaven's sake, keep me long waiting, for the suspense will be worse than death even."

" Depend upon us, my dear Rosabelle," returned her husband, " and pray keep up your spirits while we are gone. This unpleasant affair will, I daresay, soon be satisfactorily arranged,"

He kissed the pale cheeks of Rosabelle, and embraced her tenderly as he spoke, and then resigning her unto the care of the female servants, he and Rattleton followed the officers out, and stepping into the vehicle which was standing at the door, they were driven off with all possible dispatch towards the house of the magistrate.

We need not describe the state of mind in which they left our heroine. One moment she was bordering upon distraction, and the next she was comparatively tranquil, and looked forward with sanguine hope towards their quick return.

A strange and painful fatality seemed to attend their journey, and it appeared as if they were never destined to reach Holly Hall.

So many painful and trying events occurring so quick after one another had completely exhausted her patience, and worn her mind out, and it was not without considerable difficulty that she was enabled to sustain herself.

She walked frequently to the window of the room in which she was staying, and which looked upon the high road, in the hope to see them coming; but she was for some time to be disappointed, until her suspense became almost completely insupportable.

An hour and a half past in this manner, and Lady Ravensford had just made up her mind to hasten herself to the house of the magistrate which was no great distance from the hotel, and ascertain the result of Ravensford and, Rattleton's examination, when she heard the sound of the wheels of the post-chaise, and hurrying to the window, to her most unspeakable delight, beheld her husband and his friend alight from the vehicle.

As quick as her footsteps would carry her, she rushed down the stairs, and threw herself into the arms of Ravensford, who had hastened to meet her.

They had been very well received by the magistrate, and who had suffered them to depart upon their own recognizances, holding out to them, at the same time, every hope of a favourable termination of the unpleasant affair.

They did not now delay any longer than was absolutely necessary to recover themselves from the agitation and confusion into which this unexpected circumstance had naturally thrown them, and then once more stepping into the post-chaise, they, for the last time, resumed their journey.

But little conversation passed between them after leaving the hotel, and at length the neighbourhood in which Holly Hall was situated, burst upon their sight.

What powerful sensations of unspeakable delight rushed through the veins of Lady

Ravensford, and monopolized every feeling of her heart, when those scenes which she had never expected to behold again, once more burst upon her vision. The tumult of rapturous and conflicting ideas that darted to her brain were almost overwhelming, and, although her tongue was eager to give expression to her sentiments, the strength of her emotions would not permit her to give utterance to a single syllable. She looked in the countenance of her husband with an expression of the most unbounded affection and delight, and she could easily perceive that he fully reciprocated her feelings. Tears started to his eyes, and taking her hand he pressed it to his lips with eloquent silence.

Not the slightest change seemed to have taken place in everything upon which the eyes of our heroine rested, since last she had gazed upon those well known scenes. The bright beams of a silvery moon were shining serenely upon everything around, and a melancholy silence, so consonant with her own state of mind, prevailed. But alas! she reflected, what a change had taken place in the home of her childhood! That home which had once abounded with every happiness that the human mind could wish for, was now the abode of sorrow; that fond parent, whose every joy and hope were centred in her, was a raving maniac, and would be insensible to the felicity of her restoration to his arms.

This last thought was too afflicting for endurance, and overcome by her emotions, she leant her head upon the bosom of her husband, and burst into an hysterical flood of tears.

In vain did Ravensford endeavour to tranquillise her feelings; he felt how powerful was the cause she had for sorrow, and the anguish he endured was scarcely less than her own.

Rattleton exerted himself to the utmost to calm the feelings of them both, and he at length succeeded.

Ravensford, we should have mentioned before, had taken the precaution at the hotel at which they had last stopped, to send forward a person to Holly Hall with a letter to Mr. Goodman and his daughter, making them briefly acquainted with the fortunate meeting which had taken place between him and our heroine, and of their coming, so that the surprise might not be too sudden for them; and he was, therefore, fully aware that they would exert themselves to the utmost to meet the unexpected pleasure which awaited them; the more especially as the precarious and lamentable situation of Mr. Montalbert rendered the greatest care necessary.

At length the elegant, but unostentatious, mansion of Holly Hall, burst upon their vision, and Providence imbued the mind of Rosabelle with a calm feeling of joy, which she had never experienced before. Everything seemed to dance before her eyes to welcome her return to that once happy home, and the wheels of the post-chaise appeared to revolve with the most tedious slowness, as they rolled along the road, which led to the lofty garden gates.

They reached those gates; they were already open, and standing to receive them were two beings endeared to them by every affectionate and grateful feeling. Our heroine uttered an indescribable exclamation of joy, and bounding from the vehicle, was locked alternately in the arms of her dear Emily and Mr. Goodman!

Let not the too presumptuous pen attempt to describe the scene which followed; language is by far too weak to convey any idea of it! Tears, sobs, and broken sentences of unbounded transport, burst from the overcharged bosom of each individual; and then Rosabelle felt herself and her child led along the avenue which conducted to the hall.

Although her eyes were dimmed by tears, and her thoughts were so fully occupied, our heroine could yet behold several of the old domestics standing in the path, who, as she passed, raised their hands and eyes towards Heaven, and gave utterance to their simple, but forcible, exclamations of gratitude to the Most High for the restoration of their "dear young lady" to her home and friends.

Another moment, and Lady Ravensford found herself in the well known parlour, endeared to her by so many fond remembrances and associations; and sinking on her knees, she clasped her hands fervently towards Heaven, and gave full vent to the expression of her ardent and spontaneous ejaculations of thanksgiving to the Almighty disposer of all events for her deliverance.

No one offered to interrupt her, they were all too much occupied with the feelings of astonishment and unspeakable delight that filled their bosoms. But at length, Rosabelle having ended her solemn prayer, suddenly arose from her knees, and looking eagerly around the room, she said—

"But where is he?—He is not here!—Where is the poor old man?—Why is he not present to snatch his unfortunate daughter once more to his heart, and weep his tears of joy upon her bosom?—My father—my poor dear father; where is he?"

"My dear Lady Ravensford," replied Mr. Goodman; "I can fully appreciate the anxiety of your feelings; but pray endeavour to restrain them. Your father has retired to his chamber and sleeps—do not disturb him lest——"

"And think you," interrupted our heroine, with the most violent emotion depicted in her countenance; "think you that I can rest calmly one moment without beholding that unfortunate, that doating parent, from whom I have been so long and so cruelly separated?

No—no—no—I will go to him; not an instant——"

"Well, well, be it so," returned Mr. Goodman, reluctantly; "but suffer me again to advise you to endeavour to restrain the expression of your feelings, and not to wake him, lest the sudden shock should prove fatal to the unfortunate gentleman."

Rosabelle heard not the latter part of the speech of Mr. Goodman, for she had moved towards the door. Ravensford hastened to her support, and the others followed, in the most fearful silence.

Quickly up the stairs which led to the well known chamber of her father, our heroine bounded, but when she arrived at the door, she paused; a death-like faintness came over her, she breathed short, and she was unable to move a step further.

Lord Ravensford and the others entreated her to return to the parlour, and defer the trying scene till the morning, but she answered them by a look which fully convinced them of her determination, and they therefore desisted.

In a few moments she partially recovered herself, but still she had not sufficient courage or resolution to enter the chamber.

She stood and listened, supported by the arm of her husband, and her ears caught the sound of the heavy breathing of the patient, every respiration going to her heart like a stream of fire.

In a moment the breathing sounds ceased, and all was still as death.

"He sleeps," said Mr. Goodman; "he sleeps, and probably dreams of her who ——"

"Hark! hark!" hastily interrupted our heroine; "those sounds—do listen; those words—those words—my heart will burst!"

They listened with breathless attention, and Lord Ravensford supported the form of his wife, in a state of agony too powerful for description. In low and plaintive tones, sufficient to draw tears from the eyes of the most insensible individual, the unfortunate Mr. Montalbert was singing, apparently in his sleep, the words of that song Rosabelle had so often sung to please him, and which brought to the memory so many powerful and agonising recollections.

"Oh, never could that darling child
Her aged parent loved so dear,
Cause in his cheek the blush of shame,
Or in his eye excite a tear.
A comfort to his old grey hairs,
A solace in his hours of woe,
Woe brought not on by sin of hers,
Could she e'er grieve his heart?—ah, no!'

"God! God! support me!" gasped forth Rosabelle, clinging to the arm of her husband, and her whole frame convulsed with anguish.

A wild laugh, which also proceeded from the chamber of Mr. Montalbert, smote their ears, and a dismal silence again succeeded. It

was, however, only brief, and then the poor maniac was heard singing—

"Green is the turf that wraps her head,
She calmly sleeps in death;
But roses mark the cold—cold bed,
And——"

"Father! father! dear, dear father! I can hear no more!" cried Rosabelle; and tearing herself from the hold of Ravensford, she rushed into the chamber, and darted to the side of the bed.

Mr. Montalbert was sitting up in the bed when Rosabelle entered the room, and was staring vacantly around him. His countenance had undergone little or no perceptible change, the ruddy glow of health was on his cheek, and so calm and serene was its expression, that it seemed almost impossible that his mind could be in the deplorable condition in which it was.

On beholding Rosabelle and the others enter, he exhibited little emotion; but when his eyes rested upon the former, a sweet smile irradiated his features, and laughing with all the joyousness of a child, he exclaimed—

"Beautiful!—oh, how beautiful!—what a bright and lovely vision!—Her very self!—So like her! But 'tis only fancy—only fancy—Ha! ha! ha! How beautiful!"

"Father! father!—dear, dear father!—Do you not know me?—Oh, God! what a bitter trial is this!" frantically sobbed forth the distracted Rosabelle, as she threw her arms round the poor old man's neck, and pressed warm and delirious kisses upon his lips.

The poor maniac looked at his offspring for a moment steadfastly; her heart beat against her side with almost insufferable violence, for the light of reason and recollection for an instant seemed to beam in that glance; he parted the hair from her forehead—patted her cheeks with his hands, like a playful child, and then again burst into a wild laugh, and averted his face exclaiming—

"Beautiful!—lovely—very, very lovely—but mockery—cruel mockery all!—she is no more—she is no more—

"Green is the turf that wraps her head,
She calmly sleeps in death;
But roses mark the cold—cold bed,
And——"

He had gradually sunk back on his pillow; with the last word, his eyes closed, and he slept as calmly as the first slumber of infant innocence.

"Almighty God sustain me under this dreadful trial!" ejaculated our heroine; and sinking on the couch of her father, her feelings overpowered her, and she became insensible.

In that condition she was removed from the room, and taken to the parlour they had at short time before quitted, where it was some time ere, with the utmost attention, she could be restored to consciousness.

CHAPTER XLI.

THE DEATH.

WE need not enter minutely into a detail of what took place amongst the friends at Holly Hally, after our heroine had been restored to her senses, the mutual explanations that took place, and the sympathy and terror they experienced in the sufferings that Rosabelle had undergone. These the reader can much better imagine than we can possibly describe them, and therefore it would be a waste of time and space to dilate further upon them.

How much they commended the fortitude of Lady Rosabelle, which had enabled her so successfully to resist the diabolical designs and importunities of the miscreant Adder; and praised the goodness of Providence, which had at last, in so miraculous a manner, brought about her deliverance.

Then their praises were lavished upon Monckton, and Mr. Goodman and his daughter joined the others in expressing the deepest regret that a man evidently so well calculated to become an ornament to society, could not be persuaded to abandon the course of life he was at present pursuing.

One circumstance, however, caused them all the most unbounded pain, not unmingled with the most powerful apprehension; that was, the fatal duel which had taken place between Lord Ravensford and Lord Saunter, and the awkward and alarming predicament in which the former and Rattleton were placed. But Mr. Goodman and Emily stifled their real feelings as much as possible, seeing the anguish it occasioned our heroine, and the deep emotions of regret, anxiety, doubt, and fear that were excited in the mind of Ravensford. They plainly saw that the troubles of the unfortunate nobleman and his wife were far from being at an end, and they saw much more to apprehend from this circumstance than either Ravenford or Rattleton affected to anticipate.

Mr. Goodman severely reprobated the dreadful practice of duelling, so much more common at that period than it is at the present day; and, although he forbore to mention anything to Lord Ravensford, when he was alone with his son-in-law he he did not fail to censure in the most unmeasured terms the misguided impetuosity that led his lordship to imbrue his hands in the blood of that unfortunate young nobleman, whose very ignorance ought to have rendered him an object to be treated rather with pity and contempt, than

to have excited such implacable feelings of revenge in his bosom; when they must both have been fully convinced that Saunter was merely made the dupe of that most consummate and abominable villain, Adder, who had used him as the grand implement to further the nefarious designs he had concocted against the honour of Lady Ravensford and the peace of her family.

Rattleton acknowledged the full force of the reasoning of Mr. Goodman, and felt that he could not offer anything sufficiently forcible in defence of the conduct of himself and Lord Ravensford; he, therefore, contented himself by expressing his deep regret that it should have taken place, and requesting his father-in-law to avoid alluding to the subject in the presence of Lord and Lady Ravensford, as it would only cause them the deepest anguish without effecting any actual good; with which, of course, Mr. Goodman did not hesitate for a moment to comply.

That night Rosabelle slept again, after the lapse of so many months, in her own chamber at Holly Hall. Slept!—ah! no!—her mind was too much tormented by agonising thoughts to suffer her to do so. The deplorable situation of her poor father, of whose recovery there did not now appear to be the slightest hope, kept her waking, and many were the painful thoughts that crowded upon her brain, and the scalding tears of anguish she shed. The melancholy circumstances under which they met; the impressive behaviour, and every word which the unfortunate Mr. Montalbert uttered, came upon her memory in the most vivid colours, and she tossed about in a state of mind which made her look with the utmost anxiety and impatience for the morning.

During the time that Rosabelle had been separated from them in so mysterious and lamentable a manner, we need not say how unremitting were the attentions of Mr. Goodman and his amiable daughter towards the unfortunate Mr. Montalbert. They took up their residence completely at Holly Hall, so that they should be immediately at hand to render him every assistance which his situation might require, and everything which reason could suggest they did not fail to put in practice, with the hope of ameliorating his melancholy malady. But they entirely despaired of his ever being again restored to his senses; and, indeed, the eminent men who attended him gave not the slightest hope of such a circumstance taking place. His faculties were too much impaired to render any chance of his restoration to reason probable.

For the first few weeks after the disappearance of his daughter, Mr. Montalbert was so violent in his raving, that it was found absolutely necessary to keep him under the greatest restraint. At times he became perfectly furious, calling all those who approached him fiends, who had torn from him the prop of his heart, and made a hell of his brain; and even the affectionate attentions and untiring efforts of Rattleton failed to appease him.

It was awful in the extreme to see the wild phrenzy of his looks—to listen to the delirious wanderings of his wrecked mind. How piteously he would call upon the names of Rosabelle and her child, and supplicate the demon his imagination conjured up to restore them to his bosom. Then he would rave of the past, and all the melancholy history of his daughter would be recalled to the memories of the afflicted listeners in the most awful and vivid colours. In such moments as these, to pray that death would terminate his sufferings was a merciful wish; and yet, for him to die without his daughter once more beholding him was too fearful even for contemplation.

At length the extravagance of his malady, if it may be so termed, settled into that calm melancholy state of madness, which, although divested of the more glaring horrors, was scarcely less painful to witness. He would sit for hours playing with those toys which had been got for the amusement of the little Alfred, with all the artless simplicity of a child; and then he would talk in such a melancholy strain of his daughter, that it would have brought tears in the eyes of the most callous and insensible individual. But he was perfectly passive, and as submissive as a child. Emily could do anything with him, and he would frequently kiss her, and call her his dear child, but not her whose tender affections he had once known, and whose cold remains he now imagined to repose in the silent grave; although there were moments when he thought she was not dead, but that she had been again torn from his arms by the cruel arts and persuasions of the seducer.

Such was the dismal account which Mrs. Rattleton and her father were compelled to give to the eager inquiries of Lady Ravensford, and the reader may easily imagine how it wrung her gentle heart.

"Oh, Adder, monstrous villain," she exclaimed, "what hast thou not to answer for in thus destroying that happiness we were at so much pains and anxiety to restore! Curses, remorse, and misery, must surely pursue you as a just punishment for the irreparable wrongs thou hast heaped upon us."

At an early hour on the following morning after their return to Holly Hall, Lady Ravensford and our heroine arose, and descended to the breakfast-room, where they found Mr. Goodman and Mr. and Mrs. Rattleton already awaiting them.

The first eager inquiry of Rosabelle was after her father.

"He has left his chamber, as is his regular custom at this early hour," answered Emily "and is walking in the garden."

"Oh, let me fly to him," exclaimed our heroine, rising from her chair; but Emily gently laid her hand upon her arm, and arrested her purpose.

"Dear Rosabelle," she said, "let me beg of you not to do so. I tremble at the idea of the shock it might be to him. We must use, precaution and stratagem. Do, pray, be persuaded."

Rosabelle yielded.

"Come hither, Rosabelle," said Mrs. Rattleton, advancing to the window; "you can see him here without being observed by him. Poor gentleman, he is standing on his favourite spot; mark him."

With a bursting heart, poor Rosabelle did as Emily requested her, and looked eagerly towards the place to which she pointed.

Mr. Montalbert was standing near a beautiful rose-tree. It was one that had been planted by the hands of Rosabelle. Every now and then he would stoop, and appear to scrutinize every flower with the most enthusiastic admiration; then he would laugh aloud in the wildness of delight, and dance around it with the most extravagant antics. He plucked one rose—it was a white one. He looked at it pensively for a moment or two, then kissing it rapturously, he placed it carefully in his bosom, near his heart, and sighing, turned away, and moved with a slow and solemn step towards the house.

"Let me advise you, my dear Lady Rosabelle, to retire for a few minutes," said Mr. Goodman;—"your meeting with your unfortunate father had better be brought about by degrees."

"Oh, how I long to press the poor old man to my heart," sobbed our heroine; "God! what a terrible fate is mine!"

Accompanied by Lord Ravensford, our heroine retired into an ante-room, and watched the proceedings at the door, which they left ajar for that purpose.

In a moment or two afterwards, Mr. Montalbert entered, and smiling complacently upon the persons present, he took his seat in the arm chair which was placed for him.

With much fearful emotion, our heroine noticed that a remarkable change had came over the countenance of her father since she had seen him the night before. His cheeks were pale, and the expression of his eyes was strangely altered.

With the utmost difficulty she could repress the powerful emotions that rushed to her heart, and she felt as if it were ready to burst.

Mr. Montalbert paused for a moment, then

he removed the rose from his breast, gazed at it intently for a short time; kissed it often, and tears started from his eyes, trickling over the fragile flower.

Neither Mr. Goodman, his daughter, nor her husband, offered to interrupt him, and he took no more notice of them than as if there had not been any one present.

"It is very beautiful," he at length said, in a voice of the most plaintive and impressive melancholy; "it is very beautiful—so pure—so delicate! So, too, was she—but she is in Heaven now!—She was too pure for this earth, and the Almighty snatched her to His own heavenly abode. But yet it was cruel that He did not take her poor old father as well. It was hard to take her from me, and to leave the poor old man alone!—She will never come to me again!—No—no—they said she was not dead—that she had left me—deserted her poor old father. Ha! ha! ha! Liers! knaves!—they cannot make me believe them;—no—no—no—they shall not!—they shall not!—She is in Heaven, poor thing—poor thing. Heigho!—when shall I be with her again?"

"Ravensford, Ravensford," gasped forth our heroine—"can I endure this?—Oh, here's a scene to wring a daughter's heart!"

Ravensford looked at her imploringly, but returned no answer.

A short pause followed, and then Mr. Montalbert looking up at those who surrounded him, said, in the same melancholy accents—

"I had such a sweet vision last night; such a lovely dream;—but it was only a dream, and yet so lovely, that I would—I could have continued dreaming so for ever!—Methought she came to me, looking fair—oh, so fair, that my eyes were dazzled to gaze upon her. I held her in my arms—I parted the silken tresses from her white forehead, and my lips again pressed kisses upon her lips—her cheeks—her temples! But it was only a dream—mockery—cruel mockery all!"

"Father, father, dear, dear father! I am here! I am here!" exclaimed Rosabelle, unable longer to contain herself; and rushing forward, followed by her husband, she threw herself, frantically sobbing, on her knees, clasped the hands of her father vehemently in hers, and looked up in his face with such an expression, that language cannot convey an adequate idea of.

"Father—father!" repeated Mr. Montalbert; "who called me by that name?"

"Thy child!" almost screamed our heroine, "thy child; dost thou not know me, dear father?"

Mr. Montalbert looked at her for a few moments intently, and her heart throbbed with the most dreadful emotion. He parted her hair from her forehead, as he had done the night before, and reason for an instant seemed to light up his eye.

"Dost thou not know me, dear father?" repeated Lady Ravensford;—"look—look, it is no delusion—it is thy daughter,—thy Rosabelle!"

"Ah! 'tis her! 'tis reality!" suddenly cried Mr. Montalbert, in tones that thrilled to the heart;—"a light flashes upon my darkened intellect!—It is my child, my Rosabelle!—Bless, bless her Heaven—oh ——"

The poor old man made an effort to rise from his chair as he spoke, and threw his arms around the neck of his daughter. His head sunk upon her shoulder—one gentle sigh escaped him, such as an infant might breathe in its sleep. With a faint yet fearful cry, Rosabelle looked up and fixed her eager glances upon her father! Horror!—horror!—she gazed upon the pale face of a corpse! The soul of the maniac had departed to its God!

CHAPTER XLII.

THE ATTEMPTED MURDER.

No sooner was our heroine convinced of this melancholy calamity, than all consciousness left her, and after some difficulty in removing her from the corpse of her father, she was conveyed to her chamber, where medical assistance was immediately called in; but for some time her situation was considered most dangerous and hopeless. Hysterical fit followed fit, in rapid succession, and her husband and Emily stood over her couch in the most painful agony, expecting every moment that she would breathe her last.

But at last, by the exertions of the gentlemen who attended her, the alarming symptoms were abated, and Rosabelle was partially recovered, but still she remained in a state of calm insensibility, and could not be restored to a knowledge of what was passing around her. Her mind wandered, and she gave utterance to broken and insane sentences, that were quite distressing to hear.

The whole of that day and night she continued in the same situation, and Ravensford began to apprehend that her senses had fled for ever.

No persuasion could induce him to quit her chamber, and although the paleness of his countenance, his languid eye, and general demeanour, plainly showed the state of mental anguish and illness he was enduring, he was perfectly regardless of himself, in his anxiety for the distress of his unfortunate wife.

Alas! what a dreadful fatality seemed to attend them! No sooner had they escaped from one calamity, than another befel them. It seemed as if they were marked by wayward destiny to be the continued footballs of misfortune, and Ravensford almost despaired of ever enjoying real happiness again.

It was most distressing that this awful event should take place so soon after our heroine's restoration to them and to her home, and he feared that it would be some time before Rosabelle would recover from so fearful a shock as it had proved to her feelings.

Ravensford continued by the bedside of his wife the whole of the night, and paid no attention to the remonstrances of his friends, who would have persuaded him to retire to rest. But his mind was too much distressed to render the idea of sleep at all probable to him.

Towards morning a change came over Lady Ravensford, and she became conscious; but the medical gentlemen strictly enjoined that she should be kept perfectly quite, and, above all, that they should not converse with her upon the subject of her father's death.

Lady Ravensford was now sufficiently composed to reflect calmly upon her melancholy bereavement, and to listen to the consolations offered to her by the affectionate Emily and her father. But so dreadful was the blow and the shock which she had received, that tranquil as she might appear to be, she feared that it would be some time before she would be able to regain her usual composure. Such a loss as she had sustained, she felt, was completely irreparable; and never, never could the memory

THE MYRMIDONS OF ADDER SEIZING UPON LADY RAVENSFORD.

of her father be erased from her thoughts, and the melancholy, the deeply afflicting circumstances under which he had died.

The sudden death of Mr. Montalbert had caused a great excitement in the neighbourhood, and it was a subject for general lamentation; Mr. Montalbert was so generally revered by all who knew him, especially his tenants and dependants, to whom he had ever been a kind and generous benefactor. The distressing circumstances, too, under which Mr. Montalbert had expired, and the troubles which had been brought upon him and his daughter by the unexampled villany of Adder, had caused a greater sensation than probably it would otherwise have done, and great was the commiseration of all who had been made acquainted with the melancholy event.

A day of sorrow in the neighbourhood of Holly Hall was that on which the remains of Montalbert were interred; all business was suspended, and there was scarcely an inhabitant of the place that did not attend the funeral, to pay that respect to the last dismal obsequies of one from whom they had, while living, experienced so much kindness and unwearied philanthropy.

It was a dreadful trial to our heroine, and on her return to the hall, after the remains of Mr. Montalbert were consigned to their final resting-place, her emotions were so powerful, that she was almost reduced to as bad a condition as she had been in immediately after the demise of her father; but by the prompt and assiduous attention of the medical gentlemen, she was quickly recovered, and submitted to the painful bereavement she had experienced with resignation.

It was several weeks, however, before Rosabelle might be said to be restored to anything like tranquillity, or to be able to listen with any degree of patience and attention to the soothings of her dear and anxious friends; and even then it was evident that her mind had received a shock from which she could never decidedly recover, and which would imbue all her future days with a feeling of melancholy, mortal efforts must fail to efface.

A month after the death of her father, a circumstance did take place which afforded her considerable satisfaction and pleasure; this was in the arrival of Mrs. Kitson at the hall, who, having heard of the decease of her parent, by the advice of her husband, who thought that, probably, her humble but honest attentions might tend in no small degree to alleviate her grief, had resolved upon paying our heroine a visit, according to the permission and the warm invitation she had received.

The reception that worthy woman met with from Lady Ravensford must have been highly gratifying to her feelings, and more especially the heartfelt thanks that were so lavishly bestowed upon her by Lord Ravensford and the other persons immediately interested in the circumstances, for her kindness to our heroine and the little Alfred, whilst they were in the power of Adder.

Lord Ravensford was so prepossessed in favour of Mrs. Kitson, that he sincerely pressed her to prolong her stay at Holly Hall as much as she could, and he would have felt highly pleased could she have been prevailed upon to stay there altogether, offering to make every provision for her husband, and to give him a comfortable residence on his estate, and a handsome annuity, if Mrs. Kitson could persuade him to abandon his present course of life, and to settle down into peaceful retirement for the rest of his days. But, grateful as Mrs. Kitson was for the kind and liberal offers of Lord Ravensford, and happy as she would have been to have availed herself of them, she felt certain that it would be useless endeavouring to persuade her husband to accept of them, although she felt certain that he would readily assent to her passing as much of her time as she possibly could with Lady Ravensford.

Mrs. Kitson had no news to impart to our heroine. Captain Monckton had returned safe to the smugglers' place of rendezvous after he had escorted her to G——m, and nothing more had been heard of Adder, so that it was believed he had obeyed the injunctions of the former, and quitted the country, and Mrs. Kitson expressed a hope that all dread of further annoyance was at an end.

Lord Ravensford affected to think so too,

but there were times when his heart had some terrible misgivings, and he regretted that, instead of being set at liberty, the villain Adder had not been delivered into the hands of justice, so that he might have met with that punishment which was so justly his merits; and he determined to be continually upon his guard, to prevent any design that might be formed against them, and to detect Adder, if he should still remain in England, or venture at any future time to return to it.

To appease the feelings of our heroine, however, he kept his suspicions to himself, and seldom alluded to the subject at all.

Among all the persons in the neighbourhood of Holly Hall, who were gratified at the restoration of Lady Ravensford, and who deeply lamented the death of Mr. Montalbert, none were more sincere than Meriel and her husband, and they were frequently admitted to the society of their "dear lady."

The attentions and affections of these honest though humble creatures were most agreeable to the heart of Rosabelle, and, a stranger to pride, she treated them with the same kindness as if they had been her equals. For this she was amply repaid by the integrity of her own thoughts, and the gratitude of those to whom she dispensed her favours.

Rosabelle, as soon as her feelings were sufficiently tranquillised to permit her to do so, had written a most affectionate letter to Mrs. Belgrave, and warmly pressed her to visit her at Holly Hall as soon as she could. To this letter she promptly received an answer, in which, in the most feeling manner, Mrs. Belgrave condoled with her on the heavy and irreparable loss she had sustained by the death of her father, and, after stating that she had been very poorly of late, she promised to avail herself of the kind invitation of her whom she hoped in future to be permitted to consider her dearest friend, as soon as her health would permit her.

Time passed on, and now a period approached in which the anxiety of our heroine and her friends were excited in a most painful degree.

This was the approaching trial of Lord Ravensford and Mr. Rattleton, and it was with the utmost difficulty that they could appease the feelings of our heroine and Mrs. Rattleton sufficiently to enable them to meet the day of trial with anything like fortitude and hope.

The time at length came, and the result was in favour of Ravensford and his friend. The peculiar circumstances under which the duel had been fought, and the exciting events that led to the fatal catastrophe, had their due weight upon the minds of the jurors, and after a very short trial, they were both acquitted, and the suspense and apprehensions of their friends were set rest.

Months elapsed after this, without anything taking place worthy of particular notice, and the grief of our heroine had become greatly ameliorated, which happy circumstance had in a great measure been brought about by the arguments, expostulations, and sympathising advice of Mrs. Belgrave, who had become a visitor at Holly Hall, and had quickly endeared herself to the friendship of all who came in contact with her.

One great consolation to Lady Ravensford was, that her poor father had been restored to reason before his death, and had known her, and given her his blessing; and the certainty that she felt that his soul inhabited those realms of everlasting bliss allotted to those whose time has been passed in that uninterrupted course of virtue and benevolence that had ever distinguished the character of Mr. Montalbert.

A twelvemonth elapsed, and still no circumstance took place worthy of being particularized, and nothing happened to disturb their happiness. Time had served to tranquillise their sorrow, and their days might be said to be passed in one uninterrupted round of serenity and peace.

Monckton had ventured to pay them a visit, in disguise, to Holly Hall, and he was received with all those demonstrations of welcome and gratitude by Lord Ravensford, which the inestimable service he had rendered him entitled him to.

Monckton was evidently gratified at the reception he met with, and received with much kindness the solicitations of Ravensford, that he would abandon his course of life; but he positively declined adopting such a course, which he said he had then become so attached to, that he could not bear to think of retiring from it with any degree of patience.

Ravensford sincerely regretted this determination, for he saw plainly that Monckton was fully deserving of those praises that Rosabelle had bestowed upon him, and notwithstanding the errors of his past life, he would not have hesitated in honouring him with his friendship.

Monckton expressed, in terms that left no doubt of his sincerity, his sorrow at the death of Mr. Montalbert, who had been the generous benefactor of his youth, and again and again gave utterance to his regret at having abused that benevolence.

Lady Rosabelle, according to the instructions which the smuggler-captain had given to her when they last parted, had, after the death of her father, opened the packet which had been entrusted to her care, and found it to contain, as Monckton had informed her, a sum of money amounting to what he had robbed Mr. Montalbert of, and a letter addressed to that gentleman, in which, in eloquent terms, he expressed

his compunction for the act of ingratitude of which he had been guilty, and begged his forgiveness; and she now urged him to receive the money back again, but which no argument or persuasion could induce him to accede to, he considering that she was justly entitled to the money; and, therefore, our heroine was reluctantly compelled to desist from her solicitations.

Monckton promised Ravensford to keep a sharp look out after the villain Adder, and if he should ever encounter him again, to take such steps as would efficiently prevent him from doing further mischief, and then, after remaining at the hall only a few hours, he took his departure.

Every person was charmed with the urbane manners of Mrs. Belgrave; and impressed with the kindness she experienced, she needed but little persuasion to prevail upon her to prolong her visit to the hall for a considerable time after the period she had at first designed.

The circle at Holly Hall was now a most amiable one, and serenity once more alighted upon their bosoms, which they trusted would not again be interrupted; but they were doomed to be disappointed. An event shortly took place which caused them considerable alarm.

Lord Ravensford had been to transact some business at a distant town, and did not return towards Holly Hall until the shades of evening had descended upon the earth, and he was quite unattended.

He had reached a wood within a mile of Holly Hall, and was walking leisurely along, wrapped in thought upon the subject of the business he had been upon, when he was suddenly startled by an authoritative voice commanding him to stop, and looking up, he was not a little astonished and alarmed to behold himself surrounded by four desperate and ruffianly-looking fellows, who were dressed like labourers, and were armed with short sticks.

Ravensford, in an undaunted tone of voice, demanded what they wanted.

"Your money or your life," replied one of the fellows, approaching nearer to his lordship, and flourishing his stick with a menacing air; "you perceive that it would be madness to offer any resistance to us, so deliver up your cash without any bother, and depart about your business."

"Villains!" ejaculated Lord Ravensford, fearlessly; "I am not to be so easily intimidated; so, let me pass on, or you may repent this outrage."

"Oh, oh," exclaimed the ruffian who had before spoken; "that's your temper, is it, my master? Well then, we must e'en convince you of your folly."

With that the fellow aimed a blow at Ravensford, which the latter avoided by stepping aside, and then suddenly closing with the scoundrel, being the stronger man of the two, he succeeded in wresting the stick from him, and felled him to the earth.

This was the signal for an attack from the other ruffians, and they rushed upon his lordship with the utmost ferocity, giving utterance to the most fearful oaths at the same time.

Lord Ravensford fought desperately, and with resolution, and contrived to keep them at bay for a short time ; but he must quickly have been overpowered, had it not been that the heavy tread of some person or persons was heard at that moment approaching the spot, which averted the purpose of the scoundrels, and directed their attention towards the spot from whence the sounds proceeded, and directly afterwards a black man, dressed like a sailor, rushed to the spot, and called loudly upon the fellows to desist.

Seeing there was no more than one, the men were not undaunted, and they renewed their attack, cursing and swearing all the time, whilst the black man fought desperately in defence of Lord Ravensford, and having at length produced a pistol, the fellows became alarmed, and immediately took to flight.

Lord Ravensford then turned to his preserver, and warmly expressed to him his thanks for the great service which he had so opportunely rendered him.

" Do not mention it, sir," replied the man ; " I am very glad to think I was attracted to the spot, or you would have fallen a victim to the baseness of the villains."

Ravensford involuntarily started at the tones of the man's voice, which was remarkably familiar to his ears, and he gazed intently upon him, but he had no recollection of ever having seen him before.

" And pray," inquired Lord Ravensford, " to whom am I so greatly indebted ?"

" Why, your honour," replied the man, " I am only a poor fellow that has suffered shipwreck, and I have been wandering about the country for some days in great distress."

Ravensford placed a purse of money in the man's hands.

" There is a trifle for you, my poor fellow," said he ; " and if you think proper to attend me to Holly Hall, which is not far from this place, I will reward you further."

" Thank your honour, thank you," said the man, in accents of apparent gratitude ; " and since your honour has been so kind, if you please, I will attend you, and perhaps you will favour me with some food and a lodging for the night, for I have travelled many a weary mile to-day, without so much as breaking my fast, and I am, in truth, both hungry, tired, and footsore."

" Follow me, then, my good man," said Lord Ravensford, " and your wants shall be quickly attended to."

The man again expressed his thanks, in tones of apparent sincerity, and hurrying through the wood, it was not long before they arrived at Holly Hall.

The persons at the hall were not a little surprised on beholding the singular companion of Lord Ravensford, who desired the man immediately to betake himself to the servants' hall, and get such refreshments as he required : but when they were made acquainted with the adventure which Ravensford had met with, and the timely assistance which the stranger had so providentially rendered him, and which had, in all probability, saved him from a violent death, their gratitude was unbounded, and they lost no time in expressing their unqualified thanks to the man.

Rosabelle would not rest until she had seen the preserver of her husband, and personally acknowledged the invaluable service he had rendered them.

The man started slightly on beholding our heroine, but no particular notice was taken of that circumstance, but when Rosabelle heard the tones of his voice, she also started, and felt considerable emotion, for, like her husband, she thought she had heard them before, and the idea imparted no very pleasurable sensation to her bosom.

She, however, quickly recovered herself, and was rather astonished at the emotion which she had felt, certain as she was that she and the man could not by any possibility ever have met before. And yet, in spite of the service which the black man had rendered them, there was something in the expression of his features and his eyes which was peculiarly repulsive, and neither Rosabelle nor her husband could look upon him without an unaccountable feeling of uneasiness.

CHAPTER XLIII.

ANOTHER OUTRAGE.

LORD RAVENSFORD, pitying the destitute condition of the man who had preserved him from the ruffianly attacks of the fellows in the wood, and being in want of a domestic, offered him the situation, which he gladly accepted, and with many protestations of gratitude, entered upon his new capacity.

None of his fellow servants, however, liked him, and there was nothing in his general behaviour, which was at all calculated to conciliate their friendship. In his general conduct he was reserved, morose, and haughty, and he seemed to think himself above all the rest of his fellow servants.

There was something, too, in his appearance, which prejudiced Lady Ravensford against him, and she felt an unpleasant sensation steal over her whenever, by chance, they came in contact with each other.

At times he evinced manners that would seem to place him above the sphere of life in which he had moved at the time he encountered Lord Ravensford ; but he quickly appeared to recollect himself, and altered his tones to one of the most humble description.

He pretended to be an African by birth, but he spoke excellent English, which he accounted for by saying that he had been brought away from his native country when a child.

Three months had elapsed since Cæsar (which was the name the black man was known by) had been introduced to Holly Hall, and nothing more particular took place.

This state of happiness, however, was not destined to last long.

Lady Rosabelle had been visiting a village a short distance from the hall, on an office of charity, and had prolonged her stay considerably beyond the time she had at first intended, so that as soon as she had left the village it was twilight, and she was unaccompanied by any one.

Remembering the attack which had recently been made upon her husband, and her way lying through the same wood, she became much alarmed, and increased her speed, anxious to get home, and well knowing how uneasy they would feel at her absence.

It was a fine moonlight night, and the path of our heroine was as perceptible to her as if it had been the noon-day ; but she had not proceeded far, when she was startled by a shrill whistle, and before she had time to look around her, she found herself seized by two men, who were masked, while at the same moment a well-known voice exclaimed :—

"That is her ; away with her—away with her !"

She looked towards the spot from whence the voice proceeded, and to her horror and astonishment beheld standing near her and directing the men, the tall figure of Cæsar the black.

"Release me ! unhand me, ruffians !" screamed our heroine, and then turning to Cæsar, she added :—

"What is the meaning of this ? Villain ! what infamous stratagem hast thou been concocting ?"

"Thou wilt speedily know, lovely Rosabelle," replied the supposed black, in tones that thrilled to the heart of our heroine ;— "thoughtest thou that *Adder* would submit to be foiled so easily ? Ha! ha! ha!— Thou art mine—again securely mine ; nor Heaven nor hell shall again tear thee from me !"

"*Adder !*" screamed our heroine with terror, and now fixing her appalled gaze upon the features of that daring miscreant. "Oh, God! save me! spare me !"

"Away with her! stifle her cries!—We

have not an instant to spare !" cried Adder ; and immediately afterwards Rosabelle felt herself lifted from the ground and borne along with the greatest rapidity.

Overcome by her terrors, she fainted.

CHAPTER XLIV.
THE RESCUE.

OUR heroine, on recovering her senses, to her horror and alarm found herself in a close carriage, seated by the side of the villain Adder, who was still disguised as Cæsar the black man, and in a moment perceiving the danger of her situation, she screamed aloud, hoping that her cries might reach the ears of some of the passengers, and who might be inclined to fly to her rescue.

"Cease, madam," ejaculated Adder, "your cries are in vain, and may only compel me to adopt a course of violence which I have a wish to avoid. Once more I have you in my power ; —it is my last effort, and depend upon it, I will not be easily defeated."

"Lost! lost !" groaned Rosabelle, wringing her hands despairingly ; "oh, villain—miscreant."

Adder smiled exultingly.

"I triumph," he replied—"I triumph, and this time I am determined that I will not let the opportunity pass by of indulging my passions. Doubtless you thought that when the traitor Monckton (against whom I have vowed a terrible revenge) had got me in his power, that it was all over with me, and that I should fear to disobey his injunction. But thou little knewest the resolute character of Adder if thou didst, Ha! ha! ha!—I triumph!—I triumph !"

"Heartless wretch !" ejaculated Lady Ravensford, and fresh confidence beamed in her eyes ; "Heaven surely will defeat thee in thy nefarious purpose. Thy triumph will be brief."

"Ha! ha! ha!" laughed the villain ; "thou little imaginest, fair Lady Rosabelle, how deeply concocted is my plot, and what good cause I have to defy detection. Thou mayest now make up thy mind to have me for thy future partner, for thou wilt never behold Lord Ravensford or thy other friends again."

"Daring miscreant !" cried the distracted Rosabelle, "can nothing shame thee ?"

"No," returned Adder ; "I am callous to the feeling. Ha! ha!! little didst thou imagine that the attack which was made upon thy husband in the wood, was all the stratagem of that man who thou thoughtest was at the present time far away from England. Ha! ha! ha! it was well contrived, and easily have ye all fallen into the snare. Little did ye suspect, any of ye, that in Cæsar the black ye would find your bitterest enemy, Adder."

Lady Ravensford covered her face with her hands, with a sensation of the most unconquerable horror and alarm, and gave utterance to a groan of the deepest mental agony.

Adder threw himself back in the vehicle, folded his arms across his chest, and contemplated the unfortunate victim of his brutal persecution in silence.

All the exultation of the fiend was evidenced in the expression of his features, and they were alone enough to inspire terror to gaze upon them.

When our heroine thought of the desperate and determined character of the wretch into whose power she was again so unfortunately thrown, and of the many troubles which she had before endured from his persecution, the state of her mind may be much better conceived than we can by any possibility describe it. Goaded on, as he would be sure to be, by the recollection of his former defeat, through his precrastination of his diabolical designs, alas! what had she to hope? Nothing. Ruin and despair seemed to be all that was now before her.

"My God!" she reflected, "what will now be the agony of my husband—my dear friends? I shall go mad at the thought!"

The vehicle was proceeding at the utmost rapidity, and as the blinds were down, Rosabelle had no means of ascertaining in what part of the country they were, or what distance they had got from the hall, not knowing how long she had remained in a state of insensibility. But Adder was now silent, and the rumbling of the carriage wheels was the only noise that broke the stillness that reigned around.

Suddenly, however, the heavy tramp of horses' feet reached her ears, and hope flashed upon her bosom. Adder started, and quickly throwing up one of the windows of the carriage, he looked out. A loud curse escaped the lips of the wretch, and increased the hopes of Lady Ravensford.

"Ah!" exclaimed the villain, "by hell we are pursued!"

"Thank Heaven!" ejaculated our heroine, clasping her hands.

"Let not your hopes be too sanguine, madam," returned Adder, with a savage grin. "for it is extremely doubtful whether they are destined to be realised. Make good use of the whip, Burley; we may yet outstrip them."

The man to whom this was addressed, and who was driving, cracked his whip loudly, and away the horses flew with the speed of lightning.

What a terrible moment of suspense and agitation was this to Lady Ravensford. She scarcely ventured to breathe, and listened to catch the sound of the horses' feet, which, to her horror and despair, grew fainter and fainter, until they died away completely on the ear, and she had too much cause to apprehend that her enemis had, indeed, succeeded in ourstripping those who were in pursuit, and who, she had no doubt, were her friends from the hall.

Suddenly, however, the speed at which the vehicle had been going was greatly abated, and at length it stopped altogether.

The hopes of Lady Ravensford revived. Adder again put his head out of the window of the carriage, and, in a stern voice, demanded the reason of their not proceeding.

"One of the horses has crippled itself," replied the man, "and I cannot get him to go at all."

"D——n!" vociferated the enraged Adder; "urge him on—lay the whip on him—we must proceed at all hazards, or we shall be overtaken, to a certainty."

Burley did as he was ordered, and the vehicle again proceeded, but at a very slow rate, Adder uttering the most dreadful imprecations all the time.

The heart of Lady Ravensford fluttered violently, and her agitation was so great that she could not, without the greatest difficulty, sustain herself.

At length the carriage again stopped, and Adder resumed his terrible maledictions with tenfold more vehemence; but that which would at any other time have greatly shocked the ears of our heroine, now imparted a sensation of satisfaction to her bosom, and increased the hopes that the circumstance had excited.

Burley endeavoured to urge on the horses, but with little effect, and the vehicle went on at scarcely more than a walking pace.

And now once more the sound of the horses' hoofs vibrated in the ears of Lady Rosabelle, and they became louder and louder, as the pursuers were evidently gaining fast upon their track.

Adder again protruded his head from the window of the coach, and looked as far as the light of the moon, which was sailing through an almost cloudless sky, would permit his eyes to penetrate.

"Confusion!" he exclaimed, "the fellows are close upon us; I can see them distinctly; they wear the livery of Ravensford. In five minutes, unless we can increase our speed, they will overtake us. The whip again, Burley; D——n the jaded brutes, do not spare them. Horseflesh is cheap enough."

Burley did comply with the mandates of his infamous employer to the very letter, and flogged the poor horses most unmercifully. until they were absolutely forced into an increase of speed. But it was only for a very brief space of time. Suddenly there was a loud crash, and the carriage was dashed to the earth. One of the wheels had come off, and thus it had become entirely useless for the prosecution of their journey.

Lady Ravensford was violently shook, but had received no serious injury, but Adder would not permit her to leave the carriage. He got out himself, and placed a ruffian at the door to prevent her following him; and then looked back, and, to his dismay, beheld that the persons in pursuit had gained ground most rapidly upon them, and were tearing along at the utmost speed at which their horses could carry them.

"There is not a moment to lose!" cried Adder, in an agitated tone of voice. "Quick—quick!—take one of the horses out of the carriage."

The fellows to whom this order was addressed, proceeded to obey it, as quick as they could; but it was all to no purpose—they had only just got the horse out of the harness, when Lord Ravensford, attended by four or five others, appeared close in sight, and called upon them to stand, as they valued their lives.

Adder cast one bitter look of the most terrible rage and disappointment towards the quickly approaching party, and then giving utterance to a dreadful malediction, he hastily jumped upon the horse's back, and motioning his base companions to follow him, he galloped off at full speed.

Immediately afterwards the pursuers arrived at the spot, and Lady Ravensford, with a cry of gratitude for her preservation, rushed fainting into the arms of her husband, who had dismounted with the speed of lightning, and had run to the door of the fallen carriage.

CHAPTER XLV.

FURTHER DANGER THREATENS.

AT the time of Lady Ravensford's seizure by the villain Adder and his myrmidons, one of the tenants of Mr. Goodman was passing near the spot, and hearing the cries of a female, he peeped from behind a cluster of trees, and there beheld our heroine being dragged forcibly along by the wretches.

The man knew that it would be an act of madness in him, a single individual, to attempt to start forward to her rescue, opposed as he would be by numbers, and doubtless had he done so, his life would have paid the forfeit of his daring; he, therefore, adopted the wiser plan, and immediately hastened with all the precipitation in his power to Holly Hall, to make them acquainted with the circumstance.

Fortunately, he had not proceeded far, when he met Lord Ravensford, (whose apprehensions had been excited by the prolonged absence of his wife,) and four of his servants, mounted on horseback, and who had come from the hall to go in search of Lady Rosabelle.

Immediately on being made acquainted by the man with what he had seen, they clapped their spurs into the sides of their horses, and proceeded as fast as their horses could gallop, in the direction which the man pointed out as that which the ruffians, with their defenceless victim, had taken.

With the fortunate result of that pursuit, our readers have been already made acquainted.

It was some time after their return to the hall ere our heroine and the different parties so deeply interested could recover from the state of agitation into which the exciting event had thrown them, and then they returned their most unbounded and heartfelt thanks to the Most High for Lady Rosabelle's narrow escape from a fate which made them shudder even to think upon.

Lady Ravensford could not speak, but bursting into tears, she threw herself into the arms of her husband, and sobbed her gratitude upon his bosom. But when our heroine was sufficiently recovered to enter into an explanation, the surprise and consternation of them all was almost beyond imagination when she informed them that the black man, Cæsar, was the author of the outrage, and that he was the same Adder from whom they had already experienced such unparalleled sufferings.

"Gracious Heaven!" ejaculated Lord Ravensford, "is it possible?—And the villain to have been so long under this roof, and none of us to recognise him!"

"How was it possible for any one to do so, under the disguise he had taken the precaution to assume?" said Mr. Goodman.

"This, then, accounts for the strange emotion I felt when I first beheld the supposed black," observed Lady Rosabelle. "Notwithstanding I believed him to have been the preserver of my husband's life, I ever felt an unaccountable dislike towards him, and a secret dread while in his presence."

"And I must confess that the same feelings possessed my mind, my love," remarked Lord Ravensford; "but still it was not likely that the most remote suspicion of his real character could have been excited in my bosom, although the tones of his voice, and his cast of features, often struck me as being familiar to me. He could not have adopted a more secure disguise to conceal himself. Good God! shall we never be released from the villany of that abominable scoundrel?"

"He certainly is the most daring miscreant that ever I heard of," said Mr. Goodman; "and it is a pity that Monckton did not yield him up to the punishment he so richly deserves, when he had him in his power."

"Yes, that is a circumstance which I much

regretted at the time I heard it," said Mr. Rattleton, "and I was fearful, knowing the incorrigible character of the villain, that he would not quit the country until he had by some means gratified his infamous desires, or gained his revenge."

"No time, at any rate, must be lost in endeavouring to find out the retreat of the scoundrel," said Mr. Goodman, "so that he may be apprehended, and prevented from doing any further mischief; which, while he remains at large, we have so much reason to apprehend."

"Your advice, my dear sir, shall be immediately attended to," returned Lord Ravensford, "although I am extremely doubtful of our endeavours to detect Adder being attended with any success. He has, I dare say, got some secure place of concealment, or, probably, by this time he is far away from this part of the country. I will, however, give notice of the circumstance to the magistrates, who, no doubt, will despatch vigilant officers in search of him, and do everything that is in their power to secure his apprehension."

"I have no doubt of it," said Rattleton, "and I would also suggest, my lord, that a large reward be offered, which may induce some of his companions to betray him."

"That, of course, shall also be done," replied Lord Ravensford; "I should also like to make Monckton acquainted with this event, for he would, I dare say, exert himself with more chance of success than any other person for the detection of the villain."

"Very true," observed Mr. Goodman; "but what means have you of informing Monckton?"

"There I am puzzled," replied his lordship.

"And yet the means are simple enough," remarked Rattleton.

"How?" inquired Ravensford.

"Why," answered the former, "it is the intention of Mrs. Kitson, you know, to return home to-morrow, and, therefore, she can convey to the captain a letter, in which you can make him acquainted with all the particulars, and what you wish him to do."

"Certainly," coincided Ravensford, "that can be easily enough done, although the thought did not strike me. And if Monckton should by any chance discover the wretch, I have not the least doubt but that he will not fail to put his threats into execution."

This point being settled, they talked further upon the subject, and they could not but wonder at the skill with which the miscreant Adder was enabled to put in practice his nefarious and diabolical schemes, and the determined perseverance with which he followed them up.

Although Lord Ravensford endeavoured all he could to compose the feelings of our heroine after this adventure, his own mind, as well as hers, was in a state of great excitement and apprehension, for while Adder remained at liberty, however cautious they might be, he felt convinced they would be in danger from him, and it was very evident that no danger would induce him to abandon his evil projects, to which he was urged as much by an implacable and insatiate spirit of revenge as he was by desire.

Indeed, the circumstance very much disconcerted them all, and Lord Ravensford took care to have persons constantly on the look out about the neighbourhood, so that they might receive timely notice of any fresh scheme which might be concocting to disturb their quietness.

Every place where Adder was likely to seek concealment was searched, and large rewards were offered for his apprehension, without any favourable results; not the least information could be obtained of him or his companions, and months elapsed without their receiving any further interruption to excite their alarm.

Monckton had more than once been to the hall, and had been most indefatigable in his endeavours to find out the villain, but his efforts had not been attended with any better success than the others; and when a twelvemonth had passed away without their hearing more of Adder, or any event taking place to alarm them, they began to hope that the villain had at last abandoned his evil designs in despair, and had quitted the country for safety, and they became more easy; in fact, the last event was seldom alluded to, and had almost become entirely forgotten.

Our heroine having felt for some time rather indisposed, and her physician advising change of air, she was induced at last to avail herself of the frequent invitations she and Lord Ravensford had so pressingly received from Mrs. Belgrave, to visit her at Rock House; and, accompanied by the little Alfred and two attendants only, they departed for G——m, at which place they arrived in safety, and without having met with any adventure on the journey, and were most cordially welcomed by the fair and amiable proprietress.

The salubrious air of G——m soon restored Lady Rosabelle completely to convalescence, and in the society of Mrs. Belgrave, she regained that entire serenity of mind, which she had not before experienced since the melancholy death of her father.

The scenery around G——m was wildly beautiful, and romantic, and the friends would frequently enjoy long rambles amongst it, always finding plenty of food for mental enjoyment and reflection.

In this manner they had passed three most agreeable weeks, and Mrs. Belgrave warmly pressed them, and, in fact, would not take any denial, to prolong their visit for some considerable time, and they were so highly gratified that they could not refuse.

One evening, however, Rosabelle had happened to stroll from the house alone, and walking by the sea-side, became completely absorbed in the contemplation of the wide waters, gilded as they were by the bright red beams of the setting sun, and speckled here and there with a fisherman's boat, or the graceful vessels that sailed along in the distance.

At length, however, the evening air beginning to grow chilly, and knowing that she had prolonged her absence from the house beyond her usual time, she turned away from the spot, and made her way towards the Rock House.

She had just taken the path which wound round the base of a lofty cliff, when she felt her arm suddenly grasped violently by some person behind her, and looking round, we need not attempt to describe her consternation when she found herself held by Adder, who was dressed in the garb of a sailor, and his face was blackened in the same manner as when he gained admittance to Holly Hall, in the character of Cæsar the African.

"Ha, ha, ha!" laughed the wretch, his eyes

THE ATTEMPTED BURGLARY.

at the same time glaring frightfully upon her. "Once more propitious fortune throws thee in my way, and now, by all the infernal host, no power shall part us!"

Lady Rosabelle was so overpowered by her fears, that she could not speak, and Adder was forcing her unresistingly along, before she could in any degree recover herself; but at length she screamed aloud for help, and made a resolute attempt to release herself from his grasp

"This time, at any rate," exclaimed Adder, "your cries for aid will be unavailing. There is no one near to assist you!"

"Liar! d—d villain!" shouted a loud voice, and in an instant Adder was felled to the earth by a tremendous blow, and Lady Ravensford found herself under the protection of Captain Monckton.

Quick as lightning, Adder gathered himself on to his feet, and, in a voice of mingled fear and surprise, he ejaculated :—

"Hell and the devil! Monckton!"

"Yes, villain," returned the smuggler-captain, "to thy confusion, it is Monckton. Thou hast dared to disregard my injunctions, and now thou shalt most assuredly swing, if there is rope enough in the country."

In an instant Monckton placed a whistle to his lips, but ere any sound could escape it, Adder had rushed from the spot, and running with the speed of a startled deer, he was out of sight in a moment.

The signal of their captain had brought several of the smugglers almost immediately to the spot, and they inquired eagerly what was the matter.

"The villain Adder," hastily cried Monckton; "fly, quick! quick! Hunt for him in every direction; do not suffer him, if possible, this time to escape from us."

The men hurried away in different directions, and the smuggler-captain then turning to our heroine, said:—

"How happy am I to think, Lady Ravensford, that fortune conducted my footsteps to this spot, and has once more rendered me the happy means of preserving you from the power of that abominable scoundrel."

Lady Ravensford endeavoured to speak her thanks, but could not, but her looks sufficiently testified her gratitude to the smuggler-captain, and he added—

"I suppose you are staying at the Rock House?"

Our heroine replied in the affirmative, and now gave utterance to her thanks to Monckton, for the inestimable service he had so providentially rendered her, in rescuing her from the power of the miscreant Adder.

Monckton interrupted her.

"I require no thanks, Lady Ravensford," he said. "I am happy in having been so fortunately brought to your rescue at such a critical moment. But excuse me, my lady, but I certainly must say that you are much to blame to venture to walk out here alone to this strange place, especially after the narrow escape you had only a few months since."

"I own that it was very wrong and thoughtless," replied Lady Ravensford, "but such a time has elapsed since my former adventure, and all inquiries failing to ascertain anything of Adder, that, indeed, such an occurrence was the most remote from my thoughts."

"I am only afraid that the scoundrel will manage to escape," said Monckton, "although it will not be any fault of my men if he does."

"Heaven send that they may be able to find the guilty wretch," said our heroine; "for then all future apprehensions will be at an end."

"If my men had been with me at the time I encountered the ruffian," observed Monckton, "he would have been at once secured, and by this time on his way to gaol. But I fear now that he will be able to elude us, for there are so many places in this part of the country where he can conceal himself. If he is to be found in the town, or anywhere near it, however, we will have him."

"Of course, Mr. Monckton," said our heroine, "you will accompany me to the Rock House? Lord Ravensford will be most happy

to see you, and to make his acknowledgments to you for having again been my preserver."

"Certainly, I will attend you, my lady," replied the smuggler-captain, "and I hope it will not be long ere we shall hear of this most incorrigible villain being in safe custody.

Monckton looked around him to see whether he could observe any of his men approaching; and respectfully walked by the side of Rosabelle to the Rock House.

Lord Ravensford and Mrs. Belgrave were not a little surprised to behold the companion our heroine had on her return, but their astonishment and alarm exceeded all bounds when they were made acquainted with the circumstance she had met with, and the escape she had had from the power of the villain Adder, and which would not have happened had it not been for the providential arrival of Monckton at the spot, at the very critical moment of danger.

Lord Ravensford could not sufficiently express his thanks to the smuggler-captain, but at the same time he deeply regretted that his companions had not been with him at the time, so that they might have secured the villain.

In the course of an hour or more, one of the smugglers, who had guessed whither Monckton had gone, made his appearance at the Rock House, and informed them that they had been entirely unsuccessful in their endeavours to find out Adder, although they had searched every place they could think of, and where he was likely to fly for concealment.

"The crafty scoundrel," observed the smuggler-captain, "how he manages to elude my utmost vigilance I cannot imagine. But I do not think he has left the town, and, if you give timely notice to the proper authorities, he may yet be taken."

"I will attend to your suggestion immediately," said Ravensford, and he despatched a servant for that purpose to the house of the magistrate, making him acquainted, in a letter, with what had taken place, and requesting that he would afford the assistance he required, by giving instructions to the officers to make the strictest possible search after the villain. This request the magistrate very readily complied with, and immediately despatched expert officers to different parts of the country, and to examine every vessel near the place, to see whether there was any person on board answering the description of Adder.

These inquiries, however, were unattended with any success, and it was, therefore, concluded that Adder must have contrived, by some means or the other, to escape from the town, and to elude the vigilance of those that were sent in search of him.

Lord Ravensford and the others were very sorry for this circumstance, as, by securing the villain Adder, their fears would have been at once brought to a termination, and they might then hope to pass their future days in undisturbed tranquillity.

Monckton, however, entertained very strong hopes that he should yet encounter Adder again, and he promised them he would not lose any opportunity which might present itself, and which would lead to a chance of his apprehension.

Lord Ravensford and our heroine sincerely thanked the smuggler-captain for his kindness, and the interest which he took in their welfare, and the former once more tried all the powers of persuasion he could make use of, to induce Monckton to quit the life he was at present leading, and to appear in the world again as Archibald Malcolm; but he succeeded no better than he had done before.

Monckton returned his lordship many acknowledgments for the friendship which he showed towards him, and the generous feelings that evidently prompted him to endeavour to prevail upon him to comply with his request, but, at the same time, he firmly persisted in his determination not to enter again upon the more immediate scenes of the world, but to remain attached to his gallant vessel and his faithful crew, as long as she had a timber to float with. The sea had become his world, and he might be said to live only while upon it, and his rough associates had all endeared themselves to him as much as if they had been his brothers, by their honest devotedness, and could he, therefore, think for a moment even of abandoning them? No! He could sooner lay down his life; for he felt that life, apart from them, would not be worth the keeping of it to him.

In the world too, although there might not be many who would recognise him, yet those that did happen to do so, would point the finger of scorn and opprobrium towards him, and, therefore, he felt that is life would be rendered one of perpetual and vexatious uneasiness.

These arguments were such as Lord Ravensford was not prepared to combat; although he could not but admire the enthusiasm with which Monckton, as he chose to call himself, devoted himself to his associates; and there was something of a wildly romantic character about him, which could not fail to render him an object of deep interest to all who had the opportunity of being in his company for a short time.

Lord Ravensford took the liberty of questioning Monckton about the crime of which it was rumoured Adder had been formerly guilty, and with the facts of which it was believed that he (Monckton) was thoroughly acquainted.

Monckton, however, evaded these questions as well as he could, and did not appear at all disposed to gratify the curiosity of his lordship for the present.

"The time, perhaps, is not far distant," he observed, "when everything regarding that terrible affair will be explained; until which period I do not wish to converse upon the subject. Adder will, I trust, be apprehended before long, and, depend upon it, I will then on the day of trial ring such a story in his ears as will make his guilty soul quail and fill the minds of those that hear it with horror."

"I hope the time will soon arrive when you may have an opportunity to do as you say, and when justice may at last overtake the hardened miscreant," observed Lord Ravensford, and to which wish they all most fervently responded.

Monckton could not be pursuaded to stay longer than a few hours at the Rock House, but before he quitted the place, he repeated his promise to be indefatigable in his endeavours to find out the place where Adder was concealed, and he also made an arrangement with his lordship by which they would be enabled readily to correspond with each other, when they had anything to communicate.

This second meeting with Adder, had greatly increased the uneasiness of our heroine, for it showed that there was very little chance of being released from his infamous persecution while he remained at large; and from the effectual manner in which he had always contrived to elude the myrmidons of the law, it did not appear very probable that he would be apprehended easily.

A more determined scoundrel none of them had ever before heard of, and, in fact, it was doubtful to them whether the annals of crime could scarcely furnish them with his parallel.

"His heart must be entirely callous to every feeling of humanity," remarked Mrs. Belgrave, "and he is evidently a man who would not shrink from the perpetration of any crime, however atrocious. Oh, how I shudder, my dear Lady Ravensford, when I reflect how long you were in the power of that being, and at the narrow escapes which you have frequently had since of again becoming his prisoner. Alas! should ill-fortune again destine him to succeed in his nefarious stratagems, how terrible would doubtless be the fate to which he would immediately consign you."

"I cannot think of it without a feeling of the greatest horror," said Lord Ravensford; "but Rosabelle will now perceive how imperatively necessary it is that we should at times use the utmost precaution, to guard against the designs of this detestable villain, and that she must never, in future, upon any account, venture to walk out alone."

"I own," said Lady Rosabelle, "that I certainly should not have done so; it was very incautious and imprudent; but then, so long a time had elapsed since we had heard anything of Adder, and being in this strange neighbourhood, that any idea of encountering him was the farthest from my thoughts."

"Think you that he had become acquainted with the circumstance of your ladyship's staying here, and that he had been watching an opportunity of meeting with you, or that it was accident which brought him hither, and led him to encounter you in the manner in which he did?" asked Mrs. Belgrave.

"Why, that, of course, I cannot pretend to say," replied our heroine; "but, from the manner of our meeting, I rather feel inclined to think it was the effect of accident, and not of design."

"It is my opinion that Adder employs his emissaries to lurk about near wherever we may be staying, and to give him all the information he may require," said Lord Ravensford; "but is it not provoking that the fellow should carry on his diabolical career with impunity, and should apparently set detection and the laws at defiance?"

"It is indeed, my lord,' replied Mrs. Belgrave; "but, although fortune may at present seem to protect him, depend upon it, the time will shortly arrive when retribution will overtake him, and he will have to pay the dreadful penalty for the many crimes there is no doubt that he has perpetrated."

"He will, he will, most assuredly," said Rosabelle, with much emotion; "my poor father's untimely death calls for punishment on the guilty cause of it, and most certainly his spirit will not call in vain. The Almighty will not fail to visit, with the most terrible retribution, so great an offender as that terrible man."

"He must have accumulated a large sum of money by his guilty practices," observed Lord Ravensford, "or he would never have been enabled to have acted in the manner which he has done."

"He must,' coincided Lady Rosabelle, "but I imagine it must be nearly exhausted by this time, unless he has had some other means of replenishing his purse; for I do not believe that Monckton suffered him to take much away with him. when he was hurried away from the house of Gordon Desborough; and if he had any placed in a banker's hands, he would, in in all probability, be afraid to attempt to draw it, lest it should lead to his detection, especially after he became acquainted with the officers being on the alert, and heard of the large rewards that were offered for his apprehension."

"If it be as you say, my love," remarked Lord Ravensford, "and to me it appears very probable, there may be some chance of Adder's being speedily brought to justice; for he may be driven by necessity to commit some crime that will lead to his detection."

Our heroine and Mrs. Belgrave were of the same opinion, and, after some further conversation, the subject was dropped, and the friends separated for the night.

Lord Ravensford the next day forwarded a letter to Mr. Goodman, informing him of what had taken place, and putting them upon their guard to keep a strict look out in the neighbourhood of Holly Hall, and not to fail to forward them immediate intelligence, should anything occur to excite their suspicions, so that they might have every opportunity of thwarting the schemes of the villain and his infamous companions, if he had any, which there was very little doubt but he had, from the manner in which he was generally able to put his plans into effect.

To this letter his lordship quickly receivey an answer, in which Mr. Goodman warmld expressed the happiness of himself and the others, at the fortunate escape of Lady Ravensford, and informed him that nothing had occurred to them during their absence to excite in their bosoms any alarm; that a wary watch was still kept up, but that hitherto they had not met with anything to excite their suspicions that the wretch Adder had revisited the neighbourhood since the last daring outrage he had committed there; although it seemed evident, from his recent attempt near the Rock House, that he had not abandoned his bold and infamous designs.

Lord and Lady Ravensford remained another month had G——m, during which time nothing more had been heard of Adder, although every plan that could possibly be devised had been adopted to detect him. It was very evident that he was not in that locality, but in what direction he had gone, or how he had contrived to escape, no one could form the least conjecture.

Lord Ravensford, however, thought it advisable to let their departure from Rock House be as secret as possible, lest there might be a surprise contemplated by the villain, and they therefore left the house at a very early hour in the morning, and before any persons were stirring in the neighbourhood to notice their departure. They reached Holly Hall without anything occurring to them on the road; and were delighted once more to join the society of their friends.

CHATER XLVI.

ADDER AND HIS PLANS.—DESTITUTION AND DESPERATION.—THE BURGLARY.—THE DETECTION.

It may now be deemed requisite to devote some space to the villain Adder, who has already shone so conspicuously in our pages.

After he had been conveyed ashore by the smugglers, glad enough to have escaped from the dreadful fate with which Monckton had at first threatened him, and to which he knew full well he had it in his power to consign him, he was for some considerable time before he was able to come to any decision as to the manner in which he should act. The smuggler-captain had threatened him with the most terrible vengeance, if he did not banish himself from England altogether, and he was too well acquainted with the real character of Monckton to doubt but that he would do as he had said, if he should encounter him. But could he make up his mind to become an outlaw from his native land—to suffer his enemies to triumph over him in such a manner, and to abandon all further ideas of Lady Rosabelle?—No, he could not, even though the gallows should be his portion for his temerity; and now that he was once more at liberty, he did not despair entirely of yet being able to put his base designs into execution, and to be enabled to gratify his revenge against Lord Ravensford, Monckton, and all those who had excited his enmity.

He thought it advisable, however, to remain quiet for a time, until Rosabelle and her friends might fancy themselves in security; and in order the better to further his plans, he made up his mind to retire abroad for a few months, until such time as Monckton might imagine that he had acted in obedience to his stern injunctions, and would be afraid to venture to England again, lest he should encounter the punishment with which he had been threatened.

Adder had a considerable sum of money about his person, and he knew he should be able to devise some scheme or another to draw the money out which he had placed in his banker's hands when he should want it, and he, therefore, defeated as he at present was, looked forward to the future with the most sanguine anticipations.

After he had watched the smuggler's vessel out of sight, he walked hastily forward to see whether he could find any inn or tavern where he might be accommodated, and find a lodging for the night.

The place where they had put him ashore was perfectly unknown to him, and seemed to be but thinly inhabited, and very little frequented.

He saw a few fishermen's huts as he proceeded, and at one of them he knocked, and inquired whether the man could inform him of any house near at hand where he could procure refreshment, and be accommodated in the manner he required.

The man looked at Adder with an expression of the utmost astonishment and curiosity, a person of his appearance being, as it afterwards came out, quite a *rara avis* in that wretched place.

The fisherman, in reply to his interrogatories, informed him there was only one public-house in the whole place, and there the accommodation would not be found to be any of the best; but if "the gentleman would like to put up with it, he would conduct his honour to it."

Adder felt tired, and was, therefore, glad at the idea of obtaining a shelter anywhere for the night; he, therefore, very thankfully accepted of the fisherman's offer, and they walked off together at a brisk pace.

In little more than a quarter of an hour they arrived at the public-house, and certainly its external appearance was by no means inviting. Here, Adder having rewarded the man for his trouble, they parted, and the former walked into the house. Seeing no person in the front of the place, and the interior having as cheerless an aspect as the exterior, Adder made his way to the kitchen, in which he found a good fire, and seated in a large arm-chair on the side of it, and fast asleep, was a little, chubby, red-faced man, whom Adder took to be mine host of "The Dolphin," as the public-house in question was called.

The noise which Adder made in entering the room awoke him, and he looked with no little astonishment, not unmixed with suspicion, upon the intruder, any other customers than some of the poor fishermen of the place being almost unknown to him.

Adder quickly informed the landlord of his business there, and begged to be accommodated with a lodging for the night, and some refreshment.

The host of "The Dolphin" again looked at him narrowly and suspiciously, and after having apparently satisfied himself of the character of his guest, he informed him that if he could put up with such refreshment as his house could afford him, and a bed, which was clean, if but homely, they were at his service; and he then placed another log upon the fire, and waited to receive the orders of Adder.

Adder thanked him for his civility, and gladly accepted of the offer which he made him, and, as mine host had nothing in his house which he could more warmly recommend than his whiskey, Adder ordered him to bring a stiff glass of it, and invited him to keep him company until such time as he should think proper to retire to his chamber.

To this request, too, the landlord also raised not any objection, and the whiskey quickly smoked upon the table, and having brought a pipe of tobacco for himself and a cigar for Adder, they sat down, and were soon in a very fair way of enjoying themselves.

From the landlord, Adder learnt where he was,

and having stated that he had been left accidently on the "Bland," the vessel in which he was going to the south of France having sailed without him, the curiosity of "mine host" appeared to be quite satisfied.

In this manner they sat for about two hours, when Adder requested to be shown to his chamber, and having bid his host good night, he was not long in retiring to bed.

Adder did not rise very early the following morning, and then he found the landlord and his wife stirring. After having partaken of a hearty meal, he paid the landlord liberally for the accommodation he had received, and then took his departure, having received instructions in which way he should proceed to reach the nearest sea-port town, where it was his intention to embark on board some vessel going to the south of France, where he thought of settling for the present, being there the most likely not to be interrupted, and unknown.

It is needless to follow him on his voyage, as nothing worthy of notice happened to him, and he arrived at the place of destination in perfect safety.

He settled himself at Tours, and shortly afterwards contrived, through the means of an agent, in whom he knew he could confide, to get the whole of his money withdrawn from his banker's hands in London, and transmitted to him in the most private manner.

Here Adder contrived to pass away a few weeks pleasantly enough, but he soon became restless and dissatisfied with his situation, and burnt with impatience to return to England, and endeavour to gratify his revenge against his enemies, and also to devise some fresh stratagem to get Lady Ravensford once more in his power.

Through the means of the agent before mentioned, he was made acquainted with everything which transpired at Holly Hall, and it was not long ere he heard of the restoration of Rosabelle to her friends, and, while his bosom glowed with the most ungovernable rage at the success of Monckton's plans, he mentally vowed that he would not rest until he had not only ample vengeance, but also had once more obtained possession of our heroine.

Bitter and heavy were the curses that the villain gave utterance to against Monckton for the manner in which he had defeated his plans, and he often repeated that could he by any means contrive to get him into the power of his enemies, by which means he could get rid of him altogether, he should not only have his fears set at rest, as regarded the revelation of the atrocious crime of which he had been guilty at a former period, but also, at the same time, he would gratify his revenge.

How to effect this desirable object, however, he could not see at present, and he was, therefore, compelled to wait with patience, and hope that at some future period the opportunity he was so anxiously looking for would present itself.

His present life would have been insupportable to him, had he not sought after false pleasures to banish the tedium and monotony; he entered extravagantly into all the follies and dissipation of the place; was a constant frequenter of the gaming-house, where, for some time, Fortune smiled upon him, and he won many very large sums of money. The gold, however, obtained in this manner, never does any good to the winner, and so it was with Adder, for his winnings were quickly squandered in useless extravagances, and his run of luck ceasing, he lost himself several large sums, and at length found himself so much reduced, that he was compelled to abandon his former proceedings without any further delay, and to curtail his expenses, or he would soon have been entirely ruined.

During his stay here, several circumstances took place to add to his vexation and disappointment, one of which was the trial and acquittal of Lord Ravensford and Rattleton, for the fatal duel with Lord Saunter. The death of Mr. Montalbert, however, afforded the heartless scoundrel the most inhuman satisfaction, feeling convinced as he did of the anguish the circumstance would create in the minds of those he so much detested.

Adder had now been absent from England for more than a twelvemonth, and his pecuniary resources becoming extremely limited, he determined at once to make a bold venture to return to his native country, and to endeavour to put those diabolical designs into execution, upon which his whole thoughts and wishes were still fixed.

After racking his brain for some time to think of a plan by which he might more securely guard himself against detection, he assumed the disguise of a black sailor, and in that character obtained his passport, and made his way to England.

In England he arrived quite safe, and sought out the neighbourhood of Holly Hall, without any further delay, where he took up his residence at an obscure public-house, where he could hear everything that took place at the hall, and so effectually had he disguised himself, that he entertained not the slightest apprehension of any person being able to recognise him.

While staying here he frequently was amused by hearing the frequenters talk of himself, although the portrait they drew of him was by no means a flattering one, and the compliments they gratuitously paid him were anything but calculated to afford him pleasure. But the villain enjoyed their observations, and exulted when he thought of the manner in which he had succeeded in so securely disguising himself that not a shadow of a doubt seemed to exist in the mind of any one.

It has frequently been shown in the course of this narrative, that Adder was a villain who was not likely to have many moments of compunction; in fact, the misery of his fellow creatures was his delight, and consequently, he never exhulted more than when he succeeded in achieving the object of his guilty purposes.

The murder of Rose Allerton was the only crime throughout the whole course of his infamous career which he could not bear to reflect upon without feelings of the utmost horror; and frequently would her ghastly form appear to his imagination, and chill the murderer's breast, and arouse him to the certainty of the dreadful retribution which must ultimately overtake him.

Many hours of the most distracting torture would the miscreant Adder endure when these thoughts crowded upon his brain, and his agony was the more intense when he reflected that the man who had proved himself one of his greatest enemies, namely, Monckton, was well acquainted with all the particulars of that horrid deed, and that he possessed such evidence as could not fail to convict him.

He also felt confident that the smuggler captain would not fail to put his threats into execution should he again encounter him, even though it should be at the risk of his own liberty. At times like these, he almost repented the course he had adopted in returning to England; for on the Continent he might have enjoyed himself in security, and if he had been more provident, might have had sufficient money to have kept him in comfort, if not in affluence. But to resign all thoughts of Rosabelle, and to let her friends triumph, after all the trouble and expense he had been at, he could not bear to think of with any degree of patience. He thought he could almost as soon encounter the inevitable fate which was his certain doom, as to come to such a determination; and these ideas had urged him to the step he had taken. When too, he thought upon the almost utter impossibility it would be for any one to recognise him under his present disguise, he assured himself that he need only use proper precaution to remain unknown, and to meet with success in the diabolical plans he had formed.

But it was necessary that he should be quick in his plans, for his means were daily becoming more limited, and he was well aware that success depended in a great measure upon promptitude. But what was he to do when his pecuniary resources were entirely exhausted?

This was a troublesome thought, and one which he was unable for some time to answer satisfactorily in his own mind. Money he must have by some means or another, or he would not have it in his power to carry on his nefa-

rious projects with any chance of success, and the bare idea of his being reduced to poverty, after the life of indolence, luxury and extravagance he had led, made the villain shrink with dread. No—no—such a fate must not be his, and he determined to avoid it, even if by the means he should have to adopt in doing so, he should be compelled to adopt the most desperate and dangerous schemes.

From any crime, however revolting it might be, it has been very clearly shewn to the reader that Adder would not shrink; and, after deliberating for a short time within himself what was next to be done, he at last came to the determination of going for a few nights on the highway, and thus trying his fortune. If in adopting this guilty resolution, the villain should have to perpetrate murder, he would not have foreborne to do it, sooner than he would have been disappointed of his object.

Accordingly, on the following night, after he had came to this resolution, Adder, well armed, secretly quitted the house where he was lodging, and took his way to a lonely road, which was, notwithstanding, much frequented. Here he secreted himself, and eagerly watched the approach of some traveller who might possess the means about him of satisfying his wants.

Adder had taken good care to strengthen his determination by drinking deeply before he started on his guilty purpose, and he now felt fully prepared for whatever might happen. Money he had made up his mind he would have at all hazards, and, therefore, it was not a trifle that was at all likely to move him from his purpose.

The place which Adder had chosen to conceal himself, was just at the entrance of a dark and dismal lane, which branched off from the road, and was a very convenient spot for the perpetration of a deed like that he contemplated. Here, then, he seated himself on the trunk of a fallen tree, where he could have a distant view of the road for some distance, and every person that approached.

It was a very fine night; the moon shone brightly in the heavenly arch, and countless myriads of stars added their twinkling lustre to her radiant beams.

Adder sat there for some time in a state of apathy, his thoughts wandering to no particular objects, but still his mind intent upon the desperate crime he had resolved to perpetrate if the opportunity should be afforded him. At last, however, becoming impatient, and feeling rather cold, for the night air was keen, he arose and walked for some distance along the road, taking care to keep close to the bushes, that separated it from the adjoining fields, and where he was less likely to be observed.

In the course of a conversation which Adder had overheard between the landlord of the public-house and his wife after they had retired to bed, (for they slept in the next chamber to him, and the rooms only being parted by a very slight partition, he could hear every word they uttered), he had learnt that a grazier, who invariably called at their house on his way to market, and who usually had a large sum of money about him, was expected there that day, and he also was enabled to ascertain that this was the road he always came; but he could not think of making an attempt to commit a robbery in the open daylight, and when his detention would be almost certain to follow, and thus his nefarious wishes would be foiled. But then, as he understood that the grazier usually slept at the inn, the villain thought there might still be a chance left of his being enabled to rob him in the night. This, however, would be attended with considerable danger, for suspicion would, in all probability, light upon him, and should he abandon the place, it would undoubtedly be a direct confirmation of his guilt, and would put him to great inconvenience in having to quit the neighbourhood, which might greatly interrupt, if not render abortive his designs against Lord and Lady Revensford.

Reflecting, therefore, in this manner, Adder was constrained to give up all thoughts of plundering the grazier, although it was with much reluctance that he did so, for he had no doubt but that he should from him have been sure to have got a very rich booty.

The day which succeeded the night on which Adder had overheard the conversation we have spoken of, was passed by him in a state of great agitation and uncertainty, and at one time he would determine upon some daring scheme, which the next moment would serve to make him abandon all idea of.

The grazier, however, did not come to the house that day, but Adder gathered from the conversation of his host, that he would be sure to be there that night, so that he might be in time for the market on the following morning. Adder caught at this information, and his hopes once more revived; he resolved to lay wait for him, and make a desperate attempt to rob him as he had at first designed.

Adder was no coward, as that which has been already related will fully prove, and he was, therefore, prepared for any resistance which his intended victim might make, and he had made up his mind not to be defeated easily. But from what he could learn, the grazier was an old man, and one who was not very likely to offer much resistance, especially when he saw that the individual who attacked him was well armed, and a determined man, and, therefore, Adder calculated that his success was almost certain.

He had taken the precaution to provide himself with a mask and smock-frock, so that he might be fully enabled to disguise himself,

and these were the more indispensible for the villain's safety, as he intended to return to the inn after the perpetration of the robbery.

Impatient and gloomy, Adder contrived to traverse the road for some time, but he saw no signs of the traveller or any other person, and he began to despair. The place was sufficiently quiet and lonely to inspire no very pleasant reflections in the mind of Adder, and so rapidly did they crowd upon his brain, that he had not strength to endure them, and he almost made up his mind to abandon his villanous project, and to return to the inn to seek that society which might alone banish such fearful thoughts. Society! The disguise he had adopted had rendered him an outcast from any but the lowest, whom he despised; and it caused him much vexation when he was constrained, in order to prevent suspicion, to join with them in some silly argument about which he knew nothing whatever, and in which it could not be supposed that he could feel the slightest interest.

At length the solemn booming of the old village church bell vibrated on the air, tolling the hour of ten, and Adder, whose patience was now quite tired out, and whose disappointment could only be equalled by his chagrin, resolved to wait no longer, but to return to the inn.

He had just turned round for that purpose, when the low trampling of a horse's hoofs, at a distance, arrested his purpose and rekindled his hopes.

The sounds proceeded from behind him, and looking eagerly along the road, as far as his eyes could penetrate, at first he could not perceive anything, but at length he beheld a horse trotting slowly along the road, in the direction of the place where he was standing, and bearing on his back a person whom he was unable at present to observe distinctly.

"It must be him!" muttered Adder to himself, and hope once more elated and nerved him. His mind was fully made up; he would have all the money the grazier had about him, even if to obtain it, he had to embrue his hands in his blood.

Quickly the miscreant glided cautiously along the darkest and most overshadowed part of the road, until he once more reached the entrance to the lane which the traveller must pass; and which appeared to him to be the most convenient spot for the perpetration of the deed.

"But—but"—muttered Adder, "I will not harm him—no—no—I will not harm him, if I can avoid it! I do not want his blood, but his money, and it will be his own fault if he should lose his life."

Nearer and nearer the rider approached, and at length he had got to within a very short distance of the place where Adder was concealed, that by the bright light of the moon he was enabled to have a distinct view of his person.

He was a thickset man, about sixty, and carried with him a short whip with a very heavy handle. He was whistling merrily along the road, apparently quite happy and unsuspicious of any danger, and by what Adder could perceive of his features, he looked like a man who was not likely to be easily intimidated. Again he muttered to himself—

"I hope he will resign his money easily; I hope he will not make any resistance; I would not have his blood upon my conscience, but his money I *will* have."

The man had now got to within a very short distance of the lane, and Adder had no doubt, from the description which had been given of him, that this was the grazier.

He clenched his fist nervously, and involuntarily placed his other hand on one of the pistols which he carried with him.

"I will let him pass me," thought Adder; "I will let him pass me before I pounce out upon him, and then I shall take him more by surprise, and he will be less likely to offer any resistance."

The traveller had now left off whistling, and had broke into an old country ditty, which he sang in self-satisfied tones, but which were anything but harmonious. The traveller's

ADDER SHOOTS MR. GOODMAN IN MISTAKE FOR LORD RAVENSFORD.

voice was of the stentorian quality, and, therefore, Adder was enabled to make out the words, which were as follow:—

"Young Roger th' mill—er, who courted of late
A farmer's fair daughter, called beautiful Kate;
And she to her portion had fine silken gowns,
And she to her portion had five hundred pounds;
And she to her portion had jewels and rings,
And she to her portion, and she to her portion
  had many foine things!"

"St—st—st—go along Bessy, go along!"

"These glittering jewels, and money likewise,
It bother'd his heart, and it dazzled his eyes.
Which caus—ed young Roger for to tell his mind,
That if unto him she'd be constant and kind,

No other young woman shall e'er be my bride,
For thou art my jewel, for thou art my jewel, my
  joy, and my pride!"

"Good girl, Bessy—good girl; I——"

"Your money or your life!" cried Adder, in a disguised voice, rushing up to the traveller from his place of concealment, and laying hold of the horse's bridle.

The old man was, of course, rather startled, but he collected himself in a moment, and with the utmost coolness, said:—

"I tells thee what it be, young man—thee bee'st comed upon a bad errand, and I do advise thee to let go o' th' bridle, and go about thee business, before harm do come of thee."

"There, there, no nonsense," replied Adder,

in an impatient tone; "no nonsense; I am a desperate man and must have money."

"Dom thee, thee bee'st a daring rascal," cried the traveller; "but let go of the bridle, and be off, or mayhap it may not be long ere I make thee repent thy job. Leave go of the bridle, I again tell thee! Thee won't—then, dang me, if I don't soon mak' thee, and that's all about it."

With these words, the traveller flourished his heavy whip, and aimed a blow at the head of Adder with the butt-end of it, which, if he had not stepped quickly aside and avoided, would, in all probability, have deprived him of further power.

"Old idiot!" cried the enraged ruffian, "you will urge me to do that which I would rather avoid; will you deliver up your money, I say once more?"

"No," promptly replied the old man; "I'll see thee dom'd first, and all such scoundrels as thee bee'st."

"Then, by h—l! you will have to pay for your obstinacy with your life!" cried Adder hastily, groping about beneath his smock-frock to get out one of the pistols.

The old man immediately guessed what he was about, and sprang from his horse's back with the agility of a youth, and the moment that Adder got out his pistol, and before he could cock it, he closed with him, and being a strong, powerful man, the struggle threatened to be a determined one.

Adder, however, was wound up to a pitch of desperation, for it was a moment of life or death, and he was taken somewhat by surprise, as, from the age of the traveller, he had not expected such an antagonist.

Adder was also a very muscular man, and had youth on his side, and he, of course, mustered up all his strength on this occasion, and endeavoured to get his hands at liberty; but the old man had pinned them with such an iron grip, that all his efforts were ineffectual, and maledictions the most terrible escaped his lips, as the danger of his situation became every instant greater; for, as his strength decreased, so did that of the traveller's appear to increased, and he expected nothing less than that he must be overpowered. The struggle lasted for several minutes, the traveller having pinned the hands of Adder so tightly, that he was compelled to drop the pistol to the ground, and which the former was afraid to secure, for fear that, in resigning his hold of the robber, he should lose the advantage he had gained. But at length the foot of Adder caught in something on the ground, and he fell, dragging the old man with him. Fortunately, the traveller did not fall upon him, or his weight would have quickly decided the combat, and Adder would have been defeated, but he fell by his side, and consequently was obliged to leave go his hold;

and Adder, seeing the moment of advantage, and probably the only opportunity of saving his life, jumped to his feet with the speed of lightning, and, snatching the other pistol from his bosom, he sprang upon the old man, and knelt upon his chest. Pressing the fingers of his other hand tightly in his throat, until the old man was nearly strangled, he presented the pistol at his head.

"You deserve to lose your life for your infernal obstinacy, and it is at this moment in my power; but I do not want to harm you. Now, then, your money."

The old man, who was quite overpowered by the pressure on his chest, and the violence with which Adder pressed his knuckles into his throat, tried to speak, but could only make a sign to his coat-pocket, which Adder understanding, released the old man from the hold he had taken of his throat; and, putting his hand into his pocket, to which he had directed his attention, he drew forth a canvas bag, apparently well loaded, and depositing it carefully in his bosom, he secured both the pistols, and, rising from the ground, he said to the still prostrate traveller—

"Beware! You see that I have all the power of your life or death in my hands; if you move a step to pursue me until I am out of sight, that instant you die!"

The old man did not make any reply, for he had not yet recovered from the effects of the combat, and was unable to give utterance to a word; and Adder having satisfied himself that he had secured all the money in his possession, hastily retreated from the spot, and, springing into the fields, threw away the smock-frock, and made the best of his way towards the inn, which he reached in an almost inconceivable short space of time, and without betraying any emotion, entered the kitchen, as was his usual custom, and taking his seat by the fire, called for a jug of ale, and a pipe of tobacco.

He had not been there long, when he heard a loud shout and hallooing outside the house, and he immediately recognised the tones.

"Why," exclaimed the landlord, laying down his pipe, "that certainly is the voice of old Rainger! Why, what the deuce can be the matter with him?"

Adder felt a little alarmed; but he concealed his agitation, and continued, with apparent unconcern, to smoke his pipe, and to be completely absorbed in the enjoyment of that and his ale. He would have been glad to have retired to his chamber, so that he might have escaped all observation, but he was fearful that he might, by so doing, probably excite some suspicion, and he, therefore, kept his seat, and pretended to take no notice of what was passing.

The landlord having hastened to the door of the house to meet his guest, and to inquire what was the matter with him, was quickly heard returning, accompanied by the old man, who was grumbling and swearing all the way. When they entered the kitchen, the grazier looked suspiciously round upon the different persons there assembled, but appeared to take very little notice of Adder, whose assumed colour, no doubt, removed every idea of his being the robber from his mind.

"He was a most desperate scoundrel, whoever he is," said Mr. Rainger, which was the name of the old man, "and I feel the effects o' his d—n'd knuckles in my throat now. I wish I could only meet with the fellow, and I warrant me he would not escape from my clutches again very easily."

"This a bad job, a terrible bad job, Mr. Rainger," said the landlord.

"Ay, it be indeed a main bad job," said Mr. Rainger; "three hundred and fifty bright guineas be no small sum to lose, as times go."

"You are right," coincided the landlord; "but should you know the robber again if you were to see him, think you?"

"Whoy, ye'es," answered the old man, "I should, indeed; for, while we were struggling, I had plenty o' time to observe him pretty closely."

"What sort of a man was he?" inquired the landlord.

"Why, he was a tall man, and very powerful, with a very red face, and large whiskers," returned Mr. Rainger, "and he wore a smock frock."

"I shouldn't at all wonder but it is one of the poachers who infest this neighbourhood," remarked the landlord; "but, if you please, I will immediately send one of my men to the justice's, with notice of the robbery, so that he may lose no time in adopting some plan which is likely to bring the scoundrel to justice."

"Ay, friend Robson," returned Mr. Rainger, "I shall feel obliged to you for so doing; but I am afraid there is not much chance of the fellow's being apprehended, and I may reckon that I shall never see my money again. It's a bad job—a very expensive job."

"It is," observed the host; "but was it not very imprudent of you to travel at night with so large a sum of money about you?"

"Why," replied Mr. Rainger, "ye'es, to be sure it be so; but then I couldn't help it. However, I will take good care I will not do so again."

"Well, it's to be hoped that you will be able to get some intelligence of the daring robber, after all," said Mr. Robson, the host; "but I will despatch Thomas to the justice's directly."

"And, in the meantime," said Mr. Rainger, "I will take supper with you, if you please, and see if I cannot comfort myself in some measure after this affair, with a glass or two of brandy and water."

"Ay, ay, it is no use giving way to melancholy and regret," observed the landlord; "for that won't mend the matter, you know. This way, Mr. Rainger, if you please."

The landlord and his guest now quitted the kitchen, much to the relief of Adder, who soon afterwards retired to the room in which he slept, exulting in the success which had attended him, and the valuable booty he had made.

Having secured the door of the chamber, and being sure that no one was listening to or watching him, Adder took the canvas bag from his bosom, and strewing the glittering contents upon the table, proceeded to count them. Yes, it was as Mr. Rainger had stated, he had not the least exaggerated—there was exactly three hundred and fifty guineas, and the villain was very well satisfied with his night's work, as it would go far in replenishing his almost exhausted coffers.

"This sum," reflected Adder, "will do very well for the present, and if I find that I have another good chance of a similar adventure, I will not fail to avail myself of it. By Jupiter, I think I have commenced business as highwayman very promisingly; but I had a hard struggle for the money, and I think that I have fairly earned it. The old chap is a tough customer, and not to be intimidated at trifles. He was very near proving too much for me."

He locked up the money very carefully in his chest, and then burnt the canvas bag in which the gold had been deposited, thus removing every chance of suspicion or detection.

But the sleep of Adder that night was troubled and broken. Frightful visions haunted his imagination. Sometimes he imagined himself to be again struggling with the old man, and sinking exhausted beneath his power, while the latter had placed a pistol to his breast and was about to fire, when he awoke. Then again he thought that he was discovered to be the robber, and the officers of justice were sent to apprehend him, and were conveying him away, when, suddenly, the phantom of his murdered victim, the unfortunate Rose Allerton, appeared, and, accusing him of the crime, in hollow and fearful tones, breathed curses upon his head, and forewarned him of the terrible retribution that awaited him.

In a variety of other horrors, busy fancy involved him, until at length, much relieved, he was awakened by the scorching rays of the morning sun, which had arisen some time, darting across his eyes.

He speedily arose, and went to his chest, to make sure that his ill-gotten money was secure, and he found it there quite safe, as he had placed it the night before.

When he descended to the kitchen, he understood from his landlord that Mr. Rainger had departed two or three hours before to get to the market in time, and he informed Adder that notice of the robbery had been given to the magistrate, and that officers were already on the look out to find the robber and bring him to justice.

"But," continued Mr. Robson, "I do not think there is much chance of their detecting the scoundrel, now; he is far enough off by this time, and has got a booty which he can easily dispose of without exciting any suspicion, if he only acts with prudence and caution."

"The scoundrel, as you call him," thought Adder, and he could scarcely repress a smile of exultation, "the scoundrel is much nearer than you imagine, and it will be my fault if you discover him."

He then added aloud—

"It is a very bad job for the gentleman being robbed of so much money, and I hope the villain who did it may be found; but after all, it is lucky that Mr. Rainger escaped with his life from such a desperate character."

"True, so it is," replied Mr. Robson; "but I am very glad to think that the robbery was not committed in my house, or suspicion might have rested upon an innocent person; one of my lodgers, for instance."

"Yes, so it might," remarked Adder; "but then there would have been a better chance of the gentleman getting his money back again, and finding out the thief."

"Perhaps there would," said the landlord; "but, however, after all, it is a good job the robbery did not fall to the lot of a poor person to whom such a loss would, doubtless, have been their ruin; but Mr. Rainger is very rich, and, therefore, will not miss it. If I were him I would retire from business, for he has made quite enough money to satisfy any reasonable person, and I am afraid that some of these times he will lose his life travelling about, and when it is well known that he carries such large sums of money about him."

"Yes, it is very dangerous," said Adder, "and there are a very queer set of customers about this neighbourhood, I dare say."

"A queer set!" repeated the landlord. "I believe you; why, there are nothing scarcely but poachers and thieves, who would no more mind shooting a man than they would a hare. When Mr. Montalbert, of Holly Hall, was alive, and in his right senses, poor gentleman, he was the means of bringing a number of these offenders to justice, and that struck a terror to the others; but since his death they have become more numerous than ever, and they carry on their nefarious practices almost with perfect impunity. I often thought, at one time, notwithstanding the different surmises that were entertained by most people,

that Lady Ravensford had been destroyed by some of these wretches, in revenge for the praiseworthy efforts of her unfortunate father."

"I have heard something about that affair since I have been residing here," observed Adder, willing to change the topic of his conversation with the landlord from the robbery. "If I have been informed rightly, the lady you speak of was stolen away by a discharged valet of her husband?"

"Yes, a villain of the name of Adder," returned the landlord.

"He must indeed have been a villain," said Adder; "but he played a high game, at any rate, and must have been possessed of both talents and an unlimited stock of effrontery and daring."

"You're right," said Mr. Robson; "he certainly was one of the most crafty villains that ever I heard of, and it was entirely by the most miraculous circumstances that the lady was enabled to escape from his clutches."

"And what has now become of this man?" inquired Adder, in an apparently careless manner.

"Why, I am sorry to say that he was permitted to go at large," answered the landlord; "but I only hope he will yet fall in the hands of justice, and nothing would afford me greater pleasure than to see him hanged."

Adder found some difficulty in restraining the expression of his feelings, and then abruptly terminating a conversation which was anything but interesting to him, he quitted the house, and walked forth into the wood, to deliberate on his future plans.

He was burning for revenge against Lord Ravensford, and was determined that he would no longer delay putting his designs into execution, but he wanted accomplices, for he could not well expect to be able to execute his infamous designs without aid, and he was at a loss where he could find those in whom he could trust.

Several days elapsed without his being able to progress any with his plot, and at the end of that time, accident introduced him to some fellows who would just suit his purpose, and of whom he had some previous knowledge, so he was not afraid to confide in them.

The reward he offered them was liberal, and they readily agreed to aid him in anything in which he might command their services.

It was after this mutual agreement that the consummate villain concocted the plot, by which he managed to introduce himself into the hall and to the favour of Lord Ravensford, and it has been seen how well he succeeded. But it was some weeks before he could venture to make the attempt to put his designs into execution, or could find an opportunity to seize upon Lady Rosabelle, or had arranged his plans as to whither he should convey her. But, during that interval, it would be impossible to do adequate justice to the feelings of exultation he experienced when he thought of the wily part he was playing, the success which had so far attended his diabolical stratagem, and to think that he should be so near the objects of his thoughts and evil intentions without their having the least suspicion, and, in fact, looking upon him as a friend and the preserver of the life of Lord Ravensford.

Often did his deadly hatred towards that nobleman tempt him, now that he had so favourrble an opportunity, to satiate his vengeance in his blood ; but the fear of being detected, and that his designs against our heroine might be thwarted, arrested his fell purpose, and thus the life of his lordship was preserved.

What followed, his seizure of our heroine, and her rescue, the reader has already been made acquainted with ; and his rage and disappointment at that circumstance was almost insupportable, for the daring project of his constant thoughts for months past had not only been frustrated, but the expense which he had incurred by it, and which he could so ill spare, had diminished his finances, and would render it impossible for him to proceed any further with his guilty plans, unless he could meet with such a fortunate adventure as he had had with Mr. Rainger.

He had yet, however, sufficient money to enable him to retain the friendship of his guilty associates, and he, therefore, did not go far from the neighbourhood of Holly Hall, but was concealed by the poachers, and joined them in their lawless proceedings.

In this manner several more months passed away, during which time Adder had ventured to commit several highway robberies, unknown to his confederates, by which means he had got a considerable sum of money by him, and looked forward once more with sanguine hopes to the consummation of his base designs.

All that passed at Holly Hall of any interest to him he had the means of knowing, and at length he heard of the departure of Lord and Lady Ravensford from it, and likewise of their place of destination, and he immediately resolved, with two, only, of his associates in whom he could more confide than the others, to make his way with all possible speed for G——m.

He arrived there in perfect security, only a few days after Lord Ravensford and our heroine had reached Rock House, and managed to hire a place where he could secrete himself and his companions until he could find the opportunity he so eagerly panted for of seizing Lady Rosabelle. In a very short time he had devised his plans, and had made arrangements with the master of a fishing smack, to convey them over to the Isle of Wight, which being out of the track he had hitherto taken, he thought they would be secure from discovery.

He and his vile colleagues were now, therefore, constantly on the look out for a chance of seizing our heroine, but for some time no opportunity presented itself, and it was only accident that brought Adder and her in contact on the day we have mentioned, for he had not then been looking out for her, but was going to another part of the town to meet the captain of the smack with whom he had agreed for the conveyance of himself and our heroine.

At the unsuccess of this scheme, also, the rage of Adder knew no bounds ; it appeared as if there were a spell upon him, and that all his guilty designs were in future to be frustrated. But that the preserver of Rosabelle should have been Monckton, filled his mind with tenfold chagrin, and created in his bosom considerable alarm. He knew that a strict and indefatigable search would now be made for him, and he should have the utmost difficulty in concealing himself, until he should have an opportunity of leaving the town.

Still, however, let the consequences be what they might, he was determined not to give up his designs against Lady Ravensford and her husband, and would only wait for some more propitious opportunity.

For two or three days he remained concealed in the smack, when, finding a chance, at midnight his calleagues quitted the town, and made their way once more to the neighbourhood they had quitted to come to G——m.

Here Adder, who found his connection with the poachers rather more troublesome and expensive to him than otherwise, contrived to give them the slip, and took his residence in an obscure hamlet a short distance from the place, where he eagerly watched for the opportunity of gratifying his revenge, which he was now determined he would accomplish, if even he were compelled to abandon his designs against Lady Ravensford.

Nothing would appease the implacable hatred of that bad man but the blood of Lord Ravensford, whom he so mortally detested, and he watched eagerly for an opportunity of meeting with his lordship, and putting his diabolical wishes into execution. He could not, however, venture to approach near the hall in the daytime, lest he might be discovered, and, therefore, the chance he longed for was not afforded him.

At length the villain's patience being completely exhausted, he determined, at all hazards, to make a bold attempt, and to get into the gardens attached to Holly Hall, where he could conceal himself until an opportunity presented it, and he might behold Lord Ravensford.

It was towards evening when Adder ventured from his lodgings, and by a circuitous and unfrequented way, bent his steps towards Holly Hall. He reached there without having met a single person on the road, and having first looked carefully around him to make sure that no one was watching him, he scaled the garden wall without much difficulty, and with stealthy footsteps traversed the garden until he could find a convenient place to conceal himself, which he at last did in a little summer-house, and from the windows of which he could command an unobstructed view of the hall, and observe every person who came from it.

How anxiously did the miscreant await the opportunity he sought! What tumultuous ideas passed rapidly in his mind, when he thought of his proximity to Lady Rosabelle, and the man he so much disliked, and whom he had doomed to destruction! So excited was he, that he felt fully prepared for any deed, let whatever might be the result; and as he listened to the tones of the old church clock, as hour after hour passed tediously away, and the shades of evening had descended upon the earth, his impatience became almost insupportable.

The moon had now risen, and shed a mellow light upon all around, so that Adder was enabled to see objects at almost any distance quite distinctly; and, at length, he perceived the hall door opened, and two persons step forth, whom he instantly recognised as Lord Ravensford and Mr. Goodman.

The heart of the murderer panted more violently than ever against his side, and his whole frame was convulsed with the powerful effect of his excited feelings.

He watched them with eager eyes, and seeing that they turned into another part of the garden, and away from the direction in which he was concealed, he found it would be necessary for him to leave the summer-house without any more delay, or he might miss them altogether. He, therefore, cautiously quitted the place, and followed behind them, until they had reached a convenient spot, where the villain took his aim and fired! Confusion! he had missed Lord Ravensford, and shot Mr. Goodman, who uttered a cry of agony, and fell into the arms of his friend.

"D—nation!" cried the murderer, "am I ever to be foiled? There is some infernal spell upon me! But I will have my revenge! I will have my revenge, even though I swing for it the next moment! Die, Ravensford, detested Ravensford, die!"

As the miscreant thus spoke, he raised the second pistol which he had brought with him, and made a more certain aim at Lord Ravensford, who, horrorstruck and astonished at the catastrophe, was still supporting the bleeding form of his venerable friend in his arms, and calling aloud for help.

Again was the villain disappointed in the perpetration of his deadly purpose; again did Providence interpose to save Ravensford from the untimely fate with which he had been threatened. The pistol missed fire, and the next moment several of the servants were seen coming from the hall, one of whom assisted their master in conveying Mr. Goodman to the house, while the others started in different directions in search of the wretch who had been guilty of the atrocious crime. Adder, therefore, saw that there was not an instant to be lost, and uttering curses loud and deep at his failure, he bounded over the wall with the speed of lightning, and was soon far enough from Holly Hall to be out of the danger of pursuit.

In the meantime the consternation that prevailed amongst the inmates of Holly Hall may be better imagined than we can pourtray it. Mr. Goodman had fainted from loss of blood, and being conveyed to a chamber, followed by his distracted daughter and our heroine, the medical attendant of the family was sent for and speedily arrived, while Ravensford gave some hasty directions for the garden and the neighbourhood of the hall to be strictly searched for the assassin, whom, however, every person immediately concluded was Adder, or some ruffian whom he had employed, and that they had not the least doubt but that Ravensford had been the intended victim.

The medical gentleman having examined the wound, to the great relief of them all, pronounced it to be a very slight one, and not at all dangerous, and Mr. Goodman soon afterwards being restored to sensibility, desired them not to feel uneasy on his account, and was of the same opinion as the rest, namely, that it was Adder who had committed the deed, and that Lord Ravensford was the individual who he intended to have shot.

But although the circumstance created the greatest excitement in the neighbourhood, where Mr. Goodman was most highly esteemed, and the strictest search was made after the offender, they could not discover any traces of him, nor who was the person who had been guilty of so heinous a crime.

Adder had safely eluded them, and although he was not far from the spot, he had taken such precautions that his concealment was perfectly secure, and he defied detection.

In about a fortnight Mr. Goodman was almost restored to convalescence, and the excitement which the circumstance had at first naturally caused, was, in a great measure abated; but still a sharp look out was kept up for Adder, who was still believed to be the guilty party, for they knew no one else who could have been incited from any motive to commit such a deed.

At length Mr. Goodman was completely restored, and the circumstance no more caused any sensation, and, in fact, was almost forgotten, several months having elapsed since it had taken place. But another event at last occurred, which caused more excitement than anything had done before, and promised to do away with the cause of their apprehensions and uneasiness.

The house of Mr. Goodman was a large, old-fashioned structure, with no pretensions to architectural beauty; but still the gothic appearance of the place was sufficient to interest the beholder, and to arrest his attention.

It was situated about a mile from Holly Hall, and immediately on the borders of the wood. It was very gloomy and lonely; and as Mr. Goodman only kept two faithful servants, and an aged housekeeper, Mr. Rattleton had endeavoured to persuade him to give up this establishment, and to reside, for the future, in an elegant house which he had purchased on his marriage with Mr. Goodman's daughter.

This, however, the old gentleman declined, for he had resided in the house so many years, that he could not make up his mind to leave it; and latterly, when he had passed so much of his time at Holly Hall, he, more than before, did not see the necessity of it.

On his return to Beechwood, which was the name of the edifice he resided in, he was accompanied by Mr. and Mrs. Rattleton, who were going to remain with him for a few weeks, and who again tried to persuade him to give up the gloomy old house, and to come to reside with them at the mansion they had taken; but Mr. Goodman could not be induced to alter his situation, although he was fully aware how much more comfortable he should be in being constantly in the society of his son-in-law and his amiable daughter.

It was about a week only after Mr. Goodman's return to Beechwood, that Rattleton was aroused from sleep one night by imagining he heard the sound of footsteps stealing along the passage upon which his chamber opened; and raising himself up in bed, he listened attentively. All was again still, and he therefore concluded that he had been deceived, and that it was entirely the effects of imagination, and he had lain himself down in the bed, and was about to compose himself to sleep again, when he again heard the sounds more distinctly than before, and was then convinced that he was not mistaken, but that some one was moving along the passage; and speedily getting out of bed, he slipped on his morning gown, and snatching a pistol which was loaded, and placed over the mantel-piece, he silently opened the room-door, and looking earnestly in the direction from whence the sounds seemed to proceed as well as the light, which was admitted by a spiral window at the end, would allow him to distinguish, he was convinced that some one was proceeding along the passage, and holding in his breath, fearful that the least sound would betray him, he followed and watched him as narrowly as he could, certain that it was not one of the servants, and that, whoever he was, he could be after no good purpose.

The door of a chamber at the end of this passage was standing open, and Rattleton knew that it was the room in which his father-in-law had deposited his iron-chest, and he could not account for his negligence in leaving the door unlooked.

The man carried a dark lantern in his hand, and having looked around him, without being able to observe Rattleton, who had stolen into a niche in the wall, and was thus concealed from the sight, he quickly entered the room, and cautiously closed the door after him.

Rattleton paused for a few moments, and reflected what he had best do, whether he should alarm the house, or rush upon the fellow himself and attempt to take him into custody. He soon decided on the latter, and stepping lightly up to the door, he first peeped in. The light from the lantern fell full upon the man's face, and to the astonishment of Rattleton, he discovered that it was the villain Adder.

He was kneeling down by the chest, the lid of which he had raised, and was about to examine the contents, when he started, as he thought a sound reached his ears, and immediately closed the lantern.

He listened attentively, and seemed scarcely to allow himself to breathe. All this time Rattleton was watching him, with a full determination to secure him without doing him any harm, or running any risk himself.

"Psha!" muttered Adder, at length, in an under tone, "it was only fancy. I must be quick! I must be quick!"

He once more opened the lantern, and again proceeded to ransack the contents of the chest. His back was turned towards him, and that was the time which Rattleton saw afforded him the opportunity he wanted.

"Villain! miscreant!" he shouted, rushing into the apartment, and springing upon him by the collar with one hand, while he placed the pistol to his head with the other;—"resistance is vain!—You are at last detected, and most assuredly must pay the penalty of your numerous crimes by an ignominious death."

"Confusion!" cried Adder, staring aghast, and letting fall the lid of the chest;—"discovered! baulked! Ah! Rattleton!"

"Yes, villain!" returned Rattleton, "and are in my ·····

"At any rate not till we have had a struggle for it," exclaimed Adder, suddenly forcing himself on his feet, and by a quick movement extricating himself from Rattleton's hold.

Immediately he seized the hand of the latter, and endeavoured to wrest the pistol from his grasp. A violent struggle ensued, in which it was for a time doubtful which would become the conqueror, and at length the pistol was discharged by accident, and Rattleton once more succeeded in striking Adder to the floor, where he held him by the throat with an iron gripe, when footsteps were heard rapidly approaching, and it was very evident that the report of the pistol had alarmed the inmates of the house, and that all hopes of Adder's escaping were at an end. Dreadful curses escaped his lips, and he made another effort to disengage himself from the grasp of Rattleton, and inflict some deadly injury upon him, and at that moment the room door was thrown open, and Mr. Goodman and the male servants entered, armed in the best manner they could in the brief space of time which had been allowed them after hearing the report.

The astonishment of them all on beholding the villain Adder we need not attempt to describe, and the horror and confusion of the latter was more than equal to it. Of course, he was speedily secured, and placed in a strong room until the morning, guarded by two of the servants, and in the morning he was conveyed before the magistrate, who committed him to gaol forthwith, to take his trial at the next assizes, on the charge of burglary.

CHAPTER XLVII.

THE TRIAL.—THE ACCUSATION.—THE SMUGGLER CAPTAIN.—THE ESCAPE.

GREAT, indeed, was the astonishment of Lord Ravensford and our heroine, when they were made acquainted with this unexpected circumstance, and their satisfaction upon knowing that the miscreant by whom they had been so heartlessly persecuted was at length in safe custody, and would, no doubt, be punished for his crimes.

All their future apprehensions would be thus at rest, and they would get rid of the only enemy they believed they had in the world. The singular manner in which he had been taken, caused them much surprise, and they highly applauded the prudence with which Rattleton had acted, and which had rendered the escape of the ruffian impossible.

Ravensford visited Adder in gaol, and the scene which took place on that occasion needs a more skilful pen than our own to pourtray it as it ought to be. Bitterly did his lordship reproach him for the unprecedented and villanous course he had pursued towards him and our heroine; while the ruffian, on the contrary, exulted in all he had done, and the misery he had caused him, and only regretted that he should have been taken prisoner before he had fully gratified his revenge in his blood, and completed his designs against Lady Ravensford.

But reckless as Adder had appeared to be in the presence of Lord Ravensford, when alone, he gave himself up to all the horrors of despair, and the almost inevitable and ignominious death which awaited him. Whichever way he turned he could not find the smallest ray of hope or consolation, and he might, he felt certain, consider his guilty career as brought to a close.

Many and bitter were the curses which Adder invoked upon the head of Rattleton, who had detected him in the act of burglary, and upbraided himself for not having taken to his old plan, namely, a robbery on the highway, by which he had frequently made so good a booty, in preference to running the greater risk of becoming a housebreaker.

Some weeks passed away, when the assizes commenced, and Adder was put upon his trial for the attempted burglary at Beechwood, in the house of Mr. Goodman.

The prisoner had been placed at the bar, and pleaded "not guilty," and he was about to be tried, when a loud voice was suddenly heard to exclaim "Stop!" and the tall figure of a man, enveloped in a large mantle, stepped hastily into a witness-box, and confronted the prisoner.

The latter turned ghastly pale, and trembled very much, which was not to be wondered at, when the reader is informed, that in the man who had thus so abruptly entered the justice-hall, Adder recognised Monckton, the smuggler-captain.

"Stop!" he exclaimed; "before you proceed with this trial I have a wish to be heard."

"Who are you?" demanded the judge.

"Archibald Malcolm," replied the smuggler.

"Better known as Monckton, the notorious captain of a desperate gang of smugglers," added the prisoner, with a malicious grin.

"Very true," answered Monckton, coolly; "I wrote a letter to your lordships, a few days ago, offering to come forward and give important evidence if you would promise to hold me blameless, and suffer me to depart again to the place from whence I came unmolested. You were pleased to agree with my proposal, and I have, therefore, appeared before you."

"That is correct, and no harm shall come to you, if you speak the truth," said the principal judge. "What is the nature of the evidence which you wish to offer?"

"I accuse James Henry Adder of the

murder of Rose Allerton, in the village of Ashbourne, in the county of ——, about eighteen years ago," said Monckton.

Adder's countenance became instantly as pale as death, and his frame was violently convulsed, whilst every eye was turned attentively upon him and the smuggler-captain, eager to learn what would be the result of this accusation. A thrill of horror ran through the court at this dreadful recital, and the prisoner was so violently agitated that he appeared to be several times on the point of fainting. Before, however, Monckton had concluded, he had become more collected, and in pretty firm accents ejaculated—

"My lords, you surely will not believe this tale, fabricated and uttered by so notorious an offender as Monckton, the smuggler-captain? I solemnly protest that I am entirely innocent of the murder of the unfortunate Rose Allerton, and——"

"It is false! I have witnesses with me who were present when the poor girl breathed her last, and who heard her dying observations," returned Monckton.

"Let them come forward, then," commanded the judge; and Monckton having made a signal, Michael Hernwood, Ned Mayling, and Sam Kitson, instantly made their appearance in the court.

MONCKTON ACCUSES ADDER AS THE MURDERER OF ROSE ALLERTON.

"These are the witnesses I spoke of, my lords," said Monckton.

The prisoner affected to smile contemptuously; but his mind was in a violent state of agitation, and he anticipated the worst.

"These men also are smugglers, and some of his own gang, my lords," said Adder; "it surely is not possible that you can believe such men upon their oath."

"I have more evidence," remarked Monckton, producing the document which the poor illfated Rose Allerton had written in her last moments; "it is this."

"Is there any one in the court who knew the deceased female, and who was acquainted with her handwriting?" asked the chief judge.

No person answered.

"I think we had better proceed with the trial of the charge on which the prisoner is already indicted, and postpone the other until a future day," observed the judge.

The other judges concurring in this suggestion, Monckton and his associates were permitted to leave the court unmolested; and Adder, having been arraigned at the bar on the charge of burglary, it was proceeded with, and the trial, after lasting but a very short time, as the evidence was so conclusive, terminated by the conviction of Adder, who was found guilty and sentenced to death.

The wretched culprit appeared to be completely stupified when the sentence was passed upon him, and was removed from the dock in a state of utter unconsciousness.

But how terrible were his emotions when he recovered his senses, and found himself secured in a strong dungeon, without any chance of his escaping, and with the awful prospect of a violent death before him. It would be vain for us to attempt to describe them, for his sufferings were almost too intense for human endurance. All the guilty scenes of his past life were brought in vivid array before his recollection, and the eternal punishment which awaited him was depicted to his imagination in still more glowing colours. He groaned, cursed, and wept, in the utter misery of his heart; and, beating his breast, he traversed the place of his confinement with hasty and uneven footsteps.

It was several hours before he could become anything like calm, and then his reflections, from being deliberate, were, if possible, the more painful. But at length he was somewhat more aroused to action, and he began to collect his ideas, and to look around him in the hope of being able to effect his escape; but this, at first, was not attended with any encouraging prospect, and he seated himself on his bed of straw again in despair.

That night and the next day passed away without any change in his prospects, when the culprit again turned his thoughts towards escaping, and fixed his eyes upon the iron bars of the window of the place in which he was confined, but they were so strongly fixed, that there seemed not to be the least chance of any one being able to remove them without proper tools for so doing, and then not without considerable difficulty, and after much labour.

However, to remain where he was, and to tamely submit to his fate, Adder could not even think of with any degree of patience, and mad and desperate as the attempt undoubtedly would be, he determined to make it.

Looking about the room in which he was confined, Adder found a large rusty nail, which he quickly put into use, with it working away the stone in which the iron bars were fixed, until, after an immense deal of labour, he succeeded in loosening one of the bars, and ultimately in wrenching it from the window.

Having accomplished this, he gave up his task until the following day, and replaced the iron bar in the same position, so that what he had been doing might not meet the observations of the turnkey, when he came to visit him, and to bring him his provisions.

The following morning early, Adder resumed his tedious job with increased hopes, and after some hours' labour, another of the iron bars yielded, and by the time that the evening had arrived, he had wrenched out a sufficient number to enable him to get his body through.

Adder looked out at the window, and perceived that it was a very short distance from the ground only, and that he might jump it without having occasion to fear that he should

meet with any accident. But he thought it would be best for him to wait until it was quite dark before he should venture to make the attempt, when he would have every chance in his favour of being enabled to regain his liberty, without running the hazard of being detected.

Most anxiously did the wretched culprit wait for the approach of night, and at length darkness set in, and the gaoler having paid him his last visit, he listened attentively for a few moments, and all being completely still, he clambered to the window, removed the bars, and forcing his body through the opening, he gave a spring, and the next instant he had alighted on the ground in safety, and was at liberty.

CHAPTER XLVIII.

THE OLD BARN.—THE REAPPEARANCE OF ADDER.—THE RECAPTURE.

NEVER had liberty appeared so sweet to the guilty Adder as it did at that time, when he felt the fresh cool air blowing upon his face, and bracing his nerves, and he rushed from the spot with the speed of the startled deer, and made towards the most lonely part of the country, taking care to avoid the high road.

Still he was pursued by a thousand fears, and ever and anon he looked back, as he imagined he heard the voices of men behind, and which his fancy immediately conjectured were those who were sent in search of him.

He was at length compelled to abate his speed, for he was completely out of breath, and forcing his way among a cluster of trees, he threw himself upon the dank earth, and panted to recover himself.

What course to pursue he knew not, for he was entirely destitute, and had not the means to procure even a meal's victuals or a shelter. His situation, in fact, was desperate and hopeless, and it would seem, upon mature reflection, that he had but little cause to exult in his escape from prison, when he had no other prospect before him than the most abject want, or to have recourse to thieving for an existence, and it was not likely that it would be long before he would again fall into the hands of justice.

Besides, he must now abandon all thoughts of ever getting Rosabelle again in his power, or of having an opportunity of being revenged against her husband, and he regretted that he had ever returned from the Continent, where he might have lived in security and with comfort on the money then he had in his possession.

After having stretched his weary limbs for about a quarter of an hour on this spot, Adder once more arose and pursued his way, without having any settled purpose or knowing the direction in which he was going.

He had now got a considerable distance from the gaol, and for the present was out of danger, but he was weary and exhausted, and would have been glad to have found some place of shelter, even if it were ever so wretched, especially as it now began to rain, and the pealing thunder and the flashing lightning betokened a fearful night.

Adder walked as fast as his weary limbs would carry him, still hoping to meet with some place of shelter; but it was long ere those hopes were realised.

At length, however, he broke from the wood through which he had been travelling, and presently afterwards his eyes were gladdened with the sight of an old barn, which stood in a small valley, and was sufficiently secluded.

Eagerly he advanced towards it, and approaching an old rackety door which was creaking in the wind, he listed attentively, to make sure that it was not occupied already. Finding, however, that all was still, he ventured to force the door entirely open, which he did with very little difficulty, and entered the place.

It was gloomy and cheerless enough, but anything was preferable to remaining in the open air all the night and exposed to the "pitiless pelting of the storm," and Adder felt very glad that he had been so fortunate as to meet with it.

He piled all the old lumber he could find against the door on the inside, to prevent any person entering without his hearing them, and he then groped his way to the inner part of the barn, and raking together all the old straw he could find, and placing it in the darkest corner, he laid himself down and tried to sleep. But it was so cold, from the wind which penetrated through the different apertures, and his own thoughts were so much distracted, that it was some time ere he could do so, and then his slumbers were disturbed and unrefreshing.

Terrific dreams haunted his imagination, and often made him start up in the greatest terror, with the cold drops of perspiration standing upon his temples, as he fancied he was again in the power of the officers of justice. Then again he would imagine that he beheld the ghastly apparition of the murdered Rose Allerton, who pointed to the gallows and shrieked "Retribution!" in his ears. Thus it is that the guilty can never rest, and that they are doomed to endure on earth a foretaste of that dreadful punishment which awaits them hereafter.

At length, completely worn out with bodily and mental agony, the poor wretch was enabled to get a few hours' repose, and when he again awoke, the day, which was just dawning, gave him warning to quit the barn, and to make his way to some other part of the country, where he might be safe for awhile from pursuit. But what was he to do without a farthing in the world, or the means of procuring a morsel of food, and he was now most intolerably hungry? He was quite bewildered, and knew not what would become of him.

With a heavy heart he was removing the rubbish which he had piled against the door, when by the gray light which peeped through a crevice above, he saw something glitter, and, on looking closer, to his infinite delight and astonishment, he perceived that it was a guinea! Some person had evidently been there before him, and had accidentally dropped the money, and he searched still further, with the hope of finding more, but did not succeed; and after carefully depositing his money in his pocket, he left the barn, much relieved to think that he was, at any rate, provided with the means of present existence, and not doubting by the time the guinea was exhausted he should be able to devise some means of keeping out of the reach of the law.

After travelling for some time across the country, meeting only a few countrymen who were on their way to their daily labour, he arrived at a small town, where he was enabled to procure refreshments, and there also he altered his appearance as much as possible, and in order better to prevent suspicion, he endeavoured to get some employment, in which he was successful, and having been engaged as a labourer in the field, he took an obscure lodging, and then being somewhat more settled in his mind, he began to collect his thoughts, and to try to think of some plan for the future, for to remain in his present abject situation, neither his pride nor his constitution would permit him.

But what other means could he resort to than those he had before adopted—namely, to commit a robbery? And that he resolved to do without any further delay.

Night after night he was prowling the road after the people at the place where he lodged had imagined that he had retired to rest, but for some time his guilty wishes were not destined to be gratified. At length, however, ill fortune conducted a traveller, who had a considerable sum of money about him, in his way, and Adder, after knocking him down and otherwise ill-using him, until he had become insensible, plundered him of every farthing he had about him, and then immediately quitted the neighbourhood, thinking it would not be safe for him to remain there any longer.

The following morning found the guilty outcast full thirty miles from the place in which he had been living for some short time, for he had continued to travel the whole of the night, only resting at intervals, and that very seldom.

Here he lost no time in changing his appearance altogether. He washed the colour —with which he had dyed them—from his face and hands, purchased a sandy-coloured wig and whiskers, and otherwise so metamorphozed himself, that it would have been impossible for the most scrutinizing and penetrating person to recognise him. He seldom ventured out much in the daytime, and he was believed by the persons at the inn where he lodged to be some private gentleman, who had but limited means, and who disliked society.

Three weeks elapsed in this manner, and during that period the miscreant Adder had not been idle, for he had committed no less than four robberies, the whole of which had brought him in good booties. But at length the people in the neighbourhood became alarmed, and a description of the robber's person having been advertised, and a reward offered for his apprehension, Adder thought it advisable to decamp from where he was with all possible despatch ; but he did not do so until he had robbed a traveller, who had stopped at the inn, of a considerable sum of money in gold, and his watch and every other article of value he had with him.

With this booty, the daring villain managed to make his escape, and at the first town where he arrived he once more altered his disguise, and that so effectually, that it would have been an impossibility for any person to have detected him.

Having now a good sum of money once more in his possession, Adder again reflected upon what he should do for the future, and whither bend his course. At first he had half determined that he would leave England altogether, and take up his future residence abroad, where he might have the same opportunities of committing his acts of depredation, and, perhaps, with the same success ; and if he had availed himself of those dictates he would unquestionably have acted wisely, and might have escaped the fate he had incurred by his crimes, and which was afterwards doomed to overtake him. But there was some spell that still rivetted him to England ; the thoughts of Rosabelle and revenge still lingered at his heart, and he could not make up his mind entirely to abandon either.

Nay, sometimes, so strong was that feeling within him, that he was half inclined to venture again to the neighbourhood of Holly Hall, and endeavour to put his base projects into execution. For awhile, however, he was restrained by fear, and he wandered about from one place to the other, without staying long in any. At length the wheel of fortune turned against him, and he was apprehended for a highway robbery, and sent to prison, every

farthing which he possessed being taken from him. He contrived to escape, and in the utmost misery, hunger, and wretchedness, he rambled about for a day or two, subsisting alone by begging, and sleeping at night in any place of shelter he could find.

He was reduced to that state of despair, that he was almost unsconcious and perfectly careless in what direction he travelled, and, in fact, he had become almost indifferent about whether he was apprehended or not, such was the severity of his sufferings, and so little chance did he perceive there was of there being any alteration in his condition.

By a remarkable fatality his footsteps were guided to the very spot from whence he had at first fled, namely, the vicinity of Beechwood and Holly Hall; and by a strange destiny, although he was fully aware of the danger by which he was encompassed, he was urged on by an irresistible impulse to the latter place.

It was in the afternoon when Adder reached the immediate neighbourhood of Holly Hall, and it was then only that he, for the first time, looked around him, and bethought himself what he was about. But still, although destruction stared him in the face, he found it utterly impossible for him to abandon the spot, but, on the contrary, he was urged onward, until he had arrived to within a very short distance of Holly Hall.

Here Adder once more paused, and again he looked more narrowly than he had done before around him. Suddenly his eyes fell upon two objects not far from him, that fixed his whole attention, and caused a strange sensation in his bosom. It was a lady who was walking towards him, and who led by the hand a fine handsome boy, about seven years old. The lady's face was for a moment averted, for she was gazing back upon some object which she had previously passed. But Adder could not be mistaken; her figure, her very air, convinced him he was not; and, besides, the boy, he could clearly distinguish his features, and that was enough to satisfy him that his surmise was correct. The next moment the lady looked round, and almost immediately observing Adder, she gave utterance to an exclamation of terror, and appeared to be transfixed to the spot on which she was standing.

It was Lady Ravensford and her child, who were taking their customary walk, and never expecting to meet with such an adventure.

Miserable and desperate as was the situation of Adder; he no sooner beheld Lady Ravensford than all his original feelings returned, and he rushed hastily towards her, and rudely seized her arm, at the same time that he fixed his eyes upon her countenance with a mingled expression of exultation and revenge. He was about to speak, when at that moment the voices of men sounded in his ears from behind, and releasing Rosabelle from his grasp, he looked around, and beheld several rustics approaching him.

With a loud curse, Adder quitted our heroine and her child, and leaping over a neighbouring hedge, he hurried across the fields, with all the speed he could, and never once ventured to look behind, so great was his fear of being apprehended. He had soon got to a considerable distance from the place where he had encountered Lady Ravensford, and then, for the first time, ventured to look around him.

He could perceive no signs of his pursuers, and he breathed more freely.

To his astonishment, however, he found that he had taken precisely the same direction as he had done when he escaped from the prison, after his condemnation, and he, therefore, resolved to make for the old barn which had on that occasion afforded him a shelter, not doubting but that it would render him the same service on the present occasion.

He reached the barn in about another hour, and he did not perceive that there was any alteration in it since he had last been there; and after listening to make certain that no person was there, he entered, and, completely worn out with fatigue, fear, anxiety, and disappointment, he sunk upon the heap of straw in the corner, which did not appear to have been disturbed since he had been there before, and gave himself up to the most racking thought.

He had now suffered so much, and fate seemed so completely to have conspired against him, that he cared little whether he was taken or not; and yet the idea of a public death upon the scaffold, exposed to the vulgar gaze of the mob, and with their curses and execrations ringing in his ears, was too awful even for contemplation; and as these thoughts rapidly flashed across his burning brain, he arose, and once more barricaded the door in the same manner as he had before done, and then, returning to his wretched pallet, he endeavoured to seek forgetfulness in sleep.

In this he was at last successful; but how long he slept he knew not, but he was suddenly aroused by a noise, which immediately made him start to his feet, and he looked around him with the greatest consternation, cold drops of perspiration standing upon his quivering temples.

The sounds he had heard, and which had awakened him, were the voices of several men apparently immediately outside the barn, and one of whom having mentioned his name, he had not the least doubt but what they were some of the persons who were sent in pursuit of him, and who had traced his footsteps to the barn.

In a state of the utmost horror and consternation he listened, and holding in his breath, was enabled to catch the following words:—

"There cannot be a likelier place than this to find him," observed one.

"Well, then, what's the use of delaying it any longer?" said the voice of another man; "if he is here, he cannot escape us, for he must be a desperate fellow, indeed, to be enabled to prove too much for three of us. There is the door. You have got you barkers ready, both of you?"

The other two men replied in the affirmative.

"That's all right," said the man who had put the question; "then here goes. Hollo, what's the matter with the door? I can't open it; some person must be inside. Give me your help, and the door will not long be able to resist our united strength."

The three men pushed heavily against the door, and the rubbish which Adder had piled up against it began to fall down with a rumbling noise, and the crazy door creaked harshly on its hinges.

This was a moment of the most terrible anxiety and trepidation which Adder ever remembered to have experienced before; but his fate was now inevitable, and it would be vain to attempt to offer any resistance; yet with that desperate determination to make an attempt to procrastinate his fate, to which he was driven by the utter hopelessness of his thoughts, the wretched man crawled beneath the straw which had formed his humble pallet; and, covering himself over, he scarcely ventured to respire, lest the smallest sound should betray him.

Another moment, the whole of the rubbish which he had piled against the door gave way, the door itself was burst off its hinges, and the three men entered the barn.

Adder could just peep from beneath the straw, and he then perceived that they were all armed, and one of them carried a dark lantern, which he opened, and the stream of light which escaped from it cast a ghastly glare upon the wretched place, which was fast tumbling to pieces; and not having been made any use of for a number of years, it was a wonder that it had not been removed altogether.

"Well," observed one of the men, "we have got in at last, and a most cheerless looking place it is, sure enough. Hold the lantern lower down, George. I do not see any signs of a human being here: and yet any one would imagine that there must have been some person here, or else how could all this rubbish have been piled against the door on the inside?"

"Why, it certainly does look remarkable," said another of the men; "but, perhaps, whoever has been here has had to make their exit rather abruptly through some of the apertures at the back of the building."

"Well, it is very evident that there is no

person here now," remarked the man who had first spoken, "and we might, therefore, have saved ourselves all the trouble. But we had better not delay getting to the nearest village or town, with the greatest despatch, for the impression is still strong upon my mind that he has taken this way, and, if we are only expeditious, we may yet overtake him. Come, let us begone."

Adder breathed again; but his hopes were of brief duration.

"Nay, do not be in such a hurry," said the third man, as the others were preparing to go; "we have not half examined this place yet, and my suspicions are as strong as ever. That heap of straw in the corner had better be searched, for many a rogue has been able to conceal himself under much less than that ere now."

Despair again settled upon the heart of Adder; he found that it was all over with him; that his discovery was unavoidable, and that it was useless to hold out any longer. As the men, therefore, approached the straw beneath which he had lain, he started up, and in a dogged tone exclaimed—

"It is no use holding out against so unequal a power; if I am the man you want, I am here, and, I suppose, must accompany you to my old quarters."

"You are the man we want," said one of the officers, "and a pretty deal of trouble you have given us. But I'll warrant that you do not slip through the fingers of the law again."

Adder returned no reply, for his spirits were too much depressed, and the daring which had hitherto sustained him now entirely forsook him, and he suffered himself to be handcuffed, without showing the least disposition to offer any resistance.

He was then removed from the barn, and hurried on at a quick pace towards the gaol, from whence he had escaped after his conviction for the burglary, and was securely lodged in one of the strongest dungeons in the prison.

CHAPTER XLIX.

THE PRISONER'S DESPAIR.—HORRORS OF CONSCIENCE.—PENITENCE.—THE EXECUTION.

WE have shown that, by Adder having taken the direction he had, after his meeting with our heroine, he was enabled completely to outstrip his pursuers, and to reach the old barn in safety.

Lady Ravensford, having recovered from the astonishment and terror into which the miscreant Adder had again thrown her, made the best of her way, with her child, to the hall, where the surprise of her husband and her friends almost exceeded all bounds, and they were at first inclined to think that she must have been mistaken, so improbable did it appear that the villain, after having escaped from the gaol, and with every opportunity to elude the vigilance of the officers, should be so foolish as to return to the very neighbourhood, and where he was almost certain to be apprehended; but when they were convinced that Lady Ravensford could not be deceived, but that it was really Adder whom she had met, they were completely thunderstruck at his unparalleled daring, and could not be sufficiently thankful that Providence had again interposed to rescue her, by sending the rustics to the spot at the very critical moment; for they entertained no doubt but that Adder would have murdered both her and the boy. They now entertained strong hopes that he would be taken, and his fate being already sealed, they would be entirely relieved from the miseries and annoyances with which he had so long persecuted them. But after an absence of about two hours, the peasants returned to the hall, and informed them that their endeavours to trace the villain had proved entirely unsuccessful; that he had managed to elude them, and they were fearful that he would now escape altogether; but they had the good sense to make the circumstance known at the house of the magistrate, and that functionary had immediately despatched officers in all directions, with instructions not to abandon their search until all hopes of its being attended with any fortunate results should be at an end.

The manner in which the guilty Adder was recaptured we have fully detailed in the previous chapter, and, therefore, it is unnecessary to recapitulate it here; and the satisfaction of all who heard of it, and who were acquainted with all the atrocious circumstances of the villain's life, was as great as might be expected, and all agreed that no culprit had ever more richly deserved the fate which had awaited him than he did.

During the time that Adder had been at large, the most patient investigation of the dreadful charge which Monckton had brought against him had taken place, and the result was, after the corroborating evidence of witnesses, and the testimony of persons who were summoned from the place where the unfortunate Rose Allerton had resided, and who swore to Adder's being the last person who had been seen in company with the ill-fated girl, his guilt was fully established; but as he had already been tried and convicted on one indictment, for which he had been condemned to die, should he be retaken, it was thought quite unnecessary to try him for the murder.

Considering the strict search which was made, and the large rewards that were offered for his recapture, it was a most remarkable thing that Adder should have been able to elude the officers so long as he had done; and had he acted with any ordinary prudence, he might still have remained at large, and have been secure enough in some foreign country.

These were the thoughts that crowded upon the brain of the wretched culprit, now that he was again a prisoner, and several times did he curse his folly in not having availed himself of the opportunity of escaping from the terrible fangs of justice, when it was presented to him. But these thoughts were quickly succeeded by others of a very different nature. Now that every ray of hope of escaping from his awful doom was excluded from his mind, the terrible crimes he had perpetrated throughout his guilty career rushed upon his brain with irresistible force, and all the horrors of remorse racked his soul. The dreadful punishment which awaited him in eternity was depictured to his imagination with tenfold horror, and he shrunk appalled, with all the weakness of a child. Now, indeed, did penitence truly steal poun his soul, and he trembled with horror when he thought of the past, and the utter despair of the future. Oh, what would he not have given could he but have been as innocent as he was ere crime and him were acquainted; how calmly could he have died, he thought, had he but passed a life of virtue and integrity. Now, how fearful to him appeared a life of iniquity; how utterly pitiable and wretched the votaries of guilt! How happily might he have lived had he chosen honour for his guide! How different would have been his situation to what it was then; a poor condemned wretch, awaiting a violent and ignominious death, unpitied by all, despised, detested by every one. Now might he have been living honured and respected; blessings invoked upon his head instead of curses; blessed with a virtuous and affectionate wife, happy and dutiful children, and enjoying all the blessings of domestic peace.

Alas! how terrible was the contrast! The miserable convict clasped his manacled hands together, and groaned aloud in all the agony of mental torment!

Three days only were permitted to intervene ere the execution of the awful sentence which had been passed upon him, and that time he employed in repentance, and in endeavouring to prepare himself for the great change he was about to undergo. He made a full confession of all his crimes, and begged that Lord Ravensford would visit him in prison, so that he might assure him of his compunction for the injuries he had done him, and crave his forgiveness.

Ravensford, after consulting with our heroine and his friends, determined to comply with his desire, and accordingly repaired to the prison in which the guilty Adder was confined.

The interview made a powerful impression upon the mind of his lordship. Never had he beheld penitence apparently more fervent and sincere; never had he witnessed agony more acute. Deeply as he had injured him, awful as had been the days, the weeks, the months of almost insupportable anxiety, agony, and suspense which he had inflicted upon him; fearful as had been the misery which he had heaped upon his beloved wife; unparalleled as had been his acts of heartless treachery and cold-blooded villany throughout, he could not have refused to have granted his forgiveness to so wretched and so pitiable a being on any account whatever. It would have been the very opposite to Christian humanity to have done so; and, therefore, Ravensford at length assured the culprit that he did forgive him, and earnestly entreated him to employ the few short hours that intervened between him and eternity in seeking the pardon of the Almighty also; then, completely heart-sick at the intense mental torments the poor wretch was enduring, he hurried from the prison and returned home.

After his interview with Ravensford, and the assurance which his lordship had so earnestly given him, Adder felt a considerable weight removed from his heart; yet were his sufferings most severe, and as the time approached nearer when he was to suffer the dreadful penalty of the law, his fortitude entirely forsook him, and he would throw himself upon the cold stones of his dungeon, and weep like a child, in utter imbecility and despair of soul. Sometimes it was quite awful to hear his groans and shrieks, as in imagination he beheld the grizzly phantom of his murdered victim, the unfortunate Rose Allerton, and his wild ravings for mercy might be heard all over the prison, and at all hours of the day and night, making the latter still more hideous than it otherwise would have been in that gloomy receptacle for crime and misery.

The alteration in Adder's appearance, too, was as remarkable as his penitence. In a few days he looked not like the same individual. His form had become bent and attenuated, as if a century had suddenly passed over his head; his face haggard, pale, wrinkled, and cadaverous. His eyes, that were formerly very bright and penetrating, had almost entirely lost their lustre, and had become deep sunk in his head, and his looks altogether were such as must inspire pity in the most callous bosom, even while the remembrance of his enormous crimes must have filled them with the utmost horror and disgust.

But amid all the guilty man's mental anguish, he derived consolation, and felt the most unbounded gratitude when he reflected that his diabolical designs against Lady Ravensford and her husband had been frustrated, and that although he had caused them so much misery, he had been sufficiently prevented from inflicting upon them an injury which nothing could have repaired. The honour of our heroine had been preserved by her own virtuous firmness, and a perfectly miraculous chain of events, and he had the consolation of knowing that they triumphed over his iniquitous plans.

But then again, might he not accuse himself, and justly too, of being the murderer of Mr. Montalbert? Had he not been the indirect cause of that unfortunate gentleman's death? Undoubtedly he had: at least, so his conscience told him he had, and the charge was too much strengthened by reason to be denied. There could not be a doubt but that the abduction of Lady Rosabelle had caused her father to relapse into his former state of madness, and that had hastened his death; and Adder, therefore, felt himself the murderer of that unfortunate gentleman, in every sense of the word, and this thought added to the strength of the torture of mind which he was enduring.

The chaplain of the gaol and the governor exerted themselves to the utmost to calm the feelings of the culprit, and to put him in a right state of mind to prepare for eternity; and certainly, if anything can be said of the most vehement penitence, prayers, and supplications to Heaven, in proof, they entirely succeeded.

At length arrived the morning of execution, and vast, indeed, was the assemblage of persons that congregated around the fatal spot where the awful tragedy was to be enacted, to witness the last moments of a man who, by his immemorable offences and the peculiar nature of his crimes, had excited such a remarkable sensation all over the country.

Adder had slept none the night previous to his execution, but paid the strictest attention to he pious exhortations of the minister, who sat with him the whole of the time, and heartily joined in the prayers which the holy man offered up to the Most High for the forgiveness of the sins of the poor erring mortal who in a few hours was doomed to expiate his crimes upon the scaffold.

As the time approached, Adder became more firm than he had been for some days before, and it was very evident that his mind was inspired with hope.

On the dismal procession leaving the condemned cell, the culprit walked with a firm step, and continued in earnest prayer, apparently unconscious to almost everything which was passing around him, and careless about the fearful part he had to act in the tragedy.

The mournful cavalcade moved along the dark avenues of the prison, and the bell of the neighbouring church tolled the death knell.

The arms of Adder were pinioned, and the halter was round his neck; but although his face was ghastly pale, the expression of his features was more firm than it had hitherto been, and he walked with an erect form, and did not seem to tremble in the least.

When the wretched man reached the outside of the gaol, and was about being placed in the cart which was to convey him to the place of execution, and which was fixed to take place on a common about a mile from the prison, the shouts and execrations that saluted him were dreadful beyond conception, and so they continued all the way until the arrival at the gallows; but the unhappy being against whom they were directed was too deeply engaged in prayer to take any heed of them, and such disgusting demonstrations might well have been spared.

We will pass over this revolting scene as quickly as possible: suffice it to say that Adder met his fate with fortitude, and died sincerely penitent, and there were many persons present who, while they could not help feeling the most unbounded horror at the numerous crimes of which he had been guilty, with that sentiment so becoming the Christian mind, pitied his disgraceful and untimely end, and returned their thanks to the Almighty for having saved them from those guilty temptations that might otherwise have brought upon them a similar end.

Thus perished Adder, so long the secret and triumphant enemy of Lord Ravensford and our heroine, but whose wicked machinations were so mercifully thwarted by Omnipotence, at the very moment when they appeared to be more certain of meeting with success. May his fate afford a terrible example to youth, to avoid those errors that ultimately must lead to destruction.

CHAPTER L.

THE SMUGGLER CAPTAIN.—THE SHIP ON FIRE.

IT was some time ere the dismal impression which the awful fate of Adder, richly as he deserved it, had made upon the minds of our heroine and her friends could be effaced, but at length it, and the other circumstances connected with it, were remembered only by them as fearful dreams, which, now being over, should disturb the mind no longer.

Mrs. Belgrave and her friends at Holly Hall frequently exchanged visits, and the delightful intercourse which had so happily sprung up between them, was a circumstance for which they all felt very grateful.

The domestic happiness of Mr. and Mrs. Rattleton, and their excellent father, was also much increased by the birth of twins, two beautiful girls, and in due time they were further blessed with a son who was acknowledged by every one to be exactly like the father, as the girls resembled their mother, and it was strongly hoped that they would inherit all their numerous virtues likewise.

Sir Harry Spangle and his wild friend, Captain Mowbray, tired and ashamed of the numerous follies in which they had indulged, became quite reformed characters, and having married two amiable ladies, made excellent husbands, and added to the friendly circle that usually assembled at Holly Hall and the residence of Mr. and Mrs. Rattleton.

Sam Kitson, the smuggler, being attacked with an illness which terminated fatally, his widow had now no obstacle remaining to prevent her accepting the offer of Lady

Ravensford, and that honest and well-meaning woman took up her future residence at Holly Hall, and was looked upon more as a friend and companion than as a servant.

From Lady Ravensford she experienced every possible kindness, and from her husband the utmost esteem, to mark his due sense of the kindness with which she had behaved to our heroine in her troubles, and the service which she had rendered her.

Monckton, or rather Archibald Malcolm frequently visited Holly Hall, and was always received as a welcome guest. At length the persuasions of Lord Ravensford and his friends tended much to shake the resolution which the smuggler captain had formerly ex-

MONCKTON ESCAPING FROM THE BURNING SHIP.

pressed not to abandon his lawless and precarious course of life; but still he was unable to come to any positive decision, until at length a circumstance took place which at once brought about the termination which Ravensford and the others so much desired.

Monckton had lost several of the oldest of his crew by death, and the life of a smuggler was daily becoming less pleasant to him.

The friends at Holly Hall had neither heard nor seen anything of Monckton for several months, and they had begun to think that some accident had befallen him—that he had perished at sea, and that they, therefore, should not see him again.

One night, however, just as Rattleton and his lady, and Mr. Goodman, were about to leave the hall, and Lord and Lady Ravensford were thinking of retiring to rest, a servant came to inform them that a man below, who declined sending up his name, requested an interview with them.

Lord Ravensford, although he was rather surprised and dissatisfied at the message, told the servant to show the stranger up stairs, and after a short time a tall man, muffled in a large mantle, was ushered into the room.

He immediately threw the mantle aside when the servant had left the room, and they were surprised, but pleased, to behold Monckton

"Monckton!" ejaculated Lord Ravensford.

"Yes, my lord," replied the former; "Monckton no more, but plain Archibald Malcolm."

"And have you, then, at last made up your mind?" inquired Ravensford.

"I have," answered Malcolm. "I am no longer the smuggler captain, but a private individual, hoping to live by honest means, that is, if I am permitted to do so without obstruction."

"I am extremely glad to hear you say so," said Lord Ravensford, "and I think that I have interest sufficient to assure you that you shall receive no further trouble."

"I am much obliged to you, my lord," said Malcolm, "and will endeavour by my future conduct to mark my sense of your kindness."

"Anything that I can serve you in," said his lordship, "I feel it is a duty which I owe you. But what has brought you to this decision?"

"I have long thought of it," replied Malcolm; "but it is an accident that has at length brought me to such a determination."

"An accident?"

"Yes, a fatal accident."

"What mean you?" asked Lord Ravensford, eagerly.

"You shall hear," replied Malcolm, and he paused, and seemed to be undergoing some emotion; then he took a seat which had been offered to him on his entrance, and still remained silent, apparently brooding over melancholy retrospections.

Lord Ravensford's curiosity, and that of the others, was excited.

"Something particular must have happened, I am certain, by the agitation you evince," observed the former. "What has become of your crew, to whom you were so much attached?"

The emotion of the smuggler increased; he passed his hand across his face, and rising from his chair, he paced the room backwards and forwards in silence for a few moments.

Lord Ravensford repeated his question.

"Ah! my lord," at last answered Malcolm, in a voice of the deepest sorrow; "they are all gone,—all gone—not one of them left."

"All gone?"

"Yes, yes, all—all!" repeated Malcolm, "perished, poor fellows!"

"Perished!" reiterated Lord Ravensford; "what, slain in some affray with those whom—

"No—no," interrupted Malcolm, "not so;—the poor fellows—the partners of all my difficulties, met with a worse fate than that: I alone remain to tell the dreadful tale."

"Pray explain yourself," requested Rattle-ton, whose curiosity, as well as that of the others, was greatly excited.

"I will," said Malcolm; "but you must bear with for me, I confess the recollection of the event makes me as weak as a child. We had been out on one of our usual expeditions, and having shipped our cargo, were making way to our rendezvous, when about the middle of the night I was aroused by the cry of fire, and Michael Hernwood rushed into my cabin, and informed me that a fire had broken out below, and was then raging with such fury that it threatened to destroy the vessel in a very short time. Immediately all hands were piped, and we took the readiest means to extinguish the flames, but they had got such a firm hold of the vessel that all our exertions were in vain, and, in an inconceivably short space of time, the unfortunate ship, in which we had taken so many successful trips, was nearly in one mass of flames. We had now no other chance of saving our lives than by hastening to our boat, into which we all jumped, with the exception of poor Ned Mayling, who perished in the flames. But in the hurry and confusion that prevailed at that juncture, the boat was upset, and we were all immersed in the waves. I succeeded in regaining the boat, into which I got, and looked around me. It had drifted far away, and I was alone; I could not perceive one of my unfortunate companions, although the reflection from the flames of the burning ship cast a lurid glow on the waters far around, and made everything perfectly distinct for some distance. They must all have met a watery grave. I can scarcely describe my emotions at that moment. I felt like a father who had been deprived of the whole of his family by some terrible calamity, at one fell swoop. I looked around me with an eye of despair, and wrung my hands. I was now quite careless as to my own fate, and was half inclined to plunge into the deep, and thus share the fate of my unfortunate crew; but some inscrutable power withheld me from my purpose, and, after two or three hours of toil and danger, I reached the shore, in a lonely unfrequented part of the island, and with a heavy heart I made my way to the rendezvous, where I made Davey Grampus acquainted with what had taken place, and having entrusted to him the charge of disposing of the property I had in my possession, I left the place, fully determined, now that I had lost the whole of my faithful crew, that I would at last yield to your advice, my friends, if such I may make bold to call you, and abandon the life of a smuggler for the future."

Lord Ravensford and the others sincerely sympathised with Malcolm in his misfortunes, and commiserated the fate of his crew, but they all highly applauded his resolution, and Lord Ravensford repeated his promises to exert his influence to obtain for the late smuggler-captain a pardon, and entertained the most sanguine hopes that he should meet with success.

Malcolm again thanked him heartily.

"And have you laid down any plans for the future?" inquired Ravensford.

"Why," answered Malcolm, "I have hardly had time to arrange my future plans; but I am tired of the busy scenes of life, now I have nothing to charm me to them; and, as I have plenty of money, I think of retiring as a private gentleman, and by performing such acts of benevolence as my means will allow me to do, seek to make some atonement for any injuries that I may have inflicted on my fellow-creatures."

"And a worthy determination, too," remarked Mr. Goodman, "for which I sincerely applaud you, and you may depend upon it you will find ample reward for you philanthropy in the happiness of a self-approving conscience."

"I do believe you, sir," returned Malcolm; "and would to Heaven I had never swerved from the paths of rectitude and honour."

Lord Ravensford endeavoured to divert the thoughts of Malcolm into another channel, and, as it was getting late, they separated for the night, and the late smuggler-captain was shown into a chamber in the hall.

Archibald Malcolm, however, slept but little, his thoughts were harassed and distracted by the late painful events that had befallen him, and the melancholy fate of his faithful companions; his mind was tormented with doubts and apprehensions as to the probable success or failure of the plans that he had laid down for the future. Yet, upon reflection, he became more confident, when he recollected that he had such an influential friend in Lord Ravensford, and whose esteem, and that of his friends, he hoped in future to enjoy. He at last dropped into a composed sleep, and did not awake again until the morning, when he arose, and took a turn in the garden, ere he joined Lord and Lady Ravensford in the breakfast-parlour.

CHAPTER LI.

THE PARDON.—THE MURDER DISCOVERED. THE ASSASSIN BROUGHT TO JUSTICE.

IN the course of a few days after Malcolm had been at Holly Hall, he became quite reconciled to his change of life, and his natural talents being now allowed full scope, he appeared quite a different being. Well informed and highly cultivated, the different scenes he had of late years mingled in, to those which he had originally been intended for, had made

no lasting or material change in his real character.

He was a remarkably fine-looking man, just in the prime of life, and with a very handsome and intelligent countenance; and now that he appeared in gentlemanly apparel, there was something peculiarly commanding and prepossessing about him, and which was sufficient to conciliate the friendship of those who beheld him at first sight.

Until Lord Ravensford should have been able to see the proper authorities upon the subject of Malcolm's pardon, it was deemed advisable, in order to prevent idle curiosity, that the latter should remain at Holly Hall as privately as possible; and this arrangement having been acceded to, Lord Ravensford lost no time in putting his friendly design into execution.

In the meanwhile, Malcolm received a letter from Davey Grampus, whom he had apprised of the place where he intended to go, informing him that he had disposed of the rich booty which, from time to time, had been secreted in the subterraneous vaults and passages under the "Caboose," until it could be conveniently sold; and giving him a faithful account of the money it had produced, and at the same time mentioning his wish that Malcolm would make it convenient to come to him, so that there might be a speedy adjustment of the whole affair, as he had himself made up his mind to leave the house where he had lived for so many years, and to "retire from business."

To this letter Malcolm returned an immediate reply, informing Davey Grampus that he would be with him as soon as ever Lord Ravensford had succeeded in getting an answer to his application; and at the same time expressing his unqualified approbation of his conduct, and the manner in which he had transacted this difficult piece of business.

The sum which Davey had got was much larger than Malcolm had anticipated it would be, and he determined to reward him handsomely for his trouble, and also to provide for the widows of such of his ill-fated crew as had been married.

This affair settled in his own mind, and feeling more confident of the success of Lord Ravensford, Malcolm felt more at ease, and patiently awaited the issue of his lordship's application.

He had not to wait long; in about a week Lord Ravensford had made such good progress, that he succeeded entirely in gaining the gratification of his wishes; and such was the influence he possessed in the proper quarter, that he found very little, or far less difficulty in so doing than he had expected. Archibald Malcolm, alias Monckton, received full pardon, and thus he was at full liberty to carry into effect his praiseworthy intentions.

Malcolm was unbounded in his gratitude for the service he had rendered him; while Ravensford, on the other hand, as well as our heroine, were equally gratified at having it in their power of returning in some degree the obligation which they owed the former for that which he had done for them, all of them agreeing that to Malcolm she in all probability owed her life.

The next day after Malcolm had received this joyful intelligence, he took his departure to the place in which he had seen so many strange events of his past life, to keep his promise with Davey Grampus, and come to a final settlement of his affairs. On his arrival there, he found that Davey had already disposed of his house, and was only waiting to see him to leave the place.

Davey Grampus having desposited the sum of money in the hands of Malcolm, and given a strick and satisfactory account of everything, Malcolm made him a most liberal and handsome present, sufficient to keep him comfortably for the rest of his days, with the money that he himself possessed, and with which Grampus was quite overwhelmed, and could not express in terms sufficiently warm his gratitude for the " captain's," as he still called him, generosity.

The next and the last duty which Malcolm felt he was bound to perform, was to provide for the widows of his late crew, as he had previously resolved he would do, and he, therefore, desired Grampus to send for them to his place. This was soon done, and when they were assembled, Malcolm, after expressing his sorrow at the calamity which had deprived them of their partners, and himself of some brave and faithful associates, he gave to each of them a liberal present in ready money, and fixed upon them annuities for the rest of their lives.

The poor creatures, who never expected this, knew not how to express their thanks; and Malcolm, who was deeply affected by their manner, hastily pressed the hand of Grampus, and expressing a hope that they should meet again, though he must beg of Davey to forget him in the character of the smuggler-captain, hurried from the place, and proceeding for a few miles on the road, put up at an inn for the night, and early the following morning once more took his departure for Holly Hall.

Malcolm, having settled these affairs, felt more at ease, and turned his thoughts towards obtaining a suitable establishment for his future residence, which he was desirous should be at no great distance from the Hall.

It was not long before Mr. Malcolm succeeded in meeting with a compact and pleasant little villa, about five miles only from the vicinity of Holly Hall, and which was only a pleasant drive from that place,

and having engaged a suitable number of servants, he took up his residence there, and soon became perfectly happy in his change of condition. He soon became celebrated for his many acts of charity and benevolence to the people, and he gained the esteem and admiration of every one.

There were very few persons that were acquainted with what had been his former course of life, and, in fact, those who knew it not would never have imagined that it was possible he could have moved in the rough and lawless scenes in which he had mingled, and, indeed, been a principal actor. He was in his manner most accomplished and urbane, and there were very few individuals who had once enjoyed his society who would not eagerly court it again.

Mr. Malcolm was now about forty years of age, and although he was particularly attentive and attached to the ladies, he seemed to entertain an aversion to matrimony, and there were other circumstances and traits in his character that were equally calculated to excite curiosity and surprise, and from which his friends were inclined to think that his affections had been blighted in early youth, and that he had suffered some severe disappointment which had made him come to the determination that he would lead a life of celibacy.

However true or erroneous these conjectures might be, no one took the liberty of endeavouring to ascertain, or to break into the privacy of his thoughts; and as he evidently was not disposed to be communicative upon the subject, especial care was taken by his friends that it should never be broached, as it appeared to occasion him the greatest uneasiness of mind.

Thus elapsed several months, without any event transpiring worthy of being recorded in these pages, when Lady Ravensford, to the joy of all who knew her, presented her lord with a lovely girl, who was named after herself and Mrs. Rattleton—Rosabelle Emily. And now the happiness of the friends appeared to be complete, and not likely to suffer any interruption.

A circumstance shortly afterwards took place which caused a great sensation in the neighbourhood where it took place, and among all those who were interested upon the subject.

The old out-house, in which our heroine had experienced such a night of horror when she was flying from London and returning to her native place, having been ordered to be pulled down, so that a coach-house and stabling might be built upon its site, in digging for the foundation the workmen were horror-struck on beholding, buried a few feet beneath the soil, a human skeleton, with the mouldering remains of clothes adhering to the bones.

They immediately gave an alarm, and an

investigation was called upon the subject, and the only conclusion that could be come to was, that some person had been murdered, but who the individual was they were at present unable to form any conjecture.

The circumstance, as we have before stated, had naturally caused a great sensation, and having reached the ears of our heroine, the events of that night when she beheld the villains bring the body of their murdered victim, and bury it in the old out-house,—the conversation she had heard between the murderers relative to the bloody deed, and what the character of the murdered man was,—all came as fresh to her memory as if it had only been the occurrence of yesterday.

"Oh!" she exclaimed, "how neglectful have I been in this awful affair, when my evidence might probably be the means of bringing the murderers to justice."

"You say, my dear Rosabelle," observed her husband, "that you have since seen one of the murderers?"

"I have," replied Lady Ravensford. "I recognised him in Gordon Desborough, but was afraid to let that circumstance be known, confident as I was that he would not hesitate to rid himself of such a dangerous witness of his guilt."

"Gordon Desborough!" repeated Malcolm; "but are you positive, my lady?"

"I would not venture to make such an assertion if I were not certain," replied our heroine; "I can swear to him as being one of the men."

"Well," said Malcolm, "I believe that Gordon Desborough is fully capable of perpetrating such a deed, and I have not the least doubt but that he has been guilty of crimes of a similar nature before now; but it is indeed unfortunate that your ladyship did not think to make known this circumstance before, for Gordon has left the house where he formerly resided, and in which you were so long incarcerated, and he probably may succeed in eluding the officers of justice. But, at any rate, your ladyship, I would lose no time in making all the facts known to the proper authorities."

"Most certainly I shall do so," replied Lady Ravensford.

This design she immediately put into execution, and officers were despatched in every direction in search of Gordon Desborough, and bills were posted giving a full description of his person, and offering a large reward for his apprehension.

It was now recollected that about eight years before an old man, who resided in the locality of the out-house in which the skeleton was found, and who was noted for his penurious habits, and was supposed to have accumulated a large sum of money by his miserly ways, was suddenly missing from the old hovel in which he used to reside, and that nothing could be heard of him afterwards; and from what Lady Ravensford had stated, there could be but very little doubt but that he was the murdered victim.

The persons in the neighbourhood were horror-struck at the account which Lady Ravensford gave of the dreadful circumstance, at least as far as her knowledge extended; and while they execrated the base murderers in the most unmeasured terms, they deeply regretted that they had so long, and perhaps altogether, been permitted to escape the punishment that was due to their atrocious crime.

Considering the many troubles that our heroine had undergone, and the manner in which her mind must in consequence have been constantly bewildered, her neglecting to mention the circumstance before to proper authorities was excused, although it was deeply regretted, as it was feared that one of the assassins, at any rate, would escape the hands of justice.

No one, in fact, could more sincerely regret the circumstance than did Lady Ravensford herself, and she was determined that she would do everything in her power to repair the error.

Lord Ravensford employed persons to assist the officers in their search after the murderers, and was most indefatigable in endeavouring to bring the villains to punishment; and Malcolm, who. from his connexion with Gordon Desborough, was more likely to have some idea of his haunts, personally undertook to add his valuable aid to the others, and taking with him one or two persons on whom he could depend, he left his house and proceeded on his task.

Every place that was likely the miscreant would resort to was searched, but without any success; and several months elapsed without their being enabled to gain the least clue to the retreat of Gordon Desborough, or his companion in the bloody crime, although it was generally conjectured that the latter was no more.

The old out-house, in which the wretches had buried the remains of their murdered victim, and in doing which our [heroine] had observed them, was pulled down, and upon the spot where the skeleton was found was placed a stone, on which were inscribed the particulars of the event, and the names of the two individuals who were supposed to be the murderers, and the period at which it had taken place.

The poor inhabitants of the locality, with a superstitious feeling of dread, shunned the spot as much as they could ever afterwards, but more particularly at nightfall,—and the offer of even a handsome reward would not have induced any of them to venture within half a mile of it. It was reported, in fact, that the spectre of the murdered miser haunted the spot, calling for retribution on his assassins; but although plenty of simple persons were to be found who thoroughly believed that every word of such rumour was true, not one could be met with who would ever aver that he had had ocular demonstration of its veracity.

Six months had elapsed, and still not the least clue could be obtained to the retreat of the miscreants, and Malcolm had returned to his residence, and both himself and Lord Ravensford had abandoned the search in despair, when a circumstance took place which once more aroused them to action.

One of the inhabitants of the place, who was perfectly acquainted with the person of Gordon Desborough, declared that he had seen him a few miles from the village; but knowing his desperate and daring character, and being alone, he was afraid to attempt to apprehend him. He, however, made with all possible dispatch to the house of the magistrate, and making him acquainted with the circumstance, officers were sent as quickly as possible in search all over the neighbourhood, but without any successful result.

It was, therefore, concluded that the man must have been mistaken; and the story carried on the face of it the greatest improbability, it not being at all likely that Gordon Desborough would return to the very neighbourhood where the crime had been perpetrated, in which the greatest excitement prevailed, and where he would be almost certain to be taken.

The man, notwithstanding, persisted that he was right, and that it was none other than Gordon Desborough whom he had seen.

The search was now renewed with the most unmitigated assiduity, but it all proved to be entirely fruitless, and it was at last feared that Gordon had managed to escape out of the country, and had rejoined his former associate, if that villain were still living.

Another interval of several months now took place without anything occurring to excite suspicion, or being worthy of receiving a place in these pages, when an incident, more alarming than any that had happened for some time, occurred to our heroine, and which at once proved that the conjectures that had been formed as to the escape of Gordon Desborough were entirely wrong, and exhibited the daring character of that abominable villain in a more glaring point of view than ever.

Believing that she had now no reason to fear any danger, Lady Rosabelle had resumed those solitary rambles in which she was formerly occasionally to indulge, and where she could uninterruptedly ruminate upon the past events of her eventful life, and give free indulgence to the melancholy, yet salutary reflections they created.

Lord Ravensford did not offer to prevent her from indulging in her whim, although he frequently ventured to suggest to her that there was a good deal of imprudence and danger in her so doing, and advised her not to walk out alone. Our heroine, however, only smiled at his fears, and continued to follow the bent of her inclination,—indeed it was one of the most melancholy pleasures she had.

Very often she was tempted by the fineness of the weather, or the abstraction of her thoughts, to prolong her rambles, and sometimes even to extend her walks after the shades of evening had descended upon the earth.

It was upon one of these occasions that, her thoughts deeply engaged in meditation, she had wandered on, heedless of the lapse of time, until, looking up, she found herself to be at least three miles from Holly Hall, and in one of the most lonely parts of the country. Moreover, it was night; and knowing how alarmed her husband would be at her absence, she immediately turned towards the beaten track which led towards the village, and hastened on as fast as her steps would carry her.

It was a very fine night, and the moon shone so clearly in the heavens that it rendered everything as distinct and visible as if it had been broad daylight.

Lady Rosabelle had proceeded with such speed that already she saw the tall spire of the village church peeping from between the trees, and in another quarter of an hour had no doubt that she should be able to reach there.

Suddenly, however, she was alarmed by hearing the heavy and hasty tread of some person behind her, and looking back, her terror was not a little increased when the clear moonlight enabled her to behold the tall figure of a man running hastily towards her, and apparently in pursuit of her; in fact, she had just reason to suppose that he was so, for at the very moment when she looked round, he made a motion with his hand for her to stop, and increased his speed to get up to her.

"My God! what can this man want?— What will become of me?" exclaimed our terrified heroine, as she increased her rapidity, and hurried along the path panting for breath, and with all the precipitation she could.

Still, however, with even her utmost speed she was unable to outstrip the man, and she could tell by the sound of his feet, for she did not venture to look back, that he was gaining rapidly upon her; and at the very time she formed this conjecture, he called upon her, with a terrible oath, to stop, and from the sound of his voice, he was evidently close upon her.

It would be impossible now to describe the fears of Lady Rosabelle, especially as the voice of the fellow seemed to be familiar to her ears, and she had no doubt that his purpose was robbery, and perhaps murder!

Her heart sunk with every step she took, and although the village was just peeping in sight, she was so much out of breath, and exhausted, that she was afraid she should never be able to reach it before the man had overtaken her.

Still closer and closer came the heavy tread of the ruffian upon our heroine's ears, and again and again with fearful threats he commanded her to stop. But Rosabelle heeded him not, and in the wildness of her despair, hurried on as fast as her trembling limbs and the breathless and panting condition she was in would permit her.

"Merciful Heaven!—protect!—save me!" she cried, as, unable to proceed further, she sank down by the side of the very stone which was placed over the spot where the remains of the murdered miser had been buried, and gave herself up at once to fate.

"Oh, oh, so I have overtaken you at last, madam," said the ruffian, who had now come up to her, and seized her fiercely by the arm.

She looked up immediately upon hearing the tones of his voice, and her horror may be very readily conceived, when she recognised the savage and revolting features of Gordon Desborough.

"Ah! by hell!" cried the wretch, with a look of fierce exultation, "my suspicions, then, are confirmed; it is Lady Ravensford. Now then can I gratify my revenge on the spy upon my actions, and rid myself of the only witness of guilt. Here, too, on the very spot!"

As the miscreant thus spoke, he took a knife from his pocket, and opening its broad blade in the moonlight, he held it towards the bosom of our heroine with the most fearful and menacing gestures.

Lady Ravensford fixed upon the villain a look of the most impressive supplication and despair, and as she watched the glittering blade of the murderer's knife, she gave herself up entirely as lost.

For a moment or two the wretch averted his diabolical purpose, and gazed upon our distracted heroine with the most terrific looks. It was very evident, however, villain as he was, that he was somewhat moved by the imploring and despairing looks of our heroine, and was undecided in what manner he should act; but he retained his hold of her arm, and increased the strength of his gripe, although he spoke not a word.

"Mercy! mercy!" at length shrieked Lady Ravensford; "do not take my life!—I never injured thee."

"Never injured me!" repeated the ruffian, in a savage voice; "liar! wert thou not the first to make my guilt know, and wouldst thou not swear that which would bring me to the scaffold? Oh, had I but known that thou wert acquainted with my crime, while I held thee a prisoner for Adder, how bitterly would I have been avenged. But the time has now come, and here on this spot thou diest!"

"For the love of Heaven spare my life?" screamed Rosabelle, in frantic terror.

"Love of Heaven! ha! ha! ha!" cried Gordon, laughing contemptuously; "what have I to do with Heaven? You plead in vain; my own safety demands your life."

"You surely would not murder me in cold blood!" ejaculated our heroine, writhing in the agony of her fears, and looking up with clasped hands and frenzied looks at the ferocious ruffian.

"Speak low," said Gordon, again directing the knife towards the bosom of Lady Ravensford; "speak low; or by hell if you breathe beyond a whisper, or speak a word that might reach the closest ear, I will not give you another instant to live!"

"For the sake of my children, oh, do not take my life!" again distractedly implored our heroine; "do not add another so dreadful a crime to the weight already upon your conscience."

"And why should I spare you, when you are exerting yourself to the utmost to bring me to the gallows?" demanded Gordon.

"This act of mercy might save you," said Lady Ravensford; and she looked despairingly around her, but saw no help at hand, nor was it likely that she would, near that almost totally abandoned spot.

She was entirely in the miscreant's power, and what forbearance could she expect from one of his savage nature, and who was urged on to the perpetration of the bloody crime by such desperate motives? Still, however, she could not entirely banish a ray of hope from her mind, especially as she saw the ruffian hesitated, and appeared to waver in his determination, and she renewed her supplications with more energy than before.

"Oh, have pity upon me, Gordon Desborough," she ejaculated; "suffer her to depart, and make your escape, if you can, from this spot, where every moment that you loiter you are in danger of being apprehended, and expediting your fate."

"Suffer you to depart!" repeated the murderer;—"ha! ha! ha! think you I am a fool? Suffer you to depart, to give immediate notice of my being in the neighbourhood, and set the bloodhounds on my heels? No, no; I have the means of preventing that, and I am not going to be mad enough to let the chance slip through my fingers so easily. Prepare yourself, Lady Ravensford, for in another moment you will cease to live!"

"God of Heaven! shield me!—save me!"

frantically exclaimed our heroine, and again, with the desperation of horror and despair, she endeavoured to release herself from the grasp of the villain.

"You plead in vain," replied Gordon Desborough; "my safety demands it, and you die!"

"Forbear! forbear! cruel man," implored Lady Rosabelle; "as you would hope for mercy here and hereafter, spare the mother for her poor children!"

"Psha!" cried the wretch; "what a very fool am I to listen to this whining nonsense. Die!"

He raised his arm as he spoke, with the glittering knife in his hand, and was about to plunge the deadly weapon in her bosom, when, strengthened by the power of her horror and despair, she caught hold of his arm, and for the moment arrested his brutal and savage purpose.

"Mercy! mercy!" she shrieked; "spare me, Gordon, and you may expect mercy yourself."

The frenzy of our heroine's looks again made an impression upon the ruffian, and once more he paused, and looked earnestly at her.

Perceiving the hesitation of his manner, she increased the vehemence of her supplications, and hope once more sprang up in her bosom as she noticed the effect her words had upon the ruffian.

He looked at her for a moment or two, and returned no answer, but seemed deliberating within himself how he should act.

At length, in a subdued tone of voice, he said —

"I thirst not for your blood, although I have aid I did; and even now I would spare your life."

"Oh, thanks!" sobbed Rosabelle; "tell me how?"

"Swear that you will not reveal to any one that you have seen me," replied Gordon; "swear by all your hopes in this world and in the next to do that, and instantly I release you."

"Swear!" cried our heroine.

"Ay, swear!" repeated the ruffian; "every moment that you hesitate, you do but hasten your fate!"

"Oh, spare me the oath," begged our heroine, with tearful eyes.

"The oath! the oath!" cried Gordon; "not another moment will I wait!"

"I will promise you, but——" gasped forth Rosabelle.

"Swear! swear!" shouted the ruffian, again wielding the knife.

"Mercy! mercy!" groaned the agonized Lady Ravensford;—"I—I cannot!"

"Then your own obstinacy hath sacrificed

your life," exclaimed the murderer. "You die!"

Rosabelle shrieked, as the wretch raised his hand; and once more she caught his arm, and prevented the deadly blow he aimed at her heart.

Terrible was that brief struggle, and it was astonishing how our heroine could find strength to resist the murderous intentions of the ruffian as she did. But her strength increased, and in the effort which Gordon made to extricate his arm from the grasp of Lady Rosabelle, the knife fell from his hand, and stooping to pick it up, in a moment she succeeded in releasing herself from his hold, and fled with the speed of lightning from the place, shrieking aloud for help as she proceeded to the village.

"Rash idiot, you shall not escape me!" cried Gordon, as he quickly prepared to pursue her.

"Oh, help! help! save me!" again screamed Lady Rosabelle, in louder accents than before, as she felt her footsteps fail her, and her fate appeared to be inevitable.

At that dreadful moment, when certain death seemed to threaten her, she heard a loud imprecation, and looking hastily round, she perceived the villain in the act of falling, he having caught his foot in something on the ground.

He fell heavily to the earth, striking his head violently against the stone, and immediately was stretched at full length, quite insensible.

"God of Heaven!" ejaculated Rosabelle, earnestly, "I thank Thee!" and clasping her hands vehemently together, she paused for an instant only to take breath, and then resumed her flight, until she had gained the entrance of the village, where she beheld Lord Ravensford, Mr. Rattleton, and a posse of servants and villagers advancing towards her.

With a wild cry she rushed forward, and sinking in the arms of her husband, had only strength to articulate—

"Save me!— Gordon Desborough — the murderer's stone!" ere she became insensible.

Lord Ravensford committed her to the care of the two servants to convey her to the hall, and then he and Rattleton, followed by the others, hastened with all possible speed to the spot from whence our heroine had only just before escaped from the power of the murderer, Gordon Desborough.

When they reached the murderer's stone, Gordon had disappeared; but they perceived a stream of blood near the spot, and followed the marks for some distance, when they entirely lost sight of them, and could not perceive any signs of the object of their pursuit.

Lord Ravensford and Rattleton, having given instructions to their companions to continue the pursuit, with all possible vigilance. retraced their footsteps to Holly Hall, being anxious to know the condition of Lady Ravensford, and to ascertain the particulars from her lips.

When they reached the hall, they found that our heroine was restored to sensibility, but was too weak to answer questions, and they were, therefore, compelled to suspend the gratification of their curiosity, although their astonishment and anxiety upon the subject may be easily imagined.

CHAPTER LII.

THE ATTEMPTED ASSASSINATION. — THE MURDERER SECURED.—HIS FATE.

LORD RAVENSFORD had sent immediate notice of this event to the magistrate, and in consequence, officers were despatched in every direction in the hope of capturing the villain, and the utmost excitement prevailed in the neighbourhood, as well as at Holly Hall. There was not the least doubt but that the murderer had encountered our heroine at the

ADDER CONVEYED TO THE PLACE OF EXECUTION.

murderer's stone, for the knife which he had dropped, and on which his name was inscribed, was found there, which of itself was a sufficient confirmation of the fact; but how Lady Ravensford had been enabled to effect her escape from so desperate a villain, and by what means he had received the wound which had caused the stream of blood which they had seen, they were perfectly at a loss to conjecture.

They were not long kept in suspense, for after a time Rosabelle, having recovered from the effects of her terror, was enabled to furnish

them with the whole of the alarming particulars, and Lord Ravensford's gratitude to Heaven for the miraculous manner in which his wife had been saved from the murderer's knife, at the very moment when all hope seemed to be at an end, was most unbounded, and the astonishment of every one at the event was excessive.

"What a daring villain he must be to venture into the very neighbourhood of his crime," said Lord Ravensford, "and where he could expect nothing less than to be taken !"

"But he is not taken," returned Rattleton, "and there does not appear any more likelihood of his being so than there was before."

"From the short time that elapsed after his meeting with Lady Rosabelle," observed her husband, "it seems wonderful how he could have managed to escape, especially as he appears to have been badly wounded."

"It does, indeed," coincided Rattleton; "but the circumstance of his being wounded, may still be the means of his being detected."

"It may," observed Ravensford, "and it is the more likely as it does not appear probable that he can have gone far out of the neighbourhood. Your ladyship must now perceive the force of that which I have often told you, namely, how very imprudent it is of you to indulge in these solitary rambles, especially at night. The several narrow escapes you have had ought to be a warning to you."

"They will, you may depend upon it, in future," answered our heroine; "it seems as if fate had destined that I should fall a victim to the cruel designs of some villain or another."

"Nay, my love," said her husband, "I would have you banish such thoughts from your bosom, but yet to use all necessary precaution for the future."

"You may depend upon it, my lord, that I shall not fail to attend to your advice," said Lady Ravensford.

"I trust that our fears will shortly be set at rest," remarked her husband, "and that the wretch will not much longer escape from the hands of justice."

"I hope so, too," observed Rattleton; "and, indeed, my hopes are now more sanguine upon that subject than they were before this recently alarming adventure."

"The ruffian must quickly have recovered himself, or, so quick as we were after him, when Rosabelle had escaped from him, he must have fallen into our power," said Ravensford.

"There can be no doubt of it," replied Rattleton; "but it was remarkable that we could not trace the marks of blood to any greater distance than we did."

"It was," coincided Ravensford; "and it would make it appear that the fellow must have succeeded in stopping the effusion of the blood, or that he must have been concealed about that spot."

"That was not possible, nevertheless," said Rattleton, "otherwise he must have been detected, so strict was our search."

"True," replied Lord Ravensford; "and it is still my opinion that he is not far off, but that by disguising himself, like that most consummate scoundrel, Adder, used to do, he has contrived to set detection at defiance, hitherto."

"That is not at all unlikely," returned Rattleton; "but the greatest wonder is, how the fellow can subsist, as he was not very likely to be well provided with money."

"Oh, so experienced a villain as Gordon evidently is, would be at no great loss to manage the means of doing that," observed his lordship; "his ingenuity would doubtless soon hit upon some scheme to enable him to subsist, and the same power may screen him from detection longer than we imagine."

"Malcolm has again intimated his intention of going in search of the miscreant," said Mr. Rattleton; "and if anybody can find him, he will."

"Yes, of that I have no doubt," replied Lord Ravensford, "and, likewise, of Mr. Malcolm's untiring exertions to do so. He has rendered us all great service, and I shall ever regard him with the warmest esteem and gratitude."

"It is no more than your duty to do so, my lord," remarked Rattleton; "and the conduct of Mr. Malcolm is such as to entitle him to our most ardent friendship."

"Malcolm is an excellent man," said Ravensford; "and it is a pity that he was for so many years lost to that society he was so well qualified to mingle with and to embellish."

"Very true," returned Rattleton; but now he is restored to his proper station in the world, we ought entirely to forget him in his former character of Monckton, the smuggler-captain."

"Exactly so," coincided his lordship, "and you may depend upon it that I shall never remind him of it. But when does he think of departing on this errand?"

"To-morrow morning."

"When I trust that every success will attend him."

"As I said before, I have strong hopes of it," replied Rattleton, "but in the meantime we must ourselves be indefatigable."

"Certainly," said Ravensford; "it behoves us all, not only for safety, but also in justice, to exert ourselves to the utmost to bring so heinous an offender to punishment."

"Undoubtedly; and I hope that the time is not far distant when we shall succeed in our efforts," replied Rattleton.

The following morning Malcolm, accordingly, attended by two officers in disguise, left the neighbourhood, and went in search of Gordon Desborough at such places where it was the most likely he would be secreted; but after several days of the greatest exertion, and devising several schemes with the hope of accomplishing their object, without meeting with the least success, or hearing anything which could give them any idea of the manner in which they should proceed, they were compelled to abandon their pursuit, and returned to the place from whence they had come, vexed and disappointed, and bringing no less disappointment to all those who were interested in the business, whose endeavours had not been attended with any better fortune.

"I am fearful now," said Lord Ravensford, "that he will never be taken and that he has succeeded in getting out of the country."

"Oh, no, I do not think that," replied Malcolm; "I think that he is still in the country, and that he will at some future period fall into the hands of justice. I think it would be as well to abandon the heat of the pursuit at present, and probably, when he imagines that we are in a state of apathy or unwariness, he may venture again boldly forth, and thus easily fall into the snare laid to entrap him."

"A very excellent plan," said Mr. Goodman, "and one which I most urgently advise we should adopt. Nothing can be more reasonable than the observations that Mr. Malcolm has made use of:—what think you, my lord?"

"I am decidedly of the same opinion," replied Lord Ravensford.

"Then we are all agreed, it seems," remarked Malcolm; "and, therefore, for the present let us remain quiet, but at the same time be watchful and wary, and then we shall see what time will effect."

This scheme met with general approbation, and it was accordingly adopted; the officers affected to have abandoned the pursuit in despair, and the bills that had been posted about the country, offering a reward for the apprehension of Gordon Desborough, were removed, although, of course, it was generally understood that that reward would fall to the share of those who should be the means of bringing the miscreant to justice.

All went on in this manner for about two months, without anything taking place to throw any further light upon the subject, or to give them any further idea of its being likely that Gordon Desborough would be detected; but a circumstance was about to take place which brought that about more speedily than any of them had anticipated.

The winter was now drawing on apace, and the country around Holly Hall began to have a more gloomy and cheerless aspect, and with the change in the season, so did an alteration appear in the health of Lady Ravensford, who was frequently so ill as to be compelled to keep her bed.

She had, however, became so much better that she was enabled to leave her chamber, and there was every prospect of her being, in a short time, completely restored to convalescence.

It was on a very dark and tempestuous night, that Lady Rosabelle, feeling the effects of the storm on her constitution, retired early to her chamber, hoping that rest would restore her. The fierce raging of the tempest, how-ever, kept her for some time awake, until Lord Ravensford, who had to pass through her chamber to go to his own, which was the adjoining one, came to her bedside to bid her good night, previous to his retiring to rest, and he then left her, and went into his own apartment, but did not close the door, so that he might the more readily hear her if she should happen to be taken worse in the night.

Soon afterwards, the violence of the storm having somewhat abated, and being quite and worn out, Rosabelle fell off to sleep.

How low she had slept she had no means of judging, but she was suddenly awakened by a strange noise in her chamber.

It was like the stealthy footsteps of some person moving about in her room; and presently afterwards she was greatly terrified on beholding the long, dark shadow of a human form on the opposite wainscot.

Surprised and alarmed as she naturally was at this circumstance, it was with extreme difficulty she could prevent herself from screaming out; but as a sudden thought flashed across her brain that probably her life and that of her husband depended solely upon her precaution and presence of mind, she lay perfectly still, and scarcely daring to breathe, feigned to be asleep.

What an awful moment of agony was that! We cannot do adequate justice to the state of her feelings by description. Never had she probably suffered so much in her life before as she did during that brief interval.

All was quite still for a second or two, and the heart of our heroine palpitated violently against her side, as she began to entertain a faint hope that she had been deceived, and that what she had imagined she had heard and seen was only a dream.

She was quickly, however, undeceived; for again she beheld the shadow on the wall, a.. then the creaking noise of a pair of shoes they moved across the floor.

"Curse the shoes!" now muttered a voice, and the heart of Rosabelle sunk with horror, when in the tones she immediately recognised those of Gordon Desborough!

"Good God!" she thought, "what will become of me and my husband? We are lost—— we are lost!"

These thoughts were only momentary; she had not time to entertain them any longer, for the next instant the miscreant moved towards the bedside, and appeared to be gazing intently upon her. She scarcely dared to breathe, and such was the power of her emotion that her heart, which had become so violently palpitated, now scarcely seemed to throb in her bosom.

In an instant she made up her mind how to act, and taking the ruffian by surprise, she hoped, with the assistance of Heaven, to be able to succeed.

"I have been fortunate in finding the chamber," muttered the murderer to himself, as he hung over the bedside; "she sleeps, little dreaming how near she is her eternal sleep. But where is her husband? He is not here, and my business will be only half complete, if I do not have his life as well! But there is no time to lose; let me despath her, and then search for my other victim!"

The wretch removed the bed-clothes from the bosom of Lady Ravensford as he spoke, and raising the knife he held in his hand, prepared to strike the fatal blow, when, with a strength and courage which only Heaven could have imbued her with, as the fatal weapon was in the course of descent, she jumped up in the bed, and seized his arm, holding him with a power which completely astonished and unnerved the murderer.

"Oh, help! help! Ravensford!—Murder! quick! quick! Help!" she shrieked loudly, and the next moment Lord Ravensford sprang into the chamber, and seized upon the miscreant.

"Confusion!" cried Gordon, endeavouring to release himself from the hold of Ravensford, and to plunge the knife in his heart; "am I thus to be foiled—betrayed? Leave go your hold, rash fool! for you struggle with a desperate and determined man!"

"Villain! murderer!" exclaimed Ravensford, "I have you now, and will lose my life ere I will suffer you to escape!"

The struggle, although short, was most terrific, for both the murderer and his antagonist were alike determined, and in strength about equal; while the agony of Rosabelle was indescribable.

Loudly she continued to scream for help, and to pull the bell, and at length the sounds of several footsteps hastily ascending the stairs, convinced her that the servants were alarmed, and were hastening to their assistance.

"By hell, I will not be taken, to die upon the gallows like a dog!" cried Gordon, when he heard the approaching footsteps. In a moment he shook himself from Ravensford's hold, and, hurrying to the window, hastily threw it up.

"Wretch, guilty man!" cried Ravensford, "you will but hasten your death! To escape from thence is impossible!"

"Death in any shape rather than upon the scaffold!" replied Gordon, and in the next moment he sprang upon a chair, and with a stern look of determination, he took the fearful leap.

Ravensford and the servants rushed to the window, and with feelings of horror, gazed upon the body of the murderer as it whirled in the air, and rebounded from the different parapets and abutments it came in contact with in the course of its frightful descent, until it reached the earth, a horribly mutilated mass!

CONCLUSION.

WE have but little more to add in conclusion of this most eventful narrative.

The body of the murderer was afterwards hung in chains on the spot where stood the murderer's stone, and the blackened bones might have been seen but a few years since.

The last of the enemies of Lord and Lady Ravensford being now no more, they had every reason to hope that their future days would be passed in that happy state of serenity and peace from which they had been for so many years estranged.

On the anniversary of Lady Ravensford' birthday, such a scene of festivity was got up at Holly Hall as had never been celebrated in it before. There were entertainments of all descriptions, and among the rest a masque ball, to which all the gentry and nobility, as well as their most intimate friends around, were invited, and hilarity and happiness predominated in every breast.

Here, in the midst of every pleasure, we will leave them, and conclude the task we have imposed upon ourselves in recounting the adventures of Lord and Lady Ravensford and their friends.

LONDON : PUBLISHED BY E. LLOYD, SALISBURY-SQUARE, FLEET-STREET.